Cindy poked her head around a corner—and froze.

Al was stark naked, combing his wet hair with one hand and eating with the other. Holding the blow-dryer was a little silver statue; an odd sort of prop, but if it worked—

Dear God, he's a hunk. Al still hadn't noticed her; the noise of the blow-dryer must have covered the sound of her entrance. She felt like a peeping Tom.

Caught between embarrassment and an undeniable attraction, she started to back out—and ran into the corner of the cabinet instead. "Excuse me!" she blurted, as Al suddenly looked up into the mirror and met her eyes.

She froze like a deer pinned in a car's headlights. The little silver statue turned to look calmly at her, still holding the blow-dryer. The dryer cord dangled straight down, and though the dryer was running, it wasn't plugged in.

Unlike the statue's metal ones, the eyes that met hers in the mirror were emerald green and slitted like a cat's. The ears, standing up through the wet hair, were pointed.

THE
OTHERWORLD

Mercedes Lackey
with
Mark Shepherd
and Holly Lisle

THE OTHERWORLD

This is a work of fiction. All the characters and events portrayed in this book are fictional, and any resemblance to real people or incidents is purely coincidental.

A Baen Book

Baen Publishing Enterprises
P.O. Box 1403
Riverdale, NY 10471

ISBN: 0-671-57852-9

Cover art by Clyde Caldwell

First printing, February 2000

Distributed by Simon & Schuster
1230 Avenue of the Americas
New York, NY 10020

Typeset by Brilliant Press
Printed in the United States of America

Dedicated, with love and gratitude to:

Mothers—ours and others—
Who believe, nurture, and forgive just about anything

Wheels of Fire

CHAPTER ONE

Streamlined shapes of bright metal hurtled across asphalt, machines that roared, whined and howled, leaving hot air and deafness in their wake. They were without a doubt louder than any dragon Alinor had ever encountered. But instead of scales, these monsters were covered with flashy, bright endorsement decals for Goodyear, Pennzoil—

And, since the sport of automotive racing was more expensive with every passing year, such other odd sponsors as pizza and soft drinks.

The cars were no longer just racing machines; now they were, in effect, lightning-fast billboards. While these machines used many of the products they hawked, Alinor could only marvel at some of the strange connections made between the sport of auto racing and the things humans consumed.

The decals flashing under the sun only emphasized the vehicles' speed; they moved too fast to be *seen*, much less read. As car after car flashed by Alinor's vantage point, he was left with a vague impression of shapes and vivid colors. Presumably commercials had imprinted those shapes and colors in the minds of humans vividly enough that there would be instant recognition.

Alinor marveled at the sheer *power* of these metal beasts. The only other creature that could approach those speeds was an elvensteed, and then only if one wore a car's metallic seeming.

Sun beat down upon the track, numbing the brain, and Alinor yawned, pulling a red SERRA cap tighter over his head. Last night's final preps had taken more out of him than he had anticipated. Even for one of the Folk, two hours of sleep wasn't quite enough. He stretched a little and glanced at his watch; the team had been out here in the pits since just after dawn, and even the workaholics would be wanting to pull the car in and break before too long.

I hope, anyway, he thought, combating the sleepglue that formed on the inside of his eyelids. *That break better happen soon, or I'll fall on my nose.*

In spite of his fatigue, he had to grin a little as he looked around, contrasting himself with his surroundings. *Hallet Motor Speedway is not where you'd expect to find one of the Sidhe hanging out. Not even one who's a founding member of the South Eastern Road Racing Association. Strange days, indeed.*

Not that there weren't more elves and mages in the pits and driver's seats back in SERRA territory than anyone could ever have dreamed. Roughly a third had some connection with magic, and there were a few, like young Tannim, who were known for wandering feet. But for the most part, the elven drivers and mechanics of SERRA never left their home states and tracks, much less traveled to the wilds of Oklahoma.

Quaint little state, he had thought during the trip in, though "little" referred more to the size of the cities, not the square mileage of this new land. In many ways this was refreshing to one of the Sidhe, seeing so much wilderness with so few humans around to destroy it.

He hadn't had any trouble adjusting; so far as the natives and pit-crew were concerned, Alinor was just another mechanic. No weirder than most, since mechs were a breed unto themselves.

If for some reason I had to hide, this would be the place to come. There's no sign of Unseleighe Sidhe, and I haven't encountered anything hostile. I could set up a woodshop . . . maybe become a raving Baptist out here in God's country; that would really *throw any pursuers off.* He shook his head, pushing the dismal mental picture away. *Eck. What a truly frightening thought.*

Some of the Folk, the Low Court elves, *couldn't* go too far outside the influence of their chosen power-nexus, and most of the rest were content with the many challenges on their home ground. But Alinor prided himself on the fact that he was not ordinary in any sense, even by SERRA standards; the only other elven mechanic that could match his skill was Dierdre Brighthair, and she couldn't challenge his mastery of metal-magics. Even Sam Kelly had been impressed by what he could do.

Of course, I am a few centuries her senior, give or take a few decades. And I've been a mage-smith for a long, long time.

He wished, though, that he could work some other kinds of magery; a little magic that would loosen Bob's tongue, for instance. Excessive conversation had never been one of the man's character defects, not for as long as Al had known him. He *knew* Bob was no idiot, that quite a bit must be going on in the young human's mind. The problem was that what actually came out appeared to be carefully edited or just doled out unwillingly and uttered with extreme caution. If Bob had said five words since dawn, Al would be surprised.

Their car banked around a corner and screamed past them, kicking up a brief bow-wave of hot, dry, exhaust-tinged wind, motor howling like a Bane-Sidhe. Then the beast of metal and gasoline dopplered away, swinging around for another lap.

"Hot," said Alinor, strolling the few paces away from the edge of the track to where Bob sat on an oil-drum, his red coverall immaculate, despite the hundreds of adjustments made on "their" engine since it first went out this morning. He leaned up against a tire-barrier and pulled his cap a little lower over his eyes, so that the brim met the top of his Ray-Bans.

"Eyah. It's that," Bob Ferrel replied, without taking his gray eyes off the track or the frown off his lean, weathered face.

Al sighed. Bob was in full laconic Maine-mode. *Like talking to a rock. Actually, I might get better conversation out of a rock.* "Nice track, though."

"Eyah."

Considering that this out-of-the-way track was a lush little gem, that was hardly an adequate reply. *When I know people who would kill to work here. . . .* "Guys back at Fayetteville would be green," he offered.

"Eyah."

All right, new tactic. See if he's at least listening to me. Alinor tried the path of absurdity to get something like conversation out of his human partner. "I heard they're going to bring in topless camel races next Saturday."

Now Bob finally turned his head, just barely enough to give Al a hairy eyeball, despite the glasses. "There's a ping in number three cylinder I don't like," he said sourly. "I want you to look at it when they bring it back in."

Blessed Danaa, you might have said something.

Alinor stiffened and instantly became all business. When Bob said he heard something, a SERRA mech listened to him. Bob, like young Maclyn's mother Dierdre, could tune an engine by ear. "I can look at it now," he offered.

"Do that," Bob said, tersely. "We've got a reputation riding on this."

Bob took that reputation a little more seriously than Al did; after all, a High Court elven-mage like Alinor could conjure anything he wished to out of the molecules of the air and earth around him, just by studying it long enough to "ken" it. Bob, when he wasn't partaking of elven hospitality, had a living to make. *The old-fashioned way,* he once joked, in a rare instance of humor. And Bob Ferrel had every intention of dying a wealthy man.

Not that I blame him, Al thought absently. *He's the kind that hates charity.*

The elven mechanic lounged back again, but this time every bit of his concentration was bent on the car careening its way back towards them. Or rather, his attention was bent on what was under the hood; a cast-aluminum engine block of elven make from the "shops" at Fayetteville, another one of the Fairgrove facilities. Al knew this particular block so well he could have duplicated it in an hour. He should; he had kenned it himself.

Not that he wanted anyone outside of a select company of SERRA members to know *that*.

He set his mind ranging inside the inferno of the howling motor, wincing away just a little from the few parts of iron (not so dangerous now, but still uncomfortable), winding his probe into cylinder three. He gave brief mental thanks to Tannim for teaching him those human mageries that made it possible for him to probe through and around Cold Iron at all.

In a moment, he had identified the problem. As the bright red car rounded the far turn, he corrected it with a brief surge of magical energies. He pulled his mind out of the engine and looked up as the car roared by the pits.

Bob was smiling as he pushed his own cap onto the back of his head.

"What was it?" the scrawny mechanic asked, running a hand over his sandy hair before replacing the cap.

"Not the cylinder at all," Al replied. "Piston arm."

"Ah." Bob relaxed still further. It hadn't been a failure of the block, and so he was content. Bob's design had been the one used as a prototype for this block, and he took design flaws personally.

Now I'll get some conversation out of him. . . . Al waited, and Bob remained happily silent, contemplating the track with a smile instead of a frown.

Al burst out laughing, and Bob favored him with a puzzled stare. "You're incredible!" he chuckled. "Anyone else would have been throttling me to find out *what* the problem was and *how* I fixed it, when you know damn good and well the arm's steel and you know we don't handle Cold Iron happily *or* well. But you, you just *stand* there, and say 'ah.'"

"You'd tell me when you got ready to," Bob replied, unbending just enough to give Al a "man, you're crazy" look.

Al shook his head. He was far too used to the volatile temperaments of his hot-blooded Southern compatriots. *Any mech from the Carolinas would have been foaming at the mouth by now and describing my parentage in terms my*

mother would take extreme exception to. Not Bob. Not even
close. This cold fish from the rocky coast of Maine was
just as icy as the elven Nordic-derived "cousins" who'd
settled there. About the only thing that got Bob's goat
around here was the area itself: landscape and the climate.
Al thought the rolling hills were marvelous—and the heat
was a nice change from the mountainous country of home.
Occasionally the residual magic left over from the times
when the Indians flourished here came in handy. Though—
in fairness, he wouldn't want to *live* here for very long, even
if it was a nice change.

Not Bob. He couldn't wait to get back to "where I don't
bake and I don't have to look at so much damned sky."

" ' 'E's pinin' for the fjords,' " he muttered.

"Eh?" said Bob.

"Never mind. I was just thinking you're a lot like the
liosalfar that fostered you."

"Ah," said Bob, his icy gray eyes softening a great deal.
"Good people, your cousins."

Al sighed. *Another typical understatement.* At the tender age of eight, "Bobby" had been rescued by one of the
alfar from freezing to death in a blizzard. He had been
running away from a father who had nearly beaten him
black for failing to come *immediately* when called. It
wasn't the first time a beating had occurred, but it was
the last.

Acting on a tip from a human, Gundar, Bobby's foster
father to be, had put the house under snowy owl surveillance for several weeks, waiting, at times in agony, for the
right moment to intervene. The beatings had become more
severe with time, coinciding with an increased consump-
tion of straight bourbon whiskey, chased with cheap grocery store beer. Even at that age, little Bobby could see
the correlation between Daddy's "joy juice" and being
beaten; when Father was on a roaring drunk, Bobby made
himself scarce, which further angered the old man.

Granted, the father had been under a severe strain; the
fish cannery, which was the town's sole employer, had just
closed. Daddy must have suspected something going wrong
with the company long before that, for the start of the
layoffs had been when the drinking started as well.

Ultimately, though, Bobby neither knew the reasons nor cared about them. All he knew was that Dad was drinking, became a frightening, crazy man when he drank, and Mother was just as afraid of him as Bobby was.

In the end she stopped trying to protect him, instead fleeing for the shelter of her mother's house when Bobby's father became "turned on." That meant leaving Bobby alone with him, but perhaps she had trusted in the frail hope her husband wouldn't hurt his own child.

The end came on a bitter December night, when Joe Ferrel was at the end of his unemployment benefits, the cannery closed for good, and at the end of the month they'd be out of a home as well when the bank foreclosed on the mortgage—

But that's no excuse to half-kill your son, Al thought angrily, his blood still running hot at the memory, as would the blood of any of the Fair Folk at the idea of mistreating a child. *Good thing we got him out of there when we did. After the foreclosure, there was no telling what would have happened. . . . "Bobby" probably wouldn't have lived through it. How can they act like that? Treating their own offspring like possessions to be used and discarded at their pleasure—*

He forced himself to calm down; most humans loved their children, treated them as any elven parent would. And for those that didn't—well, there were other possibilities, not all within human society.

Like what had happened to Bob. Bob was grown up now, and safe—*had* been safe the moment Gundar found him. The situation had been perfect for a changeling-swap: take the boy and leave a lifeless, frozen simulacrum in his place. Easily done, and the exchange left no traces in the human world, for why run a tissue analysis on a frozen corpse when it was *obvious* why the "boy" had died?

And Bob found a new home with those who loved and cherished children, even those not of their species. A home where the rules were strict, but never arbitrary, and punishment was never meted out in anger. A place where intelligence was encouraged to flower, and where his childish delight in mechanical things was fostered, nurtured and educated, even if the *liosalfar* were sometimes baffled by the direction it took. Clockwork and fine metal-work they understood—but *cars?*

Still, he was given free rein, though he had been asked to keep his engines of Cold Iron somewhere where they wouldn't cause disruption to fields of magic, and physical pain to his foster relatives.

So things had continued, until as a young man, he eventually got a real job in the human world—for no human could live forever in the elven enclaves. Even Tam Lin had known that. The job had been at a human-owned garage whose proprietor knew about the *liosalfar* and approved of them, an American Indian of full Mohawk blood that considered them just another kind of forest spirit. Soon, thanks to native ability and understanding of physics and mechanics gained from his foster-kin, Bob became the resident automotive wizard.

Things might have rested there, but for Henry Winterhawk. He *could* have kept Bob ignorant of the existence of SERRA and reaped the benefits of having that kind of genius at his disposal. Instead, he asked Bob to bring his foster father in for a conference about his future.

Gundar knew all about SERRA, of course, but he had simply never thought of it as a place where Bob could fully realize his abilities. Winterhawk had been a little surprised that the elves knew about the organization, though—*he'd* thought the magic being practiced down there was entirely human in origin.

I wish I'd seen both their faces, Al thought with amusement. *The Great Stone Face meets Glacier-Cliff, and both of them crack with surprise. Must have been a sight.*

So now Bob was with the Fayetteville shop, and was helping Al baby-sit the first aluminum-block mage-built engine to go into entirely human hands, hands ignorant of its true origin. Keeping the secret under wraps had been a job in itself; more than once Bob had showed ingenuity in the area of creative deception.

Even if you had to pry conversation out of him with a forklift.

"Don't you ever ask questions?" the Sidhe asked, perplexed. "Not about cars, I mean, about us—*my* foster kids have been eaten up with questions every time they've run into a different group of the Folk."

Bob thawed a little more, and some of his true age of twenty showed through. "You don't mind? Gundar said not to be a pain in the ass, but you people are a *lot* different from the *alfar*."

Al laughed aloud. "Hell, no, I don't mind. Not even close. In Outremer we're Scottish Celts, for the most part, both the human fosterlings and us, and you should know the Scots—if you won't tell us something on your own, we'll find it out. That's why Scots make such good engineers. I'm used to it. Ask away."

"How did you people ever get involved with racing?" Bob asked. "I know about the Flight; Gundar told me about that—but it seems damned weird to me for you people to leave Europe because of Cold Iron everywhere, then turn around and start racing and building cars."

Alinor chuckled. "Two reasons, really. First, we've *always* measured ourselves against you. I—don't suppose you've studied old ballads and stories, have you?"

Bob shook his head.

"Well if you had, you'd find a lot of them with the same theme—the elf-knight challenges a human to a duel, either of wits or of swords, the fight goes on for quite some time, the human wins and carries off some sort of prize. Usually gold, sometimes a lover." *Lost and won a few of those myself, before I got tired of the Game.* "We did that quite a bit, although needless to say, the times when the human *lost* were never recorded in ballads." Al eased the bill of his cap up with his thumb and gave Bob an ironic look over the rim of his sunglasses.

Bob smiled wryly. "What happened when the human lost?"

"Depends on what he—or she, believe it or not—looked like, what skills they had. Usually they had to serve us a year and a day, human-time. Some of the knightly types with big egos and small brains we taught a little humility to, making them act as servants. Generally we had them get us things we needed, news, new fashions—or we had them find the kids that were being mistreated and tell us who they were."

Bob's eyes brightened. "Then what?"

Al shrugged. "Depended on the circumstance. Worst case I ever heard of was a little German town with a real high birthrate. They'd had a witch-scare and killed off all the cats, so the rats had gotten so bad they started biting the kids in the cradles. We stepped in, then, and we got rid of the vermin. But that meant the Black Death missed them entirely."

"So?" Bob said. "Sounds like a good thing to me—"

"It would have been, except that they exported dyed and woven wool, worked silver and other metals, wine—luxury goods. But after the Death, there weren't as many people around to buy their exports. Prices dropped. Food was more expensive, without serfs to till the land. Things got bad. Half the youngsters in the place went around with welts and bruises."

"That sounds familiar—" Bob ventured.

Al snorted. *It should. It's even survived into this day and age.* "Place called Hammerlein. Hamlin, to the English."

Bob shot him a glance that said quite clearly that he thought Al was pulling his leg. Al shrugged. "Ask Gundar. His German cousin was the Piper. We ended up with so many fosterlings we had to spread them out over a dozen Underhill kingdoms."

"Sonuvabitch," Bob said thoughtfully. "Say, when you Folk went up against humans in combat—wasn't that a little one-sided?"

"We did have a bit of an edge where armor and practice was concerned," Al admitted. "But when it came to a duel of swords, humans had an edge too, in that *they* were fighting with Cold Iron." Al smiled reminiscently. *I can still remember the thrill of evading an edge by the width of a hair. . . .* "Put a kind of savor to it, coming that close to the Death Metal. Well, dueling and challenging people at crossroads went out of fashion for the humans, partially because knights were like Porsches—expensive to maintain."

Bob laughed. "Eyah. You don't risk a Porsche in a back-country county-fair drag-race."

Al nodded. "That was when some of us moved. For a while we played at other things, but the Church was making it hard for us to stay hidden, and it just wasn't the same—and besides, there was more Cold Iron around with every passing year. So, in the end, almost all of us moved."

"The Flight." Bob cocked his head to one side and wiped a trickle of sweat from his neck. "Then what?"

"We 'rusticated,' as my father is fond of saying." Al sighed. In many ways, those days had been halcyon, if a little boring now and again. "Then the Europeans followed us across the sea, and rather than compete with them, we went into seclusion, at least on the East Coast. Found places we weren't likely to be bothered. Eventually we set about recreating the Courts in the wilderness." He looked out over the heat-hazed countryside. "For a long time, this was enough of a challenge. It was like starting over, and for the Indians that lived out here already, well, we fit right into their beliefs. No problem. Before the horses came up from Mexico, our elvensteeds would counterfeit deer, bear, or anything else big enough to carry us; it didn't matter that deer and bear *wouldn't* take riders. After all, we were spirits, and our spirit-animal-brothers would do things no ordinary animal would do. For some reason, perhaps that they were closer to natural power than any white man we knew in Europe, picking fights with them just wasn't any fun. It didn't feel right. So we cohabitated, in harmony, for a couple centuries."

Bob gazed at him thoughtfully. Though the human didn't say anything, Al knew the keen mind was absorbing everything he said. The young man was quite interested—probably because he'd only heard the *alfar* side of the story. The Nordic elves never moved from their chosen homes; instead, they had created places where humans passed through without noticing where they were—places that weren't quite in the "real" world, but weren't quite Underhill either.

"Then the Europeans caught up with us. At first we sympathized with them, these settlers who were trying to make homes with next to nothing, and certainly no *magic*, in the wilderness. We had done it ourselves, so we knew it wasn't easy. But with them came Cold Iron, so we had to keep our distance from them. When their settlements came too close to our groves, we played tricks on them, appearing to them as demons in order to frighten them away."

Al saw the hint of what might be the edge of a wry grin of amusement. Like a shadow drowned with sudden light, the hint of a smile faded, replaced with Bob's familiar unreadable expression.

"For a while that kept us entertained. Until they started throwing knives and shooting at us . . . which put an end to *that* silliness. Especially since a lot of their weapons used steel shot as well as lead."

"I can see that," Bob commented. "I'd say Cold Iron in that form would ruin any elf's day—and you people aren't immune to a lead bullet if it's placed right."

Al nodded. "All we could do then was avoid all humans. The Indians were slaughtered, absorbed into the white population, or relocated, so we lost our allies there. As more humans invaded the areas we once inhabited, those Low Court elves unfortunate enough to have located their groves near human cities had serious trouble. The rest of us transported our magic nexuses and Low Court cousins to places even the humans wouldn't want. Isolation, and seclusion, became necessary for us once again. And, once again, we were *bored* silly."

"Bored?" Bob said. "Eyah, I can see that. Live long enough, you do about everything there is to do."

"A hundred times. And get almighty tired of the same faces," Al agreed. "Now the story gets local, though. A few human lifetimes after that, we started seeing those new-fangled horseless carriages around Outremer. And people were *challenging* each other with them." He sighed, remembering his very first look at a moonshiner-turned-race-car, the excitement he'd felt. "Well, what they were doing—races along deserted country roads or on home-made tracks—that was just like the old challenge-at-the-crossroad game, only better, because it was not only involving the skill and wits of the *driver*, it involved the skill and wits of the craftsman. There's only so much you can do to improve armor past a point of refinement, but an *engine*—now, there's another story."

Bob's attention wandered for a moment as their car

roared past, then came back to Al. "So your lot began racing? Fairgrove, Outremer, Sunrising, that bunch?"

Al nodded. "I was all for it from the beginning; I was a smith, and I hadn't had anything to do but make pretty toys for, oh, a couple of centuries. Some of the rest wanted to use elvensteeds shape-changed, but the fighters really squashed that idea."

"Wouldn't be fair," Bob said emphatically. "Elvensteed damn near breaks Mach one if it's streamlined enough."

"Exactly. We wanted a challenge, not a diversion. So, we started making copies of cars from materials we *could* handle, learning by trial and error how to strengthen them, and copying *your* technology when it got ahead of ours." Al sent a probe toward the car, but the engine was behaving itself, and he withdrew in satisfaction.

"You wouldn't have dared let people get too close, early on, though," Bob observed. "One look under the hood, and you'd have blown it. So that's why you stuck to club racing?"

Al nodded, with a little regret. "We still don't dare take too much out of the club." He sighed. "Much as I'd love to pit the Fayetteville crews against the Elliot team, or the Unser or Andretti families, or—well, you've got the picture. Best we can do, Bob, is send you fosterlings out there and take our triumphs vicariously."

"You're here," Bob pointed out.

"I'm one of a few that can be out here," he said soberly. "Lots of the Folk can't even be around the amount of iron that's at the Fairgrove complex, much less what's in the real world. I can, though it's actually easier to handle Cold Iron magically when it's heated. That's why I try and do my modifications while the car's running. Cold Iron poisons us, but like any poison, you can build up a tolerance to it, if you work at it. I worked at it. I still have to wear gloves, and it still gives me feedback through my magic to have to 'touch' it, though. And I'd have third-degree burns if I handled it bare-skinned."

Al held up his gloved hands; the Firestone crew thought he had a petroleum allergy. That was a useful concept, since it would explain away blisters if he accidentally came into contact with the Death Metal.

"We could get only so close to the real cars in the

beginning," he added. "When the manufacturers began using alternative materials—like fiberglass bodies, carbon fiber, aluminum parts—it became that much easier. Some humans despise the concept of the 'plastic car.' We've been encouraging it for decades!"

"Eyah," Bob said, laconically. "Never could stand disposable cars myself. I always thought a car should last at least twenty-five years. The next time I see a plastic car I'll think differently of it."

Al gloated a little over the "triumph" of getting Bob to speak, with a certain wry irony. *That was actually a stimulating conversation.*

But the respite was brief. The spark of conversation dimmed, and their attentions turned to the track, the team—the unrelenting heat, the hammer of the sun, the fatigue setting over even the best-rested of them. Weariness began to settle in around him again, this time with a vengeance. *How many laps were they going to pull in that car today?* he thought, now with some irritability. *The RV sounds mighty inviting right now.*

He smiled a little at the idea of a Sidhe regarding such a vehicle as a *shelter.* He recalled the time he told Gundar about the RV, the human-made Winnie that was sheathed with the Death Metal. It took some convincing before Gundar finally believed one of the Folk could live in such a thing; Al's friend had yet to build up a tolerance to Cold Iron and shied away.

Al sat down on a stack of chalkmarked tires, a few feet away from Bob. He needed to keep his distance—not from Bob, but from the rest of the team. The Folk had a high degree of sensitivity to energies not usually discernible by humans. Since Al worked closely with humans, his shields had to be much, much better than any of the Folk who never ventured out of Underhill. He had learned when a youngster that he was unusually sensitive to human emotions. His shields had required some specialized engineering to filter out the more intense or negative feelings generated by many humans in order to be able to work around them. Even Bob had caused him a few problems. He didn't have to think about the shields much anymore; the whole process of maintaining them was pretty much second-nature. The only time he remembered the network was there was when an intense emotion somehow managed to breach it.

Like—now.

Now what? Al thought, becoming aware of a nagging feeling of someone in distress, somewhere outside his shields. He reached inside his overalls and withdrew a small package of Keeblers and starting munching absently, his thoughts drifting beyond his immediate world, seeking the source of emotion. The cookie things helped him concentrate, though he wasn't sure why. Maybe it was all the sugar.

He bit the head off an annoyingly cheerful vanilla figure and considered: *Something strong enough to leak through my defenses must be hot stuff. Where is it coming from?* He glanced over at Bob, who was apparently studying an interesting oil stain on the track.

No. It's not him.

Focusing on a broader area, Alinor *reached*, touching the members of the immediate crew. Their emotions paralleled the way he was feeling right now: exhaustion and the heartfelt desire to start stacking a few Z's, coupled with a subtle anxiety over their delicate, powerful creation hurtling its human driver around the track. That wasn't what he wanted. Nothing they were feeling would be strong enough to penetrate the shields.

Too low level. Boy, someone is really hurting *out there. Where is he? Or . . . she?*

Now Al felt a definite female flavor to the emotion, though it was overwhelmed by sheer asexual anxiety. *Ah. A clue. That should narrow the field.* He knew it was barely possible this meant there was some danger at the track, perhaps even a serious problem with one of the cars.

There's always worry, but this is close to hysteria, and we don't need that right now, he thought, regarding the other racing teams around him. There didn't seem to be anything urgent going on, though some of the teams were noticeably restless, probably from being out here for so long.

Don't blame them, Al thought, his search distracted for a moment. *I'm ready to go in, too.*

Although the world of racing remained male-dominated

even to this day, a fair number of women were on the teams. But none of *them* were particularly upset about anything.

Wives? The few who came to the competition at Hallet were not around today. During test lap days there just weren't that many spectators, either local natives or those cheering the teams.

Odd. He thought. *Maybe I'm looking in the wrong place. Who said the source had to be on the track?* A barbed wire fence surrounded the entire track, forming a feeble barrier between Hallet and the surrounding Oklahoma territory. Immediately behind them, about a quarter of a mile away, was an ancient homestead, little more refined than a log cabin, that appeared to be as old as the proverbial hills. *There, perhaps?* Intrigued, Al reached toward it, diverting his dwindling supply of energy towards the house. Immediately his senses were assaulted by—

A bedroom overflowing with fevered physical activity— brass bedposts pounding like jackhammers against slatted- wood walls pitted and dented by repeated sessions in the warm afternoons and evenings. . . .

Alinor staggered mentally backward as he recoiled from the emotional violence he had inadvertently witnessed, the steamy interplay in the farmer's bedroom. *Whoops! Lots of intense emotion there, but not quite the kind I was looking for.* He felt as if he had been drenched in a scalding shower, and put up every shield he had to protect himself for a moment.

Bob made no comment.

By degrees his mind gradually recovered from the thorough scorching it had received, and in about fifteen minutes Alinor was able to gather energies around him again, retrieving his scattered pieces of empathy from around the track.

He pulled his act together, took a deep breath and probed again. He sent his thoughts out over a wide area, hoping to pick up the source this way, a method that had proven effective before. The lethargic feelings of the pit crew were again a distraction, especially since they so nearly mirrored his own. *Echo effect*, he thought, shaking his head.

Tends to block what I'm really looking for. Maybe if I got some rest, came after this with a fresh set of eyes . . .

The moment he considered this, a blast of emotion pierced his reassembled shields once again.

This time he was ready for it; on it as soon as it penetrated. Yes, it was definitely from a female. Now he could sense some other things. The woman was a mother. Images, riding the current of the high emotion, overwhelmed him with a deep sense of loss. But not a permanent loss—the kind caused by a death or irrevocable separation. *She must be looking for something*, Al decided, wishing his powers would provide him a clearer picture. *Or someone.*

Then as if a warm, stiff breeze had blown over his mind, the final image came into focus. Al leaped to his feet, now in a fully alert, combat-ready stance, even though there was nothing here to fight.

She's looking for her child. *And she thinks he's in danger.*

CHAPTER TWO

A blistering wind dried the tears burning Cindy Chase's face as she stared at the race cars surging across the black, twisting track. She leaned against a tree in a poor parody of comfort. The oak bark pressed uncomfortably through her blue cotton blouse and into her weary muscles. This tree was the only place she had found that was even remotely cool. Her forearms, normally not exposed to the sun, were pink, probably burned worse than they looked. This served only to make her more miserable. It had never seemed this hot in Atlanta.

The heat was only one component of her misery. She'd have gladly traded her long, well-worn jeans for a pair of shorts. *Maybe even a miniskirt*, she thought in an attempt to cheer herself. *Then maybe the men would pay a little more attention than they have been*. She had never felt so totally worthless in all her life.

She'd had less than "no" luck since she'd entered the gates of Hallet raceway. Everything she'd tried had come out wrong. It seemed like the people she'd spoken with thought she was asking them for money, not help. Then again, in her rumpled clothing, washed and never ironed, and not her best, she probably looked like a homeless panhandler, or even a drunk. She had never lived out of a suitcase before and had never realized how difficult that could be. For too long she'd taken for granted things like a fully stocked bathroom, an ironing board, walk-in closets filled with clean clothes . . .

. . . and a family.

Cindy hadn't seen her reflection in a few hours, which was just as well. She knew she probably looked like hell. Her makeup had long ago melted in the heat—if she hadn't washed it away with crying.

Maybe I should go back to the car, she thought dismally, trying not to look at the little color snapshot of her son, Jamie, she clutched in her hand. *Nobody here wants to help me. Nobody cares, and they don't even look surprised! It's like little eight-year-old boys disappear all the time in Oklahoma.* She wasn't normally a vengeful person, but she couldn't help wishing some of these snots would get a taste of what it was like to have a child kidnaped by an ex-spouse and dragged halfway across the country.

Reluctantly, her eyes were drawn to the picture. The lower right-hand corner was wearing away where she had been holding it constantly for the past week. The other corners were folded and fraying. For a week a thousand pairs of eyes had stared at this picture, with varying degrees of interest, or more often, disinterest. A thousand minds had searched memories for a few moments. One by one, they had sadly—or indifferently—shaken their heads: *No, I haven't seen him. Is he your son? Have you tried the police? Are you sure he didn't just wander off?* It was as if they were all thinking: *Daddies don't kidnap their own children. It just doesn't happen. It's just too horrible to imagine.* She wanted to strangle them all.

Yes, I know. Daddies aren't supposed to kidnap their children, take them across the state line, and hide them from their mothers.

But sometimes, they do.

She had carefully mopped up a tear that had splashed on the picture, leaving behind a barely noticeable spot on the photograph's surface. It was a school portrait taken a year before at Morgan Woods Elementary, when Jamie's hair had been much shorter and their lives were much different; normal, almost. *Before his father joined the cult, anyway. The Chosen Ones. Chosen for what?*

Staring from the picture, Jamie's eyes locked on to hers,

pleading, and she knew that she wouldn't be leaving the track just then. She had to keep looking now, on this broiling racetrack, just a little bit longer. As long as there were people to ask on this planet, she'd continue the search.

Oh, Jamie, damn it, she thought, crying inside. *Why did your daddy do this to us?*

A car roared past on the track, jolting her from the quicksand of self-pity she was suffocating herself with. The race reminded her why she had come to this place to look for her son. *In Georgia we used to come to places like these, a racetrack, any racetrack, no matter how small. He loved them all, unknown or famous. It didn't matter if it was paved, or a dirt track where they banged into each other until only one was left running.*

James, senior, had been burdened with many addictions, the one most harmless being race cars. Every weekend, no matter what the weather was like, he would trudge to the races with family in tow; Jamie, too, seemed to have inherited his father's obsession. Cindy had resented the incessant trips to the races, the constant shouting over the engines, the near incoherent babble of car techese he shared with his son. "Car racing is a *science*," he had said, over and over, in the face of her too-obvious disinterest. "And a racer is a *scientist*."

"So was Dr. Jekyll," Cindy had retorted, failing then to see the eerie foreshadowing of her words. Though at the time she grew weary of the races, she now dreamed of those days and the unity of their family then. *It was a family Donna Reed would have been jealous of. At least that was what I thought. I never looked under the surface of things, never asked questions; just mopped the floors and made the beds and kept everyone fed and happy,* she thought miserably. *And it was all a lie. I'll be lucky if I ever find my son.*

She'd seen signs of danger, but she was hard-pressed to remember when exactly they had begun. James' drinking, for instance, had increased so gradually that she hadn't even noticed it.

Or, she realized in retrospect, she had chosen *not* to notice.

Then had come the mysterious "bowling tournaments" that took all night, from which James would return with a crazed expression—and a strong odor of Wild Turkey—babbling about bizarre, mystical stuff, a combination of Holy Roller and New Age crystal-crunching. At first she thought the obvious: that he was seeing another woman. Which didn't explain his *increased* sex drive, something he would demonstrate immediately on his return.

That was when she realized something was wrong, but didn't want to admit it. In the beginning she was more afraid of what was going on with him than angry—afraid of the unknown.

The man who James became was not remotely like the man she had married. His behavior just didn't fit into any of her reality scenarios. It was all just too *weird* to understand. The strange books he wouldn't let her see, the things he rattled on about when he came home drunk—it didn't fit any pattern she was familiar with, nothing she'd seen on Sally or Oprah, either.

She gave up on her friends and neighbors when they all carried on about what a good provider James was, and how she should be grateful and turn a blind eye to his "little failings." "Women endure," said her nearest neighbor, who looked like a fifties TV-Mom in apron, pearl earrings and page-boy haircut. "That's what we're put on earth to do."

As things worsened, she lived one day at a time and tried not to think at all. Her son saw that his daddy was not acting normally. She kept thinking it was a phase, like the model-building phase, or the comic-collecting phase. He'd get tired of it and go back to cars, like he always did.

Then came the call from his employer, the owner of an auto parts franchise. James had worked for him as parts counter manager for ten years. That counter had been their version of a wishing well—it was the place where they had met. She had been buying wiper blades, and he'd shown her how to put them on. Fred Hammond, his boss, was calling to see if James had recovered from the surgery, and if so when he would return to work. The place was a shambles; he was sorely missed there.

She had no idea what he was talking about.

Fred explained, in a somewhat mystified tone, that James

had taken a leave of absence from his job to go into the hospital for "serious surgery" of an unknown nature. Fred had gone to the hospital the day after the surgery was supposed to take place and, when checking with the information desk, found no record of James' stay, even under every imaginable spelling of "James Chase."

But Cindy knew that James had gotten up at the usual time and, wearing the store's uniform, supposedly went off to work in the pickup. Cindy apologized and said she couldn't imagine what was going on, but she would have him call as soon as possible. She hung up and stared at the telephone for a long, long time.

She remembered that day vividly, and she would always call it "That Day." It was the day her life changed, irrevocably. During a single moment of "That Day" the thin, tenuous walls of denial had crumbled like tissue. It was the day she realized that her husband had gone completely insane. Jamie was in the backyard when his father returned that night, and for a desperate second she considered sending him to a friend's house in anticipation of a major fight. She decided not to. *I don't know that anything is wrong*, she thought, clinging to the last, disappearing threads of hope. *It could be something like in a movie, could just be a mistake, a misunderstanding. Maybe it was even a crank call. . . .*

He had pulled into the garage, as usual, and he came into the kitchen still wearing the uniform shirt with "James" embroidered over the left pocket. He even complained about what a bad day he'd had at the store, something about an inventory of spark plugs that just didn't jive.

She quickly pulled herself together and gently, like a mother, put her hands on his shoulders and kissed him, once. Her expression must have been strained, she would later think, since a cloud of suspicion darkened his face. He also smelled, no, *stank*, of alcohol, though his motions didn't betray intoxication. He fixed her with a raised eyebrow as Cindy blurted out, "I got a call from your boss today."

"Oh?" he said nonchalantly, as he reached for a beer in the fridge. "What did he want?"

Damn you, James, she thought violently. *You're going*

to make this as difficult as possible, aren't you? "He wanted to know how the surgery went." She stepped closer, trying to be confrontational, knowing that she was failing. "Actually, I would too. What is he talking about, Jim?"

He said nothing as he started for the dining nook, paused, and retrieved another beer before planting himself firmly in his usual spot at the kitchen table. Timidly, Cindy sat next to him, touching his arm. He pulled away, as if her hand were something distasteful. They sat in silence for several moments, enough time for James to take a few long pulls of beer, as if to bolster his courage.

"I've found the glory of God," he said, and belched at a volume only beer could produce.

"I see," Cindy had replied, though she really didn't. "I thought you were an atheist."

"Not anymore," he said, taking another long drink. "I've seen the light, and the wisdom, of our leader. I haven't been at the store, in, oh, two, three weeks."

"Just like that," she said, starting to get angry. " 'I haven't been to the store.' " She couldn't believe it. "So what am I supposed to do now, throw a party? You haven't been to work and that's okay. Am I hearing this right?"

A serene, smug expression creased the intoxicated features. "I didn't say I haven't been going to work. I have been blessed with new work. I work for God now, and we will be provided for."

As if punctuating the sentence, he crumpled the empty can into a little ball, as if it were paper, and expertly tossed it into the kitchen trash, which was overflowing with the crushed cans. Cindy remembered thinking that he crushed his cans like that so that he wouldn't have to empty the trash so often.

Outside, Jamie had climbed into his treehouse, taking potshots at imaginary soldiers with his plastic rifle.

"Come with me tonight," Jim had said suddenly. She jumped at the suddenness and the fierce intensity of his words. He gripped her arm, hard, until it hurt. "Come and meet Brother Joseph at the Praise Meeting tonight. Please. You'll understand everything, then."

Reluctantly, she had nodded. Then she got up and began preparing dinner for that night.

"Jamie is coming, too," he amended. She had wanted to object then, but saw no way she could get a baby-sitter on such short notice.

"Okay, Jim," she'd said, pulling a strainer down out of the cabinet. "Whatever you say."

For now, she had thought to herself. *Until I get a handle on this insanity. Then watch out.*

Now she regretted not paying more attention to the particular brand of psychosis preached that night by Brother Joseph, the leader of the Sacred Heart of the Chosen Ones. Jamie stayed close to her the entire time, apparently sensing something wrong with the situation. They drove for hours, it seemed, far out into the country. James again said little, commenting only on this or that along the road, chewing on his own teeth, biding time. As they came closer to the place of the Praise Meeting, Jim became less talkative. A fog thicker than the alcohol had descended on him, and he stared blankly ahead. Cindy wondered if he wasn't insane but just *brainwashed*, like in a TV movie. That was something that could be reversed, she hoped, and the more she thought about it, the more the brainwashing theory began to make sense. But it made her even more afraid of what was to come; she wished then that she hadn't allowed Jamie along.

The little boy had inched closer to his mother in the front seat of the pickup truck. They had turned onto a dirt road and were immediately confronted by two armed men blocking their way. They were wearing berets and camouflage fatigues; their white t-shirts had a heart pierced by two crucifixes, with some slogan in Latin she couldn't translate. Even with the berets, she could tell they had been shaved bald. They brandished AK-47 machine guns; she knew about the guns from a Clint Eastwood movie she'd seen about the Grenada invasion. The weapon had a distinctive look; banana clips curled from under the stocks. Jim stopped briefly as the men shone blinding flashlights into the truck and quickly inspected the bed, which was empty. With maybe half a dozen words exchanged, the guards had waved them through.

"Those were machine guns, Jim," she'd observed, trying

to sound casual and not betray the cold fear that had been clenching her stomach. "Are they legal in this state?"

"You're in God's state now."

Jim said nothing more as they drove on.

Cindy had closed her eyes, wondering what the blazes she was getting into.

Finally the truck slowed, and she had opened her eyes. Ahead of them, at the top of a hill, she'd seen a huge mansion, fully lit, with rows of cars and trucks, mostly pickups, parked in front. More men in berets directed them with metal flashlights the size of baseball bats, and one led them to a parking spot. When they got out, Cindy noticed a .45 automatic holstered at his side.

"Brother Jim! Praise the Lord! You've brought your family into the blessing of the Heart, God bless," the soldier had greeted, slapping Jim hard on his back. Jim mumbled something Cindy couldn't hear, but whatever it was the clownlike grin on the man's face didn't waver.

"Momma, I don't want to go," Jamie'd said plaintively, pulling back, lagging behind. "They got guns, Momma, ever'where. They're *real* guns, aren't they?"

"It's all right, hon," Cindy'd said, knowing it was a lie. It felt like she was pulling the words out with pliers, and all the time she had been thinking, *Please God or whatever you are, let us get through this nonsense intact!*

The main sitting room of the huge mansion had been converted into a churchlike sanctuary. Cigarette smoke hung heavily in the air, amid a low rumble of voices. Jim had led them to some empty metal folding chairs on the end of a row, near a wall. There were hundreds of people there; as she glanced around at those nearest, she found an amazing number of them to be normal country folk, many of them elderly couples. Towards the front of the assembly there was an entire section of middle-class yuppies, some drinking designer-bottled spring water. And over to the side she saw what looked like homeless people, dirty, grubby, lugging ragged backpacks. Drinking out of paper bags. Salt of the Earth.

This guy has all kinds, Cindy remembered thinking, as they awkwardly made their way to the end of the row. *What is it about him that could make him so appealing*

*to these people? These transients over here, they probably
have nowhere else to go. But those guys, up in the front.
They look like they just walked off Wall Street. What
gives?*

More soldiers stood at attention here, thin, lean men
in berets, bald like the guards at the gate. Spaced from
each other like stone carvings, about twelve feet apart, they
watched those around them with their hands behind their
backs. Solemn. Unyielding. At the end of their row was a
young man, about eighteen, who still had his short, blond
hair. He looked like he had been pumping iron since he
was eight. Tattooed clumsily on his forearm was a crooked
swastika, the kind of artwork kids did to themselves out
of boredom, with needles and ball pen ink. He gazed
forward icily, solidly, as if cast in steel, looking like he hadn't
blinked in a year.

I don't like this. I don't like this at all, Cindy had
thought, holding Jamie closer. *And it hasn't even started.
This has been one big mistake. I can handle this madness
myself, but I should never have brought Jamie into this
nest of snakes!*

"James," she'd whispered urgently, tugging at his arm.
"I want to leave. Right now! These people are *crazy!*"

"Just relax," Jim had said, yawning. "It will be so much
better if you just relax. You haven't even heard what you
came to hear. It really does fall into place. It becomes very
clear, once you hear Brother Joseph speak."

At some point during her husband's little rote speech
her eyes fell on the stage, and the large emblem on the
wall behind it, lit from beneath by candlelight. It was a
heart pierced by two crucifixes, the same symbol worn on
the shirts of the soldiers around them, and was like no
church decoration she had ever seen. It had looked like
the kind of "art" that was airbrushed on black velvet and
sold at flea markets. Totally tacky.

A hush fell on the crowd and the lights dimmed, ever
so subtly. Large, silver collection plates the size of hub-
caps were passed around, supervised by the armed men
in berets. When one came their way James dropped a crisp,
new one hundred dollar bill into the till—one among the
dozens there already.

"Jim! What are you *doing*?" she'd gasped, when she saw the money drop. The plate had already passed her, she had realized in frustration, or she would have surreptitiously salvaged it as it went past. Jim said nothing, smiling blandly as the plate continued down the row. People were dropping large bills, multiple bills, watches, jewelry; she watched, stupefied, as the wealth amassed. She sat back in the creaking metal chair and folded her arms, in a mild state of shock. *We don't have that kind of money to give to a bunch of lunatics! Have they drugged him, or is he just suddenly retarded?*

"Only tithing members of the Sacred Heart will be saved. Is this your first meeting?" an elderly woman behind her had asked. Cindy made a point of ignoring her, and the woman sniffed loudly in rebuttal.

"Touchy, isn't she?" the women said behind her.

James laughed in a goofy snort. At what, Cindy had no idea.

Beside her, Jamie whimpered. "Momma, I want to go home," he said. "This place feels icky."

"It feels icky to me, too," she'd whispered in his right ear. "It will be over with soon."

"Hey, what's wrong, buckaroo?" the blond kid said, kneeling down next to Jamie. "This your first time here?"

It's his first and his last, she wanted to scream, but as the boy kneeled down, she noticed the assault rifle strapped to his back. She didn't want to argue with firearms. Jamie's sudden receptiveness to the boy didn't help either. Her son traced a figure eight over the crude swastika on the boy's forearm, apparently fascinated by it.

"It doesn't come off," Jamie said. "What is it?"

"It's a tattoo," the boy said, sounding friendly in spite of the weird trappings. "And it's our salvation." He looked up, meeting Cindy's stare with his soft, blue eyes, a disarming expression that somehow took the edge off the evil she was beginning to feel from him. He smiled at Cindy boyishly, and from his back pocket he pulled out a Tootsie Pop and gave it to Jamie, who attacked and devoured it hungrily. *He's almost normal—at least on the surface. But he has Nazi crosses tattooed on his arm and calls them "salvation." A boy Jamie could look like someday,* she thought, in agony. *Why did I have to bring him to this godawful place!*

The lights dimmed further, and from somewhere appeared the minister of the church. *Brother Joseph, didn't Jim say?* No less than four armed soldiers escorted him to the podium, knelt, and when Brother Joseph dismissed them, took their places at the four corners of the stage, glaring at the audience. The quiet was absolute. Brother Joseph had peered into the audience, his burning eyes sweeping the crowd like the twin mouths of a double-barreled shotgun. In the utter stillness, his eyes tracked through the different faces and settled on Cindy. He smiled briefly then, and continued his inspection, lord of all he surveyed. Cindy had thought she was going to collapse when their eyes locked.

Jesus! Cindy thought in dismay. *Those eyes.*

He really thinks he's God's own Gift. And my crazy husband believes him.

"Momma," Jamie whispered. "Can I have a tattoo like his when we get home?"

"Shhhhhh!" the woman behind them admonished. "Quiet. Brother Joseph is about to *speak.*"

What happened for the next three hours was a vague blur of hate images, from which she retained little. It wasn't a blackout, or even a full lapse of memory. She retained pieces, fragments, of the "sermon," and she wasn't certain if there was any coherent flow to begin with. Brother Joseph vomited a vile concoction of religion and white male supremacy that would have made a Klansman blush. That was what she remembered, anyway. The topic wavered from fundamentalist Southern Baptist preachings, to New Age channeling, to an extended foray into Neo-Nazism, sprinkled liberally with passages Cindy remembered from high school history class—*Mein Kampf.* The audience sat, enthralled; it wasn't the sermon that scared her so much as the unthinking acceptance of the congregation. Brother Joseph could have said absolutely anything, she suspected, and they would have bought it all without question.

After the sermon Cindy had made it clear to her husband she wasn't *about* to stay around and socialize, she wanted out *now*, and when she reminded Jim that she had her own set of truck keys he finally relented and, not particularly angry at having to leave, drove them home. In silence.

The next day, a Saturday, Cindy tried to broach the subject of his employment and, specifically, his income. James brushed her aside, saying that she would never understand, and asked her if she had any Jewish ancestors. She did, but didn't think it wise to tell him. He went out and spent the rest of the day playing with his son, and acted as if she didn't exist. On Sunday, he left for somewhere he didn't specify and returned late that night, almost too drunk to walk, and fell into bed.

On Monday James continued to live the lie, getting up at six and dutifully donning his uniform. He mentioned the problem with the spark plugs and other things she knew he would never deal with that day, and after he was gone Cindy didn't answer the phone, for fear it was his boss. She sent Jamie off to school, the only normal thing to happen in her life, the only thing that made *sense*.

The next day was the same, and the day after. She paid the bills out of the dwindling bank account, made sure Jamie did his homework, and watched her husband deteriorate. Cindy also began contemplating divorce, but taking the first tentative step towards breaking up, like calling a lawyer, was too terrifying for words. It was easier to live the lie along with her husband and hope they would live happily ever after.

Weeks passed, and James Chase began coming home later and later in the evening. For a while she kept track of the odometer, and going by the miles stacking up on the pickup, determined he was probably going out to that mansion where the "Praise Meeting" was held. If not that, then God only knew where he'd been. Up and on the job for Brother Joseph, every day, driving all over on errands for the church, the Sacred Part of the Frozen Ones or some such nonsense. She began to withdraw herself, never going out except to buy food, and that the absolutely cheapest she could find. She prayed the checks wouldn't bounce after every trip.

Then finally Jim stayed out overnight, then two, then

three nights in a row. Cindy wasn't terribly surprised; what surprised her was that he returned sober once or twice. Sober, yet untalkative. Whatever he was so fervently pursuing during the day, whatever his life had become as a new member of the Sacred Heart of the Chosen Ones, it wasn't his wife's place to know.

She had taken to sleeping in a bit more each day as her frustration built. She got up long enough to send Jamie off to school, then returned to bed. Sleep afforded her one way to escape the craziness the church had conjured.

She went back to answering the phone and talking to the neighbors, trying to hide the pain with makeup and forced smiles. Then one particular morning she answered the phone, after James had left for whatever it was he did during the day. It was Jamie's school; with a start she realized she hadn't seen him off that morning. The principal's secretary wanted to know if everything was all right and reminded Cindy that calling the parents was procedure when a child didn't show up for class. Uncertain why she was covering for him, she explained that he was home ill and that she had simply forgotten to notify the school. She hung up and began running through the house, calling Jamie's name, looking for some clue as to his whereabouts.

Just when she thought she was going to lose her mind she found the note taped on the refrigerator door. It was in James' handwriting and it did ease her mind—for a moment. It simply told her not to worry, that he had taken Jamie with him for the day, though it didn't specify exactly why.

Even though she didn't suspect kidnaping then, the note opened up a Pandora's box of ominous possibilities. But before she could think coherently enough to worry about what might be happening to her son, the phone rang again. The bank was calling to tell her that five checks had bounced, and that both the share and draft accounts had been closed weeks before by James Chase.

She hung up, numb with shock.

She ran for the bedroom. A brief, hysterical inspection showed that no clothes had been taken, at least that she could tell. His shaver, shotgun, a World War II Luger, a Craftsman socket set, were all still in the house, and wouldn't be if James had really left. Not wanting to even think about the notion, she decided that it was too crazy even for James. She spent an anxious day cleaning, releasing nervous energy, venting her frustration. Around noon, she had an anxiety attack, and for ten minutes she couldn't take a breath.

Jamie is with those lunatics, she thought, repeatedly. She finally calmed herself enough to breathe, but she knew she could not go on like this, day after day, wondering what twist her husband's insanity would take *this* time.

Late that afternoon the pickup pulled into the garage, its bumper tapping the back wall hard enough to make an audible *crack*. Cindy heard her son crying. She ran to find Jamie in tears, her husband drunk, and a thousand unanswered questions staring her in the face.

"Oh, Jamie, *Jamie*, what's wrong?" She'd held him, getting no sense out of him. "What *happened*? Did your daddy do something to you? Did Daddy hurt you?"

She looked around furtively to see if Daddy was around and within earshot; inside the kitchen, she heard the hiss of a beer tab.

"No. Wasn't Daddy," Jamie blurted, through the tears. "It was Br . . . Brother Joseph." He sniffled, glancing over her shoulder, apparently looking for James. "*Please*, Mommy, don't let him take me back there ever again!"

She held him closer, forcing back some fear and trembling of her own.

James stayed long enough to finish off the last of the beer and left alone with vague promises to return soon. As soon as he was gone she called a women's shelter and briefly explained her situation. Soon a motherly, older woman arrived to pick them up. At the shelter, a young graduate lawyer eager to log some court experience was waiting for them. He took down the essential information and assured her that she had a good case, and would *probably* get full custody. Cindy had a problem with that word, *probably*, but got on with the business of settling in at the shelter and quizzed Jamie on what exactly had happened at the Chosen Ones' church.

On a bed in a common room they shared with several other women and their children, Jamie sat and tried to tell his mother what had taken place in the church, describing an odd ritual on the stage in the meeting hall, in which he was the central figure. Twice her son tried to tell her what happened, getting to a certain point in the explanation, whereupon he would burst into hysterical sobs.

What happened back there? she wondered, half sick with fear that they had done something truly evil and harmful, emotionally, to her son. Divorce seemed to be the only answer, if she was going to protect her child.

Her uncertainties hardened into resolve. *Never again. That psycho is never coming near my son again!*

She steeled herself for a fight, for some attempt by James to counter her actions—but nothing happened. The court proceedings went smoothly and without incident. There were twenty or thirty other child abuse cases pending against the cult in question, some of which the police were already investigating. The judge expressed the belief that Cindy had tolerated far more than she should have, and if James Chase had bothered to show up for the hearings he would have no doubt received a severe tongue-lashing. During the week preceding the hearing Cindy returned to the house with two large men from the shelter and retrieved a few missed items, and while there she discovered that her husband had apparently left with his clothes, the shotgun, the Luger and the tools. Though the lawyer had papers served to James at the house, it now appeared he had left for good. Taking no chances, and at the strong urging of her companions, veterans of situations like these, she remained at the shelter until after the hearing. With the help of the shelter, she got a part-time job at Burger King. The judge granted Cindy Chase full custody of her son, ownership of the house, and declared their marriage null and void. Finally.

She had thought it was over, that they were safe. That *Jamie* was safe.

Then, on Friday of the fourth week following the divorce, Cindy waited on the porch for Jamie's school-bus. Just like always.

The bus squeaked to a halt, disgorged its screaming passengers, and shuddered away. There was no Jamie.

Cindy rushed inside and called the school. The teachers

told her that Jim had taken him out of class an hour before the end of the day.

Hysterical, she notified the police, but the response was underwhelming. After an hour an officer showed up at the school to take a report. If the school's principal and Jamie's teacher hadn't stayed to comfort her, she would have gone over the edge right there. There wasn't a whole lot they could do, the officer said . . . there were so many missing children, so few personnel, so little budget. She explained that this was *different*, that she *knew* her husband had taken him, there were *witnesses* for crissakes, and the cult was *crazy*, they had to do *something*, right *now* before they . . .

The officer had sadly shaken his head and told her they would do what they could. From his tone, however, it sounded like it wouldn't be much.

From memory Cindy drove to the cult's mansion, where she had been to her first Praise Meeting. She took several wrong turns, but after hours of relentless driving found the huge house. Realty signs in the front lawn declared the property for sale. The house, itself, was empty. Cleaned out.

The police, as she feared, weren't much help. She found herself in the position of thousands of other parents whose ex-spouses had kidnaped their children. Since she couldn't tell them where the cult could have gone, their options were limited. Through the parents of other child abuse victims, she learned that other members of the Chosen Ones had also vanished. Bank accounts and personal property, mostly cars and trucks, went with them. It was clear to Cindy that the cult had staged a mass exodus from Georgia. To where, she had no idea.

The only thing of value that James had left behind was the house. That, Cindy surmised, was only because it was too heavy to take with him. She needed money, lots of it, to search for her son. She double-mortgaged the house and sold everything out of it she could, all of the appliances and Jim's stereo, which miraculously had been left behind. With a certain wry satisfaction she sold her engagement and wedding rings to a pawnshop and used the money in part to pay for the divorce. Robert Weil, "Private Investigator" suggested they first begin by putting Jamie's picture on milk cartons. The Missing Children's advocacy group was very helpful.

The rest of her time and energy she spent keeping herself together. There were any number of times that she could have slipped over the edge and gone totally bonkers, and often she wondered if she had. Occasionally she slept, but most nights she did not. Her employers were sympathetic at first, but as the weeks passed, so did the sympathy. She began receiving warning "talks," suggestions by her male boss that she "pull herself together" and "let the professionals handle it." She sensed an unspoken feeling that her boss felt she was to blame for the entire mess. . . .

Robert Weil, "Private Investigator," turned out to be next to worthless to her search. He just wasn't *doing* anything, so she fired him. Then the leads began to trickle in from the Center for Missing and Exploited Children, information that was the direct result of the milk carton photographs. From Atlanta they began to track him west, from three different sightings a day apart. She stocked up the Celica with what she could from the house, quit her job (just before they were about to fire her, she suspected), and left, taking up the trail herself.

The money disappeared quickly. She checked in periodically with the Missing Children's group, and finally learned that the two had actually been spotted by several witnesses in northeastern Oklahoma. Driving all night, she arrived in Tulsa around daybreak, and after she caught a few hours of sleep she asked the desk clerk if he knew of any race tracks in the area. Not even involvement in the cult had stopped Jim's addiction to racing and cars before the divorce. The only track the clerk was aware of was Hallet; he knew there were others, he just didn't know where. She made plans to search out each one, provided her money held out.

Right now it looked like she needed a miracle. *I guess nobody's handing out miracles today.*

She stifled a sob, put the picture away in her purse, and started looking for a restroom. *If I'm going to get anywhere with this I've got to make myself presentable. A place to freshen up, maybe. I'm not going all the way back to the motel. I don't have money to stay there much longer, anyway.* She trudged towards what looked like facilities and fought back a wave of dizziness. The heat—

Her vision blurred, seeing blue sky, with the kind face of an aging man in the center, like a Victorian picture of a saint. She blinked again.

"Are you all right, miss?" the man said in a rusty voice. "You keeled plumb over."

She was lying on her back in the grass, and there was a sore place on the back of her head. The man helped her to sit up a little; from his blue coveralls she assumed he was connected to the track somehow. He held a cup of lemonade to her lips, which she gulped gratefully.

"Whoa, now, hold on! Not so fast. You'll make yourself sick again," the man said. Around them, an unwanted audience of gawkers slowly formed in the thick sludge of the heat.

"What happened?" she asked stupidly, feeling vulnerable in her supine position, the words just coming out automatically. She *knew* what had happened. Her brain just wasn't working properly yet.

"Well, you fainted, little missy! Would you like me to call an ambulance?"

"No!" she exclaimed, not out of fear for doctors, but out of concern for how much it would cost.

"Well, okay then, if you think you're all right," he said, still sounding concerned. "You know, we have a first aid tent near the concession stand," the man said. "If you're suffering from heatstroke the thing to do would be to get over there."

"No, I'm fine, really," she said, and she meant it. With the cooling lemonade her energy returned quickly. "I think I'll sit here a while and drink this, if that's okay with you. I guess the heat just got to me."

"Of course it's okay. If you want a refill, just holler," the man said, winking in a friendly way. There wasn't anything sexual about it, something for which she was glad. *He reminds me of my father, when he was alive,* Cindy thought, looking at the deep wrinkles in the man's face, which seemed to be made of stone. When he winked, the wrinkles fanned out over his face like cracks in a windshield. He leaned closer, looking like he thought he might have recognized her. "I've never seen you at this track before, have I?"

"Well, I've been here all day," she said, trying and failing to keep the frustration out of her voice. "Maybe you can help me," she added, feeling a slight surge of hope. Cindy pulled the photograph of her child out of her purse and handed it to the man. "I'm here looking for my son. His name is Jamie. . . ."

She hadn't intended to tell him her life's story, but he seemed content to sit and listen to her, shaking his head and *tsk*ing at the right moments. *Finally*, she thought, as she prattled on about her husband, the cult, and her missing son, *somebody who'll listen to me!*

Finally the old man nodded. "Miss, you ain't had nothin' but bad luck, that's for sure. Sounds to me like this fella is a pretty hard-core racing fan. And *hard-core* fans tend to hang out with the pros in the pits. I haven't seen your son, but maybe someone else has. Would ya like to come have a look see?"

Without hesitation she accepted, and soon found herself waiting for a break in the race, so that they could cross over to the pits. When the break came, another wave of heat came over her, and she thought with a touch of panic that she was going to pass out.

Not again, she thought, and willed her strength back.

The moment passed, without her new friend noticing. He escorted her—with an odd touch of gallantry—past a short cinderblock wall where a man waited, watching who came in. One nod from her heaven-sent escort allowed them through.

When she entered the pits her senses were assaulted with the sights and smells of racing. Everywhere she walked, she stepped over oil-marked concrete, bits and pieces of race cars lay strewn everywhere, usually in the form of washers, bolts and brackets—she thought irresistibly of a dinosaur graveyard, strewn with bones.

A blast of something aromatic and potent, which she identified a moment later as high-octane racing fuel, threatened another fainting spell.

Too overwhelmed by sight and sound, smell and vibration, she stood, trapped like an animal caught in the headlights.

Then the sound, at least, stopped. In the temporary absence of engine roar, she found her ears ringing, and when she turned to see where her friend had gone she saw him rushing off to a race car that had just pulled in. *I guess I'm on my own now.*

The people she saw were either frantically going somewhere in a huge hurry, or doing nothing at all, some even looking bored. It was this latter group that she tried to talk to, praying under her breath that she wouldn't get in the way. She hoped she knew enough from her racing experiences with her husband to tell when a crew was seconds away from swarming over a car, or when they were just trying to kill time.

She approached one team, who seemed more intent on barbecuing ribs than changing tires on a race car. Men stood around a portable grill, holding beer cans in beefy fists, and stepping back when the grease flared. Some of them were apparently drunk, and while this reminded her uncomfortably of her ex-husband, she went up to one anyway.

"Hi, I'm looking for my son, this is a picture," she said, holding the photograph out. "Have you seen him?"

The man's features softened briefly, but when he saw the picture, they hardened. He said curtly, "No, I haven't," and looked at her as if she didn't belong there.

Another, younger man, who might have even been the driver, smiled broadly and shook his head, and then promptly ignored her presence, as if she had faded into invisibility. She asked the next man, and the next, feeling like a scratched record.

No, we haven't seen your son. Are you sure you're in the right place?

Then, one large man staggered over to join the group, a hulk with a barrel-chested torso that could have stored a beer keg, and probably had.

"I might have," the big man said, belching loudly. *He's so much like Jim,* she thought, wondering if this man might even know him. "But then again, I might *not*. What's the story, lady?"

"He's my *son*," she repeated. *Does he know something?* she thought madly, hoping that maybe he did. *Has he seen Jamie or is he just playing with me?* "My husband, his name is James Chase, do you know him? He sort of took Jamie away, we're divorced and I got full custody. James took him out of school, in Atlanta, and they were last seen in Tulsa."

"Maybe you should go look in Tulsa," he said rudely. But then he continued, his eyes narrowing with arrogant belligerence. "And what's this crap you're saying about kidnaping, anyway? And how the hell did you get full custody? Must have cost you a lot to take a man's son away from him."

Cindy became very quiet, shocked into silence. The man moved in closer to her, exhaling beer fumes in her face.

"What kind of a mother *are* you, anyway? Jesus Christ, lady, if you were a decent mother maybe your son wouldn't have gone away with your old man. *Would* he?"

His unfairness and hostility conspired with the heat to glue her to the spot, unable to move, like a frightened kitten cowering away from a pit bull. The man continued the tirade, with angry enthusiasm—really getting into shouting at a woman half his size—but she didn't hear any of it. The heat was catching up with her again, and a race car started up and was revving loudly nearby, drowning out all the senseless noises the man was attempting to make.

But in the nightmare the day had become, she could read his lips. *Let it go. Just let it go, lady, the boy's probably happier with his father anyway. Go find another hubby and raise some more brats.*

The cars roared away.

"And no real woman would—"

That was the last straw. Unable to take it anymore, without even the noise of the nearby car to completely take away the man's unpleasantness, she turned violently and stumbled away. She didn't want him to have the pleasure of watching her cry.

She walked slowly, so that her blurring eyes wouldn't betray her into a fall, vaguely aware of the man shouting behind her, unaware of where exactly she was. The tears surged forth now, breaking through a wall she didn't even know was there. She leaned on an oil barrel, faint again from the heat, and let the tears come freely. There weren't many witnesses here, and what few there were didn't care, didn't matter. . . .

"Al, what is it?" Bob asked, moderately concerned. "Anything important?"

Alinor shrugged, feeling the source of the emotional overload coming closer. *She must be in the pit area by now. Perhaps I shouldn't involve Bob yet . . . until I know a little more about what's going on here.*

"Oh, I don't think so," Alinor said, forcing a yawn, but Bob didn't look like he believed him. *He knows me too well,* Al thought. *He doesn't look it from the outside, but for a young human he's darned sharp.*

"I'm sure you won't mind if I tag along. The car's going in anyway," Bob said slyly, as more of a statement instead of a question.

"Yeah, sure," Al said, too casually. To say "no" would certainly tip him off. *Perhaps the gods intend for him to be involved in this one after all.*

"I've got a—feeling. Not sure if it's anything," Al said conversationally, as they walked toward the core of the paddock, the pit area where most of the cars came in to refuel. "Might be nothing, but then it might be—"

Al stopped in mid-sentence as he watched Bob's eyes tracking like an alert scout's, first to the racetrack, then to a group of men clustered around a grill.

Then came the emotion again, piercing his mage-shields like nothing he'd felt in a long time, and he put one hand up to his temple, reflexively.

"Is this what got your attention?" Bob asked calmly, pointing at a large man who was yelling at a small woman holding a photograph. From the emotion and thought-energies he was picking up now, Al knew that the picture was of the child she had lost. He had seen the man before, and knew he was a first-class misogynist, a male chauvinist pig, an egotist, a jerk. A general pain in the rear.

In short, Al didn't like him. And he would be perfectly pleased to have a chance to show the bastard up.

Saying nothing to Bob, he approached the pair. He privately hoped Bob would stay back and remain out of the situation long enough for him to find out precisely what was going on.

The woman paled and turned away from the bully, obviously fighting back tears. When the man took one step after her, Al intervened, wishing he dared land the punch he longed to take, but knowing he had to be far more surreptitious than that.

You don't need to follow her, Al sent, winding the impulse past the man's beer-fogged conscious. *Go back to the party. Leave her alone.*

The man paused, shook his head, and crushed the beer can in his right hand.

He hadn't noticed Al's little thought-probe as coming from outside himself. Now Al was confident enough about keeping his powers a secret that he sent one final nudge: *She doesn't matter. Besides, there's more beer at the barbecue.*

This last item seemed to get his attention away from his victim. He turned and walked uncertainly back to the barbecue, directly for the ice chest, ignoring the ribs being served. No doubt of where *his* priorities lay.

Alinor waited a moment before approaching the woman, who had obviously taken more than she could bear this afternoon. For a moment he thought she was going to pass right out and fall into the barrel she was leaning against.

She is in such pain over her child, Al anguished with her, waiting for the right moment before going to her. *I must help her. There is more about this than is apparent on the surface.*

"Excuse me," Al said softly, coming up behind her. "Are you . . . all right?"

She sniffled, as if trying to get herself under control, then turned slowly around. Their eyes met briefly before she looked away, and he sensed she was embarrassed about her appearance. Her eyes were puffy and red; obviously, she'd cried more than once today. "Yeah, I'm fine," she said, between sniffles.

Al calmly watched her, waiting for her to respond to the fact that he was not buying her story for even a minute.

Her jaw clenched, and she choked on a sob. "No. I'm *not* all right," she said, contradicting herself, but finally admitting the obvious. "Please. I don't know who you are, but I need help. This guy helped me get in here, but I don't know how to get out. The rules. Whatever."

And then she burst into sobs again, turning away from him.

Saying nothing, knowing that there was nothing he could say for the human that could possibly help her at that moment, he took her hand to lead her to a little grassy area near the track that was reasonably quiet and shaded. He sent Bob for cold drinks and told him where they'd be. Bob rolled his eyes, but cooperated nonetheless. Al ignored him.

He'll remember soon enough what it means to help a human in distress, Al thought. *It will all come back clearly to him when he sees what's wrong. He was on the receiving end once. I don't know what it is involved in this yet, but I can tell this isn't going to be light.*

He saw to it that she was seated in a way that would keep her back to most of the track-denizens, and handed her a fistful of napkins to dry her tears.

Then he waited. The revelation was not long in coming. When she had composed herself sufficiently she showed him her son's picture and began her plea, her words tumbling over each other as if she feared he would not give her a chance to speak them. "That's Jamie, my son. My husband . . . I mean, my *ex*-husband kidnaped him from his school in Atlanta, and—"

"Now wait, slow down," Al said softly. "Start from the beginning. Please."

Cindy nodded, took a deep breath, then explained to him what had *really* happened, telling him about the cult and the eerie change that had come over her husband. The parts about her ex-husband's alcoholism reminded him of Bob's past history, and Al was grateful the young mechanic returned with the drinks in time to hear it. He saw Bob's eyes narrow and his lips compress into a thin, hard line, and knew that the human had been won over within three sentences.

The story aroused many deep reactions in him, from the near-instinctive protective urges shared by all elves, to the feeling that this was only the surface of a larger problem. There was more here than just one little boy being kidnaped.

There is death here, he thought, with a shudder he concealed. None of the Folk cared to think about death, that grim enemy who stole the lives of their human friends and occasionally touched even the elven ranks. But he knew it, with the certainty that told him his flash of intuition was truth. *There is death involved, and pain. And not just this woman's pain, or her son's.* He was not one of the Folk gifted with Fore-Seeing, with the ability to sense or see the future—but he had a premonition now. This wasn't just about one small boy.

As she finished the story, Al studied the photograph, engraving the image permanently in his mind. *Now* I must *help*, he thought with determination. *I could never turn away from something like this.* And, with ironic self-knowledge, *It was time for another adventure, anyway.*

"And that's it," Cindy concluded, as if she felt a little more heartened by his willingness to listen. "I'm just about at the end of the line. And I think I'm going crazy sometimes. Can you, I don't know, ask around? I don't know what else to do."

"I'll do anything I can to help you," Al said firmly, looking to Bob for support. The human shrugged—both at Al and at his own willingness to get involved—sighed and rolled his eyes again ever so slightly.

"I'll take that as a yes," Al told him, then turned to Cindy. "When you feel a little better, we can start asking around the track. I know the people here who would be sharp enough to notice something odd about your ex-husband and your son." He laughed a little, hoping to cheer her a bit. "Most folks here, if it doesn't have four wheels, it doesn't exist."

She looked from him to Bob and back again, grateful—and bewildered. "Th-th-thank you, Al. And Bob," she said at last, looking as if she didn't quite believe in her luck. "What can I do to, you know, pay you back?"

She sounded apprehensive, and Al did not have to pry to know what she *thought* might be demanded in return for this "friendly" help. "Not a thing," Al quickly supplied. "But I do need a little more information about your son and your ex. We know he likes races. What about some other things he enjoys? What might attract him here in particular, and where else might he go around here?"

No, he had not been mistaken; the relief she felt at his reply was so evident it might as well have been written on her forehead. *Thank God, I won't have to—he isn't going to—*

Al sighed. Why was it that sex could never come simply, joyfully, for these people? Along with the curse of their mortality came the curse of their own inhibitions.

Ah, what fools these mortals be, he thought, not for the first time—and turned his attention back to the far more important matter of a child in danger.

CHAPTER THREE

Jamie winced. Jim Chase ignored him and banged on the pickup truck's balky air-conditioner, which was threatening to break down for the third time that week. The once-cold air was turning into a warm, fetid blast, and anybody with sense would just roll down the windows. Jamie perched on the sticky plastic seat beside his father, staring glumly at the Oklahoma countryside. He counted cows as they passed a pasture, something Jim had taught him to better pass the time. Meanwhile, the hot air coming from the truck's dash made sweat run down his neck, and he was trying his best to ignore it.

Jim's large fist pounded the air-conditioning controls, which had no effect on the temperature; the interior of the truck was quickly turning into a sauna. Jamie calmly reached over and turned off the blower, then cranked down his own window. The air outside was just as hot, but was drier, and at least it didn't smell of mildew.

His father muttered something about a compressor, a word Jamie barely recognized. It sounded expensive, which meant it would stay unfixed. Jim was still a genius when it came to technical stuff. But when he was angry, or when he drank joy juice, the genius went away. Like now.

Jamie decided to see if at least he could get his father

to stop doing something stupid. "Daddy, isn't the compressor in the motor? Under the hood?"

Jim's calm words seemed to come with great effort. "Yes, son. The compressor is in the motor."

"Then why are you bangin' on the *dash* like that?"

Jim laughed, a little, at that. "Good question," he said, leaving the dash alone and unbuttoning his shirt in the heat. Jamie wished he had brought more of *his* clothes on this trip; he'd managed to scrounge around for a used tank top at the vacation place, and it was the only clothing he had that was cool enough to wear on these excursions. Even though it came down to his knees, and felt more like an apron, it was more comfortable than the one shirt he still had.

Overall, this had been the longest and *weirdest* vacation he'd ever been on, especially since Mom wasn't with them. At the vacation place, however, he had been to a kind of school, which didn't make any sense at all. *You don't go to school on vacation,* he tried to tell his dad, but his father had insisted. Jamie attended class in a single room with one strange old lady named Miss Agatha who hated blacks and Jews and had a big gap between her front teeth. She taught them her hate along with readin' and 'rithmetic, or at least tried. Hate was wrong, he knew, but since he was surrounded by adults who seemed to think differently, he didn't question them.

Much.

The classroom was filled with other children who were just as confused as he was. Most of them were there because they weren't old enough to be in the Junior Guard. The kids in the Junior Guard didn't have to go to school, so it was something Jamie wanted to join, if for no other reason than to get away from Miss Agatha. He even lied and told them his age was ten and not eight; you had to be at least ten to join the Guard and use an AK-47. But they hadn't believed him.

Jamie had thought of this vacation as one big adventure, in the beginning. But in the past couple of days, he had begun to sense something wrong. He started asking his father questions—about the whereabouts of his mother, and why he was gone from *his* school for so long. And why he didn't have any spare clothes.

He'd kept up an incessant barrage of questions, couching the questions in innocence so that he would stay out of trouble. He might only be eight, but one thing he knew was his dad. James had bought it at face value, looking pained, not annoyed, whenever his son brought up the subject of his mother.

Finally today his dad had told him that they would be seeing Mom on this trip to Tulsa. Why, Jamie had asked, didn't Mom come to the vacation place? It was a surprise, James had replied, and that seemed to be the end of that.

They had made several trips to Tulsa since they arrived here, each time loading up the truck with big bundles of food and supplies. Sometimes they had to stop at a bank and cash a CD, but Jamie had never heard of money coming out of music before. Besides, they didn't have a CD player; more mystery. James purchased canned goods, mostly; things they wouldn't use right away, food that was put away where no one could see it. This category of grocery was called "in the event of an emergency," according to Miss Agatha. The rest of the food, the "perishables," was for the other people, he knew that much, since he got very little of it himself.

Now they were going to the store again, and like the last time, the air-conditioner quit. No big deal for Jamie, he didn't mind the heat as much as his father did. It didn't matter, as long as he was outside the vacation place. It was a stifling place, especially when Brother Joseph was around. All day Jamie had looked forward to the trip, knowing that Mom would be waiting for him in town. He didn't mention her to Daddy during the trip, since he already felt like a nuisance bringing it up before.

"Miss Agatha tells me you're a bright student," James said conversationally, over the wind pouring in through the window.

Jamie shrugged. "It's not like school at home. It's too *easy*." He wanted to add that it was also pretty weird, some of the things Miss Agatha taught them. And that he was the only one in his class who wasn't afraid of Miss Agatha. He had asked her why it was okay now to hate when it wasn't before. After all, Mommy had always said that it was wrong to hate black people because of the color of their skin, or Jews because they went to a temple instead of a church.

Miss Agatha had not been amused and told him that the Commandments said he had to obey his elders and she was his elder.

Then she went on with the same stupid stuff. Only today she had also mentioned another group, the homos, but he had no idea what made them different. Miss Agatha had simply said to stay away from them, that even saying "homo" was wrong, that it was a *bad word*.

"When am I going back to the *real* school, Daddy?"

Jamie knew he had said something wrong then, by the way his father's face turned dark and his lips pressed together. But it was a valid question, after all. Wasn't it?

"Maybe it's time for you to learn what the big boys know. The truths they don't teach you at that other school, the one in Atlanta."

The boy felt a shiver of excitement. *What the big boys know. Like Joe. The things they haven't been telling me, that big secret the grownups are all excited about but don't tell us. Is it time for me to know that big secret now?*

"Listen up. This is a Bible story, but not like any Bible story you've ever heard before. Those other ministers, they don't have it right, never have, never will. We're one of the few groups of people in the world who know it straight, son, and by the grace of God we'll spread the word further."

James paused a moment, apparently gathering his strength, as if summoning vast intellectual reserves. Daddy was having trouble thinking, Jamie knew, because he had run out of beer the day before and hadn't had any since.

"Do you remember Miss Agatha telling you about the beginning of the world? About how God created the world and all the people on it?"

Jamie nodded, uncertainly. *The big secret has to do with* that *icky stuff?* he thought, suddenly disappointed.

"And the story of Genesis, in the Bible. Most Bibles don't tell you that before Adam, God had created several other species of mankind, the black man, the red man, the yellow. Some had civilizations and some had nothing. Some could live in peace because they were too lazy to do anything else, but most of the inferior races could only make war. God made all these people before Adam, long before he had it down right, you see." James sounded earnest, but he was frowning. "But most ministers, preachers, they don't know all this 'cause their churches didn't want them to know the truth."

Jamie nodded, as if he understood, but he didn't. This wasn't like any Bible story *he* had ever heard, or even read.

"Now remember, and this is important. This is before the white man. God saw that his work could be better, that all these monkey races were turning back into animals. He needed a perfect creature, and that's when he made Adam out of the river mud. Right away he knew he had something there. This one was different. This one was *white*. The color of purity, the same color as God."

Already Jamie was getting uncomfortable. This was *not* what he expected to hear. *All that hate stuff again*, Jamie groaned inwardly. *With big words to make it sound important. Brother.*

"God could see that what he made was perfect, with an intelligence higher than any creature's he had yet created. And that included the black man. The Lord God also saw that his new creation would bring peace to a world filled with war, since it was an inherently peaceful creature he had made. He was a higher being, in every way. He had to be, since the Lord God was creating a race of people to inherit the earth, to be God's direct descendants, to be his children."

"Yeah, Dad," Jamie said, forcing politeness. He didn't like what he was hearing, and he wished his dad would finish. *You made more sense when you were drinking joy juice,* he thought rebelliously.

"Then the Lord God saw that Adam was lonely, and he created Eve. She was of the same race as Adam, and it was God's intention that she bear Adam's babies, to make a perfect race. But Satan, who was an angel rebelling against God, he got involved somehow and mated with Eve instead, and gave her his serpent seed."

"Is this the same Satan the Church Lady talks about on Saturday Night Live?" Jamie asked, figuring this to be on safe ground. Mommy had let him stay up one Saturday, when his father was away, and watch the show with her.

Since then, he had always associated Satan and women like
Agatha with humor. But now, Daddy didn't look like he was
trying to be funny.

"Don't know what you're talking about there, son," James
said, puzzled for a moment. "If that's some kind of late-
night religious show, it's probably only half right. I'm telling
you what's really right, all true. Pay attention now—this
made God really angry, since this wasn't what he had in
mind at all. Eve wasn't as perfect as Adam, because she
had let Satan do this to her—which proved to God that
women were going to be naturally inferior to men. Now
God's purest race was polluted. Now Satan, since he was
part of one of the first races, is black."

Jamie stifled a snicker. *Boy, is that stupid! First he says
Satan's an angel, then he says he's a snake, and now he
says he's black.*

"Eve gave birth to two sons, but that was how God knew
they must have had different fathers, because one was
black, Cain, and the other was white, Abel. Cain was lazy
and wanted to live off the sweat of other people, through
stealth and cunning, which is typical of the way the Jew
serpent race thinks. Cain took off to Babylonia and started
his own kingdom, and this is where the Jews came from."

Now Jamie *knew* that was wrong; he knew where the
Jews came from. The little bitty squiggly place, the one
littler than Oklahoma. Israel. And he'd never heard of
Babby-whatever. Unless it was that icky lunch-meat they
gave the kids here. But James was really enjoying his
captive audience, so Jamie sighed and pretended to listen.

"Before long everyone was mating with everyone else,
mixing the races, committing sodomy—I'll explain that one
when you're a little older—and God didn't like that. So he
flooded the Earth with water, and God started a new kingdom, but as it happened some of the Jew serpent seed got
onboard the boat anyway. Before long the Jews gained
control again. The Jews and blacks are doing that to this
day."

Then how come so many poor people are black? Jamie
asked, silently. *And how come there are people putting
bombs in Israel?* He'd learned *that* in his real school.
Esther had brought in some scary pictures. . . .

"When Jesus came, it was too late. The Jews were already in control, and they crucified Jesus. The battle between good and evil rages to this day, and now the Communists are pawns of the Jews, and they're just as bad. Any day now hordes of Jew Communists are going to invade the United States, and only a select few are going to be ready for it. That's why we are called the Chosen Ones, and we abide by no laws except *divine* law."

Daddy had completely lost Jamie at this point. Was that why James drove over 70 in the 55 mph zone, because there was no "divine" speed limit? And was that why he wouldn't wear a seat belt?

James was still babbling, like a tape player that wouldn't stop. "The white race will reclaim its lost status, but it will take time, and work, lots of work. The ministers and churches today, they don't want to tell the truth, they don't want to work, understand, but it's all there for anyone to see. The other churches have been diverting energy away from the real work, and that's why we're here. This is what Brother Joseph is teaching us. This is why you're in Brother Joseph's school, instead of that unholy place in Atlanta."

"You mean, we're not on vacation?" Now Jamie was really confused.

James glanced at him sharply. "Of course we're on vacation, but it's the Lord's vacation."

"Are we really going to see Mommy when we get to Tulsa?"

Jim became silent then. It was the first time Jamie had mentioned Mommy that day, and having finally asked the question, he was suddenly nervous.

"Who told you we were going to see Mommy in Tulsa?"

The boy shrank, sensing that familiar anger which often led to his father's backhanding him. "You did," he said, meekly.

James considered this a moment, then said, "That all depends on Mommy. If she wants to see us, she'll be there. If she doesn't want to see us, she'll stay home."

But we didn't tell Mommy where we were going, and we didn't call her or anything to tell her we'd be in Tulsa today.

"What if she's *not* in Tulsa?" Jamie said, holding back

the tears at this betrayal of a promise. "What if she's still at home? What if she doesn't know we're going to be in Tulsa today?"

"Then that'll be her fault," James said. "She's a Jew woman or something."

When they pulled into the parking lot of Tom's Wholesale Discount Market, Jamie searched for his mother among the several faces he found there. Boys in jeans, shirts and vests pushed giant trains of shopping carts back to the front of the huge building, where even longer lines of carts, stuck together by some magical glue, awaited shoppers. While they were waiting to enter the store, Jamie continued the search, afraid to ask his father about his mom. James had looked ready to hit him back there, Jamie knew, and figured it was time to be quiet. Through trial and error, he had learned to gauge his father's temper.

James showed the girl their membership card and entered the store, selecting a flatbed cart. Still, no Mom. He followed his father silently, knowing that to lag behind would mean to be lost, and to be lost would eventually mean a backhand to the side of his head. And with Mommy nowhere around, there was nothing to stop James, nothing to restrain him. Jamie doubted these strangers would do anything to stop his father from hurting him; they never had before.

Tom's Discount was the only place Jamie had been to that sold stuff by the case. The store was a big warehouse. To reach some of the stuff, a forklift was necessary.

Cases of canned food began to stack up on the cart, and after a man helped them forklift some stuff down from a high shelf, they proceeded to the freezer section. Daddy had mentioned buying milk and cheese last, because it was a perishable. He hoped, also, the sample lady would be there so he could get some free cheese or barbecue sauce or wieners, he was so hungry. But she wasn't there, and he was starting to get unhappy about that when something else attracted his attention.

The freezer section was a catacomb of glass doors and frozen goods. Blasts of cold, biting air nibbled at his skin whenever someone opened a door. Over here, though, was a row of refrigerators, with milk and milk products stacked up inside the door.

His own face stared back at him.

He opened the door while his father, loading boxes of cheese, wasn't looking. The milk cartons were connected by plastic tape, so he couldn't take that one out. But he read it anyway, recognizing his school picture from the year before. It was his name, all right, and his date of birth. According to the carton, he was last seen with James Chase in Atlanta, Georgia. Jamie stared at the picture for a long time, trying to figure out how he could be on there, and why. According to the carton, he was a "Missing Child." *But I'm not a missing child. I'm right here, with Daddy. Daddy knows I'm here, so there must be a mistake. Is this what he meant about seeing Mom in Tulsa? Or does Mommy have something to do with this picture being on here?*

As he was puzzling over this, he became aware of a large presence behind him, and with a start he looked up at his father. He pointed at the carton, tried to say something, but only a squeak came out.

"What are you looking at there, son?"

James knelt down and studied the carton, taking it out of the refrigerator. He looked at the picture, then at Jamie. Then he looked up and down the aisle; nobody was around just then. The boy noticed that he had the look of someone doing something he shouldn't. He began to feel all funny in his stomach.

"That isn't you," he said, simply. "That's another boy. He's got the same name as you, but it's another boy. Got that?"

Fearful of what would happen to him if he did otherwise, Jamie nodded.

"That's good," he said, quickly going through the remaining cartons, checking the photographs on each one. Apparently, he was holding the only one with his son's picture; he found no others. "Start putting more milk on the cart. This size, here," he said, indicating a stack of milk cartons larger than the first. "I'll be right back."

Jamie tried not to look, but out of the corner of his eye he watched his father look around quickly before dumping the milk in a large, plastic-lined waste can.

When he returned, his expression was somber. "It was bad," he informed his son. "The milk was bad, so I threw it out for them."

Jamie nodded, meekly, and continued loading the milk.

"Here. Let me give you a hand with that," James said, as he helped his son load the flatbed cart.

For Jamie, the situation was becoming more frightening than he wanted to admit. His first impulse was to trust his father, without questioning him about why Mommy wasn't around, why they were far from home, why his picture was on a milk carton. It was easier to just listen to Daddy and do what he said; this gave some order to his world. It was also the best way to avoid being hit. He loved his mother, but he had to admit that during the divorce he felt very much afraid without his father. When James returned to his school to pick him up for the vacation, Jamie was thrilled, though he didn't understand why Mommy wasn't with him. The divorce was weird; Daddy explained it as temporary, and it didn't really mean they weren't married, even though that's what Mommy said it meant. She was confused, he explained. He would explain it all when she got to Tulsa, whenever that would be.

They drove away from the discount store with the loaded truck, and Jamie stared out the window at the other cars. Ahead was an Arby's, and the boy remembered his hunger.

"Daddy, I'm really hungry. Can we stop at Arby's?"

James frowned, as if the request was too much to be handled. But Jamie saw him stuff the wad of bills and change in his pocket when they'd finished buying things. Money, he knew, wasn't a problem.

"I don't know, Jamie. Brother Joseph wouldn't like it."

"Why?" he wanted to know, flinching. He expected a blow, not only for questioning Daddy, but questioning Brother Joseph, which was an even more heinous crime.

"Brother Joseph knows what he's doing," James explained carefully. "He has tapped the Divine Fire before, and through you he will do it again."

Hunger was gone, immediately, as his stomach cramped with fear. *No, not that again—*

"But Daddy," he protested feebly, "I don't want to."

James shook his head dismissively. "That's because you're just a child. When you get older, you'll understand. It's all in Brother Joseph's hands. Fasting is crucial in achieving the purity to talk to God. Something else the clergy in general doesn't know about. Consider yourself fortunate."

The Arby's came and went. Jamie could smell the odors of roast beef and french fries, and his stomach growled loudly. "Perhaps he'll let you eat something tonight. After the ritual. It will be special tonight," James said, as if savoring the prospect. "Just you wait."

They drove on in silence for several moments, while Jamie tried to concentrate on something other than his complaining stomach. *I'm so hungry*, he thought, and when he saw them pull onto the highway to get back to the vacation place, he realized he wasn't going to be seeing Mommy in Tulsa after all.

So I guess she isn't there, he thought, starting to feel a little cranky instead of being unhappy, and beginning to think he ought to push the issue. After all, Daddy had promised. He was reaching a point where he didn't care if he was hit or not. In a way, he felt like he deserved it. *I must have done something bad, or Mommy would be here by now.*

"There's something I got to tell you," James began, and Jamie sighed.

He's lying again, he thought, somehow knowing that what would follow wouldn't be the truth. He didn't know how he had acquired the talent for spotting lies, but he did know that Daddy had been lying a lot lately.

It seemed like James was waiting to get on the highway before telling him what, exactly, was going on. James gunned the motor, bringing their speed up to seventy before turning to his son.

"I haven't been telling you everything, because I wanted to protect you. You probably think it was a little weird the way we left Atlanta. Took you from your school and everything. There is really a good reason for all of that. Before I explain, I want to be certain that you understand that I do love you, and I wouldn't do anything that would harm you."

Jamie was feeling uncomfortable again, but he nodded

anyway. Whatever lie was coming, it was going to be a big one.

"Good. I trust Brother Joseph without question, and *he* wouldn't hurt you either."

Jamie wasn't sure about *that*, but he was too afraid to question it. *Brother Joseph is* really *weird, and he's why* you're *so weird, isn't it, Daddy?* He remembered the last odd ritual, the fourth of a series, in which Brother Joseph made him see and feel things he still didn't understand. Scary things. It was like a big monster on the other side of a wall, like the creepy thing he felt under his bed while sleeping or lurking in his closet. The thing that came to life in his room when Daddy turned the light out. *That* thing; a dark something that made wet sounds when it moved, the thing that watched him when Brother Joseph shoved him through the wall during the rituals. He forced Jamie to see it, sometimes even to touch it. The wall wasn't solid, he knew, but it was still a barrier. *Walls were made for reasons*, he thought, and the reason for this one was *good*. He pushed the memory away, at the same time dreading the coming ritual, where he knew it would just happen all over again.

"I don't mean for you to worry about your mother, but something has happened in Atlanta that's put us all in danger. We were going to see your mom in Tulsa, but I guess she just hasn't made it yet."

Jamie stared glumly forward. "What's happened?" he asked, resigned that whatever James would tell him would be a lie, but hoping for some truth anyway. "What's happened to Mommy?"

"Nothing," James supplied. "Not that I know of, anyway. Back in Atlanta, the police, they came and said that I did something that I didn't. They think that I'm involved in drugs; they accused me of dealing drugs in your school in Atlanta. You know what I'm talking about when I say drugs, don't you?"

Jamie nodded, remembering the cop who had spoken to their class about the bad boys who were smoking cigarettes and other things behind the school during lunch, kids who were only a few years older than him. The cop showed them the green stuff that looked like something Mommy had in bottles to cook with, and another baggie of little white rocks called "crack." That was bad stuff, the cop told them, and they had caught the man who had sold it outside their school. When the cop told them about what drugs did, Jamie was scared and decided that if he was ever offered any, he would refuse. But his dad had nothing to do with it; he knew that much for certain.

"Well, son, it's all a terrible misunderstanding. If it weren't for blessed Brother Joseph and the Chosen Ones, I'd be in jail right now. See, we've got to hide out with the Chosen Ones for a little while, until things kind of level out. I have a lawyer out there working on the case. Your mother didn't know much about this at first, but when I called her and told her what was going on, she got all nervous about me and said I'd better take you all with me; she wasn't sure if she could handle you all by herself. The police were wondering about her, too. With the drugs, and all. But don't you worry none. Momma will be here soon."

The stink of *lie* was thick. Jamie wondered why his father couldn't tell how obvious it was. The boy frowned a little, looked up at his dad, and wondered when he was going to stop lying to him.

"You know I don't sell dope, son."

"I know that, Daddy. They caught who was doin' it. I'm never gonna touch drugs. The police said they make your head puff up and your skin turn green and purple. They make you crazy and do awful things to people."

"Good, son. That's just what I wanted to hear," James replied, absently, as if he hadn't heard a word Jamie had said, once he got the initial answer. "Brother Joseph, he's going to help us through this. He's done a lot for us, and these little errands we run, getting the food for them and all, are a way of helping him back. It'll all work out, you just wait and see."

It can't ever work out, Jamie thought, getting angry at his daddy for making up stories. *Momma doesn't know a thing about this, I just know it. This is all real wrong, I shouldn't even be here, I should be in Atlanta going to my school and not this icky place with these icky people Daddy likes. Sarah would know what's right. She always knows what's right. I'll ask her when I get back. She might even know where I could get some* food, *without Brother Joseph knowing about it*.

Jamie knew they were getting close to the "vacation place" when Tulsa dissolved behind them, and the terrain became barren of civilization. There were a few cattle in this part of Oklahoma, sprinkled among the scrawny groves of native oak. The sun continued to beat mercilessly against the earth, but now that it was late afternoon, the temperatures inside the truck were more bearable. They turned off to a lesser, two-laned highway, then to a gravel road. After some time across the bumpy route they came to the front gate, a large steel barrier set in a bed of concrete. James unlocked it, and they proceeded into what the soldiers called "the Holy Land of the Chosen Ones."

Soon they reached a second gate, this one connected to a tall chain-link fence topped by barbed wire. At the gate was a sentry box, where two young men in t-shirts, camo pants and combat boots intercepted the truck. There was a brief inspection before continuing into the main compound. Above them two dozen electricity-generating windmills *thwapped*. Joe had told Jamie they were connected to powerlines leading to the vacation place.

The truck rumbled past a series of drab Quonset-style shacks. They seemed deserted; once his father had remarked that this was where food and supplies were kept, ready for the "invasion" the grownups were always talking about. Other soldiers, more numerous now than when they first arrived, were patrolling the grounds. At the northwest corner of the compound was an old log cabin that was now a sort of museum. *This was what the freedom fighters first lived in*, he remembered Miss Agatha saying on a field trip. *It stands as a monument to their holy independent spirit and is an inspiration to us all*.

Next was a cluster of plain, cinderblock buildings, and more Quonset huts that reminded Jamie of *Gomer Pyle* episodes. Beyond was the entrance to the underground shelters, the vacation place, where Jamie now lived, along with the rest of the Chosen Ones. Miss Agatha said there were almost one thousand of the "enlightened" living in the vacation place; since he was the new kid, he felt like he was treated with a little more suspicion than the rest.

After all Daddy does for them, they still don't like me.

He figured this was from jealousy, because he was allowed outside, a privilege usually reserved for the trusted few. His father's unique function in fetching supplies had its advantages. Nobody else had a membership in Tom's, and Brother Joseph didn't want anyone else to get one. He said it was a "security risk." But since Jim had gotten the membership a long time ago, there was no reason not to use it.

Jim drove the supply-laden pickup to yet another checkpoint. This was at the mouth of the underground, a gaping, dark hole at the base of a concrete ramp. Jamie knew there would be dim lighting down there that would never compete with the searing summer sun outside; his eyes would have to adjust, first. Going in always frightened him. It was like going down the gullet of some prehistoric creature.

There was some consolation, though; Joe was one of the guards working the gate today. He was just coming on duty when they had left for Tulsa, and Jamie figured by now it might be time for his shift to end. The boy had met Joe at his very first Praise Meeting, and Joe had been nice to him—he'd given him a Tootsie Pop and showed off his *tattoo*. There was something so—affable, genial about Joe; they had become instant friends. His father approved warmly, and since Joe was the only one besides Brother Joseph who would have anything to do with him, they spent a lot of time together hiding out in the nooks and crannies of the uncompleted sections of the underground.

At first Jamie thought it was a little weird that Joe could sometimes guess what he was thinking, and sometimes answered his questions before he could actually ask them. And only yesterday, Joe had predicted that they would be going out; in fact, said he would be seeing him because he was working guard duty. When Jamie quizzed him about his ability to read minds and see into the future, Joe got real scared, and said for him to never mention that again. He wasn't reading minds and he wasn't seeing into the future, said it was something called "deduction," like Sherlock Holmes did. He also said that if anyone thought he did read minds they'd both be in big trouble. It was the work of the devil, such things, and no Chosen One could *ever* have powers like that. Jamie let the matter rest.

Sure enough, Joe was standing there, at attention, looking the same as he did when they left. The boy looked up to Joe, admiring him in his uniform. He was every bit a man in Jamie's eyes even though he was barely old enough to be in the Chosen Ones' regular Guard. He was eighteen, one of the few guards who still had hair. Jamie hadn't asked why, because it seemed to be a delicate subject. The rest of the Guard were shaven bald, and it seemed to be some kind of special thing, but he didn't know what it meant.

There were a zillion other questions he wanted to ask Joe today as well, and the top of the list was: why would his picture be on a milk carton?

And besides that, why hadn't his mother shown up yet? He knew he was treading dangerously just to ask Joe, since his father had already provided an answer. If Joe squealed on him, he would be in hot water, and he'd get beaten. Jamie decided to ask anyway, as Joe's overall trustworthiness had never been in doubt, and they shared mutual secrets anyway. And if Joe's answer didn't sound right, there was always Sarah. She knew things most people didn't, and her word was golden. Sarah had never, ever lied to him, or acted as if he was bad or stupid.

James turned off the motor. This was the last and most thorough check in the land of the Chosen Ones, and was used to detect the smuggling of undesirables, spy devices or Communists into the underground bunkers. Jamie had the impression the guards trusted his father but had to do this thing anyway. They went through the truck thoroughly, examining the supplies, looking under the vehicle. His father stood by quietly; this was a sacred ritual, as was any procedure that protected the Chosen Ones from the Jew Communist enemy, who was due to invade any day now. Everything these weird people did seemed to be in preparation for a war, and Jamie didn't understand why anyone outside the compound didn't share this sense of urgency.

It must be one of those "truths" that Daddy mentioned, which only the Chosen Ones knew about.

After the inspection Joe spoke briefly with Jamie's father. "You go with Joe," Jim said, getting into the truck. "I have to go unload these supplies. I'll see you at supper, after I speak with Brother Joseph."

Go with Joe! That was exactly what he'd wanted to do. He looked over at the young man, who was grinning as he slung his AK-47 over his shoulder. Jamie had never seen him without it, not even at the big communal dinner hall, and while at first it was a little scary, now he didn't think anything of it. At the vacation place, guns were everywhere. This was not like normal life. *Things are different here.*

Before Jamie could react to the good news, his father was in the truck and starting it up, the conversation apparently finished. Joe's relief had arrived, a scowling man who looked like Daddy did a day after drinking too much joy juice.

"Hey, buckaroo," the big boy said jovially, squatting down to talk to him, "I've got something to show you."

Usually Jamie didn't like it when he knelt down like that; it made him feel like a little boy, even though he was. But this time was different, he didn't care much; there was a surprise involved this time.

Instead of a surprise, Joe pulled out another Tootsie Pop. Jamie appreciated it, as any eight-year-old would—especially with his stomach growling—but he tried to not let the disappointment show.

"That's not what I wanted to show you," Joe said, trying to conceal a snicker. "Come with me."

Joe led him through a series of tunnels and passageways, some nominally lit, which had been carved into the earth by the Chosen Ones. Some of the digging equipment was still here, Jamie noticed; he had never been down this way before, had in fact been told to stay away from this area of the tunnels, this being forbidden to those under ten. But now the restrictions seemed to have been lifted by his hero.

"You've never been down here before," Joe said, "and it would probably be a good idea if you didn't tell anyone we were here. It'll be our secret. Okay?"

"Awright!" Jamie said, with awe in his voice. "What're we doing down here, anyway?"

"Nothing we shouldn't," he replied. It was hard to keep up with him, he was walking so fast. His legs, too, were that much longer. "I talked to your daddy about this, first, so it's all right with him."

"What is this place?"

They came across a sign, with a drawing of a young soldier holding an AK-47 over his head in triumph, with the caption:

SACRED HEART OF THE CHOSEN ONES

JUNIOR GUARD

FIRST BATTALION

It took a moment for it to register; then surprise spread through Jamie. "Am I joining the Junior Guard already?" It was like a rite of passage here. It had only been a few weeks since Jamie had arrived, but he had come to recognize the importance of some of the ritual elements of the vacation place. The Junior Guard was one of them. "First Battalion? How many battalions *are* there?" He wasn't sure what a battalion was, but from the sign he gathered they important, and that there must be more of them.

"There's only one right now," Joe admitted, as they entered another large, damp room, filled to overflowing with every type of firearm he could imagine. Jim had taken him to a sporting goods store once, with what had to be a million guns on the wall, but it was nothing compared to *this*. The rifles and assault shotguns were lined up in several racks. Beyond that were thousands of wooden boxes, some of them open, filled with bullets. Along another wall, behind a huge sheet of glass, were small handguns, each with a name affixed to a tag. The room smelled like gun oil and rubberized canvas; the odor gave him goosebumps on the back of his neck. *This is for real.*

"I'm going to show you how to fire a weapon," Joe announced proudly. "Do you want to learn a handgun or a rifle?"

Jamie was struck speechless. *Learn how to use—a gun?*

Even the Junior Guard didn't start right away with guns, he knew that much. Joe was providing something special here, and he knew it.

"I want to learn *that* one," Jamie said, pointing at the assault rifle slung over Joe's shoulder, so common it seemed to be a part of him. "*Your* gun."

Joe laughed, but not in a way that humiliated him, the way the other grownups did. Joe was his friend, and his laugh didn't betray that. "Sorry, bucko, you're gonna have to work up to this one. Come over here." He led him to a rack of rifles, smaller and lighter than most of the others. "These are all the right size to start with. Hey, Jamie, I had to start with an *air* rifle when I was your age. You get to use real bullets. *You're* lucky."

Jamie studied the weapons. One stuck out, grabbed his attention. It wasn't quite a machine gun, but it looked a little more grownup than the others. It had a block-letter J carved in its stock. "That one."

"Hmmmmmm," Joe said. "Good choice. It used to be my gun, when I was little. Imagine that."

Joe unlocked the gun rack and handed him the weapon. "Never point it at anyone you don't want to kill. Don't point it up, either, when you're down in the bunkers. Always point it down. Roof's usually metal here, and if it goes off accidentally the dirt or wooden floors will absorb the bullet, but it would bounce off metal and hurt someone."

He reached for it eagerly. "All right, Joe. Is it loaded?"

"Always assume it is, even when you know it isn't. *NO— don't point it at me!* There you go, down at the ground. Good boy." Joe's voice took on a singsong quality. "What you have here is a Charter Explorer Rifle, model 9220. Takes eight .22 long cartridges. It's not *fully* automatic like mine, but it'll do for starters." Joe picked up a box of bullets, and his voice returned to normal. "Let's go to the firing range."

They walked in silence to the next room. The long, narrow area was floored thickly with sand, and the roof tapered down at the opposite end. This was, Joe told him, to deflect weapons fire into the ground. Standing in the firing area were several crude dummies, which he thought were real people, at first. They were wearing military uniforms, and some were holding staffs with flags on them. One he recognized as Russia's flag, and another held a flag with a six-pointed star. There were other items to shoot at in the sandy area, but the primary targets seemed to be the make-believe people. Jamie didn't like that very much. He hadn't associated the weapons with killing people until then, though he knew deep down that's what they were for.

Guns were something he was used to; sometimes they were used to hunt animals, but not people. His daddy had never mentioned killing when he was cleaning his Luger. And on the rare instances he had taken Jamie along for shooting practice out in the woods, he always shot at bottles and cans. Never people. And he couldn't imagine Joe shooting and killing someone else. The sight of the dummies standing there, waiting to be shot at, made him feel a little sick inside.

But he didn't say anything to Joe, for fear of being a sissy. *I'm going to do this, no matter what, so nobody will treat me like a sissy no more.*

Joe showed him three different sniper positions before he even let him handle the loaded weapon; as he lay there, belly down in the dirt, Jamie wondered what this had to do with learning how to shoot. Finally the older boy loaded the weapon with eight little bullets and carefully handed it to him.

"This is the safety," Joe informed him, lying prone beside him in the sand. "This keeps it from firing accidentally. Until you're ready to shoot, leave it on."

The lessons progressed from there, and after learning to *squeeze*, not pull, the trigger, Jamie fired his first round. It wasn't nearly as loud as he expected, but then his gun wasn't as large as Joe's. At Joe's urging he selected a target and fired a few more rounds, remembering to *squeeze* the trigger, and promptly picked off one of the objects in the sand. His first kill was a Hill's Brother's coffee can, which went *piiiiing* as it flew backwards into the sand.

"Good *shot*, buckaroo!" Joe applauded. Jamie was triumphant. "That's better than I did my first time!"

Jamie was getting ready to draw on another target when he became aware of someone standing behind them.

Another weapon went *snik, snik*. Jamie's arms turned to putty, and the barrel of his rifle dropped.

"If I were a Jew-Communist-pig you'd both be dead now, Private!" an ominous, and familiar, voice boomed. Following Joe's example, he scrambled to his feet, leaving the weapon on the ground.

It was Brother Joseph, standing there with Joe's AK-47 pointed directly at them. As if to make a point, he turned and fired a few rounds into a dummy.

"I'm sorry, sir," Joe stammered in the echo of the gun-fire. Jamie could see he was really scared; his face had become whiter than usual, which probably wasn't so bad, since these people seemed to value that color. "I was just showing—"

"*Silence!*" Brother Joseph demanded, and received. The man was wearing a strange military uniform similar to the Guard, but it had a preacher's white collar incorporated into it. Jamie had never seen this particular article of finery and assumed it was new. "On your stomach. Fifty—no, *one hundred* push-ups. Now!" the man barked, and the boy responded instantly.

Joe dropped to the ground, making his lean, muscular body rigid as he began the push-ups, using his knuckles for support. It was how the Guard always did push-ups, Jamie observed, and it looked quite painful.

While Joe was doing this, Jamie could see a thin wisp of smoke trailing out of the AK-47 and remembered his own gun, lying on the sand. He thought it best to go ahead and leave it there, to give himself time to figure out what was wrong, and what Joe had done that was so terrible. Brother Joseph was angry about something, and although the anger seemed to be directed at Joe, he did not feel at all comfortable standing in the man's shadow. Even when he *wasn't* angry.

Joe counted out the push-ups, pumping them off with ease; a slight sweat broke out down the small of his back and beaded across his forehead. The beret had been left on, as Brother Joseph had given him no permission to remove it. Slowly but surely, Jamie was beginning to understand the nuances of discipline within the Guard, though he had never envisioned Brother Joseph as the direct leader of them. The Guard leadership seemed to be comprised of middlemen subservient to Brother Joseph; now the boy knew the weird preacher was probably in command of them as well. His new item of clothing supported this.

It was in moments like these, when the cruelty shone through like a spotlight, that Jamie had second thoughts about joining the Junior Guard. Then he would look at Joe and see him endure the abuse and begin to wonder if this really was the natural order of things everywhere. It certainly was the natural order of things *here*.

Joe completed the punishment and leaped to his feet, standing sharply at attention. His breathing was hardly labored, and only the slightest gleam of sweat had appeared on his forehead. What would have been brutal punishment for most didn't seem to bother him in the least; Jamie was in awe. *Someday, I'm gonna be able to do that.*

"Very well," Brother Joseph said, sounding a little calmer. "Perhaps that will teach you never to leave your weapon where the common enemy can take it and use it against you. I know, son, it probably seems like there's no chance for a Jew-pig to infiltrate, but you never know. They're a cunning bunch, the spawn of Satan."

"Yes, Father," Joe said, looking down at the ground.

Son? Father? Is he Joe's daddy? Or do they just talk like that because of who he is?

"So tell me, young guardsman, what were you doing down here with this *child*?"

The question carried strange, accusatory undertones that Jamie couldn't fathom. Leaving the firearm in the sand didn't seem a good idea, and he wondered if now was a good time to bring that up.

"I was showing this youngster how to use a weapon, Father," Joe said, pride slowly returning to his voice. "He has a fine talent for marksmanship, if I do say so," he added.

"Glad to hear it," Brother Joseph said, and handed Joe his weapon. "Strip and clean your weapon, son," he said. "Your mother will be expecting you at our dinner table tonight. You haven't forgotten her birthday, have you?"

"Of course not, sir," Joe said. "I will attend."

Brother Joseph regarded Jamie with a bemused, patronizing expression, as if he'd just seen him for the first time. "Young James," he said. "So you have a gift. That much was obvious, that first time we touched the Holy Fire together." His eyes narrowed. "Yes. Special. And *very* gifted indeed," he said in parting, and as he walked away his laughter echoed down the metal walls.

The sound made him feel empty, and somehow unclean. As Jamie watched Brother Joseph's back recede he felt a new dread, a growing horror that had no name. The Chosen Ones didn't see it, saw only the bright side of him. They followed Brother Joseph wherever he went. Sarah was the only one who knew about it besides Jamie, that's how hidden it was. And when the preacher made him "channel" the Holy Fire, they both saw this darkness, so scary that Jamie made himself forget what he saw and touched, most of the time.

But every time he saw Brother Joseph he remembered. *And we're going to do it again tonight. Oh, no*, he thought, and shuddered.

In silence Joe finished cleaning his firearm and put it all back together. He seemed humiliated, and justifiably so. But Jamie still had questions to ask. About the milk carton, about his mother. And he was going to ask them; they were alone now, and there would be no better opportunity.

"Is he your daddy?" Jamie blurted, knowing no other way to start.

"Yes. He is. And it's nothing we need to talk about. As far as anyone is concerned, I'm just another soldier, fighting for the cause. I get no special treatment," he said, his eyes narrowing at Jamie. "And don't you treat me no different. If you do that I'll have to rough you up." He added that last, lightly, like a joke.

But in that second, with that brief, angry expression, he looked just like Brother Joseph. *Joe, Joseph. Of course. How come I didn't guess before?* Jamie knew he could get real depressed over this if he let it happen, but he tried not to. *Joe's still Joe. Even my daddy's bad sometimes.*

"Why didn't you know your daddy was coming?" Jamie asked, but immediately knew it was the wrong thing to say. Joe was looking at the ground, apparently not paying too much attention.

"Sometimes I just have to turn it off. . . ." Joe said absently, then looked at Jamie in mild alarm. "No one can read minds. Remember that. And don't call him my daddy. He's my leader, and that's all that matters."

"Oh," was all he said, and Joe looked relieved. Apparently, other people down here made a big deal over it. But then, those other people *liked* Brother Joseph. "Something weird happened today when we were out getting supplies."

"What's that?" Joe asked, brightening up. He sounded glad to change the subject.

"I saw my picture on a milk carton. It said I was a 'missing child.' What does that mean?" he said, waiting for *some* kind of reaction from Joe.

He found none, absolutely nothing. A stone mask went over his face, and Jamie knew something was amiss. It was the same mask he had worn when his father sneaked up behind them.

"Are you sure it was you?" he finally replied.

"Yep," Jamie said. "Sure was."

Joe frowned. "Did you tell your daddy about it?"

Jamie felt a little cold. "Y-yeah, and he said it was someone else."

Joe stopped and knelt again, but it was with an expression of such severity that Jamie wasn't annoyed by it; he was frightened. "Then listen to your father. Do not disobey him. It is the way of the Chosen Ones. It was wrong for you to ask another grownup when your father already told you it wasn't you." Joe held his chin in his right hand, forcing the boy to look directly in his eyes. "If your father said it was someone else, then it was someone else. *Don't ask anyone about it again.*"

Jamie wanted to cry. This was the first time his friend had spoken to him like that, and it hurt terribly. *This is still not right*, he thought. *But he isn't gonna tell me anything else, either. Maybe I'd better not ask about Mom, then. Daddy already told me why she isn't here. It's because she doesn't want to be.*

But as Joe walked him back to his room, he couldn't believe this was the real reason.

◆   ◆   ◆

Joe walked him back to the tiny cubicle that served as his home. It was in a section of the underground that was lined with sheet metal, forming tubular habitats for most of the "civilian" Chosen Ones. That meant all the women, little kids, and the few men that weren't in the Guard, like Jamie's dad. The Guard and Junior Guard lived elsewhere, in barracks-type quarters, austere living for even a seasoned soldier. At first, Jamie had thought it was a kind of jail, without the bars. Joe had showed the Junior Guard barracks to him once, but it did not inspire the awe the older boy had apparently hoped it would.

Jamie's quarters were cozy in comparison. The cult had found scrap carpeting and had used it to create a patchwork quilt on all the floors. The three pieces of furniture were all used, and none of it matched: a chair, a formica coffee table, a burlap-covered couch with the stuffing coming out in white, fluffy lumps. For the first week they didn't have a bed and had to sleep on blankets and blocks of soft foam that had been in a flood, according to Jamie's dad. The two twin mattresses they had now were an improvement over the floor, but Jamie overheard one of the men who carried them in say they had been stolen from a motel. Their lighting came from one dangling lightbulb that had no switch and had to be unscrewed each night with an "as-best-ohs" rag kept specifically for that purpose. The bathroom and single shower were down the hall and serviced the entire row of ten tiny rooms. Moist, musty air occasionally blew through a small vent, enough to keep the room from getting too stuffy. But since they were underground, the cool earth kept the temperature down.

At first the rugged environment was more exciting than uncomfortable, this secret place where he hid with his dad from the rest of the world. But as a week passed, and he began to miss his mother and wonder about where she was, the experience became disturbing. He missed his things, his toys, and especially his clothes. He missed having three meals, or even *one* meal, a day. He couldn't remember the last time he'd eaten, other than Joe's gift of candy. *It wasn't yesterday. I think it was the day before.* When he went to the dining hall, all they would give him was juice. Orange juice at breakfast, vegetable juice at lunch and dinner, and apple juice at night. Everyone *else* got to eat, but not him.

Joe's answer wasn't good enough, Jamie thought, morosely. *It wasn't even close. Didn't tell me nothin'.*

Jamie sat on his bed and leaned against the curved, metal wall. His father was not here yet, but it would only be a matter of moments before he came and fetched him for supper, which was served in a large, communal hall. *But I've got time to talk to Sarah, before he gets here.*

The wall was cool and pulled some of the heat out of his body. *Good. That'll help me to think real hard.*

He closed his eyes. "Sarah?" he said. "Are you there?"

:I'm here, Jamie,: he suddenly heard in his head. *:I was getting worried.:*

CHAPTER FOUR

Cindy looked a little better now that she was in the cool, dry air of Andur's air-conditioned interior. Her conversation was certainly more animated.

"Well, like I said, he's a car nut. That's why I was here, looking for him at the track." Cindy repeated herself often, apparently without realizing it, as Al's elvensteed, Andur, pulled slowly through the paddock.

Andur was disguised as a white Mazda Miata, although usually Andur was a much flashier Porsche 911. Andur's choice of form—and Alinor's transportation of choice—had changed through the ages. To flee the Civil War, Andur had been a roan stallion. Some years later he had manifested as a Harley Davidson, but this had attracted the *wrong* kind of attention, and Al had asked him to change to something less conspicuous. On a racetrack the little sports-car fit in quite well; though it was an inexpensive one, anything more ostentatious might have attracted questions.

Besides, Al rather liked Miatas. Their design was rounded, purposeful and sensual, like a lover's body or a sabre's sweep.

Andur in this form had only two seats, but Bob claimed there were last-minute things to do at the pits before calling it a day and sauntered off to check on his precious engine.

Al didn't spare a second thought for the man, who seemed just as happy to deal with metal and machine-parts, rather than an unhappy lady on the edge. In some ways, Al didn't blame him; Cindy seemed very close to the end of her resources—mental, emotional and physical. Bob was young and might not be much help with an emotional crisis. And he certainly couldn't be counted on for sparkling, cheery conversation if Cindy got too morose.

The summer sun was setting, casting an orange glow on the Hallet raceway, silhouetting Bob against the red-and-gold sky. He appeared solid. Someone to be depended upon. Al was very thankful Bob was here, as he pulled away from the pit area, heading for the nearby campground.

Cindy clenched her hands in her lap, as tense as an over-wound clock-spring. Al's senses told him that her anxiety attack had yet to run its course. She was not paying much attention to things outside of herself, which was all to the good for him, but that wasn't a healthy state of mind for a human.

She was surely running on pure adrenalin by now. Her hands shook slightly, and she still had trouble catching her breath, and that also concerned him. He wasn't a Healer, except maybe of metals. If she were to become ill, he wouldn't know what to do with her.

How am I to calm her down? She can't have been eating well, lately—and the heat hasn't done her any good, either. I have to get her settled and balanced, or she won't be of any use at all.

Alinor frowned as he considered her distress. From the moment they began talking he had been forced to put up an array of shields usually reserved for the most intense of emotional moments. There was no doubt that she was in dire need of some kind of release, and out of consideration for her state of mind, he allowed a small amount of her anxiety to seep through. She wouldn't know what he was doing—not consciously—but even though she was only marginally psychic, her subconscious would know that someone was "listening" to her, and cared enough to pay attention and not block her out. It was simply common manners among elves not to shut someone out completely, unless absolutely necessary; what he had done so far was enough to keep Cindy from pulling him in with her. Later, when he could concentrate on the task, he would see what he could do to apply some emotional balm to her misery.

On the other hand—so far as keeping his "cover" intact was concerned—in her present state she probably wouldn't notice that the Miata had no ignition, or that it was driving itself. Al rested his hands on the steering wheel, to make it look as if he was in control, but the elvensteed knew where they were going.

"I think I left the air-conditioning on in the RV," Al said conversationally, reaching forward with a tiny touch of magic and activating the air-conditioning switch. With any luck, it would be cool by the time they got there. *Let's see . . . Gatorade in the fridge? Yeah, plenty of that. And ice. We should be in good shape when we arrive.* "It has a shower," he added, hesitating. Al realized what this might sound like, and he glanced over at Cindy for a reaction. She offered none, gazing blankly forward, apparently unaware she was tying the edge of her blouse in a knot.

At least she didn't take exception to that suggestion. That is, if she even heard it. It wasn't as if he was trying to *seduce* her in any way—

Even though she was attracted to me, I could feel that. . . .

But he wasn't *demanding* sex—he wasn't even expecting it. It was just—

Damn. I am trying to seduce her. Am I trying to prove to her that I'm attractive, or to myself? This is something that a good session of sweat cannot fix. I should know better.

But she was very vulnerable at this point, and in obvious need of comfort. Comfort which could be physical or otherwise—and if physical, could take any number of forms. And he was skilled at offering that kind of comfort. He'd had lots of time to practice, after all—

Stop it! he scolded himself. He was tempted to reflect on the last time he'd had any kind of relationship, but he knew it would only heighten his desire. In his childhood, so many years ago, the maxim had been drilled into him by his father: *never get involved emotionally with a human, except on the most casual of terms.* There was a good reason for this guideline, as evidenced by centuries of elvenkind's experience. First of all, going by most definitions of a "relationship," the human involved would eventually become aware of the existence of the Folk and want to know what was going on. With the exception of humans like Bob, the foster children who were brought up Underhill, this was seldom a good idea. Word could get out, and if enough humans became convinced that elves were "real," the elves in question would have to go into strictest hiding. This was usually done with concealment spells, but in the more dangerous cases of hostile humans, an all-out retreat to Underhill often became necessary.

But that wasn't the real danger. One way or another, those situations could be handled. The Folk were experts at hiding from the humans, and throughout their long history had even enhanced their disguises with "fairy tales" they had written themselves.

The main reason the Sidhe avoided relationships with humans was simply that humans grew old and died.

However, when Alinor was younger, he had decided to ignore this advice. Being young, he had convinced himself that he was immune to such pain—

And I told myself that killjoy adults didn't understand love. They couldn't see how it meant more than life or death.

Or so he thought.

It had been around a century and a half ago. After falling head over heels in love with a young pioneer girl, Janet Travis, they settled in what was now North Dakota. They were one of the few settlers able to maintain a homestead in that area, as they were the only *wasichu* who could get along with the Lakota Sioux living there.

It helped that they honored the beliefs of the Sioux themselves, hunting rather than farming, never taking from the land more than they could use, never wasting anything, and giving thanks for what the land gave them. Alinor's magic, carefully disguised as earth-medicine, brought the deepest respect from the tribes.

The years passed, the seasons turned, and Alinor and

his human bride enjoyed what seemed in retrospect to have been an idyllic existence in the Plains. It was the longest stretch of time he had ever spent away from his own kind, and if it hadn't been for this periodic sojourn Underhill, he might not have survived with his sanity intact. Janet only knew that he was going out hunting—to trap furs to trade for the things they needed. He never told her that he went off Underhill to reproduce the flour, salt, bolts of linen . . . and that the few things he *did* trade for, he went to the Lakota for. Men did that, and she understood. He would go off and return with three elvensteeds laden with enough to see them through another six months or so.

The problem was, it was hard work reproducing enough goods to last six months. He could be gone as long as a month. And time did not pass Underhill the same way it passed in the real world. He never knew exactly when he would emerge. . . .

One bright winter afternoon, Alinor came back from his semi-annual trip and discovered his beloved Janet was dead.

He had never learned the cause then; and the reason was still a mystery. The Lakota might have been able to tell him, but they were in their winter hunting grounds, and no one had been near the cabin. She could have been hurt—she could have caught an illness—he had no way of telling.

She was forty years old, advanced age for humans of that era, but she had been healthy and young-seeming, without the burden of producing a child each year as women of her time usually did. She had been fine when he left her, and from the condition of their cabin, whatever had killed her had sickened her so quickly that she hadn't had time to do more than close the door, put out the latchstring, and get into her bed.

He'd thought in the first month that he would join her, dying of grief. He'd thought in the second month that no one of the Folk had ever suffered so. In the third month, he burned the cabin to the ground with his power, gave his furs and treasures to the Lakota, and returned to North Carolina and Underhill.

A little older, a little wiser, Alinor sought out the High

Court of Elfhame Outremer. He returned to his brethren
with his grief. There he learned that others had made the
same bonds to mortals as he had, and understood.

Janet was many years ago, he told himself. *I promised
myself I would never do that again.*

Still, it had been a very long time since he had taken
a human lover; despite her distress he found Cindy appealing, and sensed that she was attracted to him as well.

But not now. There is a time for everything, he thought,
and the time hasn't arrived yet.

The RV was parked on a section of the Hallet grounds
reserved for campers. The camaraderie was as evident here
as at the races; the temporary city of tents, campers and
rec vehicles provided some sanctuary from the frantic pace
of the track. The portable communities followed the races
much like the ranks of carnies did at the state fairs, and
the faces were always familiar. Al could have walked the
distance, but Cindy had seemed ready to melt—and Andur
had been right there. And, truth be told—human women
found sports-cars exciting. He'd been strutting like a prize
cock, hoping that she would admire his "Miata," and that
some of that admiration would spill over onto him.

They pulled up next to the RV, near a copse of trees
that offered some shade. "My parents had an RV like this.
A Winnie, isn't it?" Cindy said as she got out of the Miata.

"Class C Winnebago. With a bunk over the cab," Al said.
"Did you say you have parents?"

"Had. They died last year. I had to sell the RV to help
settle their estate or I'd still have it," she said. Her words
trailed off, and she seemed to withdraw a little.

I guess I'd better not pursue that one, Al thought, realizing that he'd touched on a sensitive subject. *Sounds like
this poor girl is all alone in this mess. Without even parents to fall back on.* Hearing that surprised him somewhat.
For the most part, his small sphere of friends, though far
away, were Sidhe. Al thought in terms of the Kin's longevity,
not humans'.

The interior of the RV was pleasantly cool, to Al's relief.
But as they entered the door, he found himself embarrassed
by the state of the interior. He wished that he had cleaned
the place up a little; he couldn't even see the second bed

under all the animal, vegetable and mineral flotsam that somehow migrated into the cabin, seemingly of its own volition.

I think junk breeds in RVs.

He scooped up an armload of dirty clothes—and other things less identifiable—then dumped the entire load in the tiny bathroom to be sorted. Later. Then he popped the table up, making the bed into a place they could both sit.

"Cozy," Cindy commented, but it sounded like she was trying to be polite. He noticed her nose wrinkling at an odor.

Yes, I know. The place smells, Al thought apologetically. But at the moment she looked like she didn't care too much. *Why clean the place every day when I can effortlessly make it into my normal nest?* Being one of the Sidhe had its advantages; Al could conjure whatever he wanted for the interior. On most days, his digs would make a Pharaoh envious. Silk sheets covered the beds, and intricate, woven tapestries draped the walls and ceiling of the compact RV, giving it more depth, an illusion of space it just didn't have. Bob certainly never had any complaints about it. But all that luxury would have to stay in magical "storage"; at least until Cindy was safely stowed away somewhere else.

His harem of illusory dancing girls, complete with fans, grapes and feathered garments, would also have to remain in hiding, stashed away in the netherlands of his magical universe. Only his statue, an ornamental metal reproduction of an art-nouveau Phaeton mascot, could remain the same. When "activated," it became a graceful, liquid-chrome servant. In its inanimate state, however, it looked like something that had been stolen from someone's lawn. He'd have to do without her as well.

He sighed. For the time being his home would have to remain a plain, unaugmented recreational vehicle, complete with a monumental mortal mess.

"I don't think I have to ask if you're thirsty," Al said, pulling a large square jug of orange Gatorade from the fridge. "Despite appearances, the cups are clean. I promise. And so is the ice."

Cindy settled down at the smallish table, letting the cool

breeze of the air-conditioner brush across her face. "That feels so good," she said. "I don't know how to thank you for all this. Are you sure your friend won't mind if I stay here tonight?"

"Positive. We'll work something out," Al said, though he didn't know what it would be. He sat at a second place at the table with the other plastic cup of Gatorade. "Feel better?" he asked, as she gulped the orange potion.

That much we have in common. We both need this magical stuff after all that heat. It always tastes good when you really need it.

"Much," Cindy said, sounding like she really meant it. "Tell me, what exactly do you do at the racetrack? You're not all dirty and grubby like most mechanics I know."

Like her ex, Al thought with hostility, but set the feeling aside. *You don't know he was a mechanic. Parts store, remember?*

"Originally I'm from the East Coast." *I've come from many places. I'd better tell her one she'll believe.* "North Carolina, mostly. That's where the South Eastern Road Racing Association is based. SERRA, for short. And the firm I work for, Fairgrove Industries. We're running a test-project for the Firestone team." He didn't mention he had conjured an engine block from thin air, and was here with Bob to watch how it performed.

"So what, exactly, are you doing here?" she quizzed. "This must be small time compared to what you're used to."

"Well no, not really," Al lied. "Hallet is unique. It takes skill to keep our cars on this one at the speeds we're traveling. This is a good venue to heat-stress test the cars and their engines. I'm on loan to the Firestone team as I said—what I'm actually doing is monitoring one of our cast-aluminum engine blocks. Different drivers, different conditions, out in this neck of the woods. A good way to make sure that what works at Roebling Road or Road Atlanta will work everywhere."

"I see," Cindy said, but it looked like he was losing her again. A faraway, distant look fell over her. Thinking other things.

"Do you think I'll ever find him?" Cindy finally said,

looking at him as if he was the original Sibylline Oracle, or an Archdruid.

He spoke from his heart. "Yes, I think we will. But first things first. Are you tired?"

"Exhausted," she said, yawning. "This cold air. Feel's good, but . . ."

"Putting you to sleep, isn't it?" Al observed, wryly.

"Some," she admitted. "What time is it, anyway?"

"Eight something, probably. Why don't you go ahead and crash? I have to go check some things before I turn in."

"You're sure I'm no trouble?"

"I'm certain. Go ahead, scoot. Take the bunk over the cab. That plastic curtain pulls across for privacy and snaps at the corners. I can make this table back into a bed for myself."

Which should reassure her as to the purity of my intentions.

Cindy finished off two more cups of Gatorade before she climbed the ladder into the overhead and finally gave in to sleep. It didn't take long. *She must be dehydrated,* Al decided, leaving a fourth cup of iced Gatorade in the well at the head of her bed, in case she woke up thirsty.

Before leaving the RV, Al stood in the doorway, looking back at Cindy, lying there asleep. *So trusting of strangers,* he thought. *She doesn't know anything about me, yet she falls asleep so easily, leaving herself vulnerable. Either I look completely harmless, or the poor girl is very, very naive. Or else she's so desperate she'd take an offer of help from anyone.*

Alinor left the RV, locking the door and making certain it was secure. He seldom locked it, having his own devices for safeguarding the Winnie, but this time he made an exception.

Night had fallen on the track, and locusts and crickets were out in full force, replacing the race-car roars that had dominated the daylight hours. Around him were small impromptu parties, barbecues, none of which would last very long. Racers tended to respect the next man's sleep time, and brought the noise inside after about nine or ten at night, adjourning to quiet poker games or TV. Some of them traded videotapes, and a couple had Nintendos casting *their* spell. A tranquil atmosphere fell over the little make-shift city of tents and campers at night, reminding Al of why he liked racing in general, and these humans in particular. It was as an RV marketer had advertised once, "a community on wheels," where the people next to you were your neighbors, even if for only one night at a time.

Al walked beyond the campers to an emptying parking lot. Not a lot of spectators on trial days. Only hard-core racing fans showed up for days like these, and those that were not friends of someone here were long gone. *This was a good day to look for her child,* Al thought. *If he had been here, he would have been easy to spot. Too bad they weren't here. Maybe tomorrow . . .*

Maybe—but he didn't have a lot of hope that they really would show up.

Cindy looked a lot like Janet; flyaway brown-blond hair, freckles over the bridge of her nose, direct, blue eyes. Really, allowing for the differences in clothing, she looked amazingly like Janet. He guessed that her sense of humor would be very similar too—and that if she ever really smiled, it would light up her face and make her dazzlingly lovely.

And he was afraid of the effect that would have on him.

He told himself that he had other things to think about, and plenty of them. *I will deal with that later.*

So, what should they do about this missing child? Sit around and wait for him to appear on their doorstep? It didn't seem a very logical way to handle things. *We could keep an eye out for her child tomorrow, but it sure feels like a longshot. I didn't want to tell her that, since this is her only hope. What if they* don't *come tomorrow? What then?*

Feeling tired, and just a little depressed, Al sat on a tire-wall, watching the sparse traffic on the nearby Cimarron Turnpike. His vision blurred as he gazed at the occasional retreating red taillights, and he began to see how tired he really was. His thoughts turned to his partner, Bob. *He's not going to like this one bit. And I didn't even ask him if she could stay. It's my RV, but it's his home, too. I just took it for granted that he wouldn't mind.*

But then, what else could he have done? She was alone and broke, and a child was involved. . . .

How could he turn his back on a child—or on someone as childlike in her distress as Cindy?

But then again, he didn't know exactly what he was getting into and was beginning to feel a little put out with himself for getting so deeply involved so quickly. *I know what Bob will say: leave it to the Sidhe to stick their noses in where no one else would.* But that thought simply catalyzed his resolve again. *Well, so be it! That's why we get things done.*

Al paced the edge of the parking lot; the asphalt radiated heat and the scent of baking petroleum, still warm from the day's sun. Portions were cracked and dry, the result of years of weathering. A lone Hallet employee wandered the empty parking lot with a bag, picking up litter. *If I had lost a child in this part of the country, how would I go about finding him?*

It didn't take long for him to see that he knew very little about how the mainstream of human society worked. He might as well have been from another planet. For years, especially recently, in modern times, he had relied on humans like Bob to provide a smokescreen for him, concealing him from suspicious eyes and coping with the intricacies of the modern world for him. In fact, of all the Folk Al knew, only Keighvin Silverhair in Savannah knew enough of the modern world to move about in it unaided.

Even at Hallet, Bob played interference for his partner. This was a world within a world, essentially transparent to the rest of the population. His niche as a SERRA and Fairgrove mechanic made him part of the landscape; nobody asked questions around the track if you were an insider, and SERRA automatically qualified him as that. Only outsiders were subject to suspicion. Outsiders—like Cindy, which was probably the reason she'd had so much trouble this afternoon.

When anything went wrong, if an accident happened, there was always a human there to pick up the pieces, to drive the ambulance, to call the hospital. Al had never had to do any of those things. On the rare occasions that police were involved, Al had observed from a distance, preferring to keep his presence as discreet as possible, even throwing in a concealment spell for good measure. But out here, there were no police to call—those were attached to cities, and Hallet hardly qualified as that. There was someone else in authority in these parts, but he couldn't remember who, or what, they were.

Blessed Danaa, Al thought, throwing his arms up in helplessness. *Where* does *one go for help around here?*

He had no idea. Back at the RV he had felt rather— superior. What was it Bob said? *Macho*, that was it. Macho to be able to help Cindy out like he did. Then he was in control of the situation. And he was also on his own territory, the racetrack, the Winnie. But now, faced with the prospect of going Out There, into the humans' everyday world, he was at a complete loss.

Then he remembered an ad he'd seen once. *Can't find it? Try the Yellow Pages.*

"The phone book. Of course," he whispered, barely realizing he'd spoken aloud.

Near the observation tower was a row of public telephones. Al had generally avoided such devices, even when they were in their infancy. There was something inherently wrong about one of the Folk using such a contrivance, when he could send his thoughts and messages to faraway places without them. It was like using crutches to walk when nothing was wrong with your legs. But he went in search of one, and spotted it by the lighted symbol built into it, with the phone book attached by a chain. Some of the pages even *looked* yellow.

"Let's see, her ex-husband's name was Jim Chase. That's the same as James Chase, I think," he muttered to himself. He fished out the last of his cookies and ate them while he thumbed through the book. The phone book was a bit thinner than the ones he had seen, which might have been a clue to its usefulness had he been operating on the proper wavelength.

Nothing. Not even a "Chase" was listed.

Okay, then. Be that way. Can't find it? How about "missing children" in the yellow pages?

No luck. Hallet wasn't exactly a large town. In fact, the directory listed several other towns in the same directory. Frustrated, and tired, he gave up on the phone book. *Time to find Bob*, Al finally admitted. *Maybe he'll have an idea. After all, it's* his *society*.

Bob wasn't very talkative, as usual, and suggested they tackle the missing child situation in the morning. They had both had a long day, he pointed out, and besides, tomorrow their crew had a day off. Good time to play private investigator. Al agreed, finding it difficult to stay awake. He'd been short on sleep last night, and his body knew it. A few hours from now, he'd be alert, his mind running at top form. Now was not the time to try to solve problems.

But there was the need to figure out where to put Bob—

He solved the sleeping logistics by having Andur turn himself into a white van, complete with bed—truth be told, a much nicer environment than the Winnie was at the moment. Bob volunteered for it without Al having to ask; Al retired in the table-turned-bed, with Cindy chastely asleep in the loft, and instantly fell asleep, the woman's proximity notwithstanding.

Dawn brought something besides the crowing of roosters in the nearby farmyards. There were sounds of someone stirring in the RV. Not unusual; Bob often got up before he did, and sometimes even started breakfast, if he felt motivated enough. But the sounds he heard were different, not of someone making a new mess, but of someone . . . cleaning an old one up.

This was terribly out of place. Alarmed, Al sat up abruptly.

"Good morning," Cindy greeted him cheerfully, from an arm's-length away. "When was the last time you guys cleaned this dump?"

Egads. A morning person, Al thought muzzily, as the evening's events came flooding back at him. *I took this Cindy under my wing last night, didn't I? If she's going to be awake and active this early in the morning, maybe I'd better think about putting her somewhere else.* Al fell back on an elbow, watching her sweep the narrow aisle of the RV. The place smelled strongly of ammonia and Lysol, in spite of the fact that the windows were open, the air-conditioner off.

"We have a broom?" Al inquired, yawning.

"Yes, you do," she replied. "It was in the back of the closet. Still wrapped up with the cardboard thingie on the back. Never used.'

Horrified, Al watched her sweep up the dust into a shoebox and begin wiping down the plastic runner with a sponge.

"We don't have a . . ." *What was it called? Oh, yeah*, "A mop. Didn't know you could do it that way."

She paused, then looked up with a faint smile. "I can tell. Don't worry, I'm almost done. And I guarantee you won't be able to find a thing."

"That's nice to know," Al said, uncertain of what exactly she meant. He realized that he was still fully clothed, either because he had been too exhausted to remove his garments the night before, or in his foggy state he was too modest around Cindy to get comfortable. He'd even left the track cap on, with his hair pulled back into a thick ponytail, so as to better hide his ears. *Good. Saves me the trouble of getting dressed.* He glanced out the little side window at the white van that was his elvensteed, and reached with his mind to the sleeping human within. Bob wasn't sleeping; in fact, he wasn't even there. *Must be off doing something.*

He sat up and regarded his small—but now spotless— home. The sink and stove had been cleaned, as had the microwave and refrigerator. These items were now new colors, ones he didn't recognize. Even the cabinets had been wiped clean. He was suddenly ashamed that this human had had to stay here without the usual concealing spells that made its squalor into splendor.

She deserved better. He began moving the foam-block cushions to make the bed back into a breakfast table, pondering the changes in the RV, and the more unnerving ones deep in himself.

Something was missing, but in this unnatural state of cleanliness, he didn't know what. It was all so . . . different.

My clothes! he realized, in panic, remembering the crumpled, smelly pile of fabric that was developing a life of its own, a fixture that was moved from one location to another without ever really being dealt with. *What did she do with them?*

"Bob is at the laundromat," she said, as if reading his mind. "I had to show him where it was."

Which answered two questions. "It is sort of hard to find," Al said, wondering where it was himself.

She eyed him strangely, then said, "Would you like me to make coffee?"

Caffeine! Blessed Danaa, no. . . .

"Uh, no thanks, Cindy. I don't drink coffee." Or anything else with caffeine. "Hard on my stomach. I'm—uh—allergic to it. To caffeine. Badly." Al checked his wristwatch. Ten-thirty. "It's early. And it looks like you've got a lot done. Why don't you take a break?"

"I think I will. Oh, I wanted to ask you. Where did that white van come from?"

Al feigned nonchalance. "Oh, that's ours. The crew's. It kind of gets traded around," he said, hoping she believed him. *I meant to have that changed back to the Miata before anyone got up,* he thought, and hoped that Bob told her the same, if not a similar, story.

Cindy dropped into the tiny booth the bed had become. Al opened a Gatorade, his standard breakfast fare. "How do you feel?"

"Much better. Since it was cool this morning, I went ahead and opened the windows. The cleaners, and all." Al nodded; it was still an uncomfortably strong scent. *Guess that's what clean smells like.* "Thank you for letting me stay here. Hope you don't mind the cleanup."

"Oh, not at all. I'm glad you did. Forgot what the place really looked like."

Bob came into the narrow door, first shoving in a huge laundry bag that Al was distantly aware of owning. It was stuffed to its maximum capacity with, he assumed, clean clothes. A rare treat. It caught in the doorway, and with a visible effort Bob wedged it through.

"Just set it up there," Al said, indicating the now vacated loft. "We have things to do today."

Bob looked around at the RV and the sparkling results of Cindy's work. "Jesus," he said, and sat. "You've been busy. I've been asking around about your boy, Cindy. Nobody here knows anything. Might be they've never been here."

Cindy looked down, to hide the sudden surge of despair.

Al felt it anyway. "Oh well. It was worth a try," she replied, sounding defeated. "I don't know what else to do now."

"Have you called the sheriff's office?" Bob asked.

"I've talked to the Tulsa police. There wasn't much they could do about it. Then I called the Tulsa County sheriff's office, and they were sympathetic, but not much help either."

"Eyah," Bob said. "But we happen to be in *Pawnee* county here. What you say we give 'em a call? If those nutsos that your ex is involved with set up shop around here, you can bet the Sheriff will know it. And in a place this small, everybody knows everybody else. A new man in town with a small boy is likely to get noticed."

Al finished his Gatorade and all three trooped to the pay telephones to call the Pawnee County Sheriff's office. Bob gave Al a nod and a significant look; Al shrugged and stood aside to let Bob make the call.

"Well, I think we might be in luck," Bob said, hanging up the phone. He had spoken for several minutes in a hushed monotone that was hard to listen to. The one-sided conversation shed little light on what the person on the other side was saying. "Deputy named Frank knows about some kind of whacked-out religious cult in this area. Actually, it's closer to Pawnee than Hallet, from what Frank says. He wants to talk to us."

"Well, then," Alinor said. "Let's go."

"In what? The Miata's only a two-seater," Bob said.

Al gave him the hairy eyeball, cleared his throat loudly, and continued. "The crew gave us the van. Remember?"

"Oh, yes. The *van*," he responded, while Al wondered what he had told Cindy about the elvensteed and the mysteriously appearing and disappearing van.

But at the moment, Cindy didn't seem to notice the awkward exchange, or care. She had a gleam in her eye, excitement that could only be a glimmer of hope.

Pawnee was a tiny little burg nestled among the rolling hills of Northeast Oklahoma, similar to a dozen other towns that Bob and Al had passed through on their trip to Hallet. Pawnee itself was built on a series of hills, giving it an uneven, tilted look. It looked old, and for Oklahoma, which had been granted statehood in 1907, that meant sometime early this century. The dates on the masonry of some of the buildings confirmed this: 1911, 1922, 1923. City Hall was behind an elaborate storefront, on a red brick street unevened with time. Across a street-wide gulf of time and technology was a Chevy-Geo dealership, displaying the latest Storms and Metros in the same showroom window that once must have hawked carriages, Model T's, and Woodies.

Al had a definite feeling of *déjà vu*, thinking maybe he had been here before, in his youth, when horses and sprung carriages were just starting to replace horses and buckboards. Even in modern times the town maintained a tranquil, relaxed atmosphere.

They passed a Texaco, a mom and pop steakhouse, a tag office, a Masonic temple and assorted city blocks of ancient brick structures that had no obvious function, their windows boarded or bricked over. Pickup trucks and enormous cars from the sixties and seventies seemed to be the preferred mode of transportation here. Townfolk strolled the sidewalks, casting annoyed or disdainful looks at the few hopped-up teenmobiles haunting the streets. *Lunchtime*, Al noted, thinking there was probably a high school nearby.

In the center of Pawnee was a grassy knoll, surrounded on three sides by brick streets; Al had forgotten such anachronisms still existed. The seat of Pawnee County government sat atop the knoll, guarded by a large piece of artillery, a museum piece forever enshrined on the front lawn. Behind this stood a WWI memorial, a statue of a soldier with flowers spelling "PAWNEE" at its feet. The courthouse was a three-story brick building, surrounded by a few cedar and oak trees. Carved in stone, across the top of the structure, were the words: PAWNEE COUNTY COURTHOUSE.

As they approached, Al could see a single car in the parking lot, with the traditional silver star of authority painted proudly on its side.

"This is *it* for the whole county?" Bob exclaimed as they climbed out of the van. "Doesn't seem like much."

"Pawnee County is *not* highly populated," Al reminded him, then jibed, "I thought you didn't like metro areas."

"I don't. I just expected more, is all."

Cindy held her purse closer, as if it were a teddy bear. Then she checked to be sure the photo of Jamie was still inside. "I don't care if it's a shack, as long as they can help me find my son. Is the sheriff's office in there?"

"Should be. That's where the car is. Let's have a look."

The courthouse smelled old; smelled of dust, layer upon layer of ancient floorwax, more layers of woodpolish, of old papers stuffed away in boxes and forgotten, and of heat-baked stone. There was no air-conditioning in the central part of the building. The floor was hand-laid terrazzo, cheap and popular in the thirties, and worth a small fortune today. In the hallway, handpainted signs hung over battered, wooden doors, thick with brown paint applied over the years. There was not a person in sight in the overpowering silence. Al began to wonder if they were in the right place.

"Is there anyone here?" Cindy said, as they walked uncertainly down the hallway. "No people."

"This is it. Look," Bob said, going towards a sign that said "SHERIFF'S OFFICE," with an arrow pointing down. They took a short flight of stairs to the courthouse basement, and found the Pawnee County Sheriff's office behind a glass door.

Again, the place seemed to be staffed by ghosts. They looked over a receptionist's counter into a well-furnished office. The walls were half-faded government-blue and half-wood paneling. Then, from an adjacent office, a chair squeaked, and a deputy appeared.

"Yes? Can I help you?" the young man said. "Are you . . ."

"We called a half an hour ago," Bob said.

"You must be Cindy Chase, then," he said to Cindy. "Please come in. I'm Frank Casey, I hope I can help you."

Frank was exactly what a deputy in Oklahoma should look like, Al decided. He was sizable, with short, coal-black hair, dark skin, high cheekbones. He was without a doubt part Native American, a *large* man who barely cleared the doorway to his office. He wore a dark brown uniform with tan pants, and had a deep, booming voice that commanded immediate attention. He moved slowly, as if through water, and had a gaze that suggested he was drowsy. But Al saw he was anything but dim; his eyes shone with subdued intelligence, an intensity that seemed appropriate for anyone in a position of authority. He was capable, and concerned about Cindy. Al decided that he was an ally.

Frank pushed open a creaking brass-trimmed door and led them to his office. Three ancient varnished-oak folding chairs had been set up, apparently in preparation for their visit, in front of a pressboard computer desk with a gleaming-white IBM PC sitting incongruously atop it.

"Have you filled out one of these?" Frank asked right away, shoving a piece of paper across the desk to Cindy, a form for a "runaway or missing person report."

She nodded without taking it. "In Atlanta, and again in Tulsa. Last time they said it was already in the computer."

"Good," Frank said, sitting at the computer. "That will save time. Lets see what the NCIC has to say about it."

"NCIC?" Al asked.

"National Crime Information Center." Frank tapped away, and soon a menu filled the screen. "If you filled out a report in Atlanta, then it was entered there. This will tell us if anything else has developed lately that you don't know about yet."

After a few moments he frowned and said, "James Chase, Jr. Kidnaped from school by one James Byron Chase, your husband—"

"Ex-husband," Cindy quickly interrupted.

"And last seen in Tulsa, a week ago. Hmm. And now you think he's in Pawnee County?"

"I thought he might have been at Hallet. You know, the races. They're big car fans, the both of them. . . ."

"Tell me about it," Frank said calmly. "Tell me the whole story. From the first time you thought something was wrong. There might be something there I can use to help you, and we've got time."

Al paid no attention to the words; this time he narrowed his eyes as he tried to sort out the feelings involved. As Cindy told the deputy about the changes in her husband, Al had the feeling she was somehow trying to justify the search for her son, emphasizing that James Chase was no longer the man she married, that he had become a monster and was nothing like the caring, giving father of her son that she knew. Almost . . . apologetic. *For as many years as those two had been married, there must have been some kind of ongoing emotional abuse for her to feel so responsible about the situation. Emotional abuse results in emotional damage.* Great Danaa, *look at Bob when we rescued him. Gundar thought he was autistic until he peeked out from under that thick, defensive shell.*

When she got to the part about the Chosen Ones, Frank became visibly more alert. "After that first meeting I knew I had to get Jamie to a shelter, but I was too afraid to do anything. Then, after James dragged him off the second time, he came home in hysterics. Something happened—I still don't know what. But it was the last straw."

Frank's eyes burned with an intensity that made Al think of the Lakota warriors he had known so many years ago. "I see. And the leader of this cult, what was his name?"

Cindy bit her lip. "Brother something. Brother *Joseph,* I think it was. Totally nuts."

Frank calmly got up and went to a file cabinet. When he returned he held a thick file, and opened it out on his desk. He handed Cindy a glossy photograph from a stack of others. "Is this the man?"

Cindy stifled a gasp as she looked at the picture, holding it by the edges as if it were tinged with poison. "That's him, all right," she said, half in fear and half in anger. "Those eyes. I could never forget them."

"Then it is true. More evidence. Another angle to this mess."

"What mess?" Al asked.

"This cult," Frank said, speaking the word as if it tasted vile. "They've set up shop right here in our county. There's hundreds of them, perhaps thousands. For the past three years they've been building this damned thing right under our noses and we never knew about it until recently. Here. Look at these."

Frank handed her what looked like an aerial photograph. Bob and Al, sitting on either side, leaned in closer for a look.

"What am I looking at?" Bob asked.

"We asked the State Highway police to fly in and take

some pictures a few months back." Frank's eyes continued to smolder, and Al sensed a deep and abiding anger behind the calm facade. "The construction you see there is pretty much done by now. But there you can see the equipment in use. From what I can see from these, and it's not much, it looks like they're digging bunkers for World War III."

"That would make sense," she said thoughtfully. "I remember something from that sermon, or whatever it was, about an invasion that was going to happen any time now."

Frank raised one eyebrow. "From any particular direction? Any special enemies?"

Cindy shook her head tiredly. "The Soviets, the Jews, the blacks, the gays, the Satanists, pick a group—any or all together. They didn't seem to differentiate one from the other. But from the sounds of that bunch, I don't think it would matter. He could say hairdressers or Eskimos and they'd still believe him."

Frank sat back in his chair and fingered one corner of the file folder. "We've tried to get a search warrant to kind of check things out. No luck. They have a tight-assed lawyer—pardon my language, ma'am—who has filed injunction after injunction, blocking the warrants. The judge has no choice but to grant them. We don't have enough evidence. The lawyer, as crazy as he is, knows his business. Especially the loopholes in our legal system. You'd think he wrote 'em, he knows them so well."

"What about building codes?" Bob asked. "Those bunkers look a little questionable."

"That's the sad part about it," Frank said. "That part of the county is unincorporated, so there aren't a lot of permits you have to get. We already cleared them, including the Environmental Impact Assessment, years ago, without really checking it out. The inspector in charge back then has since retired, when we found out he had serious problems of a nature I'm not at liberty to discuss. We even have the blueprints to the place they filed when they applied for the permits. It *looks* like they built more than originally declared, but it's all underground, and we can't tell from outside. And we can't get a warrant to go in."

"Can we see the—blueprints?" Al asked, though he wasn't sure what a blueprint was.

"Nothing much to see," Frank said. The blueprints were in a desk drawer, and he spread them out over the open file.

"All this here, and here, looks like living quarters. The area isn't zoned so we couldn't get them on zoning violations. The rest, I don't know. But it's legit. All of it. At least everything they actually filed for." He folded the blueprints up and returned them to his drawer. "After they scared the EPA guy off with a squad of six armed bald goons following him around, nobody wants to go in and inspect. And there's nothing leaking into the aquifer or spilling into the creek, so we can't go in there on *that* excuse."

"They had guns. Lots of guns. What do your laws say about that?" Cindy asked.

"They're legal, on private property. To own and to discharge. They're not within any city limits. They're their own city. Unincorporated, of course, but a city nonetheless. And if they ever incorporate—they can make their own laws."

"Even machine guns are legal?"

Frank gazed at Cindy a long moment. "Are you referring to assault weapons?"

"I guess," she said doubtfully. Frank got to his feet, amazingly agile for such a big man.

"I'll be back in a minute," he said.

While Frank was gone Al leaned forward and glanced through the file. On top was a map, crudely drawn, which seemed to be of the cult's hideout in relation to the land and roads around it. He leaned back in his seat before Frank returned.

"Did they look anything like this?" Frank said, brandishing a fierce-looking rifle. "It's a Colt AR-15. If they have too many of these I'll be most displeased."

"Well, they had some of those." She frowned. "But there were other kinds, too. Can I have something to write with?"

"Here's a pad," Frank said, shoving a notepad and pencil across the desk to her. "Can you draw what you saw?"

She was already sketching. Frank stowed the assault rifle and returned; she gave him the rudimentary drawing of a weapon.

He frowned. "This looks like an AK-47. The clip curled out, like this?"

She nodded vigorously. "Uh-huh. They had other guns—.45s, shotguns, 30-30s. My husband owns a World War II Luger. He has it with him. But I saw an awful lot of the ones with the curled clip."

"Christ on a crutch," Frank muttered. "Just what we need. A nest of crazies with assault guns in our hills, waiting for Commies."

"It's the same group," Bob interjected. "The same ones we *know* James Chase was with. And we know he took the boy and vanished when they did. Isn't that enough for a search warrant?"

Frank gave him an opaque look. "To search for what, exactly?"

"To search for Jamie. That's why we're here today," Al pointed out.

Frank frowned, and said slowly, "I'll talk to the DA, but I don't know. I *would* have said 'yes,' but that was a while back. I've already locked horns with these crazies and come off losing too many times. There were some things about this cult that I thought were cut and dried, but I was dead wrong. Can't shut someone down for their religion, no matter how weird, and their lawyer knows every angle of religious-discrimination law. And they've tied themselves in to being a Christian group, and Christians have the swing around here. That's the story."

"How much evidence do you need?" Cindy said, sounding mystified. Al was just as frustrated, a hard ball of tension forming in the pit of his stomach. He could not believe this group was getting away with so much, as Frank phrased it, right under their noses. *Brother Joseph is a shrewd one, to have picked this community. He did his homework.*

"I understand your frustration, Miz Chase," Frank said, rubbing his temple with his knuckles, as if his head hurt. "And I have my own set of frustrations. I'm the only one around here who wants to get excited about it. I think part of the problem is folks around here, they don't quite grasp the magnitude of what's taking place. Those people don't come into town, not even to shop. They do that in Tulsa,

by the truckload. Most of them stay cooped up in that
complex. Those that do leave, they leave their guns behind,
except for maybe rifles in the gunracks in the cab window
and big crucifix stickers, and you see that everywhere."
Frank shifted in his chair, looking thoughtful. "What I've
seen up close I don't like either. They have guards at the
gates leading into the complex, and they politely ask me
to leave whenever I show up. There are probably more
children in that place than we realize, but I've only seen
a half-dozen of the kids go to the schools here."

"They what?" Cindy said, sitting up. "Is Jamie one of
them?"

Frank shook his head, and motioned for her to calm
down. "Don't think so, ma'am. I mean, I can't be sure
without checking, but I truly don't believe they'd let him
off their grounds if they have him. I've talked to some of
the teachers. Kids seem to be from all over the country,
complete with school records. They're legit, all right. But,
the teachers say the kids are basically quiet; sort of keep
to themselves, don't say much about religion or anything
else. They don't trust the other kids. They move around
in a tight little huddle, staying together. You can talk to
them, but they won't talk to you. They just stare at you
till you go away. And that pretty much describes everyone
at the compound."

"Could *I* talk to one of them?" Cindy asked hopefully.

Frank shook his head. "Even if you could get one to
talk, might not be a good idea. Could tip them off. If they
sent your husband and Jamie out of this county, there's
nothing we could do about it. My guess is these kids are
brainwashed to the point of being 'safe' to let outside the
group. Doubt you'd get much more out of 'em than I have."

Soon, after more dead-end discussions, both parties came
to the conclusion that there wasn't a great deal that could
be done right then. Cindy's frustration was obvious even
to the deputy; Bob had his jaw clenched tight, and Al felt
the muscles of his back and shoulders bunching with the
need to do *something*. But there was nothing to be done.

Legally.

And that's the real trick, isn't it?

Frank wished them well and gave them each his card,

with his home number on it, along with instructions to call him "if anything came up." Al noted later that the deputy seemed embarrassed that he couldn't do much. Something else was holding him back, but Frank wasn't saying what it was. He also had the feeling that if *they* did something a little on the wrong side of the fence to get information, Frank would look the other way, even cover for them. He didn't come out and say that, but he kept giving both him and Bob significant looks whenever he mentioned how much *his* hands were tied.

That doesn't matter; we don't really need him now. We know their location, some of their habits, and we have a lead, he thought, plans of his own beginning to form, as they left the county courthouse. *I think I should go check out these people myself.*

Jamie was getting ready to draw on another target when ... res became aware of someone standing behind them.

CHAPTER FIVE

The day after Jamie and his father had gone to Tulsa for supplies, Jamie gave up the search for allies, especially regarding the question of his missing mother. Nobody, including Joe, wanted to discuss it.

That negative reaction from Joe had been a disappointing surprise. He'd always thought he could tell Joe anything—and he *knew* how much Joe loved *his* mother, even though he never said much about it. He was always taking her bunches of wildflowers. He'd thought Joe would understand how much he missed her. . . .

Anyone he'd even mentioned his mother to specifically forbade him to bring the subject up with anyone else; so by the time he talked with Sarah, he had already decided to keep quiet about it, even with her.

But today he was having second thoughts about that, as the situation at the vacation place began to weigh more heavily on him. They still weren't letting him eat anything, and the juice they gave him never came close to filling him up. Hunger pangs came and went, with increasing frequency and intensity. Sometimes lately he had trouble standing up, and he always got dizzy if he walked too far. If he was getting sick, he knew it would be his own fault because he didn't have faith in Brother Joseph; at least, that was what everyone else would tell him. Then they'd tell him he had to confess his lack of faith and be healed.

Not a chance! He'd rather just suffer. Brother Joseph was too frightening to trust, but try to get the rest of *them* to see that! If you had faith, everyone told him, you wouldn't get sick. If you didn't, you did.

So he didn't tell anyone about the fainting spells, but he knew the time would soon come when he wouldn't be able to keep them secret.

In the meantime, he drank all the juice they'd let him have, and lots of water. He was still allowed to do that, and if you drank enough, the hunger went away. For a little while.

He had trouble sleeping again that night, and not just from the hunger, since Daddy had brought several bottles of joy juice to their room, the strong, amber kind, in funny-shaped bottles. The only word he could read on the label was Kentucky, and why it was on there he didn't know, 'cause that was a state. When Daddy drank that kind of joy juice something happened to his throat that made him snore real loud, and he rolled around on the bare mattress in his sleep. To keep from getting squished Jamie slid off the mattress and curled up in the corner with a blanket that was covered with tiny bugs.

But that didn't really matter to him. He just wanted to sleep. The bugs didn't bother him as much as usual.

He got up before Daddy did and went down to the showers, where other kids were getting ready for school, too. He had forgotten to wash his clothes out the night before, so he would have to wear them again, with that funny smell they got when he slept in them. A week earlier one of the other boys had stolen his clothes and hidden them down the hallway while he was in the shower, but his daddy caught him and whipped the living tar out of him. Jamie overheard some of the things they said, things he didn't like. The daddy told the boy that Jamie and his dad were poor and homeless before joining the Sacred Heart, and that it was wrong to pick on needy people like that. Jamie never thought of himself as poor, and he knew they had a home; Mommy was there, or at least that was what he thought, since she wasn't in Tulsa.

Now the boy would have nothing to do with him, and had turned the others against him as well, because he'd been punished. The other kids said nothing as they got cleaned up, and Jamie started to feel a little bit to blame for the whipping the first boy got. It hurt when they ignored him, although it made him even more grateful that he had Sarah for a friend.

School that day was a little different. They didn't talk about Jews and blacks much, or Israel or the divine plan Brother Joseph had in store for them. Part of the day was spent studying a machine for making drinking water. The process was called "reverse osmosis" and Miss Agatha made them memorize it and spell it fifty times on the chalkboard. "There will come a time when we will need this," the teacher admonished; Jamie didn't understand the need for the machine when you could just turn a faucet on, but he didn't ask any questions. Miss Agatha would just have made him write something else fifty times on the chalkboard, and it would probably be nasty and full of hate.

During lunch break, Jamie was sent to a room all by himself with his juice while the other kids went on to the cafeteria. He was still under orders to not eat until they summoned the "Holy Fire," Miss Agatha reminded him.

He tried to make the juice last, but it was gone all too quickly. Funny, he'd never liked V8 before, but now he would have drunk as much of it as he could have gotten. He wished that Brother Joseph would go and get it over with. His stomach was not hurting as much anymore, but he did feel weaker today. Daddy had slipped him some crackers and cheese the night before, and that helped a little, and there had been Joe's Tootsie Pop. But sitting here alone in the empty, thick-walled room, with nothing but a chair and a lightbulb, made him want to cry. He heard Miss Agatha say something about "sensory deprivation" and this room, but didn't understand any of it. He just knew it was boring in here.

Nobody was around, not even Miss Agatha. After a while, he realized that would make it easy to talk to Sarah.

"Sarah," he offered cautiously. "You there?"

:Right here,: she said, her voice filling the space between his ears. Jamie had put a pair of stereo headphones on once, and this was the same kind of effect. *:They're all gone?:*

"To eat," Jamie said dejectedly. "There was something I wanted to talk with you about yesterday. But I was afraid to."

Jamie sensed anger, which quickly dissipated. *:You don't have to be afraid to talk to me. You know that.:*

"Sorry," he said. "It was just, I was confused, you know? First Daddy gets weird, then Joe yells at me. . . ."

:It was about the milk carton, wasn't it?:

"How did you know?"

Silence.

"Okay, okay," Jamie said, a little sullenly. After all, she was only a girl—she didn't have to rub it in how much more she knew. Everybody here said girls weren't as important as boys. "You know a lot more than I do. You already told me."

:I see more, is all,: Sarah said, impatiently. *:And you know everything else they tell you is a lie. Why shouldn't I see more than you do? Because I'm a girl?:*

He blushed with embarrassment at getting caught thinking nasty thoughts. "Sorry," he mumbled. "Just, they keep *telling* me—"

:And it's hard to keep remembering how much they lie. I know, Jamie. What's bugging you?:

Jamie had the feeling she already knew, but he told her anyway. "I haven't seen my mother in a long time. Daddy said she'd be in Tulsa, but she wasn't there. Nobody around here wants to talk about it. What's going on?"

:I'm not sure, right now,: Sarah said, hesitantly. Jamie didn't know if he could believe her or not. It wasn't like her to not know everything. *:Look, it's not 'cause I can't tell or won't find out. I need more—stuff. Think about your mother. Think about what she looks like.:*

Jamie did, fully aware that Sarah could see exactly what was going on in his mind. This once made him uncomfortable, when he remembered all the bad things he used to think about girls, and even some of the mean tricks he used to play on them at school in Atlanta. But if Sarah saw these things, she didn't let on. She accepted him unconditionally, the only one besides his mother to ever do that. He reminded himself just how much he trusted her. Hey, she'd even been nice when he was thinking girls weren't as good as boys. . . .

:*She's not here, not at their Sanctuary anyway,*: Sarah said suddenly. :*But I think . . . she's close. Nearby. She's not as far away as Atlanta, anyway.*:

Hope flared. "In Tulsa?"

:*I don't know. Don't give up, all right? I'll keep looking. Until I find her, though, you can trust Joe. I think I could even talk to him directly, if he didn't close his mind off the way he does. He has . . . things he can do, but he doesn't want anyone to know, because of what they would all think about him. They'd figure it was the work of the devil, and there's no telling what they would do about it.*:

There was a warning in her voice that made him shiver. Miss Agatha had hinted some horrible things about what was done with people who were "possessed of the devil."

"I dunno," he said doubtfully. "I mean, his daddy is Brother Joseph. I don't think he'd snitch on me, but—"

:*His father might be Brother Joseph, but that doesn't mean Joe's like him. There's a lot of good in Joe, and he doesn't agree with much of what his daddy does. He'll help you, the same way he tried to help me.*: She sounded very positive, and very tired.

But he hadn't known Joe had been helping Sarah. "What happened, you know, with you and Joe?"

Again, silence. Jamie had learned that this usually meant she didn't want to talk about something, and he let it rest. He sat on the crude chair for some time, wondering if she had left, when she spoke again.

:*Joe will see you after school. Go with him.*:

And she was gone. Her presence vanished, like a candle blown out by the wind. In the past he had tried to get her back, but once she was gone, he knew that it would be a while before she would return. He wished he could have had time to say good-bye. As usual, he didn't. That was just Sarah's way. Maybe she didn't like saying good-bye. . . .

Joe will be there, after school. We'll get to go do something, maybe go outside, Jamie thought, as the lingering traces of Sarah disappeared. The prospect of being with his "big brother" was enough to dissipate the misery, even enough to make him forget his hollow stomach. *Oh boy!*

And even though his gnawing hunger made him forgetful, so that he made mistakes when Miss Agatha asked him questions that afternoon, talking with Sarah must have brought him luck. Miss Agatha just nodded indulgently, said something to the others about "the special Gift Jamie has is coming through," and prompted him until he got the answer right. That didn't earn him any friends among the other kids, though, because Miss Agatha was even harder on them as if to make up for being easy on him—

But in the end, he didn't care. He had Sarah, he had Joe. If the other kids were going to be dumb-butts because of something *he* couldn't help, let them. They were jerkfaces anyway. If he'd been home in Atlanta, he wouldn't have hung around with any of them. All they did was parrot Miss Agatha's hateful stuff and play games like "coon hunt" and "burn the nigger." That was what they called blacks; niggers. Jamie *knew* that wasn't right—his teachers in Atlanta, the ones he trusted, said that calling a black kid a "nigger" was like calling a kid in a wheelchair "cripple" or "freak."

After school was over, Joe was waiting outside for him, just like Sarah said. It wasn't the first time Joe had met him afterwards, but since his guard duty usually ran past the time school was out, it was rare to see Joe right after class. As always, he was wearing his uniform, with his AK-47 slung over his shoulder alongside a backpack.

The other children coursed around him like a flooding river around a solid rock. Some shot him angry glances, including Miss Agatha, who sniffed as she walked past. Jamie had sensed the contempt earlier, some sort of jealousy over his relationship with Joe, and as usual he disregarded it.

"Wanna go fishing?" Joe asked right away, and instantly, Jamie's world lit up.

"Sure!" he replied enthusiastically. Then he frowned, not knowing where exactly you could fish around here. Unless Joe wanted to go to a park somewhere else; but that would mean leaving the vacation place, and he had never been allowed to do that, unless he was with his father. After drinking as much joy juice as he had the night before, James wouldn't be very good company today. "Where?" he asked doubtfully.

Joe chuckled. "There's a pond over near the north side of the complex. Only a few of us know about it. We'll have to stop and get a bow to fish with, though."

Jamie had thought the only way to fish was with a pole, or maybe even a net. But as they walked, Joe explained how it could be done with a bow and arrow, if you were good. There were plenty of hunting bows in the armory. Joe had a special bow in mind, one his dad had purchased for him when he was Jamie's age.

After the revelation that Joe was Brother Joseph's son, Jamie had begun to see that his friend had a few more privileges in the Guard than others his own age. They were, he realized, exercising some of them now; nobody else had unlimited access to the armory. At least, not among the kids.

"Let's walk," Joe said. He had talked about borrowing a motorcycle, but had apparently decided against it. "It's not as hot today. Rained this morning."

Living underground, you didn't notice things like rain or sunshine. Jamie squinted at the bright glare of the sun. It reminded him again how dim it was below. They passed by guards periodically. Joe waved and they waved back, letting them out of the complex without question. The boy knew that the story would be different when they came back through, when they would be searched. But he wasn't going to worry about that yet. When they came to the final gate, Joe told the guard they would be fishing a while and would be back before too long. The guard wished them luck and locked the tall chain-link gate behind them.

It occurred to Jamie that if they caught fish, he might be able to get a bite to eat. But eating meant cooking, and cooking meant a fire and things to cook with, things they didn't have. Jamie remembered something called sooshee that was raw fish, and before today the idea never appealed to him. Today was a different story. If Daddy could cheat and sneak him some cheese and crackers, maybe Jamie could do the same with the fish they could catch.

So he asked him, "Hey, Joe, when we catch the fish, can we make sooshee out of it?"

"Naw," he said. "We have to throw them back." Then he eyed the boy warily, as if suddenly understanding the purpose of the remark. "You know you're on a strict Holy Fire fast. I'd get in big trouble if I let you eat anything."

Somehow Jamie wasn't surprised. Even though Joe was his best friend, next to Sarah, he was still under orders from Brother Joseph. Now that he knew Brother Joseph was Joe's father, that added a new dimension to the threat. Jamie knew you couldn't get into nearly as much trouble with other daddies as you could with your own.

He dropped the subject about food, remembering the vehemence with which Joe had responded to the milk carton question. He didn't want a replay of *that* miserable scene.

The barbed wire fences receded behind them as they took a trail through the oak forest skirting the northern edge of the complex. Jamie felt a little happier, knowing the other kids, who would kill for a chance to go into the woods and play, were sitting somewhere underground dreaming about what he was doing now. Birds called and flew overhead, and something skittered through the grass and leaves along the path.

Presently they came upon a clearing.

Jamie suddenly felt cold. There was a foreboding sense of dread attached to the place, a feeling of evil, or suffering. He was sort of seeing things inside his head. The vague images flowing through his mind were shifting and confusing; having been told by Brother Joseph not to share these impressions with anyone else, he didn't tell Joe about his feelings or what he was seeing.

"You've never been to this place before," Joe said firmly. "And don't you never tell anyone you were here."

Jamie nodded, feeling a little sick to his stomach. The images grew stronger, and he began to wonder if Sarah was feeding them to him. She had done that before, when they first met, but that was a long time ago and they were good friends now. Sarah could talk to him in person now. That is, if she wasn't afraid of coming to this place.

"We had to bury somebody here," Joe said suddenly, and

the words shocked Jamie. "She died real young, but the Chosen Ones, we bury our own here."

"This is like a graveyard?" Jamie asked, hesitating.

Joe nodded absently. "Yep, but no one knows about it."

Jamie looked about in alarm. "What 'bout the head-stones?"

"Like I said, nobody knows about it. If there were headstones, everybody would know, wouldn't they? Daddy was afraid of putting tombstones up because he was afraid they'd be visible from the air—" Joe suddenly cut his sentence off, sounding like he'd said something he shouldn't have. Jamie acted like nothing was wrong, even though the bad, dark feeling was getting stronger. It was different here than it was with the Holy Fire, and not as bad. The feeling was more a terror of something that had already happened, as opposed to something that was *about* to happen to *him,* as during the rituals with Brother Joseph. But he also suspected the two feelings were related, in a distant sort of way.

They went over to a mound of dirt about as long and wide as a beach towel. The earth had been turned some-time recently, maybe this spring, but Jamie could see that it had been more than a few weeks. Wild weeds had sprung up, while the more permanent grass, which took longer to grow, came in around the edges. It was plainly somebody's grave, and the revelation left him feeling hollow and icky inside.

Joe knelt and took off the backpack. From within the front pouch he pulled out a battered bouquet of wild-flowers. *Must have picked those while I was in class*, Jamie thought, surprised. *Must have been someone important, whoever this was.*

"I hate to think nobody remembers Sarah," he said as he lay the flowers on the mound.

Sarah? My Sarah?

Joe sighed. "You wouldn't remember her. She died long before you came here."

"But . . ." Jamie blurted. He didn't know what to say, other than: *Sarah can't be dead, I just talked to her! In my head!* But that sounded too strange and unbelievable, so he didn't. Besides, Sarah was his secret, and lately Joe was showing basic problems where certain topics were concerned. Not untrustworthiness yet; but, well, there were things he just wouldn't discuss with someone who had blown up the way Joe had over the milk carton.

Joe just knelt there, staring at the grave.

Suddenly, despite the fact that he didn't want to believe it, Jamie knew this was the *same* Sarah. *Had* to be. As he looked at the mound of dirt, images formed mistily in his mind, a gust of something, a spirit, a smell, like baby powder, only a little sweeter. Sarah's scent. Jamie watched Joe in concealed horror, finally accepting that all along he hadn't been talking with a person, exactly.

He had been talking with a ghost. And ghosts were supposed to be scary.

But Sarah's not scary, he thought, in confusion. *Sarah's my friend!* He stared at the grave, while Joe bowed his head like he was praying.

The images that had been lurking at the periphery of his mind now sprang into full, vivid life, coalescing, condensing, forming a story, a kind of movie in his head. A scary story—the kind his mommy wouldn't let him watch on TV. He knew that without knowing how he knew it. And he knew he would have to watch *this* story, because it wasn't just a story, it was real.

Jamie saw her clearly now, standing just beyond the clearing on a short, grassy knoll. Sarah was a girl his age with black hair and delicate brown eyes, in a calico dress that fluttered slowly in the windless afternoon. Joe didn't see her, and Jamie knew that was only because she didn't want to be seen.

Her mommy and daddy had joined the cult, too, only they had disappeared suddenly, and nobody knew where they were. Brother Joseph told Sarah that they would be back, that they had just gone to Tulsa for a little while. Sarah didn't believe it then, but played along because she feared Brother Joseph, just like Jamie did now.

And for the same reason. Brother Joseph had been starving her just like he was being starved, and had used her as an instrument for communicating with the Holy Fire. At first her parents had objected. Then they went along with it, or at least they told her to do what Brother Joseph said, until they worked things out. Then, they disappeared. Sarah was afraid Brother Joseph had something to do with that. The weeks went by slowly, and still no parents. This was starting to sound familiar to Jamie.

Meanwhile Brother Joseph held the Praise Meetings, and the Black Thing came closer to Sarah no matter how hard she tried to keep it away. Sometimes, during the same rituals that Jamie dreaded, she actually touched that dark, horrible thing, but most of the time she pretended to see it, telling Brother Joseph what he wanted to hear.

The preacher said it was a good thing, this Holy Fire, but Sarah knew better, and kept it at bay as best she could.

Then one night it came too close, and she couldn't repel it. The hunger had been intense, and the lack of food had weakened her will as well as her body. Brother Joseph yelled at her to touch it—and, unable to fight him, she did.

The suffocating thing tried to pull her in. She cried hysterically and broke with it. Brother Joseph ordered the congregation to leave, informing them the Praise Meeting was over. When they had gone, and his personal bodyguards had locked all the doors, he turned to Sarah and grabbed her throat with his perfectly white manicured hands.

"You will do what I say, you little slut, always!" Brother Joseph screamed, and the images became shaky as Sarah lost consciousness. Then the series of images ended, and Jamie was vaguely aware of . . . a different kind of darkness. . . .

"Jamie! Jamie, what is it?"

When he opened his eyes Joe was looking down at him, his face contorted with concern. "Are you okay? What's the matter?"

Jamie's vision blurred again; he closed his eyes to keep from being sick, and he felt Joe pick him up and carry him away from Sarah's grave. He felt something wet and cold at his lips, and he drank deeply. The water had a funny metal taste to it, but he didn't care as he guzzled all that was offered.

He opened his eyes again. Joe was kneeling in front of

him, his expression a mixture of concern and fear. The clearing where Sarah was buried was in sight but further away, making it tolerable now. Above, an enormous oak shaded them from the summer sun, and nearby he heard water running.

"You passed out back there." Joe frowned. "Weak?"

"I guess," he said, and admitted to Joe what he hadn't told anyone else. "I feel funny."

Joe felt his forehead. "You're warm, but that ain't nothin' in this heat. Are you going to be all right? You wanna go back?"

Jamie sat up, finding his strength returning—as much of it as there was, anyway. He didn't want to go back, so he forced a smile and said, "I'm fine now. Let's go fishing." He looked behind him, toward the sound of running water. "That a creek back there?"

Joe seemed to be having second thoughts. "No, I'd better get you back. I don't like the way you just dropped like that." He paused, as if considering something. "You said you knew Sarah, back there. After you passed out. What didja mean 'xactly when you said that?"

"Dunno," Jamie said. "I'm okay now," he added, trying not to let the disappointment show in his voice. "We'd better hurry, if we're going to get to supper on time."

About halfway back to the vacation place, Jamie remembered he wasn't going to be getting any supper.

Frank Casey felt his tired eyes drying. He'd stared at the computer screen for a solid minute before blinking. There it was, right in front of him, all the information he needed to find a kidnaped little boy. And not a damned thing he could do about it.

The three people who had just left his office, the boy's mother and the two oddball road-warriors, were the only people in the county who seemed to care about this peculiar cult setting up shop in their backyard. When he first learned of the Chosen Ones, Frank had been willing to live and let live, until he saw the clues that people were being controlled in some obscure, sinister way. And after listening to Cindy talk about the assault weapons, and the other implements of destruction the cult seemed to take a keen interest in, not to mention the power that one man had over the whole lot . . .

It was all just too damned dangerous. Frank Casey could already hear the zipping of body bags.

The cutbacks in the department couldn't have come at a worse time. Given that the county's economy was mostly tied to the price of a barrel of oil, the decrease in revenues from real estate and other taxes was inevitable. With fewer men, he couldn't collect evidence and be discreet at the same time. But if he spent enough time—some of it his own—he would probably see something that would justify a warrant, something that their high-powered attorney couldn't block.

Frank Casey remembered the glint he had seen in Al's eye when he mentioned the stakeout, and smiled. The man was smart; so was his partner. They'd seen the hints, he was sure, just as he was certain they'd act on them. *Yeah, you're hungry for it, too,* the tall Cherokee thought. *I can't authorize civilians to do stakeouts, but if you find something I'm sure gonna back you up on it. Every inch of the way.*

Al waited, his arms crossed over his chest, projecting every iota of authority he had—not as Al Norris, Fairgrove mechanic, but as Sieur Alinor Peredon, Knight-Artificer in the service of Elfhame Outremer, who had once commanded (small) armies.

Now all he had to do was convince one human of that authority. . . .

Bob sighed, finally, and shook his head. "All right," he said, though with a show of more reluctance than Al sensed he really felt. "All right, I'll cover for you here, and I'll keep Cindy from asking too many questions, if that's what you really want."

"It's what I want," Al said firmly. "Absolutely. I don't want to raise her hopes that I'm one of your foolish movie-star corambos—"

"That's *commandos,* or *Rambos,*" Bob interrupted.

"Whatever. I don't want her thinking I'm going to charge into unknown territory and carry her boy off. I want to get the lay of the land and check defenses." Al frowned, though it was not intended for Bob. "The fact is, there is a very odd feeling about that place, even at a distance. The Native man, the deputy sheriff, he feels it too, although he considers himself too rational and civilized to admit it. I am not going to stumble about blindly in there—"

"Fine, fine," Bob interrupted again. "But while you're off with Andur, where am I supposed to be sleeping?"

"Ah," Al said, grinning with delight. "I have solved that small problem. Behold—"

He took Bob around to the side of the RV; parked there, beside the Miata, was a white van. He enjoyed the look on Bob's face; enjoyed even more the expression when he opened the door to reveal the luxurious interior. *Not* as sybaritic as the RV would have been had Cindy not been with them, but a grade above the RV in its current state.

Bob turned back to him, his incredulity visible even in the dome light of the van. "How in hell did you do that?" he demanded. "I *know* you didn't ken the van, you'd need more time than a couple of hours to make the copy—"

"This is Nineve," Al informed him smugly. "Andur's twin sister. I called her from Outremer last night, when I realized that we would need two vehicles. You rightly said that the elvensteeds can crack Mach one in forms other than four-legged; she arrived here as soon as darkness fell." He permitted himself a smile. "Now you have lodging *and* transport."

Bob regarded Nineve with a raised eyebrow. "Hope she was in 'stealth' mode, or there's gonna be UFO reports from here to Arkansas." Then he unbent and patted the shiny side of the van. "Thanks, Nineve. You're here in right good time. And you sure are pretty."

The van's headlights glowed with pleasure.

"Now listen," Bob continued, "I got an idea. How 'bout we put Cindy in Nineve, and you an' me go back to bachelor quarters, eh?"

Al thought about that; thought about it hard. Not that he had any doubt that a strong reason for Bob's request was his inherent puritanical feelings—

But with Cindy in the van, he would be able to transform the RV into something far more comfortable—so long as he remembered to change it back before she entered.

And I won't have to wear a hat to sleep, either.

He sent a brief, inquiring thought to Nineve, who assented. Andur's twin spent a great deal of time with the human fosterlings of Fairgrove and liked them. Just as she had liked Janet. . . .

"Good idea," he said, thinking happily of a long soak in a hot shower when he returned, and a massage at the skilled hands of his lovely chrome servant—small as she was, her hands never tired.

Doubtless Bob was thinking of the same things.

Better to get Cindy out of the way of becoming a temptation. Bob is right about that much.

"Well, fine," Bob said, a slow grin spreading across his face. "I'll move her things now. Soon's she gets back from the laundry with her clothes, I'll intro—I mean, show her the new quarters. That oughta keep her busy enough that she won't be asking too many questions."

"And I had best be on my way," Al observed, "if I am to learn anything of these people tonight."

Andur revved his engine a little, as if the air conditioner compressor had come on, to underscore his eagerness to get on the road. It had been a long time since he and Andur undertook a rescue mission. It would be good to get back into harness again.

Andur popped his door open as Al approached the driver's side of the car and shut it as soon as he was tucked into the seat. Al let the four-point seat-harness snake across his shoulders and his lap, and meet and fuse in the center of his chest. Not that he often needed it—but no one allied with racing ever sacrificed safety.

Or an edge.

Andur flipped on his lights, turning everything outside the twin cones of light to stark blackness by contrast. Despite the impatient grumble of the pseudo-engine beneath the hood, Andur had more sense than to spin his wheels and take off in a shower of gravel. Such behavior at a track was the mark of an amateur, a poseur, and would earn him and his rider as much respect as Vanilla Ice at a Public Enemy concert.

Instead, Andur prowled out with slow grace, making his way to the single unlocked gate for the after-hours use of mechanics and drivers. They proceeded with courtesy for the few folk still about and on their feet after the long day. Alinor thought briefly that it was much like being back at Court; it was considered good form to be socially graceful as a means of preparing one's mind before an imminent battle, and the coolness displayed gained one more status than strutting or worrying.

Al did not have to touch the steering wheel; Andur was perfectly capable of reading his mind to know where they were going. Down the gravel access-road to the roughly paved county road that led to Hallet, and from there to the on-ramp for the turnpike—

And there he paused, while Al read the map of the area and matched it with the one in his mind; the one that showed the rough details of the cult enclave. The turnpike was one possible route—

But there was a better one; so in the end they passed the turnpike and took another county road, then another. Andur knew precisely the route to take, so Al leaned back into the embrace of the "leather" seat, and let his mind roam free.

This was a land like a strong, broadwinged bird—with a deadly, oozing cancer. In this area's heart hid a festering wound in the power-flows of the earth, a place where energy was perverted, twisted, turned into something it made him sick to contemplate.

He might not have noticed if he hadn't been looking for it; it was well-hidden. He might have dismissed it as a stress headache. There was no doubt in his mind that this was the work of "Brother Joseph"; it had that uniquely human feel to it, of indifference to consequences. There was also a hate, an anger, and a twisted pleasure in the pain of others.

He opened his eyes and oriented himself, calling back the suppressed elven night-vision that made the darkened landscape as bright as midday sun. Andur had long since darkened his headlights; *he* certainly didn't need them to see his way. And now as Al watched, the shiny white enamel of the hood darkened, softened, going to a flat matte black. The engine sounds quit, too—they rolled onto a gravel-covered secondary road with no more sound than the crunching of gravel, which also quieted as Andur softened the compound of his tires. The sound of the cicadas in the trees beside the roadway drowned what was left.

Then Andur turned off the road entirely—

And Al was sitting astride a matte-black stallion, who picked his way across the overgrown fields like a cat crossing ice. The hot, humid air hit him with a shock after the cool of the wind and Andur's air-conditioner.

Al realized that his white track-suit was not the best choice of outfits for a scouting mission. With a moment's thought, he changed the Nomex to a light garment of matte black silk; then blackened his face and hands as well with a silken mask and gloves. His feet he shod in boots of lightweight black leather, easy to climb in. In this guise they approached the first of the three fences surrounding the complex.

This far from the road, there was only the patrolling guard to worry about—and the trip-wires and fences.

He felt Andur gather himself and hung on while the elvensteed launched into an uncannily silent gallop, the only sounds muffled thuds when his hooves hit the ground. Then he felt Andur's muscles bunch—

He tightened his legs and leaned forward, as Andur leapt.

No human would ever have believed his eyes, for the elvensteed began his jump a good fifteen feet from the fence, cleared the top of it with seven feet to spare, and landed fifteen feet from the fence on the other side.

Without a stirring of power-flows. The magic of good design, sweet Andur.

They passed the second fence the same way, but halted at the third, innermost fence; the one that surrounded the compound itself. This was as far as Al wanted to go right now. There was no way he was going to go nosing about an enemy camp without scouting it first.

Andur concealed himself in a patch of shadow, and Al climbed a tall enough tree that he was able to see the compound quite clearly. Whatever the sheriff might have imagined at his most pessimistic, the situation was worse.

The guards prowled within the fence like professional soldiers. There were a lot of them, and the number of life-essences Al detected below ground indicated that this "Brother Joseph" must be fielding an army.

There was Cold Iron everywhere, low quality iron which disrupted his senses; it was difficult to concentrate when using his Sight, and even more difficult to find ways around the barriers. And deep inside the complex was that evil cancer he had sensed before. It was not a spell or item, but it *was* magical. It wasn't elven in origin, nor was it human . . . no, something old and experienced had created the magical "taste" he'd sensed. There was something alive and not-alive shifting its enchanted form inside the compound.

It was quiescent when he first approached it, but as he studied it, the thing began to rouse. He drew back, thinking that *he* had caused it to awaken and stir—but then his questing thoughts brushed the thoughts of humans—many humans—in the same area, and he realized that *they* were the ones waking it.

He withdrew a little further, heart racing despite his wished-for cool, and "watched" from what he hoped was a safe distance.

The humans were gathered in one of the underground areas for a spectacle of some kind.

Could this be one of the "Praise Meetings" that Cindy described?

Something—someone—moved into his sensing area. Another human—but where the life-fires of the others burned with a smoky, sullen flame, more heat than light, *this* person's burned with the black flame of the devourer, who feeds on lives. Even more than lives, this human thrived on the *hate* of those around him. Al knew him without ever seeing his face. This *must* be Brother Joseph.

With him was a tiny, fitful life-spark, so close to extinction that Al nearly manifested in the full armor of an elven warrior-noble and carved his way to the child's side. For it *was* a child, who had been so starved, so abused, that his hold on life and his body was very tenuous indeed.

Jamie. It had to be Jamie.

And as Al held himself back, with anger burning in his heart, the evil thing at the heart of the gathering woke.

And reached for the child.

CHAPTER SIX

By the time the Praise Meeting started, Jamie was having a hard time keeping himself from throwing up even though there was nothing in his stomach but water. And he couldn't stand up for very long; he shivered and his skin was clammy, and he had to lie down on the floor because sitting in the chair made him dizzy.

He knew the Praise Meeting had started, because he heard the organ; it vibrated the walls all the way back here, in the very rear of the building. The vibrations disoriented him; he had his eyes closed when the door to the little room finally opened, and the two big guards came in to get him.

Brother Joseph always sent two huge men with AK-47s to get him. It was just one of the hundreds of things Brother Joseph said and did that didn't make any sense. But maybe it was a good thing they'd been sent this time; when one of them ordered Jamie to stand, he got as far as his knees before that soft darkness came down on him again, and he found himself looking up at their faces from the ground.

He was afraid for a minute that they'd hit him—but they just looked at one another, then at him, then without a single word, picked him up by the elbows, and hauled him to his feet. His toes didn't even touch the floor; that didn't matter. The guards carried him that way down the long, chilly corridor to the door that led to the back of the Meeting Hall.

They came out on the stage, at the rear. The four spotlights were focused on Brother Joseph, who was making a speech into a microphone, spitting and yelling. Jamie couldn't make any sense of what he was saying; the words kept getting mixed up with the echo from the other end of the room, and it all jumbled together into gibberish.

The two men didn't pay any attention, either; they just took him to an oversized rough-wood chair in front of the black and red flag that Brother Joseph had everyone pledge to and dropped him into it, strapping down his arms and legs with clamps built into the chair itself.

Jamie let them. He'd learned the first time that it did no good to resist them. No one out there would help him, and later his father would backhand him for struggling against Brother Joseph's orders.

Brother Joseph continued, so bright in the spotlights that Jamie had to close his eyes. It seemed as if the only light in the room was on the leader; as if he sucked it all up and wouldn't share it with anyone else.

Brother Joseph's voice, unintelligible as it was, hammered at Jamie's ears, numbing him further. He was so hungry— and so dizzy—he just couldn't bring himself to think or care about anything else.

Finally the voice stopped, although it was a few moments before the silence penetrated the fog of indifference that had come over Jamie's mind. He opened his eyes as a spotlight fell on him—light that stabbed through his eyes into his brain, making hot needles of pain in his head. But it was only for a moment; then a shadow eclipsed the spotlight, a tall shadow, with the light streaming around the edges of it.

It was Brother Joseph, and Jamie stifled a protest as Brother Joseph's hand stretched out into the light, a thin chain with a sparkling crystal on the end of it dangling from his fingers. Jamie knew what was coming next, and for a moment he struggled against his bonds.

But dizziness grayed his sight, and he couldn't look away

from the twirling, glittering, sparkling crystal. Brother
Joseph's voice, a few moments ago as loud as a trumpet,
now droned at Jamie, barely audible, words he tried to
make out but couldn't quite catch.

The world receded, leaving only the crystal, and Brother
Joseph's voice.

Then, suddenly, something different happened—

This was the part where the Black Thing tried to touch
him, only it didn't this time. This time he was somehow
standing *next* to himself; he was standing on the stage, and
there was someone between him and the boy strapped to
the chair.

Sarah. And she stood as if she was ready to fight something off, in a pose that reminded him of the way his
mother had stood between him and his daddy the first time
he'd come home after Brother Joseph had—

:*After Brother Joseph used you, like he used me,*: said
a familiar voice in his head. :*For that :*

The girl pointed, and he saw the Black Thing slipping
through a smoky door in the air, sliding towards the boy
in the chair.

Only now he could see it clearly, and it wasn't really a
shapeless blot. It was—like black fire, swirling and bubbling, licking against the edge of the door. Like a negative of flames.

It was bad, he felt that instinctively, and he recoiled from
it. But he found he couldn't go far, not even to the edge
of the stage. When he tried, he felt a kind of tugging, like
he was tied to the boy in the chair with a tight rope around
his gut.

:*Don't worry, Jamie,*: said Sarah. :*I'll keep it away from
you. It won't mess with me now.*:

The Black Thing moved warily past her—then melted
into the Jamie-in-the-chair.

Jamie jerked, as pain enveloped him.

Sarah stepped forward and grabbed something invisible—
and then it wasn't invisible, it was a silver rope running
between him and Jamie-in-the-chair. And the minute she
touched the rope, the pain stopped.

"Speak, O Sacred Fire," Brother Joseph cried out, as
the boy in the chair jerked and quivered. Brother Joseph's

voice sounded far away, and tinny, like it was coming from a bad speaker. "Speak, O Holy Flame! Tell us your words, fill us with the Spirit!"

Jamie-in-the-chair's mouth opened—but the voice that came out wasn't Jamie's. It was a strange, hollow voice, booming, like a grownup's—like James Earl Jones'. Gasps of fear peppered the audience when he began speaking, outbursts which the people quickly stifled. The audience reaction turned to awe as the echoing voice carried into the crowd. It said all kinds of things; more of the same kind of stuff that Brother Joseph and Miss Agatha were always saying. All about how Armageddon was coming, and the Chosen Ones were the only people who would be saved from the purifying flames. About the Jews and the blacks and the Sodomites—how they ran everything, but after the flames came, the Chosen Ones would run everything.

But then the voice said something Jamie had never heard Brother Joseph say—

"—and you, Brother Joseph," boomed the voice. "You are the Instrument of the Prophecy. You will be the Bringer of Flame. You will be the Ignitor of the Holocaust. In your hand will be the torch that begins the Great Conflagration—"

Brother Joseph began to frown, and his frown deepened as the voice went on with more of the same. *This must be new*—Jamie thought.

:*It is new,*: said Sarah, relaxing her vigilance a little, and turning to look over her shoulder at him. Even though he knew she was a ghost now, he was somehow no longer afraid of her. In fact, in his present state, he felt closer to her, like they were the same kind of people now. And it helped to be able to see her. He moved a little closer to her, and she took his hand and smiled.

:*This stuff is all new,*: she said without moving her lips, cocking her head to one side. :*And Brother Joseph doesn't like it. Look at him.*:

Indeed, Brother Joseph's face was not that of a happy man, and Jamie could see why—for out in the assembled audience there were stirrings and murmurs of uneasiness.

But when the voice stopped, Brother Joseph whirled and raised his hands in the air, his face all smiles. "Halleluia!"

he cried. "Praise God, he has chosen me to lead you, though I am not worthy! He has called me to witness for you and lead you, as John the Baptist witnessed before the coming of the Lord Jesus and led the Hebrews to the new Savior! You've heard it from the mouth of this child, through the instrument of His Holy Fire—I am the forerunner, and it is my coming that has been the signal and paved the way for the end—and *our beginning*!"

Cries of "Praise the Lord!" and "Halleluia!" answered him, and there were no more murmurs of dissent. Brother Joseph had them all back again.

:*Now comes the part they've really been waiting for,*: Sarah said, an expression of cynicism on her face that was at odds with her years. :*The miracles.*:

"Half Hi to win, Saturn Boy to place, and Beauregard to show in the second," boomed the voice. "Righteous to win, Starbase to place, and Kingsman to show in the third. Grassland to win, Lena's Lover to place, and Whatchacall to show in the fifth—"

:*Miracles?*: Jamie said, puzzled.

:*Those are all the horses that are going to win at Fair Meadows tomorrow,*: she replied. :*They're going to make a lot of money by betting on them.*:

"Fifth table, fourth seat, Tom Justin," said the voice. "Tom should get in line behind the fat woman in a red print dress and take two blue cards, two red, two yellow and two gray. Sixth table, twelfth seat, Karen Amberdahl. Karen should get in line behind an old man with a cigar, a turquoise belt buckle and a string tie with a bearclaw slide, and take one of each color."

:*And those are the people that should go to bingo tomorrow night, where they should sit, and what cards they should take. If they do that, they'll have winning cards.*: Sarah's lip curled. :*But it won't be a lot of money. They're just making the seed money for the real stuff. The horse races, and what comes later.*:

Finally the voice stopped; Jamie felt dizzy, and when he looked down at himself, he was kind of—transparent. He could see the floor through his arm. Had he been able to do that when he first found himself here? He didn't think so.

:You're fading,: Sarah said, looking worried. *:I don't know why. I think the Black Thing is using you up, some-how—:*

She didn't get a chance to elaborate on that; the guards were escorting everyone except for a chosen few out—those few filed up to the front and waited in a line just below the stage. Jamie noticed, as they arranged themselves and waited for the guards to get everyone else out, that he was getting solid again. So—the Black Thing used him up when it spoke. And if it wasn't talking, he got a chance to recover.

"All right," Brother Joseph said, in a brisk, matter-of-fact voice that was nothing like what he used when preaching, "We got the El Paso crack shipment tonight on the airstrip. Bill, you're new; hold your questions until the Holy Fire is done speaking."

What came out of Jamie-in-the-chair's mouth then, was not anything like what he had expected.

"Apartment 1014B over in the Oaktree Apartment Complex is a new dealer, he'll pay top prices to you because he's been having visions. His line dried up. Sell him a quarter of the shipment. You've got enough regulars for another quarter. For the rest, take a quarter to Tulsa, peddle it Friday on Denver, on Saturday over by the PAC, Sunday on the downtown mall. The narcs will be elsewhere. *Don't* talk to anyone in a blue Ford Mustang, license plate ZZ611; they're cops. Get off the street on Friday by two in the morning, there's going to be a bust. Take the other quarter to Oklahoma City and—"

:Is he talking about drugs?: Jamie asked Sarah, bewildered. *:Like dope? Like they said to say no to in school?:*

She nodded grimly. *:That's where the real money is coming from,:* she replied. *:Brother Joseph is a dealer, and the Black Thing knows where all the cops are, and where the best place to sell is.:*

The man Bill, who had been designated as "new," looked unhappy, and as if he was trying not to squirm. As the voice finished—and another wave of dizziness and transparency passed over Jamie—he saw that Brother Joseph was watching this man very closely. And before the man could say anything, Brother Joseph spoke, in still another kind of voice. Friendly, kind, like Daddy used to be before all the joy juice, back in Atlanta.

"Now, Bill," Brother Joseph said, "I know what you must be thinking. You're wondering how we, the Chosen of the Lord, could *stoop* to selling crack and ice, this poison in the veins of America. How we could break God's law as well as man's."

Bill nodded, slowly.

"Bill, Bill," Brother Joseph said, shaking his head. "This is part of our *mission*. The Holy Fire *instructed* us to do this! We aren't selling this to innocent children—it's going to Satanists and Sodomites, uppity Jews and niggers, Commies and hippies and whores—all people who'd poison themselves with the stuff anyway, whether we sold it to them or not. They're killing *themselves;* we're no more to blame than the man that sells a suicide a gun. And what's more, we're drying up the trade of the regular dealers, godless nigger gang members. The ones who *do* sell this poison in schoolyards."

Sarah snorted. :*No they aren't,*: she said angrily. :*That's a lie! They're* supplying *the guys who sell dope to kids. White and black.*:

Jamie nodded, remembering the stuff about "the dealer whose supply line dried up."

Bill looked unconvinced and replied, hesitantly, "But— what about the bingo games, the horse races—"

"Peanuts," one of the guards scoffed, in an insulting tone. "Grocery money."

"Now Tom, that's not fair," Brother Joseph told him, in the tones of a parent mildly chiding a child. Then he turned back to Bill. "He is right that it's really just the cash for our day-to-day expenses," the preacher said. "Bill, *you* know what an AK-47 costs these days, I know you do."

Bill nodded, reluctantly.

"And we have hundreds—thousands. And that's just one of the guns we have stockpiled. Then there's the anti-tank weapons, the grenade launchers, the SAMs—that's just weapons. We *bought* those tractors and bulldozers, out-right—"

"I was a farmer," Bill said slowly. "The gear you—we— have is about a quarter mil per tractor, and I dunno how much them earth-movers run. But—we never win big at the track or the bingo games, and I know there's big pots—"

"And there's IRS agents waiting right there at the track and the parlor, waiting for the big winner," Brother Joseph interrupted. "We *can't* let the gov'ment know what's going on here, and if a lot of our people start winning big, not even our fancy lawyer is gonna be able to keep them off our backs. Hell, Bill, that's how the gov'ment got Al Capone, didn't you know? Tax evasion!"

"Dope money's big, it's underground, and can't be traced," said one of the other men, complacently. "And nobody in this state would put dope and a church together."

Bill thought for a moment, then nodded again, but this time with a lot less reluctance. "I guess you're right—"

"It was I *who ordered them,*" boomed the voice of the Black Thing, unexpectedly, startling them all. "Holiest Brother Joseph was reluctant, but I showed him the way, the way—"

"The way to acquire the money we needed without hurting innocent children," Brother Joseph took up smoothly, when the voice faltered.

"Well, I guess it's all right, then," Bill said, looking relieved, and glancing out of the corner of his eye at Jamie-in-the-chair, nervously. "If the Holy Fire ordered it."

"That will be all, then, soldiers of faith," Brother Joseph said in his old, commanding tone of voice. "You have your marching orders. Tomorrow you will be assigned and go forth to implement them, in the name of the Holy Fire."

The guards herded the last of the Chosen Ones out, leaving Brother Joseph alone with Jamie. And the Black Thing. And Sarah—but he didn't know she was there.

Brother Joseph turned to Jamie-in-the-chair, with a terrible, burning hunger in his eyes, a hunger that looked as though it could have devoured the world and not been satisfied.

"Tell me," he ordered, in a harsh voice. "Tell me about the End. Tell me about my part in it."

The voice began again; more of the same kind of stuff it had told the crowd at the beginning, but more personal this time. About how Brother Joseph was the One True Prophet of the age, how he would lead the Chosen Ones in a purge of all that was evil on earth, until there was no one left but his own followers. How he would be made World President for Life in the ruins of the UN Building; how he would oversee the building of the Promised Heavenly Kingdom On Earth.

There was a lot of that stuff, and Brother Joseph just ate it up. And Jamie faded and faded—

Finally even the hunger in Brother Joseph's eyes seemed sated. The voice stopped when Jamie was like one of the transparent fish he'd seen in the aquarium at school, or like a boy made out of glass.

And so dizzy he couldn't even think.

"Blessed be the Holy Fire," Brother Joseph said, standing up straight and making a bow that was half adoration and half dismissal. "Blessed be the Sacred Flame. I thank you in the Name of God, and in the Name of Jesus—"

The Black Thing started to dissolve from Jamie-in-the-chair, pulling out of him, and Sarah let go of the silver cord. She stayed protectively between it and him, though; until it went into that door in the air—

The door in the air shut—and another kind of door opened behind it. And the Black Thing somehow dissolved into the *flag*.

Or the flagpole—

That was the first time Jamie had ever seen *that*—at least, that he remembered. But then, a lot had been different tonight. He'd never been shoved out of his body, either. He turned to Sarah, suddenly desperate to ask her questions—

But Brother Joseph clapped his hands three times—and suddenly he was *back* in the chair, in his body, and as nauseated and dizzy as he had ever been in his life.

His gorge rose, and he couldn't help himself or control it anymore. As Brother Joseph released his arms from the straps, he aimed as best he could and made Brother Joseph's white shoes not so white.

After Brother Joseph had Jamie taken away, the preacher retired to his private quarters. Exhausted, he stood in the clothes closet that was as long as a hallway, the aroma of cut pine overpowering in the bright fluorescents. The evening's events swirled in his mind like a lazy tornado, and he knew he was on an emotional roller coaster, swaying between doubt and conviction; as soon as he thought that the Sacred Fire had turned against him, he saw that it was, indeed, still in his court, shucking and jiving to mark his way to the top, spewing the useful information like a self-digging gold mine.

Hanging from brass rods were a hundred or so suits, worth anywhere from two hundred to a thousand dollars each, wearing a thin plastic wrap from the dry cleaners, each embodying its own, distinctive memory. Brother Joseph often surveyed his collection of expensive clothing in times of turmoil and change, to remind himself of the tribulations and triumphs that had already taken place. The suits reassured him and quelled his doubts, reminding him that he still held power, that his gifts were infinite.

Much of his preaching, especially after the founding of the Sacred Heart of the Chosen Ones, incited his crowds to violence. These suits had seen riots and marches and demonstrations against the unholy, and had born witness to his struggle. They felt like faithful supporters, always there when the important things happened; like the protest of the godless Unitarians, who questioned the Bible, slandering its very truth. The demonstration his people staged at the YMCA (so weak was their minister that they couldn't even raise the money to build a decent building!) was a wondrous thing, especially when the riot broke out. Joseph spotted the suit he'd worn that day, a conservative gray Oxford, and gloried in its cleanliness. The bloodstains which once darkened its immaculate surface were now only a memory. His suit, like his ministry, emerged from the wreckage of that incident unblemished. A good lawyer could prove—and disprove—anything.

At the end of the closet, hidden where only he could find them, were his white Klan robes, where it all began.

Ah yes, he thought nostalgically, savoring the sudden memory the robes brought. *The beginning of my struggle. The end, alas, of my youth*. The smell of gasoline and burning wood, the secret meetings, the handshakes, the passwords. The hillsides filled with the faithful, their pointed hoods aimed heavenward, toward God. The sweet hatred that flowed in the gatherings, lubricated with cheap beer and even cheaper whiskey.

Those were the glorious days.

He'd joined the KKK as a teenager, and insisted early on that he be permitted to participate in a real nigger lynching, that nothing else would hold his interest. He just wanted to kill niggers. The old-timers, they seemed to find him amusing if overly rambunctious. He had been all of seventeen when he joined. He looked older, and was able to pass as a twenty-year-old, not that it would have mattered if they'd known his true age. The Klan loved new, young blood. His raw hate sustained him for some time, but as he matured, he began to need specific reasons for the hate—he began to doubt, when he saw others his age burning with the same fervor for causes the very opposite of his.

Justification came bound in faded black leather; the Grand Dragon began quoting scripture. In the light of a burning cross, somewhere on a hillside in Mississippi, he saw the glimmer of his true destiny. The feelings of hate he had for the godless actually had a *meaning* behind them, reinforcing his beliefs. He could attach names to the things he hated, and they were impressive names, all of them: Satan's spawn, heathens, the non-believers. His soul had swelled with pride. His feelings, after all, were *justified*. And others enabled him to act them out.

It was the first time the Bible had any meaning for him, the first time its truth made any sense to him. *There is only one right way, and I know what it is.* So he had believed, and the Bible provided proof. The Bible was all the justification he needed.

After all, look at how many people lived by it.

He thought he had found his place, his kindred. But as the months progressed, he had participated in only two lynchings. *Any more, and the FBI will come after us,* one of the senior members of their Klan said.

But Brother Joseph knew it wasn't prudence that had spoken; it had been cowardice. They didn't have the guts, he knew then, and his faith in the Ku Klux Klan faltered.

By the time he had turned twenty, the Klan began admitting Catholics for the first time in its history, and he realized it was time to leave. They just didn't have it straight, was all. Time to forge a new organization, a new group.

A . . . *church.*

He never attended a formal seminary; he earned his sheepskin through a four-week correspondence course. All he needed was a piece of paper to hang in his "office," to point at when anyone questioned his credentials. He knew it was a facade, but a necessary one needed to carry out his work. He knew the *real* truth, and in his hands he held the secret to the One True Church. He stumbled across a passage in the Bible, and from this he produced a name for his movement: The Sacred Heart of the Chosen Ones.

He studied the Bible night and day, highlighting the passages which lent particular weight to his beliefs. These were the passages he emphasized in his sermons, adding some flourishes of his own.

He preached hatred. Hate was cleansing; the Sword of the Lord—didn't the Bible speak over and over about the Wrath of God? Hate purified. Hate separated the weak from the strong, the *doers* from the idle, the pure in spirit from the dissenters, the doubters. Hate separated the men from the boys—and from the women. He knew about women. They were too weak to truly hate. They were inferior to men.

There were many men who came to him just on that basis alone. And women, too, the *real* women who liked being told their place and liked a strong man who'd keep them there. Like his own wife, who went where he told her and never lifted her voice or her eyes. . . .

He claimed credit for the killing of Martin Luther King during an especially rousing sermon before a congregation of a dozen men and twenty elderly women. The next day the FBI came by, asking him to expand on that sermon. Nervously, he explained to them that he meant it in a *spiritual* sense, that he hadn't pulled the trigger after all. Not *really.*

This was back in the sixties, and the ball had barely begun to roll.

His congregation slowly built to around a hundred, and

peaked there for several years. He had masqueraded as a Baptist minister because he'd heard those people could sure fork out the money if you pleaded hard enough. With a minimum of hassle he found the necessary contacts to forge the proper documents to become a "bona fide" Baptist minister. After skimming the till for five years, stashing a good chunk of it in gold and CDs, his credentials came into question when he refused to attend an annual Baptist minister's conference in nearby Atlanta.

Before the darkness could gather completely he absconded with what he could and assumed a new identity in California, where he took to the airwaves as a radio preacher. As "Father Fact" he had enjoyed a sizable following for close to a year.

Then, as the spirit moved in him, his sermons took a more radical slant. More and more often, his true feelings began to overcome him in the midst of a sermon, raising the ire of the Federal Communications Commission. Soon "Father Fact" became "Father History," and after several unsuccessful attempts to find similar employment with other stations, he holed up in a cheap hotel in Los Angeles with one hundred thousand dollars in the bank and a fire in his gut.

At the San Jose Hotel he had a revelation, sent to him directly from God. At first he interpreted the message to mean that he was to become the second Christ. Then, as he mulled it over a bit, he decided instead that it was time to write a book, a *manifesto,* for his new church. It was time to come out into the open, to preach his new school of thought unfettered by anyone else's rules. The time of hiding behind the "established" order of religion had come to a screeching halt. He started using the name "Brother Joseph," which at first was going be a pseudonym only, since he suspected the authorities in Georgia might still be looking for him. But he liked the sound of it, and it stuck. "Brother Joseph, leader of the Sacred Heart of the Chosen Ones," was a fitting title. But the movement would need a users manual, and over the next fourteen months, with an old Underwood, he hacked out the *Manifesto of the Sacred Heart of the Chosen Ones*. Editing or retyping, he had decided, would not be necessary. After all, this was the divine word of the Lord; who was he to decide what the Lord wanted left in and what He didn't? Had the Apostles edited the books of the New Testament? Had Moses edited the Ten Commandments? Those were not choices for a mere mortal, he reasoned then and now, so he let the work stand as written.

Unwilling to trust the task of *publishing* his holy book to anyone else, the Brother Joseph purchased an old off-set press and developing equipment. Stray lumber and cardboard became a darkroom. For weeks, after typing God's Word on nine by eleven rag, he shot the individual pages directly from the single-spaced typewritten sheets.

The manifesto wasn't simple; Brother Joseph required 1532 pages to explain his leap of intellect, excluding the table of contents and index. On the "reference and bibliography" page the word God appeared seven hundred and seventy-seven times. In all-caps.

With some basic binding equipment, which was used to make cloth-bound books the old-fashioned way, he went to the next phase of his project. Between inexpensive meals of Discount Dan's macaroni'n'cheese and cold Van de Camps Pork and Beans, selected from his immense survival cache, he lovingly handcrafted each volume. They were easily the size and weight of an unabridged dictionary. On a good day, he could produce three to five books, which were soon given away. The preacher sent the very first volume to the newly elected Ronald Reagan, with a simple note reading: "Have your men read this immediately."

Six months later he signed and numbered the five hundredth volume. The four hundred ninety-nine volumes preceding it had been given away to Klansmen, defrocked ministers, congressmen, mayors, governors, shriners, a hundred right-wing organizations, and anyone else he thought would be interested. But that day, holding volume number five hundred, Brother Joseph frowned and scratched his head. Despite the address he had clearly printed on the title page, no tithes were pouring in to finance the new movement. Not even a letter or a postcard. Nothing. Although he had close to seventy thousand left in the bank, he didn't want to dip into that yet. He simply couldn't understand the lack of interest. He had thought that by now *someone* would have seen the wisdom in God's words.

Fifteen years and a thousand miles away, Brother Joseph stood in the closet of expensive suits, regarding with a sense of melancholic nostalgia the box of books marked, in purple crayon, "original manifesto." There was only one of the hefty tomes left, and it was stored here. The time would soon come when he would have to publish the full-length manifesto again. With new plates, of course—hell, in fancy, scrolled type, scanned from the original book and set by computer and fed directly into the bowels of his own printers. Now he owned his own little publishing empire. Never again would he have to type a word.

During the early years of the Chosen Ones, someone convinced him to condense the book a little, to where it was only about eighty pages long. It wasn't even an *outline* of the original masterwork—it was a mere *pamphlet*. The decision angered him, but he permitted the sacrilege in order to attract more followers.

In 1983 Brother Joseph purchased a stolen mailing list from *The Right Way,* an ultraconservative monthly which featured articles on assault weapons, Israel Identity theory, the Jewish Question, survival tactics, quilting tips and home cooking recipes. With the pilfered list he mailed, at great expense, one hundred thousand copies of the condensed *Manifesto.* The new edition contained simple instructions on how to start your own Sacred Heart chapter.

The ruse worked. Almost overnight congregations began to pop up all over the country, mostly in the South and Midwest. Ten in all, in the beginning, and he kept himself busy ministering to each. Money poured in. A few of his larger CDs, left over from his Baptist preaching days, began to mature. In the conservative atmosphere of the Reagan Administration, his church flourished. Congregations swelled. Finally, his message was receiving the attention it deserved. Humanity might survive after all.

Reluctant to end his brief jaunt down memory lane, Brother Joseph disrobed and hung his latest acquisition, a tailor-made Sacred Heart uniform with all the relevant religious markings, in a separate valet in the closet. The coat alone was a work of art, with Sacred Heart insignia, military decorations of his own creation, gold cord and epaulets. The severe black shirt and white collar gave it a religious look, and despite its Catholic undertones he let the creation stand. It looked more impressive, after all. The entire outfit cost nearly two thousand dollars to have made and it fit perfectly; it was his most treasured possession.

Nothing too good for the founder of the Sacred Heart, he thought.

As he selected one of fifteen bathrobes, each a different shade of blue, gray or black, he noticed a plaid suit. He hadn't worn this one very long because of a certain place in the trousers where it was too tight, but nevertheless, he remembered the circumstance of this particular outfit, and scowled.

That reporter will never stand on Sacred Ground again, he seethed, tying the robe. He meant to have the suit burned, to erase the bad memories it represented, but had never got around to it. He had worn it once during the early growth of the church, about six years before, when he was attempting one of the first channelings during what he would later call "Praise Meetings."

There had been a new lamb in the fold, a young man who had been to the meetings for the past three months or so. Brother Joseph had picked him to be the vehicle for the channeling session, and he had agreed. The young man was an admitted Democrat, and that alone should have tipped him off, but in those early days followers were coming out of the woodwork from every conceivable direction, and he hadn't really cared. The "channeling" went well, and the subject had shown every indication of the holy trance. The original plan was to channel John the Baptist, but somewhere it all got sidetracked and the subject recited passages from the Bible, claiming to be one of the twelve disciples. He never said which one, an omission which should have been another clue. The response from the gathering was questionable, but Brother Joseph declared the session a success and adjourned the meeting. The subject vanished soon afterward, and after a cursory asking around, nobody seemed to know who he was.

The next day, on the front page of the *Wichita Eagle*, Brother Joseph saw an article prominently displayed in the upper half of the paper. "Eagle Reporter Infiltrates 'Channeling Cult,'" read the headlines, and accompanying the article was a photograph of the reporter. He was, indeed, the same subject who had "channeled" the night before.

Aghast, Brother Joseph read on. The "sting" had taken three months, and while it had been unplanned, the leader of the cult had picked him to be channeled. In detail the reporter described the "high visibility" of firearms and the "gullibility of the audience, who seemed to come from rural, uneducated backgrounds." As the final insulting touch, it seemed that the "scripture" he'd quoted while in the "trance" was all fabricated, but had been accepted as "fact" by Brother Joseph and his followers.

Brother Joseph, staying at the house of one of the flock, packed his bags and left Wichita, Kansas, in a hurry. He left the situation in the capable hands of one of his followers, hoping the brouhaha would remain local. During the next month it appeared that it would, but the preacher had learned his lesson. To the best of his ability and the ability of the chapter members, each new member had a thorough background check.

The incident had happened many years before, but still it grated. He had been *so certain* he had a true medium sitting before him. In time it would become clear to him that a true channeling would be much more compelling and believable than an agent of Satan spouting made-up scripture.

Putting the distasteful experience behind him, Brother Joseph entered the bathroom adjacent to the long hallway, finding one of his servants sitting at the makeup table, reading a Bible. Brother Joseph recognized him as one of the Junior Guard, with beret, t-shirt and camo pants. Within the walls of his private living quarters full assault rifles were waived; this youth wore what appeared to be a WWII Luger sidearm. The young man looked up expectantly, closing the Bible.

"Your bath is prepared, Brother Joseph," the boy said, standing and bowing slightly.

The leader nodded, noting the perfect way in which he had been addressed. *I must remember to compliment his CO when I see him,* he thought complacently.

"Have a seat. Make yourself comfortable, young man," Brother Joseph said fondly. It felt good to have servants, especially the faithful young followers who were so bright, so energetic, so enthusiastic for the Church and what he wanted to accomplish with it.

To call this room a "bathroom" would be a disservice, Brother Joseph mused, as he eased into the immense marble bathtub. The bath, which was installed on a raised platform surrounded by roman columns, could have held at least five people at once. But such a thing would be wanton and sinful. This was his solitary pleasure, his just reward for serving the Lord, to be shared with no one.

"More patchouli," Brother Joseph said, and the boy poured more pink powder into the swirling baths. "More air in the jets," he added, as an afterthought, and the boy adjusted the knob to make the water more bubbly. The flowery fragrance rose from the steamy bath. To call this heaven would have been a sacrilege. But then, the preacher speculated, maybe God provided a tiny piece of heaven for his top workers.

Once Brother Joseph's needs were seen to, the Junior Guard lad bowed and returned faithfully to his Bible. *Fine young man,* the preacher observed, trying to ignore his own shriveled skin, the liver spots, the flab, and other nagging signs of aging. He thought of his age in terms of what he had told his congregation, not the date on which he was born. Instead of being fifty-nine, he was actually forty something. Nobody questioned him. Being leader of the Church had its advantages.

So much accomplished, so much more to do, he thought, glorying in the evening's events. These Praise Meetings energized him in ways nobody even suspected; he felt years younger after a successful night like tonight, and if there had been time he would hold one every night. But it was late when the meetings concluded, including the little private meeting afterwards, and his people needed rest to be able to put in a full day for the Church. The information he had gleaned from the Holy Fire would take days to process. Any more meetings, and the data would be wasted. Such a waste, the preacher calculated, could well displease the Holy Fire, and that was the last thing he'd wanted to do.

Overall it was a pretty good Praise Meeting. At least until the little brat threw up on those shoes, Brother Joseph thought, melting further into the hot, steaming bath. *I didn't like throwing that pair out, but I didn't exactly have a choice. Oh, well. Plenty more where they came from.* Adjoining the long closet was another closet, which held around two hundred pairs of fine dress shoes, each pair assigned to its own cubby-hole in the extensive shelving he'd had built.

Despite that disgusting display of nausea there at the end, the boy is a remarkable tool. The fasting had been so effective that the preacher was contemplating extending the fast until the next Praise Meeting, three days hence. No resistance to the Holy Fire this time—and that seemed to please it a great deal.

And what it *said* . . . Brother Joseph was still wallowing in that praise, an honor bestowed to *him*. Now he knew what Christ felt like: powerful, right, still the obedient servant of God, yet also the Sword in His hand.

This was, he reflected, all he ever really wanted to do, since the days of the burning crosses and the dangling niggers, and throughout his long days in the San Jose Hotel. Yes, *this* was all he wanted to do, this service to the Lord.

Especially now that he was much *more* than a mere servant. The Sacred Fire surpassed his wildest expectations tonight. It not only affirmed his position in the Church, but in the God/Man hierarchy. Tonight, his status went up more than a few notches. The memory warmed him like a fine glass of burgundy. He raised his arms out of the steamy, fragrant water, half expecting electricity to arc between his hands.

Life is grand. It's good to be the king.

Until now, everything the Holy Fire had allowed him to do had been mere parlor tricks. He reminded himself that the parlor tricks had convinced many a borderline believer in his power, and in his ability to call forth the glory of Jesus and God.

But the boy—the boy—that his key to glory should be one small boy, who might not ever have come into his hands. . . .

He suppressed that thought. It *would* have happened. The Lord willed it. Just as the Lord had willed that he find that flagstaff.

He had been looking for a suitably impressive staff for the church flag, the symbol of all they stood for, the banner under which his armies would eventually march to victory. But the stores that sold such things had only the same wooden poles, topped either with brass spearheads, eagles, or round knobs. He had wanted something more.

And something not so . . . expensive.

Surely God had directed his steps to the little junk shop in Lafayette, Indiana, a place run by two senile old people, so identical he could not tell which was the husband and which the wife. One of them had directed him to the back of the room when he answered their vague mumbles with "I'm looking for a pole."

Wedged in a space between two enormous oak dish-cupboards, pieces that would fit only in a room with a fourteen-foot ceiling, had been a selection of poles. Curtain poles, fishing poles, poles for punting—

And yes, flagpoles.

Standing tall among the others was a grime-encrusted flagpole of indeterminate age and origin. It stood taller than the two dish-cupboards that flanked it, its top ornament hidden in gloom. When he reached out to heft it doubtfully, he received a double shock.

First—it was *heavy*. Too heavy to have been made of wood.

Second—a real, physical shock, like a electrical spark that arced from it to his arm. It only lasted a moment, but in that moment, he knew he *had* to have it.

He carried the thing forward to the old couple—who, when they learned it was to be used for a church banner, refused to accept any money for it.

He remembered thinking as he carried it out that even if it wasn't *quite* suitable, the price was certainly right.

Back at the revival tent, he began cleaning his find— and discovered that under the years of dirt and grime, the pole was of hollow brass, three sections fitted together like a portable billiard cue. He had expected that the threads would have corroded together, but they unscrewed smoothly, as if the pole had just been machined and put together for the first time.

But it was the top ornament that took his breath away and made him realize that the piece had been waiting for him—for decades, perhaps even for centuries. A flat piece of brass, it proved to be engraved—with the Church's own emblem, the Sacred Heart pierced by twin crucifixes, the sole difference being that this heart was engulfed in flames. There was writing around the edge of the plaque, but it was in Latin and what he thought might be French, so he had ignored it.

And it was from that moment of discovery that the Holy Fire began whispering in the back of his mind, bringing the Word of God directly—if imperfectly—to him. It was then that he had decided to try channeling again, after that disastrous incident in Wichita. And that was the first time he had actually *gotten* something, through the medium of little Sarah.

And now, even more effectively, the Fire *acted* through the medium of young Jamie.

The boy had proven to be an effective bridge. On the very first channeling he allowed the preacher to invoke a ball of flame, which he held in his unprotected hands. The Fire spoke then, but he later learned that only *he* had heard it. The next Praise Meeting he had arranged to have a bed of hot coals ready, and at the appropriate moment, to the horror of those attending, he walked barefoot over it. Only once, though. He didn't want to try the patience of the Sacred Flame by showing preference to another, lesser flame. That one time though had been enough. The congregation flocked to the stage to examine his unblemished feet. And then, surprisingly, to kiss them.

As he thought back on his career in the light of the Sacred Fire's words tonight, Brother Joseph began to see a pattern emerge, one which placed him at the very center of things. Gradually, since the lynching days of the KKK, through his rise in the Baptist Church to the present, God had slowly but surely been revealing truth to him, and only him. Those other would-be leaders, as he was so fond of preaching, didn't have it right, never did, never would. This latest revelation, for it was truly a *revelation*, put him in a position only slightly lower than Jesus himself.

Though he hadn't felt that way when the boy threw up on him. Had Jesus had people throw up on his holy robes and sandals? At least nobody had been around to see it. If anyone noticed the condition of his shoes after leaving the altar, they had politely, and intelligently, withheld comment. Still, he didn't like how that memory played in his mind. It seemed like Satan might have had a hand in this—

No, that wasn't possible, since Satan was too afraid to mess with personal friends and agents of God Almighty. Satan's tools didn't projectile-vomit no matter what was in the movies.

It couldn't have been interference. The boy simply lost his control, and whatever it was he drank last, from the sheer excitement of channeling the Holy Fire.

At least, he hoped that's what it was. But as he considered this, an alarming thought came to mind. What if this was some kind of *signal*, sent by God, to warn him that the boy was going to be trouble? A similar signal had been sent in the case of the little brat Sarah, in the form of a sickness during one of the Praise Meetings. That had been embarrassing, and it had required maximum use of his silver tongue to quell the audience. It had looked like some sort of epileptic seizure at the time. Eventually the congregation returned to their seats, including her parents, and watched as the girl flopped around on the stage; *possession*, that's what he'd said, he remembered. This incident had happened weeks before he had to actually kill her, and now it seemed to have been a sure sign that trouble was to follow.

Time will tell, he thought, with a sigh. The water's heat was making him dizzy, but he stayed in nevertheless. He didn't feel clean, not yet. The preacher had made sure that the boy had been taken back to the isolation room, away from his father. It had come to his attention that Jim Chase had been drinking a bit heavily in his private room with his son. That just didn't seem right. Also, he wasn't sure if he could trust the man to maintain the integrity of the fast and had suspicions that he'd slipped the boy some food.

Tonight, at least, Jamie would have to be separated from his father. Perhaps the separation should be permanent. The boy seemed more exhausted and muddled than the last time, but the preacher didn't worry; God would see to it that the boy survived. His body, anyway. It really didn't matter if the boy had a mind or not. He was only a mouthpiece, to serve the Holy Fire as an object, not a thinking being. And his soul would surely be purified from contact with the Holy Fire. Why, if the soul could talk to him directly, it would probably be thanking him right now.

"After all," he'd told the boy's father, while escorting the boy to the isolation room. "Children are the property of the parent who gave them life. And now, Jim, you owe me your life. You should rejoice that I have a use for your son."

Jim had agreed, nodding numbly, shuffling off to his room after locking the door on Jamie's new home.

The Holy Fire would protect the boy, as it always had, despite the apparent exhaustion he was displaying.

The Holy Fire always survives. He knew that, as surely as he knew his own name. Brother Joseph.

If the boy became unsuitable, there would always be others. The boy could even be buried beside Sarah and her parents.

As could his father, if he objected in any way. This, however, was unlikely; the man was a faithful, unthinking servant. The best kind. Meanwhile, so was the boy, though he had little choice in the matter.

Neither did Sarah, he reminded himself.

The pitiful creature never once understood the importance of her sacrifice, and that in itself was a tragedy. It was ironic that he hadn't even been trying for the Holy Fire, didn't even know that it existed. He remembered Sarah's parents telling him how *receptive* she was, how *special.* And he remembered how the voices whispering in the back of his mind had urged him to try channeling again, that this time it would be different. So he had tried using Sarah to shoot for a garden variety prophet, like Elijah.

But instead, he got *it*. The Holy Fire. The same fire that had spoken to Moses from the burning bush.

Never, ever, had he thought he would reach something

like *that*. It had all come about so casually—almost by accident.

Channeling was very big, he had realized, after reading an article about Shirley MacLaine. Californians were making lots of money with this idea, and while he didn't believe for a second that MacLaine was telling the truth, it had a certain macabre appeal. And surely in the hands of the God-fearing, if anything happened, it would be with God's will.

So he gave it another try. Sarah seemed pliant, her parents appeared cooperative, and he staged a "channeling" one night where there were few in the audience, before he had moved all of the Sacred Heart chapters to this central location. After several unproductive tries at contacting "Elijah," it happened. The Holy Fire spoke through the girl, in a voice that made her sound like Satan. As the girl spoke, it dawned on the preacher that it was not Satan but God, the *real* God, that was talking to him directly.

Cunning, the Holy Fire was; in its first message it told the preacher what he would have to do for it so that it could aid him in his mission. It could assist the Chosen Ones in attracting new members, give them information on gambling, tip them off when the police were nearing their operations. All sorts of helpful things, meant to bring wealth to the faithful and to confound the unbelievers. And money meant power, in anyone's language.

But the girl proved a disappointment. She resisted any further attempts to channel the Holy Fire again, much to his humiliation and, later, rage. Oh, the Fire came through, but it was a struggle, and the information it was able to convey was meager compared to what he *knew* it wanted to give.

Yet Brother Joseph had not given up. He knew enough about the Holy Fire to begin seeking another suitable subject.

It didn't take long. In fact, the father had practically dumped Jamie in his lap. Jim had been attending the Atlanta Praise Meetings intermittently at first, but then he began appearing on a regular basis. He had mentioned to the preacher that he had a son, a trusting, receptive child.

Something about those words triggered an excitement in him. "Would you like to bring the boy to the next meeting?" Brother Joseph had asked, and Jim did.

Along with his mother. *She* should have been left behind, the preacher realized instantly when he first saw her. She sat stiffly in the audience, full of resistance, looking scared and angry at the same time. Over the years the preacher had learned to spot that type, the unbeliever who would always be an unbeliever, a wife or a husband who had been dragged along. The infidel who would compete with God for the ear and soul of the newcomer, and sometimes even win.

But the boy—the *boy* was special, more than Jim realized. And from the first moment he'd set eyes on Jamie, he knew that the Fire wanted him.

Jim had brought Jamie by himself one day, and Brother Joseph seized upon the opportunity. The faithful were anxious for a good channeling, and he had prayed earnestly for success before it began. He wasn't disappointed. The boy proved to be a superb conductor of the Holy Fire.

Then the mother had intervened, before he could get Jim to turn the boy over to his hands.

The divorce came as a surprise, to both himself and Jim, he had to admit. The preacher hadn't thought she'd had it in her. *The whore*, he thought, seething. The woman and her son went into hiding before he and Jim knew what was happening, but when the divorce papers were filed by that smart-assed lawyer, Brother Joseph knew what to do next: wait. Eventually, she would have to let her guard down. Just let her think Jim was gone, and then go in for the boy. Once she thought she was safe, she'd go back to the old house, the familiar surroundings. The preacher assigned a private in the Guard to discreetly watch the school for Cindy, and a few days later, after she showed up, Jim went in to pick up his son.

The father had been wired with a remote microphone, which they used to monitor the situation. Fifteen Chosen Ones waited beyond the school's perimeter in three separate vehicles, ready to go in and take the boy by force, if necessary. It wasn't; the school had no idea what was up. In fact, they had been downright *helpful*, to the delight of those listening in. Within moments Jim emerged with his son and quietly drove off in their pickup, followed close behind by a Bronco, a Cadillac and Brother Joseph's God-given stretch Lincoln. The convoy of Chosen Ones were well on their way to Oklahoma before the mother had any idea of what had happened.

A brilliant mission. Brilliantly planned and brilliantly executed, just . . . brilliant, gloated Brother Joseph. He looked up from the swirling waters, just in time to see the young guard bring a snack in on a silver tray. Cheese, crackers, caviar. A kind of salad he didn't immediately recognize. *And the police in this county* still *don't suspect a thing.*

He knew this was primarily because of their lawyer, Claudius Williams III. The old man came down with the Detroit flock three years ago, a true believer in God, Country and AK-47s. In his collection of assault weapons he had fifteen of the Russian-made rifles, all of which he has cheerfully donated to the Sacred Heart armory. As a citizen of Detroit, Williams had practiced law during the week, favoring the male side of divorce proceedings. On Saturday, he had participated in a white supremacists' organization. On Sunday, he had been a church preacher, teaching the Israel Identity to hungover auto workers. *All in all,* Brother Joseph thought, *a well-rounded individual. Even though he wanted to continue preaching. He saw, with God's help, the light of wisdom. After all, we needed his expertise in the legal field. And his performance in that capacity has been exemplary.*

Once the underground lair of the Sacred Heart was discovered by the county's law enforcement, Claudius Williams III went into action. For months prior to moving to Oklahoma, he had studied the local laws in books acquired by Guard agents, finding loopholes, exploiting weaknesses. Pawnee County turned out to be ideal for their purposes. Since the building permits had already been granted, it was a simple matter to keep the sheriff off their property. What the law didn't cover, court injunctions did. In Pawnee County, it was difficult to obtain a search warrant.

And it didn't hurt that the district judge was an old

college buddy of Claudius. The judge had been battling with the DA and sheriff for years now, over run-ins with his *own* friends and relatives, so naturally the granting of injunctions was a simple matter, reduced to a rubber-stamped formality. The judge and lawyer smiled and shook hands, the DA and sheriff fumed and scratched their heads, and the Sacred Heart of the Chosen Ones existed, more or less, as a sovereign state.

Brother Joseph chuckled at the sheer perversity of it all; his young servant looked up quizzically from the Bible. Their eyes locked for a brief instant before the boy looked away, apparently embarrassed.

"I must awe you," Brother Joseph said. "I know that service in my private quarters is a rotational thing, but you must feel a *chill* of excitement to be here. Am I correct?"

"Of c-course, sir," the boy stammered. "Is there anything I can get you?"

"My bathrobe, my boy," the preacher said. The boy scrambled for the robe, lying on a chair on the other side of the immense bathroom. "And a towel. I'm through here for the night. Secure the area and report to your CO. You will be commended."

The boy blushed when he handed the preacher the robe. *Such a young face. And such dedication to one he worships. What, Oh Lord, have I done to deserve such favor?*

Jamie was only vaguely aware of the two beefy fists gripping his arms as he was led away from the Praise Meeting. Behind him he could hear Brother Joseph talking some icky stuff to his father, none of which really made much sense. It was just more gobbledygook. More of the same.

When the man grabbed his arm he realized that his arm had gotten smaller, and that he felt lighter. These facts didn't register immediately, but somewhere along the way he saw what it meant, and wondered if he would go away if they didn't feed him. His body, he reasoned, must be feeding on itself, and pretty soon he would be all gone. Would his real body fade away like the ghost-one had during the Praise Meeting, going all see-through, until there was nothing at all? Or would he turn into a stick-figure, like the pictures of Ethiopian kids?

Then Jamie was dimly aware that he was going someplace different, that he wasn't going back to the old room. In a way that made him glad. He wouldn't have to worry about being rolled over on, and he wouldn't be using a blanket full of little white bugs. He didn't really care where he was going, though he was fully aware that it could be far worse than his room, if Brother Joseph was taking him there. His consciousness was fading, and he wondered if you could walk and sleep at the same time.

Somewhere in his schooling he had heard about the place they took bad boys who ran away from home, played hooky or used drugs, the place called "juvie detention." If that was where he was being taken, he now knew that you didn't have to do something bad to get there. But he wasn't scared about it, and he wondered why.

Finally they put him into a little room that had a little bed in it, but no carpet or other furniture. The blankets on the bed smelled clean, something he had barely noticed when they put him down on the bed; all he could do then was lie there and pant, and look at the stars that sparkled in his vision.

The darkness became absolute when they slammed the door on him. Jamie let out a little whimper before falling asleep, into a world of nightmares he was too tired to wake up from.

CHAPTER SEVEN

Al climbed a little higher in the tree, further away from the chain-link fence. The added distance he'd put between himself and the steel decreased the interference that disrupted his senses, and made it easier to get around the metal barriers, but it didn't make him feel any better about what was taking place down there at the "Praise Meeting."

In fact, the impromptu fine-tuning made what was happening down there all the clearer, and it took every ounce of his willpower to keep from dashing to the boy's rescue.

No heroics, he lectured himself. *I can't do Jamie any good if I'm shot full of holes. Lots of holes, by the look of those automatic weapons they're lugging around.* But anxiety knotted his stomach, and the urge to get over there and *do* something kept him in a state of nervous tension.

When he remembered what he looked like, in black clothing, boots and mask, he couldn't help but grimace; he looked either like a Ninja or a black-power commando. With this group, who hated black and Oriental people as much any other scapegoat, he wouldn't last very long. In the bright lights he would make an easy target. He didn't think he could dodge that many bullets, even with Andur's help. The elvensteed could run fast, but not *that* fast.

When the gathering began, and his brief glimpses into the humans' minds gave him more and more information, Alinor quickly identified this as the same kind of "Praise Meeting" that Cindy had told him about. Everything matched what she'd described, including the peculiar flag in the stage's background. What he hadn't expected was the evil thing that Brother Joseph summoned as soon as Jamie arrived. Al had not expected ritual magic, not here. He had assumed that the dark power he'd touched had been something the cultists didn't know about, or something that was using them without their knowledge. It seemed he was wrong—terribly wrong.

Given the magical power of the entity, he was still afraid that it might have detected him, there at the beginning of the ritual. He couldn't shake a sense of familiarity, a haunting foreboding that he had, indeed, seen this thing, or something like it, in the past. Alinor had to admit that it wasn't often these days that he ran across such things. One was more likely to encounter such things in the halfworld, beyond the borders of Underhill, not in the technological environment of the "real world." But here it was.

And it threatened Jamie's very survival. It would have to be dealt with, destroyed. At the moment, Alinor was most likely to be the one to face the beast.

Provided it didn't find and devour *him* first.

After he'd withdrawn his probes from the immediate vicinity of the entity, he studied its reactions. Soon he was satisfied that it hadn't sensed him, and that the humans who had gathered were responsible for its waking. And then the creature saw the tiny life-spark that had to be Jamie, and reached. . . .

But instead of devouring the boy, the child's soul *switched* with the dark thing. Alinor did a double take; suddenly, outside the boy's body, stood the boy—or rather, the boy's spirit. And speaking through the body was the evil force, in full control of mouth, tongue and vocal cords.

The elf's first reaction was awe at the expertise this human, Brother Joseph, had with the magics of the half-world. But as Alinor surreptitiously explored this "expertise" he found the preacher wasn't responsible for the shift at all. In fact, the switch took place in *spite* of the preacher and all he did. He saw the interference the emotional energies were creating: strong, gusty waves of hate and fear, intermingled with the human excitement of the Praise Meeting. Brother Joseph didn't engineer the switch, the evil force did, deftly sidestepping the waves of psionic energy the meeting generated, shunting them off.

Alinor narrowed his eyes and frowned, gathering his thoughts. His perch in the tree was getting uncomfortable, but he dared not move. If that *thing* didn't notice him, the guards down there might. The entity might even see him then, a complication he quite easily could live without.

I'm assuming too much, he decided. *I don't know that it perceives magics and energies the same way I do. In fact, it probably* doesn't *see it the same way. It seems quite alien—and it's not like an Unseleighe creature, either. The emotion-driven psychic force that Brother Joseph is raising may be acting as food to it, not a loud distraction. I wish I had someone with more experience here with me. . . .*

As the darkness enveloped the boy, Alinor became aware of yet another creature, creeping quietly out of the halfworld.

Who is she? Alinor wondered, suddenly aware of the being's gender. This was not something cut from the same fabric as the present occupant of Jamie's body.

She was quiet, yet strong. And the fact that she retained a sex, and a vaguely human semblance, finally gave him the clue he needed to identify *what* she was, if not who.

A human ghost.

Al sighed. A ghost tied to this place could only mean that it was bound somehow to Brother Joseph or the cult. Such bindings were rarely anything other than tragic. *So much unhappiness in this place, invoked by a crazed human preacher who doesn't even know what he's done!*

And now there was another complication to what had seemed straightforward last night. That this was a ghost with Jamie told him a great deal. The woman, no, *girl*, had evidently died a violent death. Spirits with that kind of ending frequently lingered near the earth-plane, still not convinced that they had died; wandering about aimlessly, knocking things over and making a general nuisance of themselves. The very tragedy of their death acted as a burden, an anchor weighing them down until the conflict surrounding their demise was resolved.

Yet even as he thought that, he knew that wasn't the case here; he could sense it. This spirit had a purpose, and the purpose involved Jamie.

Was this her way of dealing with her own death? Al wondered as he watched the flicker of light take form. The girl sent Jamie's spirit a thin tendril of energy, which began blocking the boy's pain.

Well done! Alinor complimented silently. *I hope that before this is all over and done with I'll get to meet this little one, and perhaps help her leave this plane. . . .*

But this was getting more complicated by the moment; not the simple "snatch and grab" of the usual elven rescue. His premonition had been correct. There had been death, sadism and violence here, and there was more to come.

He resisted a particularly strong urge to contact the ghost-child. Allies in this situation could only help to tip the odds in his, and Jamie's, favor. But to reach out to her could alert the beast to his presence and, conceivably, to hers. How she had managed to aid Jamie was something he would have to ask later.

Alinor listened, and watched.

The thing began to speak through Jamie, and the reaction from the audience was dramatic and varied. The thing fed on the roiling emotions of the preacher's flock. *A true parasitic spirit,* Al thought. Parasites in any world were disgusting things to him, *especially* when they attacked children. This one seemed particularly insidious, in view of the total possession the thing had of the boy's body. He wondered what would happen if it weakened Jamie to the point where it could make that possession permanent.

The entity spoke, ranting in the same vein as Brother Joseph, an outpouring of racial hate and convoluted biblical theory that was enough to make him ill. It made even less sense than Brother Joseph, something Alinor had to hear to believe.

And he could not shake the nagging sense of familiarity. *Where else have I seen this thing?* Al asked himself, now certain he'd encountered *it,* or perhaps a relative of *it,* before.

It began saying things, things the preacher seemed unprepared for. The man stood back, apparently trying to form some kind of rebuttal to what was coming out of the boy's mouth. *You, Brother Joseph, you are the instrument of the Prophecy. You will be the Bringer of the Flame.* . . . The boy's distorted voice ranted on, while the preacher just stood there, open-mouthed, slack-jawed, for once at a loss for words.

Alinor took note of how the preacher reacted to this unexpected tirade. Brother Joseph did not like what he heard—but more importantly, the words disturbed the audience as well. The congregation shifted nervously, and the deep wrinkle between Brother Joseph's eyebrows deepened.

But like the professional orator he was, he bounced back from the uncomfortable moment as soon as the entity gave him the chance to speak, replying with a rambling continuation of his previous sermon.

Within moments he had reconciled everything the creature had said with his own words, exerting a powerful charisma to charm the flock and lull them back into their feeling of comfortable *belonging.* Apparently relieved that what the Sacred Fire had to say was no real surprise, they responded with mindless shouts of "Praise the Lord," resolutely erasing any lingering doubts from their own minds.

A guard passed by the tree Al was sitting in, startling him and catching him unawares. He pulled his attention back to his immediate surroundings. *Need to watch that,* he thought, as his stomach lurched in alarm. *I am, after all, sitting in a tree in hostile territory.*

But the guard continued his patrol around one of the buildings. Apparently he had not noticed Alinor perched above him. This time he'd been lucky, but luck could only stretch so far.

Al checked cautiously for other guards, found none, and eventually sent his mental sight back to the Praise Meeting. But now the hall had been cleared of all spectators, except for a handful of men gathered at the foot of the stage. The boy continued speaking, but *what* he was saying . . .

Alinor smiled sardonically. *Now we get to the practical part of this evening's programming,* he thought, making mental notes on the kinds of information the entity produced for Brother Joseph. *Bingo. Horse racing. Gambling. What else?* he wondered. And then he heard what else—

Drugs. Information on the police. *Great Danaa, this thing has a lead on just about everything. It knows more about the humans and their world than they do. Not only that, but it's engineering the sale of drugs . . . to* children!

Now he was not only sickened, he was outraged. *The man is a monster. He has the ability to manipulate whoever listens to him—and he uses it for* this. *And beneath it all, he's still a puppet, a tool. The thing that controls him, that's the culprit, the blackness behind this entire charade masquerading as faith . . . some Christian, he hasn't got a clue. . . .*

Then, with a cold shock of recognition, Alinor finally remembered where he'd seen this *thing* before. *The church and all its esoteric trappings,* he chided himself angrily. *Brother Joseph, and all his blithering religious lunacy, should have been a dead giveaway. Of course—of course. I know where this thing came from—what it is. It's been nearly a thousand years, but I shouldn't have forgotten, no matter how long ago it happened. This dark creature, this blackness, this* thing, *this* blot of evil, *this . . .*

Salamander.

It shouldn't be happening again. But it *was.*

Only this time, the Christian soldiers weren't toting shields, swords and arrows. They were armed with the latest in automatic weaponry, killing tools designed to exterminate humans by the hundreds.

Yet how could it be happening here, now? When he had witnessed the creation of the United States, Alinor had thought that the Constitution would prevent religious crusades from destroying lives and souls ever again. The Constitution was, after all, designed to protect *all* religions, not just the Christian one. At its inception the new nation was easily the freest place in the world. It still was, though the Folk still needed to remain concealed.

The Salamander is behind it. Blessed Danaa—he thought angrily; wishing, as he had so many times before, that he had found a way to do away with the creature, or to at least send it back from where it came.

And nothing has really changed since the last time.

The last time, ten centuries ago.

I was only a child. . . .

It was his first excursion outside Scotland, to the home of his mother's people. He'd looked, at the time, like a teenaged human boy, and although he was considerably older than he appeared, he acted and thought like the sheltered youngster he was.

His father, Liam Silverbranch, had taken him to meet his mother Melisande's kin in Elfhame Joyeaux Garde in France.

His mother's mother had been Elaine du Lac, who had fostered the famous Lancelot du Lac, and both parents had deemed it high time that he meet his celebrated relatives and learn the Gallic side of his heritage. But there had been no one near his age there, not even human fosterlings, and the older elves had gotten involved in hunts and Court gossip and politics. Eventually they had left him to his own devices. He had run off on an exploration of his own as soon as the idea occurred to him.

It was his first chance to see mortals in any numbers, humans other than the fosterlings. The humans were so— bewildering. He had wanted to see them up close, to see the way they really lived; their capacity for violence astonished and intrigued him with morbid fascination. They seemed to throw their short lives away on a whim, to court injury and death for the strangest of reasons or no reason at all. He *had* to learn more.

He had slipped off in human guise when his father and King Huon were off on a three-day hunt. He had planned to stay human for several months, knowing that the time-slip between the human world and Underhill would make it seem only a day or two—five at the most—for the elves. He had even picked out a human to imitate.

His intent, originally, was to pass as a tanner's apprentice. The boy was being sent from a cousin in another village—the tanner had no idea what the boy looked like, only that he was coming. What he did not know—because his cousins didn't tell him—was that the boy was much younger than he'd been led to think; instead of being an adolescent, the proper age for an apprentice, he was only six. The cousins had hoped to fob the boy off on their richer relative; since he was already foregoing the usual apprenticeship fee, they figured once the boy was in his custody, he wouldn't turn him away. He'd lost his way and been found by one of the fosterlings, who'd taken him Underhill with her.

Alinor turned up right on schedule. For a few months all was well; the tanner was relatively prosperous, and since he catered to the wealthy with his finely tooled leather horse-goods, Alinor got to see all the violence he wanted, quite close. But in the third month of his apprenticeship, his master had died of a madness that, he later learned, had been caused by a poisonous mold in rye bread. Knowing that it would be unwise to be associated with a human who had gone mad, he attempted to return to Elfhame Joyeaux Garde.

By that time, he was weary and sick of the mortals and their unfathomable ways, and he had seen enough of the humans' world by then to extinguish any lingering desire for adventure. The bloody battling of the humans, their insatiable desire for conflict, was all very fine in a ballad or tale—but when you stood close enough to the scene of the battle to be spattered with blood from the combatants, it was another case entirely. He was tired of the poor food, the unsanitary conditions, the coarse garments. He was tired of being either too hot or too cold, and very, very tired of rising before dawn and working until the last light had left the sky.

But the ruling council of Joyeaux Garde forbade his return. And that had come as an unpleasant shock.

After all, he had left on his own, without asking leave of the ruling elven royalty, without even telling his parents. Such carelessness had led to exposure in the past—led to the deaths of elves at the hands of mortals, led to witch- and demon-hunts. Or so the ruling council said.

So he was to learn a lesson about the consequences of

selfish and unthinking behavior. Alinor suspected that his own father Liam Silverbranch had something to do with the "exile." Liam had admitted to being worried sick over his disappearance, and Liam did not care for being inconvenienced or discommoded in any way. He especially was not amused at his son's audacity in addressing the council without even a touch of humility. And since Alinor was too old for a switch to his rear, he would receive a punishment equivalent to the crime.

It was, King Huon explained (looking much like one of the pictures the humans painted in their churches of a stern and unforgiving God), time for him to get a good dose of the humans. Especially since he had left his rightful home and Underhill without regard for rule of elven law or the feelings of his elven kin.

Alinor knew that he had not been mature in any sense, back then. *I was such a little—what do they call it these days—"rug rat?" Trying to be an adult, without the mental equipment to do so. It's a wonder I didn't get into more trouble than I did.* The Court gave him a year, human time, before he could return to the elves' world, and in that year he was told to survive as a human, not as one of the Folk, and face death if he was exposed as Sidhe. Which meant, in so many words, use your wits, not your magic. Fortunately the humans were wearing their hair long in those days, and most peasants wore hats or hoods night and day, making it easier to hide his conspicuous, pointed ears.

Rebuffed, Alinor did as he was told. To a point. He wandered aimlessly, in the guise of a peasant, which wasn't too difficult since he didn't have a pot to pee in anyway. For a few days he managed to convince himself of the romantic nature of his travels, living on the edge, evading the Death Metal of humans' weapons by a hair's breadth. Great adventure for a youth, and it would have gone on for some time, except for one thing.

Alinor was cold, tired and *hungry*.

In any of the elven enclaves, food was available in abundance. But in the humans' world, starvation prevailed— at least for the lowest classes. Drought and floods regularly wiped out much of the agriculture, and what the weather left, insects and plant diseases ravaged. Small game was difficult to catch without a bow—which, as a peasant, he was not permitted to own—and it was nearly impossible to find a forest that some human noble hadn't already staked a claim to, a claim which was enforced by sword- and arrow-wielding sheriffs. His early attempts at kenning eatables resulted in a tasteless, unpalatable mush that mules would turn up their noses at. Before a week was out, the youngster knew he was in trouble, and began searching for a human he could influence and to learn the mundane ways of making a living as a freedman of some kind. Not even he was romantic enough to think of the life of a serf as something to be pursued.

Alinor had been contemplating pilfering and slaughtering a chicken, and wondering if it was worth the risk of being caught. The farmer in question had several fierce dogs guarding his property; Alinor had thought he would be able to lull them into sleep, but what if he missed one? He finally decided that it wasn't worth the risk and was going in search of a field he could loot for turnips after dark. That was when he came across an elderly man wearing a peculiar robe and a towel around his head, muttering something to himself as he trudged along a dirt highway. He was leading a sickly mule and cart, and nearly walked into the youngster.

The old man had stopped dead in his tracks and gazed at him strangely for a moment. Where he had come from, and what he was doing here, Alinor had no idea. And at the time Alinor couldn't have cared less; he was *starving*.

And whoever the old man was, he didn't speak French, Norse, Saxon English, or Gaelic, the four tongues Alinor knew. After several aborted attempts at communication, the elf finally conveyed his need for food, and to his surprise, the old man gave it to him. Though it was only a bit of bread and a stick of dried meat, gamy and heavily seasoned, Alinor had devoured it hungrily. Only after finishing the meal did he realize that, by accepting the gift, he had become an indentured servant to the man.

Not that it really mattered. Here was the help he'd been looking for. Alinor had even felt very clever, knowing he could leave at any time, since the old man was weak and helpless. Besides, he had reasoned, this had the potential to be interesting.

Over time Alinor learned that the man was known in the region as Al-Hazim, also called the "Mad Arab," though he was neither Arabic nor mad—he was, in fact, a Moor from Alhambra. After some time, he wondered how Al-Hazim escaped being set upon by the other humans— he was, after all, an infidel and fair game. He finally decided that most humans thought the old man was a Jew, not an Arab—Jews had a tenuous immunity from persecution, since when a noble needed money, he had to go to the Jews for it, his own fellows being forbidden to lend money by the Church. This led to a kind of dubious safety; no one wanted to kill the man who would lend him money, but when the debt came due, sometimes it was easier to end the debt with the life of the creditor. . . .

And those that knew the old man was Arabic had another reason to fear him and leave him alone.

He was a magician. He might traffic in demons. He might be protected by horrible creatures. No one human wanted to chance that, and by the time the local Church authorities were alerted to his presence, or the local nobleman was told the Arab was on his property—or a mob was gathered from the braver folk of the village—the Mad Arab was long gone. He never stayed anywhere that he was known overnight. Alinor had the feeling he'd probably learned that lesson early in his career as a wanderer.

Al-Hazim was an alchemist by trade and possessed a handwritten copy of the *Emerald Tablet*, a rare and eagerly sought-after book. Though the book was a famous treatise on Arabian alchemy, it had never been translated because it was knowledge that had been uncovered by the infidels, and for a fee the Mad Arab would read it aloud in broken but understandable Latin. To Alinor it was only so much gibberish, but "scientists" in the towns they passed through would provide food and shelter for the privilege of transcribing while Al-Hazim spoke.

The elf couldn't understand the reverence other alchemists paid the *Emerald Tablet*. It was all just half-mystical nonsense compounded with human ignorance, and Alinor privately thought the work and its owner equally ridiculous.

They fell into a pattern of traveling from town to town, usually in search of "scientists" and the very few churchmen who were interested in the *Emerald Tablet* and its secrets. Alinor listened to them debate the secrets of alchemy, and absorbed this "great wisdom" to the best of his abilities, at least until he couldn't stand the cryptic nonsense anymore.

Alchemy, he learned (albeit reluctantly), was considered to be more than just a science, it was a philosophy that supposedly represented mystic, occult knowledge. Al-Hazim's goal was to produce the "elixir," which could be used to convert cheap metal into gold. Alinor knew something of metals; every Sidhe did. What the alchemists were talking about was possible, but not in the way that was outlined in the *Tablet*. When Alinor was able to examine a nugget of pure gold, payment from an isolated monk from the Saint Basil Monastery, he kenned it thoroughly. The gold was the purest Al had ever actually touched, for the Folk preferred ornaments made of silver over those of gold, and the contact enabled him to ken it well enough to produce a perfect replica.

Now he could assure the prosperity of his "master"— and not inconsequentially, himself. And all without risking the exposure of his magic-use by the Folk.

Of course, he couldn't claim responsibility for doing so. It had to appear to be the work of Al-Hazim the Alchemist, not Alinor of the Sidhe.

So he produced a nugget of gold in the crucible at the appropriate moment, the next time Al-Hazim made the attempt for some of his fellow scientists.

Needless to say, it caused a sensation.

This would not have been the first time the Sidhe had produced gold for humans—though usually, it was as a gift to a mother with hungry children, or a father with girls to dower and no money. But Alinor had been specifically forbidden to work this kind of magic by his elders. . . .

He decided, rebelliously, that he didn't care. If he had to substitute gold for a few worthless lumps of lead in order to fill his belly, then that was what he would do. After all, *he* wasn't getting the credit—and notoriety. Al-Hazim was.

Word of the Mad Arab's success filtered down through

the countryside, and as they neared towns the populace cleared out of the streets, avoiding them at all costs. Only the few who sought knowledge, power or greater wealth—often at risk to their souls, according to the Church—ever sought them out. Perversely, this increased their safety. The lowborn were terrified of the demons Al-Hazim *must* have had to protect him; the highborn were well aware of the tale of the goose that laid golden eggs and were not inclined to risk either the demons or the loss of the secret of making gold to the hands of a torturer. Al-Hazim was careful with his "talent," changing only the "choicest leads" to gold, and small nuggets at that.

Meanwhile, Alinor worked the magic that created the actual miracles, while Al-Hazim conjured the "elixir" over the tiny brazier they carried with them. Chanting passages from the *Emerald Tablet*, the Mad Arab carefully heated the vessel, a small copper pot with tubes running back into it, like a still, while his tiny audiences watched.

In a trance, the Mad Arab held the vessel over the coals, sometimes for hours, often in conjunction with astrological conditions, while onlookers stared at the flames, mesmerized. Alinor became a little uncomfortable in the intense emotional energy generated at such gatherings, but he held his youthful impatience in check, reminding himself what this was all for.

He had to work stealthily, so that his "mentor," Al-Hazim, got the credit, and sometimes he was a little jealous at the attention the decrepit old Moor received. But the astonished looks and hysterical applause when a little chunk of lead "turned into gold" was well worth a little discomfort and unrequited envy. This was the most fun he'd ever had, and behind the curtains of the wagon the youngster would break out in unrestrained laughter, holding his sides, chortling until he wept.

All this, for a little lump of yellow metal. Alinor would shake his head and chuckle, as the gold was scrupulously divided between the Moor and whoever had provided the costly ingredients of the elixir. Soon they were able to buy a healthy pair of horses and a full-sized wagon, so they could ride instead of walking. They began to wear decent clothing, and Alinor took on the look of a young nobleman.

They stayed in a well-appointed tent instead of sleeping in the fields. Life was a little better, when alchemy worked the way it was supposed to.

"Everything comes from the One and returns to the One," the Mad Arab chanted from memory, as they traveled. They were on their way from Toulouse to Clermont in the southern part of the Kingdom of France, in early November of what—these days—was denoted as the year 1095. Back then, calendars were few, and dates a matter of guess. "It is truth and not lies. What is below is what is above, as all things have been from One by the mediation of One," he continued. From that he went into a recitation in what Al had determined was his native language. Al-Hazim had been particularly pleased with himself lately. They had received word from none other than the "king" of the Catholic nation, Pope Urban II, that their presence was requested in the city of Clermont-Ferrand. The messenger had been sent with a considerable sum of gold coin, with promises of more when they arrived.

The youngster had gotten the distinct feeling that the old man's excitement had more to do with who they were seeing than what they were receiving for coming. Alinor had only a vague understanding of the humans' religions at the time; to him, it all seemed completely nonsensical, whether it was Al-Hazim's brand of Mohammedism or the local variant of Catholicism.

Still, it could not be denied that the Church had considerable significance; indeed, most of the towns and villages they'd passed through seemed to be governed by the Church, with a king or lord installed as an afterthought. The Pope seemed to be a particularly important figure. Al gathered that it wasn't the man's religious significance, though, that Al-Hazim was ecstatic over. He was, after all, a follower of a different faith. It was the man's *political* power that interested the Mad Arab.

Alinor studied his strange mentor as they traveled the mountainous terrain south of their destination. *Not quite as mad as he would have us think,* he observed, wondering if this was something he had overlooked, or if the man had actually changed. The recent sessions with the "elixir"— a mixture of blood, ground pearl, mercury, sulfur, and several herbs Alinor couldn't identify—had generated vast amounts of psychic energy, powers which Al-Hazim could not see, and which Alinor had thought at first that he was probably not aware of.

Alinor had known just enough to be a bit worried about that. Such situations, or so he had been told, were dangerous in the extreme. Most humans could not see these powers, or what they could do, but that didn't stop pockets of power from forming, usually in places where they could do the most harm.

This seemed different somehow, as if Al-Hazim, in spite of his apparent lunacy, knew what he was dealing with. Alinor could not be sure, and it worried him now and again. But he was easily distracted by the novelty of their journey, and he kept forgetting to be concerned.

The last town they stopped at before Clermont was not much more than a church and an inn that served cheap ale and sour wine. Here, as at the other towns, Al-Hazim's fame preceded them, but this time the locals were less afraid and more in the mood to be entertained, as if the Moor were some kind of showman. Alinor was tired and a little irritated, and his usual envy for Al-Hazim's fame had become amplified in proportion to the size of the new audience. When the Moor agreed to perform his usual transformation ritual, the youngster decided for him to have a lapse in abilities.

The villagers gathered around, determined to see the miracle occur, as Alinor stood in the shadows. For hours Al-Hazim gazed at the little brazier, occasionally adding coal to keep it going. As night fell, more villagers, now finished with their work in the fields, wandered into the inn to witness Al-Hazim's Great Work. Some became impatient and began ignoring him in favor of the strong, sour wine, but the Mad Arab continued with his tedious task unperturbed.

Alinor gleefully listened to the villagers murmur dissatisfaction with his mentor's work.

See. He's not the great wizard you thought he was, is he? It was me all along, and I still have the power to make him look the fool!

The copper vessel simmered and boiled, and when

Al-Hazim tested the elixir on a sample piece of lead, nothing happened. The Mad Arab frowned but continued his chanting, while the villagers around him became more and more vocal in their dissatisfaction.

Alinor found this increasingly amusing. He considered giving the poor Moor a break and producing an unusually large nugget of gold. *When the time is right*, he promised himself. *Let the old fool sweat first*.

Finally the villagers got downright disgusted with the whole thing and began jeering at the old man, threatening to pelt him with refuse, although none of them quite dared to do so. The grumbling went on for some time, growing in intensity, and Alinor became a little nervous himself. Before he could give the audience satisfaction and produce the gold, the Arab's mood suddenly changed.

The old man looked up sharply from the brazier, fixing the peasants with a dagger-like glare for a moment, and the noise dropped somewhat, but did not entirely cease. Then he snarled, silently, and his chanting changed to an evil-sounding, guttural verse that Alinor hadn't heard before.

Suddenly a sense of impending danger fell over the gathering; a feeling of a vast shadow creeping over the audience, a shadow that held the chill of death in its depths. In panic Alinor tried, in vain, to exchange a large lead weight at the Arab's feet for gold, but something, something strong, was blocking him. Nothing ever raised by a mere human had ever been potent enough to do this before, and at this point Alinor was well and truly scared witless.

What is *that thing?* Alinor had thought, in a state of panic. Normally sensitive to what humans were thinking around him, his mental gifts also seemed to be impeded. But the humans' expressions of cruel mirth, now turned suddenly to fright, said it all. The evil essence seeped into every corner of the inn, sending them into silence, while the elf tried desperately to determine where it came from and, most importantly, what it *was*.

For the first time since being cast from Joyeaux Garde, Alinor considered calling for help. King Huon, certainly, would know how to deal with this thing; it was probably beyond Alinor's abilities. As the youngster considered this option, however, it seemed less and less feasible.

First of all, they might not come in time, or come at all.

Secondly, though it might solve the immediate problem, it would make Alinor seem incompetent, and very much the child the other elves apparently thought he was. *No. That wouldn't do at all. It would only show them that they were right all along, that I couldn't handle the humans' world*.

The Mad Arab turned his attention to the fire blazing in the little brazier, which itself was beginning to glow red. In the fire Alinor saw a dark shape take form, a creature that writhed and exulted in the flames. Al-Hazim apparently saw it, but no one else seemed to take notice of it besides Alinor. As the thing grew, the youngster saw what it was; it looked like a large, black salamander, moving in the fire but unscathed by the heat. Indeed, the thing seemed to thrive in the flame, and Alinor flinched when the black shape turned and *winked* at him.

He sees me, and he's letting me know it, he had thought in alarm. He remembered the elements of alchemy, in particular the animal symbols, which represented the four elements of Earth, Air, Water, and Fire. Fire was represented by the *Salamander*. Until this moment, he had thought the Salamander was a creature of complete myth; he'd never seen one Underhill, and he'd certainly never seen one *here*.

That only he and Al-Hazim could see the thing told him that it was not of the humans' world, that it was from the halfworld of spirits. So far, everything he'd seen had made him more and more alarmed. And it didn't help that it could also see *him*.

The essence of the Salamander wafted into the inn as the Mad Arab continued with his dark chants, as if he was adding power to the creature he had conjured. Fights began to break out—apparently spontaneously—over minor things, and he and Al-Hazim might just as well have been invisible. No one seemed to remember they were there at all.

Alinor knew the Salamander was behind it. And in a few more moments he watched it actually take possession of a few of the younger men, whose minds were more malleable than their elders, whose emotions flared with a little less urging. It seemed to avoid the older men altogether, perhaps because they weren't resilient enough.

The fights quickly escalated. Mugs, then bodies began to fly through the air. The innkeeper locked up the liquor, corked the keg, and disappeared.

Alinor began to look for an exit, not liking the dangerous state of things one bit. He could feel the creature probing *his* shields briefly, looking for a way into his soul—

Before he could move for the door, a newcomer blocked his way. It was a monk wearing a long dirty robe, bald and disheveled, like a hundred other mendicant friars on the road. He wouldn't have warranted a second glance ordinarily.

But there was something unique about the man and the handful of peasants that had followed him in. The monk was definitely the leader, as the others deferred to him. The monk and his entourage had an air of presence about them—

Or at least, they acted as if they were vastly more important than they seemed.

The Salamander seemed startled, as if it had seen them too—and didn't like their presence at all. Now Alinor was puzzled and abruptly changed his mind; he had to see what would happen.

The monk cleared his throat and made some kind of an announcement—

And the fighting stopped. Gradually, but it *did* stop.

The monk spoke again; it was in some tongue Alinor didn't understand. What he heard instead was the muted whispers as the inn's clientele slowly noticed the monk. "Peter the Hermit," they muttered, turning and pointing. They seemed in awe, as if he really was as important as he was pretending to be.

Now the elf noticed what he carried with him; a small copper box just large enough to contain an apple, with intricate metalwork decorating it. Alinor admired the work, but assumed it was a reliquary for a religious object and dismissed it as unimportant. There was a much more interesting conflict shaping up—between his master and this newcomer.

He still might have to run for it—so far they hadn't had any trouble with religious types, but Al-Hazim *was* an infidel, and as such, was likely to come under the censure of the Church and its agents. This Peter might just give them some trouble.

Now Al-Hazim looked up, his eyes narrowing as they met the Hermit's. They silently exchanged something between them, something not particularly polite; it was as if they had seen each other before and had some unpleasant dealings. The monk held the copper box out and opened the lid. The container was empty.

With a resigned air about him, Al-Hazim began chanting again, only this time it was something different, more intense. The foreign words did not resonate with the same dark evil as the ones before, the passage which had summoned the Salamander in the first place. But the Salamander responded, albeit reluctantly; the box the monk held seemed to act like a magnet, pulling the creature towards it.

The peasants of the inn became quiet and looked confused, as if they weren't certain if they should be angry with each other or turn on these newcomers. Dark powers fluctuated violently in the room, giving Alinor a screaming headache.

Gradually, the Salamander was sucked into the copper box. As soon as it was inside Peter the Hermit sealed it tightly with the lid, tying it with a strip of leather and a crucifix on a silver chain.

With that, the atmosphere changed again. The people even seemed to have forgotten their disappointment in the Moor's performance; seemed, in fact, to have forgotten the Moor altogether. The fights that erupted ceased, the opponents now slapping each other on the back and wandering out together.

Whatever this thing is, Alinor thought, *it brings out the ugliest feelings from humans, makes them hate. The hate was not directed anywhere, so the nearest person became the object of it*. He shook his head at the pure insidiousness of the thing. *And Al-Hazim must have had it tucked away somewhere. The peasants angered him, and he set this thing loose to cause mischief.*

He's a crazy old man, but he's dangerous. Now, I think, is the time to leave him. He doesn't know I could see what he did. After all, nobody else saw his pet. If I let on that I did, no telling what he might turn on me!

While the monk was holding the copper box, as if savoring its contents, Alinor stole away through the kitchen, leaving behind what few possessions he'd acquired while in the Mad Arab's employ.

Then he encountered another obstacle. Outside the door a large number of peasants had gathered, some with packmules.

He slipped out of their way as silently as he could, thanking Danaa that their attention was all on the inn door and not on anything else. Within moments, he had attained the road and was heading for the forest, congratulating himself on a successful escape.

Then he stopped—feeling suddenly guilty.

He pondered the unexpected reaction as the raucous sounds of the inn faded behind him, giving way to the more familiar and comforting sounds of the forest.

Where to go now? Returning to Joyeaux Garde still wasn't possible; his year of exile was barely half over. And now he had a better understanding of how the humans' world worked. It wasn't so hard to make your way about, if you were clever. Perhaps he could even set himself up as an alchemist and turn lead to gold, just as he had been doing with Al-Hazim.

I can get by just fine without him, Alinor had told himself. *I don't look like an infidel, I can speak the language better than he does, and as long as I can wear my hair long I can keep my ears concealed. Or I can even chance the spell being detected and disguise myself.* On the surface, it sounded like a good plan: ken the appropriate objects for "alchemy," perform the proper "rituals" while heating and cooling the "elixir," and he would soon be able to support himself quite well.

But—he would have to be very careful that the Folk didn't find out about his exploits.

Would that be possible? The result was tempting; to

return home dressed in human finery, showing them all that he knew how to take care of himself and that he was a real adult, not just a naughty child.

But what about the Salamander?

That was a real problem and, he had realized, the source of his guilty feelings. Leaving the situation at the inn felt like he was leaving behind a responsibility. He had heard Liam and the other older elves talk about the evil things they came across in the humans' world, and what they did to eliminate the problems before they threatened Underhill.

It wasn't just a tradition; it was something that was ingrained in each of them, Alinor realized. He had to admit that he felt a distinct tugging as he walked away from the Salamander, a tugging that became stronger, not weaker, the further he moved away.

It would be so easy to just walk away from that evil thing back there, he thought. *Nobody would know the difference. Nobody in the elven kingdoms would know that I ran from the thing. A Salamander . . . this entity, a foe far beyond anything I can handle anyway!*

Nobody would know . . . except me. I'm telling myself I'm grown up—a full adult. But can I really believe that if I don't at least try to do something about this—creature— before it becomes a danger to me and my kin?

Alinor stopped walking. Slowly, he turned back towards the inn, still visible at the side of the winding dirt trail leading from it. *Oh great Danaa*, he thought, at length. *Does this mean I'm getting a "conscience"? That thing the Court sages claim raises us above the beasts, makes us greater? Whatever it is, it makes me feel larger, stronger—and frightened. Think of the trouble it could lead me into. . . .* Alinor smiled. *Trouble indeed.*

He watched the monk leaving the inn, followed by the handful of followers who had escorted him. Outside, a hundred or so peasants gathered around him and cheered.

Who is this Peter the Hermit, with all these followers? he wondered. *Now that he has the Salamander, what is he going to do with it?* The thought of this man in control of so many people made him nervous, to say the least. Add in the Salamander, and there was no telling what would happen. *The humans' world is my world, for the time being,* he accepted, grudgingly. *I've partly caused the Salamander's summoning, and now the thing is in the possession of this monk, whoever he is. A man who had no trouble capturing the Salamander. There's no point in returning to Al-Hazim, he no longer possesses the thing. He might have other powers, but that can be dealt with later. Peter the Hermit, on the other hand* . . . Alinor frowned, knowing then what he would have to do.

Peter the Hermit had a following far larger than the group accompanying him to the inn. They were, Alinor later found out (after blending in with the rest of peasants), some of the first to throw in with him and were escorting him for protection. Alinor had no trouble joining ranks with the motley crew that wandered back to the encampment along another dirt road; they accepted anyone and everyone who was willing to follow their leader. For the time being, Alinor kept his questions to a minimum, choosing instead to look and listen carefully to what was going on around him. The bulk of the monk's people were at a camp some miles away, and cheered loudly as the ragged procession reached the edge of the assemblage of carts and crude tents.

It was just as well he had left behind what valuables he owned; from the villainous look of some of these fellows, he guessed that a fair number of "followers" were thieves as well.

He learned he was right, after fending off the plucking hands that tried to take his clothes when he "slept." And not just thieves; the gatherings that sprung up every night in the encampments were the loudest he had heard yet in this land, and the religious meetings often turned into drunken orgies once the Hermit had retired for the night. Apparently all the rules of Good Christians had been suspended for *this* lot. And the monk was a different sort from the priests Alinor was familiar with. The more he saw, the more confused he became.

After some searching—and a few misunderstandings as to his intentions—the youngster found a lad who appeared to be around his own age and fell in with him. The boy was talkative and spent most of his waking hours with a skin of ruby wine constantly at hand. He seemed to be better dressed than the majority of the Hermit's company, and Alinor soon discovered he was the son of a knight. He was quite at ease with Alinor, probably because the Sidhe was dressed in similar wealth and style, and spoke with the accent of the nobility rather than in a crude peasants' dialect. Alinor had left the Mad Arab with literally the clothes on his back—but they were fine clothes, and clothing in the humans' world marked one's status in life.

The boy had done nearly the same as Alinor, running off from home with little preparation. The boy's name was Albert, Alinor learned, and when he told the young man that he had just joined the group that day, Albert launched into a lengthy paean to the holiness and mission of Peter the Hermit.

Occasionally his words slurred, but for the most part he was coherent. Coherent in spite of the wine he gulped at every pause for breath from the skin tied at his side.

"Peter the Hermit is God's true prophet, incarnate," Albert said, though in a hushed toned that suggested that not everyone in the camp shared quite that same belief. "The Turks tortured him when he went to Jerusalem on a pilgrimage. He brought back monstrous tales of barbarians seizing the Holy Land. He'll take anyone in, as long as they follow him on his journey and pledge to fight beside him."

Where then, Alinor asked delicately, was this journey leading?

"Why to the Holy Land, of course!" Albert announced proudly. "To free Jerusalem and return it to Christian rule. He doesn't have full support of the Church yet, but he will, when he goes to Clermont. He's to see the Holy Father, the Pope himself."

Alinor remembered that Al-Hazim had been summoned to Clermont by the Pope, and wondered if this had anything to do with the Salamander. Cautiously, he inquired about the dark entity and the copper box—and the visit to Al-Hazim that had ended with the Hermit's capture of the creature.

"Salamander?" the boy said, obviously puzzled. "Don't know anything about a salamander. Today Peter went to reclaim something that had been stolen from him by that

Arab, Al-Hazim, but I don't know what it was. Some kind of power to fight the infidels, they say. Why an infidel like Al-Hazim would be in possession of it—well, who knows what an infidel will do, or why. Unless he took it to keep Peter from using it." He took another gulp of wine and grew bolder. "He should be burned. They should all be burned, the heretics, the Jews, the Turks, the Arab dogs— they're all in league with devils."

Which explains the odd exchange between the two men, Alinor thought. *The Salamander was stolen.*

When Alinor turned his attention back to the boy, Albert was happy to continue the conversation, especially when the Sidhe asked him about himself. "Where we come from, it's been dry for three years. Witches, again, I think. Drought wiped out the crops. Our fief isn't doing well, father says. He's gone back to tournaments for prize money to pay his knight's fees and everything. My older brother went with him as his squire. They left me at home, and I was sick of it, sick of hearing Mother and the rest whine about money. This pilgrimage, this *crusade,* is a godsend. I mean, besides being holy and all. Anything would have been better than staying *there.*"

The next morning, as it turned out, only a portion of Peter the Hermit's followers went on to Clermont. The majority remained as before, preparing for the long journey to Jerusalem. What they were going to do about the "invaders" once they got there was a point Alinor must have missed, since most seemed unsuited for warfare. Beggars, children, old women made up a large part of the mob, and those young men, including Albert, who were fit for combat did not seem to be armed. However, those who were picked to go with their leader were the few knights and noblemen who were armed. Alinor volunteered to go, and was offered a ride by a very young knight, newly dubbed, who had little in the way of armor. A leather tunic, a helm and a short sword was his entire outfit, so riding double on his mare would not add too much weight.

The ride took two days, with an overnight stop near a brook where all (for a wonder) bathed. Afterwards Peter the Hermit told them great stories about the holy city and the barbarians they were to battle. Alinor made himself inconspicuous, but spied on the monk whenever possible, seeing the little copper box either in his possession or somewhere nearby. He never let the creature escape while talking to his men; Alinor suspected that he was saving the Salamander for future use. He had an idea what that use might be—but he couldn't be sure. He tried not to think about the fact that once he did know, there *still* wouldn't be much he could do. . . .

The group following Peter the Hermit didn't attract much attention, as there were similar groups of armed men converging on the city of Clermont. The town was larger than Alinor expected. There were whole streets of houses and taverns, and *pavement* beneath their horses' hooves. On the other end of the town where the houses thinned, they came to a field where a large number of people had gathered. Nearby was fountain and a huge, partially built church; someone whispered that it was the Notre-Dame-du-Port, but Alinor wasn't sure if it was the building or the fountain they were talking about. In the center of the gathering a throne had been erected on a platform, where a king sat, surrounded by bishops, fully armored knights and more religious clerks and monks than Alinor had ever seen in his life. After listening to the hushed whispers, he discovered the king was not a king but Pope Urban II, the very Pope that had summoned Al-Hazim. Nervously, the Sidhe cast surreptitious glances around him, looking to see if the Mad Arab had appeared after all. Gratefully, he saw no sign of the Moor or his cart.

The Pope was giving a speech, but it was difficult to hear in the open field. Alinor caught parts of it, enough to gather that the Pope was raising an army to fight the Moslems, who had apparently invaded his Holy Land. This was a holy crusade to save Jerusalem from the hands of the infidel.

"Now that the barbarians have taken the holy city of Jerusalem, of what use is our religion?" Pope Urban II shouted over the not-quite-hushed masses. "The Church of the Blessed Mary, the Temple of Solomon, the very streets where trod Christ Almighty! Taken from us, by the godless!"

The people did not seem particularly upset by the

revelation. Alinor didn't understand why, unless they did not value their religion as much as the Pope thought they should. *More human folly,* Alinor thought. *To construct a religion, and then fail to abide by it. I wonder if their god knows about such stuff? Perhaps he's busy. This Holy Land is too far away for most of them; they're far more worried about their neighbors than the Arabs across the sea. They look ready to walk off at any moment.*

But the Pope didn't give up so easily. His voice rose as he chastised all those present for being sinners, for fighting and robbing their neighbors, for taking the Lord's name in vain. He invoked the name of a warrior of the past, Charlemagne, who had also defended the Holy Land from invading pagans. Alinor flinched at that last statement, remembering that so few of the Sidhe of Joyeaux Garde had gotten involved in that little altercation. And that Charlemagne had inadvertently mistaken a few elves for demons and had them burned at the stake when he could capture them. Only King Huon had managed to settle the mess with a minimal loss of life. The whole thing was beginning to make Alinor just a little nervous, especially after Albert's ranting about "witches and Jews and demons." Nearly everyone he'd seen in his travels had been unhappy, hungry, ill-clothed and ill-housed. It didn't take much to start a witch-hunt among people as discontented as these were.

The reactions of the people around him were mixtures of boredom and suppressed hostility; either the men didn't like being lectured like little children, or felt that the Pope could have condemned others—such as the nobles who guarded him—with greater cause. Alinor realized what the Pope was trying, without success, to do: whip the crowd into a frenzy, so that they could storm off to the Holy Land and pound others into the dust. This was exactly the kind of enthusiasm Peter the Hermit had managed to invoke in his own people, and in large numbers. But this Pope didn't seize the imagination of these people the way Peter did.

Peter the Hermit smiled smugly; there was no doubt in Alinor's mind that he was well aware that the Pope was failing where he succeeded. In that moment the monk's old face resembled one of his mules, and despite the gravity of the situation, Alinor fought to keep from laughing. *Meek and defenseless as that old monk may appear*, the elf thought, *he's managed to do what the Pope has not*.

But then his blood chilled; for without a word, Peter the Hermit pulled the little copper box from beneath his cloak.

Of course! he could have shouted. *That's why he needed the Salamander. Now he's going to release it in this mob!*

Fighting an urge to dismount and run for the wilderness outside the town, Alinor watched with dread as the monk opened the copper box.

Magic had been at work to imprison the Salamander; now the bond was released, and the creature escaped from its cage.

Alinor felt the rush of magical wind wash over him as the Salamander dissolved into the air, and its essence dispersed into the crowd. As before, it was invisible to all but himself—and the monk.

I can't let them know I see it, he reminded himself.

The effect of the Salamander's presence was immediate. It was as if the crowd had been doused with a bucket of ice-cold water from the Allier. Utter silence made the Pope's words clear and thunderous; suddenly he was the center of all attention, as if he spoke with Divine inspiration.

"Are you men, or cowards?" the Pope continued, angrily, not yet realizing that the crowd had changed its mood. Even to Alinor, the Pope seemed larger, and the throne itself began to glow, ever so subtly, drawing more attention to its occupant. "Prepare yourselves for battle. It is better to die fighting for the Holy Land than it is to tolerate this invasion of your sacred places. Arm yourselves, if you are Christians!"

The cheers were as sudden as they were deafening. Alinor could feel, beneath their horses' hooves, the ground shake with the cries for battle. Peter the Hermit stepped back at the heartfelt outcry, but quickly regained his composure. Alinor expected him to take command of the situation while the Pope was still surprised by the sudden turn of mood, but the monk remained quiet, with a subtle smile creasing his bland features. The Salamander, with its insidious power, was doing all the speaking for him—and it seemed that he did not care *who* roused the crowd, so long as it was done.

Knights rallied around the Pope, dismounted, and began taking vows on their knees, their hands shaking with fervor. Ordinary townsfolk began dismantling a cart, converting it to staves and clubs, apparently not knowing their Holy Land was thousands of leagues away. All around were cries for war and conquest. At the Pope's feet, a wooden bowl began filling with coins and jewelry, contributions for the glorious crusade.

A crusade of anger and hatred, fueled by the Salamander.

Peter the Hermit made no attempt to retrieve his little demon, and that was ominous.

Alinor learned, to his dismay, that the monk had several of the dark creatures in hiding. Back at the camp, Alinor spotted him rummaging about a wooden trunk, which contained an array of oddly shaped copper boxes. Orders among his followers were that none of these containers were to be touched by anyone but the leader. And those orders were enforced with fists and cudgels.

Before he had left Clermont, however, the monk had rallied all those townsfolk the Pope would not accept as fit for battle. Pope Urban wanted only young knights for his sacred army and would not take ordinary folk. Very well, then; Peter would take those who had been rejected by the Pope in disdain for their lowly status, and *they*, not the over-proud knights, would be God's Army, the *true* instrument of freedom for the Holy Land.

Peter sowed hate for the nobility right along with hate for the infidel, and the common folk devoured it all with glee.

The Salamander had done its work well; Jews had fled their path, for fear of being "converted" in the knights' wake. By the time they left Clermont, the Hermit had assembled a small army from those rejected by the Pope. He had led the mob back to the camp, looting and pillaging the houses identified as belonging to "Jews and heretics" along the way. "We will begin the crusade *here*!"

he had shouted. "We will first purge *our* land of the unholy, then take the purifying fire to Jerusalem!"

Alinor was profoundly grateful that he had not been with Al-Hazim; they would have arrived at the scene just in time to stand in the path of that unruly mob. And he had no doubt how *that* would have ended.

The high number of noncombatants continued to amaze Alinor. *They're going to fight some of the greatest armies in the world, and who do they take with them? Women, children, old men, boys barely old enough to think about growing beards. The Salamander has poisoned everyone with hatred and anger.*

It was insane. Utterly insane. Not even religious fervor could account for it. *This entire venture is hopeless. They gladly march into battle with this Salamander riding their backs, as long as they're promised a direct trip to heaven when they die.*

Then there was the question: Why was *he* still tagging along?

It wasn't a sense of responsibility, since now he knew he wasn't to blame for the Salamanders. Peter the Hermit had obviously been keeping several for years. In fact, the Salamander Peter released was probably not the same one Al-Hazim had conjured, judging by the collection of copper boxes.

If anything, Alinor was following the army of crazed idiots out of curiosity, or at least that was the most comforting thought for a young Sidhe not yet used to his nagging conscience. After all, what could he do? *One* Salamander was too much, never mind the nightmare stashed away in the wooden trunk. Following this ragtag bunch out of conscience—well, that was as foolhardy as their quest, wasn't it? Must be curiosity.

The army was a little better behaved when they marched to Cologne in April. Armed guards appeared when they passed through certain territories, but the townspeople welcomed them graciously, and even added more volunteers to their ranks. More armies were meeting in Cologne, most better organized and better equipped than the Hermit's. The French army started off immediately after Easter while the peasants' army organized and stocked themselves as best they could. Alinor noticed that the monk was carrying an empty copper box immediately after the French left, apparently having "seeded" their ranks.

Peter the Hermit and his army set out across Europe, gathering strength and attracting volunteers along the way. Their pace was slow; it was no trouble to keep up. Alinor stayed at the head of the group, shadowing the guards that watched over Peter, and as a result, shared in their relative prosperity.

It was amazing. Chests filled with gold and silver wherever they went. Food was not a problem. The townspeople, having heard of the looting—or holy provisioning— elsewhere, put all of their goods outside the city walls in full view, for the crusaders to help themselves as needed. Then they closed themselves behind their stout gates and city walls.

Alinor helped himself along with the rest, accumulating bedding, clothing, even weapons—but he wondered about those in the rear of the army; mostly very old or very young, female, weak or crippled. Here at the front there was no suffering, plenty for all. But there were thousands of people in this so-called army. How were the ones behind faring? This march across Europe was tiring even for him; he slept long and hard these days, and the journey was turning him from the soft, spoiled elven-child he had been into a hardened and seasoned traveler, wary and cunning. What about those for whom this was not as "easy"?

They proceeded to the Kingdom of Hungary without serious incident, their army now amounting to twenty thousand. Alinor had seen the monk release Salamanders to encourage volunteers in Vienna, and then again in Budapest and Belgrade. They ran into resistance at Nish, when a Salamander seized control of some of the knights, who in their anger set fire to houses and farms. The local militia, city guard and army responded, rounding up a fair number of the crusaders. Meanwhile, Peter hurriedly captured the renegade Salamander and returned it to its copper prison. It was the first time Alinor saw the monk lose control of one of the creatures.

It was not to be the last.

The majority of his troops intact, the "army" marched

to Constantinople, where they set up camp beyond the city walls.

And that was where the Hermit's troubles truly began.

By this time, Peter appeared to have lost control; his people looted and pillaged within the walls of Constantinople on any pretext—only now it was all the time, instead of just at the Hermit's behest. Alinor guessed there were still three or four Salamanders loose in the camp. The monk gave all the signs of being unable to catch his little monsters, and now they were inciting his troops to ever-increasing excesses and violence. Angered, the Byzantine Emperor Alexius told Peter the Hermit to take his people out of his domain. Faced with the prospect of seeing the emperor's troops—real troops, armed and trained—descend on his own "army," the monk readily complied, although it took all of his eloquence and promises of further riches to coax the mob outside the city, towards Jerusalem.

And there they stayed, camped far enough outside the walls that it was not possible for the Hermit's followers to wander into the city to loot at will. The sun beat down on them by day, and scorpions and snakes crept into their shelters by night. Food was becoming scarce even for the Hermit's followers, and when food could be found, it was full of sand, half-rotten or withered. The Hermit couldn't seem to get his troops to move on, nor could he turn back to Constantinople. Alinor became more restless as the days went on. He yearned to return to the Kingdom of France and Joyeaux Garde. By now he knew only too well that there was nothing he could do, either about the hundreds of thousands of innocents in the ranks of Peter's army, or the Salamanders that drove them here. He was no longer even curious about the humans and their ways; he was sickened to the heart by the useless violence, the pettiness and the waste of lives. As long as they were letting themselves be led about, the humans never had a clue of their potential. It was sad, so unlike the ways of Underhill. All he wanted was to go home.

Unfortunately, he had no way to get there. The army was in the middle of nowhere, camped on the shores of the Sea of Marmarra. There were no horses to be had at any price, and no ships to carry him back across the sea.

Peter the Hermit had gone back to Constantinople to parley with the emperor.

Alinor privately thought he had done this not to gain shelter for his followers but to escape the effects of the Salamanders running rampant through the camp. Isolated groups from his army began sacking and burning the Byzantine Christian churches along the shores, killing Christians and infidels with a blithe disregard for anything other than blood and loot. Alinor was deeply afraid and withdrew into himself, becoming sullen, speaking to no one. On a day when he realized he had not heard singing or laughter for a month, he decided to leave for Constantinople, trying to avoid the madmen of the crusade until he got free of them. He planned to blend in with the locals once he reached the city. The prohibition against magic—and his year-long exile—were long since expired. He could cast whatever illusions he chose, replicate some of the local coins until he had enough money to travel properly—perhaps even buy comfortable passage on one of the Italian ships. *There's nothing I can do about the Salamanders,* he told himself. *It's not my doing, and it's not my responsibility. I'd better get out of here while I can.*

He had the strange premonition that something terrible was going to happen. And he didn't want to be around when it occurred.

That night he slept fitfully under a cart in which a human couple did what passed for lovemaking. He was afraid the rickety thing would collapse, after all the stresses of the journey, but at the time it was the safest place to be. Orgiastic drunkenness ruled the camp these days, and he was soul-sick with it. *These humans are* terrifying *when intoxicated,* he observed, as the cart above him rocked and squeaked with the humans' rutting, *and there is no passion in their lovemaking in that state. They're like dogs making puppies in the fields.* Staying under the cart ensured some privacy, however dubious.

When the horizon had begun to lighten, Alinor was up and around. *Enough light to see by, at least. All I have to do is follow the shoreline back to the Bosporus. Provided the Turks don't kill me first. After what we've done to their land and their people, I wouldn't blame them.*

We?

The Sidhe slipped silently across the field of sleeping bodies. There were a few others who were slowly waking, some with more energy than others. Somewhere he heard a priest saying the morning mass to a flock of early risers.

Peaceful. And totally unlike the way the camp would be in a few short hours.

He thought he had cleared the camp when he was confronted by something in the half darkness that rose up to block his path and spoke to him, mind-to-mind.

:What are *you?:* the voice hissed. *:You can see me, where the others cannot. Who sent you here, and why have you been watching the Hermit?:*

Alinor stifled the scream that tried to claw its way out of his throat as a Salamander materialized before him, an outline against the sand that gradually became solid. There was only one, but it was enough; it grew as he shivered before it, until it was easily the size and mass of a warhorse. Half shadow, half dark fire, it seemed slightly transparent— but Alinor was not going to be fooled into thinking it couldn't hurt him.

But it's not solid, he told himself, debating whether or not he could flee the thing. After all, he had never felt its effects. Maybe he could evade any magic attacks it made so long as he ran from it rather than confronting it.

:You were with Al-Hazim,: the Salamander continued, and Alinor realized this was the same creature that the Mad Arab had conjured, and the Hermit had seized, at the inn. *:You owed him servitude, but instead you abandoned him for this,:* it hissed, and the stubby, black head jerked towards the camp. Then the creature gave him a wry, intelligent look. *:But you are not a fool. You have been following me, observing me. That you can see me means . . . you're not human? Is that why the detachment, boy?:*

Alinor fought the urge to run, barely winning.

:I cannot feed on your anger like the others. And you smell like a spirit.: It drew closer, so close that the Sidhe could smell its foul, stinking breath.

:I ask you again. What are *you?:*

It was the breath that did it. Alinor turned to run towards the beach—he heard waves pounding the shore, and that gave him direction. But then, behind him, from the camp, came screams which increased in volume and number.

What—the elf thought, and the Salamander was gone, bounding towards the screams, which were now coming from everywhere.

Without thinking, Alinor sprinted for the beach, then looked back to see what was going on.

The camp was being rushed by an army of Turks. The remnants of what must have been a raiding party were running back to the camp in terror, pursued by Turks on foot and on horse. The camp, undefended, vulnerable, not even all awake, was a prime target for a well-organized force.

And this was a real army, not a handful of Moslem traders or Byzantine monks.

Peter's followers were doomed. Alinor watched in horror as entire regiments of mounted, armored and sword-wielding Turks rush the camp, killing everything in sight. Turkish soldiers put everyone in their path to the sword, without regard to sex or age. A sea of horses poured into the camp like locusts as blades and arrows bit deeply into anything that moved.

His first instinct was to fling himself into the midst— to save the little ones from the swords, the arrows—

But he was only one. And *they* were wielding Death Metal.

A stronger instinct—that of survival—overcame his initial impulse. He could grieve later that he had been unable to act. *Great Danaa, I have to run! They'll just as quickly kill me!*

And he did run, with a desperation and speed he didn't think was possible. *Even the Salamander couldn't have inspired that run*, he would later think. But that was many years and miles later. . . . *Perhaps it was my own conscience I was trying to outdistance?*

Alinor struggled to sit up. He hadn't realized he'd almost nodded off on the tree bough until he'd teetered, and the sudden shift in gravity urged him awake. The Sidhe looked down at the ground, seeing gravel and fallen oak leaves instead of sand, wondering briefly why he didn't hear waves washing over a beach.

Time check. This is the twentieth century now, he thought, wondering why he suddenly felt so exhausted. *I must have gone into a light Dream*, he decided, still shaking the confusion. Down on the ground, in the compound of Brother Joseph's domain, soldiers stood guard, but instead of Turks waving bloodied swords, radical Christian crazies waved AK-47s and AR-15s.

Even after nearly a thousand years, it's amazing how some things simply don't change for these humans. The elf's thoughts turned grim, however, when he remembered what else was inside the Chosen Ones' complex.

Something that wasn't human at all.

What he saw the Salamander doing with Jamie was much more subtle than its crude manipulations back in 1096, when it simply reached out for young, flexible minds and started brawls in a tavern. Or, on a larger scale, when it possessed the thousands of peasants during Peter the Hermit's crusade, inciting them to go forth and reclaim the Holy Land for Pope Urban II. No, not now; the times had changed dramatically since then. A fine degree of stealth was required to operate in this modern world, where communications were instantaneous, and strong, central governments had formed, accompanied by equally strong and effective law enforcement.

To be a Salamander, one still had to find niches, gaps in the fabric of society to operate in relative freedom. Gaps like Pawnee County.

And niches like Jamie.

Alinor seethed as he began to piece together the creature's true nature; not only did it need a place where laws were not easily enforced, it chose a vehicle, a resilient vehicle, far younger than the brash, sword-toting hotbloods led by the Pope. He remembered the effect the child had had on the Praise Meeting crowd, saw it for more than the stage show he had thought it was. Using Jamie, the creature had seized control of those people just as surely as it had seized control of the crusaders, using religious hate and intolerance as the catalyst.

The girl, with as much skill as she's showing in the spirit world, must have had a medium's abilities before she passed over. Didn't Cindy say something about Jamie being sensitive? This would explain why he was chosen, and kidnaped, instead of Brother Joseph using one of the other kids who were already in the cult. The Salamander is now speaking through its vehicle, baiting its followers directly with wealth and power, something I don't remember it doing before.

I think we are all in deep, deep trouble

CHAPTER EIGHT

Al closed his eyes, and reminded himself that not even an elven warrior and magician could take on an entire army of humans single-handedly. He was not a movie hero, or a superman, who could charge through waves of men with machine guns. If his captors had *planned* to keep the boy protected against elven meddling, they could not have chosen better. He was walled away from the outside by Cold Iron; to get at him, Al would have to go inside one of the steel-sided bunkers and past several iron-reinforced walls. His magic couldn't hold up under that; iron pulled Sidhe spells awry.

And he had no real-world proof that the boy was there, nothing he could bring to Deputy Casey to invoke the human authorities. They needed evidence in order to act; a change in human legal process that now turned out to be a hindrance. *Used to be, we could stir up a population to do just about anything, just by convincing them that what we said was the truth. Damn nuisance, this need of hard evidence for due process, sometimes. Still, it means there is no room for doubt—guilty is guilty this way.*

In point of fact, there was very little he could do, either with his own powers, or with the humans'. First of all, there was the Salamander; his powers were not equal to taking it on. He had never been one of the greater warriors of the Folk; he'd never been one of the more powerful mages. *His* success these days lay in his adaptability to the humans' world.

There was nothing he had learned in all of the centuries since he had first encountered such a creature that could be used to counter it. Nothing. In fact, all he had learned was that he didn't want to meet it on its own ground. And this, without a doubt, was the creature's own ground. The last time he'd seen a Salamander, he'd turned tail and had run away. The second time, he'd headed for the nearest walled fortress. But this time he couldn't run.

He ground his teeth together in frustration. Up until now, whenever he'd had to pull a rescue, it had been a fairly simple operation. He would find the child in question, spirit it away from its parents, take it Underhill, and one of the others would cover his tracks.

Quick. Easy. Painless.

So all right, what can I do? he asked himself, angry at his impotence. *How can I at least give the poor little lad a respite? Give them something else to think about?*

First, he had to calm himself; find the quiet place deep inside himself where his power lay.

He took two long, slow breaths. By the time he exhaled the second, he had achieved the calm he needed. He called up his mage-sight, and opened his inner eyes on the world.

Everywhere he looked, Cold Iron thwarted him, standing like dull, barbed barriers against his Sight. This was the Death Metal at its worst; if his power touched it, the metal would drain energy from him, spinning his spell-traces away into shreds too fine for him to collect back. It would be very difficult to insinuate his powers into this stronghold in anything other than a passive manner. Cold Iron protected their machineries, their storage places, themselves— even their weapons were of Death Metal. And *here* was an unpleasant surprise. Even some of the bullets were sheathed in it. Now he not only had to fear a direct hit, but a *grazing* hit might poison him.

But wait—he extended his senses a little further, frowning with concentration. A headache began just at each temple, but he would not let it distract him, reaching a little further into the maze of threatening metal and humanity.

Everywhere there was Cold Iron, there was also something else that might provide an insidious pathway for Al's power to penetrate Brother Joseph's citadel; a network of copper tendrils weaving through the complex in an elaborate network of support. The electrical wiring system, of course; it hummed with the power coursing through it, and was as obedient to Al's touch as the Cold Iron was hostile.

A frail enough pathway, and one that had severe limitations, but it was better than nothing.

Perhaps Al didn't know a great deal about ordinary, day-to-day living for humans—but he knew electrical systems and knew them very well. He'd amused himself long ago with his "playing with lightning," but tonight there was nothing funny about it. He sent a little tendril of power questing curiously along the network, testing it, seeing where it went, how it was constructed. This system was mostly new, and all of it was less than five years old. Humans tended to distrust the very new, or the very old; this network of wiring was neither. They wouldn't be expecting any troubles out of it. And they depended on the electricity it carried so completely that he found himself smiling grimly.

He explored further. There weren't any voltage regulators except on the main circuit breaker; even the computers had only the simplest of surge protectors on them. Those would protect against sudden surges; they wouldn't protect against something a little more—subtle.

Al opened his mind and his magic to encompass the entire system, holding it in his metaphorical "hands" like a cat's cradle. Then, slowly, he began decreasing the resistance of the wiring across the entire network.

This was the sort of thing that happened naturally with age and generally never caused any harm. But then, few people ever had the voltage regulators that maintained the level of power in their systems fail on them.

Soon the system was running "hot"; capable of carrying voltage of around 140 instead of 110. Which didn't matter, since 110 was all it was getting. Of course, *that* was about to change.

Al carefully skirted the iron clips and bolts around the aluminum main breaker box, and adjusted voltages at it. Slowly, so no surge protectors would trip. Eventually he brought the voltage all the way up to what the system would carry—and there were few pieces of equipment here meant to operate on 140 volts.

Now motors would run faster, burning themselves out. Electrical circuits would overload and blow. Computer equipment would be fried. But none of this would happen all at once; a lot would depend on how delicate the equipment was. Whatever; they would have to replace everything that burned out—then the replacements would fail—again and again, until they thought to check voltages. They would have to replace every bit of wiring before he was through, from the breaker boxes outward. They wouldn't discover this until they had lost several more machines and had replaced everything else. This meddling was going to cost the cult a lot of money. And time, and trouble; unfortunately, it would not be as difficult to pull the wiring as it was in a normal building, but it would be troublesome enough, and they would have to do without power in the entire circuit while they replaced the wires.

If something happened that forced them to use their emergency generator, it would all happen that much faster. Al took out the voltage regulator entirely on *it*. Power levels would fluctuate wildly as pumps and air-conditioners came on- and off-line.

He contemplated his work with satisfaction. Already, all of the electric motors in the complex were running a little faster. Pressure was building in some equipment, several water-pumps, for instance.

Hmm. They are using common white plastic pipe. There is no more resistance to my magic than wood or leather would give. A little weakening of the pipes at the joints . . .

There. In a few moments, the joints would burst, at least in those portions of pipe that were under pressure. There was some kind of elaborate arrangement in one corner, for instance, that was going to go up like a water festival before too long.

Using his magic—finally *doing* something—had cooled

his temper enough that he could think again. With luck, the fanatics would be so hard-pressed for money by his sabotage that they would act hastily, perhaps get caught by the police. It occurred to him that the more havoc he could wreak that Brother Joseph *himself* would have to attend to, the more likely it would be that the bastard would believe some outside supernatural force was opposing him.

Of course, it is. And for once in his life, he will be right.

When that happened, Brother Joseph would be kept so busy trying to find the source of the interference that he would have little time for anything else.

He might leave the boy unguarded, or relatively unguarded. At the least he would leave the child alone, give him a chance to recover. If Al could not get in, perhaps the boy could escape on his own.

So, it was up to Al to make Brother Joseph's life as miserable as possible. This, of course, would make Al's life infinitely more pleasurable. A man has to have a hobby he enjoys.

He only wished he could tell the boy's mother about this—that he could tell her he knew for certain that Jamie was here. But if he did, not only would he betray that there was something supernatural about himself, he might inadvertently tempt her into going into danger to save her child.

No. No, for all that it would comfort her, he could not tell her Jamie was here. Not until he had something more concrete to offer her than that information alone.

So, back to work. *How about a bit of blockage in some of the pipes that are not under pressure? That should be amusing.* He knew those pipes that were attached to pumps, but the rest—only that they carried water. The Cold Iron interfered with his perceptions too much to be more specific than that. Right now Al could not tell whether the pipes took fresh water into the complex, or waste-water away, but in either case, there would be problems if he blocked the pipes—say, by reaching out, just *so,* and touching the pipes to make them malleable, then—pinching them, and letting them harden.

There. That should do it. Not all at once—but like the electrical failures, these should cascade.

He withdrew his senses—carefully. He couldn't detect the Salamander, but that didn't mean it didn't have ways of watching the world from wherever it was hiding. More than Cold Iron, he feared *it*.

I couldn't defeat it back then; I don't think I can do so now. The best way to deal with it for the moment is to avoid it. It can do nothing without human help and a human to work through.

He considered what he had accomplished, as he molded himself to the trunk of the tree he had chosen and scanned the area for more guards.

Another pair of them passed about twenty feet away from his tree, peering from time to time through something attached to the top of their rifles. It wasn't until after they had passed that he realized what those instruments must have been.

Nightscopes.

He belatedly recognized them from the action-adventure movies he'd watched over the years, in city after city, racetrack after racetrack, late at night when the humans slept and there was little for him to do.

Nightscopes: instruments that gave humans the ability to see like an owl or one of the Sidhe at night. He wasn't exactly certain how they worked—but he shivered, realizing that the only reason the men had missed sighting him was that they simply hadn't been looking through the nightscopes when they passed him.

And what would they have done if they'd seen him?

The answer to that question didn't take a lot of reasoning. They'd empty those clips into him without a second thought.

No illusion he knew of would fool nightscopes—

But he could reproduce—on purpose—what had occurred by accident.

He closed his eyes again and took a deep, deep breath, and as he exhaled, he *pushed* the outermost layer of his shields, expanding it outwards, slowly, until it reached about thirty feet from where he sat. Then, within that shell, he set a compulsion: *don't look at me.*

It was just that simple. Once guards reached the perimeter of his defenses, they simply would not be able to look in his direction. Any further away, and the trees would hide him, even from the sophisticated scope. He wasn't worried about Andur; if the guards saw the elvensteed, they'd simply assume he was a stray horse. They could try to catch him, of course, but the operative word was *try*. Andur would happily lead them a merry chase over half of the county before vanishing to return to Alinor.

Feeling a little more secure, he turned his attention back to the Chosen Ones' compound. There was still plenty of night left; surely he could do more than he had.

The problem is, everything I've done to them can be fixed. It'll cost time and money, but it can be fixed. I need something that can't be undone.

Well, the one thing that mankind still hadn't completely conquered was—nature. What was there about this area that Al could meddle with?

There was a spring running under the property; it was the source of the cult's water, and came to the surface to form a pond and a stream leading from it at the far end. But that wasn't the only place where it could surface, if the conditions were right.

There was a crack in the bedrock just under one of the cult's buried buildings; the building itself rested a few inches above the surface of the bedrock, on a cushion of sandy soil. If Al widened it just a bit and extended it down to the channel of the spring, the water would gradually, over the course of the next few days, work its way to the surface and emerge at the rear of the building.

This was a storage building of some kind; not one for guns or ammunition, but full of heavy wooden crates piled atop each other. The crew that had built this place hadn't known what it was going to hold, evidently, for the concrete floor wasn't strong enough to support what was resting on it. The concrete had already cracked under the weight in several places. When the spring water worked its way up through the crack in the bedrock, it would soon seep into the building through the cracks in the floor, soaking, and hopefully ruining, everything on the bottom layer. By the time they found the damage, the entire floor of the building would be under a six-inch-deep sheet of water that no pump would ever cure.

That was something they could neither replace nor repair. They would have to abandon the building. He contemplated other possibilities, but there weren't many at the moment. He could induce mice to invade, of course; plagues of bugs—

But that would mean a certain amount of hazard for the rest of the children. Mice could get into their things; *would* bite if cornered or caught. Insects could bring disease . . . some of the insects native to here were scorpions, whose sting was poisonous and painful, and could be fatal to a small child.

And there were snakes aplenty around here; he'd been warned about them when he first arrived. Three kinds of *them* were poisonous: rattlesnakes, copperheads, and water moccasins. No, he couldn't turn those creatures loose where there might be children.

Well, maybe just that one area where there seems to be a lot of plumbing, of electrical circuits. Where there doesn't seem to be a lot of people. That might be Brother Joseph's quarters, or those of his high-ranking flunkies. If it is, it's about to become unlivable over the next couple of days.

He widened cracks in foundations, opened seams, created hundreds of entrances for insects and other vermin. Then he created another kind of glamorie—one that would attract anything small, anything hungry. From there the insects, mice and reptiles would work their way into the rooms, and there were no children in this bunker. Adults, he reckoned, would get what they deserved.

That should settle the account a little more.

It was scarcely more than an hour or two past midnight. If he and Andur got out now, he'd even have a few hours to sleep before he had to get to the track.

If only he could tell Cindy what he knew. . . .

Well, he couldn't.

He opened his eyes again, on a world still dark and full of night sounds: cicadas, coyote howls, the bark of foxes, the cry of owls—

And, far off, too far for human ears to hear—footsteps, trampling methodically through the grass.

Brother Joseph's perimeter guards were still on duty.

He called Andur with a thought; the elvensteed slipped

out of the shadows of the trees like one more cloud shadow, ghosting across the fields of grass, chased by the night breeze.

Al didn't bother to climb back down the tree; he wasn't that far up. As Andur positioned himself under the branch, he simply dropped straight down onto the elvensteed's back, a move copied from late-night cowboy shows.

Then, in a heartbeat, they were away, retracing their path over the fences and out to the road.

Once again, Andur became a sleek, matte-black, Miata lookalike. Once again, Al was cradled in air-conditioned comfort. And yet it provided no real comfort to him.

He was restless and unhappy, and only too glad to leave the driving to Andur. For all that he had done, he had accomplished so little.

So damned little. . . .

He brooded all the way back to the track, by which time Andur had bleached to white and acquired headlights again. When he got out of the elvensteed, with a pat of gratitude, he remembered that Cindy had gone to sleep in Nineve, rather than the RV. In a way, that was something of a relief. It meant he didn't have to hide what *he* was, and it meant he could convert the RV into something like its usual glory—and comfort.

Ah, well. He sighed philosophically as he entered the door and locked it behind him. *Perhaps it's better this way. Bob always tells me that it is a human proverb not to mix business with pleasure—and she is business of a kind.*

He held perfectly still for a moment, standing in the narrow aisle between the stove and the propane furnace, and mustered a little more energy. It wasn't going to matter how keyed up he was; when he finished this, he was going to be so exhausted there would be no chance insomnia would hold him wakeful.

He held out his hands in the glow of the tiny overhead lamp and whispered a cantrip.

Power drained from him like water running out of a sink.

And the RV rippled and flexed, like an out-of-focus movie—and changed.

Now there was a full bathroom with a whirlpool tub behind him; he stood beside a counter loaded with the delicacies of Underhill. Beyond him was his silk-draped bed and one of his construct servants, a lovely animated Alphonse Mucha odalisque, to massage his weary shoulders. Beyond that, where a set of curtains waved in a lazy breeze from the silent air-conditioner, was what had been the overhead bunk. Now it was Bob's cubby-bedroom, with a bed as comfortable as Al's own.

Al snatched a handful of grapes and a bottle of wine from the bounty beside him, and shed his uniform and cap by the simple expedient of ordering them elsewhere. With a nod to his servant, he headed for the bathroom and the whirlpool. Between the bath, the wine and the massage, he should sleep very well.

My father, Joe Junior thought, *has finally gone* wacko.

He stormed down the narrow, steel-covered passageway that only he and a select few knew about, fists clenched. Ready to explode. Motion detectors activated lights and deactivated them in his wake. The illuminations winked on and then off, as if seeing his sour mood and sulking back into the darkness to avoid him. His boots echoed hollowly on the damp, concrete surface, as he dodged the worst of the puddles and splashed angrily through the rest. He wanted to punch a hole in the wall, but to do that down here he would need a jackhammer. He contemplated finding one.

His anger continued to simmer, just below the surface, ready to blow at any moment, as he pushed himself further and further away from the others. And, especially, away from his father.

He recalled that when digging this tunnel they had come across a small water source of some kind, a seep or a spring, and had partially rerouted the tunnel to avoid it. But the attempt hadn't entirely worked. Ahead he heard the steady drip, drip of water that had no obvious source, hidden behind one of the walls. Periodically, workers had to bail the passageway out—from the look of things, they would have to do it again soon. He remembered the fit of rage his father had when they were building the tunnel and couldn't get the drip to go completely away. *It's as if he thought he could control nature*, he thought, still furious with what he had seen at the Praise Meeting. *And it was betraying him by not doing* exactly *what he wanted.*

The boy was putting as much distance as he could between himself and the Praise Meeting, which by now was probably adjourning to smaller, special-interest groups. *Like the one dealing drugs*, he thought, biting his tongue against the anger. He was afraid to even think these treasonous thoughts around the others, in part because his body language often gave him away. In spite of the fine physique he'd been cultivating since before he could shave, he hadn't quite learned how to *control* his body, and often it revealed his emotions. A rigid stance, a certain frozen look in his face, had both conspired to betray his thoughts to his father and those close to him. He was hiding his body, at least temporarily, so that it wouldn't reveal what he was feeling *now*.

Then there was that *other* liability, the one he had been stifling since he was a little boy. It was something he tried to forget about but couldn't, because it went with him everywhere.

Everywhere, waking or sleeping. He heard what other people were thinking, whether or not he wanted to, *especially* when he, or they, were emotionally wrought up.

The ability had appeared at puberty, and for a while he was too busy sorting through his newfound raging hormones to properly assess it.

Then his thoughts began to intrude on his mother's; just a little at first, then with greater strength and clarity as he battled with the roller coaster of emotions any thirteen-year-old experiences.

He discovered to his mingled apprehension and delight that he could read his father's mind as well as his mother's. If father was angry, he knew it and could avoid him in time to save himself becoming the target of his father's frustration. That was useful; it made up in part for some of the other things he read. That his father thought about other women besides his wife was a little distressing, especially since he was a preacher, but Joe began to form the opinion that half of what his father said in church was for show anyway.

That would have been enough, but a few weeks later

came the next revelation. Not only could he read people's minds, he could decide more or less what their thoughts would be.

At first it was funny, to send thoughts into his father's head, get him stirred up and watch him make a fool of himself. After the first few trials, however, he began to feel a little sick about it. It didn't seem right, actually; as if he was using his physical strength to bully weaker people, and he stopped playing around with other people's heads—on purpose, anyway. And he began to wonder where this power came from, since his father preached that any "ESP" was the work of the devil.

Was he being influenced by Satan, or was his father just being paranoid?

Whatever the cause, Joe had learned through trial and error that whenever he was angry he ran the risk of intruding his own thoughts on the minds of the people around him. These thoughts, especially when they were as treasonous as they were now, could get him into deep trouble. They would sound as if he had said something out loud, since emotion was behind them, rather than guile and stealth.

If anyone is being influenced by Satan, it's my father, he thought angrily as he came to the end of the tunnel. Here stood a tall metal door which looked something like a walk-in safe. Joe inserted a card with embedded chip data, identifying him as Brother Joseph's son. The huge metal door swung open, allowing Joe entrance to the private health club. Here only the elite branch of the Sacred Heart of the Chosen Ones could enter.

It was empty, as usual. His father certainly never came here, and rarely did the officers of the Guard and Junior Guards. The others who came here, the first lieutenants and one of his father's personal body-guards, used the place occasionally, but that was generally before dawn, before his father had risen; while Brother Joseph was awake, they were always on duty. And during a Praise Meeting, and shortly afterwards, he was almost guaranteed solitude here.

Much of the new Universal and Nautilus equipment had been moved from their mansion in Atlanta. Other items had appeared recently, including one puzzling piece of equipment he'd never understood or seen used, which looked like something used to balance tires. The room was decorated with chrome-rimmed mirrors, red and black velvet wallpaper, and black velvet trim, reminding Joe of a funeral home.

Joe stripped out of his uniform. He peeled it off, quickly, handling it like a dirty surgical glove, now a little disgusted with what it represented. His glance fell briefly on the sloppy swastika he'd tattooed on his forearm while inspired by a fifth of Wild Turkey. *Wish I'd never done that*, he thought regretfully, now noting how the swastika had crept down his arm, almost to his wrist, as he'd grown to maturity.

Wasn't even sure what a swastika was, when I did it. Knew it had something to do with the war. Knew it had something to do with killing Jews. Daddy hated Jews, so I guess I thought it would be cool. Didn't even remember doing it until I saw it the next day. How old was I? Thirteen? No, I think I was twelve. Not a teenager yet.

He threw on some tattered shorts, not bothering with a tank top. He needed dead weight, and lots of it, to vent his anger tonight.

The fifty-pound barbells were shiny chrome, reflecting halogen light in bright arcs as he lifted them high overhead in short, intense repetitions. The wall was one huge mirror, and he stared at his own snarling face, at the veins that bulged from his temples. Muscles swelled. Perspiration broke, beaded, dripped. He repeated the exercise, this time lying back on a bench, shifting weight, working different muscles.

They warned me not to get attached to the little boy, he seethed. *Even Father, after he'd managed to kidnap Jamie. He didn't seem to mind before! He wanted me to be friendly while the poor kid had a chance to get away— but now that he's ours—he's just another tool, another toy, another magic-trick for the crowd. I played right into it!*

Weights clanked angrily as he brought them together over his head, making a satisfyingly aggressive sound. Though this was normally not good form when doing reps, he clanked them again. The sound felt good, appropriate. *Luke never liked it, the way I favored the boy*, Joe thought, remembering the reaction of one of the lieutenants, one of the first followers in the early days of their church. *He told me it was going to be a problem. He pretended to be my friend, but I know he went to my father. The first time I objected to the channeling, when Jamie was still new.* He winced when he remembered the crack of his father's riding crop, the liquid fire that poured across his naked back. He remembered his own screams exploding from his mouth, and the hoarse voice he spoke with for days afterwards. *Some of those welts never seemed completely healed,* he thought to himself, painfully aware of the ridges flexing and hurting even as he exercised. *Father said they should be a reminder.*

What he was thinking now would qualify him for such punishment again, but he guessed that next time, if it came to that, it would be more severe. If such a thing were possible.

They can't do that to Jamie again, he thought, his attention turning from himself to the boy. *I'd gladly take another whipping if that would get Jamie away.*

Normally at a Praise Meeting he would have been on the stage, guarding the proceedings with the others. But not tonight. Apparently his father, at Luke's urging, had seen what a liability he had become when dealing with Jamie. Tonight he had been given "leave," to observe the channeling if he so desired, but not to participate in any way.

Guess he figured I'd just get in the way. Weights clanked. Joe counted. *Seventeen, eighteen. Guess he figured right.*

He exhaled explosively, as weights flopped out of his hands onto the padded floor with a muffled *thud*.

He didn't starve Sarah like this. At least not for this long. The boy had become visibly thinner over the past few days, and weaker, and his eyes had developed a vacant look. *Like someone on drugs,* he thought. *Only, I know he's not on drugs.* Jamie didn't smile now, except for a few moments when Joe greeted him. Then the smile faded quickly, like a candle's flame blown out by the wind.

Joe closed his eyes. *It's the guilt, isn't it?* he thought. *I'm not angry at my father. I'm angry at me. Jamie has looked up to me like a little brother, and I haven't done a thing but manipulate him. I'm the one who's lured him*

*into this, told him it was all okay when I knew what was
going to happen. And now he's starving to death. And
worse, he's being used by that thing that Father thinks is
God. I think he's wrong. It's not God, it's not even close.*

He crawled into the bicep curl machine, sitting on the
short bench and reaching under the bar where the weights
connected. No one had used it since he'd been there; no
one else could pull eighty pounds. Luke certainly couldn't.
But Joe used Luke's image to fuel his strength, using the
anger to pull the bar up under his chin.

Luke sure has risen in status in the past few weeks, he
observed cynically. Joe had always resented the man, even
back when he was very little and Luke was still a newcomer.
He had been around their family for as long as Joe could
remember, being one of the few followers who remained
faithful to his father, even when his ideology shifted from
one political spectrum to the other. Not surprisingly, his
loyalty had been repaid in high rank within the Chosen
Ones hierarchy. Joe was beginning to see how much he
really resented that. And how much power Luke's position
had.

A year earlier, his father had suggested they form a
special security division separate from the Guard, one that
would oversee internal threats from within the United States
and the Church itself. He had hinted, rather strongly, that
Joe would be offered the position of security chief, as he
would be eighteen by then and a man. As a member of
Brother Joseph's immediate family, he would also presumably be trustworthy, more so than the any rank-and-file
Chosen One. But Joe had learned recently that when such
a division was formed, Luke would be in charge, not himself. He had yet to confront his father about this, and when
he thought about it, he knew that he probably never would.

"He doesn't trust me anymore. If he ever did," he
whispered aloud, and looked around in panic, to see if
anyone heard. Of course, no one was in the club at the
time, but he was still uneasy. Microphones were everywhere,
and he wouldn't put it past them to put one here. *None
of them trust me*, he said, this time to himself.

But Joe had something on Luke, something that went
way back, when he was only a child and still respected the

older man. He had never used it—but the time might be coming when he had to, to save himself and Jamie.

Joe's parents had gone away to some tent revival in Oklahoma and Luke was put in charge of baby-sitting. Luke didn't like being left behind, he had wanted to stand at Brother Joseph's right hand and bask in reflected glory. But, being the faithful follower he was, he accepted the task cheerfully and without complaint. Joe liked it even less, as he'd wanted to get away to see a forbidden movie, *The Last Temptation of Christ*, with a friend.

Luke's presence, of course, screwed these plans up royally. But when Luke got into Brother Joseph's liquor cabinet and started to drink, putting a serious dent in the whiskey supply, Joe thought he might be able to get away if he drank himself to sleep. He'd seen Luke do that before, and there was a good chance he'd do it that night, too.

But this time was different; Luke became drunk and started talking, saying strange things. Then he started to make advances—sexual advances. At first Joe had no idea what he was doing until the man grabbed him when he stood up to go to the bathroom, groped him, and stumbled forward.

Joe just froze, then, unable to think.

Luke's thoughts poured through the booze and struck Joe's mind at full strength; the images were so strong, it had felt like a flame had just licked his brain. Joe jumped back, squirmed out of his grasp, and found temporary refuge in a corner. But it was only temporary; he knew he was trapped.

Joe hadn't thought about his other ability, that of making people think what *he* wanted them to, for some time. It had a way of coming and going, and lately it was doing more going than anything else. But Luke's thoughts were so clear they seemed to be super-charged, and the lust that poured over Joe was a slimy thing that made him ill.

When their eyes met, Joe could see exactly what Luke wanted to do to him. The images were clear and well-defined. Joe had reached further into Luke's mind, more in a reflex than a conscious action, and saw that Luke had done this to other boys before.

It would hurt, he had realized. What Luke wanted to

do to him would hurt *real* bad. He could already feel the pain, as if it was already happening; he began to whimper, like a dog, as he froze in fear and shock. Luke had stumbled forward, one hand on Joe's leg, the other on his own belt buckle.

Joe screamed—but not just with his voice.

The old man stumbled back for a moment, as if he'd been slapped, and Joe had screamed again, but only with his mind. Luke had crumpled to the floor.

Joe scrambled away and ran for his bedroom, which had a lock. Luke lay on the floor, yelling at Joe to come back, he wasn't *finished* yet. Joe locked the door and waited, afraid to even breathe. Soon Luke fell asleep, snoring loudly from a few feet outside the door, and Joe felt safe enough to cry himself to sleep, with a pillow muffling his sobs.

Or at least he had tried to. He didn't sleep much, and when he did he would jolt awake at any little noise from where Luke was. The next morning when they woke up Luke said nothing about the incident and went about nursing a hangover. Joe was too mortified to bring it up and wondered if he would tell his parents when they got back.

That afternoon, Brother Joseph and his wife returned. Joe was watching them drive up the hill to the mansion when Luke had turned to him and said, soberly, "If you tell them about what happened last night, I'm gonna kill you. No questions asked."

Joe believed him. So he didn't tell them about Luke's attack. Then, or any time since.

After that horrible experience he began stifling his ability to see into other people's minds. What he saw coming at him from Luke's drunken brain was something he never wanted to see again. The man hadn't physically raped him, but after seeing the images of what Luke wanted to do— and had done before—Luke might as well have, since he lived through it all, every horror Luke had planned for him. He felt hollow and wooden after that night, and made a vow to himself to leave other people's minds be. He told himself that most thoughts are better left alone.

And, he had to admit then, his special power could have been the work of Satan. It sure *felt* like it.

Over the years Luke had provided several more reasons to be hated, reasons that went far beyond what happened that night while his parents were away. The way he treated Jamie was one of them.

In fact, Luke was "guarding" Jamie now, he'd overheard at the meeting. *Guarding against people who might bring him some food. But then, I have privileges. I could take him somewhere. Fishing, or—*

His thoughts stopped there, when he remembered the *last* time they'd gone to the pond, or at least in its general direction. *I could have fed him then,* he told himself. *He hinted that we could eat fish there, and I ignored him.*

He wasn't sure why, but the incident reminded him of Sarah and what his father had done to her. *He didn't know I was watching, from a distance, when he did—that.* His arms grew a little weak and he paused, forcing the image away from his mind. *I wasn't supposed to see that. No one was suppose to see that!* He had been hiding and had been unable—or unwilling?—to betray himself by bursting out and coming to the girl's rescue. He recalled with clarity the morbid fascination that had seized him, how he had watched his father grab the girl's thin, delicate neck. The blue color her face turned. The sudden weakness that came over the girl, the absolute limpness of the body. The brief surprise of his father. The lack of remorse. Then, or now.

And remembered Jamie, withering in the isolation room.

Joe saw what he would have to do. Resolutely, he put the weight-bar back down and went back to the lockers. The scar tissue on his back throbbed in a strange sort of sympathy as he thought about whips.

He's not going to do that to Jamie, he thought as he pulled his hated uniform back on. *I'll never let him do that to Jamie.*

Joe hadn't really considered how he was going to approach this. In his pocket he carried a piece of beef jerky and some dried fruit, which in itself was not very substantial. But it was *something*, and it was easier to conceal than, say, a sandwich. As he came to the sector where the isolation room was, his lack of planning now added a new, frightening dimension to what he had in mind.

He had, however, thoughtfully left his sidearm in the health club. It was a .44 Magnum and its size was enough to raise the hackles of any gun enthusiast—as any Chosen One was likely to be. Once, that model had been considered the most powerful handgun in the world. That was before .577s with Glaser slugs, and the other toys around here. He'd left his Rambo knife with the gun. He had nothing but his hands and his body—

But that body was hard and lean, in itself a formidable weapon.

Especially when fueled by *anger*.

The place where they were keeping Jamie was a hodgepodge of interconnecting rooms that originally were to be used as warehouses, but to date had only partially served that purpose. One of those huge rooms was where they kept the drugs, but he was never privy to which one—or the times they were full. He had gathered that the storage was only temporary, usually only overnight, and changed from one room to another. The blueprint of the sector, and what was actually built, never completely jived either. There were formations of rock that were either too hard to chip away, or served as strategic supports for the upper strata, and had been left alone. Where possible the rooms were paneled with sheetmetal and were further divided with chain-link fencing. The entire sector had a cold, metallic atmosphere about it. But then, Joe reflected, so did the rest of the underground complex.

Joe peered around a corner at Luke and another guard, someone whose name he didn't immediately remember, standing in front of a double door with a padlock. This was probably where Jamie was, and he ran through his mental map of what adjoined this particular room.

Back wall is solid rock; room would have been a little larger if they'd had the right equipment. Room itself is large, divided into storage bins with fencing. Jamie must be in one of the bins. Get in through the top? Joe racked his brains for what was in the level above them, and came up with: *That's Father's private quarters up there. Well, scratch that.* Other rooms beside it had sheetmetal walls, and although cutting through would be possible with a saw, the *noise* would be prohibitive. Overall, a good, secure place to imprison someone.

Time to deal with Luke and his partner, he thought, and shivered with mingled apprehension and tension.

Luke was reading a Bible; his partner, a man Joe now recalled was known only as Billybob, was reading a weapons manual on the Colt AR-15. The gun itself was lying across his lap as he sat reading. Joe hadn't intended to sneak up on them, but his footsteps simply didn't make any noise. When they finally did see him, they jumped into action and had their weapons drawn on him, cocked and ready. Bible and weapon book fell to the ground, forgotten.

"Oh Lord," Luke said, relaxing some. "It's *you*. Why you sneaking up on us like that?" He didn't seem at all pleased and continued to aim his gun at Joe.

Joe shrugged, feigning innocence. "Wasn't sneaking up on you." *You just weren't paying attention, you lazy puds*, he wanted to add, but chose diplomacy by default. "Just walk kinda quiet in these boots."

Now that the immediate crisis was over, Luke relaxed into his accustomed superior attitude. He was about forty years old with an immense potbelly that made him look like a giant lightbulb. Even after the brief excitement of being surprised, he was breathing with difficulty, and his face was flushed from the exercise of getting suddenly to his feet. *Not surprised, after seeing what he eats for breakfast. A slab of greasy bacon the size of a brick, fried potatoes, scrambled eggs. Every single day. Gonna have a heart attack before too long. Too bad it's not right now.* He didn't seem to notice the bad effects of poor health, or the fact that he was woefully out of shape. Instead, Luke put on his normal, superior sneer, an expression more-or-less permanently carved into his fatty features. Buck teeth protruded prominently from his face, and he looked like a pig doing an Elvis imitation.

"Do you have any idea what time it is?" Luke asked, slowing his breathing with a visible effort.

"I dunno," Joe replied, intentionally sounding stupid. "Late, I guess."

"It's two A.M." Luke said, arrogantly. "Any idea why your father put me on duty here?"

Joe gazed blankly and shrugged.

"To keep people away from our little treasure in there," Luke said, jerking the barrel towards the room they were guarding. "Who, by the way, is sleeping. What do you want, anyway?"

"I wanted to see Jamie," he replied. "I kind of promised him a bedtime story. I was gonna tell him about Daniel in the lion's den."

"You know what your father said," Luke said, shifting the assault rifle in his arms. "He wants no one near the boy. That includes everybody. That includes *you*."

"He's real lonely." Joe said, but he knew how helpless that sounded. "You could—"

"No. I *couldn't*."

Luke advanced menacingly, quickly, as if he was considering shoving Joe away with his own massive weight. Joe stepped back automatically as his body began to go into defense-mode, automatically tensing some muscles while relaxing others, a well-honed response due to years of self-defense training. Training, in part, received from Luke, before he'd put on the weight.

And Luke saw it. "Go ahead. Try it. I have a witness. You don't. You father will believe me, whatever you do."

Billybob made several snuffling noises that approximated laughter. Joe absently toed a rock with his right combat boot.

"That is, if you lived," Luke continued. "Why are you here, Joe? You don't mean to tell me you actually *feel* something for the little lump of shit we've got stashed away back there?"

"Well, no," he lied. Now he regretted not having a plan. *But this will only help me if it makes me look like a fool. Luke is less defensive if he thinks he's dealing with someone more stupid than he is.*

"I just wanted, you know, to study him. See what kind of effect food deprivation has on a person. Look, if we're going to be doing this we need to see how far we can push."

"Depri-what?" Luke asked, seriously confused. He always

did have trouble understanding words with more than two syllables.

"Means *starving*," Billybob informed him.

"Oh," he said, with a knowing look. But he frowned anyway while a rough, blistered thumb toyed with the safety. "Still don't like it. Listen, you go get permission from Brother Joseph and I'll let you see him. I mean, how am I supposed to know this isn't a test and all?"

"You don't. But I guess you're right," Joe said, knowing that to push now would only arouse more suspicion. "I'll go talk to my dad now."

Luke nodded. Billybob made more snuffling noises, this time sounding like a hog rooting for food, sounds that had no clear meaning.

"Where is he, then?" Joe asked, with a touch of anger.

Luke shrugged. "Back in his quarters, I guess."

Joe saw an opening. "You mean you don't *know*?"

The superior sneer faltered; Luke knew the rule as well as anyone else; *the first lieutenant must always know where the leader is, for security reasons*. Not knowing was a punishable offense. Luke stammered. "I—I—he must be in his quarters now. He is. Yes, he is. I know it."

"That's better," Joe replied, privately delighted at the tiny victory. He turned to leave, effectively terminating the conversation.

He's a fool, if you know what buttons to push. No wonder he followed Father for so long. He glanced back, catching Luke as he stood there, mouth hanging open, apparently still trying to piece together what just transpired. *You'd need a brain like a sponge to stay on with Brother Joseph all these years*.

Joe smiled—but only to himself.

Luke qualifies.

Out of range of the two idiots guarding Jamie, Joe's thoughts turned dark. He was, after all, no closer to getting food to the boy. The giant piece of beef jerky jabbed him in his pocket, reminding him of his failure.

I failed because I didn't have a plan, he reminded himself. *I can try again, but this time I'd better be smart*.

In the Guard, one was taught to use one's assets to their

fullest advantage. Being the son of the founder of the movement, he had barely scratched the surface of those assets. For example, he could go places where very few, even within the Guard, were permitted. He went to one of those places now.

Using the card again, he entered one of several remote security stations, small rooms paneled with heavy-gauge metal and stuffed to the rafters with high tech surveillance gear. Against one wall was a pickax, a firehose, and a set of bolt cutters behind a glass pane. Along the opposite wall, ten tiny black and white screens blinked back at him. This particular station, he knew, was redundant. These same feeds were going to the main security station, which had a wall of screens that dwarfed this rig. This station served only this sector of the underground, whereas the main station had camera feeds to everything. The Guard monitored the main station, and at least one member would be there now. Eventually, when they had more manpower—women didn't count—all stations would be manned, giving redundant security everywhere. The small screens here had various views of the hallways and tunnels. Some angles, he saw to his surprise, were new. *Looks like they've put new cameras up. Gotta watch that. Must assume I'm being watched at all times.*

Which prompted him to look up. *Good. No cameras here.* Every time he used his card, a record of where and when it was used was stored in the cult's computer, also located in the main station. *They'll know I was here. And they might want to know why.* He knew, however, that it would be at least a week before they ran the reports that showed security card usage. For the time being, anyway, he was off the hook. In a week, surely, he'd be able to come up with a plausible excuse.

He studied one screen, which gave the view right outside Jamie's isolation room. Luke and Billybob sat reading their respective books. The other nine screens didn't show anything particularly interesting: empty hallways and views of the storage rooms, and other things that weren't important. One screen was turned off. When Joe turned it on, a camera view from within the isolation room came to life.

Jamie was lying on a mattress, sleeping fitfully, having what appeared to be nightmares. Joe was stunned at first; he hadn't expected to find a camera inside the child's room, but when he thought about it, it made sense. Jamie was important. Jamie had to be watched. On the little black and white screen the boy seemed thinner than he'd been at the Praise Meeting. Joe remembered when, as a little boy, he'd found a kitten swimming frantically down a stream. He had plucked the animal from the water, and for several fascinated moments watched it stretch out and go to sleep in his palm. Wet, it had looked like a dying rat, its tiny lungs heaving against a frail rib cage. That was what Jamie looked like, lying on the mattress.

As pitiful as the boy looked, the sight only cemented Joe's resolve. *The question is, when am I going to be able to get in there without Luke knowing?* He debated over whether or not to wait until their shift changed over. They might even put Junior Guards down there, though this was unlikely. At any rate he might have more leverage with their replacements, being the son of the leader. Some members of the Chosen Ones held him in awe, prompting some enthusiastic followers to speculate out loud that Joe was the grandson of God.

He had never taken full advantage of these attentions, this being one of the assets he couldn't fully exploit while keeping a clear conscience. *Not that my conscience has been too clear lately anyway*, he thought, remorsefully. *Taking advantage of those people who think I'm divine might be tempting. But that wouldn't make me no better than my father. God, what a prick he is! He manipulates them so well, especially when he uses Jamie to invoke that thing. If I start doing the same crap, what's to stop me from becoming just like him? Do I really believe in what he's doing?*

Which prompted another distinct stab of doubt. *Do I really have faith?*

As if on cue, the power failed briefly, then returned. Lights in the security room blinked. As one the ten screens went to static, as if switched to a dead channel. In the distance, Joe heard an alarm that he couldn't immediately identify. Water gurgled nearby, as if a pipe had ruptured behind one of the walls.

Down the hallway, someone shouted. Running footsteps followed the shout, came near, then retreated into the distance.

Wide-eyed, Joe stood perfectly still, keenly aware of every sound around him. His faith in God, now, was completely restored.

Four of the screens flickered to life. One of them displayed the view of the hallway outside Jamie's isolation room. Luke and Billybob had abandoned their positions, it seemed; their books lay idle on the empty chairs. The two guards were nowhere in sight. Frantically, Joe banged on the screen that had the interior view, getting no results. The screen continued to display snow, with an occasional horizontal line.

He must still be in that room, he thought. *They just ran off to see what the commotion was.* Then, *There was a reason for this to happen now.* Joe eyed the bolt cutters on the wall, saw what a perfect tool it was for dealing with padlocks. Joe found a rag, wrapped it around his hand, and punched out the pane of glass. After removing the major shards from the frame, he took down the pair of bolt cutters and made for the door.

The alarm was a little louder now and seemed to originate at the end of a long corridor. The shouts became more numerous and confused, and it sounded like whatever happened would keep the two guards, along with many others, busy for some time. It never really occurred to him that whatever the emergency was could be a danger to himself or Jamie. His only impulse was to move, and move now.

Abruptly, the power went off altogether. For several moments he stood in total darkness, unable then to see his hand in front of his face. In the security room behind him, muffled by the thick steel door, several electronic gadgets whirred to a halt. The alarm cut off completely.

Good Lord, Joe thought, taking a tentative step forward. *What a time for this to happen.* During the early days of living in the underground, when all of the bugs in the electrical system hadn't yet been worked out, he had carried around a flashlight on his belt just for such emergencies. But it had been months since the last blackout, and since then everyone had become complacent about the power system, taking it for granted.

Then, further down the passageway, a light winked on. From the ceiling a thin finger of light touched the concrete floor below. *Emergency backup*, he remembered. *This is going to work even better.*

Somewhere in the underground, he heard someone shout "Fire!" followed by a scream and the blast of a fire extinguisher. Again, he felt strangely calm, although it occurred to him that maybe he should feel a little more alarmed. Since there wasn't much that was burnable in the underground caverns, not much attention had been paid to drills should a fire occur—

It didn't matter. What was important was to get a piece of beef jerky and dried fruit to a starving boy.

He knew the passageways from memory and was able to navigate back to where Jamie was being held. Emergency lights periodically illuminated the way. Still, there were sections of darkness that most people, unfamiliar with the floorplan, would have balked at. Presently he found himself in front of the unguarded double doors. Inside, Jamie whimpered.

"Jamie?" Joe said, careful to watch his volume. "It's Joe. Sit tight, I'll be inside in a minute."

In seconds he had clipped through the padlock with the bolt cutters and opened the twin doors.

Joe immediately saw by the light creeping in from behind why the boy was crying; there was no emergency lighting inside, and he had been lying in total darkness. Before doing anything else, he reached up and turned off the security camera. The power wasn't on yet, but when it did come on he figured this would be one of the first rooms security would be most interested in investigating.

"Here, partner," Joe said, holding out the jerky. "Eat this. If you see them coming, hide it. Don't let them know you have it."

But Jamie was too busy hanging onto Joe's knee to eat. "Where have you been?" the boy managed to blurt out.

The effort of sitting up and talking seemed to exhaust him. Jamie flopped back down on the mattress, sitting up on one elbow. Slowly, he took the jerky, regarded it for a moment, then started stuffing his face with it.

"Whoa!" Joe said, nearly grabbing the boy's arm to keep him from wolfing down the gift. "Slow down. You'll make yourself sick eating fast like that."

"I'm already sick," Jamie pointed out. "When did they decide to start feedin' me?"

Joe stared at the boy until finally their eyes met. "They haven't. I'm doing this on my own."

Jamie gazed at him severely. "You're gonna get your ass whipped for this."

"Probably. But I don't care. It ain't right to be starving you like this. And then making you talk to that thing. . . ." Joe froze then, wondering if he should have mentioned it. Instead of the fear he expected to see in the boy's face, he only saw blank incomprehension. *He either doesn't remember, or he's too tired to think straight now*, Joe speculated.

Jamie was paying attention to other things. "Is that fire?" he inquired innocently as he gnawed on the stick of jerky.

"It's . . ." Joe said, momentarily confused. *That was a fire back there, and I wasn't even paying attention. I was concentrating too damned hard on finding Jamie. If the place is on fire, then maybe I should get him out of here*, he thought stupidly.

Joe looked up and saw the thin film of smoke licking across the ceiling. He sniffed and smelled the smoke for the first time. But it wasn't like any smoke he'd smelled before; this stench was laden with plastic and synthetic smells, sort of like when an alternator on a car is about to go out, or when a fuse box overloads.

That's easy. It's an electrical fire, he thought, frowning. This didn't make the situation easier to handle.

This room is no longer safe, he declared. *I'm taking him out now and to hell with the consequences!* After all, this was what he wanted to do all along.

"Come on, buckaroo," Joe said, scooping him up in his arms. He felt the difference in the boy's weight immediately; ten, maybe twenty pounds. "We're getting out of here."

"Okay," the boy replied calmly. "Got any more jerky?"

"Not with me," Joe said. "Too much food will make you

sick right now. Hang loose for a while." He remembered reading about concentration camps in Nazi Germany, and the prisoners who, once liberated by the Allies, ate themselves to death. He wondered about this when he saw Jamie, but didn't think he was that far gone. *A little food. No more. At least until I figure out what kind of condition he's in.*

And what I'm doing here, and how I'm going to get him out, and what I do then.

Joe carried him out of the isolation room with a distinct feeling that he was being watched. *Paranoia*, he decided. *The power is off. The cameras are out. There's not enough light in here to see by if they weren't.*

The commotion at the end of the hall was still in progress, but now seemed farther away. From the melee he was able to pick Luke's voice out, an insistent, frantic wail trying in vain to seize control of the situation.

What is going on up there? Joe wondered, becoming a little more interested in the emergency Luke and Billybob ran off to tend to. *Soon I may just find out. Those two, they'll be back soon. I need to make this look innocent if they find me. No, when they find me. There's no way out of this place, even if I did try to make a run for it.* This last thought disturbed—and intrigued—him more than he thought it should. *Have I completely lost my mind?*

He took Jamie to another wing of storage units, where the lighting was still next to nonexistent. He found tall stacks of boxes piled on pallets, their contents unknown. *Probably food*, Joe thought. *But no more for Jamie. It could kill him.* They were well hidden here, and in the darkness he felt like it would be a less likely place for Luke to find them. *Luke is afraid of the dark. I remember that. Could be why he left Jamie and ran for the fire. The fire has light.* Had they gone further they would have walked into a highly traveled area; somewhere around here Joe remembered an access tunnel that would take them to the garage, where he could take a truck and maybe even crash the gate. . . .

There I go again. Thinking crazy thoughts. They'd shoot me and Jamie both, if I tried to get away. We'd be so shot full of holes there wouldn't be anything left.

"Try to stand up," Joe said, setting the child down on his feet. "How do you feel?"

"Sleepy," Jamie said, yawning. "But I don't wanna go to sleep." He looked up at Joe with brown, questioning eyes. "What's going on, Joe?" he asked. "Why won't they let me eat?"

Joe sat down on a bare pallet, which rocked a little as his weight settled down on it. Now they were on eye level, making it more difficult for Joe to talk to the boy. He wanted to shrink into a little ball now, the responsibility for this predicament pressing a little more firmly on his shoulders.

"I'm a little confused right now," Joe admitted. Jamie's look became puzzled. "I don't know what they're trying to prove back there, making you talk to that thing like that, but it ain't right and it's not good for you. There are some things that just aren't meant to be messed with, and that thing that took control of you tonight is one of them." *Jesus,* Joe thought. *Where are these words coming from?* He listened to his mouth rattle on, uncertain if it was him who was talking, or someone, or something, else.

"But I can tell you this," Joe continued. "It's not right what they're doing. And I'm partway to blame for it. I don't know if I can get you out of here now, but I will someday. I promise you that."

Jamie gazed at him solemnly, his lower lip curling out into a pout. Then the expression changed to anger. Eyebrows arched, his forehead wrinkled.

"Joe, *where is my momma?*"

Joe tried to gaze directly into his eyes, but his look wavered and glanced away. *He doesn't know what's up and what's down anymore. Everyone in authority has been feeding him lies, and now he knows it. He's looking to me for the answers. I've got to tell him the truth, or he'll never trust me again. And if he doesn't trust me, he doesn't have a chance in this place.*

"I don't know where your mother is," Joe said slowly. After saying it, it was a little easier to look up. "I never did. Look. The grownups around here, they haven't been telling you the truth."

Joe had expected tears; he got a dull resignation. "I

guess that means she's not coming here. To the vacation place."

He uttered the sentence with such a total lack of emotion that Joe shivered a little. *It's almost like that thing was talking through him again. Like maybe a little bit of it stayed behind or managed to burn out some of his emotions. Or else that he's so used to disappointment that he doesn't care anymore.*

"That's right, Jamie," he said with effort. "She probably doesn't even know where you are." He looked up. "You stay here a second." Joe got up and peered out of the storage room, down the corridor. The sounds that echoed through the corridor indicated that the fire was gone, but that other things were keeping the guards busy. *We're safe for a little while longer*, he decided. *Better make the best use of this time I can. After this it will be impossible to get close to Jamie again.* When he returned, he continued. "Your mother didn't know you were being brought here. Your daddy, you see, he took you away from your school so she wouldn't know, and brought you here so that you could be with him."

Jamie looked confused. *Why shouldn't he be?* Joe thought, resisting an urge to pull his own hair out. *God, I hope I'm going about this right. This had better not be causing more damage than good.*

"But *why?*" was the logical response.

A simple question with a damned difficult answer. It's too late to back out now, I'm already ass deep in this one.

"Your ma and pa stopped getting along together. You're smart, even you could see that." Meekly, Jamie nodded. "And well, he heard about the Chosen Ones and started to come to meetings. And before long he was a believer, and a follower, of Brother Joseph."

"Your daddy."

Joe winced. *You could have gone all night without saying that,* he thought, cringing inwardly. *That's one thing I would really like to forget right now.*

"Yeah. My daddy," Joe said. It felt like he was admitting to a crime against humanity. "He needed someone who could talk to the Holy Fire. Someone young, and smart, like you. Do you remember the Holy Fire?"

"I remember," he said. If the memory was frightening, the boy concealed it well. "But it was okay. I had a friend to help me out."

"Good, that's good," Joe said condescendingly. *I had an imaginary friend, too, a funny fox. Sometimes, he was the only one I had to talk to, when one of Dad's flunkies wasn't around.* "When you're hungry, you can talk to the Holy Fire better. That's why Brother Joseph is doing this. He wants to know things from the Holy Fire, things that will help the Chosen Ones."

He had nearly said, "help us out," but that didn't feel right. He didn't really feel like a Chosen One anymore. *If I'm not a Chosen One, then who am I?* came the thought, but he shelved it for later consideration.

"You don't understand, do you?" he sighed, when Jamie didn't react with anything but acceptance.

But Jamie shook his head. "Oh, I understand," he said matter-of-factly. "Sarah explained everything to me."

Joe felt the room get fifteen degrees colder. *Did he say—Sarah?*

He stared at the little boy, unsure what he should say, or what he could say; it didn't help to ask him again. He heard the name right the first time. *He said Sarah. But it can't be.*

"She's dead," Jamie supplied, with his head cocked to one side as if he was listening to two conversations at once. "She says not to worry, she doesn't blame you for what happened. But she would like to know why you didn't do anything to stop him. She says you were standing right there. When he did it."

"I—" Joe said, but the sound came out a weak gurgle, the kind of sound someone would make when strangling. *Like the sound she made. Oh God, this can't be happening! Is he talking to spirits? Spirits that can read my mind? Is this Satan's work?*

He felt the walls of his father's religion closing around him, warding off the fear of the unknown that this conversation was invoking. *I can't go back to those beliefs,* he wanted to scream. *It's all nonsense, I've already decided that, or why else would I go against him, take Jamie out of his prison and feed him. But this, with Sarah, this is what the demons do. It's what the devil does! What else do I have to protect myself with, besides the Church?*

But—once again, his father had lied.

He told me she went to heaven!

She couldn't have, not if she was talking to Jamie—

Or was she an angel, some kind of sword-wielding, avenging angel, cutting down anyone who had anything to do with her death?

Jamie continued the conversation, like he was on one end of a spiritual telephone. "Sarah says that the forces of darkness are what your daddy attracts, not what she is. She also says you aren't in danger. At first she was mad at me for telling you about her, but now she says it will help all of us, letting you know she's still around. You can help me, she says." For the first time, Jamie showed some spark of interest. "How can you help me?" he demanded.

Joe had fallen off the pallet and was now on his knees, praying. He wasn't even certain what he was saying, but he hoped the emotion of what he was feeling would convey his message.

Jamie peered down at him. "Joe, whatcha doin' down there? You gettin' sick?"

"He's going to be a lot worse off than that," a loud, booming voice shouted from somewhere behind him. Joe jumped up and turned around suddenly, habitually reaching for his sidearm, a .44 that wasn't there.

Luke. Oh good God.

From the darkness came the *snick, snick* of a shell being pumped into a shotgun. Another, softer *snick* betrayed the presence of a pistol.

"I suggest that if you've rearmed yourself to drop it. But I don't think you have. You're not that smart."

The large man's weight shifted the pallet as he stepped on one of the bare wooden platforms. The pallet creaked, protesting loudly. More footsteps; one set no doubt belonging to Billybob. A third person shined a bright spot in Joe's face, panned back and forth between him and Jamie.

"Yep. That's them. They're both here," Billybob said. It was the first coherent sentence Joe had heard the man utter.

"What the hell did you think you were trying to do?" Luke said, taking a few steps forward. The spotlight continued to shine, silhouetting the huge man. "How far did you think you were going to go with him?"

Joe glanced over at Jamie, who had—thank God—eaten everything he had given him. *If I play my cards right, I can get out of this one untouched. If.*

"Not sure what you mean, Luke," Joe replied. "I was just getting the boy clear of the fire. That is what you abandoned your post to go tend to, isn't it?"

Luke's expression wavered slightly. A flicker of concession passed over his face and then was gone.

"Guess that's what it was," Billybob said. "Wasn't sure."

"Shut up!" Luke screamed. His intensity startled Joe. "What I want to know is what you were planning to do with this kid?"

Joe assumed an expression of surprise. "I wasn't planning anything. What I did was take him to safety. It was pretty clear to me that he was in danger, and that you left him in danger."

"Enough of this crap," Luke said, cutting him off. "Billybob, you and Jimmy take the kid back to his room. I'll deal with Joe."

"But Luke—"

"But nothing. No arguments," he replied, a little softer.

Joe didn't like this one bit. It began to feel like a setup, and when he looked around at his surroundings, he had a creepy feeling he might not walk out of there alive. *This is the kind of place where people die,* he thought, trying hard not to let his fear show through.

Billybob hesitated, something Joe had never seen him do in Luke's presence. Luke's eyebrow raised in response.

"I said now," he said, quietly.

"You're not going to, are you?" Billybob asked, somewhat fearfully.

Joe could tell he was getting impatient. "Just take the kid back to the room now," Luke ordered. "I'll see about you later."

That last statement had an ominous feel to it, and Billybob took the boy by the hand and led him away out of the darkness of the storage room. Joe couldn't see

Luke's expression very well, as the light from the hallway emergency light came in behind him. Jimmy followed Billybob out, casting a glance behind him that turned his blood to ice.

He's going to kill me, Joe thought. The realization left him feeling vaguely calm, in a detached sort of way. The fear he would have normally expected just wasn't there. *He's going to kill me, and it's not going to make any difference. He'll make up some story about how I tried to take the gun away from him.*

"You've gotten awfully uppity lately. Who do you think you are, anyway? Seems like you think you're better than me these days." Luke shifted his immense weight, cradling the shotgun carefully. The barrel never wavered.

"I know I'm not better than you," Joe pleaded, trying hard not to grovel. "Its just, things are happening so fast around here. The drugs and all, seems like something's going on there all the time."

"Why don't we just talk about that," Luke said. "Why don't you help with the deliveries? Distribution? You think you're a prince or somethin'?"

"I'm just busy with the Junior Guard," Joe lied. "You know that's what Brother Joseph wants me in. There's no time for nothing else." *If I keep him talking, maybe I can get out of this.*

Luke sneered. "I've been waiting for you to screw up for a long time. I knew you were trouble a long time ago. Knew you would never follow orders from your superiors. You know what I'm talking about, *don't you?*"

He knew all too well. "I think so," he replied, not wanting to get specific. *What is he leading up to?*

"The Chosen Ones will be purified by this," Luke said, raising the shotgun to shoulder level, and taking careful aim at Joe's midsection. "You just sit still, it'll be over with before you . . ."

At that moment the power returned, at least partially, to the sector. Fluorescent lights flickered on overhead as something went *wuuummmmph* in the distance.

"Shit," Luke whispered, looking around him furtively.

Above, located behind Luke, a remote camera whirred back to life. It panned back and forth, its red LED light blinking. Luke spotted it at the same time Joe did and dropped the shotgun to his side.

"There's someone watching us," Joe said. "If you killed me now there'd be witnesses."

"I wasn't going to kill nobody," he said, forcing a smile. "Where'd you get that idea anyway, son?"

"Sure looked that way to me," Joe said.

"What's going to happen now," Luke said, starting for the entrance of the storeroom, "is this. I'm going to report to your father, see, about how you tried to kidnap Jamie and take him out of our little sanctuary here, into Pawnee. The whole story. I'll just let you worry about that."

Joe shrugged. "That's fine with me," he said, not sure where his cockiness was coming from. "But I'll tell you one thing. And I'll let you worry about this: my father is going to find out about what you tried to do to me when I was a kid. Do you remember? Or should I refresh your memory?"

Luke froze in his tracks. "What are you talking about, boy?"

"You know exactly what I'm talking about. He might understand you fooling around with little girls, but little *boys*? And his *son*?"

Luke actually looked white. "He won't believe you."

Joe kept his eyes locked on the older man's. "Are you real sure about that?"

Indecision tortured his face. Joe could almost see the gears turning, however slowly, behind the man's eyes. *Brother Joseph might not believe his own son on something like that, but then he might,* Joe imagined him thinking. *Can I take that chance? As hot as things are around here? Brother Joseph, he likes to kill things when he's under a lot of pressure. Like now.*

"I got a better idea," Luke said, after long moments of consideration. "Why don't we just forget this whole thing ever happened and pitch in and help with the mess we got going back there?"

Joe exhaled a breath he didn't realize he was holding in. "Yeah, Luke. Sure. Let's go."

Prick.

❖   ❖   ❖

Al couldn't decide if it was the massage, the bath, or the wine that put him out, but whatever it was he slept like the dead. He barely woke as Bob got up and passed his couch, chuckling over something known only to the human; he thought he said something, but then went right back to sleep. He woke a little after that, with the realization that he had only an hour to track-time.

No matter. The rest had done him a world of good, completely restoring his energies.

After helping himself to bread and fruit from the sideboard, he ducked into the bathroom for a quick shower. Then, with a sigh of regret, he tapped into one of the local energy-foci, and transformed the interior of the RV back to its usual mundane appearance.

Pity. But I can't have someone walking in on this.

He left his favorite servant, the Phaeton mascot, in animated form, however. He had his hands full with breakfast and a brush, and he needed one extra hand to hold the blow-dryer. The mascot provided that, readily enough. She never tired and never got bored; she would hold the hair-dryer for him until the Trump of Doom if he asked it of her.

A quick peek out of the curtains showed the van was quiet and the Miata was gone; that meant that in all probability, Bob had taken Cindy somewhere before track-time. With her out of the way, it was safe enough to let this little evidence of his power remain active long enough to give him a little help.

But just as he thought that, the door opened.

Cindy had gotten up early, but even so, one of the racers had beaten her. The Miata was gone—although there was evidence by the slight motion of the RV that there was someone still inside.

She was glad now that she'd talked Bob into taking back his bed last night. Al was an attractive man; *too* darned attractive. It would be easy to fall right into bed with him. And she didn't want that—or rather, she did, but not right now. If she were to indulge herself—and that was the only phrase that described it—with Al right now, she would be betraying Jamie by taking away time and energy that could be used to search for him. The fantasy also had a slight edge of fear with the desire, which fluttered madly in her stomach; her ex-husband Jim had been her first and only bed partner. Just leaping into bed with someone she had recently met, who she wasn't even in *love* with, grated against her upbringing. She could almost hear her mother lecturing her for even considering it.

But she wasn't a virgin, wasn't at home, and her mother was dead. Al seemed to be a very nice man, and he was definitely a hunk. She wasn't even married anymore—and she'd kept taking the Pill even after the divorce, as a kind of reflex. There was no reason not to—

No. No, that would only make her feel more guilt, and she had plenty of that right now; she didn't need any more.

The van had a kind of friendly feeling about it; a sheltering quality. Cozy, that was what it was, and welcoming. As if she'd spent the night in the arms of some kind of nurturing earth-mother. She hadn't slept so well or so dreamlessly since Jamie had been stolen.

But her stomach woke her, soon after dawn, reminding her that she hadn't had much lunch and only a salad for supper. Maybe Al had come back last night with a little more food. She'd even cook it for him, or rather, for them both.

I wonder what he usually survives on: Gatorade and concession-stand hot dogs? I'd hate to see his cholesterol count.

She pulled on her old jeans and another t-shirt, slid out of the van, opened the RV door, and stepped up.

She poked her head around a corner—and froze.

Al was stark naked, combing his wet hair with one hand, and eating with the other, while blow-drying his hair. Holding the blow-dryer was a little silver statue of a woman; an odd sort of prop, but if it worked—

Dear God, he's a hunk, she thought in one analytical corner of her mind. Al still hadn't noticed her; the noise of the blow-dryer must have covered the sound of her entering. She felt like a peeping Tom—

She'd seen professional body-builders with better bodies—but not many. Did racing build muscles like that?

If that was what Gatorade and concession-stand hot dogs did, maybe she ought to change her diet.

Caught between embarrassment and an undeniable attraction, she started to back out and ran into the corner of the cabinet instead. "Excuse me!" she blurted, as Al suddenly looked up into the mirror and met her eyes.

She froze like a deer pinned in a car's headlights. The little silver statue was alive and moving. It turned to look calmly at her, still holding the blow-dryer. The dryer cord dangled straight down, and though the dryer was running, it wasn't plugged in.

The startled eyes that met hers in the mirror were emerald green and slitted like a cat's. And the ears, standing up through the wet hair, were pointed.

At first, as she took in the sight of Al's reflection, she felt calm. The strangeness of what she was seeing took several moments to sink in, as there was nothing in her experience, beyond cheap horror sci-fi movies, that she could relate this to. Her mind became a total blank and unable to assign this anywhere to the reality she knew.

Then it suddenly dawned on her: Al wasn't human.

She yelped and backpedaled into the Winnebago's interior as Al swung around, grabbing wildly for—not his privates—but his ears, confirming her suspicion that he wasn't human. His elbow hit the blow-dryer and knocked it out of the little statue's hands as he lunged for Cindy; she found herself trapped against the sink, and she acted instinctively. She kneed him, right where it counted, then froze again.

He might not be human, but the salient parts of male anatomy were in the same place. He gasped and folded, giving her a clear view of his ears. They *were* pointed.

In the bathroom, the tiny silver lady had picked up the blow-dryer and was calmly turning it off. Cindy's mouth was dry and her hands were shaking—and she was sure, now, that she had somehow gotten into some place that wasn't on earth. That, and she was finally losing her mind. Or—was this RV some kind of disguised flying saucer?

Al still had her blocked in, and the moment she broke her paralysis to shove past him, he moved like lightning, recovering much faster than any human could have.

He grabbed her arms and held her, this time pinning her legs as well, his strange eyes glaring at her with an anger that made them burn like twin green flames. He was angrier than anyone she had ever seen in her life. Even Brother Joseph hadn't frightened her this way.

She shrank back, so terrified she couldn't speak, her teeth chattering like castanets, wondering when, and how, he was going to kill her—

An expression of disgust passed over his face, and the glare of rage in his eyes dimmed. Suddenly, he pushed away from her, stalked into the bathroom, and pulled the vinyl curtain shut violently.

Before she could move, he jerked the curtain back again; now he was wearing pants, at least, and was pulling on a shirt. "You try my patience and my temper more than you know, human," he snarled, his hair standing out like a lion's mane. "If there were not a child involved—"

"Human?" she blurted. "What are you, a Vulcan?"

He stared at her a moment, shirt half on and half off— and began laughing. First it was a chuckle, then a full laugh, then loud roaring howls of laughter that reverberated in the RV.

Now Cindy was confused. Hell, if he was laughing, he couldn't be a Vulcan. So much for Star Trek. She stared at him as he tried to collect himself. Was she being overly sensitive, or did the laughter have a strange hollow sound that just wasn't human? At some point his eyes went back to being "normal," but the ears remained the same. Al managed to get the shirt buttoned on, and when he looked down, it was one button off. He seemed to find this even funnier and began laughing more.

I guess he isn't going to kill me yet. He rebuttoned his shirt, still chuckling, and she amended that. *Maybe he isn't going to kill me at all.*

As some of the initial shock wore off, Cindy began to relax. But it seemed as if Al now found the situation—and her terror—quite amusing.

Cindy had been afraid, but that was shifting to anger. *She* didn't think this was anything to laugh at.

"And what is so damned funny?" she finally said, fuming. Then something else occurred to her—and her anger faded as it occurred to her what she had sounded like.

There was a long silence as Cindy sat down at the table,

and Al remained standing. The silence thickened, and neither of them could find a way to reach across it. *He sounds different now*, she thought. *He's not coming across as the techie racing mechanic anymore. I can't place his accent, but it's not from North Carolina—he sounds like he was from that Robin Hood movie. What is he?*

"Well," Cindy finally said, after she couldn't bear the lengthy pause anymore. "What are you then?"

"It would take a long time to explain," Al said, then stopped. She had the feeling now that he really didn't want to reveal anything to her, but that he didn't have much choice.

"I've got all the time you need," she said, and crossed her arms over her chest. *This should be* very *interesting*, she thought. "Go right ahead. Nothing you say is going to surprise me more than what I've already seen."

"Perhaps. But an explanation has become necessary. I would have preferred to keep it a secret," Al said, and shrugged. It appeared, at that moment, to be a very *human* shrug. "But, as you say, the cat is out of the bag."

Cindy waited for him to speak, patient as only the mother of a young boy could be in waiting for an explanation.

Al sighed and poured himself a Gatorade. "We go back many thousands of years, our folk. Your people call mine elves now." He waited, as if assuming she'd laugh at the word. She only blinked.

I suppose that makes as much sense as space aliens.

"We have . . ."

"You don't bake cookies, do you?"

Alinor glared. "No. We have known about your people from the beginning, and have always known we were a minority, and were in many ways physically inferior to humans. We have—weaknesses, vulnerabilities, that you do not have. But we have magic. We have always had magic. For a while that was a protection, and even made us superior."

"And it isn't anymore?" she asked, matter-of-factly.

He shook his head. "No, and now we are even more in the minority. As your human civilization grew, we isolated ourselves even more. Some of us were careless, were discovered. The humans quickly put them to death. We were never tolerated. We have learned the fine art of being invisible."

Al gestured to the orange jug of Gatorade, offering. Cindy shook her head. The mechanic—or whatever—took a seat opposite her, his motions careful and precise, as if he was trying not to arouse any more fear. The act was reassuring. The tale he was telling, however, was not.

"We appear in mythology, folklore, fairy tales. Some of these we planted ourselves. Some, though these are few, are true accounts that have been distorted with time. We call ourselves elves because in your language there is no other suitable alternative. 'Sidhe' sounds just like 'she,' after all."

As Cindy listened, she realized her mouth was hanging open.

"Are you sure you don't want anything to drink?" Al asked, starting to sound concerned.

Again, she shook her head. "You mean all this time you and—? What about Bob? Is he one, too?" The prospect added another uncomfortable dimension to the situation.

"No, Cindy. He is as human as you are," Al replied. "Which takes me to another aspect of our existence. The children."

Cindy suppressed a shudder and tried to make her expression as bland as possible.

Al seemed to read her mind, which did nothing to put her at ease. "No, no. Nothing sinister. We have a low birthrate, and we treasure little ones—perhaps more so than you humans do. We often step in to save them from a variety of fates, from drowning, from fires, from falling. We always have." His expression darkened. "Sometimes we save them from their blood-parents. Sometimes we save them from other things, like Brother Joseph."

Cindy relaxed a little. For some reason, she believed him. Well, why not? There was certainly no other reason for him to have come to her aid.

"Children are most precious to us," Al explained, his compassion reaching her through her fog of confusion. "For reasons that extend beyond survival of the human race. Despite some ways we have been received, we need you."

He chuckled a little. "Children. You could say that it is the way we are hardwired. No one really knows why. The children we save do grow up, of course—and if it is their parents that we save them from, it is often to other parents, loving ones, that they are given. It is true, we have human helpers, like Bob, who help us fit into society and also help keep us concealed—and some of those were human children who were so badly hurt that *we* were the only folk fit to raise them."

"Hurt, how?" she asked. Fear began again. Would this creature save Jamie only to take him away again?

"Abuse—profound abuse. Physical, emotional—" He gave her a hard look. "Sexual. You might not believe some of the stories. You would not want to. For some children, there is no way that they will find healing in your world. For them, there is ours—a world from their fairy-tale books, a world where no harm from 'the real world' can intrude to touch them. A place where they can learn that there is such a thing as love and caring, and where they can learn to defend themselves so that the real world can never hurt them again."

Cindy thought about one of the women who had shared the shelter with her—a woman with three young girls, and all four of them testing positive for syphilis. Only when the doctor had confirmed the fact—and confirmed that the children had been brutally, repeatedly, molested—did the woman believe what they had been trying to tell her about their father.

Their *father*. She had wanted to throw up. But—wasn't that the same thing that Jim had allowed Brother Joseph to do to Jamie's mind?

She swallowed. "All right," she said, "But what about other kids? The ones who've got at least one good parent?"

"Like Jamie?" He looked at her solemnly. "We would have helped as soon as we realized there was a problem. Your husband: classic case of abusive alcoholism. That alone would have qualified your son for our help, if you are in any doubt. But this Brother Joseph thing, that goes *well* beyond what we would consider acceptable. I can only hope that when we retrieve Jamie, he will be able to forget what has happened to him. If he cannot forget, then we can help him deal with it intelligently. A child must never be underestimated."

They regarded each other in silence for several moments, and the refrigerator started making sounds she hadn't noticed before.

"You must believe me when I say that we only want to help your son, and to return him to you." There was a distinct emphasis on that last that comforted her. "It is only a matter of time before I think we can accomplish this."

Cindy slumped against the backrest. There it was. Things hadn't changed that much. At least Al wasn't something from another planet, or from hell. She still didn't know how to handle the elf thing, though. . . .

Never mind. The important thing was Jamie.

As incredible as the story sounded, she knew, somehow, that it was all true. She'd seen the eyes, the ears—

The little silver lady sashayed across the floor towards Al and tapped his knee. He looked down and handed the creature a plastic cup filled with Gatorade. She took it, then hip-waggled her way to Cindy's knee and offered it.

Trying not to drop her jaw, she accepted the cup, and the silver lady sauntered back into the bathroom, hips swaying gently from side to side.

Well, there's nothing wrong with his hormones, if that's what he keeps around instead of pinups. . . .

"Is that—" She faltered.

He raised an eyebrow. "Magic? Yes. It is."

She swallowed a large gulp of Gatorade.

It could have been worse, she thought. *He could have been a giant bug in a man-suit, or something. . . .*

She saw then that his eyes had gone back to the slit-pupiled green they had been when she barged in and sensed that Al was presenting himself now as exactly what he was, and that he was no longer holding back anything that would distort the true image of himself. She noted, idly, that his ears continued to protrude through his hair even as it dried straight, and remembered that she had interrupted his grooming.

"I should let you get back to what you were doing when I came in." Her eyes fell on his right ear. It was hard to resist. "You don't mind if I—?"

Al's eyes shifted momentarily, as if he was about to object. Then he smiled warmly.

"Go ahead. But don't *pull* on it. It's very sensitive."

Gently, she touched the tip of the pointed ear, relieved for some odd reason that it was, indeed, real. It sprang back, as soft and as warm as any human's. This simple act of touching the feature reassured her that she wasn't going mad after all.

"This is going to take some getting used to," she said. "I mean, it's not every day that I meet an elf."

He chuckled. "It's not every day that I get to acquaint a human with our species."

Cindy frowned. "You make it sound like you're from another planet or something. Really, now, you don't look that much different than a human." She blushed, seeing that she was flirting, although indirectly. *What is it about him, even with the pointed ears, that is so compelling? Christ, if we ever had children they would probably all look like little pink Yodas. But then, you know what they say about men with long, pointed ears . . . or was that noses?*

"You're being kind," Al said, and Cindy looked at him askance. *Is he reading my mind, too? No, that was to something I said earlier. But what if he can read minds?* "But there is a great deal of difference between our two races. It wouldn't be wise to introduce you to all of these things now, especially the things we can do. It has already been quite a shock, whether or not you realize it."

"Of course I realize it," she objected, but she knew her words were falling on deaf, if pointed, ears. Cindy couldn't help but notice her sudden calmness and the distinct feeling of somehow being manipulated into losing her fear.

But then her thoughts returned to Jamie, and the darkness came again, swooping over her like a raven that had been waiting in the shadows to rouse her depression. And for all of Al's self-assured words, his *magic*, she couldn't see how she was going to find him, much less get him back.

Are we really any closer to saving him from those crazies? Can little magic statues do anything besides hold blow-dryers? All that talk about saving children, and holding them in such esteem—that's nice, but if Jamie's in there, there's an army between us and him! How can this elf *really help us when the county sheriff can't get inside that compound?*

"Well. Now that we've got *that* out of the way," Al said, though Cindy was not entirely certain what *that* was, "there are some things you could tell me that would help me locate your son. Unusual things. The things someone else might not believe."

"Like?" she asked.

Al waved a hand in the air. "Psychic experiences. Sleep walking. Talking in his sleep, especially if it seemed as if he was having a lucid conversation with someone. Anything at all?"

"You're talking about the Praise Meeting," she said in an accusatory tone she was trying not to use. "The weird stuff that happened there."

He shrugged. "That and, well, other things. Similar experiences that may have happened at home. But if you like, you can start with the Praise Meeting."

She sighed and straightened up, looking down at her hands while she gathered her thoughts. Though her first impulse was to reject the notion, she knew that, in a way that only Al would know, this was important. *He mentioned other abilities. Could that be why that monster wanted Jamie in the first place?* "Like I'd told you, I didn't want to go to that church thing at all."

Al shook his head. "No, not the first meeting you went to. I mean the time Brother Joseph did the channeling. You told me about it, but I don't know if you were there or not."

"I wasn't. That was the time—*he*—just took off with my son." She had difficulty mentioning her ex-husband by name, so she didn't. "When they got back, Jamie was terrified—"

Something suddenly occurred to her, a connection she might never have made if Al hadn't mentioned psychic phenomena and Jamie in the same breath. "That's really strange. Now that I think of it, that reminds me of a time a few months earlier, when Jamie had a high fever. He was having hallucinations, or something close to it, when his fever spiked. The doctor only recommended Tylenol and bed rest, so that's what we did. He was sick for a week,

but during all that time there were a few—I don't know—
incidents. And after that, after he got well, he kept having these experiences. In his sleep."

Al's interest sharpened visibly. "Could you tell me a little
more about these?"

Cindy paused, suddenly realizing how much she had
tried to forget what had happened, as if by forgetting them
she could make them unhappen. If it hadn't been for the
channeling and the whole sick mess with the Chosen Ones,
she suspected she would have managed to dismiss them
from her mind already.

She shrugged, unpleasantly aware that her hands were
shaking. "His father wasn't—interested. He kept saying
Jamie would grow out of it. But I would hear him at night,
sometimes crying, sometimes singing to himself, or even
talking to some imaginary person in the room. At least, I
thought it was imaginary. Sometimes I could rouse him
awake, but on most others, I just couldn't wake him. He
would go on, crying or singing or talking. This was after
the fever, you see, so I was a little worried that there might
have been brain damage or something, but the doctor said
it would pass, it was just a part of growing up. And Jim
said the doctor knew what he was doing and that I was
being overprotective."

"What was he saying?" Al said, leaning closer.

She shook her head, helplessly. "It was in a different
language. French, sometimes. I think it was French. I
don't speak French, so I don't know. Sometimes he sang
things that sounded like hymns in some other language.
Most of the time it just didn't make any sense at all. When
I asked him about it the next day, about the things he
was dreaming, he would tell me the most frightening
stories about dragons or lizards, and about castles and
these huge mobs of people, women, children, knights, all
marching endlessly across a wilderness. Going somewhere,
except they never got there. I never understood the
details. But then, dreams are like that, aren't they? Just
sort of vague and flowing, like someone is pulling what
you want just out of reach."

Al's expression had changed, but she couldn't put her
finger on what it had changed *to*. It was a little creepy,

seeing him staring like that, with those strange eyes—
brilliant emerald green eyes.

"Anything else?" he asked, after a bit.

Cindy thought about it. The memory popped out of
nowhere with the force of a blow, nearly hitting her
between the eyes.

"How could I have forgotten?" she cried out, with an
intensity that made Al visibly start. "The day the school
called me! Jim was at work, I guess, and so I had to go
to the school. Jamie had gotten sick or something, they
wouldn't tell me exactly what had happened over the
phone." She shook her head and put the cup of Gatorade
on the table; her hands were shaking too hard to hold
it. "When I got to the nurse's office, he was just sitting
in a chair, staring straight ahead, not even noticing me,
it looked like. The principal, he was there, and first thing
he said was he thought Jamie was on drugs or something.
I told him that was ridiculous, that Jamie would never
have done something like that. I told him we never had
anything in the house stronger than aspirin—the principal just gave me this look, but he gave up, since he didn't
have any proof anyway. But the way Jamie acted, I could
see why he would think that. He was just staring off into
the distance, like one of those little kids I'd seen on TV
that was in one of the houses that got hit by SCUDs in
Israel, like he'd seen something and was too afraid to talk
about it."

As she babbled on, Cindy wondered why in the world
she had forgotten *that*. The incident had scared the life
out of her, and she'd taken Jamie straight to the doctor.
The doctor hadn't been able to find anything, either—he'd
said something about "juvenile epilepsy" and that Jamie
would probably never have a fit like that again. . . .

It was almost as if something had come in and taken
the memory away, and it was only just now returning, bit
by bit. Was it was coming back only because Al had asked
her for details?

*Was I trying to hide it from myself, and trying not to
remember it? Or is it that something else didn't want me
to?* She wasn't being paranoid—not after elves and magic
statues, and God only knew what was being done to Jamie.

This wasn't the Twilight Zone. Or even if it was, she was *in* it, and she'd better start handling it.

"How long ago was that?" Al asked, piercing the silence that had fallen between them.

"Last year," Cindy said automatically, though on a conscious level she wasn't sure when it was. "I can't remember if it was before or after he got sick. Do you think it's important?"

"Any information is important," the elf replied. "It sounds like he went into a sort of trance." He began to say something, but visibly held back. Realizing he was probably withholding information about her son, she felt a little prickle of anger rise up her spine.

The more Cindy talked, the more concerned Al became about the whole situation. Her recollections of what Jamie had said and done were too similar to his own experiences—hundreds of years ago—to write off to coincidence.

The boy is a medium. Has been, probably all his life. Perhaps Brother Joseph, who has no real ability of his own, didn't actually select him. Maybe he was only a middleman. Perhaps something selected him, as a pipeline to a medium.

And those dreams about what could have been the Crusades . . . what must have been the Peasant's Crusade. . . .

CHAPTER NINE

In perfect formation, the First Battalion of the Junior Guard stood at attention, their assault weapons held rigidly at their sides, eyes forward, chests out. The tension was like a piano wire pulled taut, threading through the boys' tense muscles, waiting to break. Only moments before, just as they did at this time every day, the battalion of boys had scurried onto the sand-covered drill area in their underground bunker, adjacent to the firing range.

It was the same battalion, the same uniforms, the same weapons as yesterday. Only Joe was different. And he felt the difference, coursing through his veins, pulsing even at the ends of his fingers. He wondered that they didn't see it, but there was no indication that any of the boys noticed anything at all.

This was a routine drill, one they did every day. Joe had been in charge of training the boys for months now, drilling them every moment they weren't in the Junior Guard School, learning the non-physical skills they would need in the world of the New Order. His drilling had paid off, and they had become a well-oiled fighting machine, with a discipline that rivaled the Guard itself. For weeks now Joe's battalion had been the center of his life and the source of his pride—

And even after he began to doubt, at least the Junior Guard had been a diversion from the insanity that surrounded Jamie. Now, with his new vision of the way things were, they were a source of personal embarrassment.

But since it appeared that none of the boys was going to run out and denounce him, he did not dare change so much as a single lift of an eyebrow. Eyes were on him; Luke's for one. Probably others. Watching for the least sign of difference, of dissension.

Of treachery? That was how they would see things.

"Who are we?" Joe screamed into the silence.

"The Junior Guard!" the battalion screamed back, with voices that cracked with puberty, voices that were deepening, and voices that were still high and tinny with childhood. But the response became a single sound, shaking the walls, reverberating down the concrete tunnels.

"Who do we protect?"

"God and Country!"

"Who else?"

"Brother Joseph!"

"Who from?"

"The Jew Pig Commie Enemy!"

"What do we train for?"

"Armageddon!"

"WHEN'S THAT GONNA HAPPEN?"

"REAL SOON!"

The ritual followed the same script they had all memorized on their first day in the Guard. They learned the routine while half asleep and stumbling into formation during "surprise" drills in the middle of the night. Joe remembered the faint puzzlement on the boys' faces the first few times they repeated the litany, as if they were shouting slogans they didn't really grasp for reasons they didn't fully understand. But now, Joe could see as he surveyed his creation, they understood it all too well. The hate had become real. They believed it. They lived for it. And it was all they lived for; before friends, future, or family.

Brainwash complete, sir.

Today's drill took them outside, to the recently completed obstacle course. The course itself was disguised and camouflaged from the air. The ever-present guards watched for aircraft, in particular a small plane belonging to the Oklahoma Highway Patrol. When the guards spotted anything in the air, even an innocuous ultra-light, someone would blow a signal whistle and the battalion would go into hiding, concealing themselves in oil barrels and fox holes. Normally Joe would be keenly aware of anything that might be flying around in the air, right down to the ever-present turkey vultures, but today he just didn't care. The daily drill was a responsibility, nothing more. Meaningless. *Less* than meaningless. The enemy, he now knew, existed only in someone's fevered imagination.

His father's.

He hadn't slept last night, either. This wasn't terribly unusual, since he had to be up for the late-night surprise drills, and after the drills it would often be late enough that he wouldn't bother going back to bed, instead filling his time with five-kilometer runs and weightlifting. He had found a way to summon a second wind out of habit, but he was glad *he* wasn't required to run the course.

Joe watched the boys crawl under barbed wire, climb up ropes and over walls, run through tires and snake through conduit. And none of it made any sense anymore. *We're doing this for nothing,* he thought in disgust that sat in the back of his throat and made every swallow a bitter one.

Out of the corner of his eyes he saw a familiar shape. *Luke.*

He stood at the corner of the obstacle course, and all evidence showed that he had only recently awakened; he yawned frequently and had the rumpled, disgruntled look he generally had until lunch. *Father must have given him time to sleep,* Joe mused. *He never sleeps when Father is awake.* He found it disturbing, though, that Luke was here watching the Junior Guard. *He letting me know that he's watching me?*

The more he considered this, the more it made sense. Joe caught him making furtive glances in his direction, which Luke quickly diverted when their eyes made accidental contact. Then Joe saw him nod towards one of the guards in the tower. The guard returned the nod, then began scrutinizing the area where Joe was.

He's having them keep an eye on me, too, Joe realized. Dismaying, but not, after all, surprising. Unless—

For a paranoid moment the boy considered the possibility that his *father* could be reading his mind. After all, the "gift" had to come from somewhere! What if his father had known, all this time—

He mentally ran through everything that had happened so far, and his panic subsided. *They were only reading the signs,* he finally decided. *There was nothing supernatural about it. My father is still a fake.*

Still, it was unnerving to be watched so blatantly. He had hoped to be able to sneak away and get more food to Jamie, but as he stood there, watching the watchers, the flaws in that half-formed plan became evident. For one thing, it would not solve the overall problem. Jamie was a tool, one his father was going to use until it broke; and the boy seemed well on his way to breaking. He might be able to get him some more food today, but what about the next day, next week? How long before every opportunity, every chance was cut off? Not long, with Luke in charge.

And that didn't solve the real problem, because meanwhile his father was using him to talk with that godawful thing, *whatever* it was.

That wasn't the last of his problems, either. The drug dealing had also begun tugging at his attention, and he found that he could no longer look the other way and still have anything like a conscience. He taught the Junior Guard that drugs were poison—and meanwhile, his father sold the stuff to kids no older than these.

But with all of these eyes following him now, there wasn't much he could do about the drug ring, or Jamie.

As a child, he had toyed with the idea of running away. That had been when his father first began taking notice of his son, attempting to mold him into a little miniature version of himself. He resisted, at first—after all, so much of what the public schoolteachers taught him ran against everything his father preached—but obeying his father was just too much a part of him to resist. Finally he accepted his father's word completely, and whatever urge he'd had to run away seemed like the most treasonous insanity.

That had been many years ago, when he was a child of fourteen or fifteen. *When I didn't know any better.* But now he was an adult, responsible for his own actions. He couldn't hide behind "my father said" and "my father told me to" any longer. And there was another person involved, a kid, an innocent; someone who was going to die, perhaps even the same way Sarah died. That, he knew after last night, was something he could never live with.

If he could not summon the strength or the means to help Jamie from within the camp, he would have to go outside for the help. He knew enough about the outside world to realize that, once he had gone to the government, there would be no turning back. With the drugs involved, he suspected they would be all too willing to help rescue the boy in trade for busting the drug ring.

Maybe he could strike a deal.

He blinked, and for a moment his sight blurred. *Too little, too late?* he wondered. *Still, if I don't do something now, there won't be a chance to do anything at all. Luke's ready to get rid of me. It won't be long before he succeeds. And then where will Jamie be?*

Then came another horrible thought. *What will happen to him if I can't get him help? I don't have any real evidence to show anyone—just what I can tell them. That little bit of food I brought him was the first thing he'd eaten in a long time, and if I'm gone no one else will be here to help him.*

Meanwhile, the Junior Guard ran through their paces like perfect little robot soldiers. When the exercise was complete, Joe summoned then dismissed the First Battalion. For a brief but oddly sad moment, he wondered if this really was the last time he would ever lead them in exercises. If he did leave, these boys which he had helped convert into fighting and hating machines would have to come to their own conclusions about the Chosen Ones, their beliefs, Brother Joseph. Perhaps, he hoped, it wasn't too late for them to change. Would the defection of their leader make them think—or make them decide that Satan had corrupted him and vow that the Evil

One would never touch them—closing their minds off forever?

As the battalion filed back towards the bunkers, shouting a cadence his mother would have taken extreme exception to, Luke gestured for him to *come here*. The gesture seemed calculated to annoy him. It was as if Luke was ordering a dog.

Joe knew he was tired and tried to get beyond his own foul mood when he walked up to Luke. *Don't let him get to you*, he told himself. *You're tired, you're hungry, and it'd be easy for him to make you say something stupid. And he knows it. He's trying to get your goat, you know he is.*

But as he came closer, he sensed something different about the man. The sneer was a little more pronounced, smug. Luke stood in a particularly haughty pose, and there was dark laughter in his eyes.

Something happened, Joe thought. *He's talked with Father about last night, must have. Maybe it's too late for me to do anything about Jamie.* He wanted to blame the weakness he felt in his knees just then on his lack of sleep, but it was fear, and he knew it.

"Brother Joseph wants to speak with you right now," Luke said, and it sounded like he was suppressing laughter. With great difficulty. "Boy, kid, you sure have screwed up."

"Where is he?" Joe replied, completely deadpan, as if Luke's words hadn't made any impression on him.

"In his office," Luke said—a trap, since Joe knew "the office" could have meant any of three separate places.

So he asked the right question instead of charging off by himself. "Which one?" he asked. "The one near the meeting hall, the security booth, or the conservatory?"

"Near the security booth," Luke said brightly. "He knows everything."

"No," Joe corrected, meeting Luke's eyes directly. "He doesn't. At least not yet. That can always change. Remember, I was only thirteen at the time. A little *boy*."

This last statement actually seemed to frighten the man, as if it was a blow that had been completely unexpected. Luke blinked once, then stepped backwards. *As if he forgot all about last night*, Joe thought. *I'll bet this isn't as bad as he's making it out to be.*

It was, however, an effort to keep from shaking. He had been called before Brother Joseph often, as he was a high ranking officer as well as his son, in that order. Each time in the past it had always been an experience with varying degrees of unpleasantness. But today—well, he'd rather have faced a root canal.

What did *Luke say to him?*

Joe realized that Luke was accompanying him. "Did he say to escort me?"

"Why, no," Luke sneered. "We're just one big happy family. Got something to hide?"

"No, I don't. But you *are* a soldier of the Chosen Ones." He gave Luke a level stare and felt a brief flush of success when the man couldn't meet his eyes for more than a second. "Seems to me you have duties. I just thought you might have more important things to do, like see to Jamie. Who do you have guarding him now?"

"That's got nuthin' to do with you no more," Luke said. "You'll see."

Joe shrugged and walked on, pushing the pace, not looking to see if Luke kept up. Short and stocky, the older man had to walk nearly double-time to keep up with him. They entered the dimness of the complex, accompanied by the familiar *whirr, whirr* of cameras panning across them as they passed. *He's watching me*, Joe thought, with certainty. *They all are.*

They came to the main security station, the mother of the smaller one Joe had operated the evening before. *Do they know I was there?* he wondered, but he had no time to fabricate an excuse. Or—did he?

They entered a room full of video screens much larger and more numerous than the little ones he'd used at the backup station. Along one wall was a variety of radio equipment, through which senior members of the Guard monitored police, emergency and aircraft transmissions. One officer was listening to a short-wave broadcast from Russia, another monitoring what sounded like an African station. Since neither of these were in English, Joe wondered why they had it piped through. No one in the Chosen Ones spoke a foreign language, or at least admitted to it, for fear of being labeled a spy or a witch.

His father was standing in the middle of the room, arms crossed, eyes narrowed. He appeared to be displeased with everything around him, but then as far as Joe knew, he always looked that way.

"Good afternoon, sir," Joe said, his voice cracking. The fear he was trying to hide came through anyway. *He likes it when I'm scared*, he reasoned. *That way he knows I'm still under his thumb*.

Brother Joseph did not respond. He seemed to feign an interest in the screens, which displayed nothing particularly unusual; empty hallways, views of the grounds above. One showed the elementary school class, though Joe had no idea why. He cautiously looked for a screen with Jamie and saw none, although some were turned off. The silence continued, and Joe waited patiently for his father to acknowledge his presence.

In his own time, he did. He picked up a computer printout, turned it around, and held it up to Joe.

"This says you were in the auxiliary security station south this morning around two A.M. Care to tell me why, soldier?"

Joe stared at the report that he hadn't expected for days, and at first could think of absolutely nothing to say. *What was I doing in there at two A.M.? You see, Dad, I was just trying to liberate Jamie, see, and take him to the cops and tell them everything. No problem, okay?* His eyes blurred momentarily. *After that, I was helping put a fire out*, he thought, and he seized upon that as an inspiration. His father couldn't possibly know the exact timing of everything that had happened last night. If he just rearranged events a little—

"First, I had checked the storage area nearby because there were lights on down there, which there shouldn't have been at that hour. It was Luke and Billybob; they said they were guarding Jamie, so I started to leave, but there was a disturbance, and I smelled fire," Joe said calmly. "I was near the station. I entered it to examine the security cameras, to see if the detectors had picked up anything or if it was just someone sneaking a smoke. Once I was in there, I saw that there was a fire somewhere in the quadrant—and even more important, I saw that Jamie had been left unguarded, since Luke and Billybob had gone to neutralize the fire. It seemed to me that the fire might move into his room. In order to preserve our assets I took it upon myself to break him free and move him clear of the area, to somewhere secure and safe, where we could be found easily or get out if the fire started to spread."

His father stared at him for a long time. His expression then was totally unreadable.

After what seemed like an eternity he cleared his throat. "That's what Luke here tells me. I just wanted to hear it from you first. Remember next time, that whenever you enter a security station, you must fill out a report describing why you had to enter the station. File it promptly with the watch commander."

"Yes, sir." Joe waited for something else to drop, but soon it became evident that nothing would. Other things seemed to be on Brother Joseph's mind, and Joe glanced over at Luke, who appeared to be disappointed.

"I've been thinking about our new security branch," Brother Joseph finally said. "For some time now we have been lacking in some means to protect our organization from internal threats. I know, our admission standards are quite high, but there's no way to tell when Satan might infiltrate and sway one of our own. It's happened before. It will be an internal affairs matter, investigating and prosecuting those who veer from the one true path."

Joe sighed inwardly. Now that he had escaped the trap Luke had set for him, all he could feel was—tired. *Fine. He brought me all the way into the security booth to tell me that the position he once promised me is going to Luke. Swell. Anything else you'd care to rub into my face while I'm here? It'll save time and trouble to go ahead and get it over with now.*

"And it's been a tough decision, but I've narrowed it down to one." His eyes softened a bit and looked at Joe with what appeared to be admiration. "Son, how would you like to take the post? I've had you in mind all along, but I wanted to be fair to the rest of the officers. Luke here was a close second, but after hearing what you did last night, and the smart snap decisions you made, I've decided to make you the next head of Internal Security."

Joe was speechless. From Luke, who was standing off to his right, he heard gurgling sounds. Then the noises turned to grunts, which further articulated to: "But—But—But—"

Brother Joseph nodded with something approaching sympathy. "I know, Luke, this is a real disappointment. But I know you'll take this graciously. Like a man! You're still important. You're still in charge of that other little project we talked about."

Other little project, Joe thought briefly, but he was still too flabbergasted for it to really register. *He's going to make me the head of Internal Security after all Luke must have been telling him. Does this mean he trusts me after all, or is this just another elaborate test? Look at him. He's handing me the post in front of witnesses, and if this is a trick, Luke doesn't know about it. Sounds like he's about to piss his pants!*

"But—" Luke said again, but Joe's father didn't seem to hear him.

"Another thing," Brother Joseph said. "Any idea what caused all that ruckus last night? That little fire wasn't the only disturbance, as I'm sure you know."

"No, I don't. Perhaps it was the work of Satan," Joe responded automatically, not certain if he believed the words or not. "From what I saw in the security room, it all seemed to happen at once, power failures, cameras going out, pipes breaking, fires—I was concerned with Jamie's well-being and safety. Maybe—I don't know, maybe Satan wants to get at him so we can't channel the Sacred Fire anymore."

His father gave him a funny look at that. "Perhaps. Perhaps you're pushing that part of your responsibility a little too far there." He smiled benignly. "Since you are now a senior officer, let me show you your new quarters."

Joe had little to say as they walked a long corridor to the adjacent quadrant, then went up one floor to a wide, carpeted hallway that announced, with flamboyance and no subtlety at all, *rank*. At the end of the hallway was a set of flags, one American, the other, a little larger and taller, of the Sacred Heart. Not *the* Flag, that one stayed in the Meeting Hall; this was a copy. Brother Joseph unlocked a huge oak door, one of several along the hallway. Slowly, majestically, it swung open, like the gate to a castle.

Joe realized, on entering, that he hadn't really known how well the officers of the Guard lived. Now he did, and he was amazed at the luxury and opulence he saw here. Carpeting, track lighting, a computer terminal, presumably one directly linked to the main computer, and a big screen TV stood against one wall. In the corner was a small kitchen, with every modern convenience including a microwave. The place looked and smelled newly remodeled.

Luke was standing in the doorway. "But you promised me this one!" he wailed, but his words apparently went unheard.

"In here you have an added feature that the others don't," Brother Joseph said, leading him to the bathroom. Or that's what he thought it would be; when he turned the lights on, it looked like something out of ancient Rome. "A Jacuzzi, just a bit smaller than my own." And indeed it was, rising out of the middle of the room on a pedestal, surrounded by plants and Roman columns. "But no hanky panky," his father said, winking. "This is for you alone. After a long day of drill, it's good for your muscles. It'll help you keep in shape."

They walked back into the bedroom, where they found a huge antique bed with a canopy. "This was your bed in Atlanta, father," Joe protested, but his objections were a bit feeble. He couldn't deny that he had wanted digs like these all along, but never thought his father would consider him worthy enough. Within a few minutes, all that had changed.

"I will have a few privates in the Guard help you move," Brother Joseph said, watching him with an odd expression on his face. As if even this gave him power over his son.

That was *too* much. "No, please, father. Let me get some help from my Junior Guard battalion. . . ."

"You will not do that," Brother Joseph said fiercely.

"They are no longer your responsibility. You are an officer now, with full rank of lieutenant."

"Lieutenant?" Joe said, confused. That was jumping rank, something that just didn't happen. "But why?"

"Because you are my son," his father replied. "And you will be treated as such. Provided, of course, you remember where you stand in the organization." He turned to leave the room, then said, as much to Luke as to Joe, "I have the power to appoint and promote whomever I wish. The Chosen Ones belong to me first, and God second. Do not ever forget that. That applies to both of you." He hesitated at the doorway, then said, "There's something else I must show you. Come."

As Brother Joseph led them to yet another surprise, somewhere deep within the bowels of the underground, Joe tried to cope with his world turning upside down. He didn't think much about where they were being led. All his attention was taken up by these latest changes—not only unexpected, but unprecedented.

What got into him? Shoot. An hour ago I was thinking about running away, but with all this, who could? Head of Internal Security . . .

Now that he thought about it, he wasn't even qualified for something like that. He was just a foot soldier. It was so unlikely that it roused his suspicions. . . .

But his father had said that it would be an easy post, more figurehead than anything, unless a situation came up that would need his special attention. Maybe it wasn't so unlikely. After all, Brother Joseph *was* going to put Luke in charge, and Luke didn't know shit from shampoo.

Nevertheless, figurehead or not, this new job meant rank. It meant being promoted over Luke's head. *And the room! It's amazing!* Joe's present room was little more than a cubicle in a dormitory, with a simple bed on an unfinished wooden floor, a table, a lamp and a dresser. A little more than most of the Chosen Ones had, but still pretty basic. *I think I could get used to this. . . .*

But Jamie—

He tried to keep Jamie, and Jamie's danger, in the front of his mind, but with the sudden change in his status, it was becoming more difficult. He had a taste of the things that only the elite enjoyed. For a moment he was dismayed at how easily he had been manipulated—

But it was a short-lived dismay.

Now I can help Jamie more, if I can sneak behind around my father's back. That makes more sense than running off. It would be different if he hadn't promoted me, but that changes everything. And the more he thought about it, he knew he couldn't run away. What would he have on the outside? Nothing. He didn't even have a high school diploma, at least not one this state would consider valid. There were no assurances that anyone would even listen to him out there, and given the Chosen Ones' security, he knew he wouldn't be able to change his mind once he defected. They would know, immediately, what he had done. In fact, they would probably assign someone to "eliminate" him. They had done it before, killing a former member who knew too much about the organization. And the man they'd killed wasn't even an officer.

Shoot, they killed Sarah's parents, just 'cause they tried to run off. I wouldn't have a chance.

He would have to contend with Luke as best he could. It would be easier to evade Luke than the entire army. Besides, with this new and unexpected change in status, he doubted Luke would come near him now.

In fact, Luke wasn't even a real threat—no matter what he'd promised before. In order to rationalize killing him, Luke had depended on proving some questionable, if not treasonous, behavior. Now that Joe was head of Internal Security, that would be more difficult, if not impossible, to do. The game had turned completely around, this time in Joe's favor.

Why screw everything up by running away?

As he thought these things over, he had paid little attention to where his father was leading them, or what Luke was doing. Now Joe glanced over at him, walking a few feet behind his father, and saw the characteristic smug grin on the man's face. Whatever was up now, it was going to be nasty enough to revive Luke's spirits entirely.

Now what? Joe thought, but had no time to puzzle over

his expression. They had apparently arrived at their destination.

His father turned toward him with a sanctimoniously sober expression. "What you're about to see, Joe, is going to be hard to take. But just remember, it's God's will. To interfere with God's will is to do the will of Satan. And that we *cannot* have."

Then, from behind a set of double doors, he heard the whimpering of a child in terrible fear.

Jamie?

The doors opened, as if by themselves. Then he saw a disheveled, drunken man holding the door open by a crossbar.

"It's been nearly thirty minutes," the man said, visibly swaying as he struggled to stand up. Joe recognized him as Jamie's father. "Should we let him out now?"

Joe could barely see into the darkness of the room, which he now saw was a large storage facility, one of the newer ones. He smelled the damp odor of the fresh plaster and caulking. He hesitated before stepping inside, knowing that he *really* wasn't going to like what he saw. If Brother Joseph had warned him—it was going to be bad, real bad.

Behind him, Luke laughed. Brother Joseph stood in the doorway and beckoned all of them to enter.

The room was dark, except for a few Coleman lanterns sitting on the floor, illuminating two regular Guards who stood at attention. Something that appeared to be a huge box was standing in the middle of the large storeroom. But there was a dark object in the box, and when the *whimpering* came from it, he knew who it was.

"Jamie?" Joe asked, but he was more confused than afraid, since he couldn't quite see the boy or what was happening to him. Then his eyes adjusted, and the darkness retreated.

Jamie lay in the box—or at least, Joe figured he was lying in the box, though all he could see was part of the boy's head. Just the mouth and nose. The rest was covered with an enormous helmet. And the kid's body, from the neck down, was buried in some kind of white substance that looked soft.

Held this way, Jamie could breath, but he couldn't hear, see, or feel anything. If they'd blocked his nostrils with nose-plugs, and they might well have, he wouldn't be able to smell anything, either.

A sensory deprivation box—Joe recognized it from a PBS documentary. It was cruder than the one he'd seen; this one used foam or something, rather than gel or warm water. It didn't look cruel—but it was. Grownups had trouble in the sensory deprivation box. How could a little kid cope with it?

Joe immediately went for the box, but the two Guards stood in his way, holding him back with their assault weapons, denying passage.

Joe shook his head violently. This didn't make sense! Why were they doing this to the kid?

"It was God's wish," Brother Joseph said simply, walking closer, staring down at the suffering child the way anyone else would look at a tree that needed pruning. "I wouldn't worry. God will take care of him, if that is His will."

"His will?" Joe said stupidly.

"God has asked me to do this in order to make the boy even more malleable to His will. He has been resisting of late. I heard the word of the Lord," Brother Joseph said, casting his eyes up in false piety. "So I obeyed. 'The Lord moves in mysterious ways.' I'm certain the reason will become clearer, but until then I must carry out the order he has given me, and only me."

Jamie whimpered again; in that helmet, his ears filled with white noise, he wouldn't even be able to hear himself crying. Joe remembered what Jamie's father said. *Thirty minutes? How long do they plan on keeping him in there?*

Joe turned and faced his father. "May I respectfully ask how this could possibly help us? He was already communicating with the . . . Holy Fire," he said, with an effort. "The latest channeling was the most successful of all. Might this push him over the edge? He is still mortal, Father. Might this overstep the bounds of mortality?" When he finished the sentence, he found he was shaking. His voice, too, betrayed some of his revulsion.

Luke had moved closer to Brother Joseph. Silhouetted

in the light of the hallway, the two bore a striking resemblance to an evil Laurel and Hardy. Even though Brother Joseph's face was difficult to see in the dim light, Joe could sense his father's frowning. "I detect a note of protest to this situation, young man. Perhaps you had better rephrase the question."

Joe wiped sweat that had beaded on his forehead. Luke shuffled, coughed, and crossed his arms, as if trying to look important. James, the boy's father, stumbled over to a chair, where a bottle of whiskey was waiting.

"Is this deprivation supposed to help him in any way?" Joe asked carefully. *As if Jamie could take any more abuse,* he thought. *Starved till he's sick, and now this—*

"Perhaps. If the Lord wants to take him, this would be the time to do it. But I think not." Brother Joseph was looking down again at the child in the box, but his eyes were curiously unfocused. "Soon we will have another channeling, and Jamie is again to be the tool. This is, I suppose, a way to make him more receptive to the Holy Fire."

As his father replied, speaking with vague boredom, Joe realized that he had no intentions of letting Jamie out any time soon. *He's doing this because he enjoys it. He likes the fact that Jamie's scared half to death. God didn't tell him to do it, his own insanity did.*

It was going to happen all over again, the same thing that happened to Sarah, though perhaps in a slightly different form. But the end would be the same. A short struggle, then an unmarked grave in the sandy soil. Joe glanced again at Jamie, although he knew the child couldn't see him.

In his mind, their eyes met.

The boy squirmed, as if fighting the restraints. But the movement was so slight, and lacking in energy, that it was barely noticeable. Then he opened his mouth to speak, and what came out was not a whimper of pain but a whisper. *"Help me."*

"You'll receive all the help you'll need, little one," Brother Joseph said, with mock gentleness. "Joshua, take him out now. You, son, come with me."

Joe hesitated as he watched the guards moving towards the tank, reaching for the straps on the helmet.

"Come with me now!" Brother Joseph ordered. Joe flinched and followed his father out of the room. "Luke, you stay with them, make sure Jamie is returned to his new room. Remember, you're still in charge of him. Don't let anyone else near him. That includes our new head of Internal Security."

"Yes, sir," Luke said, snapping off a salute with a toothy, mindless grin. "And thank you, sir. I won't let you down."

"I certainly hope not," Brother Joseph said. The statement, uttered without emotion, had an ominous feel to it.

In shock, Joe followed his father out. After Brother Joseph closed the door behind them, he grabbed Joe by the shoulder and spun him around with surprising force.

"Now you listen to me, you little *shit*, and you listen good," Brother Joseph said, his face only a few inches from his son's. "I will not tolerate this attitude in any of my men, especially from my son! You are of my flesh and blood and you will obey me or suffer. It is clear to me that you disapprove of my treatment of Jamie. Am I right?"

Weakly, Joe shook his head.

His father slapped him once, hard. Joe's face snapped back at the impact. "Don't lie to me! You disapprove and I know it. That's why Luke is in charge of Jamie. You are now in charge of Internal Affairs, and that relieves you of *any* responsibility to the boy, do you understand me? You will have nothing to do with Jamie. You will not even look at Jamie. You will not be permitted at any channeling, and the only Praise Meeting you will be permitted to attend will be one in which *Jamie is somewhere else!* You made the right decisions last night, when we had the fire, but after that little exhibition of insubordination, I wonder if you really had my best interests in mind. If you are caught trying to communicate or assist Jamie in any way, you will be stripped of all rank and the privileges you now enjoy. There is nothing to discuss. My word is final. If you disobey, contradict or embarrass me in any way as a ranking officer of the Chosen Ones, you will be court-martialed!"

Joe stared at his father, too numb with shock to feel anything.

"Do you understand me?" Brother Joseph shouted, spraying spittle in his son's face.

Joe did not know what to say, what to do, what to think. He felt as if he was frozen in a block of ice; he felt as if he was teetering on the brink of disaster, as if merely breathing would violate some unspoken law. Any answer could easily annoy his father further, so he said nothing. Then, slowly, he reached up and wiped the spit from his cheek.

His father seemed willing to wait forever for an answer. Several long moments passed before Joe summoned the courage to respond.

"Yes, I understand, sir," he said simply.

A faint, sardonic smile creased Brother Joseph's face. He seemed, at last, satisfied. "Good. Then you are dismissed."

Joe turned to leave, and had gone a few steps when his father said, just loud enough to make him jump a little, "Remember, son, you are now in a high profile position. And you represent me, both as my officer and as my son. I keep tabs on all of my officers, in particular the ones recently promoted. This is common knowledge. You will be watched. *Closely*. Do not embarrass me!"

Cindy, Al decided, as Andur crept into his usual spot near the Chosen Ones' hideout, *is beginning to suspect something.*

It had been an uneventful day; for much of it, Cindy had seemed content to watch him, as if by watching she could comprehend him. Coping with the revelation that elves were real, Al had learned from past experience, could take some time. She had spent some time at the payphones, calling different law enforcement agencies, using a tattered calling card that looked ready to disintegrate at any moment. Nothing had turned up, and she had returned to the Winnie in a depressed and subdued state, where she scrubbed the countertops again, obviously trying to keep herself occupied. It was all he could do to keep from telling her of his own progress.

It would complicate things, he decided. *As much as I want to ease her mind and tell her what I'm up to, to do so would probably attract attention I just don't want now. This situation is more volatile than anything I've handled before. The last thing I want is for the Salamander to notice us!* He felt a twinge of hurt pride; the Salamander couldn't know such things, could it? He was just flinching from an imagined attack, scared. No way for an elven noble to act. Right?

She was getting wise to him. Earlier today was proof of that. He'd thought he was going to be able to get away from the racetrack in his elvensteed without her seeing. Around the track Andur continued to be a Miata, although there was a chance that by now Cindy had guessed the truth about the beast. After all, there were several hundred other people here at any given time, and there was no point in breaking his cover now just because *one* of them knew what he was! But as he was trying to pull out of the parking lot, Cindy stood in his path, keeping him from leaving.

"You're not going anywhere until you tell me where you're going, buster," she announced sternly, though Al detected a hint of nervousness. "Do you have a harem of elf women somewhere to tickle your ears?"

Al sighed and Andur's motor idled down. "Don't I wish," he replied, trying to keep the mood light.

She continued to block his path.

"You know, you are making quite a scene here," he said conversationally. "People are going to notice."

"Let them notice," Cindy said, coming alongside the Miata and sitting presumptuously on the driver's door, looking down at Al. "They'll just think this is a lover's quarrel. The word all over the track is that we've been seen shacking up in that so-called 'Winnie.'"

"Well, you've got me there," Al said uncertainly, unable to ignore the burning he felt in the tips of his ears.

"I do believe you're getting embarrassed," Cindy noted with a hint of morose humor. "So. These little trips you've been making at night have really piqued my interest. You want to tell me where you're going, or should I *really* start making a scene?"

"Ah, no, don't do that," he said. He looked into her determined face and felt something inside him surrender. "All right. You win."

Cindy smiled in victory, her eyebrows raised in question marks.

"I'm meeting with other elves," he lied smoothly. "It's like I'm going deep, deep, *deep* undercover, meeting other agents, you see? We're following leads. Nothing on Jamie yet. Nothing solid."

"Hmm," she said. She didn't sound convinced. "Why don't they meet you here?"

"Are you kidding?" he replied, slapping his forehead for effect. "With all this metal? You forget what an anomaly I am. Most elves shy away from human settlements, even ones like this that are easy to blend into. There's too much iron and steel around here. Their magic doesn't work. We've got to meet secretly in the woods and have conferences in the shadows of tall oaks." He folded his arms resolutely and glanced stubbornly away. "It's an elf thing."

"I see," she said, but it wasn't really clear that she did. Or that she really believed him. She stood, her expression still suspicious, that tiny touch of humor quite gone. "I don't suppose I'm going to get more out of you than that," she said. "It's better than nothing. You let me know when you find out where Jamie is, okay?"

"I will," Al said, with more confidence. *I'm not lying. I don't know where he is . . . exactly.*

He drove off, but he was aware of her eyes following him until he was out of sight. And he wasn't at all comfortable.

Her determination is disturbing. She's getting desperate, as any mother would. She suspects I'm being less than honest with her—

Well, she's right. I'm hiding things from her. She doesn't trust me. Not that I blame her. Not only am I a stranger, I'm a strange stranger.

Though it was not quite dark yet, he left Andur in his hiding place and started through the woods towards the Chosen Ones. *A thing as evil as the Salamander will be weakest at twilight, when the world of light crosses the world of darkness, and all creatures of the Earth are somewhat befuddled. At least, that's the theory. This Salamander could be one of twilight, in which case my elven behind is nailed but good.*

There weren't many guards this time of night, Al noted

with interest as he assumed his position in the boughs of a great oak. His agenda included studying the layout again, analyzing the damage he created the last time he was there, and fishing for clues to Jamie's precise whereabouts.

All this, and without the Salamander seeing me. Tricky stuff. Perhaps if I had to I could disguise my magics as something other than what they are. He remembered the girl-spirit he had seen before, during the Praise Meeting. *The child certainly was busy. If she hadn't been distracted during that out-of-body choreography she might have seen me. Let's see. Is there a meeting tonight?*

He probed the surfaces of the Chosen Ones' buildings, finding a strange absence of activity. *Not much going on. No meeting, that's for certain. The hall they met in is deserted.* He probed further, finding a few guards posted here and there through the complex. He wondered if the entire lot had just vanished, when he traced one of the power lines to the huge dining room where nearly all of the Chosen Ones had congregated. A swift scan of the people failed to turn up Jamie. But then, he remembered, the boy was being kept elsewhere, probably in isolation.

Al pulled back and thought this over. *They seem to have only a skeleton force of security during mealtime, which appears to be around dusk. If we were to go in and get the boy, a time like now would be perfect.* He froze as a guard strolled beneath the tree, and Alinor cursed himself for not throwing up another spell to help conceal him. As soon as the soldier passed, Al replaced the earlier night's spell of unnoticeability.

He reached into the complex again, this time probing a bit deeper into the complex of tunnels and rooms, a little surprised to find areas he had missed previously. *This place is enormous,* he thought. *It could hold twice as many as it does now, and with room to spare.*

Al sent his mind following electrical lines down one of the heavily modified areas and suddenly touched a sensitive mind. Now he had eyes and ears! He firmed his contact, and his elven blood chilled when he discovered that the person was one of two walking with Brother Joseph towards one of the huge storage rooms. The other man besides Joseph was overweight and radiated a strong

sense of low intelligence, but the one whose mind he had
touched was much younger and brighter.

And the younger one was very receptive to his probe.
Enough so that Al could ride along in his mind, an unseen, unguessed passenger, eavesdropping on everything.

As he listened to the conversation, he caught the younger
one's identity with a shock of surprise.

*That's Brother Joseph's son. And he doesn't seem too
comfortable here.*

They paused before a reinforced door—and when the
doors opened up, he could hardly believe what was inside.

If it had been hard for him to keep from flying to Jamie's
rescue before, it was doubly hard now. His blood heated
with rage, and he bit at the tree limb he clutched like one
of the old berserkers, to keep from flinging himself down
and taking them all on in single-handed combat. He fought
a silent battle with himself just to keep his arms and armor
from manifesting, a battle that he came within a hair of
losing.

Through Joe's eyes he saw the boy buried in a sensory
deprivation tank, a torture so barbaric he could hardly
believe the truth of his own senses.

He had to do something. *Now.*

His heart ached as he left Joe's mind and probed the
boy's mind for injuries. It was not as bad as he had feared.
The child was incredibly resilient; he had suffered no ill-
effects from the hallucinations he experienced. Oddly
enough, it was the dull gnawing of unrelenting starvation
that had helped keep him sane. It was the one constant
that the boy could cling to that he knew was real. There
was some bruising from beatings—but not as much as he'd
feared. Evidently Brother Joseph had come to the conclusion early on that physical punishment would get him
nowhere with this child.

I can send a healing to him, Al thought, grimly. *It won't
do much for the starvation, but it will help with his other
problems.*

The elf reached into the life-web all around him, summoning the power needed to reach the child and heal him,
when he became aware of something. Something that flickered like a black fire, stirring from its sleep. At first it was

only at the periphery of his powers, emerging from the darkness of its slumber, and he couldn't quite identify it. But then, as it became fully awake, he had no doubt as to what it was.

If I send a healing to the boy, it will light me up like a fireworks display to the Salamander's Sight! he thought in dismay. *Even now, with this simple contact, it might see me. If it attacks me now—*

He withdrew quickly, before the Salamander could sense him—he hoped. If he attracted its attention he could easily become history, of no help to the boy or his mother. Alinor withdrew entirely into himself, letting no betraying spark of Power leak past his shields. He made himself as dark and invisible as the night that had formed around him.

Hiding again. You'd better redeem yourself, Alinor, or your long life will be miserable indeed. . . .

He checked the area—with non-magical senses. A few more guards had taken up positions nearby, but all had the lethargic auras of men who have recently overeaten. *Something else to note. The next shift isn't very alert. Another time a move to liberate Jamie might be most successful.*

He sent a tendril of energy beyond his shields, just enough to see if the Salamander was there, but not enough to give him away. The evil creature was out there, but wasn't directing any energy his way; it seemed more interested in the suffering child—and, oddly enough, the drunken man who was watching him.

But there was something else moving within the confines of the compound, a bright and energetic something that instantly seized his attention. No, not something—someone. And he had seen her before.

The girl.

He turned his attention from the "real" world to the other world: the halfworld. There she was; a glimmer of energy, of spirit, that was quietly, diligently *watching* him. He had no doubts that she had spotted him long before he sensed her, had seen him sitting there in his precarious position in the tree in spite of the "expert" shieldings he had put up.

And she knew when he'd seen her, too.

:*Who are you?*: she asked, impudently. :*A munchkin?*:

Al didn't respond at once. He wanted to be certain that their conversation was a private one. She drew closer, to the edge of his shields, but no closer.

The nearer you are, he thought, without actually sending the thought, *the less likely that thing will overhear us.*

As if reading his mind, she dropped a portion of her own shields and stepped inside the safety of his.

:Stay away from the monster,: she warned, casting a look in the direction of the Salamander. *:It doesn't see me, and I don't want it to.:*

:I don't either,: Al said, and relaxed. *:Hey, you're pretty smart. What's your name?:*

Although she was only a few feet away, she was still a spirit hovering on the edge of the real world, and her image wavered from translucent to almost solid. She still appeared to be leery of him, a healthy caution.

Then again, to operate as a spirit in such close proximity to the Salamander, and to remain undetected, would require a long habit of caution. *She's been smart and cautious, or she wouldn't be here talking to me. She would already have been consumed, drained to nothing and sent to drift off until someone pulled her across to the Summerlands.*

"Sarah," she said. The reply was closer to speech now than the thought-message she had been sending; with such beings, Al knew, this usually meant a bridge of trust had been established. She looked down now, a little sad, perhaps embarrassed. Al was uncertain what her next move would be as her features became fluid, mistlike. She pointed down towards the Chosen Ones buildings. "I used to live down there."

She's a ghost, and she knows it, Al thought, careful to keep his thoughts to himself. *This is the spirit who was helping Jamie through the channeling. I need to get her to work with me if I can manage it.*

"What are you?" she repeated. "You can see me but you're sitting there in that tree. You're solid." Her tone became accusatory. "You're alive. But not like most people."

"I'm not," Al supplied. "Remember hearing about elves when you were a . . . well, do you remember hearing stories about elves?"

She stared at him for a long moment. "Naaaw," she finally said. "Those were just fairy tales. You can't be."

"Yes, I am," he said, then glanced down at a guard, who was walking beneath the tree. The Chosen One didn't look up, but his nearness still made Al nervous. Silently, he held a finger to his lips. Why, he wasn't sure; only he could see, or hear, the ghost.

She looked at him with unmistakable derision. "So which one are you? Sneezy, Sleepy, Stupid . . ."

Al shook his head. "Those are *dwarves*, not elves. Anyway, those are make-believe. I'm the real thing." He smiled, feebly. "You can call me Al."

"Huh. An elf named *Al*? Am I s'posed to believe that? What are you doing sitting in the tree? Are you one of *them?*" she continued in an accusatory tone, indicating the guards below.

"No. No, I'm here for another reason," he said, trying to conceal an aching heart from the girl. Just a child. And now—

She said she was from down there. Was she a Chosen One once? She must have been, so how did she die?

Jamie—had she been his predecessor? She knew about the Salamander—had she learned through first-hand experience?

How could he possibly ask her that?

"You a spy?" she suddenly said, and Al could sense a sudden surge of interest. "Like James Bond? Like in the movies?"

Whatever happened to her, the Chosen Ones must be her enemies, he thought, remembering the bizarre Praise Meeting and the careful way she had shielded Jamie from the worst the Salamander could do to him. *She was aiding Jamie during that channeling. She's good, too, because the Salamander didn't move against her. Shall I take a chance with this?*

Do I have a choice?

"Kind of. I'm here to spy on the group down there," he said. "You know, Brother Joseph's church. Did you say you used to belong down there?"

He would have asked her more, but the wash of terror that spread from her to him stopped him cold.

"Brother Joseph?" she quavered. "What do you want with him?"

"He took—stole—the son of a friend away from us. I think he's doing something with the little boy, but I'm having a hard time finding out anything." At the unmistakable quickening of interest he felt, he continued. "His mother is here, looking for him. He's from Atlanta, and he came here with his father, but his father is not a nice man. He kidnaped Jamie away from his mother, and I think he gave Jamie to Brother Joseph."

"You're looking for *Jamie*?" she asked, and the question seemed filled with hope. "Jamie's down there. You saw him, didn't you?"

"I saw him." He let his voice harden. "I didn't like what I saw." He took a brief moment to break away from the contact with Sarah to seek Jamie out, worming a tiny tendril of awareness through the complex maze. He was gone; at least he was no longer in the deprivation box.

Al returned his attention to Sarah, a little relieved. "I've got to figure a way to get him out of there. I'm not like you. Their guns can still hurt me." He hesitated. Had he said too much? Did she really *know* what she was? But it was too late to take his words back now. "I can't get through the other things, like fences and doors. But I *can* talk to you, and right now I think we need each other's help if we're going to help Jamie." He paused and tried to sense if she had been hurt or frightened by his words. "You know—you're not the way you used to be, don't you?"

She shrugged; a ripple in the mist. "It's okay, Al. I know I'm a ghost. Sometimes I don't like it, I want to go on through to the other side, but I feel like I have to help Jamie. Brother Joseph killed me." She solidified for a moment, and there was a look of implacable hatred on her face that turned it into a terrible parody of a little girl's. "I've got to do what I can to keep him from doing it again. That's why I'm still here, helping Jamie."

Then she changed, lightning-like, to an attitude of childlike enthusiasm. "So what do we do now?"

Al considered his options. *From Earthplane to Spirit to . . .*

Hmm . . . well, the next logical step would be Earthplane

*again, to someone alive and breathing. Perhaps someone
who is disgruntled or unhappy. Someone who can physically help us inside the compound. Maybe even someone
who could carry Jamie out of there, when the time is right.*

"I think I have an idea, Sarah. Here's what I'd like you
to do . . ."

:Jamie?: he heard Sarah say from somewhere in the
darkness. *:Where are you?:*

His eyes had been closed, but when she spoke the words
were like light, breaking through the pain.

He had been dreaming about being tied to a big tree
and left there for dead, when a big bony vulture in a pale
suit walked in with Joe and just stood there, watching him.
Joe didn't do anything to help, and he couldn't understand
why, since he had done everything before to make him safe
in this horrible world called the "vacation place." He trusted
Joe in all things; Joe even brought him food when no one
else would. But this must have been a dream, because
otherwise Joe would have taken him down out of the tree
or at least blown away the vulture with his assault rifle.

Jamie felt hot and knew he must be running a temperature. Otherwise he wouldn't be so sweaty all the time. And
he felt so *sick*. He could hardly move, he was so weak.
He didn't know where the restroom was, and he couldn't
get up anyway, so he just went, like a baby. He didn't like
it, and he felt a vague discomfort from somewhere deep
in the darkness, but he didn't know what else to do about
it.

His whole body had felt funny, heavy and light at the
same time, while he was hanging there in the tree, but now
it felt like everything was going back to normal. When he
tried to open his eyes, it took a minute to realize that he
had, since the room had no light.

:Sarah,: Jamie thought, his mind forming the words when
his mouth and vocal cords could not. *:What are they doing
to me?:*

:Take it easy,: Sarah said, but the words came uneas-
ily, as if she really didn't believe what she was saying. Jamie
didn't like that. *:You can go a lot longer like this.:*

:No, I can't!: Jamie protested. *:They're never going to*

let me see my mom again. They all lied to me. Joe's the only one who told me the truth. They're hiding me from her, Joe said, and they won't let her see me even if she knew I was here.: He felt tears burning down the side of his face. *:I haven't eaten in I don't know how long. Sometimes the hunger goes away for a while, but it always comes back. Then I have to wet myself and that's something little babies do. What will they do next, put diapers on me?:*

He listened to the silence, knowing somehow that she was still there.

:I'm hungry so much my arms are getting thin. If they don't give me food soon I'm going to just disappear!:

:No, you are not,: Sarah said, sounding like a grownup just then. *:Hold on. Help is on the way.:*

As hope flared, Jamie summoned the strength to sit up precariously on a bony elbow, and looked into the darkness. At first he thought the light that became brighter just then was Sarah, then he saw they were just dizzy-stars.

:Help? Who's coming to help? Joe?:

:Sort of. There will be others. Just hang on a little longer.:

:Sarah? Are you still there?:

The lights faded, and Sarah's presence faded into the darkness.

:Where are you?:

The more Joe thought about it, the more certain he was that the two regular Guard soldiers who were helping him move into his new digs were spies, working directly for his father. They were older than he was by a few years and had been around the Sacred Heart for as long as Joe could remember, and should have been promoted to captain long before now. If there was any resentment in them about Joe's new rank, they didn't show it. They paid the proper respect and subservience in his presence, and what little Joe overheard when they weren't directly under his eye did not betray feelings to the contrary.

They performed the tasks set them without a flaw, like robots, or well-oiled cogs in the machine Joe's father had built. Before, he would have been proud of his father's accomplishment. But seeing their lack of emotion, their total implied commitment to Joe and his father, made his skin crawl. If he told them to march into the pond, he had no doubt in his mind that they would do just that.

He began to doubt their facade, however, when he caught them glancing in his direction a few times as if they were trying to make certain whether he was watching them. Then, once, he saw them communicating with some sort of obscure hand signals that he didn't recognize. When he saw that, Joe turned cold. *Spies. For father, and Luke too, no doubt. Figures.*

That he was now head of Internal Security and should investigate, or at least question, such behavior, was never a consideration. For the time being, anyway, he just didn't care. After seeing Jamie that afternoon, he'd felt numb all over, incapable then of feeling much of anything.

Within the first half-hour of moving into the new apartment, he noticed two tiny microphones, each about the size of a fly, inserted into the ceiling. He wondered if there were miniature video cameras, which would have been the size of a pencil eraser, somewhere in his new place. Until he learned otherwise, he would have to assume there were. And act accordingly. In fact, he wouldn't be at all surprised if a view of his new living room was being presented to the main security station on one of the little monitors on the wall. Perhaps he should wave.

That would only let them know I know, and I don't think I want that yet, he thought, as he made a point of acting as normally as possible. *It's late afternoon now. Dinner will be served soon. I'll most definitely have to put in an appearance there. Even if I'm not very hungry, after what I saw today.*

Jamie. Locked in a box like a lab rat. Already a skeleton from starvation. The haunting memory of the boy's eyes back when he'd tried to get him free—they'd looked at each other for the briefest moment, but that moment was stamped into his memory and wouldn't let him go. It pulled at a place in the middle of his chest, stabbed at his heart with surgical precision. *He trusted me. And now look at what's happened.*

He began to wonder if he had indeed waited too long, that Jamie was doomed even if he acted now to save him.

Sooner or later Father is going to kill him. And why? For what? When Jamie dies, Father is going to lose his precious channeller. It can't have anything to do with reason. My father is simply being sadistic.

At this, Joe frowned. *Why does that surprise me?* The answer to that was not immediately clear. *Because all along I've been denying the truth. When he raised me, he smothered me with deceit that I'm still peeling away, like the plastic wrap on a choice piece of meat. But I have to face facts. My father is doing this because he enjoys seeing others suffer. He likes knowing he has the power of life and death over people. It makes him feel good and serves his own enormous ego.*

An ego that will never completely be satisfied. . . .

What a prick.

He looked around at his new place, reluctantly admiring the wealth that surrounded him, and realized that he had been waiting for years to have a place like this. To him*self.* The rank of lieutenant was also something he had dreamed of, but he had thought it would be years away, as there were so many more qualified soldiers in front of him. Now both had been handed to him, by his father, on a silver platter. Although the soldiers who had helped him move in gave no hint that they were jealous, he knew they had to be, on a certain level. *But then, all of Father's wealth has been taken without regard to right or wrong. It's pretty typical for him to hand his son all this stuff, the title, the job, the apartment, without bothering to justify it. He's God's own, right? He doesn't have to justify anything.*

He realized the hour was late and began getting ready for dinner. In the bathroom he regarded the enormous bath with mild curiosity, saw immediately that it was empty. With no obvious means to fill it. Well, it didn't matter.

He stripped and climbed into the shower.

As the hot water washed over his body, he tried to put Jamie out of his mind. But the more he tried, the more solid the memory became. *What did I see in those eyes?* he wondered at the recollection. *He was begging me, but was he accusing me, as well? He might as well have; I'm as guilty as my father.* That he was taking a hot shower in luxury brought on enough guilt; poor Jamie, he knew, was probably lying on a mattress somewhere, too weak to go to the john. *And I can't get food to him. Father made that clear. I'd be drawn, quartered and hung out to dry if I was caught near him. With all the cameras and security in this place, I'll be lucky to be able to use the bathroom without someone watching me.*

At that thought, he glanced up at the ceiling, half-expecting to find a camera staring down at him. *They'd do it, too. Especially Luke. He'd probably have a camera put in here just so he could see me without any clothes.*

Joe put on a clean dress uniform that had just arrived from the laundry and was surprised to find the lieutenant's insignia already attached to it. *Guess Father decided to dispense with the ceremony,* he thought, in a way glad that it had been done this way. The ceremony, at best, would have been awkward. He shrugged and put the uniform on with the new insignia, in spite of the fact he didn't feel he deserved it.

As he donned the uniform, a voice from deep within him reminded him of a poignant fact:

If you don't do anything to help Jamie, the boy will die.

He stopped in the middle of combing his short, blond hair in the mirror and looked himself in the eye. He couldn't remember when he had last performed this simple act of self-searching, and he found it difficult, especially when he was wearing the Chosen Ones' uniform. He felt like a monster. The uniform seemed to be alive; he thought he felt it crawling on his body, like some sort of parasite. He didn't belong in it, and he knew it.

I've got to get out of here, contact the authorities, with or without the evidence. Who knows, maybe there's a missing person's file somewhere with Jamie's name on it. If his mother is looking for him, then there would have to be. But to let anyone know about Jamie, I've got to figure out a way to escape this complex without anyone knowing, at least until I'm well clear. If they come after me, well, I'll just have to spot them before they spot me.

After making his decision, again, he felt a little bit better about himself. In the shiny new uniform, he walked straight, with his head up, strengthened by the knowledge he would soon be ridding himself of it.

◆   ◆   ◆

Dinner was a strange affair. Rather pointedly, Brother Joseph reminded him that he no longer had to eat with the "grunts," that he could now eat in the senior officers' hall which adjoined the central dining hall. He was still not invited to eat with his father, who dined separately from everyone, but that still suited Joe just fine. *The farther away I am from him, the better. What I'm thinking about here is treason, and my body language will give me away for sure if I don't watch out.*

The senior officers said little after saying grace, just a few bland comments about the quality of the food, which he had to admit was excellent and far superior to what the rest of the Chosen Ones ate. Each of them had been served an individual Cornish game hen, real potatoes au gratin and pasta salad, all delicacies and not at all what he was used to. The meal was served on china, with real silver utensils, and the dining room was furnished plushly, like his own quarters; the contrast between this room and the main dining hall was startling.

He couldn't help noticing as he ate that the atmosphere was definitely strained. No one said much of anything, and Joe had the feeling this was due in part to his presence. The ten officers were men in their forties, and as the meal progressed he felt progressively more and more uneasy. There were five captains, four other lieutenants and General Plunket, Commander of the Guard, who was an old man in his seventies who had actually served in World War II— ancient history to Joe. The general said little as he ate, and became slightly drunk on the carafe of wine as the meal proceeded, which seemed to be typical for dinner, as none of the other men seemed to notice.

"That certainly is a smart outfit you've trained there, sir," one of the lieutenants said, with a suddenness that made Joe jump. The man, Lieutenant Fisher, had been his teacher in a few bomb-making courses. More Junior Guard training, information which he had promptly forgotten. Right now if Fisher had asked him how to make the simplest black-powder pipe bomb, Joe would have had to admit that he couldn't remember. Joe regarded him cautiously, expecting his politeness to be a veil for something sarcastic, but he saw only sincerity in the man's face.

Fisher cleared his throat and continued. "I think you will make a fine addition to the senior staff."

"Thank you, sir," Joe said, almost saluting there at the table. He stopped himself in time. *Looks like I'm gonna have to feel my way around how to treat these guys.* "I'm looking forward to serving as your Internal Security head."

Fisher nodded in agreement but said nothing.

"Damned Nazis, they had the right idea!" Plunket roared from the head of the table, a response to a murmured question from one of the other men. "Train the youths. They had millions of their young 'uns trained to step in at a moment's notice. Had them running the government, the utilities, the post office. We came in through a town of about twelve thousand and all we found were teenagers and old people too feeble to walk, and the kids were running everything! Their fathers had already been conscripted, years before. He had the right idea, Hitler did. Kill the Jew pigs, and make sure the next generation understands why it had to be done!"

He pounded the table for emphasis. Silverware and glasses hopped momentarily. Joe wished he were somewhere, anywhere, else.

"Thank you, sir," he said, because he felt like he had to. "I'm certain the Junior Guard will become true fighting men when they are old enough."

"Here, here," one of the captains murmured. General Plunket muttered something else that was unintelligible. The wine appeared to be catching up to him.

Joe wanted to disappear. *I'm starting to like the compliments,* he realized. *This whole dinner is making me feel proud of them all over again. And I want out!*

One of the officers poured wine, what was left, into Joe's empty glass. "Here, have a drink," he said. Joe accepted without a word, although he didn't like the taste of alcohol, or its effects. *Even Father has a glass now and then. Said it had something to do with making the men feel more comfortable.*

But he had a lot of reasons for not liking what alcohol did to him, and one of them had to do with the walls he had carefully constructed, barriers which he maintained to keep his gift of reading thoughts a secret. *I lose control of it when I drink,* he told himself. Then, *But just one glass shouldn't hurt.* He took a sip and briefly resisted the urge to spit it out. This was a very dry and *bitter* wine, which he didn't care for at all. He would have preferred straight shots of Listerine to this.

"What exactly does your new position entail?" Plunket asked, looking as if he was struggling to get the words out clearly. " 'Internal Security.' What does that mean?"

At first Joe was a bit alarmed. *Didn't Father brief him on the new office? Plunket is, after all, in charge of the army. And my superior. Damn him!*

But the one gulp of wine had loosened him up some, and the words came tumbling out.

"Brother Joseph says that it's something we've needed for some time," Joe began. " 'Internal Security' is exactly what it says. There are threats from within this organization as well as the obvious ones without. There could be spies. There could be infiltrators. Why, even some of our own trusted men could turn out to be FBI agents or even worse, liberals."

He took another sip of the wine, not quite realizing until he set the glass down that a deathly silence had fallen over the table. Gone were conversation and the clink of silverware; everyone had frozen in place. A sickening feeling of somehow screwing up came over him; his right hand, still holding a fork, began to shake. They were all staring at him, silently.

"What I mean is, I don't think anyone in the Guard is suspect. New recruits—"

"I think," General Plunket said, with horrible clarity, "that you have said quite enough, young man. I will take this up with our leader. It would appear that you have been misguided in this endeavor."

Joe nodded, not even having the strength to speak. He felt suddenly lightheaded, partially due to the wine, but mostly to his embarrassment.

Why did I have to open my mouth? He wanted to scream. *I should have known all this crap would have been a secret even from the other officers. God, what a fool I am!*

It was then he realized that he was going to throw up.

He felt his gorge rising, and uneasiness somewhere deep in his stomach, so he had time to leave to room before it came up. *Get out of here,* he thought. *Before I puke my guts out all over this table.*

He stood and politely excused himself. Amid silent stares, which he could feel burning holes in his back, Joe left the officers' dining hall and began searching desperately for a restroom.

Moments later, after retching none too quietly into a toilet, Joe contemplated flushing himself down the sewer as well. *It would make the perfect end to this day,* he moaned, catching his breath in the stall. *If I were just a little smaller than I feel right now, it would probably work. Good-bye cruel world. Flush.*

In the washbasin he cleaned up some, still a little queasy but feeling better now that the wine was out of his system. He was contemplating a roundabout route back to his new room, so that he wouldn't have to see anybody, when he became aware that he was no longer alone in the bathroom.

He knew immediately that it wasn't someone or something that had been there when he entered, and couldn't see how anyone could have come in without his hearing them. He turned slowly, expecting to find another adult sneering at him. Instead, he saw a little girl, standing in the corner.

She must have already been here, he thought, though he couldn't see how. *What's she doing in the men's room anyway?*

They regarded each other in silence for several moments; Joe still felt dizzy from being ill, and it wasn't until his eyes had focused completely that he thought he had seen her somewhere before.

"What are you doing in here?" he asked, trying not to sound harsh. "This is the men's room. Little girls aren't supposed to be in here."

"I'm not a little girl anymore," she said, and vanished.

A light rose from where she stood, a vague, glowing mist of something that came towards him quickly before he could step back. It touched him; it felt like a child's breath brushing across his face. Then it was gone.

Joe was too stunned to react. *What in God's name was that?* he thought.

But a moment later, he decided that what he had just seen was a hallucination, brought about by the bad wine he'd swallowed at dinner. *Time to go to bed. I'm starting to see things.*

As much as he wanted to put the disturbing vision behind him, he couldn't. On his way back to his new room, he couldn't shake the feeling that he had seen that particular girl before. It wasn't until he reached his front door and turned the key that he knew, with the suddenness of a revelation, who the little girl was. And why she vanished as dramatically as she did.

No, it can't be, he thought, horrified at the prospect of dealing with a ghost. *I am seeing things. I must be.*

He opened his door in a daze of confused shock. And there was his father, Brother Joseph, sitting in an easy chair reading one of his son's books. He looked up as Joe entered and smiled a predatory smile.

"I've been waiting for you," he said calmly. "Please, come in. We have a few things to talk about."

CHAPTER TEN

"Father," Joe said weakly. "I wasn't expecting you."

Brother Joseph shifted in the chair, holding the book carefully between his two bony hands, as if it were something that might contaminate him. Joe stood frozen in the doorway, afraid to leave or enter.

"That much is obvious," he replied acidly. "Or you would have seen fit to at least conceal this work of the devil. As it is, anyone could have seen this misrepresentation of my ideals. Come. Sit. Let's talk."

Joe cautiously closed the door behind him, expecting a serious explosion to happen at any moment. His father had that sedate look about him that he had come to associate with the calm before the storm. He took a few tentative steps into the room, towards his father, then saw which book he was referring to.

For one moment, relief flooded him. "Father, that's only a novel," he protested, unable to think of anything else to say. He knew it was a mistake, but he had no idea how serious a mistake it was, until his father's face darkened with rage.

"*Only a novel?*" he spat. "Only? My own eyes have seen empires fall on the strength of a novel!"

Joe stood silently, trying hard not to fidget. The book

in question, *Interview with the Vampire* by Anne Rice, had been a paperback he'd picked up in Atlanta, before they had even relocated the Church in Oklahoma. At the time he hadn't thought twice about it. Then, later, he realized how unwise it would be to let anyone in the church see it. Vampires meant the occult, the occult meant Satanism, Satanism meant hell and damnation and evil. Even in fiction. Apparently, in the move to his new digs, some of his things had become jostled. At this point, he wasn't even sure if he'd hidden the book before moving, as insignificant as it seemed to him. It would appear that the two guardsmen who "helped" him move had seen the book and reported it directly to his father.

"Forgive me, Father," he said, with as much meekness as he could summon. "I intended no insult to the church. It never occurred to me that a book of fiction could be dangerous—that anything in it could be taken seriously. Thank you for correcting me."

"Very well," Brother Joseph said, flinging the book into an unoccupied corner of the room. It flapped like a wounded butterfly. *Paperbacks just aren't aerodynamic.*

The bathroom was beyond his father, and the illuminated doorway framed him with a soft white glow. The lighting in the room itself was subdued, mostly because the furniture hadn't been arranged yet, and many of the lamps were still unplugged. Joe thought he saw something move in the bathroom, but wasn't certain. His father continued, oblivious to everything but the opportunity to make a speech, even though his audience consisted of one.

"Vampires are creatures of the occult. Anything occult is the work of the devil. Novels in general foster mischief. Fiction by definition is a lie—something that isn't real and isn't true. There is no reason to read a lie. I would suggest you limit your reading to the Chosen Ones' Reading List."

"Yes, sir," Joe said humbly. Even sitting in the chair, Brother Joseph still managed to look down on him.

Brother Joseph gazed on him sternly before continuing. "You must understand, Joe, that as my son you represent me. I can't have you reading this fictional garbage, this so-called literature. It weakens the mind and poisons the soul.

I suggest that you cull out any unauthorized books from your possession, or I will have it done for you."

Again there was the flicker of movement, this time a little more prolonged, from the bathroom. It was obvious this time that there was something there, that it wasn't just some aftereffect of the wine. Brother Joseph looked away, as if pondering some philosophical concept. When Joe felt it was safe to divert his attention to the motion in the room, he glanced over to the side, to the bright doorway.

The corner of the luxurious hot tub was barely visible. Sitting on the edge of the hot tub was the little girl, the same one that had shown up in the men's room moments before. She watched him, calculatedly, with coldly adult eyes. Joe gulped and found himself steadying his weight against a chair.

"Son, are you feeling ill?" Brother Joseph asked, and Joe was surprised at the level of concern in his voice. "You've become very pale. Why don't you have a seat?"

Gratefully, Joe did as was suggested, sitting uncomfortably on a box.

That can't be who I think it is, Joe thought frantically. *What's she doing here? Why is she sitting in my bathroom, watching me? How'd she get there?* He felt his world turning cartwheels. *That's not a little girl. She couldn't have gotten in here . . . who am I trying to kid, anyway? That's a ghost. That's Sarah!*

The girl opened her mouth to speak, but when her lips moved he heard her voice in his mind.

:*You've got that right,*: she said. :*Very clever, Joe. Now, get rid of your father. We've got a few things to talk about.*:

"Plunket said you were acting a bit odd tonight," Brother Joseph continued, unperturbed. "How was the meal?"

Joe thought he was going to faint, or even get ill again, but he had nothing left to throw up.

As if reading his mind, Sarah continued. :*Emptied your stomach already? Now you have an idea what Jamie feels like. Only by now it's much worse for him.*:

He wanted to scream. He wanted to defend himself, tell her that he was doing everything he could to help Jamie, but there were too many obstacles—one of which was in the room with them.

His stomach writhed. If he were to become ill again, he would have to go past Sarah, this ghost, to get to the toilet. *I'd rather choke on it,* he decided.

His father was staring at him, his lips pursed. The concern had changed to something else—calculation. Joe was one of his pawns—but a valuable one. Worth caring for.

"Perhaps you should lie down," he said. "I have to admit, I did become concerned when our general, Plunket, took me aside in the hallway and said you were acting very strange. And asked me about a few things that he felt needed clarifying. Security matters. Most notably, the role of your new office."

Sarah stood up, tossing her head angrily, her little hands on her hips. It was a stance he remembered, when she was defying his father during those last horrible days. She opened her mouth.

:Jamie's going to die!: she shouted into his mind.

He couldn't take any more of it. Telling her that it wasn't his fault became the most important thing to him just then. But he had to do it in a way that wouldn't attract his father's attention. *I'll have to reach down and use that . . . gift,* he thought, but the prospect felt as horrifying as facing Luke had last night. *I swore I'd never use the gift again. Not since Luke tried to rape me. Never. . . . Jamie, I'm doing my best for him but—oh Lord, please help me through this.*

Then, incredibly, he watched her take a few steps toward them, into the room.

:DON'T COME IN HERE!: he screamed at her, but the words were silent, sent by his mind alone. One corner of his mouth twitched, that was all his father saw. That, and probably the fact that he went even paler, for he could feel the blood draining from his face.

The power inside him seemed to burst out, like a spotlight, like the sudden bellow of a bullhorn. *:Don't let him see you. You don't know what will happen,:* he continued, closing his eyes and feeling a cold sweat breaking out all over his body. *:Please.:*

She hesitated a moment, as if considering the request. He thought she'd never make up her mind. He hoped she'd take forever. He wished he could die, then and there, and get it over with.

:Oh, all right,: she said, petulantly. *:Just get rid of him. I just wanted you to talk to me, after all.:*

He wiped sweat off his forehead, considering his words carefully. *:It might take a while. Don't rush me.:*

"It wasn't my intention to reveal the exact nature of your new position until later," Brother Joseph continued, ostentatiously ignoring the fact that Joe was staring past his shoulder, into the bathroom. Or maybe he simply interpreted Joe's fixed stare as another symptom of his illness. "Until now it has been a secret, more or less. At least, as far as the senior officers were concerned."

"Huh?" Joe said, knowing he just missed something important. "I'm sorry, Father, you were right, I'm not feeling well tonight. What was that you said?"

His father fixed him with the same fierce glare that a snake would fasten on a mouse it didn't care to eat—yet. "Son, pay attention to me. I don't care if you're sick. You want to know why I don't care? Because the enemy won't care. They could attack us at any moment and it won't matter if you're sick or not. The Jew Commie pigs would probably be glad if we were all sick. You'll have to learn how to do your duty awake or asleep, sick or healthy, and you might as well start right now. Now listen up. This is official business."

Joe sat up and tried to look healthy.

"Do I have your attention?" Brother Joseph did not even try to rein in his sarcasm.

He nodded and tried to sit as straight as he stood on the drill field.

His father snorted. "Good. Show some spine, boy. Show that you come of good blood, *my* blood, that you've inherited a little stamina!"

"Yes, sir," he said, faintly. "Stamina, sir."

His father snorted. "*As* I was saying earlier, your new job as the head of Internal Security was supposed to be cloaked somewhat in secrecy. There are those who think that maybe we don't need an internal office of any kind, that our screening of newcomers is as thorough and efficient as it can be. But it's not enough. You want to know why?"

He blinked and tried to keep his expression attentive and humble. "Why, of course, Father."

Brother Joseph continued, but Joe got the feeling that he would have done so no matter what Joe's response had been. "Good. It's simple. The Evil One works in perverted and mysterious ways. We can't deceive ourselves into thinking that we're immune because of our holiness and purity. He can invade and attack us from within, working on the little hidden weaknesses, the tiny sins people think aren't important enough to confess and do penance for. The Holy Fire keeps this thing away for the most part, but it has told me that the devil is busy at work in our little community. That ruckus a few nights back, the flooding, the electrical problems, none of which were ever explained. That was the devil. That was Satan. And he didn't need permission from nobody to invade our sacred ground!"

Joe took a deep breath, preparing himself, to the best of his ability, for a long sermon. He glanced up to see Sarah had seated herself on top of the counter, patiently waiting for his father to finish whatever nonsense he was spouting.

His father stood up and began rocking back and forth, as if he *was* giving a sermon. "In retrospect, I believe that I'm glad your meeting with Plunket went as it did. I wanted that element of surprise. And believe you me, he was surprised. He's a good, experienced man, and I'm glad he's on our side. But he's one of these who believe that we are immune to Satan. His faith in my abilities to lead, govern and protect isn't misguided. I do these things well, as no other can do them. But I know better than to think that I can't be thwarted. Satan has fouled up my plans more than once. If he gets the chance he'll do it again."

"I understand, Father," Joe said, summoning as much strength as he could, trying to look as attentive as possible. But it wasn't easy.

:*I'm getting tired of waiting*,: Sarah said.

:*I can't rush him*,: he replied in alarm.

:*Well, then maybe I can*,: she said, with just enough mischief in her words to further alarm him.

She came into the room, so swiftly he didn't actually see her move. He froze as she walked past Brother Joseph;

his father continued his tirade on the wiles of Satan with a line of reasoning his son wasn't paying any attention to. Sarah took a seat on a box a few feet away from them, crossed her legs in a ladylike fashion and stared at him.

:*Well,*: she said. :*Are you going to do something, or am I?*:

His father, evidently, didn't see a thing. Joe did notice a transparency to her appearance now, which hadn't been obvious when she was in the bathroom. He could see through her, as though she was constructed of an elaborate pattern of faintly colored fog.

:*Surprise. I forgot to tell you,*: Sarah said. :*Right now I'm only visible to you.*:

Joe exhaled a breath he'd been holding in for a while. Meanwhile, his father continued to rant away, as if he was speaking before a full audience. Maybe he was practicing.

His father frowned down at him, playing the judgmental God instead of the vengeful version. "I just wanted you to know that you handled things, well, I'd say average. You'll have to stand up a little more to the officers than that. Don't disobey. But be firm. And remember who's really in control of the army." He winked and stood up, looking directly at Sarah. Or, at least, where she was sitting. The little girl stuck her tongue out at him. Joe winced, praying for it all to be over.

His father waited for him to say something, and he couldn't bear to. He held his peace, and Brother Joseph watched him in frustration and puzzlement.

Finally, after several moments of silence, he gave up waiting for a response. "I suppose I'll leave you to picking up this room," he said.

He moved towards the door—then sniffed the air with a puzzled expression.

"Do you smell something?" he asked, with one hand on the knob. "Smells like, oh, electricity in the air?"

Joe smelled it, too. He looked at Sarah, who shrugged.

:*Make something up,*: she said.

"Uh, maybe there's a thunderstorm on the way," he supplied, praying his father would just *go*.

Brother Joseph hesitated at the door. "Perhaps. Maybe I should have someone check out the breakers in this quadrant. It reminds me too much of what happened the other night." He frowned, shaking his head. "There's something else. Like perfume, maybe. Or flowers. Something sweet."

He wrinkled his brow, as if troubled with unvoiced thoughts. His eyes looked odd, as if thinking seemed to be taking greater effort than normal for him this evening. Or as if he almost—but not quite—sensed Sarah's presence, and it bothered him so much he was having trouble concentrating.

Yeah. Like I'm not?

Brother Joseph seemed to be growing more and more uncomfortable as well. Finally he said the words his son had been longing for and dreading all at the same time.

"Good night," his father said, and opened the door quickly, shutting it behind him. His exit seemed—rushed. As if something had alarmed him and he was determined not to show it.

Joe waited until he heard his father's footsteps descend the flight of stairs at the end of the great hallway. Even then, he wasn't able to look at the ghost sitting on his left. Now they were alone.

Alone, with a ghost. Or a hallucination? He only wished he could believe that.

:Okay, Joe, it's time to talk,: she said abruptly. *:Things are going to start shaking up around here real soon. I want your complete attention, as Miss Agatha would say.:*

Joe picked up a book at random and looked up at her covertly over the top of it. From the viewpoint of the spy camera, it would look as if he was reading it. Fortunately it was on the approved list.

Much as he dreaded using it, he was going to have to make use of that gift of his to talk to her. If he were caught talking out loud to empty air—well, his father would surely think him possessed. There was no "insanity" among the Chosen Ones after all—it was either "sane and holy" or "possessed by the devil."

:What kind of things? What do you mean, shaking up?:
:That's not important to you. Jamie needs your help. Remember what he looked like last time you saw him?:

Joe shuddered. He suddenly wished she would just go

away. :*You know, I don't need this! I was just fine until you came along. I was going to defect. Squeal to the police. Things my father would have me shot for. And probably will, if he has a chance. I can't help the kid by myself; I have to get outside and tell the police what's going on here. It's the only thing that will keep Jamie alive.*:

Her expression remained hard and firm. :*That's not the attitude I was picking up back there at the dinner table,*: she informed him. :*You were starting to feel a little too comfortable, if you ask me. Proud of your "men"! They look more like boys to me. And you trained them to hate as well as fight.*:

Joe could feel himself withering under her gaze. :*Don't remind me,*: he said. :*I know what I did. But I can't help the way I was raised.*:

She had no mercy on him whatsoever. :*Were you raised to kill innocent people?*:

Like Jamie, did she mean? Or—herself? :*No, but—*:

She glared at him, her eyes full of accusation. :*You stood there and watched him kill me. Don't you remember that? What did I ever do? Was I a Communist? Was I even a Jew? Would it have been right even if I was? How old was I? Ten? You've gotten to live eight more years than I did!*:

He flung the book across the room and huddled inside his arms, away from her angry gaze. :*Shut up!*: he screamed inside, resisting the urge to jump to his feet. :*I know what happened! I know what I did and didn't do! I couldn't help it! You can't possibly know what it's like to have him as a father!*:

The words came tumbling out, like rocks cascading down a hill in an avalanche. Then the words ran out, and he buried his face in his arms, sobbing. That he was talking to a ghost no longer mattered to him, and somewhere in the back of his mind was the suspicion that he had gone certifiably crazy. :*You're right, I was going back on my decision to leave, to help Jamie. But how can you know what it's like? For me or for him?*:

She shifted to a place right above him, where he had to look up to see her. :*How do I know? Do you really want an answer to that?*:

Did he? But her attitude demanded an answer, and irked

the hell out of him. Who did she think she was, anyway? Who put her in judgment over him? *:Yes, I do. What are you, a mind reader or something?:*

Joe wasn't sure if it was a frown or a smirk that passed across her childish features; at this warped angle, her misty composition made her expression especially difficult to read. It also became difficult to tell if he was really talking to a child, or a very angry adult.

:Okay, smarty-pants,: she said. *:Here's how I know.:*

She drifted across the room before he could make a move to stop her—though he hadn't any idea how he could possibly manage that. Reaching down, she touched him on the forehead.

The room dissolved rapidly around him, burning away in an instant, and all that was left was black space. He felt the space in his mind expand outwards, and he could no longer feel his body. His emotions of grief, confusion and fear all fell from him; broken glass, discarded shards, leaving a neutral vacuum in their place. All was air and non-light; he floated in nothingness. The strangeness of it, of what he understood or couldn't even begin to grasp, triggered the deepest level of fear he had ever experienced. He sensed a loss of bladder control, but his bladder and the plumbing connected to it was nowhere to be seen or felt. He wanted to scream, but couldn't.

Where am I? Where's my body? The thought formed from the purest distillation of fear. *What did she do to me?*

Sarah was invisible in the blackness, but suddenly Joe knew she was nearby, watching, orchestrating this strange dance in the spirit world. Then gradually, the pinpoints of pain from a tormented soul entered his senses, and he felt himself unfolding into a tiny, frail body. A body that wasn't his own.

The pain increased, gnawing at his belly, as if there was a monster trying to eat its way out of his stomach. He was aware of another being, reminding him the body he was in touch with was not his own but belonging to another. Like a parasite, he saw and felt the torment, but at a distance.

His arms were encased in something soft that held them completely, he felt, as two eyes struggled to open. It felt like a nightmare, but he knew it wasn't. The eyes that weren't tried to see and saw only darkness. Finally, another kind of eye opened and looked *through* his head, seeing people who were standing above him; a man he recognized as Jim Chase, Luke, Brother Joseph, and . . .

. . . himself.

Help me out of here, Jamie was trying to say. *My tummy is hurting. I can't see and I can't hear.* But he just didn't have the strength. The Joe standing above him seemed so capable, so strong, yet so helpless. His objections meant nothing to the ones around him, the ones really in charge. The thoughts blazed through Joe-from-beyond and burned away all pretenses.

Joe watched himself protest—feebly, it seemed from down here—to his father. He could have easily overpowered all of them right then, and he knew it; from Jamie's perspective, it seemed the only thing to do. Consequences didn't seem to matter in this state of starvation and agony; that he was conscious at all was a small miracle.

:No!: Joe screamed, from somewhere beyond himself he couldn't locate just then. *:Sarah, no more of this! Please!:*

:You had to see what Jamie was feeling,: she said without a hint of emotion. *:You had to, for you to understand. You do understand now, don't you? Or do I need to show you what I went through?:*

Joe considered this, wondered briefly what it would be like to be the victim of a strangling. And for a moment, he could actually contemplate the idea in a strangely detached mood, temporarily barren of fear.

But that moment passed.

He felt the tightness around his neck, of his own father's hands crushing his windpipe, of the futile gasps after air, the struggle to get free—felt his lungs burning for air they would never have—his throat collapsing—his eyes bulging—

He wanted to scream and couldn't. She released him before the moment of her death.

He floated in the blackness, numb with overload. *:Too much, too much,:* he heard himself thinking. *:I can't go through any more with her. Sarah, let me out of this place!:*

The silence was maddening. Had she forgotten him? Had she abandoned him to this?

Then—:*When you leave the church,*: she said, :*go to Pawnee and talk to a county sheriff named Frank Casey. He'll help you. And tell him about Jamie!*:

Then Sarah was silent. He sensed that she was gone now, leaving him alone in this place that he could only describe as hell. He was all alone with what his father had done to him, his righteous father who was so convinced that he was right all the time.

He felt Sarah's absence now, though he wasn't certain how he had felt her presence.

He lost it, then, control, sanity, everything—he thrashed wildly against nothing until he was exhausted and consciousness slipped away from him.

Jamie can't hold on much longer, was his last, exhausted thought, *I don't have much time*—Then he slipped into oblivion.

When Joe woke he was laying on his back in the middle of his new living room, spread-eagled like a sacrifice. He sat up suddenly, expecting to see Sarah sitting there, wearing that sly, adult look she had used to wither him.

Sarah was nowhere to be seen. He was completely alone in the new place, and this felt more unsettling than sitting with the ghost.

When he struggled to his feet, the memory of Jamie and his experience in the tank came rushing into him like the wind of a hurricane. The sudden movement, and the recollection, instantly unsettled his stomach, and he had to dash to the toilet, where he heaved into the porcelain god until his stomach and lungs ached.

"Please help me through this," he whispered to no one in particular, as the porcelain cooled his forehead. "Help get me out of this place."

He stripped and got into an icy shower, which helped his queasy stomach. It wasn't until he reached for the soap, dropped it, and had trouble retrieving it, that he realized he was shaking.

I've got to get out of here tonight, he thought, the certainty of it now so absolute that it felt branded on his mind.

Question is, how?

Several plans came to mind, most of which he rejected because they would probably result in several pounds of lead perforating his flesh. He considered just walking out, flashing his new rank if anyone gave him any hassles. But— no, not a good idea. That would be reported right away, and someone would come after him, and he would have nowhere to hide except the forest—that was a dubious haven at best. No, he needed a way out of the place that would not be visible to anyone, or to cameras.

This place is designed to keep people out, not in, he thought frantically. *There has to be a way.*

He toweled himself dry and then thought of one idea that might delay things. He went out into the room and turned off all the lights, as if he was going to bed. Hopefully the tears—and the collapse—would be put down to his sickness. He went to his bureau drawers in the dark, felt for certain textures, then began putting clothes on—street clothes, not the new uniform or the undress "uniforms" of camo-clothing. The jeans were worn, a little too tight, and had holes in the knees, but were clean, as were the plain white t-shirt and old battered combat boots he pulled on. He packed a few essential items, things he couldn't leave without. The small backpack was easily overlooked; if he walked out with a suitcase, however stealthily, he knew he would be asking for trouble.

While he packed, he put together a plan to get out. The trash collector came around three A.M. every morning and emptied three dumpsters the Chosen Ones had leased from the refuse company. The dumpsters were inside the perimeter of the complex, but beyond the buildings, so he wouldn't have to attempt an escape either through the gate or over the fence, both of which were risky propositions. The trucks were rear-loaders, if memory served him correctly. Perhaps he could sneak onto the truck somehow, in that rear compartment, as it pulled away. It was the only way out he could think of that stood a chance of working.

The hour was already late, and the hallway lighting was subdued. No one was in sight as he silently closed the door

behind him and made his way down the grand flight of
stairs. Instead of going down the well-traveled corridor,
which was monitored by cameras, he turned right and
entered a maintenance hallway. There were few of these
tunnels, because of the expense of blasting the rock, but
this section had been dug out of the red Oklahoma dirt.
Maintenance tunnels, though they varied in size, all inter-
connected. And one of them surfaced near the road which
would take him to the dumpsters.

The exit was located at the top of a ladder set into the
wall. The door opened up, like a storm shelter. He opened
it a crack and peeked through the slit, studying the night.
A thunderstorm was brewing on the horizon, licking the
clouds with snake-tongues of light, giving the air a wet
smell.

*There should be a guard down—yeah. There he is. If
I'm careful, he won't see me. And there are the dumpsters.*

The large cubes of metal were very nearby, at the edge
of a gravel parking lot, which had a few trucks and earth-
moving equipment. When he could see the guard looking
the other way, he scurried out of his hole, carefully letting the door close behind him, and sprinted for a large
dump truck.

Joe concealed himself in the wheel well of the huge
beast and began a long wait.

As the minutes ticked by, he considered his decision and
knew it to be a good one. But he was scared, and knew
it. He was leaving behind everything he had known for a
complete unknown. *They might not even believe me,* he
thought. *But what choice do I have? I've gotta go through
with this. If Jamie dies, and I don't do anything to help
him, I'm just as guilty as my father.*

He wasn't sure if he had dozed off or not. All he knew
was that he snapped to attention, his senses sharpened with
fear, at the sound of the garbage truck trundling up the
way. As it backed up to one of the units, he was dizzily
relieved to see only one man working it tonight. It would
make it all the easier to hop into the back undetected.

Once the last of the three dumpsters was empty, the
refuse man put the truck in gear and began the slow drive
to the gate. Joe wondered, fleetingly, if the truck would

be searched going out. But this caused only the slightest hesitation; he was already running for the retreating truck, the tag-light giving him a reference.

Like a cat, he hopped into the foul-smelling cavity where the day's garbage had been deposited and pushed into the deeper recess of the truck. He lay down, pulling stray refuse over him for cover. And prayed.

What began as a simple test drive of Cindy's battered Toyota Celica turned into an expedition into Cleveland for supplies.

Cindy commented to Bob after Al left—over microwaved dinners—that her '82 car had been running a little rough, and before she could bat an eye Bob had grabbed a toolbox and had the hood open.

"Eyah, I see the problem here," he commented in the waning daylight, pointing to a thingie that looked obviously loose. "Mind if I have a look to see if anything else is wrong?"

Of course, she didn't mind at all. In fact, she was a bit taken by his offer, which made her blush. One of her fears in buying the car was that she would get all the way out here in God's country and the thing would quit running. When she drove it into Hallet, what seemed like an eternity ago, it sounded ready to do just that. With her limited money, she had little to spare for a mechanic. This offer, like all the help Al and Bob had extended, was a blessing she could ill afford to turn down. Besides, there had been something about Bob's demeanor, which was often cold and icy, that suggested he was thawing a bit.

Was there a hint of, well, softness in his voice? she had wondered, but if there was it was so subtle as to be questionable. Bob was twenty, but a mature twenty, so his age wouldn't necessarily eliminate the possibility of involvement.

But . . . Bob?

It was a concept that almost made her laugh. *It would feel like incest,* she thought. He had seemed like a younger brother in many ways—

Until tonight. Now he was out working on the car. She hated to admit it, but he was reminding her of Jim, before he'd gone bonkers. She couldn't leave him out there on his own—it didn't seem fair. She joined him, holding the light, passing him tools, bringing him rags or something to drink. There was a bond forming between them tonight, reminding her even more of Jim, especially when he started explaining what he was doing.

But it wasn't painful. It was a reminder of the old Jim— a man who might have done something kind, considerate— who would have done something like fix the car of a lady whose resources were wearing thin.

As she watched him, she became aware of a curious current running between them—and her thoughts turned serious. *Would Jamie like this man?* The answer to that was yes, she decided without a moment's hesitation.

When Al returned from his mysterious journey and she turned in that night, Bob was still clanking away under the hood, with a determined, almost robotic tenacity. He looked like an exotic, half-human plant that had sprouted from the car's motor.

"How long does he plan to stay up doing that?" Cindy asked, before retreating to the van.

Al had sighed in response. "As long as it takes," was all he said, and shrugged.

The next morning Bob suggested she take a drive. "Be careful," he warned. "It has a bit more power now than it did."

Then he smiled shyly, handed her the keys as if he was handing her a rose, and ambled off towards the racetrack without saying another word.

Al suggested they go into Cleveland and pick up some odds and ends they all needed. Groceries, toiletries, and the like. Cindy offered to contribute, but Al would have none of that. "Save your money," he ordered as they got into her car. "We've got plenty. Fairgrove's paying for this."

As they drove to Cleveland—strange to see a sign for Cleveland, *Oklahoma*—she couldn't help but notice the new power the car had. She had to consciously drive slower than what she was used to, as the Celica seemed to have a life of its own now.

"Migod—this car can *go*," she commented to Al, who

just nodded. "You didn't do anything with your . . . abilities, did you?"

"Oh, no," Al said calmly. "This is all Bob's doing. No elven magic here. Not this time. Just good old mechanical ability. Bob's a natural." He gave her one of those obtuse looks she had trouble reading. "He's not very good with words, but when he likes someone, he tends to do things for them. He'll appreciate it a lot if you tell him how impressed you are with his work."

A natural—something Jamie would admire, she found herself thinking, uncertain why.

But the mention of his elven origins brought back the fears she was trying desperately to deal with, or to at least bury. *Just give it time—sooner or later you'll get used to the whole thing, like being around someone from another country who might seem a little weird at first. Like that guy I met from Iraq, that James used to work with. He didn't change. I guess I did.*

She cast a wary glance at Al, and at the vague outline of the pointed ears in his long, blond hair. *Somehow, with this one, I don't think it will be the same as getting used to an Iraqi. They're human. Al isn't. Though he comes close.*

Remembering the view she had of his sculptured body made her shudder. *Real close.* Somehow, by contrast, Bob seemed more attractive, not less. Al's perfection was *too* much. A reminder of how inhuman he was. Bob on the other hand, was *very* human. Very . . . attractive. . . .

They stopped at the Quic Pic for a badly needed tank of unleaded and proceeded into Cleveland, dropping well below the speed limit in the busy afternoon traffic. "You know, Al, it occurred to me that maybe some of these people have seen Jamie. While we're here, I'd like to show the picture to a few people."

"Sure," Al said pleasantly, but it sounded to Cindy as if he thought the effort would be wasted. *As if he knew exactly where he is, but isn't telling me,* she thought suspiciously. He shifted in his seat when she thought that, raising another uncomfortable question.

Does he know what I'm thinking?

If Al was reading her thoughts, he gave no indication

of it. He was gazing absently out the passenger window, apparently with a few thoughts of his own occupying his time.

"Any suggestions on where to stop?" she asked, seeing nothing on the main street that looked even remotely like a supermarket.

"Keep going all the way through Broadway. There'll be a large store on the right, I think." For a moment he lost some of that smug self-assurance, became a little less perfect. "Bob always came along on these trips. He always seemed to know where all the stores were, and what to get."

Cindy suppressed a snicker. *If it weren't for Bob, Al, you wouldn't know how to tie your shoes.* This was a thought she hoped he *could* pick up.

"I hope you have a list," she said, and Al held up a scrap of paper.

Presently they found the Super H discount market on the other side of the business district, as predicted. As they entered the supermarket, Cindy noted that Al blended right in with the crowd. His clothing and demeanor, which was that of a simple mechanic, made him virtually transparent. But as she observed him, there was more than that; she caught a faint glimmer of something surrounding him, something that nobody else noticed. In fact, nobody seemed to notice him at all. Natives walking toward them in the aisles didn't even look up, but smiled warmly at Cindy when she passed. Instead of walking straight into him, however, people walked around him. His movements were fluid, and without any apparent effort he wove through the crowded market, unnoticed. And, she was beginning to speculate, unseen. She'd have to ask him about that later.

Soon the cart was full, stocked with everything from motor oil to Gatorade. Al seemed to know where everything was in this store, so Cindy was content to let him lead the way. Occasionally she dawdled over this or that item, as Al patiently waited for her to come along. In the check-out line she saw a tabloid newsrag with the headlines proudly proclaiming "Phantom Elves Invade White House; Bush Scared." This apparently caught Al's attention, and he winked at her as he dropped a copy into the cart. Cindy rolled her eyes in response.

As they were wheeling the bagged groceries into the parking lot, Cindy looked up to the street, where a line of five cars and trucks were waiting for a Volvo to turn. Something about the sight disturbed her, but nothing really registered as she pulled the cart up next to the car and began handing Al bags.

After the third bag, though, she looked up again. There was the pickup truck, the same one she remembered.

The truck. Their truck.

Jim.

Sure enough, a haggard James Chase was at the wheel. She couldn't quite see his expression at that distance, but his posture suggested exhaustion. Or a hangover?

"Cindy?" she was vaguely aware of Al saying. "What are you looking at?"

"It's him," she said, but it came out a whisper. "Look. Over there. That's our truck! That's Jim!"

Without making any conscious effort, she found her feet moving her in the direction of the truck. *Jamie, where's Jamie? If he's in the truck with Jim, I wouldn't see him unless he sits forward or stands up and looks out the back window like he always does. Please, let him be in that truck!* The Volvo evidently found the gap it was looking for and sped into the parking lot. The truck began edging forward, merging with the traffic.

"*No!*" she heard someone screaming, not knowing the scream came from herself. "No! Jim, you get *back* here, dammit!"

The truck drove on, with Jim probably unaware of the frantic woman running through the parking lot, trying to catch up with him. "Stop, you sonuvabitch! Where's Jamie? *Where's my son?*"

The next thing she remembered was dropping to her knees on a little strip of grass, a block or so away from the supermarket, sobbing loudly. The truck was nowhere in sight. *He didn't even see me*, she thought, through tears of frustration. *He's going to pay for this!* Cars slowed, and moved on. Nobody seemed willing to get involved.

"Cindy!" Al said from behind her. "What in the seven hells has gotten into you?"

Al's anger seemed to dissolve instantly when their eyes met. "Let's get the car," she said weakly. "Let's go after them." But even as she said the words, she knew it would be futile. The truck was nowhere in sight, and it could have gone in any number of directions.

"After who?" Al asked, helping her. Then realization seemed to dawn on his face. "You mean you saw Jamie?"

"Not Jamie. My husband. He was driving our truck."

They started walking back to the car. Al's expression, however, did not suggest that he was convinced. "Are you sure?"

"Hell, yes, I'm sure!" she said, unleashing all of her frustration and anger on him. "I was there when we *bought* the damn thing. I was *married* to him. We could have gone after him! Where were you, anyway? They could be in Kansas by now!"

Al said nothing. The silence weighed heavier with every passing second, until it became uncomfortable. She began to feel ashamed for her response when Al finally said, "Sorry. I was chasing you."

"I know," she sighed. "I know. Don't be sorry. I'm the one who should be apologizing. It's just that I was so close to confronting that bastard!"

Alinor put the cart into the corral, and they both climbed into the Toyota. He acted like he wanted to say something, then changed his mind.

She prompted him. "What were you about to say?"

Al turned the ignition. She wasn't aware when they had decided he would drive, but somehow it seemed to be the thing to do just then. Her knees were still shaking.

"That might not be such a good idea at this point," Al said as they turned onto Broadway. "To let them know we're in the neighborhood, I mean."

She was about to ask, when she saw why. *They'll just disappear again,* she realized. *Then I may never know where they went.*

"At least we know for certain he's in that crazy place," she observed. "We do. Don't we?"

"We should probably leave this to the sheriff," he replied,

without really answering her. "Let's put away the groceries and take a trip out to Pawnee. Let Frank know what we saw."

They drove in silence. Cindy stared out her window, her heart leaping whenever she saw a pickup truck. Then it would turn out to be someone else's, and she would sink back into herself, doing everything she could to keep from bawling.

The last thing Al needs is a crying, hysterical woman to deal with, she thought wretchedly.

But by the time they reached the Cleveland city limits, that's exactly what Al had.

Comforting crying women wasn't one of Alinor's favorite duties, but he seemed to be doing a lot of it lately. And truth to be told, he was beginning to prefer the company of his constructed servants to Cindy. At least they knew how to smile and look pleasant no matter how unpleasant the circumstances. The human seemed to spend most of her time wrapped in gloom or in tears.

Bob was at the RV when they arrived at the track, and when they told him who Cindy had seen in Cleveland, he insisted on going with them to Pawnee to talk to the deputy sheriff, Frank Casey. "Work at the track is done," he said, not expanding on that, in spite of Al's questioning gaze. They were putting away groceries in what Al would later realize to be record time. "This sounds more important, anyway. Did you go after him?"

Al gave him an ugly look. "She only saw Jim Chase, not Jamie. Do you really think that would have been a good idea?"

"I see. So Jamie wasn't with him. No telling what would have happened there." Bob seemed to shrink away from the discussion. "Do you want me to go with you, or would you rather I stay here?"

"No. You come with us," Cindy said resolutely, taking Bob's arm and escorting him out of the RV. "You've been cooped up here long enough."

Al lingered in the RV's kitchen, a bit perplexed. The action of taking Bob by the arm and leading him out as if he were some kind of date was a little confusing. *Cindy and Bob?* Al thought, trying to imagine the two together, and promptly shook his head against the thought. *No way.* Al laughed at himself as he locked up the RV, trying to figure out why something so ridiculous and improbable would annoy him.

Somehow Al ended up sitting in the back, with Bob and Cindy in the front. He hated sitting in rear seats—they never had enough leg room for him—but he kept his complaints to himself. Few words were exchanged between the two, though Al did observe a sort of silent communion. They seemed content to ride in quiet, without the need to fill the void with meaningless talk.

Frank was in the building somewhere, the receptionist told them when they arrived in the Pawnee County Courthouse. She led them back to his office and told them he would be with them soon.

It was tempting to lean over and study what was on the desk, as intriguing as all the maps and charts were—and how much they excited his curiosity. He would have to content himself to studying the maps at a distance. Not all that difficult, after all. . . .

One of the maps was the same one he had memorized and used to find the Chosen Ones' hideout earlier. The other ones were different, but seemed to represent the same area. He couldn't immediately see what all the lines and diagrams represented, and why they were drawn the way they were. Then he saw it: *he's working up a strategy to raid the Chosen Ones!*

Al held his face expressionless, no mean feat when considering how much this disturbed him. *If they go in it could be a massacre,* he thought. *All those children. It wouldn't be the first time a religious cult had held their people as hostages, and down in those bunkers, they would be in a perfect position to hold out until everyone was dead. It's what they've been training for! All the food and supplies they need are down there.* He frowned as the whole picture, with all its frightening details, clicked into place. It would take no great leap of thinking to turn those people against law enforcement agencies. As it was, they perceived themselves as acting beyond the law anyway. The government of the United States was not truly *their* government.

Brother Joseph had the One Answer given to the congregation. What the sheep didn't know was that it was an answer from a hideous monster, through the deteriorating body and soul of a young child. They were beyond the law; they were divine.

They're looking for an imaginary enemy. First opposition to come along will do.

"Hi, folks," Frank said amiably as he entered. His great size still caused Al to look twice. The big deputy toted a coffee cup, tiny in his hand, and yet another map, partially unrolled. "Didn't know you were coming or I would have been here sooner. What's up?"

"I saw James, my ex," Cindy blurted. "In Cleveland this afternoon."

Frank scooped up the maps and diagrams lying on his desk. The only purpose Al saw in this was to conceal the documents from them, confirming his suspicions that the law enforcement agencies involved in this would act secretly and tell them about the results later.

The question is, when are they going in?

"Is that so?" Frank said, but he didn't really sound surprised. "We had already concluded that he was with them, but I'm glad we have a sighting. Cleveland, you say?"

"In front of the supermarket. Discount H or something, wasn't it?" she asked, turning to Al.

"That's where we were," Al said, nodding.

She turned away and stared at Frank Casey with accusation in her eyes. "So when are you going to get a search warrant and go in and get him?" Cindy asked. "Don't you have enough evidence now?"

"You saw him in Cleveland, Miss Chase," Frank said, soothingly. "That's a long way from the Sacred Heart property. I doubt I could convince a judge to issue a warrant on the basis of that sighting. Especially this judge. I told you I thought something odd was going on there. To be blunt, the judge doesn't want to help."

"Why not?" Cindy cried, losing her hold on her temper and her emotions. She was shaking in her chair now, wiping away tears. Bob touched her arm; Cindy recoiled from him.

"Am I to understand that you're not making any plans to raid that place?" Al asked, unsure if it was a good idea to show this particular card just yet. "I had the impression, from odds and ends lying around in this office, that you have precisely that in mind."

Frank looked directly at Al, apparently trying to look unruffled and doing a reasonably good job. "Don't know where you got that idea," Frank said. "Such an operation would require information and evidence that Pawnee County doesn't have."

Bob's chin firmed, and it was his turn to turn accusing eyes on the deputy. "But what if the State of Oklahoma has evidence? Or the FBI?"

"Nobody said they were involved," Frank said coolly. "Perhaps you should examine your source of information a bit closer."

Al raised an equally cool eyebrow. "I didn't want to seem nosy, looking closer at what was on your desk. It was difficult not to notice the maps."

Frank sighed. He didn't seem the least bit angry, just tired. Tired and restless, as if something big was going down, and he was running low on the energy needed to bring it off.

"Look," the big man said, leaning forward over his desk. "I'm in a very delicate situation here. Other people have been contacted regarding this cult, individuals we are going to be needing to testify. You are one of these people, Miss Chase. This is a police matter and will be handled by police *only*. I don't want civilians fooling around with this cult. They are lunatics with a cause, and they are all well armed. *All*. I'm not saying that we're going in to get your son, but I am saying that I might not be at liberty to discuss it if we were."

Cindy sniffled and looked at the floor. This was, obviously, not what she wanted to hear.

"Do you understand what I'm saying?" Frank said softly. "I'm trying to juggle ten different things at once here. Please don't make this any harder for me."

"Okay," Cindy said, however reluctantly. "You win. You said other people. What other people? Who are they? Are they parents looking for their children, too? Can I talk to them?"

Frank threw up his arms, his palms outward. "I can't discuss it. Sorry, Miss Chase. Please be more patient. For a little while longer, anyway." Frank got to his feet, a signal which they all followed. "For a few days longer, at least."

A *few days,* Al thought, alarmed. *Whatever's going to happen will happen in a few days. I need more time!*

From the grim determination he saw on the deputy's face, he saw that he wasn't about to get it.

For the second time that week, Frank Casey watched the sad trio leave his office empty-handed. He wished that he could tell them everything, including the plan to bring in the FBI SWAT teams, and get it over with. Every time he had to dance around the facts like this, he felt disturbed and guilty. Particularly when a mother and child were involved.

But he was under strict orders to keep the operation a secret. Not that the orders were necessary; he understood the wisdom in keeping a lid on any pending raid. When information like that got out in advance, to the public or press, cops died.

A plan as big as this would surely involve casualties. The question was, how many and on whose side.

He wasn't getting enough sleep, and he knew it. It was already noon, and he had spent the entire night on the phone with FBI SWAT leaders, coordinating logistics. Fortunately the bulk of the army they were assembling was going to hole up at a National Guard depot in Tulsa, so as not to alert the Chosen Ones. They would begin moving in under cover of darkness and strike a few hours before dawn, when armies were traditionally the most vulnerable. He hoped the plan would work. But given the apparent luck of the lunatic cult lately, he had his doubts.

If I'm going to be worth a flip during this thing, I'd better get some rest. It will either happen two or three days from now. If I'm going to sleep, this will be about the last chance I'll have.

Frank was on his way out the door to take care of exactly that when the phone rang.

"I'm not here," he said to the secretary. "I'm going home."

He was halfway to his squad car when he realized he'd left his keys on his desk. When he went back into the office, the secretary frantically waved at him, the phone pressed to her ear.

Frank groaned. *I knew I shouldn't have come back in here. It would have been better to just curl up in the backseat and go to sleep. Better yet, in the trunk. No one could see me there.*

"Who is it?" he asked. "I hope it's important."

"I'm not sure," she hissed. "He says he's from that camp of crazies over there at that church. Chosen Ones, I think he said. You wanna talk to him?"

Frank stared at her. His exhaustion was temporarily forgotten as he went into his office.

"Line four," she said, and he picked up the phone.

"Yes?" Frank said. "This is Deputy Casey."

There was a pause, just long enough for Frank to think it was a crank call after all. He was about to hang the receiver up when a young-sounding male said, in a trembling voice, "Are you Frank Casey?"

"That's me," he replied. "What's on your mind?"

The gulp on the other end of the line was audible. "Everything. I'm an officer of the Sacred Heart of the Chosen Ones. I want to leave the group, but I need your protection."

"Is that right?" Frank said conversationally. *Good Christ, this is a kid I'm talking to!* "For what purpose?"

"My father is crazy," the unknown said. "He's going to end up killing someone."

Father? Crazy? Who am I talking to? He broke into a cold sweat, but managed to maintain his casual tone. "Oh? And who is your father?"

"Brother Joseph."

Frank sat up in the chair, rubbed the sleepiness from eyes. *Did I hear that right?* he thought. *Or is the sleep deprivation making me hallucinate?*

"Are you still there?" the boy asked.

He took a deep breath and rubbed sweaty palms on his pants. "Oh, I'm here. I know who you're talking about. You said you need protection. Why?"

The boy sounded desperate enough to be authentic.

"Because they'll come after me. They'll come after me and kill me. I'm not joking."

"I don't doubt it," Frank said, not entirely sure he was believing this conversation. "How do I know this isn't some sort of a trick?"

It was the other's turn for a long pause. "Well, I guess you don't know. You'll just have to take my word for it."

"I'm afraid that's not good enough," Frank said evenly. "We can get you the protection," he said, thinking, *Yeah, the jail cell is a pretty safe place. Iron bars. Concrete walls. Reasonable rates.* "What are you willing to give us?"

"Anything you want," the boy said without hesitation. "I know everything there is about the Chosen Ones."

"I suppose you would," Frank said, "if this man is your father." *If this is true, this boy can tell us what to expect. Layout of the bunkers. Who's there. Or, it could be a trick. Do I take a chance?*

What would it cost me? Another few hours of sleep?

"So tell me," he continued, "what do I call you?"

"Joe," he said. "That's short for Joseph. Junior."

"Of course it is," he replied inanely. "What would you like to do about this, Joe? Could you come down to the station—"

"No!" was the immediate reply. Then, "I mean, they'll be watching for me there. Too risky. I meant it when I said they would try to kill me. They should know by now that I'm gone, and they'll be looking for me. Do you have any extra bulletproof jackets?"

Frank considered this a moment. "Perhaps. Do you really think that's necessary?"

There was no hesitation in the answer. "Yes. I do."

In the silence that followed, Frank decided the boy was serious. *The risk might not be real, but he certainly thinks it is. What I've seen of that bunch, though, it wouldn't surprise me to see them hunt down and kill one of their own. Especially if he's serious about squealing on the whole rat's nest.*

He sighed. "Okay, then. I can't promise a vest because I don't know who has them checked out. There isn't exactly a lot of call for them around here. But I will meet you someplace. You name it."

A moment's pause. "There's a steakhouse out here. Called Granny's something. You know it?"

"Granny's Kitchen?" Frank asked. "Out on Highway 64. Would you like me to pick you up?"

A sigh. Of relief? "No. That's all right. I can see the place from here. Granny's Kitchen it is."

Frank did a quick mental calculation. "I'll be there in ten minutes."

With bells on.

CHAPTER ELEVEN

In spite of the fact that *he* wasn't sure about taking the kid's paranoia seriously, Frank found himself calling in a few tags, some out of state, on vehicles he didn't immediately recognize. He told himself that he did have to admit he'd seen more strange faces lately. But there were always a certain number of strangers around, especially around race-time down at Hallet. He'd never made any connection with the Chosen Ones—if that was really who they were. What surveillance the PCSO had done indicated this group pretty much stayed on their own land, with only a few of them going out for supplies.

While he'd been trying to dig up information, he'd even questioned the trash collection agency that went out there and turned up nothing. One or two men went in with a single truck at night when the place was dark, passed a guard on the way in and out, and that was it. The guys on the truck never saw anything but a parking lot, the guard and the dumpsters. He'd come to the conclusion a while back that if anything suspicious was going on, it was either kept out of sight of watchers from the edge of the area and from above, or it was happening down below, in the bunkers.

Every tag he called was clean, but that didn't do much

to calm his jitters. Shoot, now *he* was getting paranoid! Too much coffee, Frank diagnosed. *Too much coffee and not enough sleep. It's enough to make any man jumpy.*

He pulled in the parking lot of Granny's Kitchen, a quaint little restaurant he remembered fondly, though he hadn't been there in some time. *I've been with the department now for what, ten years? Where has all the time gone?*

Nothing that he'd ever been through or been trained for had prepared him for what waited for him inside. *What am I walking into here?* Trap—or hoax—or the break he'd prayed for?

The diner was exactly as he remembered it; not a stick of furniture had been moved. The old formica and vinyl booths still lined the walls, each with their own remote-jukebox selector dating back to 1957. The floor was worn through to the concrete foundation in places; the scent was of home-cooking, with an aftertaste of Lysol. The cash register sat atop a wood and glass case, which enclosed candy and cheap, locally made trinkets.

The place was oddly silent for the time of day. From the kitchen came the sounds of an ancient Hobart dishwasher, the *tinkle-clank* of glasses and coffee cups being placed in racks, plates being stacked, silverware being sorted.

On duty at the open grill, Old George flipped hamburgers; when he saw Frank he smiled a toothless grin and waved, a greeting that hadn't altered since the deputy was fifteen.

And there was someone else on duty who knew him almost as well as Old George.

"Good God, you look like hell," Peggy said, putting an order pad away in the pocket of an immaculate bleached apron. The waitress looked like she'd walked off the cover of a 1955 issue of *Life,* complete with blond bouffant. Like the diner, she hadn't changed since the fifties.

Frank had dated her briefly in high school, but the romance never advanced past petting, and Peggy had married a real estate agent the same month Frank went into the academy.

She's the kind of girl who can be your best friend, Frank had once observed. *Too damn few of them around.*

She frowned at him, hand on one hip. "Don't you believe in sleep anymore? Or are you too busy catting around at night?"

"Have pity on me, Peggy. It's been one helluva long week," he said awkwardly, glancing around the diner to see who else was there. Two high school girls, one of the locals, named Russ, and a National Guardsman he didn't immediately identify. But no young man. He took a seat at his usual booth. "Coffee, please. For now."

Maybe the kid's waiting outside, he thought, hoping this wasn't a wild-goose chase.

"You looking for someone?" Peggy asked, pouring a cup of coffee, and dropping a plastic-covered menu on the formica table beside him.

He decided to play it cautious. No point in setting himself up to look like a fool to more people than just himself. "Not sure yet. Have you seen a boy—a teen-ager—hanging around here lately? Not one of the local kids, a stranger." Peggy knew every kid that hung around here—and their parents and home phone numbers. God help them if they acted up when she was on shift. Mom and Dad would hear about it before they cleared the door.

She pursed her lips. "Well, yes I have. Early this morning. Saw him walking along the road. Just thought he was passing through, but he showed up again and made a phone call over at that pay-phone." Peggy pointed to a gas station with a phone booth, across the highway. "He looks kind of like a runaway. That who you're looking for?"

"It likely is," Frank said. *Has to be.* "What did he look like?"

"Blond, looked like a jock. About eighteen, nineteen. Holes in his jeans, wearing a white t-shirt. If it weren't for the military haircut he'd look pretty scruffy. Like you did when you were that age." She grinned. "Or can you remember that far back?"

Old George yelled, "Order up." Peggy winked mischievously and trotted off to the counter, pink uniform skirt swishing.

Military haircut. Could be, though most of those guys were shaved bald. I'll have to ask him about that. If it's him. If he shows.

The door opened, jingling the little bell fixed to it. Frank looked up as he took his first sip of coffee.

Son-of-a-gun. Looks like I've got my chance now.

He came into the restaurant slowly, a predator moving into new territory, feeling his way with all senses alert for trouble. Coolly, professionally, he scanned the patrons sitting at the booths, apparently deciding after a cursory examination that they were not a threat. And that *they* were not who he was looking for.

His eyes alighted on Frank. Frank nodded, warily, and the boy returned the nod. Just as warily.

"You must be Frank," the boy said, walking over to the booth. "I'm Joe. We spoke on the phone just now?"

The boy kept his voice low, just barely audible. Frank followed his example. "Yes, son. Have a seat."

Joe carefully set his pack down on the bench and deposited himself opposite Frank. They regarded each other uncomfortably for a moment before the deputy suggested, "Would you like something to eat? I'm buying."

Indecision passed over the young face, as if the boy was afraid to ask for a handout. "No thanks. I'm not hungry," he replied, in a tone that wasn't very convincing. Then suddenly the boy's stomach growled, loudly; people in the booth next to them gave them a sideways glance.

Frank couldn't suppress a grin of amusement. "Are you *sure?*"

The youngster shifted, uncomfortably. "Well, sir, I am hungry, but I don't want any handouts. I was raised funny that way."

No handouts? If his father really is Brother Joseph, why would that be a problem? That's how the entire circus over there was financed. But then, the boy probably has a pretty distorted viewpoint.

Frank shrugged. "Consider it a loan, then. We can work it out, somehow."

Relief washed over the youngster's face. "Okay then," he said, reaching eagerly for a menu. As Joe studied the selection, Frank was impressed with the boy's fine physique. It took work and dedication to get a body built up that way. Muscles bulged from under the tight shirt, with thick, meaty arms that suggested years of free weight training.

Frank's eyebrows raised when he saw the crude swastika tattooed on Joe's forearm, though the boy was deep in the menu and didn't notice. From the symbol's location on the youngster's arm, though, Frank had a shrewd idea that it had been done a few years earlier, before a rapid spurt of growth.

For the rest, Joe was shaving, but just barely. A fine blond stubble was visible on his upper lip and chin, but nowhere else. He was dirty and smelled, and looked like someone on the run, right enough. But this was no teeny-bopper runaway; for all Joe's apparent youth, this was a full-grown man. And one who, from the dark circles under his eyes, was having a serious crisis.

Peggy appeared with two glasses of ice water, raising an eyebrow at Frank. A silent response from his eyes asked her to save her questions for later. She nodded knowingly and said only, "What will you have, sugar?"

Joe looked up at her and licked his lips, his hunger showing. "How 'bout the chicken fried steak with fries, a hamburger—you got a chef salad? Yeah, I'll take the salad with a side of cole slaw, a large milk. . . ."

"You have quite an appetite," Peggy noted with a grin, continuing the order on another ticket. "How about you, Frank?"

"Just a hamburger and a ginger ale," he replied. "Put it on one ticket. I'll pick it up."

Peggy left with the order. Joe drained his ice water in one gulp. Frank edged his glass over. "Have it. I'm not thirsty. When was the last time you ate, anyway?"

"Yesterday—yesterday morning, actually," Joe replied. "I've been moving ever since this morning around four."

Interesting. Either the Chosen Ones were keeping their folks on short rations, or something had happened to kill the kid's appetite for a while. Maybe the same thing that had caused his defection? "You waited a while before calling the office. You almost missed me."

Joe toyed with the glass of ice water. "I had to lay low today. I knew they were going to be out looking for me as soon as they knew I was gone—by breakfast at the latest. There's always an early Praise Meeting around noon, so I figured now would be the best time to get in touch." He looked up, under eyebrows drawn together in a frown. "I wasn't kidding when I said they were going to kill me."

"Don't worry, you're safe here," Frank said placatingly, still not altogether certain there was anything to really worry about from the Chosen Ones. So far all he had evidence for was an overactive imagination. "Would you like to tell me what this is all about?"

Joe took a deep breath, let it go. "Not sure where to start."

"Why don't we start with your father," Frank urged.

"Yeah. My father." He made a face, as if the words tasted bitter. "It took a while to figure him out."

I bet it did. "So tell me about it. And just for the record, how old are you?"

Joe sighed. "I just turned eighteen. I've been training in paramilitary since I could walk, it seems. Guess what I need to do now is go into the army or something."

Frank nodded, slowly. "Not a lotta call for Pizza Hut delivery guys that handle AK-47s." That was a test, to see by the youngster's response—or lack of it—if what Cindy Chase and her backup band had told him was true.

The kid didn't even flinch, and that made him one very unhappy cop.

"I guess so." He sighed again. "But there are some things I need to take care of first. Will you give me the protection I need?"

"Of course we will," Frank said smoothly. "We've got assault weapons, too."

The deputy let that last statement dangle in the air, like bait. *The question was, would he take it?*

"Yeah I bet you do," Joe replied levelly. "But not as much as what we've got down there."

Frank was now a profoundly unhappy cop. "Would you care to expand on that?"

Joe shook his head, but not in denial. "I guess it's not 'we' anymore. I don't know, its just that a lot of weird stuff has been happening to me lately. Things you wouldn't believe. Things I'm not sure I believe."

"Start from the beginning," Frank advised.

Joe nodded. "As long as I can remember, Daddy was a preacher. He kept talking about the second coming of

Christ, the Armageddon, the Sword of God—and this direct phone line he had to God Almighty. Like a Heavenly Hotline or something. Only thing is, he never told me why he could hear God, and I couldn't."

"Well, I'm not too surprised about that," Frank said cautiously. "We gotta lot of guys like that out here in the Bible Belt. Not real big on explanations."

Joe grimaced. "Yeah. I just took it for granted that he was right and I was wrong, as usual, and the only right thing I could possibly do was to obey him and serve whatever church he had created that day. I didn't dare contradict him, even when the contradictions were so obvious that any fool could see he was making this stuff up as he went along. I kinda got to the point where it didn't matter, you know? Like as long as he was handing down the line, I'd swallow it and not even think about it. Then he started the Sacred Heart. Sacred Heart of the Chosen Ones, he called it. God's chosen people. And the only chosen people."

Peggy showed up with a pitcher of water and filled both empty glasses.

Joe emptied his for the third time. "Hot day. Nothing to drink, either," he offered.

Frank let him take his time. It was obvious that this wasn't comfortable for him.

Joe took up the thread again, in a softer voice now. "Funny. From the time I was thirteen I dreamed of being Rambo. I only saw *First Blood* one time, but I remember every line in the movie. I worshipped Rambo, I guess. I kind of felt like I knew where he was at, because I was an outcast, too. But I never told Father that, since I was only allowed to worship two people, him and his Jesus. So when he sent me to a military academy, I was happy. The other kids, they saw the academy as some kind of punishment. Not me. I thought it was great. Like summer camp, training for the Olympics and getting to join the army all in one. I did pretty good, too, until one day they just pulled me out of class and sent me home. Father had a disagreement with the dean over the religious part of our training, wasn't to his liking or something, so I went back to Atlanta."

That much could be checked. Frank nodded, and Joe took that as encouragement to continue.

"I got a big surprise, though. After only six months, the Chosen Ones had grown. There were ten congregations in the south and east, instead of just the one I remembered. And everybody had started wearing guns everywhere." He grinned, disarmingly. "I started thinking that coming back to Atlanta wasn't that bad a deal after all."

"So you could play Rambo?" Frank said cynically. Joe flushed, but nodded.

"Father changed some time while I was gone. He was always crazy and weird anyway, but now it looked like something else was pulling his strings." The kid leaned forward, earnestly. "He would talk to himself when he didn't think anyone could hear him, and he would have these *conversations* with something, only it was like overhearing someone on the phone. You only heard one side of the conversation. He started calling this other thing the 'Holy Fire,' and he said it was telling him the direction the church would go. Like, it told him to begin all the other congregations. It told him to begin the Guard, and then it told him to start training for the war of all wars. Armageddon, with the forces of God toting assault rifles, you know?"

"Excuse me," Frank interrupted. "The Guard? Is that what you call your army?"

"The Guard of the Sacred Heart," Joe supplemented. "Then there's the Junior Guard, which I used to be in charge of."

"Tell me a little more about that," Frank said. "The Guard, the Junior Guard. I'm curious. How many are there? What kind of weapons do you have back there?"

For a moment Frank was afraid pushing for that kind of information might have been premature, but apparently Joe had warmed up enough to be willing to talk. *Poor kid,* Frank found himself thinking. *All these years, and he never really had someone to talk to. Already he feels comfortable enough around me to unload.*

It surprised him to feel pity for the boy. It surprised him more that he wanted to.

Joe frowned, absently, his lips moving a little as if he was adding up numbers in his head. "There's around two hundred fifty foot soldiers. Everyone has an AK-47; Father and General Plunket like them a lot. We have stockpiles of ammo, fourteen thousand rounds per rifle last I counted. Grenades, launchers, AR-15s, M2A2s, six .50-cals."

Frank couldn't help but utter a low whistle. "You're not pulling my leg, are you? That's an army down there."

"You bet it is," Joe replied brightly, but the sudden pride in the Guard seemed to embarrass him. "But—it's bad. I know that now. I don't hold with any of it anymore. Ever since . . ."

The boy looked away, evidently struggling with what he had to say. "Ever since my father killed Sarah. She was just a little girl."

Killed a little girl? Jesus—Frank waited in stunned silence for him to continue. When Joe didn't, he prompted, "What little girl?" *Let him be wrong. Let this be hearsay, God, please. . . .*

Joe swallowed and turned pale. "I—I saw him do it. I helped bury her."

Well, so much for it being hearsay.

"It had to do with that Holy Fire thing. It told him to do it, I think. Her parents were part of the church. They disappeared, and I don't know what ever happened to them."

They're probably dead, too, Frank thought, still in shock, but he didn't say anything. Likely the boy knew it, but was just hoping it wasn't true. *Look, you've dealt with murders before. People die. People kill. It happens. The important thing now is to get the damn evidence that'll put this bastard away.*

Joe shook his head and traced patterns on the formica with the water that had run down the side of his glass. "The church began to center around that Holy Fire thing more and more. It began calling the shots. First we'd train ten men to use a gun, then it would tell us to train fifty. And when that was done we'd get the orders to train a hundred."

Frank didn't like any of this. It sounded like some kind of carnival sideshow—except that people with high-powered firearms were taking it seriously. "And you never actually saw this 'thing,' did you?"

Joe shook his head again, emphatically. "It all came through Father. But then the thing wanted to talk to us directly. The little girl, Sarah. She was used to talk to it at first, and what came out of her would scare anyone. Ugly sounds. Grunts. Then it would talk. Like something out of a movie."

Frank nodded, wondering where reality ended and fantasy began. He had to act as if he was taking it seriously, or he'd lose the boy. He sure thought it was real. *We should be getting this on tape,* he thought. *There's time for depositions later, but I wish I had a recorder going now. This Brother Joseph guy must be one hell of a con artist to convince a little girl to play along with this little parlor show, not to mention the rest of this group. There must be hundreds more down there. And they're all under his thumb.*

Correction. All except his son, now. I've never seen anyone spill their guts like this. He sings like a cage full of canaries. Or like someone with a guilty conscious.

Joe raised his eyes to Frank's again, and the earnestness on his face could not be mistaken. "This wasn't just my father playing like a ventriloquist or something, you've gotta believe me. This *thing*, this Holy Fire, it's the real thing! It ain't—isn't—anything I've ever seen before. But it's real, real as you or me. . . ."

Frank nodded, but his skepticism must have shown a little. The boy frowned.

"I bet you'd like to know where we get our money, right? The Holy Fire, it would give us information on the horse races and the bingo games in Tulsa. And the information *would always be right*. But we couldn't attract attention by scoring big every time we went out there, so the 'luck' was sort of spread around." He swallowed, hard. Frank tensed. Something big was coming. "That wasn't where the real money came from. That was just seed money."

Here we go. Time for the nitty-gritty.

"Drugs. That's where the real money comes from. I never got involved in the sales, but I knew what they were doing. They used the money from the horse races and stuff to buy coke from the big guys in South America. It got delivered at night about three times a week. Then they would have to move it the next day, out into the street."

Frank cleared his throat. "What kind of large quantities? How much are we talking about here?"

"Oh, three, four hundred kilos a shot," Joe said casually. "Comes in by private plane, mostly. There's a landing strip and camo-nets out on the land. Or when the plane can't make it, they bring it in by truck."

Christ almighty, Frank thought. *All that coke, right under our noses. If what he's saying is true, it's hard to believe that we didn't get a line on any of this. He might be exaggerating the amount. But even if it's one ounce, we can bust them but good.*

Joe caught his attention again. "Now *listen* for a minute. They never got busted, not even once, because of what the Holy Fire would say right before we went out. Like the other night, it told us about the Oaktree Apartments. That there was going to be a bust, and when. *Exactly.*"

Frank squirmed. Which, for a man of his size, was not an action easily concealed. "Oaktree Apartments. In Cleveland?" He had been involved in that stakeout. And the resulting raid had produced zilch.

Every residence on their warrants had been sanitized. Not a shred of evidence, not a dust speck of coke. Nothing. And no explanation. One day before the bust, the place was red-hot. Day of the bust, nothing but empty rooms.

"Cleveland? I guess. But there's more, the reason why nobody ever gets busted. The Holy Fire warned us about the police. There was something about a blue Mustang."

Frank knew about the Mustang; he'd driven it once. The Tulsa County sheriff's office had loaned it to Pawnee last winter for a drug bust related to one on their turf. *But how in the world did that quack know about it?*

The first thought was that there had to be an informant working from within the department or even the state's attorney's office—

But how could someone cover county cops and Tulsa City stuff? And *state* busts?

Someone who had access to warrant information right across the state? But that was coming out of a dozen different offices—oh, it could be done, but only after the busts were over and the warrants filed—

More than one informant. It was the only explanation.

And it was the least believable. *When a cop goes bad, it's generally an isolated event.* A statewide coordinated effort of counter-informers—run from the sticks?—that was too much to believe.

They knew somehow, he thought in shock. *There's no denying that.* For one moment, he wondered if it was possible this Holy Fire thing was real—

No. It couldn't be. There was some other explanation. Meanwhile, he had to play along, because the kid believed, even if he didn't. . . . "It sounds like this thing needs a medium to talk through," Frank said, thinking quickly. He'd heard of the psychic medium scam, some with a kid hypnotized for good measure.

"A child," Joe corrected. "At least, that's according to my father. That was why Sarah. But Sarah began to resist this medium thing too much, and—"

Frank waited. And waited. "And what?"

"He got angry," Joe said in a soft voice. "He—strangled her. Six months ago or so."

A thin line of ice traveled down Frank's spine. "You did see this?"

Joe nodded, and his haunted eyes begged Frank for forgiveness. "I can show you the grave."

Evidence. "That will help. Is it on Chosen Ones' property?"

"It's hidden, but yeah, it's on our land. Their land." He shook his head. "I'm glad to be out of there, but at the same time I feel sorta lost. Like I don't know where I'm going now."

"Don't worry," Frank assured him. "You're doing the right thing." *Damn bet you are, kid.* "But if the girl was murdered six months ago, then who's he been using for the go-between since?"

Joe stared at the back of his hand. "That's what I'm getting at. This family started showing up at Praise Meetings in Atlanta, before we moved everything out here. There was this little kid—he was kinda like the way I was when I was that age. I think one of the reasons I liked him from the start, now that I look back, is 'cause he wasn't caught up in all that crazy Sacred Heart stuff like everyone else was. And he liked me, I think he kind of thought

I was like a big brother. The kid needed someone to look up to, and I just sort of fell into the role, I guess."

Frank was getting an eerie feeling about this, a sense of *déjà vu* that he couldn't quite shake. *Why does this sound familiar?* he wondered, but saved his questions for later.

The back of his hand seemed to fascinate the boy. "The father, this drunk named Jim, got roped into the Sacred Heart real good. My father convinced him to bring his son to the Praise Meeting. The kid turned out to be better than Sarah."

"The man's name was Jim?" Frank asked, knowing now why this all seemed familiar. And he didn't want it to. "Was his last name Chase?"

Joe frowned. "Might have been. Everyone there is on a first-name basis, but it'd be on record somewhere."

Frank knew he had to ask. "What about the boy? What's he called?"

"Jamie," Joe said. "The boy's name is Jamie."

Oh Lord, Frank thought, keeping his face as bland as possible. *How do I tell Cindy Chase this?* The answer came to him quickly: *You don't. At least, not yet.*

"He grabbed the kid—actually, he got Jim to grab him and bring him here. He had Jim kidnap the kid out of school, and lie to him, told him that the compound was a summer camp or something. Then they started using Jamie all the time as the medium thing, and they started starving him to keep him quiet, make it easier for the Holy Fire to talk through him. All he gets is juice—" Joe faltered, then picked up the narrative again. "That was when I started to feel bad about my position in the Guard, the whole Sacred Heart thing. Last night—Father made me a lieutenant with a new promotion, head of Internal Security. He must have figured something was wrong, 'cause all of a sudden he started dangling all this stuff in front of me. New apartment, new rank. But—I just can't take it anymore."

"You couldn't take what happened with the little girl?" Frank asked.

Joe shook his head, guiltily. "No, I mean, I know that sounds bad, but I didn't know her. She was kind of a puppet

for Father, and it was like what was happening wasn't real.
No, it's what he's doing to the kid. For weeks they've been
starving him, to be a better channel for this Holy Fire, and
he keeps getting weaker and thinner—he can't hardly stand
anymore. It's torture. I got some food through to him, but
it's not enough to save him. I was up against too much in
that place. I had to go get help."

Joe shuddered. "Sir, you've got to go in there before
it's too late. Father's been putting him in a sensory deprivation tank for some godawful reason, which is just hurting
him more. It's something I don't understand at all, it's like
he does it just 'cause he *can*. And whatever else happens,
Jamie can't go on much longer!"

Joe's eyes were pleading, glistened over with tears not
yet ready to fall. "I'm responsible, too. Arrest me if you
want to, but go in and save him."

Suddenly all the barriers broke, and Joe put his head
down on his arms and sobbed—tiny, strangled sobs that
sounded horrible, as if the boy was choking.

Frank was amazed. After all that control, he hadn't
expected the boy to break down and cry. The other patrons
in the restaurant had already left; now it was just them and
Peggy, who turned the front door sign to "Closed," then
came over with a box of tissue.

"Sorry," Joe said, after composing himself in the face
of a strange female. "I didn't mean to—lose it like that."

"Its okay," Frank told him, feeling a little better now that
he knew the kid still had some real emotions. "Cry as much
as you want to. We'll figure this mess out somehow."

But the control was back, at least for the moment. After
a while, Peggy began bringing their food over. Old George
was watching, covertly, his face lined with concern.

"Hope you're still hungry," Frank said. "There's a lot of
food here."

Joe's appetite did not seem to be dampened at all by
grief; the boy devoured everything in front of him.

"Don't worry, son, we're not going to arrest you," Frank
assured him, between mouthfuls of his own hamburger.
"For one thing, I don't see evidence yet of any wrongdoing
on your part. I doubt any judge in the country would hold
you responsible for what happened to the little girl or to

the boy, either, as long as you're willing to turn state's evidence. Would you be willing to testify against your father?"

Joe didn't answer right away. He seemed to mull over it, but only briefly. "Yes. I—I know I shouldn't think twice about it, but my father scares me, sir. He has too much power, and what he says goes. If you haven't got a bullet-proof jacket lying around, I think maybe you should find one, if you want me alive long enough to testify. Even then it might not make any difference."

"I'll see what I can come up with," Frank said. Now it seemed like a pretty good idea. *Assault weapons. I guess death squads and assassins is a logical next step. After all, this Brother Joseph has killed at least once. . . .*

"Surely he left something behind?" Brother Joseph said carefully.

He had been eating lunch alone in his private dining room, when Luke had interrupted the meal. He didn't like being interrupted at meals. Especially not with news like this.

Joe. Gone. No—not possible.

"No note?" he persisted. "No clues? Nothing at all to tell you about where he went?"

"Nothing," Luke said simply, his eyes staring at the wall over Brother Joseph's head. "He left nothing behind, sir. Some clothing appears to have been taken, but none of the Chosen Ones' uniforms. He vanished, apparently, as a civilian. No one really knows where he is."

The preacher's eyes narrowed at the news. *I knew the boy was up to something,* he thought coldly, a slow rage building. *The devil must have had his claws in him for a long time now. Why else would he turn against me? Haven't I shown him the way? Didn't I give him more than any other father would? I gave him one of the most prestigious honors he could ever hope to achieve. And this is how he repays me? How dare he?*

Then the rage—paused for a moment. *Or—did he? How could he dare?*

"This is simply not acceptable," he said to Luke. "I think that your conclusion that my son has abandoned us and gone to the authorities is premature. He could be testing us, you know. That would be just about his speed." That made more sense. Surely the boy would never dare run off. *He's probably trying to impress me.* He smiled as the logical explanation unrolled before him. "I can see it now, flexing his new muscles as the new Internal Security head, hiding in some corner we've forgotten about, waiting to see what precisely our reaction would be to this. If you think about it, our response would be rather revealing. It would emphasize our ability to handle—or not handle—a defection."

Luke shook his head, stubbornly. "No, Brother Joseph, I just don't think so. Haven't you noticed how peculiar he's been lately? Especially around Jamie. If you ask me, it seems he's had a change of heart about the Cause. The devil's in his heart, and he's not listening to the voice of God anymore."

"Well," Brother Joseph said, smiling thinly. Luke's statement touched a raw nerve, and he tried to conceal it as much as possible. "I'm *not* asking you. Use your head, man! This is my flesh and blood you're talking about! I suggest you organize a thorough search of the complex. If he wants to play this little game with us, we'll show him we can play it better."

"As you wish, sir," Luke said, but it didn't look like he was pleased with the assignment. "We will conduct a thorough search of the complex. Again."

"You do that," the preacher said. "And I suggest you not report back until you find him."

Brother Joseph watched the retreating back, a bit surprised that Luke had actually contradicted him. Nobody in the organization had ever done such a thing.

For that matter, Luke was the only one who could do it and escape serious punishment. His loyalty was unquestioned, and he was totally devoted to his leader and the Cause. But it wasn't like the man to think for himself; usually he just followed blindly, a quality Brother Joseph encouraged in his followers.

But there had always been an unspoken competition between Luke and his son. *Competition and animosity. They've tried to conceal it from me, but I saw it anyway.*

Interesting that Luke seems eager to declare my son a traitor.

Never mind. It wasn't going to ruin his day. He had much to look forward to tonight. This particular Praise Meeting was going to be special, he knew. The Holy Fire had been restless lately, an anxiety he could feel in his bones, suggesting that a spectacular channeling was in store for them all tonight.

Alas, it would probably be the last one, at least with Jamie. The boy had been pushed to his limits, though for a good reason, the only reason necessary: *the Holy Fire desired it.* Now the boy was closer to death, which took him closer to God. Brother Joseph had estimated yesterday that the boy had perhaps a week left to him, before starvation and the Holy Fire finished him off. After tonight, he would either be a vegetable or dead, most likely the latter.

The preacher sighed, staring at his unfinished meal. He wished there was some way to do this channeling so that he didn't have to go out and find another host every six months. It was so . . . inconvenient. Jamie in particular had been far better than Sarah, who was, he now saw, a mere container. She had been to Jamie what a hatchback coupe was to an exotic sportscar. The boy was a perfect vehicle, and the only thing that had kept him from disposing of Sarah when she started to resist and substituting the boy immediately had been Jamie's whore of a mother. Cindy had been a nuisance from the very start. It was a good thing she had been left behind in Atlanta.

Why, he wondered now, had Sarah begun to resist? So far Jamie had been quite complacent about the whole thing. Perhaps it had been the girl's age. He noticed that she had begun to mature, a little early, at ten. *That has to be it!* he decided. As soon as girl children began to mature, they took on the attributes of any whore. This womanhood, this *contamination,* must be the evil that made her resist the holy touch.

It was all he needed to formulate a brilliant theory. *If it weren't for men, all women would be spawn of Satan! Why are most preachers men? Didn't Eve succumb to evil, not Adam? And of the church's staff, how many women fulfill any kind of useful role?* The only one that came to mind was Agatha, the retired schoolteacher whom he'd won over years before. And *she* was old, well past menopause. Sterile. Pure. The rest of the women in the place were cattle. *Baby producers. Preferably, boy producers.*

He glanced up at the clock on the wall and frowned when he saw the time. Ten past one. *Looks like my wife isn't going to join me. Wonder what's gotten into her? I'm going to have to check into that. This is the fourth meal in a row that she's taken elsewhere.*

He finished his solitary lunch and went directly to Joe's room. The door was open, evidently left that way since the first search. Frowning, he saw the sinister paperback he'd flung across the room the night before, displeased to see that Joe hadn't destroyed it. *How dare he defy me?* he seethed, poking through the boxes that remained. *When I see him again, I will have to punish him severely for this.*

His pager went off at his waist, and when he checked the number saw that he was being summoned to the central security station. *Ah! Maybe Joe's decided to report in. Mystery solved.*

When he arrived, however, he could see from the expressions on all assembled that this wasn't the case. There were half a dozen security officers there, immaculate in their uniforms, plus Luke. They jumped up from their consoles and saluted as he entered. But nobody seemed willing to meet his eyes, and that alone was enough to stir his wrath.

"Well?" he said impatiently, when no one offered to explain why he had been paged. "What is it?"

Luke was standing in the middle of the cluster of guards. They glanced covertly at the man, deferring the answer to him. He cleared his throat, and with an effort met his leader's eyes.

"One of our people has seen Joe," he began. "In town."

Then he stopped, and the silence was infuriating. "Yes? And?"

Luke coughed. "He was seen talking to a sheriff's deputy. He was not wearing the uniform of the guard. Apparently, they spoke for a long time."

Brother Joseph stared at him, stunned. He didn't know how to respond. *Who saw him? There aren't too many*

*people it could be—only a few of us go out at a time. No
one who really knows Joe. . . . It must be a mistake, either
that or it's an outright lie!*

"Who says he saw Joe? I want to speak to him personally."

As if on cue, the group parted, revealing a man in the
back who looked like he wanted to become invisible. He
didn't look well; actually, he was obviously suffering from
a hangover. But then, he usually was. Lank blond hair
straggled greasily and untidily over his ears; his eyes were
so bloodshot you couldn't tell what color they were. His
skin was a pasty yellow-white, and his forehead was creased
with a frown of pain.

"Jim Chase?" Brother Joseph said. "On your honor, now.
Did you see Joe today?"

"Ah, yessir. I sure did," Jim said, though his eyes never
quite met the preacher's. He seemed to be studying the
wall behind the preacher instead. "Like Luke said, he was
talking to this big Indian deputy, there at this diner. I pulled
into the parking lot and was going to go in and take a leak,
when I saw him through the window with his back turned
to me, talking to the cop."

Brother Joseph frowned. "If his back was turned to you
how do you know it was him?"

Jim shook, but didn't back down. "I saw his profile a
few times, when he looked out the window. It was him."

Brother Joseph stepped closer and examined Jim's
disheveled appearance carefully, letting Jim know he was
taking note of the state the man was in. He sniffed, once.
His nose wrinkled at the reek of bourbon.

"I see," Brother Joseph said, turning away. "You have
a strong odor of liquor about you. I've told you before that
I don't mind my flock imbibing from time to time. But in
your present condition, how can I be certain you weren't,
how shall we say, seeing things?"

Jim didn't seem to have an answer to that. "Sir, I wasn't."
He shook his head. "I know your son; you know yourself
he's spent a lot of time with my—with Jamie. Besides, I
saw his tattoo in the window. The swastika."

Brother Joseph felt himself blanche; he'd always wanted
his son to have the blasted thing taken off. It just wasn't

politic to be brandishing symbols of something that had failed, no matter how noble their cause had been.

"Seems cut and dried to me," Luke said calmly. "That must have been him, then."

Brother Joseph knew that his tranquil facade would dissolve completely if he stopped to think. And he knew that he'd lose some of the power he had over these men if he didn't take back control; in fact, he could feel the power crumbling now.

Get a grip on yourself. And deal with this. "We must consider Joe a renegade and a traitor," he said, emotionlessly. "He is to be shot on sight, provided it can be done anonymously. Luke, would you kindly dispatch an assassin to eliminate him?"

"Yes, sir," Luke said. The preacher thought he saw a smirk forming at the corners of the man's mouth.

You would enjoy that, wouldn't you, you little toady? he thought, but retained his own cold smile. It didn't matter. Command had been reestablished. *You see, my followers? The importance of my own flesh and blood pales in comparison to the importance of our mission. I'll sacrifice my own traitorous son without a hint of regret so that we may march on unimpeded!* He nodded, offering tacit approval to Luke to do the job himself. The rest of the guardsmen seemed frozen in shock at Brother Joseph's decision.

Saying no more, Brother Joseph left to visit Jamie in his cell.

After all, didn't God sacrifice his own son?

CHAPTER TWELVE

These mortals are ineffectual fools, Al thought, during the long ride back from Pawnee. *I can't believe this has gone on for so long without a resolution. Our ways are better.*

It was a judgment he had made a long time ago, but the whole sad situation with Cindy, Jamie, Frank and the Sacred Heart of the Chosen Ones simply reinforced it. After this latest encounter with the sheriff's office, he'd just about decided that unless he intervened, the outcome of this was going to be bleak. *The wheels of justice turn in this county, true, but only slowly. If this were a violation of an elven law, the matter would have been resolved long ago, by spell or swordpoint. If it hadn't been for the Salamander, I'd have found a way to take care of it myself.*

All the way back from the sheriff's office, they were ominously silent. Gone was the hopeful mood during their trip out to Pawnee; Cindy oozed depression. Any moment Alinor figured she was going to break down and cry. It was all he could do to keep his shields up and his mind clear. At this point in the game, he needed everything working in top form.

Keeping Cindy's emotions out, though, wasn't the real

311

problem. His own simmering anger threatened to over-whelm him. *Now I know why I deal so little with the humans' world,* he thought. *I would go mad with all that . . . that . . . red tape!*

Frank had been no help at all. It only confirmed what he suspected all along: that the sheriff's department, though with all the right reasons for their actions, had no inten-tion of including them in any move they might make against the group. That alone rankled him. After all, hadn't he already been in the camp and gotten closer to the situa-tion than any law enforcement officer? *I know more about what's going on in there than they do—or could. They have no concept of the universe beyond their own, immediate physical world. They wouldn't know a ghost if they walked through one!*

He couldn't begin to consider explaining the Salamander to the cop. *He'd probably have me committed or jailed or something,* he thought, shuddering at the possibility of being surrounded by all that cold steel. *They have no idea what they're up against. The Salamander could come in and pulverize anyone's mind without much effort. Great Danaa—it would happily pit all of its followers against the law enforcement people and gorge on the resulting carnage. . . .*

In fact, that was probably what the Salamander had in mind.

What he doesn't know—couldn't know—is that Jamie is being exposed to this thing regularly. If his mind isn't destroyed yet, it will be soon, perhaps even the next time they have their little "Praise Meeting." At the sheriff's rate of progress, Jamie isn't going to last long enough to be rescued.

He considered another nagging possibility. *The Sala-mander is going to see this raid a mile away. It probably knows about it already. Then what? Is it going to instruct Brother Joseph to fortify the underground complex of bunkers even more? Short of a bombing run with napalm, there would be little chance of getting to the soldiers. And if we did, what would be left? Too risky to the children to even consider it.*

They pulled into Hallet raceway in the late afternoon,

and Al reached forward with his mind to make sure the air-conditioning was on in the RV. The temperature was up to at least a hundred now, a county-wide sauna. Heat like that that would only aggravate already touchy tempers. Al would have to be careful lest Cindy blow up in his face; he sighed with the realization that she probably would anyway, regardless of how much caution he exercised around her. *How can I blame her, though? If it were my child—and I'm beginning to feel like it is—I would be frustrated to tears, too.*

Fortunately all at the track had been running perfectly since that last minor fix on the engine, and the team had given them as much time as they needed off. *Thank Danaa,* he thought, wishing that all racing gigs had gone as well mechanically as this one. *If we'd had to deal with a balky engine, I doubt we would have had the time to do as much as we have.*

After they had parked the car, Cindy excused herself. She said she had to go make a call to her bank in Atlanta. Al suspected she just wanted to be alone for a while and didn't say anything. She'd probably go hole up in the ladies' room over by the stands and cry her eyes out.

Bob looked tired and slouched back on the couch-bed with a Gatorade and a *Car and Driver* magazine. Not surprising, after being up most of the night working on Cindy's car. Al didn't really want to burden his friend with what was on his mind, but they had made promises to each other that no matter what they would be there for each other. It was a pact encouraged by every one of the Folk who'd joined SERRA, for experience had shown that their kind didn't always do very well going solo in the humans' world.

Especially, Al thought tiredly, *when a Salamander is involved.*

He took a seat across his companion and pretended to study the table top for a moment. "You know, Bob," Al said conversationally. "This, ah, sheriff's office doesn't strike me as being all that efficient in dealing with this mess."

Bob lowered the magazine and gazed steadily at his partner, his eyes narrowed, with a slight frown on his lean features. "Eyah?" he said, but the glint in his eye suggested

he already knew what to expect. But he added no more
to his comment. Instead, he waited patiently for his friend
to continue.

"I mean, look at it. They have all the evidence they need
to raid the place, or at least investigate the cult a lot closer.
If they did, they'd *find* Jamie, you know they would! But
their own laws are preventing them from doing it!" He felt
himself snarling and clamped control down on himself. "The
laws that were designed to prevent this abuse are indirectly
condoning it," he said a little more calmly. "What sense
does that make?"

Bob took his time responding, as usual. "I don't pretend to be a part of the humans' world," he replied, slowly.
"I know, I am a human, but I don't understand it. I feel
like I'm sorta caught between the human and the elven
worlds, and to tell you the truth, most of the time Underhill
seems a lot more sensible. This is one of those times when
it's especially true." He sighed wearily. "I think I know what
you're getting at. You want to go in. Like Rambo. Play
Lancelot. Do you really think, though, that you can take
on this thing by yourself?"

Al bristled at the suggestion, however true it probably
was, that this was out of his league. "I don't know if I can
or not," he said. "We don't have a choice, and I'm going
to have to try. The law enforcement people involved in this
deal are blind to the Salamander; they wouldn't believe in
it even if we told them about it. How could they hope to
combat something they can't even see?"

"Right," Bob said, and shook his head. He knew that
no matter what he said, Al was going to go ahead and do
what he was planning on doing anyway. And Al knew that
he knew. It had never changed anything before, and it
wouldn't this time, either. "Had it occurred to you that
maybe you should call in some help?"

Al snorted indignantly. The problem was, he had. The
Low Court elves he had contacted—hundreds of miles away,
in Dallas—had shown polite interest in the Salamander
project, but nothing more. He had explained carefully to
them how imperiled the boy was, pushing all the proper
elven buttons to rouse their anger. But those he talked to
had sadly shaken their heads, telling him that there was

nothing *they* could do. There simply was no nexus close enough—even if they had been able to transfer themselves to it in time to do any good. They couldn't operate that far away from the nexus in Dallas. There were no High Court elves there, and while the Low Court was sympathetic to his plight, they were helpless. They simply could not survive more than fifty miles from their grove-anchored power-pole. And he hadn't been able to contact any of the High Court elves of Outremer or Fairgrove. Al checked again, working through his anger—but once again he could touch no one. He released the fine line of communication he sustained and refrained from beating his head against the nearest convenient wall.

"I see," Bob said, as if reading his mind. "No luck, huh?"

"None."

The discovery left him feeling empty, reminding him how different he really was from the other elves. Traveling the world, intersecting with the humans' universe whenever necessary, was for him a way of life. To the rest—except for those in Fairgrove and Outremer, and some rumored few in Misthold—it was an esoteric and dangerous hobby. *They're probably behind shields or Underhill. Damn. Why didn't I tell them about this when I first realized the Salamander was involved?*

"So what do you suggest?" Bob said. "Waltz in there all by yourself, politely inform them you're there for Jamie and then walk out with him?" He sat up, setting the magazine aside, and faced Al. "You really think they're going to go for that?"

"No, no, *no!*" Al said, a bit of his anger slipping past his shields. "Just what kind of a fool do you think I am? I'm going to pull out every trick I can conjure just to get through this one alive. What choice do I have? You know that child hasn't a chance unless I go in after him! Frank Casey is a good man, but he's only one sheriff, and he's the *only* one who knows or cares about Jamie! How much will you wager me that he's the least senior man involved in whatever it is they're doing about the Chosen Ones? I *have* to go in there because no one else will!"

"God," Bob said, wearily. "Listen, Alinor, I'm not blind or deaf. I saw the maps and all, and the way Casey hid them. It's just that you're going to have to go up against that thing, and there is nothing on a magical level I can do to help you. I want you to *think* about what you're doing and not just charge in there like every other macho warrior in Outremer, thinking you can conquer the world just because you can work a few magic tricks. I'm afraid for you, even if you won't be for yourself. This thing scares me."

Al snorted. "Don't think for a minute that it doesn't scare me. I told you, I'm not a fool. Anyone else might act like a 'macho warrior'—but they don't know what they're up against. I do. Believe me, I do."

Near their RV, a barbecue party was in noisy progress. In the distance was the dim roar of race cars, the muted bark of a PA system. Around them the world was functioning normally, while they discussed—what? A raid on a crazed madman and his army—confronting a supernatural monster. Life had progressed way beyond surreal.

But he had a sudden idea. "There is something you can do to help me. Keep a close eye on Cindy when I go in there." Bob flinched at the mention of "there," but Al continued. "Keep her occupied. I don't want her to know what I'm doing."

Bob gave him the Look. "What, exactly, will you be doing? And don't forget the cops. They can still come after us if they find out we're interfering. Remember, the deputy told us to stay out of it."

Al expelled a breath as he gazed at the floor. *What, indeed?* "Here it is. *If* they find out, it'll be after I've gotten in and out. At that point dealing with them will be the easiest part of this whole mess. I play games with Frank's memory, make him forget 'Al,' replace what he knows with memories of some crazy human antiterrorist or something. Let him spin his wheels trying to find someone who never existed. I've done it before. It's the Chosen Ones we need to be concerned with the most."

"No kidding," Bob muttered. "So how are you planning on keeping yourself bullet-hole-free?"

Al shrugged. "I'll go in with James' face, or someone else they'll recognize."

Bob nodded. "Okay. And once you're in, then what?"

Al shrugged. "I wing it, I guess."

Bob groaned.

Jamie came awake in the darkened cell, suddenly aware that someone was sitting in the room with him.

:Sarah?: he sent, but there was no answer, and the presence was solid. It smelled, sweat and dirty clothes and mildew—real.

And another odor that could only mean his father. That smell. Joy juice. *Oh, no, I'm going to get sick again.*

He had barely enough energy to turn over and vomit into a small trash can that had been left there for that reason. A man named Luke had told him to use it if he got sick again, and if he missed it he was going to spank him with a rubber hose. Long welts on his legs and buttocks testified to his poor aim. It was difficult to hit the bucket when you saw two of them.

When he was finished he leaned back on the bed. From the sound his vomit made, he knew he'd hit the bucket, so he knew he wouldn't be beaten this time. But he was still afraid. He looked up through the fog that clouded his vision at the face in front of him he dimly recognized as his father's.

"Daddy," he whispered, since that was all he had the strength for. "What did I do wrong? What am I being spanked for?"

It was always possible that to ask such questions would only solicit more beatings, either from his father or another adult nearby. It didn't matter. It seemed like whatever he did, it was wrong, and it was his fault.

Always my fault.

"Don't talk back to your daddy," Jim said angrily. "Don't you *ever* talk back to me. There's a reason for all this. I know it, you don't have to. Just you wait and see."

Although Jamie heard the words, there wasn't much sense he could extract from them. Another question formed, then slipped past his teeth.

"Where's Mommy?"

Stars exploded in his vision as Jim hit the side of his face. Jamie saw stars and felt his whole face spasming with pain, then aching right down to the bone, his teeth loosening. His head jerked to the side, stayed that way. He had no energy to cry or scream or protest or agree to what was going on. All he could do was to lie there in terror and wait for whoever was inflicting the pain to go away, however temporarily; they would always return, he knew.

"I'll beat the devil out of you yet," Jim said, but his voice sounded like he was further away, though he hadn't heard his footsteps retreating. Jamie heard another voice then, one that sounded like Luke's.

"Tonight's the night," he heard Luke say, further away, beyond the open door where light spilled into the room.

"There's too much of his damn mother in him," Jim Chase said, as if that was Jamie's fault. "He won't believe in anything! He always has to ask *questions!* It's his damn mother, I tell you—"

He heard footsteps as they left the room. "It don't matter," Luke replied. "Holy Fire can use him now whether he believes or not, and anyway, after tonight it'll be all over with." Luke laughed, nastily. "Until then, we'll let him see what *questions* buy doubters. He gets to see what the darkness of hell is like."

The light went out.

Darkness used to mean terror, now it was welcome. Darkness usually meant the beatings would stop.

:Sarah. Help me,: he called. *:You promised you'd help me.:*

Long moments passed as he waited for his companion. As always she appeared, faithful as ever, this time as a ball of bright white light at the outer periphery of his vision. Her presence, over the last several visits, seemed to be getting stronger. Jamie didn't know what to think about that, except that maybe he was getting closer to becoming a ghost like her.

She hovered there a long while, longer than usual, which made Jamie nervous.

:What's wrong?: he asked.

:I can't stay,: she said, sounding afraid. *:It's getting stronger. If I stay too long it will see me, and I don't know what will happen yet. I came by to tell you . . . :*

The light flickered, dimmed, threatened to go out.

Jamie panicked. :*Sarah! Don't go away.*:

The light brightened. :*. . . to tell you help is on the way. Joe ran away and told the police what was going on. And . . .*:

He waited for her to finish, but he sensed she was struggling against something, like there was a hard wind where she was, blowing her away.

The light surged back one more time, for a brief moment.

:*. . . that I love you.*:

And the wind blew the light out.

Bob stood in front of the white van with his hands planted on his hips and a frown on his face. Cindy stood beside him, holding his arm tightly, but trying to be so quiet she was holding her breath. "Look," he said—profoundly grateful that it was after sunset and there was no one near enough to see that he was talking to a grill and a pair of headlights. "You know he and Andur went over there with no backup. You *know* he's not up to this! So who's left to do anything? You and me!"

The lights glowed faintly for a moment. Bob wished—not for the first time—that he was one of the human fosterlings with the power to speak mind-to-mind. But then Nineve was probably just as frustrated with this as he was. None of the elvensteeds could speak audibly—and in fact, none could transform up to anything larger or more complicated than a cargo van. Nineve's interior modifications were all due to the same magic Alinor used to modify the Winnie. Otherwise, Bob would have had her shift into a nice solid M-1 tank.

"Here's what I figured," he continued, hoping desperately that what he had *figured* was going to work. "I've been playin' with the scanner Les Huff's got in his trailer; he's got this book on police freqs, and I've been listening every night, tryin' t' see if there was anything goin' down with the cops, okay? Well, just after Al left, there's all *kinda* stuff, radio checks, code-words—sounded like somebody was gearing up for something real big. Well, when we visited that Pawnee County Mounty, he covered up what we thought was plans for a big raid. I figure that big raid's about to happen. And Al's right smack in the middle of it. But—*but*—if you ask the owls where it's all coming from—and then we catch them gearin' up—well, maybe we can force their hand. If we get them to kick off that raid early, while Al's in there, maybe that *thing* he's going up against'll pay attention to them and not him."

Nineve's lights came on and stayed on—and her motor started up abruptly and the driver's-side door popped open. Bob could have wept with relief.

Cindy released his arm and started for the passenger's side as Nineve revved her engine. Bob grabbed her elbow before she had gotten more than a step away. "No," he said, holding her back. "You stay here."

She whirled, balling her fists, her eyes flashing in sudden anger. "No? *No?* What the hell do you mean, *no?* That's my *son* you're talking about—"

"That's the police from a backwater, redneck, prehistoric county we're talking about," Bob replied levelly. "Plus the FBI, the state cops, maybe the DEA for all I know. All good ol' boys *frum roun' ear.*" He imitated the local accent mercilessly. "You're not *frum roun' ear.* You're not military, you're not even male. If you can think of a bigger bunch of macho ass-kickers, I'd like to hear it some time. *Your* son isn't gonna mean squat to them, Cindy. You show up, and if you're lucky, they'll just dismiss everything you tell them as female hysterics and shove you off into a corner to make coffee. If you're *not* lucky, they'll throw you into the county clink to keep you out of their hair!"

She fell silent and stopped resisting his hold. He continued, a little more gently. "Cindy, it's not fair, but that's the way these guys are gonna be, and we've gotta deal with it. I'm a man, I speak their language. I'm a National Guard MP with a security clearance, I know how to handle a gun, I've got grease and oil under my fingernails—if I go in there and find Frank first, I think maybe I can convince him to deputize me and bring me in with them. If I'm deputized, he can *assign* me to find Jamie. And figure I've got a better than average chance of not getting shot in the ass."

He took a deep breath, as Cindy slumped and put her hand to her mouth to keep from crying. "Cindy, Frank's not a bad guy—he wants to help, but he's got his job to do. He may even be happy to see me. More important, though—if we start a ruckus while Al's in there, we'll be giving him cover. If between us we can't get Jamie out, no one can. But if you go, that's not gonna happen. We'll *both* wind up in the county slammer. You for showing up, me for bringing you."

"All right," Cindy said, in a small voice. "I guess you're right. But—just sitting here, not doing anything—"

"I know it's hard, Cindy," Bob told her earnestly. "It's the hardest thing in the world. I've done my share of waiting, too. Not like this—but I've done a lot of it. Will you stay in the RV and trust me?"

She nodded, shyly—and to his surprise and shocked delight, kissed him, swiftly. Then she turned and ran into the RV.

"Did that mean what I thought it meant?" he asked Nineve. The lights blinked twice, and he touched his lips, a bemused smile starting at the corners of his mouth. "I'll be damned. . . . Well, hell, this isn't catching any fish. Let's get going!"

Bob faced Frank Casey with a stolid, stubborn expression he knew the deputy could read with no mistake. Casey, in his camos and blackout face-paint, looked absolutely terrifying; bigger than usual, and *entirely* like a warrior. If they'd let him wear feathers, he'd probably have one tucked into the cover of his helmet.

Casey was trying to intimidate him with silence and a glower. Bob refused to be intimidated. Casey tried a little longer, then deflated.

"Christ," he muttered, removing his helmet and passing his hand through his hair. "I don't know how you found out about this—but you're here now, and Captain Lawrence says your ID checks out—shit, I can use another hand, I guess." He shook his head. "Consider yourself deputized. Goddamn. At least you got more sense than that hothead buddy of yours with the hair."

Behind Frank, the Air National Guard hangar at the tiny regional airport was as full of feverish activity as a beehive at swarming time; it had been bad *before*, when he first strolled in. But now—

He'd almost been arrested on the spot, until he cited Frank Casey as his contact. Then he'd faced an unfriendly audience of DEA officers, National Guard officers, FBI agents and police. They hadn't liked what he told them about Al.

And I didn't even tell them a quarter of it.

"Yeah, well," Bob coughed. "I couldn't stop him. Tried, but—" He shrugged. "He's real worried about that kid."

"So'm I," Frank said grimly. "But I've got the FBI, the DEA, the County Mounties, the state boys—and half the local National Guard to worry about, too. They made me local coordinator on this thing, they've been letting me call some of the shots. And your buddy may just have blown our raid."

"Maybe," Bob said cautiously. "Maybe not." *How do I play my ace in a way he'll believe? He sure as hell won't believe me about the Salamander. . . .* "Seems to me these guys've got ways of finding out things—like they've been able to screw things up for you before this." The flinch Frank made cheered him immensely. He was on the right track! "So, okay, they may even know about this one. Except you're gonna jump the gun on them. So maybe *now,* 'cause we forced your hand a little, you got a chance of catching 'em off-guard." He cocked his head to one side. "So that's why I asked you to bring me in on this. I know what he looks like; hopefully I can find him before he catches a little 'friendly fire.' *That* sure wouldn't look good on the report."

Frank shook his head slowly. "Man," he drawled, "I haven't heard a line like that since *Moonlighting* got canceled."

Bob almost grinned and stopped himself just in time.

"Right now, the *only* reason your ass isn't in the county jail is because I convinced *my* superiors that *you* are somebody I've worked with before. Your Guard record helped, but basically they're going on my word." Frank looked back over his shoulder at the half-dozen Blackhawk helicopters being loaded at double-time. "Don't push your luck."

"No, sir," Bob replied, with complete seriousness.

"You've got three assignments," Frank said, holding up

three fingers, and counting down on them. "Find your buddy. Find the kid. Try not to get ventilated. When you accomplish one and two, get down and *stay* down so you can accomplish three."

"Yes *sir!*" Bob didn't salute, but he snapped to a completely respectful attention. Frank nodded, apparently satisfied.

"Now get your ass over there," he said, nodding at the third chopper in line. "You're with Lieutenant Summer; you can't miss 'em, he's the only black officer in this crowd. He knows you're with his bunch. One of his men turned up sick, so lucky you, you get to ride. And buddy, that's all you got. You manage to liberate a weapon from the enemy, *then* you've got a piece—otherwise, you got nothing."

Bob nodded. He hadn't expected anything else. There wouldn't be any spare weapons on this trip—and even if there had been, there was no one here who'd take responsibility for signing him out on one. If an assault rifle turned up missing after all this was over, and then guys in charge found out an outsider had been brought in at the last minute—there'd be no doubt of where the gun went (whether or not that was the real truth), and the one who'd authorized issuing it to Bob would be in major deep kimchee. And in theory, given his assignments, he wouldn't *need* one. Not having a gun would make him concentrate on those assignments instead of playing Rambo.

Frank looked him up and down one more time. Bob knew what Frank was thinking, given his "nonstandard" clothing. When he'd headed out in this direction, he'd had a small choice of outfits. Instead of going for concealing gear, since he figured he wasn't going to be in the first wave, Bob had chosen to suit up in *real obvious* clothing—his bright red, Nomex coverall. There wasn't a chance in hell that any of the Bad Guys would be wearing something like *that,* which meant that the Good Guys—in theory, anyway—wouldn't mistake him for a lawful target. Al would recognize him if he saw him, even at a distance, even during a firefight. Hopefully Jamie would recognize racetrack gear and trust him. Nomex was fire-proof and heat-resistant; he might be able to make a dash into or out of a burning building if he had to.

Of course, this same outfit made him look like a big fat target for the *Bad* Guys—

Frank shook his head. "How come you didn't paint a bulls'-eye on the back while you were at it?"

"Reckoned all they'd see was a red blur goin' about ninety, and figure I was a launched flare," Bob drawled.

Frank's mouth twitched. "Deployable decoy. You're either the bravest bastard I ever met, or the craziest. Get over to that chopper, before I change my mind."

This time Bob *did* salute, and did a quick about-face before Frank got a chance to respond. A huge black man in camos was supervising the loading of his men; as Bob quick-trotted over, he looked up and waved impatiently at him.

Bob broke into a run—hoping he wasn't about to make the biggest mistake of what could turn out to be a very short life. . . .

The gloomy, empty hallway would echo footsteps, if Alinor had been so careless as to make any noise. Wherever the Chosen Ones had gone to, it wasn't *here*, and Al was perfectly happy to have things that way.

But he was going to have to find somewhere to hide for a little, while he got his bearings. There was so much iron and steel around him that his senses were confused; he needed to orient himself—and most of all, he needed to find where the Chosen Ones all were—and where Jamie was.

He slipped inside the door marked "Cleaning Supplies" and closed it behind him. He waited for his eyes to adjust to the darkness, and made out a mop, a bucket, and a sink with two shelves over it, with one gallon jug of cheap disinfectant cleaner on the top shelf. Nothing else.

Not a lot of supplies. I suppose it's easier to punish someone by making them clean the floor with brute force than to buy adequate supplies. Then again, any penny that goes to buy a bottle of cleaner doesn't go to buy bullets— or steak for Brother Joseph. That's the Way of the Holy Profit.

Getting in had been much easier than he had thought it would be. First of all, he'd gone in right after dinner, when the guards were torpid from their meal. He slipped in with Andur's help over the first two sets of fences at some distance from the compound, then he'd walked around to the third checkpoint openly, as if he'd been out for a stroll. He'd altered his face to look like Jim Chase's—then, as he approached the third set of security guards, he'd planted the false memory that they had seen the man going out—supposedly for a walk—about an hour before. They waved him in after no more than a cursory question or two. He continued his stroll towards the main bunker, as the sun splashed vivid reds in fiery swaths across the western sky.

But the next problem confronted him immediately, in the form of a technological barrier. Illusions weren't going to fool video cameras, and there was one just inside the bunker door. He would *have* to pass it to get inside.

Well, there *had been* one. Technically, there still was one, it just wasn't working right now.

He had paused just out of range, loitering for a moment, as if enjoying a final breath of fresh air before descending into the dank bunker, and had checked out the circuit the camera was operating on. To his delight, he had discovered that they hadn't replaced the wiring of that line after his initial tampering. He had used a fraction of his powers to create an electrical surge that had fried the camera just before he turned to face it. And with the corridor beyond empty it had been child's play to penetrate into the lower level and find this closet to hide in.

Now, as he braced himself carefully against the wooden support-beam and sent his mind ranging along the electrical circuitry, he discovered they hadn't replaced *any* of the wiring, despite all the damage his tampering had been causing. Evidently none of these folk associated the cascading equipment failures they'd been cursed with to an overall failure in the wiring.

Maybe it wouldn't occur to them. They may be the "plug and play" type, using things without understanding them. Al found that kind of attitude impossible to put up with, but most humans seemed to be like that. He had learned that if you asked the average mortal how something he used every day (a light bulb, for instance) worked, most of the time he would not be able to tell you.

Mortals relied on others more than they ever dreamed—even the Chosen Ones, who prided themselves on being self-sufficient. It was a false pride, for without the outside world to support them—in the apocalyptic world they seemed to dream of—their entire way of life would fall apart within weeks.

Never mind that. Just take advantage of it.

He located the shielded security circuits and sent surges along all of them, blowing out every security camera he could find. There was more he could do—he hadn't done much in the way of starting electrical fires yet, except by accident—

Not yet. I might need the distractions to cover me.

The first thing he needed to do was to locate the bulk of the Chosen Ones, using the wires to carry his probes. He found them, as he had expected, still in the communal dining hall. Good; he wasn't likely to run into any stragglers for a while yet.

And now for my enemy. He searched for the Salamander, then, sending his mind cautiously out into the emptier parts of the building complex to look for it. He had a fair idea of where it might be. The room of the Praise Meetings. Hopefully, it would be drowsing.

He recoiled swiftly as he touched it, realizing by the difference in the tension of its aura that it was *not* half aware, as it had been before when there was no meeting. It was awake — but it was preoccupied, as if something else had its attention, and it had little to spare to look about itself.

It was in the Praise Meeting room. In fact, as he examined its energies from a cautious distance, it actually seemed to be *bound* there somehow, as if it had been tied to something that was physically kept within that room. Was that possible? Could a being of spirit and energy be confined like that?

It had been possible during his ill-fated excursion into the world of the humans in the time of the First Crusade. The creatures had been imprisoned within the little copper boxes. They would be freed only if Peter the Hermit actually broke the spell binding them—which he had, so that several of them could travel with other armies than his own. That had been a mistake—as Peter had learned—for once released, there was no controlling them. Even the ones still bound to their containers would seize the opportunity to run amok when released temporarily.

That made another thought occur to him; this creature had actually felt familiar when he'd first encountered it. He had dismissed that feeling as nothing more than the reawakening of old memories. Now he wondered if he really had sensed the presence of an old adversary. Was it possible? Could this creature be one of the Salamanders that had *not* been released, one he knew? Could it still be tied to something physical? If that were true—

That would explain how the damned thing got over here. Most magical creatures cannot just buy a plane ticket, but they can invest themselves in a transportable object, which also gives them the advantage of a physical storage nexus for their power. That could be it. Hmm. The last time I saw those creatures they were spreading violence through the Middle East.

. . . which might partially explain why the Middle East was still, to this very day, a hotbed of violence, if the Salamanders were still there, still spreading their poison. . . .

If this creature has a physical tie, then I can do something about it. I can force it back into its prison, or I can dismiss it from this plane altogether!

He slid his back down along the wooden support-post until he was sitting on the cold concrete floor of the closet, his knees tucked up against his chest. He would have to probe very carefully. He did not dare catch the Salamander's attention; bound or not, it was still dangerous, and he was no match for it in a one-on-one fight.

He still didn't know if it truly *was* bound, either. Even if it was, there would only be a very limited window of opportunity for him to act against it. And he had to know *what* it was bound to.

He allowed his perception to move slowly through the electric lines, extended his probe into the room beyond, testing each object on the room for the peculiar magic resonances that had been on the Hermit's enchanted containers.

Nothing. Nothing again.

But wait. How about something quicker—searching for copper?

Still nothing.

There was nothing there but chairs, a little bit of audio-visual equipment. Nothing that could possible have "held" the Salamander, and certainly nothing that had any feeling of magic about it at all.

Wait a minute—what about on the stage?

He moved his perception to the circuits running the footlights, and "looked" out across the wooden platform. It seemed barren; it held only the podium, a single chair of peculiar construction, a flag—

He recoiled as he touched the Salamander's dark fire. *Blessed Danaa!*

The flag—no, the *flagpole*—radiated the peculiar dark power of the Salamander. There was no doubt, none at all. The creature was bound to the brass, sculptured flagpole.

I don't remember any flagpoles! Copper boxes, certainly, but no flagpoles—

Besides, the pole couldn't be more than a single century old. Two, at the most. And if there had been any human mages capable of imprisoning a Salamander these days, surely he would have heard about them; power like that couldn't be concealed in an age of so relatively few mages and so much communication.

There wasn't even anything of copper, which was the only metal that he recalled the Hermit using for his containers. Copper, not brass—

Brass. But brass is an alloy of copper, isn't it? Maybe it wasn't the shape that mattered, it was the metal. . . .

Blessed Danaa. What if someone found one of the boxes and used it for scrap? That must be it; someone smelted the damned thing down. They smelted it down and made . . . that.

He pulled all of his senses back, quickly, and sat quietly for a moment, calculating his next move. Now would be a very good time to call in an ally.

He closed his eyes again and reached out with his mind, but this time in an entirely different direction.

:*Sarah?*: he called, hoping he was doing so quietly enough to avoid the attention of the Salamander. :*Sarah? It's time*—:

CHAPTER THIRTEEN

:Hush!: The little girl literally popped into the tiny closet out of nowhere, surprising Alinor into a start. *:I got Joe to run away. Don't call me like that! It's not listening for us now!:*

:I don't think it'll hear us,: Al replied, after a quick check. *:It's real busy with something.:*

:Jamie,: Sarah said angrily. *:It's getting ready for Jamie. It wants to kill him and take his body, and it can this time! Jamie's real sick—and I can't fight it off now, not when he can't help.:*

Al elected not to ask just how sick Jamie was; he couldn't do anything about it, and there was no point in worrying. If he succeeded in banishing the Salamander, Jamie would be with his mother by dawn. If he didn't, they'd both be beyond help.

:Sarah, what exactly happens when Brother Joseph calls the monster?: he asked. *:Describe it as closely as you can. I think there's going to be a point where you and I can stop this thing, but I have to know exactly what it does, and when.:*

She wasn't an image so much as a hazy shape, but he could tell she was thinking very hard. There was a kind of fuzzy concentration about the way she "looked." *:Well, he has to kind of get everybody all riled up.:*

:Yes, I saw that,: Al agreed. *:Does that anger make the monster stronger?:*

The image of a little girl strengthened as she nodded. *:I think so,:* she said. *:If he doesn't get them riled up enough, it can't come out of the door.:*

:Whoa, wait a minute: Al exclaimed. *:What door? What are you talking about?:*

She faded for a moment, as if he had startled her, but her image strengthened again immediately. *:What? Can't you see the door?:*

He thought quickly. *:Not that I recognize what you're talking about. Look, I'll try to stop interrupting you, and you tell me everything that happens, the way it happens, as if you were describing it to someone who hadn't seen it.:*

:All right,: she agreed. *:First he gets everybody all riled up. Then there's a kind of—door. It's kind of in the flagpole. The monster sort of opens the door and comes out, and that's when he's in this kind of world, where I am.:*

She seemed to be waiting for him to say something. *:The halfworld,:* he said, *:That's what elves call it. The place that's half spirit and half material.:* He thought for a minute. *:This door—is it kind of as if you were standing right at a wall, and somebody opened a door, and then the monster kind of unfolds out of it?:*

She brightened with excitement. *:That's it! That's exactly what it looks like!:*

So the Salamander was being confined in the flagpole, much as it had been confined in the copper box. Because there was no summoning spell involved, it required the energy of Brother Joseph's congregation to pry open the "door" of its confinement place.

:Then what?: he prompted.

:Well, then the door goes shut again, and I don't think it can get back in until Brother Joseph lets it go again. So it stays there, and that's when it starts feeding on Brother Joseph. When it feeds enough on him, it can push Jamie out of his body and take over.:

He chewed on his lip for a moment. He tasted blood and wrinkled his nose, remembering *now* why he'd started carrying packets of cookies around with him. It was a lot less painful to carry around a few cookies than it was to regrow lips and nails.

So, there was a moment, as he had hoped, when the Salamander had to feed before it could take over the boy, a moment when it was in the halfworld. Perhaps because there was no longer anyone who knew the summoning spell it could no longer enter the material world directly. In the spirit world of Underhill, it would be too powerful for him—in fact, it would probably be too powerful for anyone but a major mage, like Keighvin Silverhair or Gundar. In the material world, it would not only have the powers it possessed—fairly formidable ones—but it would have command of all of Brother Joseph's gun-toting ruffians.

But in the halfworld it was vulnerable. In fact, if he could *keep* it in the halfworld, blocked from power, it would probably starve away to a point where he could bottle it back into the flagstaff permanently.

:Sarah, can you protect Jamie from the thing if I keep it away from his body?: he asked. *:I promise I'll keep Jamie strong enough that the thing can't feed on him, but I need you to keep him safe from it.:*

:How?: she asked, promptly. *:I will if I can, but how?:*

Now he hesitated. *:The Salamander—the monster—can't kill you. It can hurt you, but it can't kill you. If you keep between it and Jamie, you can keep him safe—:*

:But it might hurt me?: She tossed her head defiantly. *:Well, maybe I can hurt it, too! And I will if I get the chance! Besides, Jamie hurts a whole lot worse than me.:*

:Sarah—: he hesitated again, deeply moved by her bravery. *:Sarah, you are the best friend anyone could ask for. I think you're pretty terrific.:*

The hazy form flushed a pleased, pale rose color. *:They're gonna start the Praise Meeting pretty soon,:* she warned. *:If you're gonna sneak in there, you'd better do it now.:*

:Thanks, I will.: He uncurled, slowly, flexing his muscles to loosen them. *:See you there?:*

There was a hint of childish giggle, and a cool breath

of scent, like baby powder; the glow bent forward and brushed his cheek—

—like a little girl's kiss.

Then she was gone.

The room where the Praise Meeting was held had been constructed rather oddly. There were places, little niches, behind the red velvet curtains covering the back wall where a man could easily stand concealed and no one in the audience (or even on the stage for that matter) would know he was there. Al wasn't quite sure what they were there for. Were they some construction anomaly, an accident of building the place underground?

Probably not, he decided. The niches were too regular and spaced too evenly. They were probably there on purpose, places where helpers could be concealed to aid in stage magic tricks in case the "channeling" ever failed.

Or maybe they were there to hold backup guards in case the loyalty of any of the current guards ever came into question.

Whatever, Al was grateful that they were there, although his hiding place was so near to the Salamander's flagpole that he was nauseated. He managed to slip into place without attracting its attention and concentrated on making himself invisible to the arcane senses, as the first of the Chosen Ones began to trickle into the hall, avid to get good seats in the front row.

He couldn't see much; his hiding place was directly behind the chair he suspected they would use for Jamie, and he didn't want to chance attracting mundane attention by making the curtains move. But his hyper-acute hearing allowed him to pick up good portions of the conversation going on out in the audience, and the gist of it was that something special was supposed to happen at the channeling tonight. Brother Joseph had promised something really spectacular.

And—so one rumor went—the Guard had been placed on special alert. That rumor hinted that a confrontation with secular authorities was about to take place.

"Well, if they want a war, we'll show those ungodly

bastards what it means to take on the Lord's Finest!" said one voice loudly, slurred a little with drink.

Al felt a chill of dread settling into the pit of his stomach. *A war—*

"Those godless bastards think they can come in here with the Red Army and march all over us! They think we'll lie right down, or maybe poison ourselves like Jim Jones' losers!" someone answered him, just as belligerently. "Well, they'll find out they haven't got the Lambs of God to deal with, they've got the Lions! When they come in, we'll be ready!"

This could only mean one thing. The Salamander *knew* about the plans to attack the compound, and just as he had feared, it had passed the warning on to Brother Joseph. But did it know when the raid would start? *Blessed Danaa—could it be tonight?*

Before he could even begin to add *that* to his calculations, the noise of a considerable crowd arriving and the sounds of boots marching up to the stage made any other considerations secondary in importance. He sensed the Salamander's rising excitement and knew by that sign that Brother Joseph had arrived to get the evening's spectacle underway.

He tensed and readied his first weapon of the night.

There was the scuffling of feet, and the sounds of two people doing something just in front of his position. He guessed that they were binding Jamie down in the chair, using the canvas straps he'd noted. That was all right; when the time came, those straps might just as well not be there for all that they were going to stop him.

Suddenly lights came on, penetrating even the thick velvet of the curtains, and the crowd noise faded to nothing but a cough or two.

"My brothers and sisters, I am here tonight to give you news both grave and glorious." The voice rang out over the PA system, but from the timbre, Al sensed that even if Brother Joseph had not had the benefit of electronic amplification, his voice would *still* have resonated imposingly over his flock. The man might not be a *trained* speaker, but he was a practiced one.

"The time the Holy Fire has warned us of is at hand!

The time when the evils of all men shall be turned against us is near! Even now, the Forces of Darkness ready their men—and yes, brothers and sisters, I do not speak merely of the demons that have infested even my own son and sent him running to betray us to the ungodly!"

There was a collective gasp at that, as if the news of Joe's defection came as a surprise to most of Brother Joseph's followers.

"No, my Chosen Ones, I speak of men, men and machines—armed as we are armed with guns and bullets— but they are not armored as we are armored, with the strength of the Righteous and the Armor of the Lord! Say Halleluia!"

A faltering echo of "Halleluia," answered him. Evidently the arrogant, belligerent attitude of those two early arrivals was not shared by the majority of the congregation. But Brother Joseph did not seem in the least disturbed by the lackadaisical response.

"Yes, they plan to fall upon us, like wolves upon the sheep!" he continued. *"But they do not know that the Holy Fire has warned us, even as the Virgin was warned to flee into Egypt, even as Lot was warned of the destruction of Sodom and Gomorrah! Say Halleluia!"*

This time the chorus took on a little more strength. And it was very nearly time for Al to think about launching his first attack.

"Yea, and the Holy Fire will tell us all, tonight, the time when the Army of Sin will seek to destroy the Holy! The Holy Fire will do more than that, I tell you! Tonight, the Holy Fire will take shape and walk among us, even as Christ Jesus took form and walked among His Apostles when He had risen! Say Halleluia!"

This time the shout of "Halleluia!" was enough to make the floor vibrate under Al's feet.

"The Holy Fire will lead us to victory! The Holy Fire will be our guide and our General! The form of this boy will be transformed into the Chariot of God, the vehicle for the Voice of God and the Sword of the Almighty! Say Halleluia, thank you Jesus!"

Cacophony ensued, and Al sensed that Brother Joseph

was about to turn the energy of the crowd from positive to negative.

"And who are these Godless Enemies?" Brother Joseph asked.

The response was a roar in which Alinor picked out the words "Jew," "Communist," "Liberal," and "Satanist," as the most frequent.

"And what do we do about them?"

Someone started a chant of "Kill, kill, kill," which was quickly picked up by the rest, until the entire room—probably the entire building—resonated with it. The energy coming from them made Alinor shudder, even though he was shielded from most of it.

And the Salamander was—literally—eating it up. Al sensed that the creature was prying open its prison from within. Like a man forcing a door open against a heavy spring.

He's forcing it open against the binding spell, Al decided. *He needs the energy of the crowd to do it, as I thought.*

He waited, as the Salamander slowly forced its way out of its prison, opening a doorway into the halfworld, bit by bit, until it stood free in the halfworld and moved away from the flagpole—

:Now, Sarah!: Al "shouted," and cast the spell that permitted him to "step" out of the physical world into the halfworld. He placed himself squarely between the Salamander and its home, before the creature was even aware that he was there. As he got into place and launched a levin-bolt at the creature, Sarah flung herself between the Salamander and Jamie, covering him with her own insubstantial body.

The Salamander saw her just as Al's levin-bolt struck it from behind. It turned—its eyes were pits of fire, and its black body hunched as it snarled with rage and prepared to attack—

And Alinor cast the second spell he had readied. The one that reinforced Sarah's protections, bolstering her powers—sealing Jamie away from its reach.

As the Salamander lunged for him, he cast his third spell—reaching the absolute limits of his ability as a mage—and eluded it by a hair, stepping out of the halfworld and back into his hiding place behind the curtains, with scarcely a ripple in the cloth to mark his movement.

Weakness flooded through him, but he dared not pause, not even for a moment. Timing—that was going to be all of it.

Outside the curtains, Brother Joseph had no idea that anything was going wrong.

He was about to find out differently.

Thank Danaa this isn't spell-casting as such—The thought was fleeting; hardly noted as Al attacked the breaker boxes, fusing everything in sight, so that nothing would protect the lines beyond, and surging every circuit, every wire—

A full lightning strike couldn't have wreaked more havoc. Every bulb in the hall exploded in a shower of sparks—electricity arced from raw sockets and dozens of fires burst into existence as wires shorted out. The Salamander's energy-source fragmented as the crowd itself fragmented into a chaos of screaming, frightened humans, each one clawing for an exit and paying no attention to anything else. Now they showed their true colors, panicking, trampling over each other, ruled only by fear; a selfish fear that cried out from each wizened little soul that *he* was more important than anyone else here, that *he* should be saved—

Brother Joseph screamed at them, howled orders at them, but the sound system had died a fiery death with the first surge, and not even he could shout loud enough to be heard over the screams of his congregation.

Alinor took advantage of the chaos to dash aside the curtains and fling himself at Jamie's chair, pulling out the only physical weapon he'd brought with him, a silver-bladed knife. Jamie's guards had been the first to flee, and Brother Joseph was temporarily paying no attention to anything behind him. Alinor slashed through the straps holding Jamie to the chair; the boy started at the first touch, then stared at his rescuer in numb surprise. Not that Al blamed him; he wasn't wasting any energy on a disguising illusion.

"Sarah sent me," he said in the boy's ear, as he slashed the last of the bonds. He glanced briefly into the halfworld; with no energy-source to help it, with Sarah and Alinor protecting the boy in the halfworld and the physical world, there was only one logical place for the Salamander to go—back into its prison.

And once there, Alinor could see it got no further chance to escape until he delivered it to a greater mage than he; one who could seal it there for all time.

The Salamander had other ideas.

It shrank away from Sarah, the child-spirit incandescent with a cool power far beyond anything that Alinor had sent her, standing between it and its prey like an avenging angel. It didn't even try to confront her—but instead of leaping for the protection of its prison-home, it turned, snarling, and leapt in another direction entirely.

Straight for Jamie's father.

Alinor snatched the boy up and ran with him as the Salamander made brutal contact and the drunkard's face and body convulsed. Where the Salamander had found the energy to make the leap into an unprepared, unsuitable body, Al didn't know—but he had to get Jamie away, and now, before anything else happened. Once Jamie was safe—

The fires were spreading; one whole corner of the hall was ablaze, giving more than enough light for Al to see his way to the exit with Jamie. He jumped over fallen chairs, kicking others out of the way, as he bullied his way through confused and terrified humans to the door that led to the outside corridor.

But suddenly someone blocked his path, deliberately. A man with a shaven head, in the Chosen Ones' uniform, stood in an attack position and brandished an enormous, unwieldy knife at him, blocking his way.

The man Al cared nothing for. His weapon, however—
Cold Iron—

Al acted instinctively, without thinking, lashing out with his mind and throwing an illusion of nightmares straight into the man's thoughts, bargaining that he might be marginally sensitive. It worked better than he could have hoped, sending the man screaming to the ground, clutching at his head, howling that his brain was being eaten by serpents.

Alinor kicked him in the side as he passed, to ensure that he did not follow, felt the crunch of broken bones beneath his heel, and ran on.

He shoved his way through the last of the panicked Chosen Ones—old people, mostly, too frightened and bewildered to know where to go—but once he was out in the corridor leading to the bunker entrance he met with a new tide of humans, this time pushing and shoving their way *into* the depths of the underground building.

What—

The answer came with the muffled, staccato *crack* of automatic weapons' fire just beyond the entrance. He shoved his way into the middle of the corridor just as an explosion blew the doors off the hinges and deafened him.

The people at the farthest end of the tunnel were flung into the air, backlit by the fires outside; they flew at him and hit the ground, in a curious time-dilation slow-motion. Those nearest him cowered away, hiding their faces in their arms. Jamie started and began shaking, but neither cried out nor hid his face.

The raid—great Danaa, they've started the raid—

His ears weren't working right, though he doubted the humans could hear anything at all. Explosions and the sound of gunfire came to him muffled, as if his head was bracket in pillows. He held the boy to his chest and forced his way through the crowd; it thinned quickly as noncombatants fled into the depths of the bunker.

He burst out into a scene straight from a war movie.

Fires roared everywhere; helicopters touched down and disgorged troops wearing SWAT team, DEA and FBI vests, who poured from the hatches and took cover. *They* didn't seem to be firing until they had sure targets; all the random gunfire was coming from sandbagged gun emplacements and the weaponry of the Guard, Junior and Senior.

One of the helicopters hovered overhead, flooding the area with light from a rack of lamps attached on the side. And in the light, Al caught a flash of familiar color—something that didn't belong in this chaos of camouflage and khaki.

A red jumpsuit.

Bob!

The mechanic wasn't that far away, thank the gods. He dashed across the open space between himself and the chopper, praying that the invaders would see he was carrying a child and that he was unarmed, and would hold their fire. Bob recognized him as he was halfway across and ran to meet him. He thrust the child into Bob's arms before the human could get a word out.

"Get him out of here!" Al shouted—and before Bob could grab his arm, he turned and ran back in the direction he had come.

He had unfinished business to attend to.

But the unfinished business was coming to him.

He sensed his enemy's approach before he saw it—then saw, as the Salamander emerged, that his enemies were two, not one. Jamie's father emerged from the mouth of the bunker and beside him was Brother Joseph with something long and sharp in his hands. The drunk's expression had completely changed, his eyes pits of fire, his face no longer remotely human.

So much for James Chase. He was half brain-dead already, from the alcohol; it must have been easy for the Salamander to take him.

The preacher spotted Al first and pointed, his mouth opening in a shout Al couldn't hear. But the Salamander did; its mouth twisted in a snarl, and it made a lashing motion with its arms—

And the razor-wire surrounding the compound came to life, writhing against its supports, trying to reach Alinor. He backpedaled into the temporary safety of a helicopter, but the stuff was still coming, and if it bound him—

A hellish noise right beside him pounded him into the dirt, as the door-gunner in the chopper let loose a barrage against a trio of gunmen that caught Jim Chase and cut him in half. Brother Joseph must have seen the gunner take aim; he hit the dirt in time to save himself, but Jamie's father had only seconds to live—

Seconds were enough for the Salamander.

As another munitions dump exploded on the far side of the compound, light flared and danced around the two men, one dying, one alive—and when it faded, the Salamander glared at Al from out of Brother Joseph's eyes.

The man's eyes swept the space between them and found him, stabbed him. This time Alinor did not run from the challenge. He faced it; walked slowly toward it, oblivious to the gunfire around him, to the explosions as one of the munitions dumps went up in the near distance, a giant blossom of orange flame. None of that could touch him now—not in this moment. There was only one enemy that mattered. The Salamander: ancient as he, perhaps more so—and his enemy since the moment he'd first seen it.

:Al!: Sarah's voice rang inside his head, although he didn't sense her anywhere in the chaos. *:Jamie's safe!:*

That was all he needed. There was one thing he had not yet tried with the beast to defeat it—and it was now, or see the thing loose in the world again, jumping from host to host like any parasite, bringing rage and chaos wherever it went. This fragile world could bear no more of that—

The monster was hanging back for some reason—

Waiting for more power?

Well, then, he'd give it power. He'd cram power down the damned thing's throat until it choked!

He rushed it; the monster wasn't expecting *that* and tried to elude him, but he grappled with it. It reverted to its old ways and tried to manipulate him as it manipulated the humans, but this time instead of fighting it, Al let it happen. The Salamander infused him with anger, but it could not direct that anger, and in a sudden surge of rage-born strength, Al tore the flagpole from its hands.

And with the pole in his hands—he *knew* what it was. Not just a prison, but a *ground*, a focal point for the Salamander's hold on the physical world.

And any ground could be shorted out.

I've learned how electricity works, and magic and electricity are related in every important way. Only you don't know that, do you, monster? Come on, give me all you've got, you're getting it back!

Again, he did not think, he simply acted; linking into every power source available to him, whether the physical fire, the arcing electrical current—

:Here!: Sarah cried, and a new source of power surged

into him, a power so pure, clean, and strong he did not want to think of what its source might be—

He plunged the staff into the Salamander's chest—and the creature laughed, for how could he expect to harm it with its own ground? He held to his end of the flagpole as the Salamander closed both hands about the other end and opened itself up to drain him of power.

And the moment it opened itself, Alinor leaped back and poured every bit of power he had available *into* it.

The staff shattered as the massed electricity of the compound's power grid arced into it; the Salamander convulsed, its mouth gaping in surprise, and Al loosed the magical power Sarah was channeling into the raw wound.

Its mouth formed the word "No!" but it never got a chance to utter it. Its eyes glared like a fire's last glowing coal, defiant before its death, and between one breath and the next—it vaporized.

Brother Joseph fell to the ground, hardly recognizable as human, a burnt and twisted human cinder. The last charred sliver of the staff dropped beside him.

As Al stood there numbly, a bullet ricocheted off the building nearest him and buzzed past his ear, startling him into life. He glanced around; the Good Guys seemed to be winning, but there was no reason why *he* had to stay around to help—

A hint of movement on the other side of the fence gave him enough warning to ready himself; in the next moment, Andur launched himself over the tangle of wire and slid to a halt beside him. He grabbed a double-handful of mane and hauled himself aboard as another bullet buzzed by, much too close for comfort. He watched a SWAT officer level a pistol at him, then lower it, amazed—then Andur was off like a shadow beneath the moon, leaving the noises and fire far behind. . . .

All Al really wanted to do was get back and into a bed, any bed—but he reached back and touched one mind in all the chaos.

I was never there. You never saw me. Bob ran in and rescued you. It was all Bob. . . .

Then he allowed himself to slump over Andur's neck.

❖   ❖   ❖

"Hey, Norris!"

Alinor looked up from beneath the hood of the car to see one of the Firestone boys waving at him.

"Yeah?" he said, standing up and wiping his hands on a rag. "What's up?"

"There's a cop here, he's looking for a mech named Al. Big blond guy, says he wears black a lot. Know anybody like that?" The Firestone pitman eyed Al's scarlet Nomex jumpsuit and raven hair with amusement.

"Not around here," Al said truthfully. "The head of Fairgrove looks like that, but he never leaves Savannah." *And that'll teach you for not answering my aid-calls, Keighvin Silverhair.*

"Well, he's with Bob, so I guess it must be something about the raid on those fundie nuts they pulled the other night." His curiosity satisfied, the pitman turned back to his stack of tires, and Al returned to his engine. He was paying only scant attention to it, however; most of his attention was taken up with the four humans heading for the pits.

Frank Casey didn't know it, but the moment he'd passed out of Alinor's sight, Al's appearance and name had been altered. And in the stories he'd told the rest of the crews, the actions that should have been ascribed to Al had mostly been attached to Bob—with the exception of those few that could not logically have been transferred. *Those* Al left alone, taking on a new persona, entirely, of Norris Alison. The story was that Al had gotten into the Chosen Ones' compound and sabotaged their electrical system, giving the impromptu army good cover for their invasion. Then he had somehow slipped past the sentries outside and had vanished.

Bob's *other* partner, the sable-haired "Norris," had shown up the next morning, after Bob supposedly called for extra help on "Al's" disappearance.

Cindy's memories had been altered, though not without much misgiving on Al's part. He hated to do it, but the memory of her discovery of Alinor's species had been temporarily blocked. The not-so-surprising result was that her growing emotional attachments to both Al and Bob had been resolved into a very significant attachment to Bob alone. And now that Bob was the sole rescuer of her child—

Al sighed. *Well, he certainly seems to be enjoying his new status.* His loss was Bob's gain . . . and Cindy *was* mortal; he was her kind. There would be no conflict there.

If anything more permanent ever comes of this, he promised himself, *I'll take the block off her real memories. By then she'll have learned about us all over again, and she'll know why I had to take them.*

Frank Casey wore the look of a very frustrated man as he searched pit row for someone who didn't exist. Finally he gave up and allowed Bob to bring them all over to the Firestone pit for a cold drink.

Al waited while Bob fished soft drinks out of the cooler, watching Jamie out of the corner of his eye. This was the boy's first day out of the hospital, and although he was still painfully thin, he had some of a child's proper liveliness back. When they had all been served, he stood up and sauntered over himself, pulling out a Gatorade before turning to face the others.

"Miz Chase," he said, tugging the brim of his cap. "Well, so this is the little guy, hmm?"

Cindy nodded, and Jamie peered up at him, a little frown line between his eyebrows, as if he was trying to see something and having trouble doing so.

"I don't know if Bob told you, but we're all through here after the race tomorrow. We'll be packing up and heading back. Did you have any plans?" Then, before she could react to what could only be bad news, he added, "You're welcome to come along, of course, if you've nowhere you need to go. We can tow your car, and the boy can sleep or play in the RV. You, well, we could use another driver to switch off with. Our boss, Kevin—well, he might maybe need another hand in the office. If he don't, likely one of the test drivers can dig up a job. Tannim's got a thumb in about everything."

She hesitated for only a moment before saying, with a shy glance at Bob, "If you really don't mind, I think I'd like that. There isn't that much for me in Atlanta except the house—"

"Can always sell it," he suggested.

Then he turned away as if he had lost interest in the conversation, pausing only long enough to drop his race-cap over Jamie's head. The boy lit up with a smile that rivaled the Oklahoma sun and ran to his mother.

The quartet drifted away after a final futile effort to find "Al," and before too very long, the rest of the crew departed in search of dinner and a nap before the long night to come of last-minute race-preps. The only sounds in the pit were those of reggae on a distant radio, cooling metal, an errant breeze—

But suddenly Al had the feeling that he was being watched.

He turned abruptly.

For a moment there was nothing behind him at all—then, there was a stirring in the air, a glimmer—and there was Sarah, watching him with a serious look on her face.

:I've come to say good-bye,: she said solemnly. *:Jamie doesn't need me, and all the Chosen Ones are in jail, so I have to go.:*

He nodded gravely. "I understand," he told her. "You were a very brave fighter out there, you know. A true warrior. I was proud to be on your side."

She looked wistfully at him. *:You're nice,:* she said. *:I wish I could say good-bye right.:*

It might have been that exposure to the Salamander made him more sensitive; it might simply have been that her lonely expression told him everything he needed to know about what she meant by "saying good-bye right."

Well, after all, he *was* one of the Folk.

He triggered the spell and moved into the halfworld with her.

She clapped both her hands to her mouth in surprise and delight. *:Oh!:* she exclaimed—and then she ran to him.

He held out his arms and caught her, holding her, hugging her for a long, timeless moment, trying to make up for all the hugs that she had never gotten. He thought she might be crying; when she pulled away, wiping away tears, he came near to tears himself.

:I have to go,: she said. *:I love you.:*

She faded away, or rather, faded *into* something, into a softer, gentle version of that blinding Power she had been linked with when she protected Jamie and helped him. Alinor wasn't certain he could put a name to that Power. He wasn't certain that he needed to.

"I love you, too, Sarah," he replied, as the last wisp of her melted away.

He waited a moment longer, smiling in the last light of her passing until he was alone in the halfworld, and finally sighed and triggered the magic to take him back.

With his feet firmly planted on mortal cement, he pulled the windblown hair from his face, packed up his tool kit and headed back to the RV.

After all, there was a race left to run.

When the
Bough Breaks

CHAPTER ONE

Maclyn, Knight of the High Court of Elfhame Outremer, leaned forward over the steering wheel of his classic '57 Chevy and flicked on the radio. Q-103 FM was playing two-fer-Tuesdays and had just finished up a set by Fleetwood Mac. The DJ cut into the fadeout, chattering, "Coming up for all you April Fools—two-fers by Phil Collins, The Beatles, and Grim Reaper. But first . . . a Guns N' Roses two-fer. . . ."

"Aw Gawd, not Guns N' Roses. If I want to listen to a garage band, I'll find a good one. . . ." The engine growled and downshifted as his convertible pulled out of the secluded dirt road into traffic. The driver of a late-model Ford Taurus glanced over at them and did a classic double-take, jerking her head around to stare. Mac flashed a grin in her direction, and she waved before driving on.

His elvensteed, currently taking the form of a Palomino-gold '57 Chevy convertible with cream trim, was a traffic stopper. Rhellen didn't cause quite the disruption to traffic he would have in his regular form, Mac reflected, but he was still impressive. And women loved him.

With any luck, he would impress the socks off of Lianne McCormick.

Mac pushed his troubles with the Seleighe Court out

351

of his mind. There would be time to deal with Felouen and her demands. The present, as far as he was concerned, wasn't the time.

"Okay, Rhellen, let's make some time," he told the car. "Tonight—we *party!*"

The elvensteed growled affirmation and accelerated past two Fayetteville city policemen and one North Carolina Highway Patrol trooper, hitting seventy-five without causing so much as a chirp on their radar.

With Rhellen in full charge, Mac made it to Lianne's apartment complex running seemingly just under Mach One. *She*, the current human lady of his interest, if not his dreams, was sitting on the deck of her apartment grading papers, a tiny frown of concentration on her face. He pulled up silently and vaulted out of the car in equal silence, which gave him a chance to admire her before she spotted him. She was slender, with short, soft chestnut hair, deep blue eyes and pale, flawless skin—she had the fragile, ethereal look frequently attributed to one of his own people. She had, too, the blazing energy of a human—she was, he thought, one of the delicate mayflies of the sentient world.

Like all humans.

Here today and gone tomorrow. He felt a moment of poignant loss and suppressed it. *But today will be a lot of fun, anyway.*

He intentionally crunched some gravel on the walk to let her know he was there.

She looked up, and her face lit with an amazingly sweet smile. "Hey!" she said. "Glad you made it. I was beginning to think you'd changed your mind. Or come to your senses or something." She grinned when she said that, but Mac felt the pain of old rejection masked in her voice.

"Stand up a gorgeous gal like you?" he asked. "Not in this lifetime."

She chuckled and arched an eyebrow. "Yeah, yeah—sure, sure. So are we going to go someplace, or am I going to spend the rest of the evening checking math tests?"

He smirked. "You won't even remember what math tests are."

"I could live with that." She shoved her papers inside the front door of her apartment and locked it. "Let's go."

He showed her to the Chevy, and waited for her eyes to light up. Which they did, as predicted.

"Wow!" she whispered, and ran her hand slowly along one gleaming fender. "What a beauty. I've never seen one this color—or in such perfect condition."

Mac felt Rhellen's pleasure and grinned. "Custom job. I'm pretty proud of him."

"I'll bet." A puzzled expression crossed her face. "Him?" she asked. "I've never heard anyone refer to a car as *him* before."

"In this case, it's appropriate," Mac assured her.

Lianne stood back and crossed her arms over her chest. She tipped her head to one side and studied the car. She went down on one knee and carefully examined the undercarriage. Finally she nodded. "You're right. Definitely a him."

He'll love you for that, Mac thought. *I think, lady, that you've just won yourself a friend.*

Rhellen preened under all the attention.

"By the way," she said, as she climbed into the passenger's side, "you haven't forgotten the field trip tomorrow, have you? I hope you're ready for it; you're going to need all the help you can get."

He laughed. "Forgotten, no. Worried? Also no. What's to worry about a herd of kids who're probably car-crazy to begin with? It'll be a snap."

She didn't reply; just smiled, the kind of enigmatic smile found on the Mona Lisa. The smile that said—"I know something you don't know, but you're going to have to find out for yourself."

The kind of smile his mother Dierdre would give him—

For a moment, he was taken aback by it, enough for a nagging little worry to intrude.

Then he dismissed it. What could this mere human know that he, with all his centuries, didn't? Ridiculous. He'd enthrall her little flock, dazzle her with his cleverness, and it would all be a pleasant day for everyone concerned.

Right now, he would concern himself with *tonight.* Tomorrow was not worth even thinking about. . . .

❖   ❖   ❖

Looks like the troops have arrived. "Hey, beautiful!" Mac shouted across the parking lot at Lianne as she jumped out of the first of the two bright yellow school buses to arrive at Fayetteville International Speedway. "What's a babe like you doing in a place like this? Sweetheart, where have you been all my life? Come, let me take you to the Casbah, where we will make beautiful music together. We will make lo—"

She made a shushing motion at Mac and blushed. "Like tigers," he finished. Neither the gesture nor the blush escaped the noisy herd of children who followed her out of the bus.

"O-o-o-ooh!" yelled one boy. "Miss McCormick has a boyfriend!"

"Miss McCormick has a boyfriend," someone else repeated.

A chant started. "Miss McCormick has a boyfriend—Miss McCormick has a boyfriend . . . ."

Maclyn regretted his impulsive teasing. He had obviously just made things difficult for her, and he suspected she didn't appreciate the attention she was getting.

A teacher from one of the other buses, a good-looking woman in her mid-thirties, stared at him curiously, then walked over and whispered something to the beleaguered Lianne. Lianne nodded slowly, and the other woman raised an eyebrow. She gave Mac an appreciative once-over as she returned to her own flock of children.

He was used to getting those calculating looks from women. Usually, he enjoyed them. This time, for some reason, he felt embarrassed.

Lianne got her class lined up and led them across the pavement toward him. She sent him a killing glare as she and the rowdy fifth-graders advanced.

"Lianne, I'm sorry. I didn't realize that they would do that," he said.

"I'll bet." The kids behind her had taken up a whispered refrain of "Miss McCormick sitting in a tree, K-I-S-S-I-N-G," and Lianne did not look mollified in the least by his apology. "The only way you wouldn't have known they would do that is if you'd never been a kid in the fifth grade before."

And there, he thought, *you have it. I haven't* ever *been in the fifth grade. So how was I supposed to know? It's not my fault your class is a mob of little barbarians. I'm innocent—this time. Unfortunately, there is no way in the world that I could convince you of that without blowing my cover.*

He smiled at her, shrugged helplessly, and tried to look boyishly ingenuous. "What can I say?" he asked. And then, in a louder voice that carried to the last kid in the back of the last line, Mac introduced himself to the class. "Hi. I'm Mac Lynn, and I drive race cars."

:Och, and he drives the maidens wild, he does, too!: came an impish, entirely uninvited thread of Mindspeech. *:You have only to ask him, and he'll tell ye so!:*

:Mother!: he snapped, trying to regain his aplomb.

:So gallant, so regal, so handsome. And so modest he is—his hat sometimes even fits him these days! Why, he drives race cars, does he? Sure and what a fine man he must be!:

:MOTHER!:

Despite Dierdre's teasing, it was a good opening line. The kids calmed down and studied him, checking, he suspected, to see if they recognized him from television.

Mac didn't mind. It wasn't likely that they would, but the moment of their uncertainty would buy him their attention. He could take it from there. He drew on his years of racing experience, and with purely elvish fervor, translated his enthusiasm into terms that drew the sixty-plus fifth-graders in front of him wholeheartedly into the world he loved.

"What do you watch on television?"

Mac was answered by a barrage of titles—almost all of them cop shows or adventure cartoons. "See, now, on all of those shows, you get to watch car-chases, or the heroes drive hot cars. Think of Don Johnson without the Daytona, or Magnum without the red Ferrari—it just doesn't work, right? Hey, your folks drive cars, you see ads on TV, there are roads practically everywhere—people are in love with cars. Some of us love 'em so much we want to drive 'em for a living. Think any of you would like to do that?"

A chorus of "Yeah!" and "Sure!" came back at him.

They were in his pocket. It was time to get them moving—show them the sights. He asked them, "So . . . . do you want to go look at some race cars, or what?"

They cheered.

Nice kids, he thought. *I'm glad I decided to do this.*

Gruesome bunch of larvae, Mac thought. He'd spent the better part of two hours showing the kids garages and pits, the medevac helicopter, the infield and starter's tower, and introducing them to mechanics and crew chiefs and various race drivers. Including his mother.

They'd enjoyed his mother, who just happened to be his crew chief. D.D. Reed (not as close to Dierdre as Mac Lynn was to Maclyn, but it would do) was ninety-five pounds of lightning and thunder, all wrapped up in one coveralled, pony-tailed, hellcat package. She took no guff from anyone and handed out twice the grief he ever gave *her*. She also looked half his age.

She gave him lip mental *and* audible, the mental over Lianne and his ego, the audible over everything else—much to the entertainment of the rest of the pit crews: his, and everyone else's within hearing. His crew knew the secret, of course, and thought it hilarious. Of the rest, there were a few more SERRA mages nearby that had a notion—and to those left, it was *still* funny to hear a "girl" giving hotshot Mac Lynn a hard time. Those who couldn't "hear" the telepathic comments were very nearly as amused as those who could.

The kids—*little sadists*—had loved it.

He'd also spent the better part of two hours watching them stick chewing gum on walls and under ledges when they thought no one was looking, kick each other in the shins, poke and prod each other and then stare off innocently into space when someone screeched. When he'd joked that some cars were held together with bubble-gum, one kid actually, sincerely, offered him his. Freshly chewed. Mac couldn't believe it.

He had no idea how many lug-nuts would be missing by day's end. He'd listened to their gross jokes. He'd answered their weird questions. He'd had more than enough. Finally, it was time to sit down on the small stands and watch the drivers speeding alone around the track in the time trials.

Mac was ready for the break. As kids wiggled and squealed and squirmed and passed notes and stuffed paper down each other's shirts, he knew a moment of sheer gratitude that he had been spared the indignity of fifth grade.

:They'd not have had you. You were worse than any of them.:

He sighed. *:Thank you, Mother.:*

His mother might have been right, he reflected. Nevertheless, he felt admiration for the guts of the teacher who had to put up with this sort of nonsense on a regular basis. He rolled his eyes and grinned over the kids' heads at Lianne.

She raised her eyebrows in a mime of disbelief at her class's behavior and grinned back.

Cars roared around the track, and from their front-row seats in the pits, the smell of oil, gasoline, exhaust, and hot rubber numbed the nose while the howling of engines numbed the mind. The few fans in the stands screamed and cheered at their favorites, as if by sheer volume they could push the drivers to better times. The palpable electricity in the atmosphere always got to Mac—that excitement was what had originally pulled him out of the timeless magic of Underhill and into the very human world of auto racing.

In between runs, the kids asked *more* questions.

One stub-nosed kid with bright brown eyes waved his hand in the air at Mac and bounced up and down on his bleacher seat until Mac was sure it was going to have a permanent bow in it. "Yes?" he asked warily. He'd already had more than a taste of what fifth grade boys considered reasonable to ask.

"I want to drive a race car when I get out of school, but Mom and Dad say I have to go to college. Did you have to go to college?"

That question seemed pretty harmless.

Lianne, however, gave Mac a warning look.

Oh, yeah. College. That great baby-sitter of the post-adolescent masses. Naturally Lianne is going to want me to be strongly in favor of it.

Mac shrugged helplessly. "No. I didn't go to college, but I wish I had." It was an easy lie. With luck it would mollify Lianne. "A college education is a good idea. If nothing else, it will give you something to fall back on if racing doesn't work out."

The look in her eyes when he said that, though, made him think he should have quit with a simple no.

And just then, D.D. popped up. "Mac doesn't need college," she said, with a sly look and a toss of her blond ponytail that told him she was going to zing him again. "He doesn't even need a brain; he never uses the itty-bitty one he's got. He has the rest of us to think for him. We don't believe in overstressing anything that weak. Now *me*, I needed every mechanical engineering and physics course I could cram."

The kid looked confused. "Why?" he asked. "You're just a mechanic."

D.D. cast her bright green eyes up to the sky. "Gloriosky. *Just* a mechanic? Sweetie-pie, I not only have to know *how* every part in that car works, I have to know *why*. This is leading-edge technology here; what we've got on our cars your daddy won't be able to buy for ten, maybe twenty years. There's no manual for what we're doing; we're working real automotive magic out there."

"I'll say," one of the crew called out. "And D.D.'s the great high wizard of Ah's. She can tell you what's wrong with an engine just by *listening* to it."

"And you don't get *that* kind of expertise working on a dune buggy in your back yard—right, Mac?" she finished triumphantly, and vanished back behind a stack of tires.

:There. Saved you again.:

With the sinking feeling that he was getting deeply mired in something he was never going to escape from, he sought a graceful out. A flash of deep blue on the track caught his eye and promised sudden salvation.

"Much as I hate to admit it, my crew chief's half right. Here's the other half. There's more to racing than driving fast—" he told them "—more even than winning races. Racing is a business. And it's a tough one. If you can't make that business pay off, you won't be racing." He waved over to the starting line. "Look at Number Fifty-eight, the car getting ready to start now. That's Keith Brightman. He's driving a '93 Lola Wombat right now. He owns it himself. He has an efficient crew and a talented mechanic, and he's a very good driver—but if he didn't know how to run a business, he wouldn't be able to race his own cars."

D.D. appeared from somewhere else. "And if he didn't know his engineering, he wouldn't be able to trouble-shoot his vehicle while he's driving it. Half the time he tells his crew what's wrong, which is a heckuva help, let me tell you, and more than Tom Cruise here can do."

She vanished again. Mac chose to ignore her.

"Keith is a good example of somebody who is doing what he wants to do because he has the smarts and the guts, and because he isn't afraid to work hard. If you want to be a driver, use him as your example."

"Does *he* have a college education?" the school-hater asked with a hopeful glance towards the deep-blue Wombat.

"You bet," Mac said. He'd picked Keith as his shining example of racetrack virtue for precisely that reason. It was going to pay off, too, he could tell. Lianne sent an appreciative glance in his direction. "College was where Keith learned about mechanical engineering, and probably learned how to run a business," he added. "And had fun doing it."

"*Brightman, K. Mech-E, Rose-Hulman Polytech, class of 1987, cum laude!*" screeched a voice that was getting tiresomely familiar, from just behind Mac.

The Wombat took off with a roar, and the questions stopped. The kids watched the car intently. Maclyn could tell they were impressed. Hell, he was impressed. More than it ever had before, the Wombat *moved*; Keith was putting on a real show. Mac could hear a difference in the engine, a rich, deep throb of power that grabbed deep in his gut and twisted; the rookie's mechanic had made an exotic modification somewhere. That damned Wombat was flying like it thought it was a fighter plane and had forgotten the ground.

What has Brightman done to that engine? Wonderful stuff, Mac mused. *Magic with gears and cylinders—and maybe something Mom can duplicate. I hope she's listening.*

:I am—what do you think I am, tone-deaf? I also happen

to be Watching it. Teach your grandmam to suck eggs, why don't you.:

Maclyn had to give the Wombat's crew credit. On a shoestring budget and what amounted to little more than native genius, they were putting themselves in a position to give the big boys a run for their money.

Mac's ears followed the car even after it was out of sight. *:He's taking seconds off of the best time we've had so far.:* Mac commented to his crew chief.

:I'm paying attention, Mac.: D.D. retorted. *:Unless someone else comes up with a miracle, he's just gotten the pole.:*

The car did a flawless lap and dove into the final curve as if it owned it—and there was a sudden hollow, popping sound. It wasn't much of a noise really, but Mac's throat tightened, and his mouth went dry. The sudden hush of the crowd in the stand across from the pits was the first indication of the seriousness of the problem—then the car became visible from the right side of the pits, and Mac saw a tiny trail of smoke and sparks that streamed out from beneath the front wheels.

D.D.'s voice was in his head, all humor gone. *:Sweet Daana—Mac, a control arm just sheared! The lad's going to lose her any second—:*

For one timeless instant, the car continued as though nothing was wrong, and then it seemed to bunch itself like a wild animal crouching for the attack. It swerved wildly to the left, then fishtailed back to the right, and in the middle of its rightward spin, collided with the outside wall. It rebounded and launched itself into the air, bounding end over end like a skier doing stunts off a ramp. The Lola disintegrated just as it was designed to, but in the direction it was heading, it was going to hit the low retaining wall in front of the pits nose-first at around a hundred miles per hour. And it was going to do it a mere twenty yards from sixty-plus school kids.

"No!" Mac heard someone bellow, and realized the voice was his own. *Gods and demons,* he thought. *Oh gods above—Keith isn't going to make it out of there, and we aren't going to make it out of here!*

A deep bass *whump* marked the car's impact. Bits of

car ricocheted back towards the crowd, and others came over the retaining wall; flames spurted from the engine pinwheeling across the asphalt. Screaming fans saw impending disaster and panicked. They jumped off the sides of the stands and tumbled to the ground, packing and running like frightened cattle in a slaughterhouse pen.

The roll-caged cockpit skidded upside-down in the middle of the track, trailing sparks. It followed the flaming engine unit as though they were strung together, its trajectory matching the engine's—one of the worst possible scenarios Mac could imagine.

They're built to come apart to save the driver, dammit! Mac thought in anguish, as he watched the cockpit collide with the engine right in front of the stands. Fuel spurted from the ruptured fuel-cell, torn open lengthwise, next to the limp driver. The spreading puddle of fuel inched nearer the shooting flames. *I can see the flames. Gods, I can see the flames—alcohol fuel should burn almost invisibly—this is even worse than it looks. Keith's gotta be dead by now.*

Mac could only watch numbly. His puny magics were useless here. From the paddock, vehicles were gunning to intercept the wreck before it had even stopped moving. He heard a metallic whine, building in pitch, as the track medevac helicopter started its engines. *Now the whole tank goes*, he thought. *We have to get the kids out of here—*

There was no way. Shrapnel would be filling the air in a second, and it would fall everywhere, even in the paddock. "Get them down beneath the seats," he shouted; he, Lianne, and the chaperons started pushing kids down.

He became aware of a tingling at the base of his skull. The hair on his arms was standing up—and he realized that he had first felt this sensation right after the car started to go out of control. His mind gave the sensation a name. *Psi. TK.*

D.D., the Healer, the Empath, Mindspoke with quiet amazement. *:No one has been hurt yet by the flying debris. The car hasn't exploded yet. It's coming from near you, Mac—but who's responsible? There isn't a SERRA Psi out here, and no elves but us, and none of the mages have the right spells. . . . :*

Somebody nearby was keeping the car from blowing.

Mac Looked around him. One fragile-looking little girl sat, transfixed, watching the disaster. Motionless, silent, unblinking, she could have been a statue of a fifth grader, except for the breeze that blew her wispy blond hair around her face and caused her plaid skirt to ripple around the tops of her white kneesocks.

And from her poured incredible power.

In the crowd across the track from the paddock, one woman ignored the people milling around her—seemed even to ignore the accident. She read the face of a meter whose needle was in the far right-hand side of the red zone; she wore a cool, satisfied smile. Then she locked long, perfectly manicured fingers around a voice-activated mini-recorder and whispered into it.

"The accident went off flawlessly—shouldn't be enough left of the car to prove sabotage. Rumors were right—definitely telekinetic activity here. Localized it to the pits across from where I'm standing, but too many people around to get a definite fix. TK is preventing the explosion of the car, though—bet anything on that—think one of the racing people must be our target. This explains why the Fayetteville track has such a good record, maybe. I'll try to move in for a closer read."

She stuffed the meter and the tape recorder, still on and ready, into her bag, and worked her way out of the crowd.

The fire crew sprayed foam on the blazing engine block and the spreading puddles of fuel; Heavy Rescue cut away bits of twisted metal. Mac stood transfixed, watching the kid who stared at the wreck.

:*Catch her before she leaves—I want to talk to her!*: D.D. ordered.

He agreed absently—then his attention was drawn to the racetrack, where one of the rescuers gave a triumphant shout.

They pulled Keith Brightman out of the car—and he stood on his own.

A number of things then happened at once. From their hiding place beside the stands, the crowd went wild. The rescuers and the young driver sprinted for the pits and the little cover they provided. Lianne noticed that one of her students was still in the path of potential danger, and Mac saw her pull the girl down behind the bleacher.

And that was when the fuel cell blew.

Shrapnel flew across the infield and into the pits. Mac winced at the sound of metal-on-metal as pieces of car went into the mesh that protected the stands. The crowd's cheers became terrified screams.

:Dammit!: Mac thought as he huddled for cover behind a stack of tires. *:The kid's got to be a line-of-sight TK. Lianne broke the contact when she moved the kid.:*

There was a pause. Then D.D. told him, *:I can still feel the child, Mac. She's controlling the shrapnel. And no one's been badly hurt yet.:*

Mac looked through the huddle of scared fifth-graders for the girl. Sure enough, she was peeking over the bleachers, still intent on the wreck.

The air cleared, and the crowd started climbing back into their seats. Several young soldiers on leave from Fort Bragg organized the mob of fans, then moved quickly through the crowd, looking for wounded. They escorted the three folks with small lacerations down to the infield medic.

There were no other injuries.

Down in the pit, Lianne McCormick and the other fifth-grade teachers efficiently rounded up their own crowd, herded them into a raggedy line, and marched them toward the exit.

"Lianne!" Mac bellowed. "Wait a minute!"

Lianne came back—the rest of the field trip contingent kept going. "We have to leave, Mac. This is the sort of thing parents have heart attacks over—we want to have the kids safely back to school before any footage shows up on a local newsbreak."

"But I really wanted to talk to—"

"Gotta go, Mac," Lianne interrupted. "See you soon?"

He forced a smile. "As soon as possible."

She hurried after her students.

Mac's watched his little TK trooping away, way to the back of the line—when, as if she felt his stare, she turned and looked directly at him—and the look in her eyes became one of startled recognition.

"Elf—" he read on her lips. "You're an elf—"

He nodded, staring past her young face into her old, old eyes.

:*My name is Maclyn of Elfhame Outremer. My mother Dierdre Brighthair and I need to talk with you.*:

She didn't respond to his Mindspoken request. She did, however, start to walk toward him—

And her face changed. Mac would have sworn that her eyes had been dark brown—but they weren't. They were light green. The appearance of age and wisdom, the look of recognition that had been in them, were gone. Instead, her face reflected pure terror. She wrapped her skinny arms around herself and stared at him in wide-eyed dismay. Then she fled. She disappeared into the crowd of kids, leaving Mac standing open-mouthed and bewildered.

:*Mother,*: he noted, :*That was, I believe, the strangest encounter I have ever had with a human being.*:

D.D. had witnessed the last part of the odd exchange, and for once she had no sharp comeback. She only nodded, and replied, :*Something is very wrong there, Mac. I don't know what it is, but there is something seriously wrong with that child.*:

CHAPTER TWO

Although he was attuned to his crew well enough that he would have *known* if any of them were hurt, Mac checked on them anyway. Everyone was fine, though one of the boys had sustained bloody knees from a slide across cement. D.D. was on the ground beside him, hands full of gauze, with a roll of adhesive tape in her mouth.

:If you don't hurry up, you're going to lose our TK:, D.D. said acidly, as he slouched against a tire-wall to watch her.

What was the rush? He knew where the child was. She wasn't going to escape them. *:She's in Lianne's class. I'll find her later, it's no big deal.:*

He felt his mother's impatience at that assumption, and if she'd been acidic before, her reply could have etched glass. *:I want to talk to her now, Maclyn. That makes it a "big deal.":*

The times Dierdre had taken that tone with him could be counted on both hands, with fingers left over. It instantly became a big deal for Mac. He hurried after the vanished fifth-graders, determined to hold up the buses long enough to borrow Lianne's TK student for a few minutes. Instead, he careened into a woman who'd been reaching to open the door Mac burst out of. She fell off her four-inch spike heels and landed on her rump on the cement.

"Why don't you watch where you're going, idiot!" she snapped.

She was gorgeous, in her early thirties, with porcelain-white skin and a flawless figure. She glared up a him through a tangle of waist-length red hair and snarled, "You could kill somebody that way."

Real red hair, too, he thought, distracted. *Not bottled.*

"I'm sorry," he said, and offered his hand. "I was trying to catch someone."

The woman was fidgeting with something in her purse—some sort of little black box. Suddenly she looked up, and seemed to actually *see* him—and her glare melted.

Eh?

"She isn't too bright if she didn't let you catch her," the redhead drawled. She gave him a slow, sensuous smile and extended her hand, allowing him to help her up, taking her time about it, too. She was slow to let go of his hand, holding onto it while she tested her ankles to make sure they still worked. Mac suspected that the little wiggles were also so that she could make sure he took a good look at her legs—which, painted into brown leather jeans, were admittedly worth looking at. She flipped her hair—he found himself thinking of it as The Hair—out of her face, and giggled.

"I suppose I'll survive." She looked up at him through her eyelashes. "You're one of the drivers, aren't you?"

Mac was wearing his Nomex suit. It was a bright red one. He might have had "RACECAR DRIVER" carved on his chest, and been a little more obvious, but he doubted it. He sighed and nodded. *Takes a real genius to figure that out,* he thought. *Lovely package, but I don't think there's anybody home inside the wrapper.*

He had lost interest in empty-headed humans a few hundred years before this one had been born. There was one advantage to the Folk; the rare cases with nothing between the ears but air tended to fall prey to Dreaming, which took them effectively out of circulation. "I'm glad you weren't hurt," he told her, doing his best to exude polite, *distant* sincerity. "I've got to run, though. I've got to catch a kid."

She pouted. She actually *pouted.* "If you wanted any of

the ones on those school buses, you're too late. They just pulled out."

"Damn!" Mac muttered aloud, without thinking.

She used his immobility as an excuse to come closer, and laid her hand on his arm. "What's wrong? They steal something?"

"No," he said shortly. "Hell—probably . . ." He shook his head, then looked down at her hand as if he was unpleasantly surprised to find it there.

She was observant enough to take the hint and removed it.

I know where to find the girl. And D.D. knows I can't outrun a bus. She should be reasonable. "It doesn't matter, really," he told the woman. "Sorry I ran over you."

"You're the best-looking thing to run over me all week." She flirted with her eyes shamelessly and giggled again, though she didn't make a second attempt to touch him.

The giggle grated on Mac's nerves. It sounded false— and anything that false made Mac very wary. It felt like— bait. And bait meant a trap.

And a trap meant that there was a lot more under The Hair than she was letting on.

"I'll let you get back to whatever you were doing," he said, taking a cautious step backwards.

"Oh, you don't need to leave. I was lookin' for you anyway . . . Mr. Lynn." She looked at him with those big blue eyes, and leaned towards him, exuding a sweet sexuality.

That's bait, all right. Wonder how many poor fools took it?

He took another step backwards; she was oblivious to his sensitive nerves. "I . . . write—free-lance, y'know. And I just had to interview someone who knew about racing after that accident. It was just like *magic* the way nobody got hurt, don't you think? I mean, that looked like a *terrible* accident."

What is she getting at? What's she after? "It looked worse than it was," he murmured, looking for a way to get past her without knocking her over again.

She ignored his remark as if she hadn't heard it. "And the way the driver walked out of there—I've never seen

anything more *unbelievable* in my life. And all that metal
flying everywhere, and not hitting anyone—well, I simply
have to know how often a thing like that happens. You'd
have to have *nerves* of *steel* to have a job like yours and
run the risks you do every day. And I just knew you were
the person to help me, Mr. Lynn. I mean, I've always been
a big fan of yours."

"I'm sure you have." *Big fan of mine, eh? So why have
I never seen you at the track before? And why didn't you
recognize me? And what were you looking for in here, if
it wasn't me?*

She finally paused long enough to take a breath. "So
will you let me interview you? I can't promise national
publication, but I'll do my best. And the publicity would
be wonderful for you, I'm sure."

She was lying, and he knew it. It wasn't just her tone,
or his shrilling nerves. He'd seen her eyes flickering to the
name tag on his suit just before she called him Mr. Lynn;
he'd caught the awkward pause in her speech when she
told him what she did. And he didn't believe for one minute
the Sweet-Southern-Honey Vapor-Brained-Belle routine she
was laying on him. She was no more from the Deep South
than he was. That accent was as assumed as the one
Dierdre used among mortals. The odds that she was a
writer were slim—the odds she was a free lance were even
slimmer. She was working for someone. And that look in
her eyes—no, she wasn't anywhere near as dumb as she
was playing. But now Mac was . . . curious.

:*Curious? Curious, are you! Is that what you're calling it now? Were you curious with Lianne last night, hmm?
An' would ye be carin' what was between this one's ears
if ye had her between the sheets, then?:* His mother Sent
him a wicked laugh. :*I think not. Och, my laddie! He's a
curious one for sure. Always mighty curious with the ladies.*:

:*Mother, you* will *die young if you keep that up.*:

:*Too late for that, child. Besides, I'm only trying to teach
you something—the next trap might be baited so attrac-
tively that you forget it's a trap.*: But then his mother's tone
became serious. :*I saw you couldn't catch the child. Another
time for that, then. If you really want to know about this
little fishie, though, reel her in. I'll have a look at her.*:

:Right.: And suddenly Mac was all warmth and admiration. "Call me Mac," he told the redhead, and held out his hand. "Come on back and I'll introduce you round."

She shook his hand and turned up the wattage on her smile. "And you can call me . . . Jewelene. Jewelene Carter."

:Yeah, sure,: D.D. snickered. *:And you can call me Dolly Parton.:*

Gawd, what a day.

Lianne unplugged the hot-air popper and carried her buttered popcorn into the living room. She sprawled on the couch and stared out the sliding glass door at the dappled sunlight on the grass of the apartment quad. *I ought to go outside and sit in the sun on the deck and grade papers and listen to the birds,* she thought guiltily. *It's a gorgeous April day, and they're singing like mad, and love is in the air, and tomorrow it might be too cold or too wet to sit outside.*

I need to unwind. Fresh air will do me good. I'll regret it if I waste this weather. Platitudes exhausted, she sighed, but she didn't move. She was too wrung out to move.

She couldn't concentrate on grading papers. She couldn't concentrate on averaging out grades. She was still mentally at the racetrack, with Mac shouting for everyone to take cover, a car about to blow up in their faces, fire, smoke, people screaming—and Amanda Kendrick sitting up on the bleacher staring at the disaster and trying to commit suicide. The entire business ground one more time through the seemingly endless loop it had worn in her memory.

It had been close. Amanda was no more than behind the bleachers when the motor blew—and there had been hot metal flying *everywhere*.

Except where there were people, Lianne mused. *But that was luck. Amanda isn't stupid—not really. She had to know she was in danger. So why did she just sit there like a— what?*

It was a bizarre accident. Everything had been stacked against them. It was a wonder somebody wasn't dead. She'd heard later that only three people had been injured, and those had been fixable with a stitch or two. It seemed impossible. There had been no dead kids whose parents had to be phoned, no trips to the emergency room in the back of a wailing ambulance holding some bloody little hand, no six-o'clock news rehashes with plenty of gory film. There could have been. In fact, she didn't see how any of those nightmares had been avoided. Lianne decided she was about ready to believe in miracles.

So, really, it had ended very well.

I'll never go on a field trip again, though. Anybody who takes fifth-graders on one of those things should automatically get a prescription for Valium from the Board of Education.

Lianne sighed again and snuggled further into the plush cushioning of the couch. Her mind flicked back to Amanda Kendrick.

Something is wrong with this picture, kiddo. Amanda wasn't frozen in shock at the sight of the accident. She was watching—fascinated—eating it up. She was furious when I pulled her down from her seat. And after the explosion, she was watching again.

Lianne munched popcorn and pondered. It wasn't the first time she'd caught Amanda doing something odd, only it was the first time it had been anything so ghoulish.

She needed to talk to Amanda's family. Again. Her nose automatically wrinkled at the thought. The Kendricks were one of Fayetteville's *good* families. Daddy was a corporate lawyer, Mama was Vassar, Junior League, Arts Council— and raised champion Arabian horses. They were both Old Money, and both times Lianne had talked with them, she walked away from the conference feeling undereducated, poorly dressed, that her hair was messy, her makeup was smudged, and she had runs in her hose.

That's not being fair to them, though. They're also concerned, attentive, and determined that their kids won't get a hothouse view of the world from education in Fayetteville's exclusive—and sheltered—private school. They want both of their girls to get a real-world education.

The Kendricks were always frustrated and somewhat at a loss when they discussed Amanda. Lianne could understand that. Amanda's IQ and achievement tests said she ought to be the hottest thing in school since the handheld calculator—and her grades were erratic, to put it kindly. She was slipping through the cracks of the educational system in spite of her family's concern, in spite of her teachers' attention—in spite of everything.

As she thought about the family, something finally clicked.

Mama was actually Step-Mama, wasn't she? Doing yeoman work, as far as Lianne could tell—but not even Super-Step-Mom could work miracles if Amanda was getting twisted ideas from somewhere else. Lianne wondered if the problem might stem from the real mother or the step-father.

It would be worth discussing with the Kendricks at their next conference. She decided she would set that up in the morning.

Better yet—I have the number here somewhere. Why don't I call now? Then I'll be able to work.

The phone rang only twice.

"Kendricks'." The voice was female, cultured, and clipped.

Ah, joy, Lianne thought. *None other than Amanda's stepmother.*

"Yes, Mrs. Kendrick. This is Amanda's homeroom teacher, Lianne McCormick. I've called to see if I could set up an appointment to meet with you and Amanda's father."

"*Again*, Miss McCormick? I'm beginning to wonder where the problems *are*. Andrew and I have visited with you more this year than we have with all of Amanda's other teachers put together. I think there is something significant about that."

Great. Obviously the assumption now was that Amanda's problems were her teacher's fault. Lianne took a deep breath, prayed for patience, and sternly stepped on the nasty little thought whispering that they might be right. "I regret having to call you. However, I'm noticing some odd behavior from Amanda, and I'd like to discuss it with you."

"I'm not sure I have the time to get away," the voice on the other end of the line said. "There's been some trouble with the horses, and we don't like to leave the stable unwatched."

Lianne saw an opening to get a closer look at Amanda's home life. She leapt at it. "I do understand that you've both been in a great many times this year, and I appreciate the difficulty that causes you. I'd be happy to come out to your home after school and talk with you. In fact, I think that might reassure Amanda that I do care about her progress."

There was a long pause. "Well, that's kind of you, Miss McCormick—"

Lianne heard an evasion coming and headed it off. "I don't mind. In fact, why don't I stop by tomorrow—say, six o'clock?"

There was another pause. "I do have plans tomorrow— I've scheduled an afternoon with the trainer to look at my two-year-olds—we're getting ready for some of the national shows." Then, perhaps realizing that she'd just put her horses' show status in front of her child's welfare, she immediately added, "But the day after tomorrow, I'm free, and I'll see if Andrew can wrap up with his clients in time to be home by six. Does that sound suitable?"

Lianne smiled. "That will be fine, Mrs. Kendrick. I'll see you at six on Friday."

She hung up the phone and pressed her back against the wall. *Feels like I just won the first round of the International Chess Championship.*

The room was enormous, beautifully decorated, absolutely immaculate—a sweet, perfect, peach-and-white little girl's bedroom as envisioned by a top designer. Stranger was unimpressed. Stranger knew the cost of the perfect bedroom. Downstairs the battle raged, and soon it would be time to pay the price.

Gods, they're fightin' again. That bodes no good for her. Stranger bit the bottom lip, tried to figure out a strategy that one of the others would be able to carry out.

Strategy was what Stranger was best at; even before— hundreds of years before—Stranger had been able to plan, to devise—to win. But a winning strategy required a willing army. The three-year-old, even if she could be lured out of hiding, would be no help—but if the three twelve-year-olds could be introduced to each other and enlisted, Stranger might be able to work something out. Stranger thought the elf would help—if the others could be made to go to him. They wouldn't trust *anybody*, but then, they didn't believe in elves. Maybe they would trust someone they thought didn't exist.

Her name wasn't really Stranger. It was Cethlenn. But she was a newcomer, and at first, the others refused to acknowledge her existence. Then she'd done them some favors. They'd reacted by giving her a name. To them she was Stranger. It was her badge of honor, and she wore it proudly.

Stranger's eyes watched twelve-year-old hands form numbers on the paper, carefully shaping out a long division problem. Stranger didn't know a thing about long division, and didn't care. The math could wait. Someone else would come along later and do it. Stranger was more interested in the fighting downstairs.

The Father was raising bloody hell, the Step-Mother was cold and hateful.

The Father's voice carried clearly up the long, curving stairwell and through the carved wood door. "You don't do a goddamn thing with her. That's the reason her teacher keeps calling, wanting conferences!"

"She's yours—not mine. I didn't marry you so I could be caretaker for that psychotic little rodent, Andrew. You deal with her." The Step-Mother didn't like Amanda, but that was nothing new.

"She needs discipline from you, too, Merryl!" The Father's voice dropped an octave. A bad sign.

The Step-Mother sneered; she had wealth enough on her own that the Father couldn't cow her. "I'm sure she gets more than enough *discipline* just from you—and I have Sharon to look after. I can handle normal children."

"Sharon is getting big enough that she could stand a bit of discipline. You coddle her too much." The Father's voice turned threatening. Stranger had heard that tone of voice before.

The Step-Mother's voice could have frozen boiling water—and was just as threatening. "You keep your hands off of Sharon. I won't have you turning her into another Amanda."

"Worthless, useless, frigid bitch! If you were any kind

of a woman, we wouldn't be having this problem with Amanda!" the Father yelled, losing control, thus losing the argument. The Father wouldn't like that.

The kitchen door slammed. Then Stranger heard the tread of heavy footsteps on the stairs.

"Amanda," the Father's voice shouted from the other side of the door, "Your pony is standing in filth. Get down to the barn and clean out his stable. Now."

Stranger tried to hang on, tried to control what happened next, but the others were panicked. They pushed to get in. Stranger tried to tell them what to do, but they wouldn't listen. They were too scared. They hid in the closet, wrapping their arms around themselves, and ignored Stranger.

"No, no," they whispered. "No, Daddy, no." The little voices crying inside Stranger's head made the hair stand up on the skinny little-girl arms. Stranger shivered and screamed at the others to listen, to run, to get away—to find the elf. She was so preoccupied with trying to rouse them that she ignored the real enemy standing outside the door.

But finally, when the Father got tired of yelling outside the door and came in to get Amanda, Stranger went away instead.

"Mel, I've got a winner on this end."

Melvin Tanbridge rocked back in the soft glove-leather chair and watched the sun set over the ocean through the tinted glass wall in his office. "Secure line?" he asked.

"Scrambled," the other voice affirmed.

"Then tell me more, baby."

"Our target, I'm almost certain, is a racecar driver named Mac Lynn. I had too big a crowd to eliminate all the noise, but he's the best possibility. I got a chance to talk to him later, and even latent, he flicked the needle on the meter. I don't think he's too bright—all glands and no brains—but he has plenty of talent. And, my Gawd, Mel, the film I have of this accident—you'll have to see to believe. There's no chance that this one's just a fluke. Besides, the readings on your little monitor were all red-zone. I'm FedEx'ing the film, some taped notes, and an 'interview' I got with the driver to you—it will be on your desk tomorrow."

"Fine." Mel tapped one manicured nail on the ebony desktop and smiled. "Nobody said we needed a nuclear physicist anyway. If he's stupid, he'll be easier to control. So—get a little background on him so we know what we're dealing with—then bring him in."

His agent chuckled. "On it already. I'm running a couple of goons that I brought with me today on the off chance I'd get lucky—maybe I'll be able to FedEx *him* to you tomorrow."

Mel laughed. "Sounds good. Who are you running?"

"Stevens and Peterkin." The voice sounded pleased.

Mel nodded and shifted the phone to his other ear. He picked up a pencil, started writing on a yellow legal pad. "They'll do. At least for pulling in a dumb jock."

"I'm going to need an alibi, and my clearance."

"First make sure he's the one. I don't want to have to feed any more mistakes to the sharks." Mel made another note under the first on his paper. "You set for money?"

"For the time being. If things get expensive, I'll let you know. But the cost of living here is nothing compared to California."

Mel's attention drifted from the phone to the scene outside his window. A girl in a wetsuit rode her board in on the crest of a breaker.

"Mel? You still there?"

He dragged his attention back. "Yeah. I'm here. Report in tomorrow, let me know what happens." He hung up the phone, and pulled a dull black box identical to the one the woman at the racetrack had from the top drawer of his desk. He aimed it at the girl on the surfboard and depressed the switch. The needle on the meter didn't twitch.

He shrugged and put the box back in his drawer.

Mac sat on a folding chair beside the Victor III while D.D. and her current human boyfriend, a twenty-six-year-old engineer-turned-biker, tinkered on it. They lay underneath the car, only visible from the knees down. An occasional *thunk* issued from under the car, but the three were otherwise, to all appearances, companionably silent. The human boyfriend—Redmond something-or-other—was concentrating on the car. And probably, Mac thought, sneaking an occasional grope of D.D.

None of it interrupted D.D.'s inaudible conversation, but then she had a lot of—skill. Mac wondered if the boyfriend knew how old she was. . . .

Probably. D.D. didn't believe in keeping that kind of secret from someone she let into her bed. Chances were he was one of the changelings from another Elfhame. Maybe Fairgrove, birthplace of the Victor III; they grew a lot of mechanics down there.

:Your little fish is no fish at all,: D.D. remarked.

No surprise there. *:I knew that. But what is she up to?:*

:My impression, laddiebuck, is that she's out a-hunting— and with you her quarry. Nathless, you needna think 'tis your handsome body she's lusting for. Nor your mind, though I doubt that occurred even to you. I'd say from the smell of her, 'tis magic she's hunting.:

He tightened his jaw; that was unwelcome news. *:Dangerous?:*

Mac heard an audible snort from under the Victor. *:Not to such as you and me. Merely amusing. But to another human, now—aye, there's danger there. And I'm not for certain that she knows her target. There was, after all, the child today. Not a shield on her, and projecting like a woman full-grown. Sure, I'd wager you were nothing but a convenient bit of misdirection.:*

:So much for my *masculine charms, hey, Mother?:*

The snort this time was derisive. *:I always thought you sold yourself too dear.:*

D.D. rolled out from under the car and stared intently into her son's eyes. "Go make yourself useful somewhere," she told him out loud, and added in Mindspeech, *:Lead your little not-fish a merry swim. No doubt she's waiting for you. Be sure she thinks you're her quarry for true. While she's chasing you—who are old enough surely to take care of yourself—you'll be keeping her away from that child—who cannot* protect *herself.:*

:A good point.: The woman had looked expensive, from the clothing to the perfume. Someone was paying her well,

if she was a hunter. A child would have no chance against her.

:*And no forgettin' now!*: she reminded him. :*About that child; you may deceive the woman all you like, but we need to find* her.:

He headed through the parking lot with the late afternoon sun baking his back and the glare of reflection angling inconveniently into his eyes from the few cars that were left there.

And as D.D. had anticipated, the woman *was* waiting, Hair and all.

Mac suppressed a smile. The self-named "Jewelene" lurked in the shadows of a closed concession stand near where Rhellen was parked. He couldn't actually see her—but her anticipation was palpable. She wasn't going to be a problem—

A tingle at the base of his neck slowed him down.

No, she wasn't going to be a problem. The two men who were sneaking up on him from slightly behind and to either side could have been, however, if he hadn't been expecting something.

How to play it?

A vision of the Three Stooges, chased by villains, succeeding by sheer ineptitude, came to him from his last hotel room cable-TV binge. He smiled slyly.

Rhellen, old friend, you and I are going to have some fun.

His step became jaunty. He whistled a cheery rendition of "Laddies, There's Trouble, Oh, Trouble A-Comin'." The tune was one he and Rhellen had used as a signal when tavern-hopping back in his days as a colonial rakehell. It had always been useful for assuring a backup or, if need be, a quick getaway.

He took in the slight change in attitude in the elvensteed, and felt his partner signal that he was ready.

Mac grinned and, without warning, bolted for the concession stand. "Jewelene!" he yelled. "Hey, baby! You waited around for me! Fabulous—and, gorgeous, it's your lucky day. I've got the whole afternoon free."

The two gorillas who'd been casually working their way

through the parking lot, following him, changed direction. "Jewelene" looked wildly for some place to hide, and realized there wasn't one. She looked straight at him, made an "Oh-what-a-surprise!" face, and smiled.

He caught her lightly by one wrist.

"Mr. Lynn," she said, and forced a bright smile, "I didn't expect to run into you again."

He leaned against the concession stand and gave her his best come-hither look. "Baby," he purred, "we both know that's not true. Why else would you be waiting around by my car after everyone else has gone home? And it's Mac—remember?"

"Right—Mac."

He slid an arm around her waist and moved her towards Rhellen. "You don't have to pretend with me. The first time I saw you, I knew we were meant for each other. And I could tell that you knew it, too." He gave her a quick little one-armed hug that threw her off balance. She fell against him.

Out of the corner of his eye, he caught the panicked glance she threw at her two goons.

"Uh, Mac . . ." She tugged ineffectually at his arm, then gave up. "I'm glad to see you. Really. But I was waiting to talk to some of the other drivers—for my interviews. I think I can sell this story to *Playboy*, but I need more, ah, input."

"Honey—Jewelene—why didn't you say so? None of the drivers are here right now," Mac lied fluently. "But I can take you to a bar where most of us hang out. I'm sure we can round up some other drivers for you to interview. And the atmosphere of our hangout will be great for your story. And I can give you any kind of 'input' you want." He tugged her toward the Chevy.

"Well, hey, that's—ah, really nice of you. Go ahead, and I'll follow you in my car."

Mac laughed. "I'm a professional driver, babe. You couldn't keep up with me if you wanted to."

Her goons were finally in position behind Rhellen, crouched down against his rear fender. "Jewelene" relaxed.

"Okay then, Mac. Thanks. Very much."

Mac had a hard time keeping himself from laughing

aloud. He wrapped his arms around her tightly and pulled her into an extended kiss. "Wonderful. And after you get your interviews, we'll go home and interview each other."

She smiled back, and he noted a vindictive gleam in her eye. "Yes," she agreed. "We'll do that."

He escorted her to the passenger side of the car and opened the door for her. She climbed in, completely confident. He walked around the front of the car, and noted the movement of one of the men around to Rhellen's driver's side. The other, of course, would be sneaking around behind him. He patted the hood.

Everybody ought to have an elvensteed, he thought— Rhellen radiated satisfaction and chuckled in agreement.

:Ready?: he asked the elvensteed. He waited long enough to catch Rhellen's assent, and then made the single step forward that changed him from target to missile.

As he rounded the front of the car, both men lunged for him. The driver's door swung open and flung the first one back, and Rhellen edged forward just enough to knock the second one down. Mac slipped into the seat to find "Jewelene" trying with all her strength to open her door and get back out. He grinned. His door closed, the car started itself up, and "Jewelene's" head jerked around.

"The weirdest things have been happening around here lately," he told her, as he drove Rhellen away from the two bewildered goons, who were scrambling for their own car. She stared at him, wild-eyed and open-mouthed. "I've found out it never pays to let your guard down." He laughed. "So, beautiful, are you ready to get your interviews?"

She was staring behind them at the dwindling parking lot. Mac glanced into the rearview mirror; there, two hairy guys in jeans, t-shirts, and ball caps were jumping into an incongruously clean, expensive navy-blue sedan. They came tearing out of the parking lot like they'd been bitten by denizens of the Unseleighe Court.

She nodded slowly. "Yeah. Yeah, let's go."

"Okay, Rhellen," Mac drawled. "You heard the lady. Let's go."

Rhellen accelerated to his top speed. They launched into Raeford Road's six-lane roller derby, shouldering aside a steroidal poser-mobile and causing the owner of a brand-new Mercedes to jam on brakes to keep from marring its expensive paint job.

Mac rested his hands lightly on the steering wheel but let the car do the actual work. "Jewelene" yelled, "Jesus, slow down!" and started fumbling around the seat and the doorframe.

"What are you doing?" Mac asked.

"Looking for the seatbelts. Slow down! Where are the damned seatbelts?"

"Honey, this is a mint-condition fifty-seven Chev-ro-let," he drawled. "There ain't no seatbelts. They were an *option* back then."

Rhellen dodged a Porsche, weaved on two wheels past a semi, darted into a hole exactly two inches longer than he was, then bolted in front of a cop car and accelerated. Mac casually took one hand off the wheel and flicked on the radio.

"Come on, baby, come on! You've just got to release me—" Wilson Phillips sang cheerfully.

His passenger was white beneath the painted blush, and looked as if she agreed wholeheartedly with the trio. "Jesus God! Mac, slow down or let me out of here!"

He chuckled, exuding machismo. "Relax, baby. I'm a professional. I do this all the time."

She turned to him, pupils wide with real fear. "Not with me in the car!"

He gave her his best impression of a man whose masculinity has been called into question. "Look, baby, if you don't like my driving, you can walk."

She grabbed his arm and shook it. "Dammit, that's what I already said! Let me walk!"

Rhellen whipped out of traffic into a Kwik Stop parking lot and hit the brakes so hard he almost stood on his grille. "Jewelene" was flung against the dash, then back into her seat. The contents of her purse erupted into the interior of the car and bounced everywhere.

Mac hid his delight. Under the auspices of throwing things back into the bag to get her out of his car, he managed to pocket her driver's license and also got a look at some very esoteric toys she was carrying.

Voice-activated tape recorder, stun gun, brass knuckles, Mace, thumbcuffs, little packet of fake ID's . . . all sorts of neat stuff—plus the mysterious little black box. Interesting. I'd love to get a look in her closet sometime.

Then he shoved her toward her door—which opened smoothly.

He sneered at her. "Have a nice walk. It's too bad about your attitude, baby. You would have had a terrific time—but it's your loss." He slammed the door on her heels. "Have a nice day, bitch," he called after her.

"Arrogant pig!" she screeched. Or at least, that was part of what she screeched. The rest was incoherent, and probably not Webster's English. She spun away as he laughed at her, then flounced toward the road.

Several G.I.'s leaned out of the windows of a passing car and yelled. She shot them the bird, and they retorted with a jeering obscenity. Another car full of G.I.'s right behind them slowed and tried to offer her a ride. He saw her take out her can of Mace. The driver of the car shrugged and grinned, and he and his friends drove on.

Her goons would probably find her soon enough. And if they didn't, Mac figured she would enjoy her little hike in the nice April weather. Especially in *this* neighborhood, and with sunset coming on—and looking the way she did. That wouldn't be the last offer of "temporary employment" she'd get before she found a cab. This was a G.I. town, and G.I.'s have two things on their mind when they get off base. . . .

And "Jewelene" was certainly dressed for the part. Between The Hair and the Spandex, she'd be lucky if the cops didn't pick her up and run her in just on general principles.

Mac looked at the driver's license he'd stolen. "Rhellen," he told the elvensteed, "I think Ms. Belinda Ciucci of Berkeley, California, is going to *love* Fayetteville—what'cha think?"

The '57 Chevy rumbled a deep chuckle of affirmation and cruised on.

CHAPTER THREE

Thank heavens it's only an hour till lunch.

Lianne eyed her students with weariness that bordered on desperation. *And I'll have several minutes of blessed silence while we do the spelling test. Of course, I could have a lot more silence if I just shot them. Nice idea. I like it a lot.*

The three-minute pencil-sharpening break was over. It was time to get everyone back in order.

"Sit down *in your seats, facing forward.* Be quiet, get out your pencil, get out your *paper. Use* your pencil to write on the paper—write the following things. Your name—yes, Keith, when I say your name, I *do* mean the name your parents gave you, not any name you think is really cool today. The date. Today's date. It's on the board. Look at the board. Copy the date. Get it right. Your life depends on it."

Lianne tapped the blackboard with a piece of chalk for emphasis and counted mentally to ten. The fifth grade Mafia had apparently declared that today was Silly Day— every simple chore required detailed instructions. Even usually well-behaved kids like Latisha McKoy and Marilee Blackewell were misbehaving. The first time she told the class to sit down, almost all of them sat on the floor. It was a bad moment—for the continued existence of the kids, as well as for her.

She hadn't done anything to them—yet—that would lose her this job. Her guardian angels were probably taking bets on how much longer that could last, though.

"Fold the paper neatly in half, *longwise*. Write the numbers one through twenty-five, down the left side of the paper—Arabic numerals, William, not Roman numerals—no, Snyder, you may not go to the bathroom during a test—I don't care if your big brother *did* tell you it's your Constitutional right. He lied. Write the numbers twenty-six through fifty down the fold in the center of the paper."

Because we have learned never to say the words "center fold"—in any context—in a room that holds fifth-grade boys, haven't we, Lianne?

"Jennifer, Latisha, you do *not* talk at any time during a test. Not even if you dropped your pencil, Jennifer—getting it back does not require conversation. Maurice, close the book!"

Ten minutes of orders. Now, finally, she could give the test.

"Number one—concentration. CON-cen-TRA-tion. School work requires *concentration*."

Not murdering you little monsters requires CON-cen-TRA-tion. Lianne felt her teeth grinding and tried to relax her jaw before she splintered something. Crowns were expensive, and they didn't come under the heading of "injuries in the line of duty."

She studied her charges. Twenty-six heads bent over their papers. Twenty-six hands wrote out creative versions of the spelling words, some that would bear no relationship to any word ever written in the English language. The Death Row Five snuck surreptitious glances in her direction to see if it was safe yet to use their microscopically handwritten cheat sheets. If they spent half the time studying that they did in cheating, they'd be straight-A students. Beth Hambly sat primly in the front row, carefully guarding her (surely perfect) answers from the prying eyes of less perfect classmates. William Ginser, foiled in his plan to number his paper with Roman numerals, was misspelling his words in some ornate style that bore a striking resemblance to German Blackletter.

If he'd just put that kind of energy into learning to spell the damn words in the first place—She sighed. *Then he wouldn't be William.*

Amanda Kendrick, sitting in the back corner of the classroom, stared out the window.

"Eight. Contradiction. CON-tra-DIC-tion. If you say something that means the opposite of what I have said, that is a *contradiction.*"

Amanda didn't move. Lianne had noticed, on and off during the morning, that Amanda was quieter than usual—but *usual* was awfully quiet. Now, though, she looked closer.

The total absence of expression on Amanda's face made Lianne shiver. *Is she breathing? Yes, she is—a little. Good God, she looks dead. She is breathing—but she sure as hell isn't here. And I don't think I'd want to be wherever she is right now. She hasn't done a single spelling word—no, screw the spelling test. I don't want to call her down in front of the rest of the class. Not right now. She doesn't look like she feels too well.*

Lianne cruised through the words on the test, making up sentences on autopilot. She couldn't stop looking at Amanda.

The dead look is in her eyes. They're glazed—could she be having some sort of a seizure? Maybe I need to call a doctor. But she doesn't look physically sick. And the few times I've called on her, I have been able to get an answer out of her—she just drifts away right afterward.

Lianne bit her lip.

We're going to take a break after this test, and I'm going to talk to her.

"Thirty-nine—" Decision made, her attention snapped back to the rest of the class. Her loss of vigilance had not passed unnoticed. "Snyder, Maurice—I'll take those papers, gentlemen, and you may sit out the rest of the test. You've just earned yourselves F's. Anybody else like to try? No? Thirty-nine. Interception. In-ter-CEP-tion. What you have just seen, folks, was the *interception* of two cheat sheets."

The rest of the test went without incident.

Lianne got everyone started reading Thomas Rockwell's

How to Eat Fried Worms, a book she had fought long and hard to get on the fifth grade required reading list. It proved to her students that reading really was fun—she'd converted more book-haters with that—plus *A Light in the Attic*, and the *Alvin Fernald* books—than with anything else she used. They wallowed in the gross-out joys and Machiavellian plotting of a kid who got dared into eating a worm a day and the friends who'd bet him he couldn't.

With their attention fixed on their books, she was free to take care of Amanda.

She walked to the back of the room, squatted down beside Amanda's desk, and waited. Amanda kept staring out the window. There was no sign that the child knew she was there.

"Amanda," Lianne whispered. "I need to talk with you."

She got no response.

Lianne rested her hand lightly on Amanda's shoulder, and said, "Amanda, is something wrong?"

The girl's whole body shuddered, and her face turned toward Lianne—and Lianne pulled her hand away, horrified. Pale, pale jade-green eyes stared back at her, stared *through* her, lips pulled back from teeth in an animal expression of fear, or rage—or both. The face was not Amanda's face, not a child's face—if it was human at all. The expression was fleeting—there, and gone so fast Lianne wondered if she'd really seen it—then one of the girls behind her and towards the front of the class started shrieking. Others yelled, desks squeaked, and something hard hit Lianne on the back of the neck. She spun towards the front of the class, started to yell at the kids to stop fighting, and froze.

Impossible.

Loose chalk flew from the chalkboard as if thrown by an angry child. Closed chalk boxes opened themselves, spewed their contents into the air—the liberated chalk rained against walls and ceiling and floor and kids. Bulky blackboard erasers pelted students and furniture, fell to the floor, and leapt up to attack again.

The neatly stacked spelling tests on her desk launched themselves into the air, to join with piles of loose construction paper from the bulletin board corner and reports on

The Planets of Our Solar System that had suddenly come to life.

Books fell off of desks to the floor. Pens and pencils leapt from desks to smack against the windows. The classroom door opened, then slammed shut, then opened again to allow a stream of paperwork to escape out into the hall.

The children's screams didn't cover the sound of paper snapping in the nonexistent wind.

Lianne had just enough time to realize that what she saw was *real;* it actually was happening. Then it stopped.

Projectiles in mid-course slammed into some invisible wall and dropped to the floor. Papers swirled downward like rainbow-colored autumn leaves. The door shut with a soft click.

There was silence.

Everyone waited. Scared, big-eyed kids looked at her for direction.

She didn't know what to do. So she cleared her throat, bent down, tentatively picked up a piece of chalk, then another. They didn't attack. She picked up a handful of paper.

"Okay, folks—everyone all right?" There were tentative nods from the kids as they looked themselves over and made sure they were still intact. "Good. Then let's . . . let's get this mess cleaned up." She tried to sound brave. God knew, she didn't feel it. "Whatever happened, it's over now. When we've finished, you can all read until the lunch bell rings."

Lianne's knees felt weak. She made her way to the front of the class, put all the chalk and loose erasers around her desk back on the blackboard, then sagged into her seat and rested her head in her hands.

Two days in a row. Right now, I could be convinced to give up teaching forever. The racing accident, the Attack of the School Supplies, Amanda's weird behavior—

Amanda! I forgot about her!

Lianne looked up, expecting to see Amanda frozen at her desk. Instead, she saw the girl chatting with Brynne Lassiter as the two of them cleaned up one corner of the mess.

Amanda glanced in her direction, saw Lianne watching

her, and smiled brightly. She bounced up to the desk, and handed the young teacher her gold Cross pen.

"Your pen fell beside my desk."

Lianne tried to smile. "Thank you, Amanda," she said.

"That was really strange, wasn't it, Ms. McCormick?"

"Strange doesn't begin to describe it." Lianne looked closer at the girl, then closed her eyes and rested her forehead against the back of her hand.

"Are you okay, Ms. McCormick?" Amanda asked. She sounded so normal!

"I'll be fine, thank you. Just—just go back to your desk now, please." Lianne felt herself struggling to breathe, felt the room starting to reel, but her skin felt cool to her touch. *No fever.*

She was light-headed—certainly sick. She had to be.

Amanda's eyes are blue.

Mac woke up with sunlight streaming through the sheers in the window of his hotel suite.

Dammit. Forgot to pull the drapes again. What time is it?

He looked at his clock on the tacky vinyl-veneer almost-Scandinavian dresser that sat in a puddle of sunshine. Green digital numbers, muted to pastel by the light, glowed reassuringly back at him. He stretched with feline grace. *Eleven-fifteen. No hurry. I've got plenty of time for room service.*

He rolled over to the phone that rested on the equally cheap nightstand and dialed. A bouncy-sounding girl at the other end took his order for French toast and bacon and orange juice and the fruit plate. It would be up shortly, she assured him.

Mac smiled and rolled over on his back. *A nice hot shower, I think, while breakfast is getting here—then maybe a little TV. Out in time for the maid to straighten the place up, take Rhellen for some exercise down Bragg Boulevard, drive over to the school to see where Lianne works. Then a stop by the track so Mother doesn't think I've vanished into the ozone. I'll tell her about the outcome of the Belinda Affair. She'll enjoy that.*

It felt like the start of a wonderful day.

Of course, any day that started out with room service and a maid couldn't go too far wrong. Maclyn approved of room service.

He lolled in bed, not quite ready to plunge into the pounding spray of a shower, when he noticed a flash of blue and a dull gleam of gold on the other side of the open door that led to his usually-dull-beige suite living room. Curious, he crawled out of the bed and went to take a look.

:Not a very early riser, are you?: The Mindspeech was female, frosty—condescending, too.

Felouen—beautiful, irritating Felouen—lounged on his couch. She wore a cobalt blue silk Court jerkin heavily embroidered with gold over a soft, pale-blue silk blouse. Gold-and-sapphire chains draped around her neck and wove through her pale amber hair. Her long legs—in matching blue trews—were thrown indecorously over one of the couch's overstuffed arms. She hadn't bothered to take off her knee-high blue leather boots. She lay her head back on a cushion and stretched, sending a languorous, sexy smile in his direction.

"A little overdressed for the area, aren't you?" Mac remarked.

:And you're a little underdressed.:

It was a legitimate comment. Mac was stark naked. "You didn't make an appointment. You don't let me know you're coming, you take your chances."

She smiled. :And this time I won.:

Mac refused to be amused or flattered. "I have plans for the day, Felouen. Go home."

:I have plans for the day, too, Mac. I want you to come Home with me.:

He glared at her. "What is this? You can't get me to play warrior for the Court by guilt, so you fake lust? I don't believe you, dear."

She laughed out loud, delighted. :Fake lust! You'd suspect that, with every other elvish maiden sighing after your broad retreating back? My bonny lad, I needn't fake lust.:

She sat up. :But the Unseleighe Court—:

He blanked out her Mindspeech and turned his back on her. "I won't play defender of the lands with you, Felouen. The lands don't need a defender."

Unable to continue her conversation in the more compelling Mindspeech, she shifted with bad grace to physical speech. "It isn't play," she snapped. "The minions of the Unseleighe Court surround you, even now."

"Ooooh, *minions,*" he mimicked. "I'm terrified." He crossed his arms over his chest. "They don't bother me, I don't bother them."

If anything, her voice grew colder. She sounded like his old sword-instructor, Siobhan: deadly, deathly serious. "You know evil doesn't work that way, Maclyn. The Unseleighe Court grows stronger with every back that's turned to it. The darkness has spread to our corner of Underhill—the filth is leaking through even there. Soon enough, it will be able to conquer even the strongest and best of those who could have defended against it. If you don't face it now, you will face it later—on its terms."

There was a knock at the door. "Room service," someone called.

"Yeah—just a minute." Mac pointed into the bedroom. :*Get in there—then vanish*:, he told the elven warrior. He pulled his bathrobe off of its hook on the coatrack, put it on, and opened the door.

A smiling busboy pushed the cart into the room. "Mornin', Mr. Lynn," he said. "All ready for the race Saturday?"

"You bet, Sam. You gonna be there?"

"Nah." The young man shook his head, disgusted. "Cain't. I'm scheduled to work. I'm pulling for you, though."

"Thanks." He signed for the food—on the Fairgrove account, of course—and grinned as the busboy left. But the grin vanished with the closing of the door. Mac turned and stalked into his bedroom, expecting to find Felouen waiting for him.

She was gone. *Good,* he thought. *The day is looking up.*

But the feeling of Presence hadn't abated—

On his bed, gold gleamed. He could feel it. He didn't need a closer look. He knew exactly what she'd left.

Shit. The day is looking down.

Mac felt pretty much the way someone who'd just found a leaking radioactive canister in his house would feel. He stared at the lovely gold circle and swore creatively.

Finally, he picked it up. *Uh-huh. I should have known*

she'd pull something like this. One of the Rings. He pulled a scrap of silk out of a drawer, and carefully wrapped the bit of jewelry in its insulating folds. Then he shoved it into the leather pouch he kept with him. *Well . . . maybe D.D. will take it off my hands.*

In spite of Mr. Race-Driver's machismo, he doesn't drive so damn-all fast. That stupid shit yesterday must have been to impress me. Ooooh, ooooh, I was so impressed. Gonad-brained jerk-off!

Mac Lynn's '57 Chevy with its custom colors was about as easy to keep track of in traffic as if it sported strobe-lights. She'd always been good at tailing—this was so simple it was dull.

My commission is the same whether I have it hard or easy. I guess I shouldn't knock it.

Belinda downshifted and slipped in behind a pickup as her target slowed and turned into the elementary school parking lot. She chose an unobtrusive spot about a hundred yards down the road, U-turned, and parked. Then she settled back with a bottle of mineral water and a packet of fresh sliced vegetables to wait Mac out.

Her old partner in the Berkeley P.D. had given her endless grief on her choice of stake-out munchies. Ed had hated rabbit food. His idea of stake-out rations was a cold Philly steak sandwich, a stack of Domino's pizzas, and a carton of Mountain Dews. Of course, Ed had given her good-natured hell about almost everything. Sometimes she even missed him.

She missed him at that moment. He would have loved trailing a race-driver with a classic car. He would have known Mac's racing stats and would have tried endlessly to get her to be interested in them. They could have had a wonderful argument about racing, and what it did to the environment. That argument would have segued into solar versus fossil fuel, and Middle Eastern politics, and even—she grinned thinking about it—psychic phenomena. Ed wouldn't have believed the accident yesterday was anything but an accident. He would have argued until his last breath—in spite of her neat gizmo, in spite of the lack of casualties, in spite of everything. Ed had loved to argue.

Debate, he'd called it.

She bit her lip, and glared out the window.

In the end, he had died arguing—debating. He'd had a lot of practice, and he was very convincing, too. She'd wanted to believe him. But he hadn't had as much practice lying as he had at arguing. He'd caught her with the dead mark in the alley, taking her cut to look the other way, and no matter what he said, old Honest Ed could not have meant it when he said he wouldn't turn her in.

She'd hated killing him.

The job wasn't the same after that—it was ruined for her. She bit viciously at the carrot stick.

Damn Ed, anyway!

She could have been happy in the police department for years.

It was Moonchange, tide change, sea ebb at Fayetteville's Loyd E. Auman Elementary, where the thundering outrush of the pounding surf of children battered against the lone swimmer-to-shore, who was Mac Lynn, Mighty Racecar Driver—

Or maybe it's more like the charge of the lemmings, Mac thought, as he watched small children trample all over each other in their race to leave.

Fascinated, he stopped to watch.

Teachers bellowed and directed and commanded in voices that would have done a drill sergeant proud—Mac wondered how many of them joined the Marines following a few years of teaching so they could get a vacation. Parents leaned out car windows and screamed for their youngsters to hurry up. Kids shrieked and yelled insults and questions and promises to call each other, fighting to be heard over the general uproar. The school bus engines rumbled bass counterpoint.

The odors of asphalt and bus fumes and new-mown rye grass mingled with the smells of books and stale baloney sandwiches and sweaty gym clothes. Noise, commotion, odors: all were overpowering. For a moment, he wished he was Underhill.

But if I went there right after all of this, it would feel like someone had plugged my ears and my nose, muffled my brain in silk, and put dark glasses on me. It would be too subtle, like that awful French food.

There was rarely anything subtle about the world of humans.

The buses filled slowly, then, abruptly pulled away—little pockets of traveling riot. Parents drove off with their young, the few walkers vanished into the distance—and quiet returned suddenly, like the descent of the theater curtain. Mac watched as teachers sagged with relief against the building or their cars, or turned with slow and tired steps to head back inside.

He went inside after them.

Lianne's head rested on her desk. Her eyes were closed and her hands were locked over the back of her neck. To Mac, she looked pale.

"Bad day, huh?"

The teacher looked up at him, blearily, too exhausted to register surprise at his appearance. "Hell day."

Mac grimaced by way of showing sympathy. "I'm sorry. You want a back rub? Or maybe you'd prefer that I drive you home?"

Lianne buried her head in her hands again. "I want to crawl into my bed and die."

Mac shook his head. "The first part of that idea doesn't sound too bad. Tell you what. We'll go over to your place and crawl into bed, and I'll bet I can get you to change your mind about dying."

"I doubt it," Lianne groaned. She sounded sincere. She sounded *frightened.*

Mac leaned his palms on her desk and waited until she looked up, then stared intently into her eyes. "It can't be that bad. What's wrong?"

Lianne pushed away from her desk and started gathering up her things. She turned her back to him. There was a long pause, filled mostly with the sounds of her stacking papers and breathing rapidly. Finally, she said, in a small, hesitant voice, "Mostly, it seems that my classroom is haunted."

Mac started to laugh, but stopped himself when he noted the tension in her shoulders. "You aren't kidding."

"God, Mac, I wish I were." She sighed and turned, and he could see the brightness of impending tears in her eyes. "You're—you're going to think I'm crazy, but it happened! All the kids were so scared—"

And so were you—"Tell me," he urged. "Lianne, I've seen plenty of things that seemed crazy at the time." He grinned at her, the lopsided, *very* Celtic grin that always won women's trust. "I may not hang crystals in my car like Bill Gatlin, but I'll go along with Will Shakespeare."

" 'There are more things in heaven and earth, Horatio, than are dreamt of in your philosophy'?" She managed a tremulous smile. "You know, I think I believe you. . . ."

Mac said nothing, only continued to smile encouragingly.

She took a deep breath and relaxed, just a little. "Partway through reading today, papers and chalk came to life and started flying around the room on their own, attacking people. The door opened and slammed shut—it was a madhouse in here. Then it just stopped. I was terrified."

"I'll bet." He put warmth into it, so much that Lianne smiled at him. Mac felt a twinge of excitement. Something was up—it seemed a bit of a coincidence that he should be hunting a telekinetic kid when inanimate objects suddenly came to life in that kid's homeroom teacher's class. Mac was willing to bet that something about the visit to the track had triggered the girl. Maybe the accident.

Time to do a little fishing, he decided.

"What were you doing when it started, baby?" he asked, urging her to keep talking. "Do you remember?"

She nodded. "Oh, yeah. It was weird. One of the kids in my class had been lost in space all morning—I'd assigned everyone to read, and I went back to her seat to talk to her. I didn't get the chance to, though. I hadn't any more than gotten Amanda's attention when the classroom just—blew up."

That name sounded familiar. "Amanda . . . is the name of the kid?"

Lianne didn't notice his increased interest. "Yeah. You might remember her from our little disaster yesterday. She was the skinny blond girl who wouldn't get down behind the bleachers. She's an odd kid."

Mac felt a surge of triumph. *There are no coincidences. I knew it. Same child—and the accident was the trigger.*

He nodded casually. "I remember her—she always act like that?"

Lianne picked up jacket, bag, and papers and headed out the door. Mac followed.

"Yes, no, and maybe," she told him. "Nothing about her makes sense. Her aptitude tests indicate that she should be one of the smartest kids I've ever taught. . . ."

"And?" he prompted, taking her elbow.

Lianne sighed. "And sometimes she is. One minute she's sweet and chatty and willing to discuss the lesson, and the next she doesn't even seem to realize there is a lesson. Her spelling tests are a trip. She'll either slaughter the words entirely, or she'll get them all perfect—and sometimes she'll kill the first half of the test and ace the second half. As far as I can tell, she has no attention span. And sometimes she really likes me, and sometimes she really hates me—and I don't have any warning before she goes from one attitude to the other."

Mac frowned; there was something about those symptoms. . . . "That is strange."

"She has parents that care—they have lots of money, she has all the advantages—" Lianne shrugged. She waved to another teacher who was coming down the long hall toward the stairs from the other direction. "I'm not the only one she's this way around. Her health teacher says she went into a rage during sex ed the other day. Said that she started screaming that anyone who could do something that disgusting was a whore or a slut or worse—I guess Amanda used a few words Nancy had never heard before. What's funny was, they were talking about where babies come from. Really low key, really mild—and all of a sudden, there goes Amanda, right off the deep end."

A sick feeling had started in the pit of Mac's stomach when Lianne began describing Amanda's behavior. It grew worse with every detail. By the time she'd finished, he was sure something was horribly wrong with the child. He just didn't have any idea what.

They walked out of the hot hallways, redolent with chalk

dust, ink, schoolgirl perfume, and sneakers, into baked-asphalt parking lot heat.

Mac held onto her elbow as she started towards her own car. "Let me drive you home," he urged. *I have to find out more about this child—or better yet, get Lianne to take me to her.*

But Lianne shook her head with a stubborn determination he was beginning to know well. "Mac, I appreciate it—but I'll be fine. I have to get some groceries, and I want to go home and just soak in the tub and think for a while." A bit of breeze touched the little tendrils of hair that had escaped from her French braid. Not enough breeze to cool, just enough to be annoying.

Azaleas, dogwoods, and a goddamned heat wave, all blooming at the same time. Welcome to April in North Carolina, he thought.

He persisted, in the forlorn hope that she had been worn down enough to give in to him. "Are you sure?"

This time her nod was quite determined. "I'm sure."

Mac shrugged. "Okay. I really guess I ought to stop by the track before D.D. sends out search teams, anyway." *Try a different tactic.* "May I see you tonight?"

She finally gave in to his persistence, yielding with a willing heart, if the smile that answered his was any indication. "I'd like that. But—how about just an evening in? I'm too tired for anything that involves going out in public."

He pretended to consider it. "Hmm. Never tried one of those before. . . ."

She lifted a skeptical eyebrow, and he laughed. "It's a date," he said, and gave Lianne a tight hug and a kiss. She returned the kiss with startling enthusiasm, and Mac caught his breath.

They are so warm, so bright . . . so enchanting—
And so fleeting—

He pulled away quickly and forced a grin. "Gotta run, babe. See you tonight," he told her, and turned away. He didn't want her to see the pain in his eyes.

—And they die so soon, he thought. *So soon . . . and anyone who loves them dies a little bit with them. Not again. I won't ever let myself hurt that way again.*

✧   ✧   ✧

Redmond Something-or-other was pawing Mac's mother again, back in the corner behind the tire stacks. Mac heard D.D. giggling and whispering, and her young lover's erratic breathing. It was, he reflected, a hard life that gave a man a mother who looked ten years younger than he did—when she was nearly two hundred years older.

"Hey, D.D.," he yelled. "You're never going to get my car ready doing that. Chase your stud-muffin off with a nice big tire iron and get out here."

"There's more to life than cars," she yelled brightly, but she and the stud-muffin appeared. Redmond, looking flushed and flustered, was struggling with his buttons. Mac suspected he'd gotten the zipper back in place before he came out of hiding.

D.D., of course, was unfazed. "I didn't think you were going to join us poor peons today," she said, flaunting her pony-tail. "And Redmond and I didn't see any reason to waste a perfectly good day if you weren't even going to show up."

"Mmmm-hmmm." Mac looked over at the dark corner of the garage. "Fooling around on the cement behind the tires has got to be one of the more romantic ways I could think of to spend a day."

She laughed at him. "We pump grease our own way, we do. You're too stuffy, Mac. You wouldn't know a good time if it bit you on the ass."

Mac smiled agreeably and made a tsk-ing noise. "That's the difference between you and me, D.D. If it bit me on the ass, I wouldn't call it a good time."

D.D. laughed and flipped him the finger. "You'll never know what you're missing."

He cast his eyes up to heaven, as if asking for help. "Gods, I hope not. You're one short step above delinquent, and if you weren't such a good mechanic—"

"But I *am*," she replied impudently. "So you indulge me."

"So I do. Hey, D.D.—I just remembered. A friend of yours stopped over at my place this morning—she had a present for you, but she couldn't find you, so she left it with me." Mac fished the scrap of green silk out of the bag in his pocket, and started to hand it to D.D. . . .

But D.D. kept her hands shoved firmly into her pockets.

:Bullshit, Maclyn, my love.: "What friend was that?" she asked out loud.

"Felouen," Mac said. He saw no point in lying. *:I'd appreciate your help here, Mother.:*

:No doubt—but I'm not going to interfere in your relationship with the Court. You have some responsibilities that you're evading—I won't force you to live up to them. I also won't help you get out of them.: Out loud, D.D. lied for Redmond's benefit. "Felouen and I can't stand each other. I wonder what she's up to."

:She stuck me with a Ring, Mother. Won't you please take it off my hands? Before it calls too much attention to me?: Mac proffered the silk again. "She wants to be friends, D.D. Why don't you just take her present? You can always give it back to her later if you don't change your mind about her."

:You deal with it, kiddo.: "If she wants to be friends, she can find me herself. If you see her again, give her present back to her. And tell her what I said. I'm sure she'll be seeing you again."

Mac muttered, "I'm sure she will."

He held the Ring in his fingers and wished that it would go away. It radiated warmth, power, assurance—and a broadcast beam that would tell every Unseleighe thing in the area that a Seleighe warrior was among them.

Just exactly what I needed for Christmas.

CHAPTER FOUR

Elementary school. The racetrack. Penney's at the mall. Barnes' Motor and Parts. Three count 'em, three—fast food joints. No—she thought, watching with disbelief as Mac pulled into a Kentucky Fried Chicken, *Make that four fast food joints.*

"You sure know how to show a girl a good time, fella," Belinda muttered. "If this is how hot-dog race-drivers spend their days, I'll pass."

She'd never tailed anyone duller in her life. She'd spent her entire afternoon driving in circles around Fayetteville, watching Mac gorge on junk food and run apparently pointless errands. It was getting dark, she'd put monster miles on her little silver Sunbird, she had to go to the bathroom, and she was, for the second time, almost out of gas. Mac hadn't taken a potty break or fueled up his accursed Chevy once. Belinda would have given anything to know how he'd accomplished that second trick. Those beasts were supposed to guzzle gas, everyone knew that. His gas tank couldn't be *that* big.

He hadn't spotted her. She knew he hadn't spotted her. Except a suspicion kept nagging that nobody, absolutely nobody, could or would spend a day in such a boring manner unless he was trying to mislead a tail.

But finally, at about seven-thirty, Mac's aimless wandering ceased, replaced by apparent commitment to a single direction and increased speed. *Now we're getting somewhere,* Belinda rejoiced.

She had to fall further and further back as they left the center of Fayetteville and traffic thinned. For twenty minutes, they sped along roads that became increasingly deserted. Suddenly, on a narrow country lane, Mac left the pavement entirely, bounced along a sand two-rut through a fallow field, and screeched to a halt in front of a stand of stunted hardwoods along the field's back perimeter. There were no buildings anywhere around. There were no cars passing by.

This is going to be good, Belinda gloated. *If he has something going on back there, I'll make sure he finds a nice little surprise waiting for him the next time he drops by.*

Belinda saw him creep out of the Chevy and sneak into the woods. She turned off her headlights, drove in as close as she dared, then rolled down her window. She left the keys hanging from the ignition in case she needed to get out fast, crawled out of the window to keep from making any unnecessary noise, then trailed him on foot.

Bless him for wearing light colors, she thought. His white windbreaker nearly glowed in the dark. She edged past the Chevy—*cautiously*—she still couldn't explain the incident with Stevens and Peterkin—and slipped into the trees. She moved quietly. She'd had plenty of woods experience. Mac apparently hadn't. He sounded like a buffalo dancing on potato chips—she'd never heard such a racket from one person. She could have followed him blindfolded.

He worked his way up a rise and into a clearing. She saw him plainly. He stopped, illuminated by the light of the half-moon riding almost overhead. Then he turned. Fifteen yards behind him, she froze.

With preternatural clearness, she saw him look right at her. She saw him grin. His eyes fixed on hers, he mouthed the words "Hi, babe," and he waved at her—

Then he vanished. Poof. He didn't hide, he didn't move, he just—plain—vanished.

For one stunned moment, she couldn't think at all.

Then her mind started working again, beginning with a long list of things she'd like to call the sonuvabitch.

The boss, Belinda thought with some bitterness, *ought to be thrilled by this.*

From back where she'd parked, she heard a whinny and the sound of horse's hooves on dirt. She heard the "ding, ding" sound that could only be caused by someone opening her car door with the keys in the ignition. Still in a state of shock, she listened as a motor—her motor—kicked over.

What?

Mac had vanished and now someone was stealing her car!

Released from her trance, she turned and broke into a full-out gallop, screaming, "Get the hell away from my car, you thief!" as she ran. Branches slapped her face and tore at her clothes. Thorns ripped at her hands and tangled in her braid. Full-sized trees seemed to jump in front of her. She arrived in the field in time to see her car, headlights on, back out into the highway. The driver flipped the interior light on for a moment, just so she would be sure to recognize him. It was Mac. He waved, and tooted her horn, and drove off.

There was a light-colored horse running behind him. Pacing him, she'd have said.

"Give my car back, you bastard!" she shrieked. She pulled her gun out of her shoulder holster and fired one shot in sheer frustration. She heard the crack of shattering glass, and a laugh. Red tail lights disappeared in the distance.

Now her nice little rental car had a bullet hole in it. And a broken window. For which, no doubt, she'd be charged the worth of the entire car.

Shit! But, no—it doesn't matter. He stole my car, he didn't have anyone with him—therefore, he had to leave his. The Chevy. He'll have taken the keys—but I learned a lot from the P.D. I'll just hot-wire his damned Chevy.

She turned to walk back to Mac's car—and found hoofprints and emptiness.

There was no car.

✧   ✧   ✧

Mel Tanbridge grinned and fished out a pen and a yellow legal pad from his desk. He'd just mined a new sure-thing cash-crop angle out of his latest issue of *Science News*, and he wanted to get it down on paper while the idea was still fresh. The members of Nostradamus Project's auxiliary organization, Nostradamus Foundation International, paid well to get their pseudo-science delivered to their doorstep, and he worked hard to make sure it arrived full of juicy tidbits that would keep the money rolling in.

He looked over the *SN* article, which, in very careful terms noted a variance in the ability of rhesus monkeys to pick symbols shown on a computer screen when the symbols were chosen by a human researcher compared to random assignment of the symbols by the computer. The article, "High-Level Pattern Recognition in Rhesus Monkeys," noted that the monkeys picked the correct symbol from a random stream about 13 to 17 percent more often when the human researcher was choosing the symbols. The article noted that this happened even when the monkey was not able to see the researcher, eliminating the chance of visual cues from the human. The article suggested that the human researchers' attempts at randomness displayed a subconscious choice pattern picked up by the monkeys, and noted that the rhesus monkeys had a strong affinity for pattern recognition.

Mel snorted.

"Telepathic Contact Between Humans and Monkeys Confirmed In Independent Studies," he scratched down on the legal pad. "Rhesus monkeys are the first non-human species to demonstrate telepathic abilities—reading the minds of researchers in carefully controlled double-blind experiments conducted by—" He paused. One wanted to be very careful about naming names in these things. Some of his pet flakes, he suspected, also read *Science News*. "—by an independent simian research facility in Florida." He carefully copied in the statistics and a few, slanted quotes, referred to *Science News* as a "professional journal for scientists," and hit his pitch.

"Nostradamus Foundation International must raise—" He thought about it. How much did he want to raise this time? A couple million dollars would be nice. A couple million dollars would permit him to put out glossy four-color fliers and advertise in all his favorite magazines and expand his carefully cultivated list of fools who could be parted from their money. It would also permit him some breathing room to continue with his covert and highly illegal, but real, search to acquire a stable of TK's and other psi talents. "—two point four million dollars to continue its exciting research into projects like this." "Like" was an important word in Mel's vocabulary. He used it a lot. With that one little word, he could infer, without actually stating, that his foundation was involved in simian psychic research. *My ass!* Simian psychic research. What an angle. God, I love it.

"Finally, paranormal phenomena have become a legitimate domain of scientific exploration, and NFI is spearheading that exploration. Your participation has been essential to NFI's research in the past. We need your help now."

He drafted out a series of boxes, starting with twenty dollars and ending with a thousand, and noted that he wanted a place at the bottom of the fund sheet for "participants" to check "current areas of research" they would particularly like to see expanded, with a write-in line for "other." Those little mini-surveys were great. He'd been on the lookout for an animal project ever since some lady had written requesting that NFI expand into "telepathic research with other life forms." She'd added a long, hand-written letter (on pink cat stationery), with her check for twenty dollars, stating that she firmly believed her cats could read minds. Mel made sure she got a nice note back stating that NFI thought psychic cats were a good subject for research. He'd added "non-human psychic research" to his list immediately.

Mel loved New Agers.

He spun the soft leather executive chair to face out the window, leaned back, and laced his fingers behind his head. The taste of success was sweet. The last letter, scavenged from a *National Geographic* article on Eskimo shamans, had netted him about a million-five. This one, his instincts told him, was good for easily that much.

"Fran!" he yelled.

His secretary leaned in the door. "Yes?"

He indicated the legal pad. "Get Janny to set that up in bulletin format—yellow paper and black ink, a line drawing of a telepathic monkey—tell her to keep it understated and scientific-looking. Make sure the drawing is of a rhesus monkey," he added. He closed his eyes and sighed. "Some of these people might notice."

"Okay. Mel, do you want to look at your mail? You have a FedEx package, some bills, some junk, and a few responses from the last mailer."

"Bring 'em in." The bills would wait, the responses he loved to open personally—money in the mail was a wonderful thing. And the FedEx package ought to be Belinda's TK film. He felt a rush of adrenalin. There might be nothing to what she had—but Belinda wasn't one of the true believers. She thought the whole Nostradamus Project was a dodge. If she was convinced she had something real—

He suppressed that line of thought. No sense setting himself up for a disappointment. "Bring in the VCR from the conference room while you're at it."

Lianne opened the door, wearing an oversized pink t-shirt with Garfield on it and a pair of tight blue jeans, minus knees. Her deafeningly pink socks bagged around her ankles, and her hair was tucked behind her ears and held in place by barrettes. She looked about twelve. Mac had really been hoping she'd be wearing something from Victoria's Secret—or maybe nothing—but he hid his disappointment bravely.

"Hey'ya!" She looked him over and grinned. "You look like a man who expected to be greeted by a woman wearing Saran Wrap." She winked. "I don't go to the door that way, you know. If I did, my mom would be on the other side."

Mac squeezed her to his chest and kissed her passionately. "That wasn't what I was thinking at all," he lied. "I was just thinking you were the prettiest bag lady I'd ever seen."

He followed her into her apartment, admiring the way

she walked, and kept close as she led him to her television set.

"I went for comfort, I'll have you know. I had a very bad day." Lianne gave him a wan little smile and a tight hug. "I'm glad you're here. I rented a couple of movies, got a huge bag of popcorn, and I've got all the makings for daiquiris—unless you'd rather have diet soft drinks—?"

"Decaffeinated?" he asked cautiously.

"Nah—I like my caffeine." She made a face. "Why have a cola without caffeine? You might as well not bother."

He answered her face with one of his own. "Whereas I like to sleep at night. No, really, I'm allergic to caffeine. Daiquiris will be fine."

She pointed out the bag on the TV cabinet. "So. Pick the movie you want to see and get it ready—I'll do the daiquiris."

She vanished into the little apartment kitchen. Mac pulled three clear plastic boxes out of the paper bag she'd indicated and studied the titles. He grinned as he peered at the first label. *The Man With One Red Shoe.*

He'd seen that one at least a dozen times. He closed his eyes, replayed the opening credits, recalled the slinking, skullduggerous beat of the score, and chuckled softly. *Tom Hanks, Lori Singer, Carrie Fisher, Dabney Coleman, Charles Durning and Jim Belushi. A casting miracle,* and *a great script,* and *hilarious, too; elvish nominee for an all-time Oscar.* He put the movie on top of Lianne's VCR. *Probably that one,* he decided.

Violent machinery sounds ground out from the kitchen. Mac's smile took on a bemused air. What was she *doing* in there? Was that making daiquiris? It sounded more like chainsawing down a Buick. He shrugged. The ways of humans were inscrutable.

He glanced at the next title she'd rented. He liked Bette Midler a lot, and Danny DeVito—*nasty little man, in this one at least*—was well cast. *Ruthless People* wasn't quite in the same league as her first choice, but on the whole, he approved.

When he saw what her third pick was, though, he dropped the other two movies back in the bag without another thought. He put that cassette into the VCR's slot, checked to make sure it was rewound—gloating all the while at his competence with human machinery—and flashed a Cheshire grin at Lianne when she came out of the kitchen with a mammoth bowl of popcorn balanced in the crook of her elbow and a bright pink daiquiri in either hand.

"Strawberry," she said. "Fresh strawberries my mom picked and dropped off yesterday."

"Sounds tasty." It did—and it smelled tasty, as well. The fresh strawberry-smell was mouthwatering.

She smiled at his expression. "I already tried mine. It's pretty good. I can't think of a better combination than strawberries and popcorn. So—what are we watching?"

He set the bowl of popcorn and one of the frothy pink drinks on her coffee table, and hit the on button of the remote. "Just wait and see." He favored her with a sly smile.

"I rented them, you doofus. I already know what the choices are." When he still wouldn't tell her, she rolled her eyes and snorted. "Mysterious men just give me goosebumps."

Belinda sat on the berm of the dark, lonely road, reloading the chamber of her handgun and wishing Mac were standing in front of her so she would have a target. Reloading was mostly an excuse to sit down for a minute. After all, she'd only used the one bullet. But she'd been hiking along the road for nearly an hour and a half. Her feet hurt, she was tired, she was pissed off, and she really would have liked to have taken time for a good long scream, but that wasn't practical.

Besides, police training had left an indelible mark on her subconscious when it came to firearms. She firmly believed that one empty chamber would be the one she needed—so it would never, never stay empty.

I hate him, she thought, rage coloring everything she did. *If he wasn't worth a ruddy fortune to me alive, I'd kill that two-bit jock just for the fun of it.*

But he'd proven to her that he was exactly the person she was looking for. His psychic tricks verged on the magical—that vanishing act, even more than the business he'd pulled with his car doors—had guaranteed his fate in Belinda's book. That slimy little shit Tanbridge would be willing to pay through the nose for Mac Lynn. And soon. Real soon—because her patience wasn't going to hold out much longer.

She sighed and got up. She was spending a lot of time walking on this job—something she would pay Mac Lynn back for. At least *this* time when he stranded her, she hadn't been wearing high heels and tight leather pants.

Ten minutes further down the road, after a wide detour past an abandoned house that would have to be repaired before it would even be suitable for ghosts, she spotted a gleam of silver off to her right, reflected in the moonlight. As she drew nearer, the gleam resolved into the shape of a Sunbird.

My car! she thought. *I don't believe it!*

Suspecting a ruse, she dropped into the woods and edged up to the vehicle from the passenger side, working her way through grass and weeds that reached to the Sunbird's door handles. He hadn't locked the car. She checked for booby traps, held her breath as she opened the passenger door, and—heart racing—eased herself onto the passenger seat and across to the driver's side.

My God, the keys are in it. And the tank still shows half full. She smiled, bemused. *I'll be damned. Maybe I won't have to skin the soles of his feet with a rusty knife after all.*

She turned the key in the ignition, and the motor kicked right over. She put the car in gear and gave it some gas. It moved—sluggishly—onto the pavement.

Flop-flop-flop-flop, flop-flop-flop-flop.

She hit the brake, turned the motor off, and leapt out.

She stared for a full minute at the car's tires, tires that had been completely hidden by the tall grass. Her anger grew to monumental proportions. In a blind fury, she kicked the door, and screamed "You *son-of-a-bitch!*" into the empty night.

"I'll kill you," she ranted. "I'll kill you, I'll kill you, I'll kill you! I don't need the money this bad—I don't need anything this bad. You bastard! You rotten, stinking, stupid, sneaking *bastard!*"

She stared at her car again, and hot tears of pure rage rolled down her cheeks. The tires—all four of them—were flatter than soggy pancakes.

After the ordeals of the day, Stranger watched the children with apprehension. They huddled, separate and isolated, in the darkness of the beautiful little-girl room and wept in silent, tearless rage. Her heart went out to them.

Och, if there was but a way to show them each that they are not alone—she thought.

She knew all of them—Anne, battered and abused, always angry, who lived only to deal with the Father in all his giant horror; Abbey, the sheltered, the brilliant, charming scholar who loved learning; Alice, the repressive puritan who hated everything that failed to meet her impossible standards of righteousness—and the silent, frozen, tortured husk that was all that remained of the original Amanda. Each of the first three would acknowledge *her* presence—none would admit that their "sisters" existed. The three-year-old Amanda was unreachable, hiding forever inside her frozen shell of fear. Amanda would never come out, without a miracle.

But they need each other sa' badly—if they could only come t'gether, they'd be whole again. And then—Stranger stared up at the milky reflection of moonlight on the wall—*then they could fight back, couldn't they? For all that they're only children.*

Well, then, it's up to me to introduce them, isn't it? A bloody nightmare that's likely to be, but best begun is soonest done.

Abbey was the easiest to reach. She stayed in the frilly pink bedroom, and did not ring her world with guards and traps. Alone of all the girls, she still retained the childish wish to please. She would listen to the ancient voice of Stranger.

:Abbey, can you hear me?:

Abbey, blue-eyed and blond, sniffled and nodded. *:Yes, Stranger. Wh-what do you w-w-want?:*

Cethlenn made her thoughts as gentle and persuasive as she could. *:I have a surprise for you.:*

Abbey perked up a little. *:Is it good?:* she asked hopefully. She alone of all of them retained the ability to hope.

Stranger reflected on the answer to that and sighed. Was it good that there were four little girls and one ancient Celtic witch living in the body of one child? Probably not—but it felt necessary. Stranger had come late to this little drama. She had her own ideas about what had shaped the weirdling child in whom she found her own spirit suddenly awakened. She had ideas, too, of what cures there might be.

:Och, it's good enough, I suppose. I've a giftie for you, little Abbey. Secret sisters, hidden from all the world save you. Would you like to be meeting them, then?:

The child pondered. *:Are they little kids like Sharon?:*

:Not at all,: Stranger assured her. *:They are like you—almost magical.:*

That was the key word. Abbey's eyes widened. *:Oh, yes, Stranger. When can I meet them?:*

Cethlenn, the Stranger, smiled grimly. *:Come with me, child. I think now would be a good time.:* She enveloped Abbey's spirit in her own, and with some difficulty slipped both of them through tiny cracks in the barrier that grew between the children. On the other side, Anne curled in a ball, silent, rocking back and forth, staring at nothing. Anne's world was unremitting gray, with all the shifting featurelessness of unformed nightmare—except for the walls. Everywhere in Anne's world, walls crawled up and up and up until the eye couldn't see any further. They were brick or stone or shiny black glass, but they were everywhere.

When Stranger and Abbey appeared, Anne looked up and shrieked with fear. Her eyes dilated, and she jammed herself up against one of her omnipresent walls.

:Anne, I've brought a friend for you,: Stranger said, her voice soothing. *:You don't have to be alone anymore.:*

Anne cowered and stared. *:A-lone,:* she crooned. *:A-lone, a-lone, a-lone . . .:* Objects materialized in the hazy space that surrounded the three of them and began to spin through the air. Lit cigarettes and burning matches, ropes and riding crops—all took up a stately waltz around Abbey's thin body, then darted in one by one, charging closer and closer to the other child's face. Abbey winced away.

:*Stop it, Anne,*: Stranger demanded, and moved next to the child under attack. :*This is Abbey, your sister.*:

:*Sis-ter, sis-ter, sis-ter,*: the green-eyed child chanted. :*I—don't—want—a—sis-ter.*:

The flames grew bigger, the coals at the ends of the cigarettes brighter and more menacing. The riding crops became bullwhips that cracked like thunder. The ropes coiled and struck out, serpents of hemp. All of them wove around Stranger and Abbey in a tighter and more lethal dance, faster and faster, until Abbey began to scream.

:*Out!*: Cethlenn commanded, and with the flick of her fingers, she and Abbey were through the barrier, back in Abbey's safe haven.

Abbey sat on her bed and sobbed, while Cethlenn sat next to her and stroked her hair. :*I don't want any more surprises, Stranger,*: the child told her gravely.

:*No,*: Stranger replied softly, :*I rather imagine you don't.*:

Cethlenn sat, the tearful child cradled in her arms, and stared off into space. *Well then, lassie,* she thought to herself, *will ye be havin' any more bright ideas this evenin'? Let's hope not.*

"I love *The Princess Bride.* I could watch the sword fight scene all by itself a million times." Lianne snuggled deeper into Mac's shoulder and munched popcorn. On the screen, the fight raged. Inigo made a remark about Bonetti's defense. The Man In Black laughed. The swordsmen battled across the rocks, near the cliff—Inigo switched the sword from his left hand to his right, and the tide of battle turned.

"Probably reminds you of your job," Mac drawled.

Lianne's left eyebrow flickered upward, and she snorted. "I should have it so easy. Even the Fire Swamp and the Rodents of Unusual Size would be a piece of cake compared to fifth grade at Loyd E. Auman."

Mac punched a button on the remote and the TV went off.

"Hey," Lianne yelped. "You can't turn off *The Princess Bride!*"

He turned to her wearing the most serious expression he could muster. "We've already watched the whole movie once and the sword fight three times. Lianne, I want to hear about what happened in your class today. This is important."

Lianne sighed. "I know, but . . ."

He shook his head. "No 'buts'."

She considered his expression, then stiffened her shoulders. "Okay. It just sounds ridiculous, but it was real. Stuff was flying around the room, Mac—books, chalk, pens and pencils, paper—it couldn't have been a draft or a breeze. I don't know what it could have been. I have no logical explanation for what happened."

"Life doesn't require a logical explanation, Lianne," he replied as persuasively as he could.

But she shook her head, violently. "Yes, it does. I refuse to sink to the level of the Shirley MacLaines of the world. I don't flitter after every goofball anti intellectual guru who promises the keys to universe—no math required. I don't approve of all this New Age mumbo-jumbo. The real world doesn't need it. The real world needs mathematicians, scientists, artists, builders, writers, teachers, nurses—the real world doesn't need any more flakes." She drew a deep breath. "There are already enough of those."

Mac grinned wryly and hugged her closer. "Oh, I don't know, baby. I think the real world could use a bit of magic. You know, a few elves and fairies, some bogans to play the bad guys, some ghosties and ghoulies. . . ."

"Life's too short to waste on fantasy," she said, but he could tell she was weakening.

This, from a woman who watches The Princess Bride? "Life's too short to waste on math. Anyone who tells you otherwise is selling something." He grinned.

She frowned. "You'd make a great fifth-grader."

"The world will never know." Mac kissed her cheerfully on her nose, then took a more serious tone. "This morning you were as upset by your student, Amanda, as you were by the stuff flying around in your room. Why?"

Lianne rolled over and looked directly into Mac's eyes. "I want to understand what's the matter with her. As a matter of fact, I'm going out to her house on Friday to talk with her folks. You'd know the place, I'll bet. Kendrick's Bal-A-Shar Arabian Stables. I know it is going to sound silly—but you know what bothered me most today? I just had the craziest feeling, with that *poltergeist* business going on in my classroom, that *Amanda* was really the one responsible." She stopped and pursed her lips. She was watching him for a reaction. "Now I really sound nuts, huh?"

Mac brushed his finger along the line of her eyebrows and slowly shook his head. "Nope—you sound like you have good instincts."

"You think Amanda *might* have had something to do with—oh. Stupid me. You're humoring me." She turned her back to him, grabbed the remote control, and turned the TV back on. The Man In Black leapt from the cliff, did one great swing from a vine, followed up with a back-flip, and landed next to the sword he'd tossed point-down into the sand.

"Who *are* you?" Inigo pleaded.

The Man In Black smiled. "No one of im—"

—Click.

"Don't turn the TV off, Mac," Lianne snapped. "I want to watch this."

He snapped back. "Don't pout. I can't talk to you with the TV on, and I want to discuss this."

She rounded on him, fury in her eyes. "Well, I don't! I don't want to be patronized, I don't want to be humored— I don't want to be remembered as that amusing little schoolteacher you dated once upon a time who had a problem with poltergeists in her classroom and bats in her belfry! I'm going to watch the movie. If you don't want to do that, you can just leave."

I don't want to leave. I had a lot of other plans for this evening, Mac thought, and sighed, mentally. *Give up on the child for a moment. Now that I know who and where she is, there are other ways of reaching her.*

He slipped his hands under her giant t-shirt and nibbled gently along one side of her neck. He felt her shiver, then start to pull away.

"I wasn't making fun of you. I *believe* in poltergeists and fairies and—" he dropped his voice to a low whisper

"—even elves. I think that part of the universe is real, even if you don't. But you're tired, and you probably want to forget about work for a while. I'm sorry I brought it up. Let's find something else to talk about."

"Like what?" she asked, suspiciously.

He breathed into her ear. "Oh, you—and me—and maybe a little snuggling."

Lianne smiled and rolled over against him. "I have a better idea," she whispered. "Let's skip the talking entirely."

It was painfully early. Mac stared at the dull green glow of the alarm clock, then rolled over to look at the woman asleep by his side. She slept on her stomach, the sheet tangled around her knees, her face buried in the crook of her left arm. Her breathing was soft and regular, almost inaudible. Even asleep, she glowed with vitality.

Fascinated, Mac stroked the soft skin of her back and lightly caressed the smooth curves of her buttocks.

She wriggled against his touch, moved closer—and her breathing told him she was awake.

"Hi, there," he chuckled.

She squinched one eye open, smiled at him, and sighed. "Hi, yourself," she said softly. "It isn't time to get up yet, surely?"

"Not really. And don't call me Shirley."

"Oh gawd. It's too early for Zucker jokes."

He softened his smile and caressed her cheek. "I was just watching you sleep."

"And so you decided to wake me up." Lianne giggled. She had a charming giggle. "Mac, you are such a fink. But, boy-oh-boy-oh-boy, I don't want to get up yet—"

An idea occurred to Mac. "Tell you what. I'm completely awake, and I won't get back to sleep again. Why don't you go back to sleep, and I'll put together a terrific breakfast for you—you can eat in bed, and then the two of us will take a nice long shower together, and then we'll go off to work. Okay?"

Her muffled response reached Mac through the baffling of her pillow, under which she had buried her face. "How could I refuse an offer like that?"

He laughed. "You can't, so don't try."

Mac rolled out of the bed and started to walk to the kitchen.

Lianne's voice stopped him.

"You didn't really mean it about the elves, did you?"

He looked back at her. She was propped up on her elbows, studying him intently.

"Mean what about the elves?" he asked carefully.

Her eyes were wary. "That you believed in them."

Mac grinned at her and winked. "Of course I meant it."

She snorted and buried her head back under the pillow. Mac laughed and went on into the kitchen.

Bacon, an omelet, hot croissants, some waffles—or maybe crepes covered with powdered sugar and fresh whipped cream—fresh-squeezed orange juice . . . mmmmm. Sausage. Link sausage. What else? Mac's imagination reviewed the possibilities. *I think I'll do this one without magic. No point in wasting the power when there is a kitchen full of human food to use.* He flipped on the light in her kitchen, wandered over to the fridge, and opened it. *Wonder where she keeps the croissants.*

None were evident. In fact, he didn't see any bacon or link sausages either. No waffles. No crepes. The orange juice was plainly marked, but when he tasted it, it most definitely wasn't fresh-squeezed. He found eggs, but the steps necessary to change them from raw egg to tasty omelet eluded him.

He did see a Betty Crocker cookbook. *I've seen June Lockhart making breakfast for Timmy and his dad on Lassie. How hard can it be?*

He picked up a cookbook at random, opened it, and paged through the index.

Eggs And Cheese—page 101. He thumbed through the pages until he found comprehensive descriptions on how to buy and store eggs, how to measure and use egg equivalents, and a mass of information on cheeses. There were pictures of a woman's hand over a big, flat pan, and instructions that described the making of poached eggs, shirred eggs, fried eggs, scrambled eggs, souffles, egg foo yong, and dozens of varieties of omelets.

Good enough. He rummaged through the kitchen until

he found a pan that resembled the one in the picture. He put together as many of the listed ingredients as he could locate. He couldn't find any fresh green peppers, but he did find a jar labeled "Hot Red Chili Pepper—Ground." In the tradition of the cookbook, he substituted a cup of red peppers for the suggested cup of green peppers. Lianne had an eight-ounce can of tomato sauce in her cupboard, but it didn't have a pop-top on it, and Mac couldn't figure out how to open it, so, with the competent smile of a man who can adapt, he added eight ounces of tabasco sauce—which, he reasoned, was bright red and should be the same thing. He broke the three required eggs with enthusiasm, and very carefully picked out most of the pieces of shell. There didn't seem to be enough omelet for two people though, so he added another three eggs.

Satisfied, he stirred his ingredients around in the little flat pan, and following instructions, located the knob on the stove that said "oven," and checked the instructions. It was supposed to take forty minutes to cook an omelet, but he really didn't want to spend that much time on it. He thought for a moment. The instructions called for 350 degrees. If he doubled the temperature, he should be able to halve the time. But the oven wouldn't go any higher than 550. Well, actually, it did go to BROIL. *That must be about 600–700 degrees.* He turned the knob to broil. Carrying his embryonic omelet carefully by the pan's plastic handle, he placed it into the oven.

Nothing to that. I might as well see what else I can whip up.

He paged through the cookbook. Pictures of delicious roasts and beautifully prepared fowl caught his eyes. He read down the instructions for some of the dishes. *I could do that,* he thought, fascinated. The world of humans was amazingly accessible, if one simply knew where to look. Page after page of substantial human dishes—that anyone could make.

He became absorbed in pictures of London Broil and Sweet-and-Sour Meatballs, Broccoli-Tomato Salad and Swedish Tea Rings. The time slipped past.

The sudden shriek of the smoke alarm brought him out

of his reverie. The kitchen was redolent with the stench of burning plastic. Smoke roiled from the front of the oven.

"Shit," Mac muttered, admiring the succinctness of human vernacular. With a glance, he silenced the smoke alarm. With another, he formed the smoke into a compact ribbon and sent it trailing out the entryway in a neat, steady stream. He pulled open the oven door, surveyed the melted ruins of the skillet handle and his prodigiously grown and dreadfully blackened omelet with dismay. He made a gesture of dismissal, and skillet, omelet, and mess vanished.

Lianne called from the bedroom, "Was that the smoke alarm?"

So much, he thought, *for doing a fabulous breakfast the human way.*

"That was your imagination."

"I suppose it's my imagination that I smell smoke, too."

"Absolutely. I'm bringing breakfast in now." *To blazes with it. I'll do it my way.* Mac visualized his own breakfasts from the hotel, and out of thin air and elven magic, recreated an exact duplicate of the best one he'd ever had, down to the little rose in the cut crystal bud vase. Then he doubled it. He lifted up the heavy silvered serving tray he'd materialized, and trotted into the bedroom with it.

Lianne rolled over and sat up, and her eyes grew round. "Wow! When you talk about breakfast in bed, you aren't kidding." She looked over the steaming croissants, the huge, cheese-filled omelet, the two steaks—broiled, medium rare, the big crystal glasses full to brimming with fresh-squeezed juice, and the bowls of fresh fruit. "And where did you get fresh cherries this time of year?" she asked.

Mac shrugged and grinned. "You like?"

"I like." She took one of the cherries and bit into it, and closed her eyes with ecstasy. "God, that's good." She looked at Mac with eyes that seemed to see right through him. "I'm beginning to realize why you believe in magic, though. The fancy trays and the cut crystal aren't a bad trick, considering I've never owned anything like them in my life, but these—" She indicated the little bowls of rich red fruit. "There won't be any cherries available around here till the middle of June. I know, because I haunt the grocery stores for 'em every year. If you found these—that's magic."

"You bet it is." Mac dug into his omelet and steak. "Stick with me, kid. You ain't seen nothing yet." He grinned at her. The wincing he saved for inside.

Carelessness like that, he thought ruefully, eyeing the out-of-season cherries, *will blow your cover all the way to Elfhame Outremer. And beyond.*

CHAPTER FIVE

D.D. had MIX 96 turned way up. She was sprawled under the engine of the disassembled Victor, tinkering with something, singing along at the top of her lungs with a Creedence Clearwater Revival cover of "I Heard It Through The Grapevine" that Tank Sherman had dug out of the Golden Oldies box. Mac grinned. He wouldn't admit it to her, but D.D. didn't sound too bad on backup vocals.

He waited until the song was over and something odious by Madonna started to play—then he turned the radio off.

"Hey!" D.D. yelled without looking up. "Turn that back on. I'm listening to it."

:*Mother, Mother, what would they be sayin' back home if they could see you right now? The shame—och, the shame of me own fair mother disgracin' herself so.*:

:*Can it, kiddo.*: Dierdre was unfazed. She stood, wiped her hands on her overalls, and turned to face her offspring. "I'm not believin' me own eyes," she said for the benefit of everyone. "Mac Lynn, the perennially late, is in here at eight o'clock in the morning. Ye gods, man, fetch me water before I faint."

"Ha-ha." :*Stopping in to let you know—I found the homebase of our little TK. I'm going by there later today to see if I can talk to her.*:

D.D. turned back to her engine block and returned to her tinkering. Mac sat down on a stack of tires to watch her.

:*Good,*: the pony-tailed terror remarked as she loosened bolts. :*'Bout damn time. I may graduate you to nearly-competent.*:

Mac grinned. :*Actually, there is something you can do that would be a lot more help.*:

:*If you're still hoping I'll talk to Felouen for you—*:

Mac snarled out loud, and realized a comment was necessary for the benefit of the non-elven who were present. "While you're working on the steering, D.D., tighten it up. It felt like you had it patched together with rubber bands and wishful thinking on Wednesday." Inwardly, he added another snort. :*Not even close, Mother. I think I know how to take care of Felouen. This is something else entirely. I suspect Belinda Ciucci will be back. And after last night, she's going to be looking for my hide nailed to a board. Unfortunately, that might put an edge on her. Entertain her and her two goons for me, if you would. I don't want her getting close to the kid.*:

Dierdre chuckled. :*She still haunting your backtrail, is she? That I'll be happy to help you with.*:

Maclyn was out on the track when Belinda showed up. D.D. spotted her making nice to Brad Fennerman from the SpelCo team, batting her lashes and leaning forward just enough to give him a really clear view of her cleavage.

D.D. wrinkled her nose with disdain. The woman was a menace—and an embarrassment to both her species and her gender. She decided to watch, though, to see what Belinda's angle of attack would be.

It was only when she caught the girl's gaze skim past a point in her own pit area that she noticed a pale, hulking shape hovering in the shadows over Mac's thermos holding a little baggy full of something white and powdery. *Interesting. No doubt Mac's young admirer has a Borgia event planned here. Probably not true poison—I suspect they want darlin' Mac alive.* D.D. grinned and made sure the intruder thought she was far too involved in her work to notice him.

White powder went into the Gatorade. She saw a steady stream of it pour in—saw the man carefully twist the cap back on the thermos, then slink out along the row of stacked tires—saw him signal Belinda. The girl didn't acknowledge the signal, but she abruptly looked at her watch, gave a dramatic sigh, and wriggled away on her high, high heels.

She'll be around a while yet, D.D. figured. *She's got to have some plan for draggin' him out of here under everyone's noses. Och, this ought to be delightful.*

Mac did three more laps before he roared in.

:She's been by,: D.D. informed him without preamble. *:Such a sweet, innocent lass she is, too, I canna imagine why you're suspectin' her at-all. Be sure to drink all your Gatorade—your friends went to such trouble to drug it for you.:*

Mac smiled slyly. *:Did they now? Well, then—:* He went straight to his thermos, groaned, "God, it's so hot out there today, I could drink almost anything," and drained the contents in two long gulps.

:Now, Mother, do I pretend that it affected me and bug the hell out of them when I disappear from their car—or do I just go about my business and drive them really nuts?:

D.D. shrugged and grinned. *:Your call.:*

Tucked into a dark corner of the pits, Belinda waited. Mac had swallowed every blessed drop in his drugged drink—she tried to keep her glee in check, and failed—and Peterkin had dumped a whole twelve hundred milligrams of Seconal into the stuff just to make sure the jackass got enough to knock him out even if he only drank half. In fifteen to thirty minutes, according to Belinda's drug reference, Mac should start getting sleepy. In an hour or two, if they didn't get him to a doctor, he'd end up in a coma. In between that time, she needed to get him out of town.

She had her story worked out to perfection. The line would be that she and the boys were one off-duty EMT and two friends who just happened to be racing fans—they could take good care of their hero, the big racecar driver, and get him to the E.R. faster than an ambulance could hope to arrive. They would claim expertise and supplies on hand. There would not be anyone who would doubt that Mac Lynn was on his way to the hospital. There would be no interference from the airhead mechanic or any of the other crew. The first of several switch-cars was waiting outside. The plan was perfect. She didn't doubt that Mel had a doctor on his payroll somewhere—she wondered, however, how long she could leave Mac in a coma without Mel considering the package he received "damaged goods."

She entertained herself with images of what she was going to do to Mac when he was helpless and in her care. She wondered briefly about the mechanics of castration. The idea appealed to her, and it wouldn't damage his TK ability any—would it? *With my luck, it would finish his talent off for good. After all, that's where men's brains are.* Maybe she should leave his balls alone and just cut off his head.

Feeling more cheerful, she glanced at her watch. With a shock, she realized that almost an hour had passed. Mac was still working—and there was no visible sign that the drugs were affecting him. She looked over at Peterkin and Stevens in their hiding place across the pits. Both shrugged.

She bit her lip and stared at the wide-awake driver. *He drank it, dammit! I know he did. I saw him with my own eyes.*

Could Peterkin or Stevens have double-crossed her? Yes, obviously—but why would they?

Unknown. However, the easy way to tell would be to try an equal dose of Seconal on them and see how it worked. If there was something wrong with the prescription she'd finagled out of the doc-in-a-box in LaJolla, Peterkin and Stevens would be fine. If they had double-crossed her, they would get what they deserved. Either way, she didn't lose anything.

She made a curt signal and slipped away from the pits. Her two stooges followed her out to the parking lot.

Felouen, in a cream silk blouse and tailored cashmere skirt and blazer, her hair pulled back in a classic chignon, appeared behind Maclyn and D.D., smiling wryly. "What charming friends you have. No wonder you'd rather spend your time here than in Underhill."

D.D., her face and overalls dirt-smudged, torque wrench in one gloved hand, smiled politely. "We all have our little hobbies, dear." Her smile widened as she watched Felouen wince away from the Cold Iron wrench. Mac wished he dared smile.

Instead he sighed. "Still overdressed, hey, Felouen? Why don't you go home and change into something more appropriate?"

She frowned. "I'm here on business. Dierdre, you've served your time on Council—I really do not need to speak with you. But I must speak with Maclyn for a moment."

D.D. nodded, and lost the smug smile. "I'll leave you two, then." Whistling a Killderry reel, the delicate mechanic moved back to her prized auto, leaving her son to fend for himself.

:Thanks, Mother.:

:You know where I stand on this.:

Mac shrugged and turned to glare at Felouen.

The elegant warrior gifted him with a frosty smile. "I need your company for a few moments, Maclyn. Please come Home with me; I'll show you what you need to see, and then, if you still feel that I am imposing needlessly on you, I will take back the Ring and the Council will decide on your standing within the Court."

Maclyn didn't quite grimace. "More signs and portents?"

Felouen didn't change her expression by so much as a twitch of her eyelid. "Please—just come with me. If you choose to scoff *after* you have seen what I have to show you, so be it."

Maclyn sighed. "You are so damned irritating—you and your bogeys and doom-crying." But he followed Felouen into the office, and through the temporary Gate she'd formed there.

They appeared at the border of Elfhame Outremer, where the edges of order collided with the infinite black Unformed, next to the Oracular Pool. The border, usually firmly fixed and still, billowed unsettlingly while Maclyn watched, pushing dark tentacles into the shield that walled the Ordered Land. The effect looked enough like something big trying to break through that Maclyn cringed when one tentacle brushed within a few inches of his thigh. More tentacles pressed suddenly from the same spot, as if they had become aware of his presence.

"What's doing that?" Mac asked, more disturbed than he cared to admit.

"There's nothing out there that I or anyone else can find," Felouen said. "That's all just unformed energy—and a feeling of fear and rage and hatred. It's been getting worse."

"I see where you might be worried," he admitted.

She shook her head. "Not yet, you don't. I'm afraid there's more. Look into the Oracular Pool."

Mac turned and studied the flat, deep blue sheet of water nestled in its shallow concave of mossy rock. After a moment, his reflection disappeared, replaced by darkness. For a long moment, nothing was visible in the Pool; then, with jerky, shambling movements, blood-spattered horrors streamed out of the Unformed—misbegotten nightmares with gape-jawed lopsided heads jammed neckless onto narrow shoulders, sticklike arms and legs terminated by terrible claws, sketchily formed bodies that bore no resemblance to anything Maclyn had ever seen, or ever heard of. They bared monstrous fangs and ran screaming after tall, blond, graceful runners that fell before them, bleeding from jagged, terrible wounds—and the Pool dimmed, and once again Maclyn looked at his own reflection.

He stood, speechless, staring into his own eyes.

"It's time to let go of the memories, Maclyn," Felouen whispered. "It's time to stop pretending that you'll find her again, and come back to your own kind. We need you here and now. *I* need you. Those humans do not, nor do you need anything of theirs."

"I still love her," Maclyn said, still staring stiffly into the Pool. *That isn't the only reason I stay, but it's a reason. I know you wouldn't understand the others.*

"She's dust these last two hundred years, Maclyn," Felouen said, reasonably, calling up a despair he'd begun to forget. "Sure and she loved you—'twas your own folly you loved her, too. You were both young, but she grew old and died, and you're still young—and still searching for her among mortals who are destined to leave you just as she did."

Despair turned to anger, and he turned on the source of that anger. "Have you ever loved anyone, Felouen?" he snapped, restraining his wish to strike that impassive face. "Has anyone ever really gotten through to you?"

For a time, Maclyn got no answer. Finally the slender warrior responded, turning a face full of a loss that matched his own, speaking in a dull, lifeless whisper. "Yes. I've loved without hope for more than two hundred years—" Her voice cracked, and she fell silent.

Maclyn turned and studied her. She had her back to him; her shoulders were stiff and her spine was rigid and erect. His hands clenched and unclenched. "I'll hold on to the Ring, Felouen. I have something else I need to take care of now—and it may be important; I don't know yet, and I'm not taking on anything else until I do know. The fact is, I'm not sure what this thing I'm involved with means, or how much trouble it's going to entail for all of us. There *is* a child involved, and you know I can't turn my back on a child. I'm not promising to get involved in this problem here. But I won't say that I won't, either."

Felouen nodded but said nothing, and kept her back to him.

Maclyn Gated back to the garage, and the Gate closed off behind him.

In the office, he stared at the plain round wall clock that ticked off the seconds and minutes and hours that formed the limits of humans' lives, and he bit his lip. He could not keep himself from remembering that one of the elves that fell to the shambling things in the Oracular Pool's vision had been Felouen.

Amanda-Anne slipped off the bus and hurried down the lane, between the long lines of neatly painted fence, the gentle green, clovered swells of pastures, black and bay and glossy chestnut Arabs who stood head to tail, grazing peacefully and swatting flies from each other's faces. She detoured around the stables, moving carefully along a route that not only hid her presence from anyone working in the

barns, but also from anyone who might be in the house
or the yard. Sharon was still in primary and got home from
school half an hour before she did; it was essential to keep
close watch for her. Sharon would tell the Father and the
Step-Mother where she went. Sharon was a big tattletale,
but she couldn't help it. The Step-Mother made her that
way.

The grass grew taller back of the stables. It edged a
woodland dark and cool and quiet even in summer, with
stands of pines marching in long, neat rows, bordered and
filled in by scrub oak. Amanda-Anne moved across the beds
of pine needles in near-silence, being sure she went a
different way than the times before, consciously leaving no
path. The pines merged with swamp on the right, full of
snakes and cypress, with older hardwoods on the left—not
first growth, but large, sturdy trees nonetheless: oak and
magnolia and sycamore, ash and gum. Amanda-Anne went
to the left, up a gentle incline.

At the top of the little hill sat an immense, ancient holly.
Patches of pale green moss spotted its dappled silver-white
bark, a few red berries still hung on in defiance of the
season. The old tree's branches bent so low they touched
the ground, and spiny evergreen leaves formed a screen
so that the base of the tree became a fortress, well protected, with only one narrow entrance. That entrance,
invisible except from a difficult approach through a stand
of scrub oaks and blackberry canes, was formed from a
branch that arched higher than the others and left a narrow gap that could be crawled through by a small, determined child.

Amanda-Anne, experienced in the delicate negotiation
of thorn and thicket, got inside without snagging her school
clothes or getting dirty. Once inside, she breathed deep
and stood up straight. Amanda-Anne retreated to the
background and Amanda-Abbey came out.

Things sparkled under the tree—decorations hung on
bits of thread and string that decorated Amanda-Abbey's
magpie nest. Tiny glass beads scavenged from an outgrown
pair of Sharon's moccasins and a green carved glass bead
saved from a broken necklace that was the only token she
had of her real mother hung next to little round mirrors

glued back-to-back, rescued from a favorite sweater that Daddy had ripped apart when he was mad once. Bluejay feathers, bits of fragile shell brought back from trips to the beach house at Ocean Isle, a broken, but still pretty, stained glass suncatcher of a hummingbird, the cut glass baubles from a pair of discarded earrings, one rhinestone pin—all swayed and glittered and turned with every scant breeze. There were comic books wrapped carefully in plastic and hidden in the tree's only reachable knothole. A worn saddle blanket served as a rug.

Amanda-Abbey leaned against the tree trunk in her secret home and watched her collection catch the light. Amanda-Anne's fingers stroked the cool, almost smooth bark, her ears drank in the hushed murmurs of safe, isolated, protected woods. No one would find her; no one would hurt her—not while the tree guarded her.

The child closed her eyes and felt the warmth of the sun on her face and studied the cozy speckled yellow glow of the inside of her eyelids. A few birds chirped and fluttered; squirrels raced along aerial throughways and chattered pointed squirrel insults at each other.

The light that flickered through her closed lids grew brighter—much, much brighter.

She opened her eyes.

Something was happening in front of her. Her green carved bead was glowing with warm, glorious inner light. A swirling mist began to curl out of it, emerald-green shot through with flecks of gold bright as tiny suns. The mist stretched and grew, and within it a form took shape—a form wrapped in rich green-and-gold tapestries, taller than anyone Amanda knew and handsome and smiling, with eyes bright as new leaves, long blond hair held back by a gold, jewel-studded circlet, and the neatest pointed ears Amanda had ever imagined.

"Wow," Amanda-Abbey whispered. "That's really cool."

Amanda-Alice sensed something that required her attention. From her white, pure castle, she stretched out feelers, then, finding what she sought, withdrew them again in shocked disgust. *It's magic. Magic is evil.*

❖   ❖   ❖

The green man produced a shimmering wand and waved it in a circle in front of her. Sparkles of light scattered and danced in front of the child, weaving patterns in the warm spring air.

"Magic," the child whispered. Then, *There's no such thing as magic,* she thought. Amanda-Abbey was sure of this. *So this isn't a real elf. It's just imagination.*

Amanda-Anne kept quiet, watching, paying close attention, taking notes. Appearing out of thin air was a good trick. If she could learn it, she could hide from the Father. The magic lights were pretty, but they didn't look useful. Even so, Anne could sense power in them. Power was something she wanted.

The amazing man seemed to look right through the scrawny child in the tartan plaid skirt who stared at him— and then, silently as he had come, he folded into the scintillating fog from which he had emerged and was drawn back into the glowing bead. The light in the bead gleamed an instant longer, and then flickered and died.

"Gone," Amanda-Abbey said, wistfully. "I want him to come back." She thought. *If I can figure out why he came here, maybe I can bring him back.*

She inched over to where the bead hung. She blew on it once. Nothing happened. She walked around it, staring. It remained just a bead on a string. She pushed it once with a single index finger, and watched it swing in a few short arcs, then stop. Still, nothing happened. She closed her eyes and wished the magic back into the bead again, without luck. Tentatively, she reached out and broke off the fine strand of thread at the branch, then tied the makeshift bracelet around her wrist. Almost immediately, the single bead on its weathered thread sprang back into glowing life, and the mist spiraled forth once more.

The green-garbed man reappeared right in front of her and winked at her, then laughed soundlessly and hid behind the holly's trunk.

She walked around the tree, stooping under low branches and her dangling decorations. He was gone.

A flash of green light from behind her alerted her, and

she turned to see him again, this time on the outside of her tree-fortress. He waved, and she waved back and watched him, but she did not follow him beyond the protective circle of the tree's branches.

Stranger's voice broke into her thoughts, making herself known. *:Don't fear him, lass—'tis good luck to meet one of the Fey folk.:*

:He isn't real, Stranger.:

There was gentle laughter in her head. *:Of course not, child. 'Tis still good luck.:*

Amanda-Abbey giggled at the apparent nonsense in that, and when the green-garbed elf vanished again, she rubbed the bead on her wrist, like a waif summoning a genie from a bottle.

The bead glowed again, and the elf reappeared in his gorgeous robes and glowing green cloud, but this time he settled cross-legged in front of the girl, floating an inch off the ground.

He smiled shyly.

Amanda-Abbey smiled back. "Can you talk?" she asked.

"Of course," he answered. "Can you?"

She giggled. "What a silly question. I just did."

"And so did I," he retorted, and winked.

"But you aren't real," she pointed out. "So I thought maybe you couldn't talk. Do you have a name?"

The elf pulled back his shoulders and in solemn tones, announced, "I am Prince Maclyn Arrydwyn, son of the fair Lady Dierdre Sherdeleth and of the Prince of Elfhame Outremer. I am rider of great metal steeds and horses of air and magic, guardian of the Twilight Lands, immortal walker among mortals." Maclyn bowed slightly from the waist. "And who are you?"

"Everyone calls me Amanda—but my name is really Abbey." Amanda-Abbey returned the bow gracefully.

The elf—Maclyn—nodded seriously. "I see. So then, shall I call you Amanda, as everyone else does, or shall I call you by your true name?"

The child grinned. "Call me by my true name. Nobody else but Stranger knows it."

"Very well." Once again he bowed, gracefully. "And who, by the way, is Stranger?"

Amanda-Abbey giggled. "If I knew that, she wouldn't be Stranger, now would she? Do you grant wishes, like in fairy tales?"

He considered her request. "Hmm. I do magic. Would that be good enough?"

"Magic isn't real," she insisted.

:Magic is wicked, wicked, wicked!: A voice screamed in Amanda-Abbey's head, but Amanda-Abbey refused to listen to it. Magic was just silliness and tricks with mirrors. Everyone knew that.

"Isn't it, now? Let me show you, and you be the judge." Maclyn touched the string that held the bead to Amanda's thin wrist, and it glowed softly. When he pulled his hand away, the bead was strung on a beautiful, intricate gold chain.

Yes-s-s! Amanda-Anne watched closely and whispered to herself. The elf pulled energy from somewhere, made it do things. *I can . . . almost . . . see how—but . . . whe-e-e-re?*

"Oh," Amanda-Abbey gasped. "How beautiful, and how wonderful. Do something else."

But Maclyn smiled and vanished.

"Wait!" Amanda-Abbey cried.

The elf reappeared in the woods a little way off. He beckoned, and the girl hurried out of her hiding place, heedless of the thorns and the briars. Her blouse snagged, and she got some pulls in her sweater, but the elf had vanished again and reappeared still farther off, and she couldn't take time to be worried about mere clothes.

She darted through the woods with the elf always appearing and disappearing in the dimming light just ahead of her. Suddenly Amanda-Abbey noticed that she was moving through fog that got thicker with every step she took, and that she didn't recognize anything about the part of the woods she was in. The trees were farther apart, and taller than any trees that she had ever seen, and incredibly beautiful. Leaves of silver and gold brushed against her and rang gently with every touch or puff of the faint breeze. Lights in soft greens and muted blues, gentle reds and bright yellows, flittered and danced through the branches high overhead, and the sound of a tiny waterfall somewhere nearby tinkled merrily in her ears. Voices whispered from above her, and at a distance, there were sounds of laughter, and dancing, and a jig played inhumanly fast by virtuoso performers.

:*I know where this is,*: Stranger told Amanda-Abbey with a satisfied voice.

Amanda-Abbey whispered, "Really? Where are we?" Suddenly she was no longer so certain that elves and magic were impossible. She was no longer certain of anything.

From right beside her, Maclyn said, "Welcome to Elfhame Outremer, Abbey. This is my home."

"It's beautiful," the child whispered, in a voice full of wonder.

Evil, evil, evil, thought Amanda-Alice. *Only the devil does magic; that's what the Sunday-school teacher said. This green man is the devil, and this place must be hell. I'm telling Father about this. He will know how to punish the devil—I know he will.*

Amanda-Abbey felt a vague sensation of disquiet. It seemed as if part of her mind wanted to rebel, to run away from the lovely haven in which she found herself.

"Yes, it is beautiful," Maclyn answered. "I thought a special girl like you would be able to appreciate such a magical place."

Amanda-Abbey raised her eyebrows. "Why me?"

He spread his hands wide. "Because of the magic you do," he said, and his words had a ring of sincerity about them.

She stared at him, puzzled. "I don't do magic. Magic isn't real."

He shook his head. "Wasn't it magic that kept the race car from hurting anyone at the track the other day? Wasn't it magic that sent all the erasers and papers in your classroom flying?"

Amanda-Abbey giggled; where had he gotten these stories? Race cars? Erasers? What was he talking about? She didn't remember anything like that. "I don't know what you mean."

Amanda-Anne, satisfied that she had figured out the elf's magic tricks, looked up and noticed the darkened, twilight sky. Fear gripped her. The Father would be furious—the Step-Mother would tell him that she was late. She shoved her way to the front, grabbed control of the body, and stood, rigid and trembling. Her eyes met those of the elf, and she shivered. "Home!" she wailed, suddenly terrified. *Late! I'm . . . late! Home!* She used the information she'd garnered from watching the elf to draw in the earth-energy that pulsed through Elfhame Outremer, and promptly removed herself to the safety of the holly tree hide-out.

Amanda-Abbey was back in control and back in familiar surroundings. She didn't even flinch. "Wow!" she whispered, crawling out of her nest in the muted sunlight of early afternoon, still impelled by a powerful urge to get home, "What a neat dream." She studiously avoided noticing the green bead on the gold filigreed chain that hugged her wrist, or the dirt and snagged threads on her school clothes.

Amanda-Anne took over control as Amanda walked through the woods. She trotted home by a different route, alert for watchers of any kind.

Cethlenn had been aware of the elf's presence, but she had been unable to wrest control of the body away from the children long enough to beg for help. Now, hurrying back to the child's terrible home, she swore softly and wondered what she could do to save her child host.

Lianne drove up the long, winding lane past carefully tended fences and manicured pastures, well-maintained, picturesque old barns, and a riding ring set up for trail training, with jumps and bridges and barrels. Over to her right, a young man put one lean gray filly through her paces on a lunge line, while two hawk-faced men in tweed jackets and caps watched and commented.

She noted the exquisitely kept ornamental gardens, the flawless landscaping, the elegant half-timbered home that bespoke good breeding and old money—and she shook her head in bewilderment. This Eden was more than she could ever hope to aspire to. In her whole life, she could never hope to live so well, to have so much. Where was the worm that gnawed away at Amanda? And how could it survive in such a place?

She parked her little yellow VW bug to one side of the house, clambered out of the car, and smoothed her skirt nervously. She felt suddenly shabby and plain—and on very shaky ground.

Stomach in knots, she strode up the walk and rang the bell. After a long wait, she heard the click of heels in the hall. The door swung open noiselessly, and Lianne pasted a confident smile on her face.

Merryl Kendrick gave her a cool, polite nod and said, "Won't you come in, Miss McCormick? Amanda is upstairs doing her homework—I can call her if you would like."

"Not just yet, please," Lianne answered, and found herself following Merryl through a long, perfectly kept maze of glossy mahogany halls and decorator-perfect rooms. She studied Mrs. Kendrick's back and winced. Merryl Kendrick would have been a good six inches taller than Lianne in flats. In heels, the other woman towered over her. Amanda's step-mother was casually dressed, the elegance under-stated—but every article of clothing spoke of more money than Lianne could put into her wardrobe in an entire year. She shouldn't let all that money have a psychological effect on her, Lianne knew, and knew at the same time that *should* was a meaningless word. All that money, all that power, did have an effect on her. It weakened her position, it weakened her credibility. As much as she would like to pretend otherwise, she was not an equal among peers in this world. And she would have to act as if she were, for Amanda's sake. Because whatever was wrong with Amanda was wrong in spite of all these evident advantages.

"Tea?" Merryl asked.

"Thank you." Lianne took the seat the other woman indicated and glanced around the sun-room. It seemed to her that she had seen it in a *Better Homes and Gardens* spread. With its Mexican tile floor, hand-adzed timber-framed beams, and walls of glass looking out over a scenic view of the estate and a lovely, wild patch of woods, it was breathtaking.

And sterile.

There were no family pictures, no knickknacks, no personal touches whatsoever to mar the carefully conceived vision of the designer. As she ran her memory back over what she had seen of the rest of the house, she realized it was all the same. The house was lovely, but it looked as if no one lived there, or ever had.

That's a middle-class prejudice, she told herself. *Only the middle class insists that a bit of disorder is healthy.*

Merryl returned and placed a heavy pottery teapot and a matching cup in front of Lianne.

"Thank you." The young teacher poured herself a cup of tea and sipped at it gratefully.

"Of course." Merryl Kendrick nodded gracefully. "Andrew will be home any time. In the meantime, we can drink our tea, or you can fill me in on what you perceive to be the problem."

What I perceive *to be the problem. That's nicely put. The problem is no doubt going to be my* perception, *and not the problem. Ah, well, face it right out.*

She decided on a frontal assault. "To the best of your knowledge, Mrs. Kendrick, is there any history of mental illness in Amanda's family?"

The other woman's lips curled in a faint smile over her own cup of tea, and one eyebrow raised slightly. She leaned back in the peach-and-mint wing-backed chair and crossed her legs. After a moment, she chuckled. "Well, that's certainly getting to the point." Merryl Kendrick sipped slowly at her tea. "Actually, yes—there is. Funny you should ask. Andrew's first wife had a long history of psychological problems—paranoia, delusions, depression, psychoses. She was hospitalized—Andrew obtained a divorce, but made sure she was well taken care of until her death."

At Lianne's startled expression, Amanda's step-mother nodded slowly.

"You see, she died about two years ago. Suicide. I understand these problems are sometimes . . ." Merryl picked delicately around the word ". . . hereditary."

Lianne held her breath, closed her eyes, and let it out again, slowly. "Sometimes," she agreed.

"Dana's parents—Amanda's natural grandparents—aren't quite normal, either. We've done the best we could for Amanda—limited her contacts with them ever since her mother's death. . . ." Merryl Kendrick seemed to be actually relishing this. "It doesn't seem to be helping, does it, Miss McCormick?"

Lianne blinked, choosing her words with care. "Amanda is having serious problems in school this year, behavioral as well as academic. I'm not the only teacher that has noticed this. It's in her records, if you'd care to see them." *There. So much for "my perception."* "I can't say that her problems stem from her mother, or her mother's death, or heredity, or anything else. All I can say is that she needs help, and I don't know that I am able to give her the help she needs."

There were thundering feet on a stairway, and Amanda burst into the room. Her sweet, blue-eyed face lit up when she saw her teacher, and she ran over and hugged her vigorously. "I didn't know you were coming over tonight, Miss McCormick. Don't you like my house?" The child turned to face her step-mother, still smiling. "I got all of my homework finished, Mother. May I go outside for a while?"

"Not now, Amanda," Merryl said. "I'm expecting your father home any minute."

"As well you should, darling," Andrew Kendrick said from the doorway, slipping a cigarette pack into his crisp breast-pocket. "I'm sorry I'm late—one of my clients was quite distraught and needed a bit of extra time."

Lianne had been watching Amanda, bemused by the girl's cheerful countenance and normal manner—so she didn't miss the change. Amanda's face turned from her step-mother to her father, and a series of unreadable expressions flashed across her features. Her mouth fell slightly open, giving her a dull, witless look.

And her pale, pale green eyes stared at the man in the

doorway with a cross between canny hatred and stupefied terror.

The flesh stood up on Lianne's arms, and chills raced up and down her spine.

There was a crash from another room. Andrew and Merryl looked at each other, and Merryl cleared her throat. "You evidently let one of the cats in with you again, Andrew."

His eyes focused on his child. "No doubt," he agreed. "Amanda, I see you've been playing in your school clothes again. You've soiled them and ruined the fabric. Please go upstairs and change into your stable clothes, then go clean your pony's stall. I'll be out to check on your work when your mother and I have finished speaking with your teacher."

"Yes-s-s . . . Father," the child said. Her voice grated; low, animal-like. She was as much a different child as if Amanda had been picked up and physically replaced.

Lianne felt her pulse begin to race. *Wrong*, her mind screamed at her. *This is wrong! It's weird! It's awful!* It took every bit of control for her to keep her seat, to keep smiling while Andrew Kendrick crossed the room, took a seat next to his wife, and smiled at her and said, "Well, ladies, what solutions have you reached?"

His voice was cheerful, his eyes bright and kind and concerned—so why did every nerve in Lianne's body insist that some invisible force was dragging monstrous talons across a giant blackboard?

"Miss McCormick deduced Dana's problem from Amanda's classroom behavior." Merryl looked into her husband's face. Her body posture and gestures indicated sincere concern. "She *says* she isn't the only teacher to have seen problems with Amanda."

Her husband dropped his eyes. "Dana," he said, and Lianne would have sworn she could hear real anguish in those two labored syllables. Her instincts told her that, no matter what she saw, or thought she saw, Andrew Kendrick was a phony. Merryl was the perfect foil for him, and the two of them had snowed her from the beginning— would have kept her convinced that the problem was in other directions. But Lianne knew kids. She'd been well acquainted with thousands of them in her eight years of teaching, and she'd seen that unguarded expression of Amanda's before. The look in her eyes, the little girl's actions, the abrupt change in her attitude—those things had given Lianne a name for the sick feeling that weighted her down and dragged on her every breath.

Child abuse.

She needed to get out of the house, get help—but first, she needed one more tiny reassurance that she'd really seen what she thought she'd seen.

"I think Mrs. Kendrick and I have stumbled across the problem. And I think I may have thought of a solution." She had to have parental permission for this first step. Unless the child revealed something on her own, or there were physical evidences, there wasn't anything that could be done that Andrew Kendrick with his money and influences couldn't counter. "I can't promise anything, but I'd like your permission anyway. I'd like for Amanda to be seen by one of our counselors. I think there are a great many things troubling her, probably related to her mother's death, and I think that having some time with the counselor, starting on Monday, would give her a chance to talk those problems out. It would at least give us an idea of what we're dealing with."

Lianne waited. She watched concern crawl across Merryl's features like a spider, watched Andrew's eyes harden, watched them glance at each other—*we have to keep our secret* expressions that gave the teacher her answer.

"I don't think so, Miss McCormick," Andrew said, still smiling—but with the smile artfully condescending. "I think you may be right, that psychological help would be in order for Amanda—but I don't think that a school counselor who works for peanuts and sees his, ah, *clients* in the sardine-can atmosphere of public education would be of much use. While we want Amanda to be mainstreamed in a public school, and not sequestered away in a private and privileged academy, I don't think my open-mindedness runs to welfare-quality counselors. I'm sure we can find someone much more suitable through our contacts."

Bingo, Lianne thought. *And dollars to donuts she'll never go to see anyone, because they can't take a chance of Amanda talking to anyone.* Outwardly, though, Lianne kept her expression neutral. "Of course, Mr. Kendrick. I wasn't suggesting that our counselor could provide therapy—only that she might be able to give us a direction in which to look for the problem. However, I'm sure that *your* choice of counselor will be even better. Just let me know when you come up with someone."

The teacher stood. "I've taken enough of your time. Thank you for talking with me. I think we've come up with some positive avenues to explore, and I'm sure Amanda will benefit."

Merryl and Andrew walked her back through the maze to the front door and showed her out, making small talk all the while.

And when I get home, you creeps, I'm calling Social Services. And we'll see if you get away with blaming your kid's behavior on your ex-wife to them.

CHAPTER SIX

"You didn't ask to be excused," her step-mother called from the dining room.

"Amanda Jannine Kendrick, get back to this table at once!" yelled Daddy.

Amanda-Abbey, halfway up the steps to her room and running headlong, reluctantly turned and plodded back to the dining room.

"Where were you going in such a hurry, young lady?" her daddy asked her.

He glared at her from the head of the table. Her step-mother, lingering over hot tea and a wafer-thin slice of pound cake, shook her head with annoyance. Sharon sat next to her real mother, looking secretly pleased that Amanda was in trouble again.

Amanda-Abbey looked from one adult to the other, and her fingers twisted against each other. She took a deep breath.

"May-I-please-be-excused-I-have-to-go-clean-the-pony's-stall," she said in a rush.

Her step-mother nodded curtly. "Wear your coveralls. I don't want those clothes ruined any more than they are."

Her daddy just smiled, playing with his lighter, tumbling it end-over-end between two fingers.

"I won't get them dirty. Promise."

Amanda-Anne took over, hurling the child's scrawny body out of the dining room and up the stairs two at a time and into her room at breakneck speed. She grabbed worn coveralls from their spot behind the hamper and darted into the closet, closing the door behind her. Trembling and breathing hard, she flung on the coveralls in the darkness, then crept to the door. She listened, soft ear pressed against the cool, white wood. On the other side, there was nothing but silence.

Silence, Amanda-Anne knew, was very bad.

There were two sets of steps, one on either end of the hall. Both had landings halfway, and closets at the top and the bottom—

Amanda-Anne closed her eyes and *thought*. No answers came to her, no pictures. And every minute she wasted gave the Father one more minute—

She bolted out her door and to the left, heading for the front stairs, which were farthest from the dining room, praying that she had guessed right.

Past the top closet and down the stairs—safe.

Around the landing—still no sign of Him.

Down the rest of the stairs—only a little further to go.

Past the partly-open door of the closet at the bottom of the stairs—and an arm shot out and grabbed her and dragged her into the closet.

"Boo," the Father whispered. He laughed softly in the darkness of the closet, and his hands pinned her against the smothering piles of coats. "You're lucky I'm not a monster."

Amanda-Anne struggled to get away from him. The Father tightened his grip until her arms hurt. "Monsters wait in the dark for bad girls, Amanda. Getchells and morrowaries, slinketts and fulges. Big, drooly monsters with bloody red teeth and sharp claws and white eyes that glow. Slimy, slippery shapeless things that slither and drip burning goo and won't even leave your bones behind for anyone to find you, *Amanda*. And it's almost dark outside, *Amanda*. They'll be there any minute. Hungry monsters. When you go outside to clean your pony's stable, be sure the monsters don't get you."

❖   ❖   ❖

Someone picked up after the seventh ring. A masculine voice said, "Hello?"

Lianne closed her eyes and leaned her head against the wall next to her phone. Getting through to the government agency after-hours had been a morass of answering machines, people who were home but not on call, and people who were on call but not at home. The hospital emergency department's Cumberland County Social Services' after-hours emergency phone numbers were one week out of date. The person she'd finally reached, after an hour of trying, had given her four numbers that *might* put her in touch with the person she needed. She had tried three of the numbers, and they hadn't. This was her last hope, and she clenched the receiver in her hand until her knuckles went white. The real live voice on the other end of the line wasn't getting out of this until Amanda's rescue was guaranteed.

"Hello," she said. "This is Lianne McCormick—I'm a teacher at Loyd E. Auman Middle School."

"Don Kroczwski. What can I do for you?"

Lianne took a deep breath. "I suspect that one of my students is being abused. I want her family checked out."

"What kind of evidence do you have of the suspected abuse?" The man on the other end of the line sounded tired; bone-tired and heartsick.

Lianne's voice went tense on her. "Evidence?"

"Do you have reason to expect imminent danger to life or limb?" he asked—or rather, recited.

This wasn't what she had expected. "For example—?"

Kroczwski sighed deeply. "For example, does the kid say either of his or her parents said they were going to kill him or her? She or he have any old cigarette burn scars, rope burns, broken bones, bruises on the face or body, brothers or sisters who have died or been hospitalized in the last few weeks—anything like that?"

Lianne's stomach contracted at his list of horrors. "*She*. Her name is Amanda Kendrick. And no. Nothing like that."

The voice on the other end of the line sighed. "You got any reason to think the kid will be dead tomorrow if I don't go over there tonight?"

The teacher bit her lip. "No," she said softly. "She shows psychological damage—personality problems—but nothing that makes me think her parents will murder her."

"Okay. That's a problem, Ms. McCormick. I know that you know your students. I understand that you probably can tell when something is wrong, and I trust your judgment and your instincts, but I have to have something tangible. Bruises, something the kid told you, something I can show a judge. I can't walk up to her parents' house and tell them they are being investigated for child abuse because their kid's teacher has a bad feeling."

"But I know something is wrong."

"Ms. McCormick, I believe you, but let me give you an idea of how wrong things can be. I have a neighborhood outbreak of syphilis among three- to nine-year-olds that I'm investigating; I just got a call from the Cape Fear Emergency Room about a little girl whose mother dumped hot oil on her because she wouldn't be quiet. I have a five-month-old baby with broken arms and broken legs that the mother's boyfriend threw across the room and whose four brothers and sisters have to be gotten out of that situation. I have a dead kid who showed up in the morgue whose body hasn't been claimed. I have a list of call-in's from concerned neighbors and teachers and relatives as long as my arm with complaints that may or may not end up with a bunch of little bodies in little body-bags if I don't take care of them yesterday—and it's already almost tomorrow. Child abuse is the year's biggest growth industry. I understand *wrong*—I really do. You give me something to go on, and I'll be out there to check on your kid in a heartbeat. Okay?"

Lianne's throat tightened. "Okay," she whispered. "If I can find anything, I'll call you back."

The voice sounded even wearier. "Day or night."

Tears started down Lianne's cheeks. "Okay. Thanks." She hung up the phone. Images of infants with arms and legs in plaster casts, little children with burns given to them by the people they wanted to love, with bruises and cuts and old scars and new wounds—kids who'd been shaken, beaten, screamed at, starved, tortured, raped, neglected— those images swirled around in front of her eyes, blurred by tears. And all those children began to have Amanda's face.

Amanda's pony was not kept in the main barn with the pedigreed Arabians Merryl Kendrick raised. It had its own quarters—a neat little doll-house version of the bigger barns, one Andrew Kendrick had ordered to be built for Amanda when she was five. It sat next to the main stables but did not connect with it in any way. Its cheerful, red-painted sides and white trim gleamed in the twilight; warm, yellow light spilled out of the opened top half of the front Dutch door. The neat, cedar-chip path crunched under Amanda-Alice's feet as she scurried down to finish cleaning the pony's stall.

"Lazy slut," Amanda-Alice muttered under her breath. "You should have cleaned the barn when you got home from school. Then he wouldn't have made you come down here now. Stupid, wicked, worthless tramp—out chasing evil elves when you should have been working. You deserve to be punished. You deserve it."

Amanda-Anne didn't have time for guilt. In the near-darkness, things moved. Shambling phantasms pressed close, deformed grotesqueries chittered in her ear, and—"Come to us, Amanda—we're hungry," unseen things whispered from the shadows, while their awful stomachs growled.

No! Amanda-Anne thought, and lurched into a gallop.

Out of the corner of her eye, she saw that the darkness gained. The horrors were almost upon her—she could feel their breath on the back of her neck—

"No!" she shrieked, and heard them laugh.

And then somehow she was through the barn door, intact and uneaten, and the door was closed behind her. The heavy wooden bolt dropped into its brackets, and Amanda-Anne was safe from the monsters.

In the stall, she picked up the pitchfork and began loading manure and straw into the little wheelbarrow. Her pony, Fudge, poked his head into the barn from the pasture entrance and whickered.

"Vile, filthy beast," Amanda-Alice snarled. "You leave these messes to get us in trouble, don't you? You don't deserve supper."

She ignored the bin of sweet feed in the corner, avoided looking at the little Shetland, and continued mucking the stall with short, sharp, angry jabs.

Andrew Kendrick paced the living room floor. Merryl curled in one of the overstuffed chairs, contracts spread on the floor around her.

The man punched one closed fist into the palm of his other hand. "That child is a disgrace. When I was a child, my behavior was excellent. I never had a visit from one of my teachers. And for that woman to suggest school psychiatrists—"

"Counselors," Merryl corrected. "Only counselors. Public schools don't keep psychiatrists on staff."

"It doesn't matter. How dare that child cause me this sort of humiliation? How dare she?" A scowl carved itself deeper into Andrew's face, and his complexion flushed a hotter, uglier red. "She obviously hasn't had enough discipline," he growled.

"Jesus," Merryl muttered. "Leave the kid alone for once."

Andrew turned his anger on her. "Stay out of it, you bitch! She's my child, my responsibility. As you keep reminding me. It's up to me to make sure that she grows up to be a useful adult. She won't if you ruin her with your lax attitude. Look at Sharon. She's getting old enough that she needs firm discipline, and you let her run wild. She'll be worthless when she grows up."

Merryl's voice went flat and dangerous. "Leave Sharon alone."

Andrew stiffened and glared at his wife. "We'll see," he told her. He walked heavily toward the outside door. "I'm going to make sure Amanda does a good job on that stall. She's going to clean it until it's done right, even if she's out there all night—she's going to learn that I'm in charge around here. And she's going to learn that she has to do what I expect." He stopped and stared at his wife with cold, ugly rage. "That's something you could stand to remember, too, Merryl."

He stalked out, slamming the door behind him.

❖   ❖   ❖

Belinda sat cross-legged on the bed in Peterkin's shoddy hotel room, two decks of cards spread in front of her on the cheap polyester bedspread. "Black three on the red four . . . okay, and that opens up the red jack to the black queen . . . hah! Moves that to *there*—yes!" She briskly restacked, completed, and removed piles of cards.

A rustle from the foot of the bed distracted her. She looked over from her game of Napoleon's solitaire to the floor, where Stevens and Peterkin were turning blue. "Oh—hi, guys." Her voice was bright and cheerful. "I thought you were dead already. Would you mind hurrying it up a little? I have plans for the evening." She grinned—perky, sexy, and charming, obviously a woman having a good time—and turned back to her cards.

She played a few more moments and sighed with minor annoyance. "Dammit! I almost won that one." She riffled the cards together, staring at her two thugs.

"Seems my prescription was okay, huh? At least it's working pretty well on you two. Well, fellas, I don't know why you wanted to double-cross me, but I guess we've proven that wasn't a good idea." She smiled at the dying men and began laying out the cards again. "Jerks."

She spread out a deck of poker cards and began another game of solitaire, latex-gloved hands shuffling with some difficulty.

Peterkin made strangling noises, then quit breathing. Froth foamed out of his mouth. Belinda smiled and flipped her hair back out of her face.

"That's good—that's very good. You did that nicely, Joe. One down, one to go, Fred-ol'-buddy. Let's see if you die well, too."

Fred Stevens lay on the dingy green carpet, sucking air like a beached fish for over half an hour after his partner threw in the towel. When his breathing ceased, Belinda folded up her cards, took both men's wallets, changed the ID's and other important papers, and dumped the wallets back on the dresser. Then she walked down to her car. When she came back, she carried a large shopping bag. She emptied the bag onto the bed and strewed her purchases around the room: a small packet of crack cocaine and the attendant drug paraphernalia, a white feather boa and a large, skimpy leopard-spotted negligee, a queen-sized pair of fishnet hose and patent leather shoes with six-inch spike heels—sized 12EE—a black leather men's bikini, battered handcuffs, and a well-worn bullwhip.

Then she cut the clothing off of both men with a pair of heavy-duty bandage scissors, the kind EMT's and paramedics used, rolled the clothes into a ball and stuffed them into her now-empty bag. She rolled Stevens onto Peterkin in the best "compromising position" she could manage, considering he was the smaller of the two corpses and weighed more than twice what she did. But police training came in handy. When she had them more or less posed, she put the shoes on Peterkin's feet and the handcuffs around his wrists, and draped the feather boa once around Steven's neck. Then she stood, breathing hard, and chuckled softly.

"That ought to amuse the investigators for a while," she whispered, and grinned cheerfully. She looked at her watch. *Time to see what my race-driver is doing. I need to be able to collect him tomorrow.*

The front doors of Amanda's barn rattled. The child was busy shoveling manure into the wheelbarrow and didn't notice the noise the first time. The second time, however, she stopped and cocked her head to one side, listening. The noise did not recur a third time, and after waiting a moment, she nodded with satisfaction and resumed her cleaning.

She didn't realize the Father had come into the barn through the pasture door until she heard the top Dutch doors click, and the heavy thud as he carefully dropped the door-bar into the brackets.

Inside the pony's stall, all the Amandas stiffened. Cethlenn noticed the change in their attitudes and froze, listening.

A series of light clicks followed—the sound of a key in a lock, the sound of light furniture being moved, the clink of metal.

Suddenly, Cethlenn realized that Amanda-Alice and Amanda-Abbey were gone. The only one who remained with her was Amanda-Anne.

Thud, thud, thud—the Father's heavy steps left the storage room, walked slowly closer—

Then the Father was right there, standing in the doorway of the stall, completely filling it. Cethlenn watched with Amanda-Anne, staring up and up and up at the huge form of the man.

"The stall looks very dirty, Amanda," the Father said. "What a very lazy, nasty, dirty little girl you have been." He smiled, his lips pulled back across his teeth so that they gleamed in the light of the naked, dangling light bulb.

Inside their head, Amanda-Anne made a mewling sound that died before it reached their lips. Cethlenn shuddered.

"I ought to make you lick the floor clean," the Father said. "Would you like that?"

Knives and whips and ropes and sharp, hot things danced in Amanda-Anne's head, and dull red rage blurred the child's vision. Cethlenn was forced back by the spreading fury, and fear clutched at her.

The Father's smile got bigger, and he took a step toward them. "I said," he whispered, *"would you like that?"*

Oh, gods, just answer him, child, Cethlenn thought.

"No," Amanda-Anne said.

"No," the Father mimicked, his voice a chilling falsetto. "Oh, no. You wouldn't like that. But you're a dirty little girl, aren't you, Amanda?"

The child stared at him, silent.

"I said, you're a dirty little girl, *aren't you?*"

"Yes," Amanda-Anne said.

"And we know what dirty little girls really like, don't we, Amanda?"

Amanda-Anne wrapped her frail arms around herself and stared up at the Father in silent terror. Cethlenn felt sick.

"Don't we, Amanda?"

"Yes," Amanda-Anne whispered.

"I can't hear you."

"Yes," Amanda-Anne said.

"Dirty little girls like to make their Daddy happy, don't they?"

Amanda-Anne's throat tightened, and she nodded.

"Good," said the Father. "Then come here. I know what you like, don't I, you dirty little girl? Tell me you like it."

Amanda-Anne walked forward, moving like a creature drugged.

"Say, 'I like it, Daddy.'"

The child was silent.

The Father grabbed her and shook her. "Say, 'I like it, Daddy.'"

"I like it . . . D-D-Daddy," Amanda-Anne croaked.

"I know you do, you little whore." He picked the limp child up and carried her into the storage room.

Oh, gods, Amanda, I'm sorry—I can't stay here—I can't watch this! Cethlenn shrieked, and vanished.

Lianne sat at her little kitchen table and dried her eyes. She had done what she could for Amanda for the time being. It was Friday night—she couldn't do anything else about the child until the next morning at the earliest—so she needed to get herself under control.

I've been under an awful lot of stress lately, she thought. *It isn't like me to cry like this. There have just been too many unexplained things happening in the last few days.*

She leaned back in her chair. *I've taken care of this now, though. Things will get back to normal. I know they will.*

Her eye strayed to the kitchen sink—to a rainbow sparkle and a flash of white metal.

And the feeling of otherworldness returned. She got up and walked over to the sink, and picked up the crystal carafe that Mac had produced—seemingly out of thin air—for their delightful breakfast in bed. She hefted it in both hands, studying the flawless faceting of the crystal and the incredible quality. One eye closed, she gnawed on her lip as she appraised it, and a whole number followed by a surprising quantity of zeros ticked off in her brain. She fingered the silver serving tray, and then picked it up and studied it. It was *real* silver, and solid, too, not plate—and Lianne pondered the odds of finding such exquisitely crafted silver with nary a maker's mark on it. She picked up a cherry pit and studied it as if it were something likely to burn her fingers. She tilted her head, and her eyebrows furrowed, and then, with a thoughtful expression on her face, she turned out the kitchen light, went into the living room and plopped down on her couch and stared off into nothingness.

"When you have eliminated the impossible, whatever is left—no matter how improbable—is the truth," she said softly to no one.

Amanda-Anne lay in the bathtub, staring up at the ceiling. Steam swirled around her, and a thick layer of sweet-scented bubbles pressed against her skin like fat kittens. Amanda was oblivious to the warmth and the sweetness and the light. Her mouth still tasted of oily cotton, her wrists and ankles still stung and chafed, and she *hurt*.

And in her mind's eye, nothing existed but the storage room, with its little cot and its dim light, and its supply of ropes and rags, and its awful locking door.

She rubbed absently at her wrists—and her fingers brushed across her real mother's bead, still strung on the lovely gold chain.

And the image of the elf pouring himself out of the bead in a stream of green mist came to her. She sat up in the tub and stared at the bead. Let Abbey pretend that the elf wasn't real. Let Alice complain that he was evil. And let that goody-two-shoes Stranger think that the elf would help them. They didn't know about Anne, but Anne knew about them. And she knew better than to believe their silliness. Amanda-Anne knew that Alice was stupid, that Abbey was wrong, and that Stranger meant well but was looking for help in the wrong direction; the sweet-faced elf was too soft and too gentle to do what was needed. But he had shown her the trick of his magic without meaning to. Without even knowing that he had done so. Her eyes narrowed as she considered the possibilities of the scene that played itself out in her mind, and softly, the child began to laugh.

Don't want . . . the elf, she thought. *Just . . . the smoke. And the wind.*

She stared at the bead, forcing unfamiliar patterns into the rhythm of her will, and slowly her green eyes glowed.

For a moment, nothing changed.

Then a flicker of light came to life in the heart of the bead—not the pure green light of earlier in the day, but a throbbing, pulsing, angry red light. Without words,

Amanda-Anne spoke to the red light and carefully explained to it exactly what she wanted. Then she waited.

The bead grew brighter, and the bathroom was suffused with the ugly, bloody red glow. Then heavy smoke poured out of the bead and hung over the bathtub. It swirled around the child, threatening, menacing.

Amanda-Anne's eyes grew lighter, her pupils constricted to pencil-points of darkness in the centers of the white-green, and as if it had suddenly seen something to fear, the red cloud recoiled. With a kind of reluctance, it crawled in a thin line up the wall and out of the bathroom through a slight gap in the window high overhead.

Amanda-Anne held her breath as the last traces vanished from the bathroom. She listened, every muscle tense and straining to catch the slightest sound in the still night air.

Then, from the direction of her barn, there came a very satisfying crash, followed by thunderous clattering and the scream of a full-sized hurricane compressed into a tiny box. The noise and the destruction raged for as long as Amanda-Anne could maintain her concentration.

When she reached the point of exhaustion, she released the storm she had summoned, sending it back to wherever it had come from. Then, a diamond-hard smile on her tiny face, Amanda-Anne settled back into the bath-water and relinquished her place to Amanda-Abbey, who actually liked stupid, childish bubble-baths.

Mac left the track late and with too much on his mind. There was Felouen, with her strange and completely unexpected intimation of unrequited love, and the Oracular Pool, with its images of terror and disaster. There was the sensation of intangible evil at the border of the Unformed World, and the turbulence of the shield. There were his problems with the Seleighe High Court, and with that low and vile woman who had tried to poison him. There was beautiful, ephemeral Lianne, whom he suspected was falling in love with him. And last, but certainly not least, there was the child, Amanda, who had followed him into Underhill without flinching, and who had then promptly returned to her own world on her own power and of her own accord—in spite of the fact that there was no way she should have been able to do that. Maclyn was tense, and unsettled, and somewhat scattered.

And so, for the first time, he failed to notice a sleek brown Ford Thunderbird that maintained its position four cars behind him all the way from the street beside the racetrack parking lot to Lianne's apartment.

Lianne answered the door with an unnervingly perceptive expression in her eyes. "Hi," she said, gave him a brusque kiss, and immediately asked, "Where's the movie?"

"The movie?"

"The *movie*. C'mon, Mac—just this morning you said, and I quote, 'I'll pick up the movie tonight. I think I'll get *The Man With One Red Shoe,* since we didn't watch it last night.' After breakfast, and before we headed out the door. Remember?"

"Of course I remember," said Maclyn, who remembered no such thing.

"So where's the movie? You forgot it, didn't you?"

"I just forgot to bring it in with me. It's in the car. I didn't forget to rent it."

Like hell, I didn't forget, he thought while he trudged back to Rhellen. *What in Oberon's name was I thinking this morning?—I burned breakfast, I fixed something else, we rolled around on the bed awhile, we took a shower, we ran out the door—I still* don't *remember anything about a movie. At least,* he mused, *I promised one I've already seen. Be a bitch to pull it out of thin air if I hadn't.*

He opened Rhellen's door, concentrating hard, and a VCR cassette in a clear plastic cover appeared on the seat. He picked it up and returned to the apartment.

Lianne's expression as he handed her the tape was decidedly weird. He started to ask her what was wrong, then thought better of it.

She walked over to the VCR without a word, and pushed the eject button. A movie popped out. She opened the plastic case of the tape he'd provided for her, and turned her back to him.

She stood silently for a long moment, while Mac grew more and more tense. "Jesus, that's a neat trick," she said finally, and turned around. "Who are you—really?"

Maclyn hedged. "Why do you ask?"

She smiled. "You were very close with this. Your label is almost perfect, except you're missing the copyright date, and there's only a gray box where the small print would be—if I hadn't had an original here to compare, I bet I never would have noticed the difference."

He nodded, maintaining a calm exterior while his brain raced wildly. In her hands she held two copies of *The Man With One Red Shoe*. One of them had been obtained from a video rental store. The other—well, it *hadn't*. He felt the tempo of his pulse increase. "Maybe the copy I picked up was pirated."

"Oh, I'm sure of it," she said with a wry smile. "Out of thin-fucking-air. We never said anything about movies this morning, Mac. I only said that to see what you would do—because there is something very odd about things that have happened in my life since you showed up. It strikes me as uncanny, for example, that neither of us said a word about you picking up this movie, and yet, when I asked you about it, you happened to have it in your car. Wherever this came from, Mac Lynn, it wasn't a rental place."

He stalled for time, trying to think, but unable to make his mind work. This wasn't the way it was supposed to happen—it wasn't supposed to happen at all, actually. "I see. So I was correct in thinking I hadn't said anything about movies in our rush this morning? How interesting. You see, I have an imperfect memory for minutiae. It usually isn't a problem."

Her arms were crossed in front of her chest. "Perhaps more of a problem than you realize. There is, of course, the silver tray—real silver, of incredible quality, with no maker's mark. I don't buy it. There are the out-of-season cherries. And of course we can't forget your willingness to believe that papers were indeed flying around my classroom of their own accord." She took a step toward him. "You are very interesting, Mac Lynn. You are charming, you are handsome, and you are great in bed. But you are not what you seem to be. Now I want an answer on this, and I want it right now. Who—or what—are you?"

❖   ❖   ❖

Finally, she was getting somewhere.

From her position behind the shrubs outside of the apartment window, Belinda stared through the slatted mini-blinds at Mac Lynn and his girlfriend. She recognized the girl—had seen her before, in connection with Mac Lynn. She frowned, determined to remember where she had seen that face, and suddenly she recalled the girl striding across a parking lot—

Bingo! She's one of the teachers at Loyd E. Auman. I followed him there that one time—and that explains why he was over there in the first place. That's where his piece of ass works.

Belinda's face lit up with a beatific smile. His girlfriend could give him to her. Just grab her and stash her someplace, then tell him his girlfriend was dead unless he did exactly what she said, and have him follow instructions that would deliver him voluntarily to Mel's doorstep.

Voila, she thought, *a nice paycheck for me and a well-earned vacation that doesn't involve chasing spookies—preferably someplace far away, with mountains and ocean and deferential waiters.*

Cozumel, she decided, *or maybe Greece.*

They appeared to be arguing. That was good from Belinda's point of view. *He might stomp out, leaving her alone tonight. In which case, I'll just knock on the door and grab her when she answers it, thinking he's come back to apologize. If he stays the night, of course, I'll just pick up Little Miss Teacher sometime tomorrow—or after school Monday.*

That seemed like a good, sound, workable plan, and much less complicated than trying to drug him again. It also meant she didn't need to sit in the damp shrubbery catching a cold. Belinda stood up and headed back to her new rental car. Stake-outs were much more pleasant when accompanied by Perrier, Bach, and croissants.

She moved into the area of darker shadow that lay between the teacher's apartment and the parking lot, and noticed two disturbing things as she did. The first was that Mac's car wasn't in the parking lot anymore.

The second was that what had seemed, out of the corner of her eye, to be laundry hanging out between the apartments, wasn't. It was a big, light-colored horse.

And no sooner had she identified the horse for what it was than it had her jacket between its teeth, and she was flailing through the air to land on the beast's back. She reached for her gun, the creature bucked, she grabbed the beast's mane to keep from hitting the ground—

And things got a little hazy from there.

Belinda decided pretty promptly that she must have fallen off the horse anyway and knocked herself silly and wandered around a bit. It was the only explanation that made any sense. Otherwise, she would have had to admit that the horse had turned into a car that drove itself, and that it had driven her onto the street in front of the old abandoned Fox Drive-In, and dumped her by the side of the road before cruising off into the night. It would have implied that the car had *chosen* to abandon her where hookers plied their trade and G.I.'s and out-of-town businessmen and restless locals went looking for action.

It would have implied that the fight Belinda got into with the pimp and the big buxom blonde and the transvestite and the two horny guys in the red Camaro was the fault of a goddamned '57 Chevy.

And no matter how spooky things got, Belinda wasn't ready to admit that.

Mac faced Lianne, and swallowed hard. Humans weren't anywhere near as gullible as they'd once been—at least some of them weren't, he decided. The room felt uncomfortably warm.

"I'm a racecar driver," he said with an ingenuous smile.

Lianne nodded, her expression grave. "A racecar driver is the least of what you are, Mac Lynn. I've always made it a point to date within my species before this, but I think I've not even managed to live up to that one simple rule this time. Have I?"

Maclyn stood, studying her, thinking fast.

Lianne saw the evasion coming and headed it off. "Mac, I'm to the point where I won't believe anything but the truth. And please give me credit for being able to tell the truth from a lie—remember, I deal with ten-year-olds on a daily basis." She smiled wryly. "Besides, I doubt that the truth is going to be anywhere near as ludicrous as what I've suspected."

"Wanna bet?" Mac muttered.

Lianne heard him. "No," she said. "But lay out your cards anyway and let me take a look."

"Okay." He took a deep breath and studied her. "You've heard of Faerie, of course."

"One of my best friends is one."

"Not that kind of fairy."

"I was being facetious. I've heard of Faerie. Up to this point I've found its purported existence likely to be the product of hallucination and overdoses of wheat-smut, but I'm a logical soul. Presented with sufficient proof, I'll believe just about anything. I suppose you're going to tell me you're the elf-king of Fairyland or something."

Mac's right eyebrow arched up. "I'm an elf. Not 'or something.' And I'm fairly high up in the line of succession, but I'm not the king, or even the prince."

Lianne sighed and said to whatever higher powers inhabited the ceiling, "I'm taking this rather well, aren't I?" She studied Mac for a long, silent moment, then said, "Granted I've already seen enough to convince me that you aren't normal—but would it be too much to ask for some proof that you are what you say you are? Seeing that we've been sleeping together and all?"

Maclyn gave her a very Gallic shrug—and his human seeming faded away. He presented himself to her in his full elvish glory, from the gold circlet on his head to the sweeping white folds of his ermine cloak, to the rich white-on-white textures of his silk-embroidered tunic and velvet leggings. He showed her himself, pointed ears, pale green slit-pupiled eyes, and inhuman smile.

"My lady," he said, inclining his head with courtly grace. "Is this sufficient proof?"

Lianne sat down sharply on the coffee table. Her eyes went round and she whistled softly. "I'll be damned," she whispered. "An elf. A damned sexy one."

She cocked her head to one side and studied him closely. "A question, then."

"I'll answer it if I can."

"What are you doing hanging around me?"

And isn't that just *the question?* Maclyn thought. *I wish to hell I knew the answer.*

CHAPTER SEVEN

Andrew Kendrick heard the first sounds from the barn just as he was locking up the house for the night. He ran to the window and stared out at the hellish red glow in the dark that held the stable area. It was clearly coming from the pony barn. At first his mind couldn't recognize the disaster for what it was—but then he shook himself out of his paralysis and reacted.

"Fire!" he shouted to Merryl. "There's a fire down in the pony barn! Call the fire department, *now!*"

He pulled on boots and sprinted out the back door. If anything, it looked and sounded worse now that he was outside. He could barely hear the terrified whinnies of the pony above the roar that came from within the shed.

He goaded himself into a run, heading down to the barn, wondering if he would be able to get into the secret storeroom and thinking of the money that was going up in smoke in there. Thinking of all the—special things—that were going to be destroyed, and that were going to be even more difficult to procure the second time than they had been when he'd first obtained them.

Merryl passed him on the path, flew to the right and to her own barn, full of pedigreed mares and foals, her prize stud, her champion filly—the objects of her real passion and her love. Andrew heard her throwing open her barn doors, chasing the horses out into the pasture and away from the impending disaster. He clenched his fingers into tight fists, outraged at her care for the animals and her indifference toward him.

He watched her working frantically, momentarily distracted from his goal. *She has a lot of nerve, ignoring me. Amanda's* mother *learned what happens to people who ignore me. I've been too easy on Merryl.* He fumed with smoldering rage as he raced towards the pony barn, wondering if he could save anything without Merryl seeing it. He wasn't really thinking about the barn, nor about the fire—not, at least, until was he nearly at the structure.

Realization that there was something very strange going on stopped him like a stone wall. *I don't smell any smoke,* he thought. It sounded like there was a war going on down there, and it certainly *looked* as if the place was being overrun by the fires of hell—wind that screamed like a damned and tortured thing, the crash and thud of heavy objects hitting against the walls, the screech of nails ripping loose from beams—and the terrible red light still gleamed through cracks, but there were no tongues of flame visible and no smoke to smell.

What the hell—? he wondered.

A piece of board blew past him, and some unidentifiable bit of shrapnel grazed his cheek—and Andrew watched dumbfounded as gaps appeared, as if something or someone from inside battered away at the barn. The night air was thick with a sense of rage, of hatred so dense and palpable he could feel it brushing against his chilled skin like damp, drowned hands. His heart pounded with fear that was not even his own, and his mouth went dry and his breath came fast in spite of his struggles to control his emotions. He found himself backing away from the barn, and found that he could not stop himself, could not make himself walk back toward it.

From behind him, he heard the wail of sirens and the squeal of tires turning into the lane. The fire engines' flashing red lights joined the peculiar illumination that came from the barn—the night pulsed red. *Blood,* he thought, clutching his arms around himself. *The world is bleeding.*

The firemen were unrolling their hoses, shouting to each other, pointing out their target. Merryl was still loosing horses out into the field.

Andrew saw none of it; instead, he had been inadvertently thrown back to his own childhood.

He saw the little beagle puppy he'd "bought" when he was eleven from the kid down the road—bought with marbles and a brand-new baseball glove and a brand-new football. The puppy he'd smuggled home and made a wonderful soft bed for and hidden under the house because his father had said, "No dogs," but he'd wanted it so bad—

His puppy, laid out on a board, belly up; its little muzzle wired shut, its eyes wide and staring, its paws nailed into place. And his dad, furious, shouting at him, "Now you'll know to listen to me, won't you, you little bastard! Next time you disobey me, this will be you!" And the knife, in his father's hand, slitting the little beagle's white belly open, and the pup's eyes rolling in terror and pain—

And the blood pulsing red and redder around his father's fine doctor hands, pulsing like the lights from the fire engines—and again he tasted the anguish and the fear—

And the red glow in the barn just—went away.

Thick, suffocating silence crowded in to fill the void and darkness. The firemen paused, and stared. The horrible noises that had been coming from inside had stopped, abruptly, almost as if a switch had been flipped. The terrible feeling of rage and fear made the same abrupt departure.

Then sounds rushed back and revived the night: the chirping of crickets and the whinnies and stompings of the horses out in pasture, the stamp and crunch of one fireman's boots as he walked, flashlight in hand, down to the barn, and pulled the battered and sagging door open.

And his voice, awestruck as he aimed his flashlight into the dark recesses of the structure—"Je-e-e-e-ZUS, Johnnie, get a load of this!"

The rippling motion of the border had lulled her into a near-trance. Felouen sat, her back pressed against the smooth rock base of the Oracular Pool, staring into the nothingness, and she worried. Maclyn might come around. He might help against whatever was coming. Then again, enchanted by his other interests, he might leave her to fight and die alone.

There had been more to the visions of the Oracular Pool than the one brief glimpse it had shown Maclyn. War was coming—a long and savage battle with the outnumbered elvish forces lined up against hordes of Unseleighe unlike anything the Kin had ever seen before. Her friends would fall, and she would fight on, uselessly, would herself be gravely wounded, would flee and be captured, would suffer at the hands of the unstoppable things from the Unformed. And only then would she die. She had seen her own death. It was not a good one.

She had seen another vision as well, an alternate future in the inscrutable reflections in the Pool. Maclyn would stand at her side, with the battle raging as before—but the enemy would be fewer and weaker, the tide of battle would turn in the Kin's favor, and she would live. So she sat and pondered, staring out into the non-place on the other side of the border with loathing.

Felouen sensed the change before she saw it.

A presence born of fear and rage and hatred swirled into being in the Void, reached out and clawed at her from that nothing-world. It sent her to her feet, recoiling from the tentacles that reached with sudden intent directly for her.

From the Nothing, flickers of blood-red light began to glow.

". . . so you see, she was human, and I loved her, and when she died, I thought that everything about me that had mattered had died, too," Mac said. He sat on one side of Lianne's couch, again wearing his human seeming. "Everything about her was so brief and so painfully fleeting, and the harder I tried to stop time, to hold her life in my hands and keep her with me, the faster I saw the years tear her into shreds. She died nearly two hundred years ago, but there are still times when the thought crosses my mind that if I went back to Tellekirk, I'd find her there."

He locked his hands together, and he stared at his shoes. "In you, I see that same frightening beauty, that same—

life—that burns so hot and so fast. I cannot stay away from you. And I find myself longing for your brief, blazing beauty, and wondering how you can burn your life so fast."

Lianne pursed her lips and blew a soft sigh through them. She got up and walked over to one of the bookcases that lined the walls of her bedroom, and perused the shelves. Finally, with a nod, she pulled down a deep green leather volume and flipped through the pages.

"We've done some thinking about that ourselves," she said, and looked down at the page she'd chosen. "Here—" she pointed, and read aloud.

"For a man cannot lose either the past or the future: for what a man has not, how can anyone take from him? These two things then thou must bear in mind: the one, that all things from eternity are of like forms and come round in a circle, and that it makes no difference whether a man shall see the same things during a hundred years or two hundred, or an infinite time; and the second, that the longest liver and he who die soonest lose just the same."

She paused to let the quote sink it. "Marcus Aurelius— a Roman philosopher and leader from way before *your* time—said that, and I suspect he's right. Even though I'll live—at most—a hundred years, and you'll live God-only-knows how long, we were both born, we will both live the span of our days, and we will both die. I mean, you *will* die *eventually*, won't you?"

"It's been rumored," Mac said, a faint hint of the beginning of a smile at the corner of his mouth.

She gave him a real smile. "Don't pity us humans, then. Time runs at a different pace for you and me, but my life will be as full as yours. It will just happen faster. It won't seem to me that I got cheated—I'm doing things with my life that matter to me and to other people. I'm teaching children, and to me, that is an important and meaningful job. I have friends who care about me, and a family that loves me, and I'm doing what I can to make the world a better place. And as for your long-gone love, I guarantee you that if she *lived* her life, and could see where her presence made a difference, she didn't feel cheated either."

Lianne sat back on the bed, put the book down beside her, and pulled her knees up to her chest so she could wrap her arms around them. Now was the time for a little noble self-sacrifice, and it made the smile she had given him fade away entirely. "I think you're doing yourself an injustice hanging around humans, though, Maclyn." She did her best to hide the tears that brimmed in her eyes; she didn't *want* to give him up. She really didn't. But it was for his own good. "Look for someone who exists in your own timeframe—who won't get old and die between two blinks of those gorgeous eyes of yours."

She did her best to look brave and happy—but all she could manage was a smile as transparent and empty as a soap bubble on the wind.

Maclyn listened to her words and tried to find some hope or comfort in them. She looked so beautiful. Mac's gaze roamed from the curve of her ankle to the full swell of her breast, to the plainly-written pain in her eyes, and words surged from his lips before he could stop them. "You don't have to get old so fast. I could take you into Elfhame Outremer, Lianne. There, you would live at the pace of *my* years." He faltered, and further brilliant suggestions died in his throat.

What in all the hells of the Unformed Planes had he said that for? Did he love her? Really, truly *love* her—as an equal and a companion with whom he could sustain interest for some significant span of his own long life? Was he infatuated with her humanness? Or was he—even less noble—burning with desire to fix the long-dead past?

An unbidden memory of Allison—fair, dainty, dark-eyed Allison, two hundred years dust—choked his throat and stopped his tongue. To Allison he had said those same words, had begged her to let him stop time for her. Allison had refused him, had told him about her God and her Church and her Bible, about God's demand that only he had the right to count the measure of a man's life. At first he had argued with her—fruitlessly, and then he had stayed at her side, using what time she let him have, while she grew old quickly. Allison had not lived her life fully. She had spent her days railing at an unjust Deity who gave life unequally. He had watched her turn bitter, as she wrinkled and fattened and her tongue went acid. Suffered, as she

studied him secretly from beneath her lashes, hoping some
sign of age would scar him. Mourned, as eventually she
hated him because it never did. Yet, often enough, even
in the old woman, the young girl who loved an elven prince
could be found. And in those moments, Maclyn had felt
his heart ripped to tatters.

He remembered Allison while he stared at Lianne,
wondering at his motives, trying to guess what she hid
inside her shielded thoughts.

"That's a hell of an offer," the young teacher finally
breathed. "What's the catch?"

He shook his head. "I'm not certain. For Allison, it was
her religion. She didn't think God would forgive her for
thwarting death."

Lianne grinned, a devilish, teeth-bared grimace that was
half humor and half wry self-deprecation. "Not my problem." The strange smile vanished, and the woman rested
both hands on his thigh and stared into his eyes. "Let me
think about ramifications—especially what this would mean
to the two of us. And give me a while, okay? I've got a
kid in school who's in trouble, and that's left me with a
lot on my mind."

Mac heard only the first part of what she said and
nodded. Then her last statement she'd made caught his
attention. "What do you mean, 'a kid in trouble'? You
haven't said anything about it to me before, have you?"

She frowned a moment. "Sort of. Do you remember
Amanda—the little girl from the racetrack who wouldn't
get out of the way of the explosion?" She looked at him,
her eyes uncertain.

Only too well. "I remember her."

She grimaced. "Yeah. Probably you do. That was pretty
bad. Well, I went to talk to her parents today. Something
is very wrong there—I suspect abuse. I called Social Services and reported it, but the guy I talked to said that, since
I don't have any hard evidence, he can't go out there to
check on her."

Chills ran along Maclyn's spine. "Abuse?" he asked in
a voice gone ominously flat.

Lianne must have heard the change in his tone and
laughed without any humor. "That's how I feel, too. Every

time I see something like this, I want to kill the people responsible. God, I wish I could *prove* she was being abused, to get that guy out there—but I'm on such thin ice. I've never seen any bruises, she's never *said* anything to me about it—although *that's* normal for abuse cases, actually—she doesn't miss a lot of school. It's just, her personality isn't right. Not right at all."

What would happen, Mac wondered, if he told Lianne everything he knew about Amanda? Would she be able to believe in Amanda's magic?

Why the hell not? he decided. *She believed I was an elf easily enough.*

"I'm willing to bet Amanda is the reason everything in your classroom came to life on you the other day," he told her. "I know for a fact she is the reason nobody got seriously hurt at the racetrack."

Lianne gave him a long, clinical look. "What—exactly—do you mean by that?"

He licked his lips. "She does magic—controls inanimate objects. Makes them move."

"Tele—um—telekinesis?" Lianne asked. "Moving things with her mind?"

He nodded. "I think that's the term."

Lianne's expression grew harried. "Aw, c'*mon*," she snarled. "I bought you as an elf. You don't want me to believe in that, too! Next you'll be insisting on the validity of Bigfoot, flying saucers, and the effectiveness of the two-party political system."

Mac snorted. "No, I won't. I'll just want you to believe in your student. She's special—but she *is* hiding something. She wouldn't admit she could do magic."

"Mac," Lianne replied as if she were talking to one of her students, ". . . maybe that's because she can't."

"Sensible, logical theory—except that I saw her," he persisted stubbornly. "I watched—and sensed—her work her magic."

"*Ergo sum ergo,*" Lianne muttered. "It is, therefore it is."

"Don't get grouchy. While she was looking at Keith's car, she kept it from exploding. As soon as you pulled her out of the way, it blew—but she was able to see it again at that point, and she controlled almost all of the shrapnel. *I saw her.* More than that, I sensed the flow of power."

Lianne still looked skeptical, but Mac sensed she was weakening. "So what you're saying is that if I had left her alone, the car wouldn't have blown up at all?"

Mac shrugged. "Who knows? I am saying that the SERRA drivers were lucky she was watching the race that day. Keith owes his life to her."

"Great. Fine. She's a helpful little brownie. So why did she send everything in my classroom flying?" Lianne set her jaw stubbornly.

Mac sighed. "I don't know. There are a lot of things about her that I don't know. But I think we can find some answers. Tomorrow—well, I'm racing tomorrow—why don't you come out and watch me? You can keep my mom company in the pits—"

Lianne forgot about the child entirely. "Your *mom?*" she said, her jaw dropping.

"Oh . . ." He smiled weakly. "I forgot to mention that, didn't I? Uh—D.D.'s my mother."

Silence for a moment, while Lianne absorbed the information. Then—"She looks five years younger than *me,*" Lianne wailed.

Mac deemed it time to get the discussion back to more serious subjects—or, at least, subjects he could do something about. Getting D.D. to change her apparent age was not one of them. "Don't let it bother you. She looks at *least* that much younger than me. Anyway, after the race, we can all three go out to Amanda's house and poke around a little. We'll see if we can find out anything. D.D.'s been concerned, too, ever since the day of the accident."

Lianne flung herself backward and down onto the bed and slapped herself dramatically on the forehead. "Gosh, what a brilliant idea! It becomes obvious why elves rule the world. Why didn't *I* think of that? I mean, why would Andrew or Merryl Kendrick ever notice two racecar-driving elves and their daughter's schoolteacher tromping around on their posted, private property, looking for magical mystery clues like something out of Scooby Doo—on a Saturday, no less, when they're probably home all day?" She scrunched her eyes closed in mock-agony.

Mac formed his will into a familiar shape and draped that shape around himself. "I don't see the problem," he said.

"You're kidding." Lianne opened her eyes to stare at him, then looked all around the room. She sat up, and her expression became more and more puzzled. "Mac?"

"I'm right here," he said from the spot he'd occupied since the moment they both sat down.

"I don't see you."

He took the little "I'm not here" spell—pirated from a human mage named Tannim—off of himself, and smiled at her as her eyes went round. "And I don't see the problem."

She sighed and flopped back again. "Maybe there isn't one."

Mel Tanbridge waited three hours beyond his absolute cut-off time, and still neither of the two calls he was expecting came. With growing disbelief, he acknowledged that they might never come.

He was more than willing to accept the fact that either Stevens or Peterkin could be bought off, if enough sweeteners were added. He was not willing to admit that Belinda could buy them *both* off—not on the money he was paying her, and certainly not at the same time. He knew they weren't the brightest guys in the world, but he couldn't imagine them making the sort of world-class bumble that would alert her that they were *both* reporting to him on her activities, even if she realized that one of them was.

And they didn't realize that he was paying each of them the same bonus to report on the other.

So why hadn't at least one of them called in?

The answer was fairly obvious.

The three of them had captured Belinda's race-driver TK, and he was even better than anyone had hoped for. Belinda had seen dollar signs and had convinced Stevens and Peterkin that they could make a lot more money if they joined forces with her and kept their catch to sell to the highest bidder, instead of handing him over to the man who rightfully owned him.

Mel considered that scenario from all angles. It was the

only one that made sense. Considering the healthy mix of bribes, threats and terrorism he'd used on Belinda's two assistants, they should have stayed loyal under almost any circumstances. Therefore, Belinda must have convinced them she was coming into an unbelievable fortune to get them to double-cross him. For that matter, knowing what he had on her, she had to have convinced herself of the same thing, in order to forget how important it was for her to remain loyal.

None of them had stayed loyal. Therefore, Mac Lynn was the biggest telekinetic find ever—and Mel was more determined than ever to own him.

Belinda had only had two days to hide her trail and her booty. However, with both Peterkin and Stevens in her camp, all three of them knew how many bases he'd had covered, and how little he'd trusted any of them. They would be more than careful, they'd be paranoid.

He glared out his smoked glass window at the night and watched the ghost breakers run up the beach, the white of sea-foam all that was visible in the clouded dark. He planned for ten minutes, and when he was satisfied, he dialed a number from memory. Moments later came a drowsy hello.

"This is Tanbridge. Set things up to fly to North Carolina tonight. I'm going to Fayetteville. I'll meet you on the strip in two hours."

He hung up, then glanced around the office. Not much lying around that he'd need to take with him. As a matter of fact, there were only two things in the office that he was going to need. The TK meter.

And the gun.

Andrew forced himself to walk to the barn. He stood next to the fireman with the flashlight and stared in at the devastation. It was all-encompassing and complete—but his first feeling, on looking in at the destruction, was one of relief. Nothing inside of the barn was recognizable anymore—including his large collection of special items. The pony's stall was ripped to shreds, and the pony had evidently kicked through the back doors to escape; he was out at the far side of the pasture cropping grass. *Lucky for him,* Andrew reflected. *He wouldn't have survived whatever did that.*

Whatever it was, it hadn't been a fire. Vandals? Only if they had come equipped with a log chipper and managed to run every item in the barn, including tack, feed barrels and hardware, through it in a matter of minutes.

The presence of other people around him, talking to him, gradually seeped into his awareness. He turned and found that while he'd been lost in his shocked reverie, two sheriff's deputies and the sheriff himself had arrived.

"Can you think of anyone who would want to do this to you, Mr. Kendrick?" the sheriff asked.

Andrew thought for a moment. "Dozens of them," he said. "Merryl won't sell her horses to just anyone—maybe someone who didn't measure up to her standards wanted to see if he could force her to lower them. For that matter, I've helped my clients acquire a number of profitable enterprises through hostile takeovers in past years. I've made enemies on the way. However, I can't think of any of them who would be able to *do* . . . that." He nodded back toward the barn.

One of the deputies said, "We've seen it, sir. It's pretty unbelievable. I don't know how they could have been so destructive."

The other deputy said, "The firemen said they saw red light coming from inside the building, but that it went out suddenly."

Merryl spoke up. "We all saw it. Apparently, whoever did this wanted us to think it was a fire. It looked like one."

Andrew agreed. "It was a very convincing special effect. The whole setup was very realistic, and very frightening— I'm not ashamed to admit I was terrified. However," he yawned "it's over now, and it's late, and we all will have plenty of time in the morning to hash over the details of this. I don't think there is anything more we can do tonight. So if you don't mind, I'd rather deal with it tomorrow."

"That's reasonable, sir," the sheriff said, "It's a clear night. Any tire tracks or other evidence will still be available in the morning. We'll be out first thing. Until then, I'll be glad to leave someone here overnight to keep an eye on things."

"Not necessary," Andrew said dryly. "There's an old line about horses and unlocked barn doors that seems appropriate right now—"

The sheriff shrugged. "That's up to you. If you see or hear anything out of place, though, let us know right away."

Andrew nodded shortly. "I'll do that."

Watching them leave, Merryl said, "I think you should have let them post a guard."

He sneered. "Do me a favor and don't waste your time on thinking. It isn't what you're best at. I had reasons for not wanting them here."

The knowing look she turned on him made him suddenly uneasy. "I'll bet. What were you hiding in there?"

He reacted to his unease by issuing threats. "Don't push your luck, Merryl. Don't ever forget, you can be replaced."

From her bedroom window, Amanda-Anne watched the police cars leave, and watched the Father and the Step-Mother trudge slowly toward the house. She smiled. The Father's secret place was gone. Now he couldn't hurt her anymore. He would never hurt her again.

She felt the power of her own dark magic coursing through her and savored the sweet taste of revenge. No one, *no one*, would ever hurt her again.

Under the covers, Lianne tossed and turned. Mac's warmth next to her was, at the moment, more disturbing than comforting. She almost wished that he hadn't spent the night. She would have liked to sit up, to drink hot tea and stare off into space knowing that she wouldn't have to try to explain to him why she wanted to. She would have liked to pace—but stalking around the apartment would wake him up. She listened to him breathe, slow and steady, deep in sleep, and tried not to resent his presence.

He's not human, she thought. *He's very wonderful, but he's not human. No matter how well we get along, there are things we can never see in the same way. His mother is hundreds of years old, he says. She's still young—he says she'll live until she gets tired of it. My mom and dad are nearing sixty, and might have another twenty.*

What about children? Could we have them? What would

they be? She winced, rolled over and buried her head under her pillow. *That's unpleasant, thinking of your own possible children as "what," not "who." More than likely, from my understanding of genetics, there could be no children.*

He loved children—he said the elvenkind intervened in the lives of battered and abused human children because they rarely had children of their own, and they valued them so. He would want to have them someday, wouldn't he?

He said that time in Underhill was changeable, that a day there could be a minute here, or a day, or a year, or a hundred years. Lianne tried to imagine dropping into Elfhame Outremer for a quick visit with the in-laws, and returning to find everyone she'd ever known dead a hundred years ago. Like the old fairy tales. She shuddered and tried to think of something else.

When I divorced Jim, I thought I could save myself from stupid mistakes. I promised myself, "I'll never fall for someone who's wrong for me again—I'll never let myself get hurt like this again." I was so goddamned sure that I knew something finally, dammit! I thought I'd learned my lesson, that I was only going to go out with men who wouldn't lie to me, who could be trusted. Now look at me. I'm in love with the wrong person again.

That was the worst of it—never mind that he wasn't human, never mind that he would live damn near forever and she would be gone in no time, never mind all her doubts and her confusion. The cold, bare fact that scared her the most was that one: she really did love him.

She burrowed deeper into the covers and pressed her back against his. It was going to be a very long night.

Mel Tanbridge surveyed his hotel room with distaste. At four-thirty a.m., anything should have looked good, but the fact was, he expected quality. No, dammit, he expected *the best*. The best he could do on no notice wasn't good enough—he hadn't been able to get the penthouse in Fayetteville's Prince Charles hotel, just a suite—and while it was a nice old hotel, it wasn't a nice old five-star hotel. He hadn't stooped to anything below five-star accommodations in years. The service was good and the suite was clean and spacious, with furniture of excellent taste, but the room didn't have a private jacuzzi—and there wasn't a sauna in the entire hotel. He hadn't had time to check out the amenities in the gym—or even if there was a gym—but he doubted that they would be of the technical level or variety he was used to. After all, this was a military town. He doubted that a military town would have accommodations anywhere that he would find acceptable. That was just the way they were.

There would be a gym somewhere, he decided. And he would find it in the next day or two. After all, he needed to stay in shape. A healthy body equaled a healthy mind—and he had the healthiest. It was his competitive edge.

That edge was important, especially in light of his subordinates' betrayal. Their trail was probably a full two days cold. All the more reason, he decided, not to start down it without sufficient sleep. A healthy body, and all that. . . . He left a wake-up call at the front desk for noon, climbed into bed, and was instantly asleep.

Belinda checked herself out of the Cape Fear Emergency Department and slipped into the waiting cab. She gave the driver the address to the school teacher's apartment complex, then sank into the back seat, thinking ugly thoughts. The stitches in her scalp throbbed, and knowledge of what the wound looked like hurt her just as much. She'd borrowed a mirror from one of the nurses to check out the damage to her hair, and had been appalled. A patch the size of a monk's tonsure had been shaved around the slash that guy in the miniskirt and fishnet hose had made when he brained her with a handy beer bottle. She wore a huge bandage of white gauze and bulky pads that covered the shaved spot for the time being, but when it came off, she was going to be left with an awful mess. She'd been eight the last time she'd had short hair.

Mac Lynn and Mac Lynn's girlfriend, and Mac Lynn's car crew, and anyone else Belinda could think of were going to pay for her hair.

Soon.

However, the anesthetic was wearing off, and she felt dizzy and sick and tense. She needed to find a drugstore to get her pain medicine and her antibiotic prescriptions filled, and then, she had to admit, it would be really nice to take a day off. Maybe even two. The idea of lying in a soft bed taking drugs and not getting kidnapped by horse-cars, beaned by drag-queens, or scalped by bored young doctors was an idea she found appealing right now.

Maybe she could consider her time off the clock as workman's comp. Mel could basically go screw himself if he didn't agree. After all, he was taking it easy out in his beach complex in California. What was he going to do about it?

Her immediate future more or less settled, she closed her eyes and tried her best to ignore the breaking day. *The motel and bed,* she thought. *And no more stinking adventures, not for a while.*

A few drops of rain spattered on the cab's windshield, mixing the fine coating of dust into thoroughly opaque mud. Belinda looked at the sky, startled. It had been clear the last time she'd seen the sky. The clouds must have moved in really fast.

She smiled. Rain was a good omen for her. People didn't look around when it rained. They ran to their cars and got straight in. They didn't sightsee. She considered revising her morning plans. She'd take a free ally any day.

Mac's car was parked where she remembered it. The cabbie pulled up where she directed him, but suddenly Belinda found that she didn't want to get out of the cab. *I'm almost convinced that damned Chevy is* watching *for me. Which is ridiculous, except that I don't have any other way to explain what happened last night.*

I have to pick up my car, though. I need it.

The cabbie gave her an impatient look. "You're on the clock, ya' know," he drawled. "No big deal for me—but you're gonna find it right expensive. I ain't gonna sit here all mornin' for free."

"Yeah, right," she answered. The rain was no longer just a few splashes on the windshield. Now it slashed down in sheets, whipped across the front of the car by gusts of wind. "Drive closer to that brown Thunderbird." She prayed that nothing had happened to the latest of her rental cars. She couldn't afford to experience too much more of Mac Lynn's version of fun and excitement.

The cabbie rolled his eyes, but moved his vehicle so that it formed a screen in front of the T-Bird's driver-side door.

Belinda paid him off, then jumped out of the cab. Once in the T-Bird, she locked the doors. She ignored the cabbie's raised eyebrow. He hadn't had her night. He wouldn't understand.

Belinda sat in the dark safety of her car, watched the raindrops sheeting down her windshield, and listened to their soothing thrumming on the roof. Outside, the world lightened in tiny increments, gray on gray on black, revealing shrubs heavy with water and pines swaying in the driving rain.

The monotonous brick-box apartments were laid out in a grid, with parking lots with separate entries at each square. She moved to the last parking slot three rows away from the teacher's place, cut off the motor, and watched. She was comfortably hidden behind cars parked in the lines ahead of her, and scattered tall Carolina pines—trees that reminded her of the California palms with their trunks that soared thirty feet before the first limb sprouted. Her position gave her a clear view of anyone leaving the apartment.

It couldn't have been more than fifteen or twenty minutes before Mac and his little teacher came flying out of the apartment and dove into the Chevy.

A good, hard rain will never fail you. I knew it. Belinda smiled and, when they pulled out, followed them at a discreet distance.

At the Fayetteville International Speedway, the first fat drops of rain hissed onto the tarmac. More followed, faster and faster, and the patterns made by the first drops were obliterated by water that fell in steady streams, and then sheets, and then in waterfalls that whipped sideways in the steadily increasing wind.

Dierdre, already at the track and doing final pre-race work on the Victor, sighed with resignation at the roaring deluge outside of the garage. The weather station had hinted at this—but torrential rains weren't supposed to be part of the picture until Sunday. She closed her eyes and concentrated on feeling the shifts of air currents and pressure cells. After an extended time, she opened her eyes again, and surveyed the rich red Victor with dismay. *Surprise,* she thought. *We're going to have a whole weekend off, whilst the be-damned weather craps on our heads. Oh, joy. 'Tis not a natural rain, either. This has been pulled in by heavy magic somewhere nearby.*

Time to call her son, the slug, and tell him he wasn't going to have to get out of bed.

She headed to the phone, then stopped. She could have sworn that she'd just heard Rhellen's familiar rumble from the parking lot—even over the rain. She queried her own elvensteed, who was leaning against the back wall keeping dry.

Afallonn rumbled her surprised affirmation.

D.D. looked up at the wall clock, just to make sure time hadn't slipped past without her noticing. It was six-oh-four in the morning, a good three hours before Mac's earliest voluntary wake-up hour. *Will miracles never cease?* she wondered.

Maclyn swung into the garage, a sheepish grin on his face. Behind him was his schoolteacher girlfriend, and the expression on *her* face was patently unreadable.

"Well, Mac, shouldn't surprise me that the first day you show up early for a race is the day they're sure to cancel the whole show."

"Hi, Mom," he said.

:Mom?: D.D. was sure her jaw had hit the floor. *:What the bloody hell—?:* she asked for his ears only.

He sighed. "Rule number one, Mom—never date a pragmatist. Slips of logic and technique convince them that the impossible isn't, whereas girls who operate on blind faith never will believe you're anything but what you appear to be. She figured the whole thing out."

Well. The cat was out of the bag—for now. It wouldn't take but a wee spell to put it back in, but she doubted Maclyn had told his girlfriend that. No harm in waiting to see if she might be a useful addition to the SERRA folk. "In other words, you dated somebody smarter than you for a change." D.D. snorted. "I keep telling you you've not the brains to keep company with any but the dim girls—but you won't listen to me, will you?" She grinned at Lianne.

"Sons know everything, whether they're elven or human, I imagine."

"My mom made a few similar remarks concerning my brother," she said.

"All this came as a shock to you, no doubt," D.D. added.

"Oh," Lianne agreed. "Rest assured."

D.D. gave Lianne a wary look and braced herself for what she felt sure was the impending "big news." "Well, if you're here with my brilliant son, and you know our wee bit of a secret, I expect there's something the two of you will be wanting to tell me."

Surprise flashed in Lianne's eyes. "Uh—not really—ah, D.D. Nothing like *that*, in any case. Actually, Mac mentioned that you were interested in a student of mine. Amanda Kendrick. He said you wanted to find her because she was, um, telekinetic."

Dierdre tried not to make her relief too obvious. "Quite," she said. *I sense the need for a spell of forgetfulness, once we have the wee bairn.*

But Lianne's next words drove all that out of her head. "I have reason to believe her father is abusing her. Mac is going out with me today to her house. He thought you might like to come along."

D.D.'s face had flushed at the mention of abuse. She swore softly in Gaelic, then said slowly, "That explains a great deal, my dear. This—wouldna be the first time I've seen something like this. It breaks my heart, lass, that humans who do not appreciate children have them and hurt them because they don't want them, while we, who would give anything to be able to have more, cannot. Aye, I'll go with you. Do you plan to take the child, Maclyn?"

Maclyn frowned. *:Not now, Mother. She doesn't know about the changelings yet.:* "No. Lianne has the Social Service people taking care of that. She simply wants to get information that will hurry them out to Amanda's house faster. I showed her Tannim's spell-gift, so we can stay unseen."

:Well, we'll see,: Dierdre told him. *:If the situation's bad enough, we'll take the child and befuddle your light-of-love.:*

He winced.

"This rain won't stop today, nor tomorrow either, most

likely," D.D. said. "There won't be a race. So we might as well leave."

Belinda pressed the button on her little black box as Mac hurried by, and the needle waggled to around nine-point-five and stopped. That was only what she expected. She couldn't get excited about Mac anymore. He was too-fucking-much trouble. She pressed it again at the teacher, and nothing happened. No surprises there, either. But when she tried a third time on Mac's little blond mechanic, the needle danced like a fish on a line and dove across to ten.

"I'll be damned," she muttered. It couldn't be any harder to get hold of the mechanic than it had been to abduct that son-of-a-bitch Lynn. Granted, she hadn't seen the mechanic *do* anything—but after the demonstrations she'd gotten from the driver, she was willing to trust the meter, skip the dog-and-pony show, and just collect the warm body and go home.

She waited as the three pulled out of the speedway's parking lot, then followed them again.

Visions of herself as Marlin Perkins on safari danced in her imagination, and she wondered momentarily if it would be possible to get Mel to send her one of those hypodermic dart guns and a big supply of knock-out dope. *Probably not. Mel was starting to get cranky about finances the last time I talked to him.*

She wasn't worried about that, either, though. The FedEx people would be trotting in with her next cash payment, as well as Stevens' and Peterkin's money, on Monday. Since she didn't have to pay either Stevens or Peterkin this time—*and since I haven't mentioned their unfortunate demise to Mel yet*—she could just hang on to the whole thing. Their cash would make a nice addition to her finances.

That reminded her that she really needed to call Mel and assure him that things were progressing nicely. It would be a shame if she didn't keep this job long enough to collect her bonus—especially after all she'd suffered through to get it.

CHAPTER EIGHT

Cethlenn "woke" with no memory of anything since her escape from the Father in the barn. It was early morning, she knew—light came through the bedroom windows in the morning. Whether it was the next day, or a day in the next week, or in the next month, she had no way of knowing. Time was a fluid thing to her in this body; hard to catch, impossible to hold. She wondered if she would ever get used to it.

Rain poured down outside of the little pink-and-white bedroom, framed in the ruffled curtains like an illustration from a child's book. The teddy bears sat on the windowsills, just so—the Step-Mother insisted that they stay in the windowsills because that was where the decorator had placed them. The expensive handcrafted doll-house was filled with porcelain dolls which smiled with sweet insincerity. Everything in the room, in fact, was just so except for Muggles, the terrycloth dog a child had traded to Amanda-Abbey for a small, exquisite porcelain figurine. Amanda-Abbey had smuggled the figurine out of her room for show-and-tell when she was in first grade, and made the deal in the school cafeteria. Muggles looked like the last remaining survivor of a battle between Cethlenn's own folk and the Roman invaders, but he had three advantages none of the other toys in the room had. One, he was eminently huggable. Two, he could be smooshed down to fit in the tiny space between the headboard and the wall, where no one could see him. Therefore, he couldn't be thrown away. And three, he belonged to no one but Amanda, and she could do anything she wanted with him. He did not have to be kept nice—he was not a decorator dog.

Cethlenn liked Muggles, and since she had been left in control of the body, she hid him carefully in the place Amanda-Anne had shown her. Then she slipped into the closet and listened to the sounds from Sharon's room next door. Sharon's television was on, and the chaos of Teenage Mutant Ninja Turtles reverberated off the walls— Saturday noise. *Saturn's Day. Proof that the gods-be-damned Romans won.* She frowned, briefly wondering at the events that had changed the world from the place she'd known to the place she now found, and wondering what she'd missed. Then she shrugged off her curiosity.

The last thing she remembered from her own life was taking a knife in the gut, and pain. The next moment, she woke in the body of a child a long, long way from home. Even though the devices and customs in this land were alien, it was better being an unhappy child than a woman with a knife in her. Better than being a woman in a world ruled by Romans.

So it was Saturday. Good. Then perhaps it *was* the next day, and she hadn't lost much this time. She dressed in the closet—clean white cotton underwear, blue jeans and a white t-shirt, white socks and red Halston designer hightops. Dressing was one of the things that had improved greatly since her days with the Druids. Most everything else was worse—but houses were better, and so were clothes.

She debated the merits of going downstairs for breakfast versus staying hungry. She decided against breakfast— there was no telling where the Father might be, or what mood he might be in, and she would just as soon not remind him of Amanda's existence. Instead, she nibbled on cheese crackers bought from another schoolchild, purchased with scavenged and stolen change and carefully hidden.

Thinking of the Father brought back fleeting images from what she suspected had been the night before. She wondered how Amanda-Anne had fared in the barn—and was fearful for the child. She could feel bruises and raw spots that hadn't been there before, and dull aches that she knew the meaning of well enough. It was strange that she should wake up "alone" in the body—usually when she was awake, she was watching Amanda-Abbey or looking over Alice or Anne's shoulder, so to speak. She decided to see if she could find Amanda-Anne, just to check on her. Cethlenn peered cautiously into the walled-off space that Amanda-Anne kept for herself.

At first, what she found puzzled her. Over the wall, there were usually more walls, towering constructs of brick that enclosed and protected the child and kept everything away from her. But the scenery wasn't like that this time. It stretched away in all directions, vast nothingness, gray and empty without ground or sky, without markers—except for the single wall to Cethlenn's back.

It was, the witch realized, a part of the Unformed Plane, although how the child had reached into it and made it a part of herself, Cethlenn had no idea. Initially, she couldn't see the child anywhere. Gradually, however, faint movements off to her left convinced her that something was there.

Cethlenn blended herself with the mist. Her last confrontation with Amanda-Anne on her own territory was still fresh enough in her memory that she had no wish to repeat it. As part of the mist, she floated toward the place where the movement seemed to originate.

Sure enough, Amanda-Anne was there, as happy as that child ever got, contentedly humming some monotonous tune in a minor key. There was no sense of fear or anger—instead, the child gave the impression that she was extremely pleased about something.

Without doing anything that would alert the little girl to her presence, Cethlenn thinned herself out to a fine thread of pure consciousness and eased closer.

The child was working on something, a sort of a doll, perhaps—

Cethlenn focused on the details of the "doll" until she

realized what she was looking at. What had seemed innocent child's play became sinister. The "doll" the child made was nothing of the sort. It was a creature formed of fury, molded out of all the darkness in Amanda-Anne's soul—Cethlenn felt the ancient magic like a fire in her chest, felt a horror from memories burned into her centuries before. It was something derived from the magic of the Sidhe—and it must be linked to the visitation by the elven warrior the other day.

The child had copied the elf's magic by watching him, Cethlenn realized. She had discovered how to use the energy of the Unformed Planes to create a thing of order out of the chaos—but what she formed was horrifying. The user of such energies had to take her will and her experience to form the energy into whatever she desired. Cethlenn knew the strength of will it took to do such a thing—and in Amanda-Anne's short life, she had experienced no joy, no love, no laughter—nothing but pain and humiliation and fear and hatred. The thing she molded between her fingers was a misshapen nightmare formed of those emotions, and only those emotions.

Cethlenn watched the child with growing unease, as she played with the stuff of the Unformed Plane as other children would play with dough. She had molded a round, lopsided, lumpy head, rolling it into a rough ball, poking in eyes and a nose and scratching a gash of a mouth with a fingernail. She had formed the body in the way children made dough snakes, and then jammed the head onto it. The arms and legs she created in the same fashion while Cethlenn hovered and watched. When the thing was finished to the child's satisfaction, the little girl stared at her homunculus, all of her concentration and focus centered on it. At first, nothing happened. Then Cethlenn saw that the seams where the arms and legs and head were joined to the body had become thinner and smoother. The arms and legs began to move with weak, spastic shudders, and embryonic digits grew out of the flattened pancakes that were hands and feet. With a sudden flash, the thing's eyes flew open, and glowed with white light. Red fangs sprang from the wide, grinning mouth; a wet, pink tongue darted between them along the lipless rim. Fingers and toes sprouted black, rapierlike claws, and hair sprouted from the round, neckless head as if it had been scribbled there with a pencil.

Amanda-Anne giggled, and the thing giggled back at her: a high, empty, chittering imitation of a little-girl laugh. The child stood her creation on its feet and sent it walking. As it walked, Amanda-Anne stared after it, muttering "Big-ger—big-ger—big-ger," in her whining, nasal voice.

And it grew bigger, and stretched and filled out so fast that it seemed the creature, walking away, grew nearer with every step. First it was tall as a child, then as a small woman, and then as a large man.

The golem shambled off into the mist—and Cethlenn knew that the movement that had led her to Amanda-Anne had come from another of its kind, moving out. Once she knew what to look for, she realized there were more of them moving around in the mist—impossible to mark and count because of their aimless drifting and the perpetual fog of the Unformed Planes, but still . . . many. Cethlenn repressed a moan as, cross-legged and happy, Amanda-Anne began to build yet another one.

Oh, gods, Cethlenn thought. *Oh, gods, I've got to get help.* She left the child sitting in the gloom making her monsters and singing her discordant songs and shot toward the wall that marked the boundary of Amanda-Anne's space.

Once free from the eerie gloom of the Unformed Planes, Cethlenn discovered she was still alone and in control of the body. She would have worried about the whereabouts of Amanda-Abbey and Amanda-Alice if she had more time, but she had to admit there were things she could accomplish more easily if she didn't have company. Setting up a spell that would summon the Seleighe elves was one of those things.

Cethlenn dug through the closet and found galoshes and a neon-pink raincoat in the back. There was a part of her that dreaded the raincoat as too bright, too much of a beacon for the Father, who might see her moving through the woods and follow her. There was another, more practical part of her that insisted that the Father would want no part of the pouring rain, but that she would surely regret whatever happened if she came back into the house soaked to the skin and dirty from the rain and the woods. She decided on a compromise. She rolled the raincoat up in a ball and stuffed it in her black nylon book-bag. Then she gathered up her kit—cords of various colors, a white candle, one of the Step-Mother's filched cigarette lighters, a bright blue crayon, and a vivid green crayon. Last of all, she looked around the room for a gift. The tales she remembered of elvenfolk, and incidents from her own rare dealings with them, all indicated that they were shifty and tricksy, and a favor asked had to be a favor repaid. She recalled tales from her childhood in the old world—tales of the fey folk who appeared, offering the heart's desire, and desiring in return the one thing a human had that an elf didn't: a soul. She wanted to have something to offer that wouldn't cost her *that*. Her own continuing existence was proof enough to her that her soul might be a real thing, after all, and worth hanging on to.

Gifting elves was a chancy business by all accounts. Stories indicated that there was rarely anything one was likely to have that the elf didn't already have, and of better quality to boot.

She thought back on her mother's tales. Elves were supposed to be fond of silver and gold, fine fabrics, good music, good drink and good food. She had, quite frankly, nothing to offer in any of those categories—except, she thought with sudden joy, for the giant chocolate bar Amanda-Abbey had bought from one of the band students who was selling them to raise money. The last time Cethlenn had been around, none of the Amandas had yet gotten a chance to eat it. Perhaps it was still intact.

She rummaged through the school pack, and indeed, it was still there. She pulled the blocky gold-wrapped bar out of the pack. It was somewhat wrinkled and battered from its trip home on the bus, and she could tell that it had broken into several fragments, but it was good chocolate. Chocolate, she decided, was a gift worthy of elves, being the *other* thing about this era that was an improvement over the days with the Druids. And since it was the best she had to offer, she hoped any elves she might draw in would give her credit for effort.

With her pack slung across her shoulders, she opened the window on the right side of her room and scooted out of it. Then she pulled the window closed, slid around until she dangled off the sill by her fingertips, and dropped the final six inches between her feet and the sun-room roof which ran out at right angles from her own room. She scurried like a lizard along the peak of the wet, slippery roof to the very end, then slid down the steeply pitched side and shinnied down the old pecan tree that had grown too close to the house.

From there, she kept under the cover of the evergreen azaleas and the rhododendrons, which took her straight into the woods. The Father hadn't found her escape route yet. She hoped he never would.

Once in the woods, she put on the loud pink raincoat. Her t-shirt wasn't too dirty, she decided. The Step-Mother wouldn't like it, but she wouldn't fuss terribly, either.

Cethlenn beelined for her tree, not following the usual devious route. She didn't have time. Amanda Anne was still sitting in the Unformed Planes making golems as far as *she* knew, and that had to be stopped. At least the creatures were still *there*, but for how long?

Inside the safe barrier of the holly tree's limbs, Cethlenn took out her prizes. She wondered if the spell she'd learned for summoning the Faerie folk was any good anymore— or if it ever had been. After two thousand years or more, maybe the elvenkind wouldn't pay attention to cords and candles. Maybe they preferred the new technologies—the answering machines and car phones of this strange age. That would be unfortunate, the witch thought—because she didn't have access to car phones or answering machines. She just barely had access to cords and candles.

She spread out the cords—one green, one red, one black and one white. From the hollow of the tree, she removed Abbey's forbidden comic books. She placed the candy bar and the candle inside the hollow, wedging the candle in so that it stayed upright. She put the cigarette lighter beside it. She lay the blue and green crayons at the base of the tree.

Preparations made, she offered up a quick, sincere prayer to her Lord and Lady, then took the green cord in hand, and took a slow, deep breath to steady her nerves.

While her fingers worked the cord into the patterns of a Celtic knot, she sang in the Old Tongue:

"Fair folk who have danced in the wood, on the green—
I would call, I would beg, to your king, to your queen,
To you who listen, all unseen,
I bind your ears with my knot of green."

She lay the elaborate knot at the periphery of the tree and pressed it firmly into the dirt with her foot.

Next she took up the black cord, walked one quarter of the way around the tree, and while working the cord into her second pattern, chanted:

"Faerie folk with the strength I lack,
I dare not run, nor dare attack,
But I summon you still, and call you back—
I bind your eyes with my knot of black."

She took up the red cord, walked to the far side of the tree, and with her fingers weaving, sang:

"Fey folk drawn from board and bed,
Gifts I offer to quick and dead,
Think of me kindly whom I have led;
I bind your oath with my cord of red."

At the fourth quarter of the tree, she took up the white cord, and knotted it, and said:

"Old ones come from the long twilight,
Brought to the world of day and night,
I ask your aid to make wrong right;
I bind your power with my cord of white."

When the last knot was in place at the periphery of the tree, she moved back to the candle and lit it.

"Now you who are drawn from your Faerie mound,
And led by my beacon to this ground—
To my circle shall you be bound
Until my knots are all unwound."

She melted the tip of the blue crayon in the flame and drew a protective rune on the palm of her left hand. With the melted tip of the green crayon, she copied the same device on the palm of her right hand. Then she picked up the chocolate bar, huddled on the ground in the incongruous pink raincoat, and began her vigil.

❖   ❖   ❖

Gwaryon, one of the original settlers of Elfhame Outremer, sat beside Felouen at the side of the Oracular Pool and stared with her at the ominous changes in the curtain of the Unformed that rippled in front of them. He was going through an Egyptian phase, and was at the moment dressed as an ancient pharaoh—from the massive amber scarab pendant around his neck to the draping see-through robes which Felouen found annoyingly pretentious, though she had to admit they showed his body off to good effect. His gold bracelets jangled with a flat heavy sound as he rested his arm around Felouen's shoulders.

She sighed. The effect was so completely—*Gwaryon*.

"I am grateful," Felouen told him, and rested her head against his shoulder. "Your presence here is a comfort to me—the visions from the Pool these last few days have left me feeling very much alone."

Gwaryon smiled, happily. "You are never alone, dear one. You know I would be with you always if you would say the word."

Felouen sighed and studied the lean, sinuous elf with deep sadness. "I know. And I cannot give you reason to hope in vain for that day to come—it will not. You are dear to me, but you are not the one I desire the most."

Gwaryon laughed and sprawled on his back in the deep, soft grass that grew beside the Pool. "Och, dearest lady, I know that well enough—but still I hope. You cannot extinguish hope, while we both breathe. And even if you don't want me forever, surely a moment's dalliance would relieve your mind of the weight of your duties." His grin broadened, and he arched his eyebrows suggestively.

She tried a smile, but it didn't feel convincing. "Ah, Gwaryon, you are ever considerate of the weight of my burdens," she told him with heavy irony, and absently stroked the hilt of her jeweled dagger. She ceased that, point made, and rested her chin in her cupped hands. Gwaryon's offer of pleasure didn't fit well with her mood. Her worry was even stronger and more pressing than it had been. The red glittering of the Unformed had deepened and seemed angrier, somehow. And at rare intervals, she was almost sure that she could see shapes moving through that fog-shrouded realm of nothing, where no living things should be. Not even the Unseleighe creatures wandered at will through the Unformed—it was more a state of mind than a place, and it welcomed only madness with open arms.

Something was going to happen—she was sure of it. And soon.

"Ho!" Gwaryon whispered. "Feel that?"

Felouen stiffened. "A pull . . ."

He nodded emphatically. "Human magic. I haven't felt its kind since long before you were born."

"I want to go toward it." She glanced at Gwaryon, and her eyes filled with worry.

He nodded. "Once it would have been very dangerous to do so, but now—" He sat up and shook his head. "The knowledge is there, but not the strength. We aren't being summoned by some great mage, nor anyone whose power will overwhelm us. And sometimes these things were calls for help from those who had no other recourse."

Calls for help? "Should we arm ourselves for battle?"

Gwaryon laughed. "I would guess that the human who dug that ancient spell out of an old tome doesn't even suspect that it is real—much less that we exist. Such a human won't be a threat to us. Let's just go and take a look."

A stirring in the forces she had woven into her net of hopes roused her from her trance of concentration. Cethlenn turned from her spell-making to find herself staring into the faces of two of the Old Folk, who were studying her with mixed bemusement and disbelief.

Well, she thought, mouth agape, *At least I know it still works.*

Lianne McCormick was keeping a wary eye on her companions, when both of them suddenly started, as if they had heard something she couldn't. D.D., perched on Rhellen's sumptuous back seat, cocked her head to one side, birdlike. "Oh, my," she whispered. "Maclyn, my love, my darlin' boy, do you feel that?"

Maclyn ground his teeth audibly. "All over, Mother. It's coming from out where we're heading, more or less."

She looked grim. "And a good thing, too. I think otherwise we wouldn't be able to go there—it would pull us to wherever it was."

"What are you two talking about?" Lianne asked.

D.D. rubbed both temples with her knuckles, as if she had a headache. "Mac feels something tugging at him, but he isn't old enough to recognize what it is—*I* haven't felt this particular sensation in so many years, I would have thought I'd forgotten what it was. And I've *never* felt it on this side of the ocean. I thought such summonings were left behind in the Old Country."

"Summonings?" Lianne asked, startled.

D.D. nodded. "Oh, aye. Someone has cast a spell to draw and bind the elvenkind. Such binding spells were known to a few priestesses and witches in the Old Country long ago, and to even fewer mages—but those who were willing to demand our presence were rare. We grew weary of being drawn into the world of Cold Iron against our wills, and we began to attack first and ask questions later. It took only a few toasted humans before that spell fell out of favor."

Lianne rested her head against Rhellen's door. She stared at the neat subdivisions they drove past, and at the stands of tall pines and the orderly young rows of cotton and soybeans that grew in the square, predictable fields. "Witches," she muttered, speaking to no one but herself. "And spells. Elves and telekinesis. Magic. Did I mention that I never cared about magic when I was growing up? Did I ever say that *I* was the kid who didn't give a damn about unicorns? I like science: nuclear physics, math, chemistry. I always liked the world when it was rational. Didn't I make that clear?"

D.D. looked at her son with concern.

Maclyn shrugged. "She's had several difficult days. She'll snap out of it."

"I *thought* I was dating a human," Lianne said, as Maclyn turned the Chevy down the dirt road that paralleled the Kendrick's property. "I thought this was a guy I might potentially take home to meet my folks."

"This is bothering you, isn't it, babe?" Mac asked, flippantly.

Lianne quit talking to the four winds and centered her attention on Mac. She glowered at him with disbelieving eyes. "No-o-o-o-o!" she drawled. "Having elves screw with my brain is just my favorite thing ever. Having my world-view and all of science refuted in two days' time has done *wonders* for my morale. You ought to try it sometime."

"You're welcome to keep thinking that the world is a nice, logical, rational, safe place," Maclyn said with a helpful smile. "You'll be wrong, but that hasn't stopped anyone else who thinks the same way."

Lianne growled something profoundly obscene, and Maclyn and Dierdre both laughed.

"If it makes you feel better, Lianne, magic works by laws, too. Think of it as another kind of science you don't know yet."

Lianne fumed.

Maclyn drove Rhellen up to the very edge of the woods, out of sight of the road or any houses. Behind them was a fallow field, standing tall with weeds. Maclyn got out of the car, and Lianne slid out after him.

"She would be safer here with Rhellen," D.D. said, as if Lianne wasn't there. Lianne hated being talked around.

"I probably would be," Lianne agreed, studying the woman who would probably not end up as her mother-in-law. "But I don't intend to stay here with the car—with Rhellen."

"Only until we see who has summoned us," D.D. said, placatingly. "Then you can join us and help us find the wee child's home."

"No thanks. I'd like to see that myself." Lianne pulled her gray mackintosh tight, noticing that the rain fell all around her but not on her. The cold and the damp still blew straight through her, and the low keening of the wind gnawed at her nerves. *Great day for this sort of thing*, she decided. *Make a believer out of even the staunchest pragmatist. Wind sounds like a banshee, and I think I could see ghosts in broad daylight on a day like this.*

She had to remind herself that this was an attempt to find information that would rescue an abused kid—not a midday ghost hunt. *Amanda needs help*, she reminded herself. But it made her nervous that Mac and D.D. were being drawn against their will toward something that called from the same direction as Amanda's home. Could that bastard of a father be summoning them?

Bad thought, Li. Very bad thought.

Lianne watched the two of them walk, faces grim and tense, ducking around the dripping greenery—scrub oak and sassafras and willow; blackberry bramble, grapevine and kudzu—that made up this part of the woods. She walked a step behind them, staying quiet. They did magic, and this was something that frightened them. She was out of her element, way out of her area of experience, much less expertise. It was as if there was something out there that didn't *want* them to help Amanda and was trying to prevent them from interfering. That made her profoundly nervous.

Cethlenn stood with her back pressed against the trunk of the tree, the chocolate bar in her outstretched hand. Though it still rained all around her, no rain fell on her, nor did any fall on her—guests. She stared at the two elves, the woman in clothing similar to that which elves had worn in her earlier life—the man in a foreign-looking gown of some gorgeous filmy material she would have killed for once upon a time, and covered with gem-crusted gold jewelry.

"Child," the male elf said, "the last time I heard that bit of doggerel was a good two thousand years before you were born. And it had become uncommon then."

The female elf shook her head. "I didn't realize anyone could summon us."

Cethlenn shivered. She would have preferred to have been less of a novelty. She held out the chocolate bar and waggled it a bit. "I gift thee, lord and lady."

The female—one with the look of a warrior about her—studied the proffered bar, and shuddered. "Oooh, chocolate. Loaded with caffeine, and you wouldn't believe the empty calories in that thing."

"Summoning price has gone down a bit since the old days, Felouen," the male muttered with dry amusement. "It used to be that they greeted us with baskets of gold and jewels and fine silks and rare spices. But then we needed a bit more placating back then—too many calls for no good reason. No, child," the elven male added. "We won't take your candy. There is another gift we will require instead, for having come when you called us forth."

Och, and there goes my soul, Cethlenn thought with dismay.

Her face evidently mirrored her fear, for the female elf said, "We won't hurt you. We don't hurt children."

The strangely dressed male looked into Cethlenn's eyes and said, "That isn't what she's afraid of—oh, this is rich. Just rich. They used to think we stole souls, and that's what she is afraid of. It *is*! Look at her—that's exactly what she was expecting." He grinned at the witch in the child's body, and said, "Kid, if you had a really hot 486 with a VGA monitor, a solid keyboard, and a ton of software, I'd steal that in a heartbeat. But you can keep your soul. I *would* like to know where you found that old string-and-knot song and dance."

Cethlenn could hardly believe her ears—or her luck. "That's all?"

The elf nodded. "That's my trade. Information for our arrival."

Cethlenn smiled, confidently. "I learned it from the MacLurrie's first witch, when I earned my place as one of his advisors."

The elves stared at each other, and the female elf mouthed the name "MacLurrie?"

"An old warrior and rake who was a bit before your time, child," the male elf said, and nodded to his female companion. "He was a bit before *her* time. I remember the young boaster well enough, but I can't imagine how you could."

Cethlenn drew herself up as tall as she could stand—which was not very—and said, proudly, "I am Cethlenn, daughter of Martis and witch at MacLurrie's circle. I was not always this child, though how I came to be here, I know not."

The male's brow creased with thought, and he absently played with a great beetle of amber that hung about his neck. "Cethlenn . . . hmm. I vaguely recall a charming, dark-eyed creature named Cethlenn from around the time of the battles of the Gauls and the Gaels—as a matter of fact, now that I think of it, she was sharing her favors between MacLurrie's bastard son and one of our folk. Bryothan, was it? Or Prydwyn?"

"Eodain was my other suitor," Cethlenn corrected. "Eodain. But he wasn't elven."

"Eodain . . . Eodain . . . It's been so long, I've forgotten." He stared off into space, while his long, graceful fingers twined in the many layers of his gold jewelry. "By Oberon's steed, girl, I believe you're right. It . . . was . . ." His eyes narrowed and fixed on Cethlenn, and he glared at her from beneath lowered brows. "Eodain. Who was one of our folk, although you certainly couldn't expect him to tell a mortal like yourself that. No tales of his little tryst were barded about—it was mere court gossip, which means—"

"That she either made an extraordinarily lucky guess, or she is what she says." The one called Felouen frowned.

The male gave his companion a somber look. "Then the price is met and our oath is bound."

"No!" Felouen snapped. "If this is not a child but a witch of the Old Country, then she has not called us in idle sport. She would have known the dangers. No matter how unlikely, and no matter how innocent she seems, she is a danger to us. You stay, I'm leaving."

The elven woman shimmered, but stayed solidly within the child's hiding place. She made another obvious attempt to leave, and when that, too, failed, she turned on her companion with a snarl. "We're trapped here, Gwaryon!"

The male elf shrugged. "She means us no harm."

But there was veiled panic in the female's expression. "I don't care! I want out of here!"

Gwaryon looked at Cethlenn, and his face grew stern. "I also dislike this spell that holds us here."

There was no point in acting contrite. Not with those—things—out there, shambling around in the Unformed Planes. "I've met your price. Besides, 'twas the only way I knew of callin' the Fair Folk," Cethlenn said. "I need help. I am not the only one in this child, you see. . . ."

Cethlenn's voice faltered in mid-sentence, and a furious presence pushed her back and usurped her control of the body. *:No!:* Amanda-Anne screeched to the ancient witch. :*You . . . c-c-c-can't . . . tell . . . them about . . . us!*:

:*They could help,*: Cethlenn said, soothingly. :*They could take you away from the Father.*:

But Amanda-Anne was not about to be soothed. :*No-o-o-o! Stopping . . . is . . . not helping! They . . . w-w-w-would . . . only call us . . . bad girl. Make us . . . weak again. They would take . . . our m-m-m-magic.*:

:*No, Anne,*: Cethlenn told the child, her thoughts pleading. :*Let them help you. They can take you away from him, make the bad things go away—they can hide you someplace safe.*:

Amanda-Anne had quit listening. She looked at the elves who were held—trapped—in the circle, and her voice rose in a shrill sing-song. "I m-m-m-made me . . . gletchells and . . . sl-sl-slinketts . . . and m-m-m-morrow-w-waries . . . and . . . f-fulges. F-f-friends of me . . . friends . . . of me. And . . . *you* . . . w-w-want to hurt my . . . f-f-friends," she wailed on a rising note.

The elves stared at each other, amazement and confusion written clearly on their faces. *Oh, Lord,* Cethlenn thought. *What have I done?*

Amanda-Anne knelt in the dirt, and rubbed her fingers across Mommy's green bead on its new gold bracelet. Without words, she summoned her "friends" and brought them through the bead and out into the charmed circle that was Amanda-Abbey's safe place.

The homunculi spewed into the haven under the holly tree in a cloud of black smoke, giggling as they took solid form. Their wide, grinning mouths split open, and their fangs gleamed red. They shambled and staggered on uneven legs, ducking gracelessly under the sheltering boughs of the holly. Their scimitar fingers grasped toward the elves.

Amanda-Anne waited until five of her pets were through the bead-gate. Then, laughing, she slipped out of the tree-shelter, and darted home.

To Felouen, her arrival in the child's spelled circle had been discomfiting. The spell was carefully wrought, so that her eyes saw nothing but the world inside of the magical boundaries, and her ears heard nothing but the sounds of

the child's voice and the few creakings that the old holly
tree made. Its branches blew in a wind she knew to be
present, but neither felt nor heard. Her world narrowed
to the tree itself, which soared upward, its dark, leathery
leaves contrasted with the brilliant light green of new spring
growth, and with the startling reds of the few remaining
berries not yet picked away by the birds. And in the center of the circle, the child: frail, blond, brown-eyed, with
skinny arms and legs covered by wet clothes, who stared
at her with awe—but not surprise. All else was hidden in
the obscuring darkness of the spell. Her senses and her
magic were bound—she could not leave. She was trapped—
by a child who, in all sincerity, said that she was a witch
from the Old Country.

And then the witch in the child's body changed—no,
change was not the precise word. The witch, Cethlenn,
disappeared, or was abducted, and was replaced by someone—terrible. Felouen felt the newcomer, the child—for
this one was a child—arrive, full of rage and fear and
confusion. This green-eyed human, who was terrified of the
elves without knowing fully what they were, knew only that
she wanted to hurt them. Wanted to hurt everything.
Felouen felt her slashing, unfocused rage like a blow to
the face, sensed her hatred and wondered, in the brief
instant before the child brought forth her monsters, what
could have twisted the youngling in such horrible and
deadly ways.

After that, she didn't have time to wonder about anything.

It was not the vision from the Oracular Pool—Felouen
wasn't defending the Elfhame Outremer grove. She and
Gwaryon fought to save their own lives. There were no
armies of elvenkin at her sides; but neither were there
armies of the great shambling things.

Her own situation, however, was no less grave than the
vision of the Pool.

The Pool had made a true showing of the monsters.
They were just as malformed and frighteningly senseless
as they had appeared in the glassy surface of the water—
and the ratio by which they outnumbered the elves was
as bad.

Felouen regretted Gwaryon's casual response to the summons and her own willingness to follow along. Now, between the two of them and the child's nightmares-made-real were only two little silver elven-blades, knives pitifully small when compared to the claws of their opponents. Felouen and Gwaryon scrambled up the trunk of the tree into its upper limbs, hoping at best to escape the monsters' talons completely, and at very worst for a defensible place in which to make their stand.

Unfortunately, the things could climb—and they did. Their glowing, pupilless white eyes gleamed in the pouring rain, and their high-pitched and horribly childlike giggles carried over the pounding rain and the low moans of the wind. They were slow climbers and clumsy, but deliberate, and they seemed to stick to the tree as they moved upward.

The leading monster reached a point just under Felouen's ankles. It screeched with sudden wild intensity and slashed out at her legs. Its talons ripped through the sturdy leather of her boots as if it was silk, and dragged into her flesh. Felouen cried out once at the sharp stab of pain and pulled her feet higher. Gwaryon threw his knife, and Felouen saw the little blade bury itself in the pallid thing's eye.

The monster grabbed for the knife with both hands, lost its balance, and fell. Even falling, it giggled, until the noise was cut short by the *thud* as it hit the ground.

Felouen slashed at the next golem within reach. The blade cut deeply and lopped off three of its fingers, but the wound didn't bleed and the creature showed no signs of pain. It kept climbing, and she was forced to climb still higher, onto a weak, green branch that bent alarmingly under her weight. The golem stopped and looked up at her, and its giggling became shriller. It grasped the branch to which she clung and began rocking it back and forth.

"Stop it!" she screamed. "Damn you!"

Beneath her and to one side, Gwaryon was fighting his own battle. He had wedged himself tightly into a crotch of a sturdy branch and was kicking the monsters in the head as soon as they were within reach. His legs were bloody ribbons, and his sandal-clad feet were unrecognizable as feet. His skin, at least that which wasn't bloody, was gray.

Felouen saw the beads of pain-sweat standing out on his forehead—but his face never lost its determination. She watched one golem fall to the ground as Gwaryon kicked it loose from its perch. It hit heavily, lay still for a moment—then rose, and begin its climb back up the tree. It had already been replaced by the next monster.

Felouen realized with horror it was the one that had taken Gwaryon's knife in its eye. *They're unkillable,* she thought with sudden, overwhelming despair, and clung tighter to her branch. The monster beneath her kept rocking it, swinging it in faster and further arcs. Its hysterical laughter never stopped.

"Stop it! Damn you!" someone screamed from ahead of them, and the sounds of a desperate struggle and a blood-curdling chittering made the forest sound like something out of a horror story. In front of her, Maclyn apparently heard it, too. He started to run. "Weapons and armor," he told his mother. Silver swords materialized in their hands, and chased and enameled armor appeared around them.

God, I wish I could do that, Lianne thought, breaking into a run behind them.

They were faster than she was. They ran effortlessly, appearing to do no more than jog—yet they pulled away from her at an impossible rate. She ran flat out, putting everything she had into the effort, yet she fell further and further behind. The two elves darted through a thicket without slowing, and she stopped completely to disentangle herself from the inch-long thorns that held her clothes in fast embrace.

By the time she was out of the thicket, the elves had disappeared from sight, but she still heard the fighting, and the—other noises. The sounds came from the other side of the small hill she was climbing. She slowed to a trot, by necessity picking her route more carefully than the elves had. She wondered now what in hell she was doing out here. What good was she, an unarmed human, in a fight where at least two of the combatants were well-armed and armored elves? She suspected she would be more of a liability—someone who would end up needing to be rescued. By the time she'd reached the crest of the hill, she had decided to find a safe spot in which to wait out the fight.

Close up, it sounded even worse. Unfortunately, she couldn't see much. The holly's leaves blocked most of her view, but a steady green glow from the tree's center backlit shadowy forms; the fight was more terrible than she could have anticipated. In the cramped space under a holly tree's branches, Maclyn and Dierdre battled misshapen horrors that looked from the brief glimpses she got like the most awful nightmares the folks from Industrial Light and Magic could have concocted. She saw two elves she didn't recognize, stranded in the thin upper branches of the tree, fighting more of the things. She saw one of the white-eyed monsters then, and squeezed her eyes shut until she realized she couldn't wish the nightmare away. The elves in the tree were wounded and bloody—the monsters they fought appeared unscathed.

Lianne saw Maclyn bring his sword straight down on top of one monster's head in a two-handed blow that should have split the thing in half, but the monster never fell.

A scream of pure anguish drew her attention back to the treetop. One of the monsters had overcome the male elf and had severed one of his arms. It dropped like some macabre fruit to land against the tree roots. The elf screamed once more as the horror gnawed through his remaining forearm. Lianne shoved her fist against her mouth to silence her own screams; one last slash of the thing's claws and the elf's severed head hung from its grip.

The body tumbled from the tree, with unreal slowness. The golem threw the head in a lazy overhand toss that sent it soaring in a slow, graceful arc toward Lianne. As it passed beyond the spread of the holly tree, it winked out of existence as if it had never been.

Lianne stared at the spot where it disappeared and shuddered.

It was only the steady repetition of someone calling her name that brought her out of her stunned reverie.

"Lianne? Lianne? Can you hear me?" Dierdre shouted. Lianne could make out her shadowy form, back pressed against Maclyn's, keeping the monsters at bay with a steady barrage of swordstrokes.

"Maybe she ran off," Maclyn yelled. He parried a talon-strike aimed at his face and landed a stop-thrust that did no apparent damage to its victim.

"Maybe we just can't hear her because of this damned spell. I hope that's the case."

"I'm right here!" Lianne yelled from her hiding place. None of the combatants paid her any attention.

Certain that she was exposing herself to attack by the monsters, Lianne did the bravest thing she had ever done. She stood up and ran toward the fight, again yelling, "I'm right here."

It was if she didn't exist to those battling under the tree. And that was as horrible as all the rest combined.

"Lianne," Dierdre yelled between swordstrokes, "if you're there, listen—a spell traps us in here. Look for knotted cords around this tree—probably four or five. If you—"

One monster got inside her defense, and the sound of talons raking across armor screeched through the woods.

"If you find the knots, untie them!" Dierdre yelled. "And hurry!"

Lianne heard the elves parrying claws and Maclyn's voice asking, between panted breaths, "What if she's not out there?"

She heard Dierdre answer, "Then we die."

Lianne stared at the headless, armless torso that lay under the tree, and then through the branches, at Dierdre and Mac. Then she looked up at the bleeding, exhausted elf stranded in the upper branches. The one tireless monster who was trying to dislodge her had shifted tactics and was scraping across the branch with his claws. Bits of wood flew away with every stroke. It wouldn't be long until the branch broke.

Cords? she wondered. *Made into knots that I should untie?*

She could not imagine what good untying knots would do—but she was willing to concede that this was not an ordinary situation, and that the rules she knew didn't apply. She ran to the periphery of the tree and scouted around the branches.

In a moment, she had located one knot. It was tied in a heavy, glossy black cord, and it wove in and out around itself half a dozen different ways. It took her a bit of fumbling even to discover where the ends had been tucked, and once she had found them, even longer to return the cord to its unknotted state.

As soon as the knot was unraveled, however, Lianne heard Maclyn yell, "There she is!" One of the monsters suddenly noticed her, too, and charged toward her. Mere inches away, it broke through the branches and was brought up short by an invisible barrier. It shrieked in frustration, and charged again.

She backed away frightened.

"Get the rest of the knots," Dierdre shouted.

"What will happen when they are untied?" Lianne asked.

Dierdre looked puzzled, then shouted, "I can't hear you."

Lianne shrugged and hurried around the periphery of the tree. A flash of red caught her eye, and she stopped. The monster that charged at her as she pulled the red cord out from under the branches sent her heart leaping into her throat, and the other creatures' incessant chittering giggles made it almost impossible to concentrate—but with trembling fingers, she managed to untangle the second knot.

"If we survive this," Dierdre suddenly remarked, "I'm going to severely damage the person responsible."

"I know how you feel," Maclyn agreed.

There was a creak, and the branch that supported the third elf sagged. "Felouen!" Maclyn yelled, "Hang on!"

"I'd figured that out already, thanks," Felouen shouted back.

Giggles grated along her nerves. *Third cord*, she thought, and refused to let herself consider what would happen when all the cords were unwound.

It took a bit of digging in the spot where she thought it might be, but she did locate the third cord. It was white.

She ignored the crash that indicated the branch had broken through, ignored the scream of fear and pain and the heavy thud that followed. Lianne fumbled with the complex knot and worked it loose.

"Magic works again," Dierdre muttered, and that terse statement was followed by a flash of brilliant blue light and a loud sizzling sound.

Lianne ran to the fourth quarter of the imaginary circle the unknown magician had laid out, and within seconds had discovered a twisted length of green cord. Familiar now with the permutations the knots had taken, she quickly pulled it apart.

There was a low rumble, and the air around her shimmered like air over pavement on a hot day. For an instant, the situation under the tree continued unchanged. The monsters slashed at the elves, the one who had broken the hapless Felouen loose from her tree clambered down after her, chuckling evilly. The monster that had been charging at Lianne broke free of its circle and came straight for her, and Dierdre and Maclyn fought their way toward the body of their fallen comrade.

Then, with a resounding "crack," the monsters and the dismembered remains of the dead elf vanished.

Dierdre looked around as if she couldn't believe it was over, then sagged against the tree trunk. Maclyn charged to Felouen's side.

Lianne crawled through the holly's low-hanging branches with some difficulty and joined him.

Felouen was badly hurt. She lay, unresponsive, on the woodland floor, her breathing ragged and irregular. Dark blood seeped into the fabric of her shirt, and through a tear in the cloth, Lianne could see the white gleam of ribs and the dark bubbling of a large, open wound.

"Mother!" Maclyn's voice was hoarse. He knelt beside the downed woman, probing for hidden injuries. "Hurry!"

"Do you need me to get an ambulance?" Lianne asked. She felt foolish asking that question when, looking at the woman, the answer seemed so obvious—but she wasn't dealing with humans, she reminded herself. Elves might have other ways of dealing with emergencies.

"D.D. will take care of her," Maclyn said.

Lianne watched D.D. moving around the tree toward them. Her armor flickered once, then vanished, replaced by clothes that looked like the ones the other woman wore.

D.D. bit her lip and knelt beside her son. "How bad?"

Mac's voice was without expression. "We may lose her."

The elven woman nodded and rested her hand on Felouen's shoulder. "I'm taking her back. You and Lianne find out what you need to about your child. I'll meet you in the Grove when you're done."

Maclyn did—something. He sketched a kind of arch with his fingers, anchored on one side to the holly tree. Lianne watched the air around the two elven women shift and darken.

Something about that arch made her feel queasy.

But beyond that arch were hints of unearthly beauty. Was that the elven world?

The images of wet forest and misty, enchanted grove blurred over each other and shifted disconcertingly until the teacher had a hard time looking at the Gate. D.D. pulled Felouen through, and both of them took on the same hazy, half-there appearance of the world beyond. Then Mac spoke a few quiet syllables, and they were gone.

"Come," he said, turning to Lianne. "We still have to find out about Amanda."

CHAPTER NINE

Belinda concealed herself and the entirely too fancy T-Bird along a riding path just out of sight of the Chevy and her targets. There was no way she was going to get out of her vehicle around that hexed Chevy again. There was no telling what might happen to her. She remembered the incongruous picture of a horse trotting through the night behind her first rental car, after the damned race-driver stole it—and the way the Chevy was mysteriously missing when she went back to try stealing it. She recalled the odd behavior of the '57's doors the time she ended up as Mac's captive. Certain pieces of her last few days began to form a picture—one she didn't like at all.

In a sudden burst of curiosity, and with some trepidation, she took the little black meter out of her pocketbook and flashed it at the car. The needle quivered and moved steadily across the scale, wavering slightly as it hit 3.71 P and came to a halt. Goosebumps rose on her arms, and the hair on the back of her neck stood on end. *A car sitting in a field doing not a goddamned thing rates higher on the psi scale than any people I've ever checked—except that bastard Mac Lynn and his blond bimbo mechanic.*

It figures, she thought. She panned the psi-meter in a semicircle that encompassed the general direction in which

Mac and company had been heading, and left room over for error. Sure enough, she picked up one narrow burst of activity at about 8 P's of intensity—mid-scale, and another of about the same reading. That would be the two of them, she thought—Mac and the mechanic. She scanned beyond them from force of habit, letting the meter play across the field at the dreary mix of scrub-oaks and long-leaf pines—

About fifteen degrees west of her two identified targets, the needle dove all the way across into the red zone, hitting 30 P, then kept moving until it vanished into the out of range sector. It stayed there.

Belinda leaned her head against the headrest and stared at the little ventilation dots in the car's headliner until her eyes unfocused and the dots blurred and appeared to move toward her. *What the hell have I gotten myself into?* she wondered. *The car, the driver, the mechanic—and something huge out there in the woods. Either this place is a hotbed of psi activity—or something is wrong with my meter.*

Now, *that* was a genuinely comforting thought. She knew she didn't even raise a .01 P blip on Mel's scale—she shuddered to think what might have happened to her if she had—so maybe her meter was screwed or picking up something else. Something cars and normal people and whatever radiated.

She pointed the psi-meter at herself and pushed the button.

The needle didn't budge. *Zip. Nada. Nothing.* Her eyes narrowed, and she pointed at her own car. She obtained the same results. To her left, coming from the same general direction as all the psi activity, a kid in a pink raincoat shot through the woods at high speed. She was heading straight for the fancy house with all the horses and pastures. *Testing, testing,* Belinda thought, and aimed the meter at her.

"Shit. Shit-shit-shit-shit-double shit!" Belinda snarled. The needle had again shot all the way across the meter and buried itself in the out of range zone. She flung the black box across the seat, and stared at the galloping kid. *What are the odds?* she wondered. *Just what are the fucking odds of running into that many TK's in one place?*

She bit her lip. *The odds are probably better than running into them one at a time and spread all over,* she decided after long contemplation, *if their being here was no coincidence. Do psychics attract psychics?* And another thought, straight out of a Spielberg movie: *Do adult psychics track down kids?*

Her head throbbed, and the thinking she was forced to do was making it worse, but the pain pills would make her fall asleep if she took any. *Live with the pain,* she told herself. *You may be about done with it anyway, champ. 'Cause kids are little and weak and naive—and they don't drive haunted '57 Chevys. And I'm betting you can heist a little kid way out here in the sticks without anyone being the wiser.*

A thought occurred to her. *There were kids all over the racetrack the day I did my little set-up. Wouldn't it just be a bitch if the kid was the one I was looking for after all?* She started her engine and pulled carefully out onto the road that led past the kid's house.

"Kendrick," the mailbox said. And the flowing script on the sandblasted wooden shingle read, "KENDRICK'S BAL-A-SAR STABLES—FINE ARABIANS."

Horses, huh? I can fake it with the horsey set. Oh, yeah, kid . . . I can find you with no trouble at all. A new haircut, and a pair of jodhpurs and riding boots, and I'll be back.

Mel Tanbridge drove through Fayetteville accompanied by his constant companion, distaste. Military towns annoyed him. The entertainment wasn't classy enough, the architecture was just plain drab, and the people themselves—well, he decided, the less thought about them the better. Rude, crude, and obnoxious were the kindest adjectives he could come up with for these peons.

Take the maids at the hotel Stevens had been staying at, for instance. Stevens' room was paid through the end of the week, and they knew he'd been staying there, but they refused to tell him anything about the man—whether he'd left in a hurry, who he'd been with—anything. They'd told him hotel visitors were confidential guests (the way they pronounced "confidential" positively made Mel's skin crawl), and even when he'd flashed a couple of twenties in their direction, they'd blinked their stupid cow eyes at him and said they didn't know anything. He was ready to believe them—the bitches. He'd gone on to break into Stevens' hotel room and had scoured it with a thoroughness that would have left the simple-minded maids chartreuse with envy. He came out with more questions than he took in.

The room was beyond nondescript. That fit well enough with Stevens' character. The thing that puzzled him was that most of Stevens' belongings were still in it. The money was not to be found, of course—except for a bit of change on the dresser that made his stomach twitch in uncomfortable ways. Nobody *left* change if they weren't intending to come back—and pretty promptly, too, in cheap hotels. His bags were present, his clothes still balled up in the drawers. The bed was made, and the maids had placed the pile of dirty clothes neatly on the room's single chair next to the ubiquitous round hotel table under the equally everpresent hanging hotel lamp.

He left carefully, feeling that he had missed something important, but having absolutely no idea what that something might have been.

On his way to his next stop, Peterkin's hotel, he puzzled over the scene and came up completely empty. The room was a blank—there was nothing incriminating, nothing that gave him a clue to what might have happened to his employee.

He hoped for better luck at Peterkin's place.

His hopes fell with his first sight of the place. Stevens' hotel had been bland—but Peterkin's was positively tacky. It was one of those "adult" motels with twenty-four-hour hot and cold running movies and beds that wiggled for a quarter—no doubt so the rented rubber dummy would feel like it had a bit of life to it, Mel thought with disgust. While he might have more luck bribing the help, he doubted that he would find anything useful in a dump like the one in front of him. *Then again,* he thought, *I doubt they* ever *sweep under the beds here. I might find something useful.*

He obtained the room number from the blowsy, rumpled tub of a woman who sat at the front desk. He went back to his car and watched until no one was on the breeze-way. Then he slipped up the steps and, ignoring the "Do Not Disturb" sign hung on the door, used one of the little tricks he'd learned from the burglar he kept on staff. He broke in without so much as a sound.

He closed the door quietly behind himself and waited for his eyes to adjust to the darkness. When they did, he wished they hadn't.

"Christ!" he yelped. Peterkin and Stevens were in the middle of something he would never have credited them with having the imagination for—or rather, he noted, as their silence and stillness caught his attention, they *had* been.

The moment that he took a deep breath, he knew that they were dead. What had caused their deaths seemed pretty evident, too. Drug paraphernalia was laid out on the dresser, and they didn't have any visible wounds—

He walked through the room, careful not to touch anything until he'd taken a towel from the bathroom. He used that to open drawers and look over the IDs lying on the dresser. They were false ones, he noted, but not the same false ones Stevens and Peterkin had left California with. *Interesting,* he thought. *Those are the ones Belinda had on hand for emergencies.*

There were only a few low-denomination bills and some change in the room, and Mel left all of the money. It wouldn't do to make this look like they'd been robbed. He left the false ID's, too. They were very good and very solid—he even had a couple of "widows" who would be only too happy to collect the insurance on their late "husbands." Best of all, they wouldn't be traced back to him.

Mel backed out of the room and closed the door behind him. He heard the lock click into place. Immediately, he began beating on the door and yelling, "I know you're in there, Kraft! I want my money, dammit! Open the door! You owe me eight hundred bucks, you flake! Pay up!"

Hotel management, in the form of the overweight woman, appeared at the foot of the stairs. "Sheddup or ah'll call the cops," she yelled. "Don' you go raisin' hell aroun' my place."

Mel took on a menacing air. "Lady, that S.O.B. owes

my company eight hundred bucks—and he skipped town
to keep from paying it. I'm the collector—I tracked him
down here, and now I want my money. You see these
papers?" He waved several sheets of paper at her from his
safe spot at the top of the steps; papers that were actually contracts with his brochure printer back in California.
"These say I have a right to collect that money, and if I
don't get it, I'm going to call the cops and have them raid
this dive."

The woman studied him from the foot of the stairs, her
bright black eyes nearly hidden in the rolls of fat. She
grimaced and mumbled, "Aw, shee-it. Ah don' need that
again." She waddled back toward the office, muttering over
her massive shoulder-pads, "Jes' wait a dam' minute while
ah git my keys."

After she returned and moved her vast bulk up the
narrow cement staircase, Mel took his expectant place half
a step behind her.

He waited, feigning impatience while she pounded on
the door, then fumbled with the keys when she got no
answer. He pretended not to watch her closely as she
opened the door and flipped on the light. He noted, however, her absolute lack of shock as her eyes took in the
room, its inhabitants, and the attendant sex toys and drugs.

"Oh, my," she whispered, her eyes gleaming with vicari-
ous pleasure. "Oh my, oh my! Will you jes' look at that!
Imagine them doin' that in mah nice clean *mo*-tel!"

"Dammit," Mel said, making sure she heard him. "There
goes my eight hundred dollars."

Mel slipped back to his car and drove off before the
police could arrive. He returned the Lincoln, took the
shuttle to the Fayetteville airport, then another to a second car rental agency, where he used an alternate alias to
pick up a car as different from the previous one as he could
find—a bright blue Geo Metro. He didn't want to be
bothered with the police in a town that had the two strikes
against it of being military—and Southern.

Then he drove out toward Belinda's last reported
address. The situation so far was not at all what he had
anticipated. He didn't think for a minute that Stevens and
Peterkin had died in the way they appeared to have. He

felt the touch of his favorite redhead stamped all over their dead bodies. But there might be extenuating circumstances. It might be that he wouldn't have to terminate her from his payroll—he chuckled at that euphemism—as soon as he'd anticipated. But he would be careful. After all, she was dangerous—part of her charm—and one never knew.

Mac was as weary as he had ever been. The rain died down to a cold, sullen drizzle, punctuated by cloudburst exclamation points that showered the woods around them. Lianne and Mac trudged through the ugly weather, untouched.

"That was Amanda's hideout," Mac noted abruptly, breaking a silence that had carried them from the tree to the edge of the woods behind the child's house.

"Really?" Lianne said, sounding surprised. "How did you—oh."

Mac did not ask her what the "oh" meant. Perhaps she remembered catching sight of bits of bright junk that had hung on strings from the branches, decorating the tree like treasures in a magpie's nest. Perhaps she simply deduced—correctly—that he had been here before.

Lianne shuddered. "You don't suppose she was anywhere around those—things—do you?"

I would bet she had something to do with getting them here, Mac thought, but he didn't say it. There were so many things about the kid that didn't fit. She knew he was an elf, then she didn't. She did magic but didn't believe in it. She walked out of Elfhame Outremer on her own—a pure impossibility. To Lianne, he only said, "I hope not." That at least was the truth.

He covered the two of them with his "I'm not here" shield, and they moved out of the woods and across the yard.

"God—the police are here!" Lianne froze, then started backing toward the woods.

Mac grabbed her arm. "They can't see us," he whispered.

"Are you really, really sure?"

He gave her a half-smile. "Well, don't run up and pinch them on the noses to test this—but yes, I'm sure. We still show up on film and video, still leave footprints, but some-one looking right at us won't see us. Wonder what they're doing here—"

"Rummaging through that little barn. Obviously." Lianne started forward. "Come on—let's take a look."

Maclyn lingered back as Power, twisted and sick, hit him like a board to the front of the head. "Gods," he whispered, "what happened in there?"

Lianne looked up at him and arched her eyebrows in a silent question.

"Are you familiar with the human term 'bad ju-ju'?" he asked.

She shrugged. "I've heard it. Means—oh, black magic, or something."

Mac watched the police with wary eyes. "Or something, actually. Well, bad ju-ju is stamped all over that little barn in glowing letters ten feet high. Something happened here, but not what the police see."

She shook her head, obviously confused. "The monsters under the tree again?"

Mac closed his eyes and stood very still, his head tipped to one side. "Funny—" he started to say something, then fell silent. Finally, he shook himself and looked at Lianne again. "You are almost right about comparing this to the battle this morning," he told her. "The traces of magic in the barn have some of the same touches as those golems had—but this magic is tied in to someone else as well. It almost feels like some kind of a ritual—group magic, or something involving a group." He wrinkled his nose and walked toward the barn.

"Bad ju-ju," Lianne snarled behind him, and followed his lead.

Mac's nerves screamed with every step that drew him nearer to the barn. The little building reeked of power drawn from pain—but the signatures of the magic-wielders and the victims were so tangled that he couldn't get a clear picture. When he glanced inside, his stomach twisted like a knife-pinned snake, and he drew in a breath between clenched teeth. The contents of the structure had been shredded apart fiber by fiber—he had seen the results of a food processor on occasion and had no difficulty imagining that the inside of the barn had been through one. The taint of Unseleighe work reeked through the place. And where, in all of this, did *they* fit in? So far, his dark kindred hadn't shown so much as a hair.

Mac and Lianne stayed to the shadows and watched the policemen digging through the mess.

"You find anything?" one of the officers asked.

"Sawdust," the other answered. "Plenty of sawdust. And I'll tell you something, Sammy—if we rake through this shit till the end of forever, that's all we're going to find."

The first speaker straightened and groaned. "Yeah. I think you're right. This place gives me the creeps. Feels like something's watching all the damn time."

Lianne gave Maclyn a worried look. He grimaced and shrugged.

The cop continued. "Why don't we check outside—maybe we'll find tire marks or something."

"After all this rain?" the second policeman snorted. But then he grinned. "Hell, walkin' in the rain is a damnsight cozier than pokin' around in here. Let's go." Both policemen headed for the door.

Lianne heard one mumble as they stepped outside, "Wish to hell I knew what could do that."

Mac leaned over and whispered in Lianne's ear, "I know what did it—I just wish I knew who'd summoned one up."

Lianne shuddered under his hand. "So tell me, what *does* do more damage than Hell's Cuisinart?"

He almost wished he didn't know. "A banesidhe wind—deadly, borderline intelligent, called up from the lairs of what you might call the Dark Elves. They're pure destructive energy. Pain and hatred born of torture on this plane create them out of the raw stuff of the Unformed Plane—but to 'create' one here, to call it out from its Unseleighe hiding place, the magician has to know it, to know that fear, that hate, that pain. And there aren't many magicians strong enough to call one out who are willing to be tortured to make one."

Outside the barn, they heard Andrew Kendrick talking with the policemen. He was not happy. "You mean to tell me you've spent all morning poking around in my kid's barn, and you still don't know who vandalized it?"

An unhappy voice answered. "Mister Kendrick—we can't even begin to figure out how they did it. Given a few hours, maybe somebody could wreck things that completely—but not in a few minutes."

"Dammit," Kendrick snapped. And after a pause, he added, in a voice thick with sarcasm, "I can tell my tax dollars have been well spent on you two."

It's Amanda's barn. It was Amanda's hideout tree. Her classroom. And the magic signatures in all of these places have been the same. They haven't been Amanda—but they have all been the same! Who is with her doing Unseleighe magic? And why?

A different man walked into the barn and was framed for an instant in the dreary outdoor light at the doorway. He was tall, with sandy hair and light eyes, broad shoulders and the very early signs of a potbelly to come. He would have been a handsome man, but his expression was ugly, his lips clamped firmly on a smoldering cigarette, his demeanor cold and calculating. The man scanned the interior of the barn, his eyes fixing on Mac and Lianne and flicking quickly past them. Mac felt Lianne jerk once beside him.

The feel of this man was in the barn, too. His was the second signature present—and Mac would have taken him for the magician and maybe the torturer—but while the man had strong magical potential, it was completely latent. Still, the man carried a store of repressed hatred so deep-burning and all-consuming that the elf felt it as a physical presence.

Father and daughter in league with the Unseleighe Court? Maybe—but somehow none of the pieces fit—

Kendrick walked to the back left corner of the gutted building and started digging through the drifts of debris.

Father and daughter—and torture . . . there has to have been some kind of torture to have conjured the banesidhe wind. Mac clenched his hands and glared at the man across the little barn from him. *It's sure that the child didn't torture her father—but there was torment wrought here, and it has his signature on it. But stress has brought out mage-powers in humans before. . . .*

Latent mage torturing developing mage. That matched.

He took a deep breath to calm himself and leaned back against the wall.

There's my *proof of abuse.*

Belinda walked into her hotel room, and reacted an instant too late as the cold, heavy barrel of a gun was pressed against her ribs, preventing her from backing out of the room. A leather-gloved hand clapped over her mouth.

"Don't move or you're dead," the voice in her left ear said in an equitable and utterly reasonable tone of voice.

"Mel?" The word sounded muffled through the heavy padding of the glove.

A delicate snort, and the gun-muzzle didn't move a hair, but the glove moved enough so that she could talk, at least. "In the flesh. That was quite a nice little tableau you left at Peterkin's hotel. Very artistic. I always have liked your style."

"Why are you here, Mel?" Belinda couldn't feel, in her heart of hearts, any deep urge to be chatty.

"You haven't brought me my TK yet," he chided gently. "And then Stevens and Peterkin vanished off the face of the planet, and you hadn't called in days—I started feeling a little lonely. And I thought you might have reeled in the TK and then found a higher bidder." His hand tightened over her mouth, and the gun began moving in slow, gentle circles over her side, and the glove covered her mouth again. "You haven't found a higher bidder, have you, dear?"

Belinda tried to clear her mouth of the glove, and failed. "Foo-fif fiff-feff!" she spat.

"Beg pardon?" Mel chuckled softly in her ear and lessened the pressure on her mouth.

"You stupid shithead!" Belinda repeated. "Do I look like I've been rolling in somebody else's money and taking it easy at your expense?"

Mel said, "Stay still." He released her and moved to one side of her. Now they were both reflected in the mirror across from her. Out of the corner of her eye, she could see that the gun was still pointed steadily at her midsection. She kept her hands away from her sides and stared straight into the mirror on the far wall. She could see him taking in the bruises, the bandages on her head, the dark circles under her eyes and the gaunt hollows in her cheeks that hadn't been there when she left California. "Now that you mention it, you look like you've been dancing with trucks. What's been going on?"

She snorted. "You didn't tell me how dangerous hunting down a telekinetic could be."

Mel's eyes narrowed. "I didn't know. The racecar driver did all that to you?"

She shrugged. "Yes he did, in a roundabout fashion I would rather not discuss. I've got you a better prospect. I've found a child who is a sure thing—an even stronger talent than the driver. I'll get her for you—she's bound to be less dangerous to rope in than Mac Lynn. I'm going to kill him after you have the girl." Belinda smiled and rubbed absently at the bandage on her head. "Unless I have the opportunity to do it beforehand."

"You've really found someone else?" Mel's voice sounded eager.

Belinda eased into the Naugahyde chair beside the bed. "Just today—a little girl. Lynn led me to her. Probably, oh, eight or ten years old. A kid would be very easy to work with, wouldn't she? I figure whatever you have planned, it would be less hassle to do with someone smaller."

In the mirror, Mel's eyes brightened. "Check her out. TK ability is supposed to show up right around the time puberty strikes, and is supposed to be more common in girls. This kid fits the profile."

Mel ran one hand along the line of his jaw and stared at a nonexistent point somewhere over Belinda's left shoulder. "A child would be good—very good. Little girls are pliable and agreeable; I could probably obtain her cooperation with a few grand in toys—whereas getting cooperation from an adult male for what I have in mind would require . . . more complicated measures." His voice faded off into nothing, and he refocused on Belinda. "Why did you kill Stevens and Peterkin?"

She yawned. "They double-crossed me. I don't take that from anyone, especially not from the hired muscle."

Mel sat on the long dresser that also acted as the motel room's writing desk. He crossed his arms and let the muzzle of the gun dip toward the floor. "The word 'double-cross' is open to a wide range of interpretations. Be more specific."

She spread her hands wide and gave him her most innocent expression—hard to do with all the bruises. "I should have had him on his way to you in a bag yesterday. They withheld a drug that would have knocked Mac Lynn out, then lied to me about it. I can't figure out what they hoped to gain by that maneuver, but there is no doubt that they lied to me. I tested the remainder of the drug on the two of them, just to make sure it wasn't faulty— you found the results, apparently."

Belinda went into greater detail, stopping only when Mel asked questions. She went over each point until she was sick of talking about it—and finally Mel seemed satisfied.

Mel lay the gun on the dresser top. "You aren't lying about this. I can always tell." He pulled one knee up to his chin and rested with his arms wrapped around his leg. He looked genuinely bewildered. "Why the hell would they turn traitor on me? They knew what I would do to them if they tried—God knows, they carried out my sentence on a couple of their colleagues."

Belinda leaned her head back and tried to relax enough to get it to stop throbbing. "I have no idea. I searched their rooms, their possessions, their car, their pockets—everything I could think of. I couldn't find anything incriminating." She sighed. "Whoever bought them kept the whole deal very well hidden—and they must have been offering a fortune. I just can't figure out why anyone would pay so much for such a ridiculous thing as a TK." She glanced at Mel through half-lidded eyes. "No offense intended."

Mel's face twitched into a slimy smile. "None taken. *I* know why someone would offer a fortune—you haven't seen the private offers that come across the desk of anyone who might have access to, ah, commodities like Mac Lynn. Believe me, dear, he's worth more to you on the hoof than in the bag."

"Pardon me for not giving a flying fuck." Belinda laughed. "I guarantee you he's worth more to me spread-eagled on a rock somewhere with a white-hot poker in his ass."

"Tch-tch," Mel said, shaking his finger reprovingly at her. "Language like that is not becoming a lady."

Belinda made a full-forearm gesture at him and ignored her boss' raised eyebrows. "I'll get you a TK. But I've gone through hell you wouldn't believe"—*quite literally couldn't believe,* she thought—"trying to get this one. You'll get the kid. And I'm going to take that creep out all by myself."

Mel patted the gun that lay beside him. "We really must talk sometime about this habit you have of killing people who annoy you, Belinda dear."

Belinda's laugh was short and harsh. "You should bloody talk."

He chuckled. "Not at all. I would never think of killing someone just because he—or she—has annoyed me. For example, Belinda, you annoy me, but you are useful. I only kill those people who are dangerous to me or who are of no further use to me alive." He smiled gently. "I thought you had passed that line, dear. I truly did."

A cold knot formed in Belinda's belly, and she repressed the shudder she didn't want Mel to see. "Friends again?" she asked with false cheerfulness.

His smile was just as false. "Of course—now that I know you're still playing on my team. I make it a point to stay friends with the people on my team. Get me my kid tomorrow or the next day, and we'll even be best buddies."

Belinda nodded, and winced as her hair moved with the nod. There were a lot of bruises under that hair. "I'll go out tomorrow. I already know how I'm going to get close. First, though, I've got to get some sleep, and then I'm going to the beauty parlor. I'm not going to be able to get anywhere near her looking like this. I'll have your kid for you in a day or two."

"Fine." Mel's eyebrows furrowed, and he looked down at his shoes for a long, silent moment. "I think I might like to go along to pick her up," he said when he finally looked up. "I want to have a good look at my merchandise."

Belinda sighed. "Hey, it's your party. Just so long as you still intend to pay me the full price, you are welcome to come along."

Mel chuckled. "You mean you aren't inclined to give me a discount if I come along and help out?"

She gave him a look of disdain. "You came along too late to earn a discount. Hell, I deserve a bonus just for pain and suffering incurred."

"We'll see." Mel stood, and they watched each other warily. Then Mel slipped the gun into the holster hidden beneath his windbreaker, and keeping his eyes fixed on Belinda, he eased out of the room. "I'll be in touch. Or if you need me, call me at the Prince Charles. I'm listed as Mel Tenner," he said just before the door closed.

Oooh, that's creative, Belinda thought. *Nobody would ever connect Mel Tanbridge with Mel Tenner. Idiot.* She listened to the click of the latch and held her breath until she heard Mel's measured tread moving away from her door. "Shit," she whispered.

The room would be bugged, of course—Mel would have kept his options open, even if he had fully intended to kill her. *"Do nothing irrevocable until the last possible moment,"* he'd told her more times than she cared to think about. *"And always leave yourself an out—two, if you can."* So he would have the room bugged, and he would now have someone keeping track of her movements.

What else? Threatening her family? Maybe—and if he tried it, he would find out how little that meant. Her lush of a mother wouldn't even notice a bullet between the eyes, her bastard stepfather deserved one, and if Mel's goons could locate her real father, who had skipped before she was even born, she hoped they'd make his life exciting. Threatening her, then? If she screwed up, she was dead. But she already knew that. She was dangerous to Mel—she just had to make sure she kept herself useful. Well, as long as she was the only one who knew who—and where—the little girl TK-wonder was, she was useful. And after that, she'd get out of his reach. Fast.

In the meantime, she hadn't seen the inside of her eyeballs in far too long. She double-locked the door, then stripped and eased herself between the cold sheets.

Life was giving her real cause to consider another line of work.

Andrew Kendrick sat in the kitchen, staring out the window at the policemen who wandered around his property accomplishing precious little. He was satisfied that they wouldn't find anything incriminating in the barn. There *was* nothing—absolutely nothing—left. How that could be, he didn't know, but the fact that it seemed impossible didn't in the least change the fact that it was true. And with the worry of discovery of his questionable activities behind him, he could relax a bit. And since they hadn't found the person responsible for destroying his barn, he wished the police would just get the hell off his property.

He would have to rebuild the barn. Rebuild the little windowless locking room, he thought. For the time being, the other barn would serve—but not as well. It had its private places, and its private times, but they were less frequent, and less convenient. Convenience had become important to him.

He could see Amanda and Sharon playing Barbie dolls in the den, doing something that was not meant for adult eyes and whispering with their heads leaned close together. He watched them without making it obvious that he was doing so—something had just occurred to him as he sat there. Amanda was growing up.

He sniffed with sudden distaste. Amanda had once been an enchanting child. She had been innocent and vulnerable and tractable. Now, as she sat next to the delicate and fragile Sharon, whose hair still tumbled loose in a five-year-old's baby ringlets, whose face was sweet and round and whose eyes were gentle and uncomprehending, Amanda was a gangling and ugly colt. She looked plain and scrawny, Andrew thought—and she looked hard. She had lost the childish innocence of Sharon. She seemed somehow adult, as she sat there making sly little comments while the two girls changed their dolls' clothes.

His attention was suddenly riveted by something his older daughter did. Amanda's face and mood had changed, and her eyes glittered green in the dim light. She tied the Barbie doll's wrists behind her back and placed the Ken doll behind her in a pose suggestive of—

Andrew's fingers tangled around the tablecloth in unconscious rage. He knew what Amanda was telling the little girl—he knew what she was showing her. Sharon was watching her older sister, fascinated, hanging intently on every word. Andrew couldn't hear the words hidden in the hushed whispers, but he knew anyway that she was exposing his secret—exposing *him*. And in the same burst of insight, he knew something else.

He knew that he was going to have to get rid of Amanda.

What she told to her little sister was of no real importance. Sharon wasn't old enough that any rational adult would take her seriously if she repeated what her sister said. Assuming she even understood half of what Amanda was telling her, or that she considered it anything other than a scary story. But Amanda could talk to adults as easily as she talked to the little girl. She could walk out the door and tell the police in his side yard what he had been doing—and what would come of that? Where would his law practice, with his high-powered corporate clients, be? Merryl would leave him, and worse, she would take Sharon with her—sweet, beautiful, obedient Sharon.

It would only be a matter of time until Amanda let something slip—he saw it coming with terrible clarity. He could see it in the crafty, loathsome eyes of the homely creature in the other room. He would have to get rid of her as soon as possible, in some way that would leave him completely above suspicion.

With the police department's newfound interest in his home, that was going to be damned difficult.

Dierdre felt the Gate pull in behind her, felt it drain her of some of her energy as she bore the brunt of the snap for both herself and Felouen. Felouen was near death. She hovered there, suspended over the chasm of nonexistence by the finest of gossamer threads.

Dierdre stood in the sacred grove of Elfhame Outremer, and felt the magic flow into her—magic she had cut herself off from voluntarily for a very long time. The great trees seemed to bend over her, welcoming her home, and their acceptance changed her subtly. She dropped her lighthearted human persona, her years of human acclimatization. She seemed to stretch, becoming something both more beautiful and more terrible than the human-seeming creature she had hidden herself in for all those many years. Her human colleagues, who had never seen the ancient elven noblewoman she truly was, would not have recognized her—and would have felt the strong compulsion to kneel and beg mercy in her presence for ever treating her with anything less than deepest respect.

She knelt next to her wounded comrade and gently rested her hands on the torn and broken body. A soft, golden glow gathered around her; a faint sheen that grew in glittering bands until she became the pale, lovely center of a brilliant light warmer than any homecoming. Her lips trembled just a little as she sang, over and over:

"Gathwaloür muelléiralra elearai ao;
Elearai, pallaiebaroa, ailoaüé houe.
Tué, atué escobeieada—
Tué, atué,
Tué, atué—tué."

The song was ancient, one of the oldest magics of the elvenkind—so old that its language was far removed from that spoken by the Seleighe Court. To a people whose lives stretched thousands of years, and whose language had not changed in tens of thousands of years, this made it a tongue of unimaginable age and power. Singing it, she gifted her strength and her health to Felouen. And as she sang, pain spread through her body, and Felouen's wounds healed under her fingers.

She kept singing until the pain blinded her and her voice faltered. She had no more strength to give—she could only take some of the damage to herself. Too much, and she would die in Felouen's place.

As her voice fell silent, though, another voice picked up the song, and other hands rested on Felouen's body. The Grove had felt her need and had summoned help. She fell back and lay in the soft velvet grass, and the Grove fed her and comforted her and promised her renewal.

She listened, unable to move, as the voices over Felouen changed; strong voices becoming weak, then being replaced by other strong voices, over and over. She felt like a child in her cradle again, rocked and safe, with others singing the old songs and whispering in the language of her childhood, the sounds familiar but the meaning of the words just out of the reach of her tired comprehension.

Homesickness, long foreign to her, overwhelmed her as

she lay in the eternal twilight in the hallowed place between the worlds. The elven-tongue, so beautiful and long neglected by her, sang through her veins like hot brandy. Dierdre felt tears welling in her eyes, felt the uprush of repressed longing for a place and a way of life she had voluntarily forgone.

Homecoming—in such a way, with the death of one of her folk and the near-death of another riding her shoulders like a close-fitting cape—was bittersweet. The bitterness was only in the pain she brought with her from the low and dirty world of the humans, the unbearable sweetness in the touch of friends too long neglected, too long put aside.

Felouen would live. Her people had come to the call of the Grove, and her wounds had been shared by them.

And over Dierdre as well the elves began to sing, dispersing among themselves the agony that she had taken on alone when there was no one else to help her.

At last she was able to sit again, to hold her head upright, to look around her. She saw Felouen moving restlessly in the grass, her head tossing and her arms jolting out at intervals to stop the fall her mind would not release from present memory. Around her moved the beautiful folk in their flowing robes, their pale faces grave.

"Welcome home," said a rich, deep voice from behind her. "Too many years have you been apart from us, fair lady. Your home weeps in your absence."

Dierdre looked up and to one side. The elven lord had once been a friend and a comrade, had fought at her side under Dwylleth's leadership—and had been, with other friends, sadly neglected of late because of her other interests. "Yes," she said sadly. "I've been away a while."

She glanced around the Grove, and back up at her old friend, and touched his iridescent green robe. "But I'm home now."

CHAPTER TEN

Amanda-Abbey "woke" to find herself playing Barbie dolls in the den with Sharon. Daddy was in the other room—she could just barely see him in the kitchen corner with his long legs stretched out under the table, while he sat and watched her. She had no memory of where she had been, or of how she came to be playing with Sharon—and the dolls in her hands were doing something that made her stomach twist, although she didn't know why. It looked naughty and *felt* naughty. She moved the dolls apart and stared at her hands with dismay.

What happens, she wondered, *when I'm not here? Why doesn't Sharon notice that I just woke up? What,* she thought with a shudder, *has my body been doing without me?*

She busily started putting clothes on her dolls, so that Sharon wouldn't interrupt her while she was thinking. She thought about Stranger.

Stranger had always seemed to be just a funny voice in her head, one that talked oddly and used a lot of words she didn't recognize, but Amanda-Abbey had always assumed Stranger was part of her imagination—like the elf had been. She had to wonder about the elf, however. Amanda-Abbey looked at the gold bracelet on her wrist and at her real mother's glass bead, and she wondered—

Maybe the elf was real. And if the elf was real, maybe Stranger was real, too.

Amanda-Abbey put down her dolls and dug her fingers into the cool, deep carpet. She stared at her hands, her odd, unpredictable hands, now pulling little bits of fiber out of the rug and rolling them into pills. *Suppose—just suppose—Stranger is real. Then the place where she took me, the place where that awful girl with the flying knives and whips and stuff was hiding behind her walls, was real, too.*

Stranger is inside of me. Is the awful girl? Is that what happens to me when I'm not here? The awful girl comes out?

"Don't pick at the carpet," her step-mother said, walking into the room. "That's destructive."

Amanda-Abbey stopped and began to put her dolls away. She needed to get away, to think. There were things going on that she didn't understand, but she wanted to find Stranger and talk to her if she could. She wanted to be alone when she started looking for her. For some reason, it seemed important to be alone for that.

"You said you'd play with me," Sharon whined.

"I already did play with you," Amanda-Abbey said, hoping this was true.

Now the whine was joined by a pout. "Not long enough."

Amanda-Abbey decided that it was time to be firm. "Yes, long enough. I have stuff to do." When the pout continued, she tried coaxing instead of ordering. "Why don't you watch Turtles, now? I bet they're on."

The pout turned scornful. "I already watched Turtles— they were on this mornin', dummy butthead. They're not on in the afternoon."

Amanda-Abbey shrugged and finished shoving her dolls and doll clothes back into their storage case. "Watch something else. I gotta go clean my room." She got up and started for the stairs.

"I want someone to play with me," Sharon wailed.

From the kitchen, Daddy leaned around the corner and looked past Amanda-Abbey to Sharon. He said, "I'll play with you, honey. Just give me a minute to finish my coffee."

Something about Daddy wanting to play with Sharon all

of a sudden worried Amanda-Abbey, but she didn't know what it was. Her stomach twisted, as it had when she saw what she was doing with the Barbie dolls. Confused, she walked to the stairs and up them, trailing her doll case. The stairs, too, made her feel a little funny. It seemed that today everything in the house made her feel a little funny. Amanda-Abbey decided that she was probably getting the flu like Bobby Smithers in her art class, and next she'd have a fever and be puking on everybody.

She'd worry about that when it happened. Right now, she wanted to find Stranger if she could. She wanted to see if Stranger was real.

In her room, she stretched out on her bed and looked out her windows. The clouds outside were low and dark, and for a moment she expected to see rain—but there was none. She didn't know why, but this surprised her.

She lay very still. If she were someone else hiding in her body, where would she hide? She watched the clouds scudding by and wiggled her fingers tentatively. :*Stranger?*: she asked.

There was no answer.

:*Stranger?*: She closed her eyes and tried to hear the voice with its funny accent. :*Stranger? Are you there?*:

:*Aye, lass, I'm here. What are ye' huntin', then?*:

:*I was looking for you*—: Her thought faltered. It occurred to Amanda-Abbey that it was probably rude to ask someone to prove that they were real. Still, if she didn't ask, she wouldn't know. :*Are you just my imagination, Stranger?*: she asked.

:*Nay, I'm not that. I'm as real as you are—how real that is, I've no more way of knowin' than you.*:

With her eyes still tightly closed, Amanda-Abbey tried to see where the voice was coming from. She got impressions of a shadow, the outline of a woman—

:*If you're wantin' to see me, I'll give you a light, child. Before this, you nay wanted to look at me.*:

Amanda-Abbey considered that. It was, she realized, quite true. She never had wanted to see the face that went with the odd voice—not even the time she had seen that horrifying other girl, the frightening child behind all those walls. She had not looked into Stranger's eyes even when they had escaped, not even when the woman's arms had been around her, comforting her.

White fire cascaded in waves from the darkness, until she saw Stranger clearly. Amanda-Abbey stared at her, devoured the woman's features with her eyes—and suddenly knew why she had been afraid to see her.

Somewhere, in the back of her mind, she had been afraid that Stranger would look just like her, and that this would prove what she had suspected when she first started hearing the voice—it would prove that she was crazy. Amanda-Abbey knew stories of people who heard voices and were locked up.

Like my real mama. That's what Father said.

But there had been another fear, equally deep, equally bad. She had also been afraid that, even though the voice belonged to a stranger, the face would belong to her mother—her real mother, who was dead—and that this would mean she was seeing ghosts. She wanted her real mother back, but did not want her back as a ghost.

Stranger looked like no one she had ever seen. The woman was short and extraordinarily pale, with a long dark braid and a pointed, pixielike face; her clothes were funny, too, like they were made out of kitchen towels or horse blankets pinned together. She smiled, and Amanda-Abbey nervously smiled back.

:Hi. I'm Abbey.:

The woman nodded politely. *:I know you. Merry meet,:* she added. *:I am named Cethlenn.:*

Cethlenn. Not Stranger, Amanda-Abbey thought. She rolled the name on her tongue a few times. The woman looked real enough standing there in that short cape that was nothing more than a horsehide with round pins holding it on, with her boots looking like something she'd made herself. *Yes, she does look real enough,* Amanda-Abbey thought, *At least while my eyes are closed.* Experimentally, she opened her eyes. The woman vanished. She closed her eyes. Cethlenn still stood there.

:Prove you're real,: Amanda-Abbey demanded. Inside, what she was hoping was that Cethlenn would prove she was not crazy.

The woman nodded. *:Fair enough. Get up and walk to*

your mirror. Look at yoursel' in't, an' say what ye see.:

Amanda-Abbey followed these directions—and found herself staring at her reflection. *:I see me, of course.:*

From over her shoulder, it seemed, Cethlenn said, *:Quite right. Now, close your eyes and imagine that ye stand behind my shoulder, and let me look in the mirror.:*

Amanda-Abbey found this difficult to accomplish. Several times, right when she was sure she had it right, she opened her eyes just at the wrong moment and found that nothing had changed. When finally she got it right, she didn't even know it until Cethlenn said, *:There. See?:*

She opened her eyes and discovered, to her surprise, that *the* eyes had opened already. She had the feeling that she was standing behind Cethlenn. When she moved her arms, they felt just fine, but *the* arms, the ones attached to the body which she could see quite plainly in the mirror, did nothing.

:Oh!: she cried out, and no sound came out of *the* mouth. The face that was and was not hers said, "See? I'm real."

She looked on in fascination as the arms moved without her will, as the lips smiled, as the eyes—*brown* eyes—blinked in a rhythm different from her own. The face in the mirror looked unaccountably fierce, and though the hair was still blond, and the skin still had a little of last summer's tan to it, she could see that the person inside was Cethlenn.

:Oh, Cethlenn, you are real!: she said, with a rush of joyous relief. And, suddenly bewildered, she asked, *:But why are you here?:*

The face in the mirror looked back at her, and the uncertainty reflected there matched her own. "Och, child," Cethlenn whispered, "I have na' the faintest idea to that. I dinna even remember how I got here. I only wish I knew what I was supposed to do now that I'm here."

The trip back to Lianne's apartment was mostly silent. Maclyn stared at the road that unfolded ahead of them—Lianne leaned back on Rhellen's soft gold upholstery with her eyes closed and pretended to sleep. Maclyn didn't expose her pretense for what it was—he didn't particularly want to talk anyway.

Old Gwaryon was dead—weird old Gwaryon, with his

fascination for ancient human cultures and his reputedly bizarre personal habits—who had been a part of Maclyn's life since his birth. Dierdre had liked Gwaryon, had seen some value in his tedious memorization of long-dead human languages and his eccentric love of human books and his freakish emulation of long-outdated human fashions. She'd thought the old elf bright and funny and clever, and so Maclyn had grown up surrounded by his elvish imitations of human worlds that—Mac suspected—bore only a faint resemblance to the long-gone realities. Dierdre had lent these suspicions some truth when, to young Maclyn's unending questions, she would admit nothing but that Gwaryon preferred to see only the good in every human culture and work.

Old Gwaryon had, in his way, been a friend. He had died bravely—but not well. In Maclyn's estimation, there was no way to die well. Dead was dead, and the longer one put that state off, the better.

And that brought him to Felouen. What of Felouen?

The image of his mother dragging Felouen's unmoving body through the temporary Gate he'd made into the Grove of Elfhame Outremer left a queasy hollow in his stomach and made every breath painful. What of Felouen? He felt she was still alive—he thought that surely her death would have left a bigger ache in him than the one he carried right then. She had said that she had been waiting for the one she loved for hundreds of years and had implied that she loved him. He glanced anxiously over at Lianne, whose eyes were still closed—and he allowed himself to acknowledge the deep and painful yearning for Felouen he intentionally ignored, the one that came roaring back to life every time he saw her.

It was a yearning, he had to admit, that invariably and promptly got quenched by Felouen's stiff-necked, hardheaded, do-it-or-die approach to every damn thing. Witness her insistence on dumping him with a Ring.

Unconsciously, his fingers made their own way into his jeans' pocket and pulled out the scrap of silk in which the Ring resided. Felouen was wounded, maybe dying—he didn't know if she would survive. She had wanted him to wear the Ring, had wanted him to be her knight.

He started feeling a little guilty. It hadn't been that much to ask of him—just that he accept the role of one sworn to uphold the Seleighe Court's edicts. It wasn't as if he had to start walking perimeter on guard duty if he wore the damn thing. It would, he thought, have made her happy if he had worn the Ring. Hell, Korindel, over in Misthold—California—wore *his* Knight's Ring openly and constantly, and *he* spent most of his time in the human world.

Against his better judgment, he slipped the carved gold band on.

Nothing happened. *There*, he thought, *that wasn't so bloody difficult, was it? Show a bit of respect for your own folk, show a bit of backbone, stand up against the Unseleighe things—you'll still survive it. Plenty have before you—that's how they earned their high places in the Council.*

It isn't driving race cars—but then, what is? It's probably less dangerous to be one of the Ring-wearers than it is to drive race cars.

The dull gleam of the gold ring on his right index finger mocked that last assertion.

Rhellen pulled into the apartment parking lot.

"Wake up, baby," Mac said, in deference to her act.

She barely stirred. "Mmmph."

He shook her, gently. "We're home. Time to get moving."

One slit eye glowered at him. "I'll wake up in a minute."

"Okay." He paused, on the brink of delicate negotiations. "Lianne, I know you have some classwork you need to finish. And we didn't find out anything that we can use to get Amanda out of that house a minute sooner—but maybe Felouen did. She was out there at Amanda's tree before we got there, and somehow all of this feels tied together. While you grade papers or whatever it is you have to do, I'm going home to check on Mother and Felouen. If I find out anything useful, I'll stop by later and let you know."

Instead of looking disappointed, Lianne looked relieved. "That sounds fine, Mac. Tell you what—unless you find out something earth-shattering, why don't you just stop by tomorrow morning. I feel like making an early night of it."

Perversely, Maclyn's feelings were hurt. "I'll be happy to spend the night—" he started.

She waved him off with one slender hand. "Actually, Mac, the idea of having the bed to myself for a night sounds appealing. I want peace and absolute quiet. I want to think for a while—and I also want to scrounge around the house and not have to worry about how I look or how I act or what I do. I'm a bit too tired to be social."

"Well," he pouted, ignoring for the moment the fact that the outcome was exactly what he had hoped to accomplish, "if that's really what you want . . ."

She nodded. "Yeah, I think so. Gimme a kiss and I'll see you tomorrow."

When Maclyn drove off, he noticed that she hadn't even stayed outside long enough to wave good-bye—something she almost always did. *Maybe,* he thought, *she's mad at me for something.* He pondered that notion while he and Rhellen drove toward the permanent Gate the elves had hidden in the center of the Grove on 15-401, out back of the Beauty Spot Missionary Baptist Church.

Maybe, he decided at last, *she's pissed off at me because I didn't thank her for saving my ass out there in the woods today—and neither did Mother.* That, he thought, was a good possibility. He would have been pissed if the situations had been reversed and no one had thanked him.

It was just that elves didn't often have occasion to think of frail human women in the role of rescuer. Ah, well— he supposed in this case, he'd better show up with an apology offering first thing in the morning.

The Grove spread in front of him. Rhellen drove off-road, carefully picking his way. As soon as the car was well into the trees, Rhellen shifted, and the two of them charged through the Gate into Elfhame Outremer.

Even though the on-again-off-again rain might be annoying if one had to be out there in it, it made ideal sleeping weather, Belinda decided. Too much of a good thing, though, would get her in trouble. She rolled over and stared at her clock.

It was a bit past two in the afternoon, and she had just finished a well-earned nap that had left her feeling better than she had anticipated, by a long shot. Her head still ached, but less than it had when she went to sleep. Still, she was going to have to get all her hair chopped off, which was damned depressing.

And Mel wasn't happy with her, which depressed her more. An unhappy Mel was a dangerous Mel. She couldn't spend a great deal of time worrying about him, however. She had her afternoon plans mapped out. Worry wasn't on her list.

Screw Mel, she finally decided. Then she laughed. *It would probably solve a few of my problems if I did. I'll bet the little bastard is kinky as hell, though; that's one of those personal details about my employer I'd rather not discover firsthand.* Belinda's personal sexual preference was abstention—a fact that would have surprised any number of people. Including, no doubt, her employer.

Ah, well. She stretched, then lay under the covers a few minutes longer, lazing. She had to spend some time with her modem and laptop computer. She needed to access files on the Kendricks and see what bounced. Then she needed to get herself looking good again. There was a salon out by the mall that was open nearly all the time. She could go there without an appointment and get her hair clipped and styled in some fashion that hid her new bald spot. Then she could get the kind of clothes that would make her look like a well-heeled member of the horsey set, and she could visit the Kendrick stables—get a close-up look at her target and the obstacles she would be facing.

Let's see: to do this right, you gotta walk the walk and talk the talk. Belinda had spent some time on a job pretending to be a rich woman who wanted to be part of California's moneyed crew, and that meant an interest in horses. And not just any horses, either. She rehearsed vocabulary. *Breeding terms: broodmare, stallion. Buying terms: colt, filly, yearling. Good on those. How about words for things to look for when buying. Ah, good legs . . . hmm. Yeah, that includes fetlocks and hocks, pasterns, withers— no, the withers is that hump on the back up near the neck. Riding things: good gaits—brisk walk, comfortable trot, springy gallop, and . . . easy canter. Performing things— uh—dressage training, jumper, cross-country—*

She carried on mentally in that mode for several more minutes, then called up an online encyclopedia from her laptop computer. She searched by keywords—horse, Arabian, Andalusian, stud, all things she'd need with an Arabian breeder—and scrutinized the entries until she was sure she could pass herself off in that unused persona again.

Then she stretched and crawled out of bed.

Out of habit, she scanned the room, and her attention fixed on the door. It bothered her that Mel had broken in with so little difficulty, had caught her off guard so easily. While she showered, she wondered if she was losing her skills. God knew, she hadn't managed to pull in the racecar driver, whose IQ had to be on a par with that of a Boston fern or cold mashed potatoes. She didn't give herself any breaks because of the extenuating circumstances. There were *always* extenuating circumstances.

While she dried herself off, she entertained herself with the television. A news teaser caught her attention with the "bizarre drug-related death" of "two gay men" whose bodies had been found in a roadside motel—details at six. She cheered up again. After all, she decided, for every one wrong thing she did, she also accomplished a multitude of right ones.

Once she was dry and dressed, she hacked around the Fayetteville school system's computer setup, running one up and one down from the long list of phone numbers, until she got in. Security was weak, and very forgiving of errors—for that, she grinned. It was so much easier to break into schools than into, oh, police departments, say, or restricted installations.

Once she was into the system, she ran a search for any Kendrick files, cross-reffing with the Bal-A-Shar Stables address. In a moment, she had a match.

Kendrick, Amanda, was the name of the kid she'd seen. She was on the verge of adolescence; her records indicated plenty of personality disturbances, some of them pretty odd, her grades and teachers' comments marked her with all the stigmata of the erratic genius. And she was part of a "blended family"—a term Belinda considered a euphemistic hype.

Blended family. *Right. Mom has one, Dad has one, and now we are four. Sure we are.* More stress, which, according to Mel, made for psi-powers popping out.

Plus you made my little black box happy, kid.

The information she had turned up was good enough for Belinda. She disconnected her modem and reconnected the hotel room's phone, then picked up the Fayetteville phone directory and located "Kendrick's Bal-A-Shar Stables" in the Yellow Pages. "By Appointment Only," the ad announced clearly. Belinda called.

A clipped, feminine voice answered on the other end after the third ring. "Bal-A-Shar Arabians, Merryl Kendrick speaking."

Belinda affected her persona from the old California job. "Mrs. Kendrick, this is Alessandra Whitchurch-Snowdon," she said in the upper-class Brit accent that could only be obtained by speaking without moving the lips. "I've recently moved to the States, and I'm looking for a yearling filly, probably green-broken, with good conformation and potential as a dressage contender. Your stables were highly recommended to me, but I'd like to come have a look, informally, before I go any further. Even if you don't have fillies suitable now, if your establishment impresses me, I'm willing to wait to look at the new crop in the fall." Belinda grinned at the phone. *Come on, snob appeal,* she thought. The Brit accent had never failed to get her access among the wealthy yet—something, she suspected, to do with making the local upper-class feel like provincials who needed to prove themselves.

It didn't let her down this time, either. "Yes, certainly, Ms.—ah?"

"Alessandra Whitchurch-Snowdon. But it's *Lady* Rivers."

"I *see.*"

Belinda saw, too. She could see the dollar signs clicking merrily in the other woman's eyes, but more, she could see the other woman sampling the prestige factor possibly offered by her name. "Oh, yes, Lady Rivers rides Bal-A-Shar Arabians," she pictured Mrs. Kendrick imagining telling her other clients.

The woman came very close to concealing her eagerness—but not close enough for Belinda. "When would you like to see the horses?"

A little more pressure. "Have you an indoor theatre?" Implying that anyone who didn't wasn't worth visiting.

Eagerness became avarice at the hot prospect. "An indoor arena? Certainly."

"Splendid," Belinda replied. "Then would tonight be too much of a bother—say, nine?"

Avarice became anticipation. "That would be fine."

Belinda allowed her voice to warm. "Lovely, then. I'll be off."

Anticipation swelled. "Ah, yes. I'll look for you at nine."

Belinda hung up the phone and laughed merrily. One every minute—and, boy, did she know how to jump 'em through the hoops. P.T. Barnum would have *loved* her.

She slipped into some dressy clothes—for shopping later in the "right" stores—and trotted off for the hairdresser's, happy as a blacksnake in a nest of baby rabbits. *We're back in business, now, babe*, she thought. *Oh, yeah.*

As soon as Mac was out of sight, Lianne darted out of the apartment and took off for the discount bookstore that was hidden away in one of the town's indoor malls. When she got there, she hunted down Jimmy, her favorite bookseller. She found him crouched down inside the cash wrap, sorting special orders.

"Lianne McCormick!" His eyes lit up when he saw her, and he gave her a warm smile. "Nice to see you again. Dare I hope that you have given up dating car jockeys?"

She flushed. "I'm still dating, uh, Mac Lynn."

He sighed. "So the answer to my question is 'no.' What a waste of a woman with brains." He stood and leaned against the counter, his expression mock-wistful. "You ought to give some of us bright guys a chance."

Lianne glared up at him. "I've seen those creatures you date. All big bleached hair and legs up to their ears—so don't you feed me that line about looking for 'women with brains.' Now, I want everything you have on child abuse."

"Change the subject, why don't you?" Jimmy stroked his goatee and stared off into space. "Well . . . child abuse? Ugh! That's a nasty subject." He propped his elbows on the cash wrap. "Not thinking of taking up another new hobby, are you?"

Her glare became truly vicious, and he backed down.

"Just a joke," he said, and tried a placating waggle of the eyebrows. "Really. I don't normally make jokes about that subject, but you looked so—ah—threatening."

"The books."

"Foot-in-mouth, huh? Sorry. I won't joke anymore." He headed back toward the psychology section. "I think we actually might have a few. They'll either be in Psychology, or True-Crime, or—um, Biography. I just remembered one that's pretty highly recommended."

He pulled a thick paperback off a shelf and handed it to Lianne.

"*When Rabbit Howls*," she read aloud. "By the Troops for Truddi Chase?"

He made a "you've got me," gesture. "Abuse, a woman with multiple personalities—all kinds of stuff. I haven't read it, but several of my customers have. They told me I ought to, but I wasn't into getting depressed right then. It's apparently all true. And pretty awful."

Lianne nodded. "I'll take it. Anything else?"

He pursed his lips and thought. "We have a couple on adult children of abusive parents, one on alcohol and abuse—and a few novels have started dealing with the subject, even fantasy stuff from Baen." He pulled the books that the store stocked and handed them to her with a sigh. "There isn't a great deal on that subject available yet outside of special order or hardbound." He jammed his hands into his pants pockets and rocked back on his heels. "Why the sudden interest?"

She decided it was better not to let the cat out of the bag yet. Kendrick was a lawyer—and there was such a thing as "defamation of character." "There's a kid in one of my classes—I'm just suspicious, you know?"

He nodded. "I hope you find what you need."

"Thanks." She paid for her small stack of books and got ready to leave.

Books in hand, Lianne felt a sense of relief related to the feeling that she was beginning to accomplish something. She looked at the bookseller with her sense of humor renewed. "By the way, that pinstriped suit makes you look like a gangster," she remarked.

Jimmy grinned and bowed with mock-gallantry. "Wanna see my violin case?"

Lianne returned his grin and headed out the door.

Maclyn found Dierdre just behind the Gate of a Thousand Voices, sitting next to the singing water-flames and staring into their depths.

"How are you, Mother?" he asked, resting a hand on her shoulder.

She kept her eyes turned to the blazes that darted through the fountain in their ever-changing dance. "I'm better than I was, but feeling my age."

"You aren't looking it."

Maclyn was rewarded by the soft half-curve of her smile, seen in profile. "Ask what you're wantin' to ask, laddie, and spare me your silver-tongued flatteries."

He came straight to the point. "How's Felouen?"

Dierdre—he couldn't think of her as D.D., not when she looked like this—sighed. "In pain—more of the spirit than of the body now, I suspect—but pain hurts no less when it stabs the soul."

Maclyn recalled seeing Gwaryon with Felouen a time or two and remembered the infatuated expression the older elf had worn on those occasions. "She and Gwaryon were—?" Maclyn couldn't bring himself to finish the question.

His mother understood him anyway. "No. Gwaryon loved her; she was his friend. But his death hurts her more than her own remaining wounds."

He rubbed his temple, wondering which would do the most good—leaving her alone, or going to her. "Where could I find her?"

Dierdre nodded to her left. "She was still resting in the Grove when I left."

Maclyn swung onto Rhellen's back with a fluid motion. "I'll find you later, Mother. We need to talk—but I want to see Felouen before then."

He found her where Dierdre had said she would be. She was alone. She knelt with her forehead pressed against the base of the Grove's heart-tree, still dressed in the tattered remains of the clothes she'd worn earlier. He saw her shoulders heave and realized she was crying soundlessly. His chest tightened and he felt a lump in his throat. He wanted, at that moment, to put his arms around her and hold her.

The cynical voice at the back of his brain commented that this was most likely because this was the first time in his life that he had seen her looking like anything but the seamless and indomitable warrior-maiden.

He quelled his doubts and knelt beside her. Hesitantly, he rested a hand on the small of her back. Felouen froze. Maclyn had seen the same response in deer caught in Rhellen's headlights. "It's only me," he said.

She looked over at him quickly, not relaxing even slightly, and he saw that her eyes were red and swollen. "I—I—" she started, and her voice faltered. "G-g-gwaryon—" she choked out, and fresh tears streamed down her cheeks.

Aw, hell, Maclyn thought, and pulled her against his chest. "I know," he whispered, holding her and rocking her against him.

She cried against him like that for a long time. When finally the tears were all wrung out of her, she started to talk, still keeping herself pressed firmly against him.

"We felt the summons together," she said. "He was watching at the Pool with me." She gave him the details, what she and Gwaryon were talking about, the things Gwaryon had said. Maclyn let her ramble.

"This child called us," she said, and abruptly he found himself listening with complete interest again. "She looked like a child, but she wasn't really—she said she was Cethlenn, a witch who had lived back when the elves were still only on the other side of the sea, back when someone named MacLurrie was a leader of the Celts."

"I don't know that I've heard of him," Maclyn waffled. History had never been one of his strengths.

A single faint flicker of a smile crossed Felouen's lips. "Don't feel too bad. I didn't remember hearing of him, either. He was, according to Gwaryon, a pompous, over-blown human warlord who died long before we were born—in the days when you could call yourself a king if you commanded more than a dozen men."

"Ah," Maclyn said. "That explains it." But her choice of words in describing Amanda puzzled him. "What about the child, though? You said she was . . . a witch?"

Felouen looked just as puzzled and confused. "Her body was a child's body, that was what was so strange. She was very young, even by human standards. Very thin and frail-looking, with pale hair and brown eyes. But she knew the old magics, and her speech was from the Old Country. She talked about people that Gwaryon recognized. I did not feel that she intended us any harm. Truly."

If Felouen hadn't sensed any intended harm, there hadn't *been* any. "Then what happened?"

"That was the strangest thing of all." Felouen pulled away and leaned against the heart-tree, gathering strength. "She started to tell us why she had called us—but something stopped her. There were two voices warring in her, and a sort of awful battle that I saw going on in her face. It was frightening. Her face seemed to change as I watched, so that one instant she was one person, the next, someone else entirely. The closest I can describe, is that it was as if we were watching a possession, a war for control between the witch and something else. And in the end, the witch lost the battle. When the child looked at us again, she looked like someone completely different—completely mad—and her eyes had become a green so pale they were almost white. *That* mad creature summoned the golems from a bead she wore around her wrist—from the Unformed."

"That *was* Amanda," Maclyn whispered, his uneasy feeling confirmed.

Felouen turned to stare at him. "You know her—or them?"

Maclyn pulled at a tuft of grass near his knee. "Them . . . yes. *That* explains the day at the racetrack. *That* explains everything—" He hugged Felouen again, this time in relief. "There really is more than one person in that child's body. I've met several of them, but I don't know if they've met each other."

Felouen put a hand on his cheek, then hugged him back. "I'm glad you came here," she whispered.

"I was worried about you," Maclyn admitted, serious again. "I was afraid you were going to die."

She shuddered convulsively. "I almost did, Mac. I was standing with the Abyss in front of me, and I started to step onto the glowing bridge—but the singing called me back." She started crying again. "I wasn't going to come—but somehow, standing there, I remembered you. I suppose it wasn't time for me yet."

Mac found his voice suddenly hoarse. "Don't leave again. If you face the edge of the Abyss, walk away." He held her tighter.

She pressed her face into his chest, trembling. "I will, Maclyn. I promise."

Amanda-Abbey lay on her bed with her eyes closed and talked silently to Cethlenn. *:The other one, the crazy one—is she one of us, really?:*

:Aye,: came the grim reply. *:She's real enough.:*

Amanda-Abbey shuddered. *:She's so—bad.:*

:She is that, too. But she has been through things you canna' imagine, child—she has taken all the pain in your life so that you wouldna' have any. Fear and pain are all she knows, and if she has learned to fight, she's paid, and plenty, for the knowledge.:

Amanda-Abbey remembered the sick feelings she'd had earlier. *:I don't know what you mean,:* she said.

Cethlenn's expression darkened. *:There are times when you have bruises—when you hurt and don't know why—when things that you don't understand scare you—:* the witch began slowly.

Amanda knew what the witch meant now. *:Like the Father.:*

Cethlenn nodded agreement. *:Exactly like the Father. You don't know how you got those bruises, or why you hurt, or why the Father scares you—but she knows. Her name is Anne, and she is very frightened, and very brave. And in her own confused way, she loves you.:*

Amanda-Abbey wrinkled her nose. *:I didn't like her. She scares me.:*

:You ought to be scared. She's very dangerous, and sometimes she doesn't know who is trying to hurt her and who is trying to help her. The only person she trusts is herself, because that is the only person she knows won't hurt her.: Cethlenn sat closer to Amanda-Abbey and whispered, *:She scares me, too.:*

Amanda-Abbey sighed. That was an uncomfortable revelation. *:Is she the only other one?:*

Cethlenn shook her head. *:No. There are others.:*

That was even more uncomfortable. *:Are they all like her?:*

:They are as different as you and I,: Cethlenn assured her.

Amanda-Abbey thought about that for a while. At last she said, *:Are there any I could meet?:*

Cethlenn considered the question. *:Those of you who I know are Anne, Alice, you—and Amanda. There may be others who are hiding. Anne hid from me for a long time, until she realized that she was stronger than I am.:* Cethlenn seemed to think of something, and she frowned abruptly. *:You can't meet Amanda, I'm afraid.:*

There was something ominous in Cethlenn's expression. She was afraid to ask, but she did anyway. *:Why not?:*

Cethlenn answered, after a reluctant pause. *:Amanda stays in a very cold place, and she never moves, and she never speaks—I'm not sure that she's really still alive. She is—or was—very young. Something terrible happened to her when she was three, and that was when she went away, and you and Anne were born.:*

Amanda-Abbey's body tensed. *:What about—um, Alice?:*

Cethlenn seemed relieved that she didn't ask anything else. *:Alice goes to church with Them on Sundays, and keeps your room all cleaned up, and makes sure you don't get your clothes very dirty. There are many things that she, too, has done to protect you. But I don't know that you will like her. Still, I think that you must meet her. If you can work together, I think we can beat Them.:*

A thought niggled at the back of Amanda-Abbey's mind, which grew larger and uglier and began to worry her deeply. *:Cethlenn,:* she whispered, *:if they have these things they do to protect me, what do I do for them?:*

Cethlenn smiled sadly. *:You're the one, child, who learns her school lessons, plays with her friends, and makes everyone outside of your family believe everything is all right. Anne decided that you couldna' tell what you didna' know, and protected you, so that you could protect them.:* A tear formed at the corner of the witch's eye, and she wiped it away with a preoccupied swipe. *:Alice protects you by*

*believing things you might ask questions about, so that you
don't get into trouble there—and by keeping your room and
your things exactly the way the Step-Mother wants them
so that there are fewer reasons to punish you. They have
no life except for keeping you from the ugliness and the brutality and the pain that they know. You keep up the disguise tha' keeps them alive. Even so, they want to live.:*

Cethlenn's voice grew hoarse, and her expression grew
far away. *:It's the only thing any of us wants, at the end.:*

The red-haired woman who stepped out of the late-model
Thunderbird and strode across the gravel to the Bal-A-Shar
barn bore little resemblance to the somewhat battered
woman who had left a cheap hotel room for the beauty salon
only a few hours earlier. "Alessandra Whitchurch-Snowdon,
Lady Rivers," complete with expensive-looking business
cards, wore her shoulder-length hair in a neat french braid,
and affected riding boots, jodhpurs, a lean tweedy jacket
with leather patches on the elbows, and a high-necked silk
blouse. She carried herself with the effortless confidence
that access to unlimited funds and a high social standing
seem to confer. She managed to convey, in her cool, clipped
accent, wry amusement at American cars which had their
steering wheels on the wrong side, American roads which
were positively rampant with insane drivers and impossible
rules, and American restaurants, which didn't know how the
hell to serve tea ("they serve it over *ice*, my dear, and
sweet!"), or what went with it ("*everything* over here tastes
like it's been bathed in sugar"). She saved her compliments
for the horses.

Within ten minutes, Merryl and "Alessandra" were on
a first nickname basis, ("Dear, I'm only Lady Rivers to the
poor—my closest friends call me Bits,") and were comparing points on the three two-year-old fillies Merryl was
offering. "Alessandra" narrowed the choices down to two,
and then it became a matter of pedigree.

They returned the horses to their stalls, "Alessandra"
making sure she watched gait and conformation even as
they were led away, and then headed back to the house
to flip through the pedigrees that Merryl kept up with on
her computer.

After a thorough study of the pedigrees, for both of which the delighted "Lady Rivers" received laser-printed hard copies—"Want to see what both of the girls could offer to my breeding program before I settle on one, don't I?"— Merryl gave her a guided tour of the house.

"Cozier than the ancestral pile back home, don't you know?" the ersatz noblewoman offered about halfway through the tour. "You wouldn't believe the chilling effect suits of armor have on one if one happens to be wandering about the place in the wee hours. But nobody will let me change the bloody decorating scheme. National Trust, don't you know."

Prices for each of the two horses were discussed and agreed upon in between rooms—there was no dickering. This appeared to hearten the seller greatly.

The two women parted with "Bits" promising to make up her mind in the next day or so, and ring back with her decision. Both women were smiling as they went their separate ways.

Lianne skimmed the abuse texts first, and was surprised to find that they were more help than she'd anticipated. They outlined signs and symptoms of abuse that went farther than just noting bruises with regular outlines, or a high incidence of broken bones, E.R. visits, or days absent from school. They also outlined personality traits—from constant timidity, clinging behavior, or a desperate search for anyone's approval, to erratic school performances.

One book focused almost exclusively on child sexual abuse, and Lianne was surprised to find that sexual abuse of children did not have to include intercourse. Inappropriate touching or kissing, verbal abuse with sexual overtones, and some forms of humiliation were all forms of sexual abuse. She was appalled to find that a shocking number of children were sexually abused—statistics varied slightly, but according to her books, by the time they reached adulthood, roughly one out of every five girls and one out of every nine boys would have encountered sexual abuse. Most sexual abusers were also alcoholics, and almost all of them were men.

Abuse of all kinds ran in families, with a high percentage

of abused children growing up to be abusers. It was agreed in all of her sources that the biggest hope for eliminating child abuse of any kind was to treat the children who had been abused, *soon*, so that they in turn would not continue the cycle.

Lianne curled on the couch, lost in the horror of the raw numbers. The odds were that Amanda was being sexually abused—she fit many of the characteristics of abused kids, though not all at the same time. Even worse, the odds were incredibly high that Amanda not only wasn't the first abused child Lianne had in her class, but that she wasn't the only abused kid in her class right then.

I didn't know, Lianne thought. She felt sick. *Dammit, I just didn't know.*

There had to be something she could do. *Maybe I could lobby to have some sort of abuse-detection program added to our curriculum. Let the kids who are being abused know that abuse is not their fault—never their fault—and find some way to tell them that they aren't alone.* The books had said that children felt—or were told until they believed it—that they had somehow caused the abuse. It also said kids thought such things had never happened to anyone but them. And sometimes—this made her gorge rise—they thought it was normal. That things like this *did* happen to everyone else, and that there would be no reason why anyone would help them. They were often told no one would believe what the children said. Those were apparently the biggest reasons why kids didn't go to someone for help.

Another was that they were afraid that something bad would happen to their parents. They didn't realize that the abuse was as bad for their parents as it was for them—that their parents needed help, too.

They could come to me, Lianne thought. *And there are always a few teachers in any school that the kids know they can trust. Those are the people they should tell.*

Lianne stretched out on the couch, staring out the glass doors of her apartment at the quad and the faintly greening trees, and the few bits of dull gray sky that showed around the other apartment buildings. *Someone would listen— someone would believe them. And then they would get help.*

She felt emotionally depleted, but she picked up the Truddi Chase biography anyway, and was drawn into it almost immediately.

When she finally put it down, hours later, it was dark outside, and the wind had picked up again. She shuddered and drew the curtains across the glass doors.

That Truddi Chase had managed to survive her ordeal in any form whatsoever spoke for the strength of the human spirit. That she had gone on to make a life for herself left Lianne feeling very weak and insignificant in comparison. *I feel almost guilty that I had such an easy life.*

Lianne had a bad moment when she realized she could see similarities in things she read about Truddi Chase and things she saw in Amanda. Changes in personality, in abilities, in attitudes toward her and other teachers and the girl's classmates—she'd seen all of them.

Could Amanda be a multiple personality case? It seemed more than a little farfetched. But if she was, what sort of life could have fractured her into those multiples?

The door rang, and Lianne sighed with relief. *He's found something, then. Good.* After reading *When Rabbit Howls*, she wasn't as eager to spend the night by herself as she had been.

She opened the door with a grateful smile on her face.

"Hi!" a masked stranger said, and wedged her riding boot into the door. "I saw your boyfriend wasn't here, so I thought I'd pay you a visit."

She shoved her way inside with her gun aimed at Lianne's midsection the whole time, and closed the door before Lianne had any time to react.

"Just us girls together," the intruder said cheerfully, and pulled back the hammer with an ominous *click*.

CHAPTER ELEVEN

Feeling guilty is not the best way to start the day, Mac told himself, driving slowly toward Lianne's. He worried about telling her how out of hand his comforting of Felouen had gotten, then rationalized that hang-ups about monogamy were a mostly human obsession. But then he reminded himself that he had known about that human quirk before he started dating a human—

Finally he made up his mind that he would just pretend nothing had happened unless Lianne accidentally found out otherwise.

Besides, he told himself in an attempt to soothe his aching conscience, *Felouen really needed me there last night. It made her so happy to see that I'd accepted the Ring's geas. She looked at me the way human women do when I've just won a race. And after Gwaryon's death, she needed comforting.*

And since when does "comforting" include jumping the bereaved's bones? his conscience snapped back.

So much for that approach. He dragged his feet as he walked away from Rhellen, heading as slowly as he could up the walk to the apartment. And he knew immediately that there was something very odd.

She's left the door standing open, he thought when he

stepped into the apartment entryway. The heavy gray door stood about an inch ajar. He could see that the chain lock wasn't on, either. *Considering the day she had yesterday, I'm surprised she doesn't have the whole apartment locked and barred. What did she do, just go collapse on the couch? Or maybe—maybe she left it open for me this morning. So I'd just come straight in.* He shook his head, puzzled, and knocked.

"Hey, Lianne!" There was no answer. He pushed the door all the way open, and looked inside.

Fear overwhelmed puzzlement.

He stared at the living room. It had been thoroughly and expertly trashed.

Oh, gods, he thought, *oh, shit!* With inhuman strength, he clamped down hard on the doorknob; it broke off in his hand. Before him, two living-room chairs lay on their sides with books scattered across them. The shattered television lay on the floor, one of the shoes he had last seen Lianne wearing resting in the debris. In the connecting kitchen, shards from broken glasses and dishes sparkled in the light of one errant sunbeam. A Rorschach blot of blood traced obscene patterns down one wall.

"Lianne! Lianne! Where are you?" he shouted. He ran from room to room. Beyond the living room and the kitchen, nothing had been disturbed. Lianne's jewelry was intact, her stereo and her computer were where they belonged, her clothes still hung neatly in the closet.

Only Lianne was gone.

In the sinister hush of the empty apartment, his sharp, irregular breaths and the tick of the kitchen clock were the only sounds. He stretched his psychic feelers—and came up empty. No magic had touched this room except his own. No demon creatures from the Unformed Plane had stolen Lianne away.

Scenes from a hundred TV cop shows played in his memory. Robbery wasn't the motive—and it wasn't magic, either Unseleighe or human. Rape? Kidnapping? Worse? Mac started looking for a message, a note, anything—going room to room and searching inch by inch.

When the phone rang right next to his ear, Mac

jumped. "Gods, let it be her," he whispered. "Let this be some stupid mistake."

He picked up the handset and held it to his ear. "Lianne?" he asked.

"Not a chance, babe. It's Jewelene. I've got her." The voice on the other end of the line was muffled, the laughter in his ear was coarse and vicious. "You owe me. You owe me big time, baby—and you're going to pay. You know what?"

A dull ache gripped Mac's chest. "What?"

"You stole my car and slashed the tires. So I stole your girl. You don't want to know what I've slashed." The voice was laughing again.

Belinda Ciucci.

"What do you want?" Mac whispered.

The voice was full of obscene gloating. "I'm going to kill her. And I'm going to enjoy every long second of it."

Think, fool! What can you bargain for her? "You don't want her."

Belinda made a *tsk*ing sound. "Sure I do, babe. You know what they say about a bird in the hand and all that."

Convince her. Somehow convince her. "You want me. Not her."

Deep breathing for a moment, as his heart raced and fear clogged his throat. "Yeah, but I've got her. Right now, pal, I just want to hurt somebody. She put up a fight— I've already hurt her a little. She's not as pretty as she used to be."

Gods, Lianne. What in hell have I done to you? Mac thought. *What did I get you into? How can I get you out again?* "You tell me what you want me to do, and I'll do it. Just let her go. Don't hurt her anymore."

"Damn shame you didn't have that attitude a day or two ago. Everybody would have been a lot happier." Maclyn twisted a butter knife lying on the counter into a knot. *Damn Belinda Ciucci,.* he thought. *I should have wiped her memories instead of playing games with her.*

The woman cleared her throat. "First, don't call the police. I'll kill her at the first sign that you've involved them. For now, you get to wait. You're going to meet me somewhere, but I haven't decided where yet. Stay by the phone. I'll call you back when I make up my mind."

Mac clenched his hand on the handset. This woman was not sane. "When?"

Belinda laughed, and the note in her voice confirmed that she was not sane. "Who knows?"

"Let me talk to her," he pleaded.

"Nope." There was a click. The woman had hung up.

Mac refrained from smashing the handset to shreds. Instead, he set it gently back in the receiver. Then he put his fist through the wall. "Dammit! Dammit, I should have *been* here, dammit! I should have been *here*. Not with Felouen. Here. If I'd been here, none of this would have happened."

He stared at the phone, his only link with Lianne. He hadn't thought through the possible consequences of angering Belinda, then leaving her to her own devices. He could have taken care of her by himself earlier—that would have been the end of it. No one would have suffered. Now he needed help, and needed it badly.

And Dierdre and Felouen and all of his other potential sources of help were currently Underhill gearing up to wipe out golems. In fact, he should have been going straight from Lianne's place back to Elfhame Outremer. Instead, he was locked in place in the apartment.

He would have to construct a Gate in the apartment, he decided—one that he could leave up and use to shuttle back and forth between Underhill and Lianne's telephone. The energy drain would be bad, worse since his resources were already low. He was tired, he was needed by both his own people and a seriously disturbed child, he'd just lost a friend and had another seriously hurt—and now Lianne was a hostage somewhere. He was pulled in too many directions.

Which is exactly when people get careless and get themselves killed, he told himself. *Not that my state of readiness matters. There's no looking back.* He started pulling in the energy that would form the Gate.

Amanda-Anne sat like a spider in her web, centered in the Unformed Plane, singing loudly and off-key, making monsters.

She had started to vary them—somewhere along the line,

she had gotten tired of the stick-men. She made a few two-headed stick-men, but even that was too boring. She made some things with four legs and long, spiky tails and huge teeth, and she rather liked those. She made a few more, similar but with wings. When the first of her winged monsters flew through the air, she laughed and clapped her hands—and began adding wings to everything she made from then on. Her monsters started getting bigger. One had dozens of legs and three heads on long, snake-like necks; it flew with less grace than a winged tank might have, but it did fly.

No one bothered her in the Unformed's nothingness. The Father couldn't find her. The nasty things that lived there were more afraid of her than she was of them. Nothing could touch her, nothing could hurt her. She had never had so much fun in her life. She had never had so many friends, either.

She rubbed the green bead strung on her wrist. "My m-m-magic door," she whispered. "J-j-j-just like the g-g-genie's lamp." She crowed with delight. To have been so weak, to be so strong—it was wonderful.

And the best thing was that her magic door could take her back into the elf's world. She thought about this as she worked on her current creation, an eight-legged nightmare with hundreds of eyes and a fanged mouth that ran the length of its belly. If it weren't for the goody-two-shoes elves, that place would have been perfect. The Father and the Step-Mother couldn't get there. In among all those trees, with all that magic, she would be safe. She could hide there forever—if it weren't for the stupid elves, who would make her go home.

She thought yearningly of how nice this place would be without bossy elves, about how much she would like to hide here forever.

She sang to herself and made another monster.

Lianne woke to a blaze of pain, with the tang of blood and a filthy rag in her mouth, bathed in the stench of car exhaust and gasoline. She felt as if she was lying on a bed of nails, with another one slowly descending on her. Her head throbbed, her eyes would not open, her face burned horribly and screamed with pain. Her ribs crunched ominously against hard cold metal and stinking carpet when she rolled off to the left. She felt the bones of her face shift relative to each other when she moved, and white-hot searing agony shot through her skull. She sobbed, and the movement of her rib cage stabbed fire along her nerves.

What have I done? she wondered. *Where am I?*

She fought to retrieve foggy memory.

She remembered elves fighting the monsters—or was that a true memory? She remembered magic, too—and Maclyn doing magic. And that was crazy. Absolutely crazy. Impossible. Everyone knew that magic couldn't exist.

Mac Lynn. Not Maclyn. He's a racecar driver. Not an elf. Something has happened to my mind—amnesia or something—to make me think of magic. However I got hurt like this—it's confused me.

But that wasn't so, was it? Maclyn, not Mac Lynn, wasn't human. She'd figured that out all by herself, using logic, using reason—and she'd caught him out. So the elves were real. That meant the monsters were real, too. The elves had won their fight with the monsters. Because of her. *I'm a hero—whoopee. Look where it got me.*

What happened next?

She remembered books. Child abuse books—she'd been reading, and she'd just figured out something about Amanda. Yes. It was coming back. She remembered the knock at her door, but it wasn't Mac waiting on the other side.

It had been a strange woman with a gun.

The woman had barged in—but Lianne hadn't reacted the way she'd expected. Lianne had grabbed a heavy ashtray and bashed the intruder in the face—*God knows where the courage for that trick came from, or how I managed it*—and blood had spurted down the inside of the pantyhose mask the bitch wore. A second bash, this time to the gun-hand, and the gun had flown across the room.

I got first licks in—but she had obviously had training. Lots of it.

Lianne was starting to remember the other things, as well. Very unpleasant things. The woman was good at hand-to-hand combat—she'd probably used it on other people, given the way she acted. When she dove at Lianne, she took her down and flipped her on her stomach, slapped handcuffs on her—*what the hell was she doing with handcuffs?*—and then started kicking.

Lianne knew she had broken ribs. She remembered hearing them crack when the woman's riding boots struck, and she could feel them now, hurting more than she'd ever thought she could hurt, screaming with pain with every breath. Her nose was broken, too, and probably her jaw and her left cheekbone—those injuries had occurred after the woman retrieved her gun, when she started beating Lianne in the face with it.

Her eyes wouldn't open because they were swollen so badly. *I could go blind from this,* she realized with horror, then wondered if she was going to live through this to *be* blind. She couldn't move her arms—the handcuffs were still on. Her ankles were tied together.

The rag in her mouth tasted of blood, old and new.

Why I'm here doesn't matter. What matters is—how do I get out?

From her almost-fetal position—which she could not change without bumping solid obstacles or causing even more pain than she already endured—from the smells, and from faintly heard road noises, she figured she was in the trunk of a car. She did not remember how she got there. *She must have knocked me out, dragged me to the car—she was a hell of a lot stronger than I would have guessed.*

The car door slammed so hard right then that the shock wave jarred her head and rattled through her teeth. The driver's weight as she (or was it a he now?) bounced the vehicle around, confirming the fact that her cage was, indeed, the trunk of her captor's car. The engine started up, and Lianne was thrown from one side to the other as the driver accelerated and turned corners at high speed. The teacher debated making some noise to let the driver know she was awake—then decided against it. There was nothing in the woman's attitude last night that made Lianne think she would let her get a drink of water, or go to the bathroom—if the same woman was still the one who had her. Lianne figured if she made any noise, she was more likely to be beaten with a pistol again. A drink of water wasn't worth the pain.

Mac will know I'm gone today. No one else will miss me until tomorrow, but Mac will know. I hope he finds me soon—I think she's going to kill me if he doesn't.

Elves with mage-blades and gleaming gold armor sat on the grass next to elves in Kevlar who carried Steyr AUGs, shotguns, or high-tech graphite compound bows—and these sat next to elves whose only weapons were their expressions of scorn or amused disbelief. Felouen tried to contain her dismay at the meager attendance. Less than half of Elfhame Outremer's fighting force had seen fit to show up for her briefing. The few warriors present had listened in polite silence while Felouen described her ordeal. She began with the spell that had drawn her and Gwaryon in and ended with Dierdre's entrance. Dierdre took up the tale then, describing what they found, Gwaryon's death and the rescue by the human woman.

Felouen thought that she had done well—and Dierdre certainly sounded convincing enough—but it was obvious that the warriors were unimpressed.

One of the younger elves, who wore no weapons, sprawled in the grass, nonchalant. He'd listened with a bored expression on his face. When she finished speaking, he indicated that he had a question with an indolently raised finger.

"Yes?" Felouen asked him.

"I felt the spell you're talking about yesterday. I warded against it as soon as I noticed it, and it didn't bother me. If you hadn't been hanging around old weird Gwaryon, you would done the same thing, and then we wouldn't have been out here earlier using a lot of valuable energy saving your life." He shrugged and turned his palms up. "Not that I resent helping you out—but if you had taken a few reasonable precautions, it wouldn't have been necessary."

One of the older elves nodded. "You should never have answered a summons unarmed."

"How in all the hells would I know that?" Felouen snapped. "Humans stopped summoning elves long before I was born. And Gwaryon didn't mention it."

One of the others grunted. "He should have."

"Granted," Felouen snarled. "However, you are all missing the point. The witch-child who summoned us wasn't the threat. The other child and the Unseleighe things *she* called were the threat."

A mail-clad woman who sat near the front sighed. "I find it hard to believe that they are even a fraction of the threat you make them out to be, Felouen. The sort of weirdlings a child is strong enough to conjure would have to be pretty feeble. I know they killed Gwaryon, and I'm not discounting the injuries they did you—but neither of you were *armed*. Neither Dierdre nor Maclyn were harmed."

Felouen felt her frustration building. She hit her fists together, wishing each of them held one slow-brained elvish skull in it. "The only reason they were unhurt is that the human woman broke the containment spell and sent them back wherever they came from."

A shrug of indifference. "Yes. Precisely. We're talking about monsters that one *human* can banish."

"We're talkin' about five beasties that four elves couldna' kill—couldna' even scratch, Ymelthre." Dierdre, cross-legged to one side of the standing Felouen, leaned forward, her eyes glowing with contained rage. "With our enchanted blades, we couldna' even make them cry out. *And neither Gwaryon nor Felouen could break the binding spell that held them helpless*. A spell a 'mere human child' set. Felouen has seen these things in the Oracular Pool, and she says they are a threat to us. And I've fought them, and I say they are a threat to us. We need to stand a watch. We need to be ready."

Felouen watched them as the group broke into a debate over standing watch versus not standing watch. *I know what the problem is. Nothing really scares them anymore*, she thought. *They have been the fastest and the strongest and the best for so long, they believe they can't be hurt. Except by our Unseleighe kin, and this time they aren't involved.*

When the group announced its decision to post a bare-bones watch so thin that she knew it was merely a token thrown in her direction because she was the warriors' chieftain, she smiled bitterly. *Well, I hope they're right.*

After the main group had drifted off, several of the Ringsworn, who had waited in silence, came up to stand in front of her. She recognized all of them from long-ago campaigns together, or from more recent social meetings. Of the group, considered by most of the elvenkind in Elfhame Outremer to be dreadfully conservative, Amallen was nominal leader. Amallen bent one knee slightly—Old World manners—and briefly bowed his head.

"Lady," he said in grave tones, "do not think too badly of them. They have not fought beside you—and they cannot imagine a human child who could bring forth anything that could endanger them. We," and with a nod of his head he indicated his companions, "have decided among ourselves to stand a separate watch. We will begin at once; we have already set our shifts. The others will realize that they were wrong later—and some may die learning their folly. We don't need to see the monsters to smell their taint. There is something sorely wrong here—and though we cannot fathom it, we cannot doubt it."

Felouen smiled gratefully, as relief so profound it made her knees weak washed over her. "Those who will later owe you their lives will thank you. I know that thanks is due now." She hugged each of the nine who had supported her for so long. "I wish this were idle worrying. As it is, I know you won't be standing your watches alone for long."

Belinda grinned at herself in the rearview mirror. *The worm turns—that's the phrase, I think. The worm turns.* She readjusted the mirror and stretched the stiff muscles in her shoulders.

The worm has certainly turned in my favor now. The light changed from red to green, and Belinda headed through the intersection and pointed the car out of town. She'd spent the night in the Thunderbird, unwilling to move her captive out of the security of the trunk, and equally unwilling to leave her in the trunk while she slept inside her motel room. No sense taking a chance on the teacher waking up and making enough noise to get herself rescued. And she couldn't think of anyplace to keep the woman— until she remembered the abandoned building out in the middle of nowhere that she'd hiked past the night Mac Lynn stole her car.

It would work well enough, Belinda thought. Tie the teacher up, steal her clothes so that she didn't get the urge to do any wandering even if she got loose, and leave her.

Of course, killing her immediately would be a lot less complicated. There was nothing to connect her with the woman; nothing left behind to incriminate Belinda. It would be just one more senseless abduction-murder—probably wind up on "Unsolved Mysteries." If she killed the teacher, there wouldn't be any witnesses who might cause trouble later, and Mac Lynn didn't need to know his little slut was dead—hell, the whole purpose of this business had been to get him by the balls. Belinda smiled. The tone of his voice over the phone told him she'd accomplished that. So Miss Teacher had served her purpose. He'd go where Belinda told him to go, hoping that his girlfriend would still be alive.

The abandoned house would *still* make a good destination. It could be weeks or even months before someone found the body—Belinda and the child and Mel Tanbridge would be well away from North Carolina by then.

She retraced her trip from that night carefully, stopping and backtracking on a couple of occasions as she missed a turn. It was a long drive, made longer by the fact that she felt obligated to drive the speed limit right then. It would be a stone bitch to get pulled with a well-beaten kidnap victim in her possession.

The sun rode higher and the day started getting hot— a nice enough change, Belinda thought, after the cold, wet crap of the day before. She drove past hundreds of little rural houses, all of them ordinary, all of them quiet—which suited her just fine. But none of them was the one she wanted.

Finally she spotted the place. Weeds had overgrown the drive, and kudzu, greening as the weather warmed, covered everything else. In another month, the house would be completely invisible under its kudzu blanket.

Perfect. I'll have to thank Mac Lynn for helping me find this dump.

Now, what to do with little miss schoolmarm?

Belinda considered only an instant, then decided. Hostages were risky, and too much trouble to take care of. Dead bodies, on the other hand, were very little trouble at all. She'd rather deal with corpses than captives any day.

So, she'd get the woman out of the trunk, march her into the place. Shoot her in the head, shove the body through some loose floorboards—there were bound to be some loose floorboards in there somewhere. Then she'd find a phone, call Mac Lynn, have him meet her—where?

Why not out here? Torture the bastard, dump him next to his girlfriend while he's still alive and can appreciate it—then kill him. That would be fair after what he's done to me.

First the girlfriend.

She pulled into the weed-choked drive, and the Thunderbird bumped along, weeds and sticks hissing and thumping against the glossy brown finish. She stopped the car when she was right behind the house. It was going to be hell to get back out again, she thought with displeasure.

The place was dilapidated, the wrap-around porch sagged to the ground in several places, and the only part of the structure that looked slightly solid were the boards nailed over the windows. There had been something nailed over the door, too, but that had been ripped away. The actual door hung on one rusted hinge, partway open. The place was a perfect haven for snakes and rats and God only knew what else. *At least that probably keeps the riff-raff out*, she mused. *More than that ludicrous little sign, anyway.*

The building was posted, "NO TRESPASS—G BY ORDER OF T—." Rain and sun and wind had bleached the yellow sign to bone white on one side and obliterated much of its message. *Dump looks like the place where the universe goes to die.* It gave her the creeps worse in the daylight than it had at night. She realized that was because she could see it better in daylight.

Belinda pulled out her gun. It was a good, reliable weapon. She didn't use it often—guns weren't subtle enough for her taste most of the time—but it had never let her down.

Still, she didn't much like the idea of killing the teacher—it would hurt the bastard race driver, but it was extra. She wasn't getting paid for it—and that made it dirtier, somehow, than killing for pay. Or for revenge.

Belinda looked out at the bleak ruin. *I'll be doing her a favor,* she decided. *It would be worse for her if I left her here alive.*

She slipped the gun into its holster and pulled the keys out of the ignition. It would be a long time before she made the mistake of leaving them in it again—no matter how little time she intended to be gone. She popped the latch on the trunk, got out, and walked around to the back, fighting her way through burrs and thorns and tenacious stickers.

She pulled her shoulders back and took a deep breath. The gap between the trunk and the hood looked odd for a moment. Peculiar. It gave her the shivers for just a moment, like someone had stepped on her grave.

She shook off the feeling.

Ah, well. Showtime, she thought.

She reached down to release the latch.

Cethlenn flew Abbey across the slick ice-barrier that Alice had created to protect her domain, then floated both of them down to stand in the long, white-on-white corridor.

Amanda-Abbey studied the high-arched ceiling and the unadorned walls that ran, unbroken, to the vanishing point. "She's in there?" she asked.

"Somewhere," Cethlenn agreed.

Abbey stared at the nothingness, puzzled. "How will we find her?"

Cethlenn didn't seem concerned. "We won't. She'll find us."

"We're just going to wait here?" Abbey asked, hoping that Cethlenn had some plan.

Cethlenn gave the girl a weary smile. "I wish it were so easy. No—we'll walk. Make lots of noise."

That made no sense at all. "Why?"

"You'll see," Cethlenn promised.

The two of them started down the corridor, stomping on the floor as hard as they could, sending the clamor of their footsteps ringing on ahead of them. Amanda-Abbey started hopping, and her heavy thumps increased the racket—until she noticed the noise becoming muffled, and the floor on which she jumped becoming springier.

She looked down at her feet. "Cethlenn," she whispered, "look! The floor is growing carpet!"

"Aye." Cethlenn did not seem surprised. "She always does that after a bit. Now we must sing. Know you a bothersome song that we can sing together?"

" 'One Hundred Bottles of Beer on the Wall,' " Abbey offered after a moment's thought.

Cethlenn shook her head. "Sing a bit of it for me."

Amanda-Abbey did, while the witch listened.

"Oh, for sure—" Cethlenn laughed. "That will drive her to distraction."

They resumed marching while they bellowed through nearly forty verses of the song. Again, Abbey noticed a change, as their singing echoed less and less, and seemed closer and smaller—though she knew she was making just as much noise as she had at the first.

Cethlenn looked up and pointed at the ceiling.

Amanda-Abbey's gaze followed the gesture. "She's lowered it."

"Now we bring her to us," Cethlenn whispered. "Here. Take this." The witch made a gesture, and a pail of bright yellow paint appeared in her hand. She offered it to Abbey, who took it and stared at it in confusion.

Cethlenn created blue and pink paints for herself, in the brightest tints imaginable. She took the pink pail, and slung it against one wall. Fluorescent streaks spread in gaudy profusion, and dripped messily down the surface of the corridor. The witch followed the same procedure with the blue.

Amanda-Abbey watched, appalled. "That's not very nice, Cethlenn," she said.

"It had to be done." The witch shrugged. "Now you do yours."

Abbey bit her lip, then tipped her can and dribbled just a bit of the yellow onto the floor.

"*Not on the carpet!*" a shrill soprano voice screeched, and a child raced out of hiding and yanked the can away from Abbey.

Abbey and Alice stared at each other. Abbey thought

that the girl appeared to be about her own age—but that similarity was the only one Abbey could find. The other girl was as white as the walls around her—white hair, white face, white lips, white clothes—no hint of color touched any part of her except for her eyes. The girl's eyes were gray, but they were neither the bright and lively gray of kittens nor the safe gray of the bark of old maple trees, nor the firm and dependable gray of the stones in good fireplaces. They were the dismal gray of drizzly late afternoons when the sun hadn't been out all day. They were the flat gray of institutional paint, the kind Abbey saw used on garage floors and storage rooms, and the kind she suspected prisons would be painted in.

"I'm Abbey," she said, lost in the hopelessness of those gray, gray eyes. "I'm—I'm your sister."

The gray eyes narrowed. "*You made a mess!*" Alice fumed. "You tracked on my carpet, you were noisy, you were *singing* in my hall!" She glared at the two of them, then pointed her finger at Cethlenn. "*You* have come here before. I don't want you here."

"*Alice!*" Cethlenn took the authoritarian posture and voice of a demanding adult. "You are being rude to your guest. You have not properly introduced yourself to your sister."

Alice wasn't fooled for a second. "I'm not the one who went into peoples' houses and stomped and screamed and sang wicked songs and threw paint on the walls and tracked it into the carpet. That's evil. Evil! I don't have to be polite to evil people—the Bible says not to countenance wickedness."

Abbey raised an eyebrow and looked at the witch. :*This is my sister? She's awful. Why would anyone ever let her come out?*:

:*She's very good at cleaning up messes. That's something neither you nor Anne have managed yet. Adults think she is a very good child, she knows manners—and she is very organized and very patient. And she doesn't mind being alone.*: Cethlenn rested a hand on Abbey's shoulder. :*She also knows things you don't know. You need her.*:

:*Then we shouldn't have dumped paint on her carpet.*:
Cethlenn waved her hand at the paint that still marked

walls and floor. It vanished, along with the paint cans that had contained it. :*Now she doesn't have as much to be upset about.*:

Cethlenn jammed her thumbs into the braided belt that wrapped around her narrow waist and leaned down until her eyes were on a level with Amanda-Alice's. "If you want to stop real wickedness, come with us," she told the pale girl. "You have yet another sister, who protects both of you. She thinks the way to protect you is by making monsters—and that is what she is doing now. She has to be stopped."

"Making—monsters?" Alice looked at Abbey. "You are going to stop her?"

Abbey shrugged helplessly. "Cethlenn says the two of us can't. We need more help."

Alice's eyes lit with a zealot's glee. "I'll help. When we've stopped her, I'll tell her about the Bible."

Amanda-Abbey, who had met Anne once before, had doubts about the wisdom of that, but she kept them to herself. She figured Alice would reconsider, too, once she'd met the other "sister." So she said nothing, just nodded.

Cethlenn said, "Excellent. I'm glad you're joining us, Alice. We can put your talents to good use."

Abbey tried not to be bothered by the fact that, where she had only had herself and the faceless voice of "Stranger" to rely on a few days ago, now she had the bossy presence of Cethlenn and the bizarre Alice. And Anne, who scared her badly, and whom she did not like at all, was yet to come.

Maclyn finished the Gate and sagged against the living-room wall, gray with exhaustion. :*Rhellen—stay put, and if the phone rings, come through and get me,*: he Mindspoke to his elvensteed—hoofprints in the living room were the least of the damage that had been done here. :*The Gate is in the kitchen—get me as fast as you can, and get me back here before it stops. I'll leave the side door open.*:

The elvensteed sent back affirmation, and Maclyn stepped toward the kitchen and through the Gate.

He stepped out at the periphery of the Grove and

immediately looked toward its center. He had expected to see the fighting forces of Elfhame Outremer assembled, or at least to have been met by armed guards.

But there was no one. The Grove was devoid of warriors, devoid of elves of any walk of life. He listened and heard the gentle laughter and the music of normal days coming from Elfhame Outremer itself, and he frowned. Surely Felouen and Dierdre had brought their message to the city. Yet the sounds he heard were not the sounds of a people preparing for war.

"Ha, Thaerry, you almost had me," a light female voice called from the other side of the Grove.

Maclyn saw a red-clad beauty dart out from under the sheltering boughs of the trees, followed closely by her lean swain, elegantly robed in gold-shot blue.

"Droewyn, you minx—I'll have you yet," the would-be lover answered. He caught the girl and tripped her into the grass, and the two of them rolled together, laughing and fondling each other, oblivious to Maclyn's presence.

"Pardon," Mac said, stepping into the open arena of the Grove with them, "but have Felouen and Dierdre not been here?"

Droewyn straightened her bodice with some annoyance, and said, "Aye, they've been, Maclyn gone, too, I hope. Old buzzards, prophesying their dismal tales of doom."

Thaerronal chuckled and nibbled on his companion's neck. He gave Maclyn a pointed stare and said, dryly, "They headed back toward the Oracular Pool, no doubt to bathe themselves in more of their gloomy worries. Why don't you follow them?"

Maclyn bit his lip and withheld the criticism he wanted so badly to give. Thaerry was about his own age—and one of the few Elves of the High Court even less inclined to involvement in Court affairs than he had been. Droewyn was Low Court, tied to the Grove—Maclyn wouldn't have expected any better of her.

So he nodded stiffly and ran in the direction they'd indicated.

The rich woodland scents, the soft whisper of his boots on the forest loam, the warm, moist breeze that brushed his skin, the twilight gleam of the eyes of the beasts that watched his progress along the path—all those things said "home" to him, reassured him—

:Halt, Maclyn, Ring-sworn Friend of the High Court of Elfhame Outremer.: The crisp Mindspoken command cut through the exhausted reverie into which he'd drifted. Maclyn skidded to a stop and watched the forest around him.

From behind a massive tree, an armed and armored elf stepped into view. The Uzi hung casually at her side; the Kevlar body armor fit her like a seamed skin. Her soft gold hair streamed like a river from the silver coronet that held it out of her eyes. She grinned at him. *:Nice to see you've finally joined us.:*

Maclyn smiled with relief. *:Hallara. Good to see someone standing watch.:*

The woman, one of his mother's contemporaries, laughed. *:Some of us know Felouen—and Dierdre. They have better things to do than chase imaginary bogans; if they say the Unseleighe—or anything else—are about to bite us, we won't wait until we feel the teeth. So. There are enough of us to cover the permanent Gates, with a few left over to raise the alarm throughout Elfhame Outremer. We may be caught short, but we won't be caught sleeping.:*

He nodded. *:Mother around?:*

:Checking the Oracle, I think. The omens were very bad, last time I got any news. Crisis impending, any second— of course, that's the Oracle. Damned imprecise. Makes you wish something would happen, just so you could get past the waiting.:

Maclyn's laugh was bitter. *:Don't you believe it. The waiting is a hell of a lot better. Things have broken loose on my side—someone kidnapped my girlfriend.:*

:The human? Is it related to all of this?:

:I don't think so. This crazy woman has been following me for about a week. I don't know what she wants, but she's not Unseleighe, just mad, and evil. A bad combination, but there's none of the feel of magic to her.:

Hallara nodded, then whistled—a low run of rapid notes with a liquid trill at the end. The whistle was answered and repeated.

I really ought to keep up on the codes, Maclyn thought as he listened to the brief message making its way through Elfhame Outremer. *It would save a hell of a lot of footwork.*

In almost no time, Dierdre, astride her elvensteed, galloped into view.

"That red-headed bitch kidnapped Lianne," Maclyn told her without preamble. "I need help finding her—and some backup for her rescue."

"The timing on this couldn't have been worse. The Oracle is showing imminent disaster, Mac. None of us dare leave—it appears that an attack is going to be launched against us through one of the Gates within mere minutes. I'm afraid I'm going to have to leave you on your own where Lianne is concerned."

This was not only unexpected, it was disastrous. "Dammit!"

Dierdre shook her head, implacable. "I'm sorry. We're thin here as it is."

"I know—" he pleaded, "but I'm afraid for Lianne's life."

"And I'm afraid for all of ours." Never had he seen his mother look so drawn, so torn by conflicting duties. "I'm sorry, Maclyn. Go back, do what you can—I'll come and help you search if I survive this."

Mac stared at his feet, then looked into his mother's eyes, anguished. Conflicting loyalties and loves tore at him as well. "She's in trouble because of me. I can't stay and help you fight. I can't abandon her, Mother."

She nodded slowly. "Go. I understand. A single fighter more or less isn't going to make a difference. An army, now—but an army isn't going to have time to come to us. We've called on Fairgrove, but they're depleted and down after their last to-do. Nobody else is near enough."

Maclyn's shoulders sagged, and he turned and began the walk back toward his own Gate.

Amanda-Anne shivered. The cold mists of the Unformed Plane seeped through to her very bones, and the things she had made had grown restive. They looked at her with edgy calculation in their glowing eyes—circled around her along an ever-shrinking perimeter, snapped their toothy jaws and hissed at each other, slashed and growled. But always, they watched her.

And the closer they moved, the more she ached for a safe haven, and the more she yearned for safety, the more restless and dangerous her monsters became. Suddenly, making them didn't seem like such a good idea after all.

They grinned at her, the awful things, and they suddenly looked hungry. She didn't know what to feed them, but she suspected they would be only too happy to eat little girls. And now Amanda-Anne felt very much like a frightened little girl again. The Unformed Plane wasn't fun anymore. Making monsters wasn't fun. She wanted to be warm, she wanted to be protected, she wanted to be—

—in a safe place. Where the elves lived!

She "stretched"—reached out to take control of the body she shared with the others. It wasn't occupied—all the others were elsewhere, and the body itself was in Amanda's bedroom, curled on the bed. Amanda-Anne took control, opened her eyes, wrapped stubby fingers around Mommy's green bead. The first of the monsters appeared in her bedroom, following her.

Amanda-Anne shrieked and carved a road that drove straight into the heart of the elves' stronghold, and safety.

CHAPTER TWELVE

The trunk was so hot that riverlets of sweat ran down Lianne's face, back, and chest, stinging in her cuts. The metal handcuffs around her wrists slid up and down her forearms, and every time they did, it felt as if they added another set of bruises. Everything hurt. And what didn't hurt, she greatly feared might not be working anymore.

She squirmed a little, trying to find a more comfortable position. If only her hands were in front of her—wait a moment. Maybe this bitch wasn't used to kidnapping people Lianne's size. *Well*, she thought, *there are a few advantages to being both skinny and flexible*.

This might be something the bitch that caught her hadn't reckoned on.

She ignored the pain that movement caused her, and scooted her hands down over her hips, curling her back as she did. That hurt so bad she almost quit—but the promise of not being thrown forward on her face every time the car jolted was more than she could resist. She waited for the worst of the wave of agony to pass, then pulled her knees up to her chest and tucked her feet through the handcuffs as if she were jumping a very short rope.

A *very* short rope. The cuffs caught on her instep. *Better,* Lianne thought. *I always figured my twenty minutes of*

*yoga at bedtime would come in useful for something. But
I never thought it would be for dealing with a kidnapper.*

The pressure of her feet on the links of the handcuffs
had pressed them halfway down Lianne's sweat-soaked
hands. They hurt, but when Lianne experimentally shoved
her thumb joint hard into the palm of her left hand, the
cuff slipped down further.

The possibility that she might actually get the things *off*
hadn't occurred to her until that moment. *I'll be damned!
I think I can get out of these things!*

She pressed the bones of her left hand together as
tightly as she could and pushed with all of her strength.
The combination of her sweat, the looseness of the cuff,
and her flexible joints worked a minor miracle. The cuff
slipped off, scraping skin as it went.

She pulled the foul-tasting rag out of her mouth and
reached down to fumble with the knots that tied her ankles.
When they came loose, she got to work on the other side
of the handcuffs. The right one proved to be more intrac-
table than the left—her captor had shoved it tighter when
she put it on.

It doesn't matter, the teacher thought. *I can move now.
I'll bet that will surprise the hell out of her.*

In fact, Lianne realized, *it might surprise her enough
to save me. That is, if I can get the rest of me to function. . . .* She tried to open her eyes again. Although they
were badly puffed and swollen, she felt the lids of the left
one move apart.

There was nothing but blackness.

Oh, God—I'm blind!

For a moment she felt panic clawing at her.

Then, hard on its heels, dry humor. *No, idiot. You're in
the trunk of a car.*

Lianne considered her situation. She probably wasn't
blind. She was within the confines of the trunk, but completely free. She hadn't made any noise that would carry
over the road and engine sounds, so the driver wouldn't
know this—wouldn't even know whether she was awake or
not. She had a length of rope, the handcuffs, one of which
was still attached—was there anything else in here she could
use as a weapon? She felt around in the trunk and stopped

when her fingers wrapped around the smooth metal length of a tire iron. In the darkness, Lianne grinned. Hot damn.

Those were her advantages.

She enumerated her disadvantages. She wasn't likely to have very long to make use of her element of surprise. Her captor, if she ever decided to open the trunk, could do so at any time. The only warning Lianne was likely to get was the click of the key in the lock. Also, she was hurt—the broken ribs were going to be the worst of it. She wouldn't be able to run away. Wouldn't be able to put up much of a fight—though, she thought with wry amusement, the tire iron had the potential to be a great equalizer. And finally, she didn't know where she would end up, while her captor would be on her own chosen ground—possibly with allies.

I've got a damned good chance of getting myself killed if I put up a fight. Lianne considered playing dead, or going along with whatever the woman wanted her to do, and hoping for a chance of escape later on, when she was alone. But her dad had spent a very short time as a P.O.W. in 'Nam—before he'd escaped. He had, in the course of years of later conversations, mentioned a fact about the art of escaping from a P.O.W. camp that Lianne considered applicable now.

"Baby," he'd said, with the air of one imparting the wisdom of the sages, "the sooner you attempt to escape after they've captured you, the less they'll be expecting it, and the better chance you'll have to succeed. When you're first caught, you're usually hurt, and damned confused—and you keep thinking someone is going to come from outside to rescue you. It isn't until later that you realize no one is coming, and you'll have to get out by yourself. So you take care of it while they're thinking you're still too messed up to take off." Then he'd winked at her and grinned his broad, easy grin. "Works in most any situation. You remember that, okay, baby?"

A kid in on her daddy's joke, she'd grinned back and had said, "Sure, Daddy. I'll remember."

Well—I remembered. Okay, Dad, she thought, *I'll go for it, first chance I get. Let's hope for baby's sake you knew what the hell you were talking about.*

The car bumped wildly, throwing her against the front with a vicious thump that sent every bruise and broken bone into fresh, screaming agonies. Lianne shoved her fist into her mouth to keep from howling. She heard grass and branches dragging on the sides and undercarriage. *Shit— we're out in the middle of nowhere, then, I'll bet. Not likely to be anybody friendly around. And no witnesses to see what happens next.*

She planned her tactics with that in mind. Readied her weapons. Stilled her racing heart. Positioned herself as best she could in the cramped space.

Waited.

The Gate appeared with an unnatural shriek as time and space themselves were shredded. Winds raged out of the raw wound that opened in the middle of Elfhame Outremer, whipping the delicate silk hangings and bright pennants into a frenzy. Out of the pocket maelstrom raced a child, tiny, blond, green-eyed, with a fragile beauty obscured by the fear on her face, who ran like one pursued by all the devils of hell.

The elf who reached out and caught her, a patroness of the arts on her way to the premiere of Valyre's production of "Nine Lives of Woldas Toklas," could not imagine how the little human child had arrived nor what could have frightened her so. Her confusion cleared up an instant later, as the first of Amanda-Anne's monsters followed her through the Gate, to be followed by another, and another, and another.

The child wriggled free of the elf's suddenly nerveless grip and darted off among the trees.

The last thing the elven matron heard as the monsters leapt on her was the seldom-sounded attack-alarm, a clarion call that echoed from the top of first one tree, then many.

When the trunk lock released, Lianne tensed. *Wait for it, wait for it,* she chanted in a silent mantra. She gripped the tire iron like a sword.

She heard the door open, heard footsteps swishing through the grass.

Wait for it, wait for it.

Her eyes adjusted to the meager light that came through the tiny space between trunk-lid and body, and she discovered she really *could* see. She watched fingers sliding along the inside of the trunk, feeling for the catch.

Wait for it, wait for it.

"There it is,"—a faint mutter, followed by the click of the latch, and light so bright it hurt.

Now!

Lianne stabbed with the tire iron and hit the woman in the throat, pumped full of adrenalin and with her attention focused someplace where the pain wasn't. The woman gagged, one hand flying to her throat as she staggered back a step, her expression one of shock.

If Lianne had a little more strength, it might have ended then and there. Instead, she only stunned the woman long enough to get the upper hand.

Lianne loosed a banshee scream, the accumulation of her rage and pain and fear tied into that savage howl, and tumbled out of the trunk. Her grip shifted slightly, and she backhanded the tire iron across the woman's face, then with both hands brought it down on the top of her head. The handcuff that dangled from her right wrist swung staccato accompaniment against the metal of the tire iron.

The woman threw her hands over her face and head to protect them, and Lianne staggered toward her, the tire iron held like a quarterstaff in front of her. Then she swung again, overbalanced, and fell forward, catching the woman across the chest with the tire iron. They tumbled to the ground together.

Lianne screamed with the pain of her broken ribs, but she forced herself to sit up, forced herself to hit the other woman until the bitch stopped struggling and her arms dropped to her sides and she lay still.

It was a pity, she reflected, as she sat on the ground and panted with pain, that she was so weak that it had been the weight of the tire iron that had done most of the damage. The woman lay like a lump in the weeds, a red welt rising on her cheek—but she was breathing, Lianne noted, with mingled disappointment and relief. She was still breathing just fine. Lianne poked her in the side once with the pointed end of the tire iron. She didn't move.

"I wish I was the kind of person who could do to you what you did to me. I'd beat *your* face in with your gun and kick *you* in the ribs." Lianne was so angry she shook, as conflicting emotions warred within her. *Damn, I wish I could do that!*

She looked down at the woman, lying unconscious and helpless. *Well, I can't.* She sighed, her adrenaline fading away. *Time to get out of here—wherever here is.*

Lianne went through the woman's pockets. She came up with the keys to the car, but none for the handcuffs. She toyed with the idea of taking the gun, then decided against it. At least she could take the clip out of the gun— leave her without bullets. That would work. When the police found the woman, Lianne wanted them to find plenty of evidence that would make it easy for them to throw her into a cell forever.

With the keys in hand, she pushed herself shakily to her feet and surveyed her escape route. She would have to retrace the other woman's path, which would mean backing the car down the long, overgrown drive to the road. She would have to twist around in the seat to back the car, which ought to hurt like hell, considering her broken ribs. She looked at the redhead, lying in the track broken down by the T-Bird, and sighed.

"I ought to just back over you, dammit. I really ought to."

But she didn't. She pulled the woman out of the middle of the drive, swearing with every step. An instant of weakness and the opportunity for revenge overcame her, though, and she dragged the woman over to the edge of a huge blackberry thicket, rolling her as far into it as she could, without getting caught in the vines herself. Limping over to the car, still suffering, Lianne wore the smile of the vindicated on her face.

She shoved the trunk down with difficulty, and leaned against the car itself to keep herself from falling as she stumbled over creepers and vines and fallen branches toward the driver's side door. She opened the door, leaned forward, wheezing; doubled over at the sudden stab of pain in her side, and fell onto the seat. Falling saved her life.

She heard the crack of the other woman's gun, a surprisingly unimpressive noise, at the same time that the driver's side window, in the precise spot where her head had been, flowered into an array of tiny concentric cracks.

Damn! Another clip? That's what I get for not killing you, isn't it! I should have taken the gun, she thought, pulling her legs in quickly, and closing the door as fast as she could.

Better yet, I should have left you where I could run over you. She shoved the keys in the ignition and curled low on the seat. The car started easily, and she slipped it into reverse and pushed lightly on the gas. She sprawled across the bench, as low as she could get and still reach the pedals, facing the rear of the car, her left hand clutching beneath the headrest of the passenger seat for balance, her right steering the car. *Thank God the thing's not a stick, anyway.*

She curved the car around the side of the house and aimed toward the road, praying like a gift wrapped nun at the devil's birthday party. The car wallowed over a bump at the same instant that a bullet hole appeared in the front passenger window, and Lianne's foot slid farther down onto the gas pedal. The T-Bird accelerated wildly.

"Shit, shit, shit—oh, shit!" Lianne wailed, as various small trees and other obstacles loomed in the rear window, vanished at high speed and were replaced by others. She swerved and kept right on going. *I wish I could close my eyes*, she thought. *I doubt it would make much difference in my—oh, shit!*—she dodged another tree—*driving!*

She heard two sharp *pings* in the windshield behind her head. *Two more of the bitch's bullets. When is she gonna run out?* Lianne didn't dare look back. As long as she was still alive, anything else could wait.

The car bounced again, and a small tree splintered across the rear bumper. *Oh hell*, Lianne thought for some reason, *it's only a rental.* She didn't even remember the joke that punchline was from.

There was a crunch of metal and one massive heave—and Lianne felt the smoothness of pavement under the tires, heard the scrape of what must be the entire exhaust system under the car. A quick spin of the wheel, and she backed the rest of the way into the road. To her right were the dilapidated ruins of the house, and the red-haired woman, taking aim yet again. Lianne threw the car into drive and hit the gas. *What a persistent snake you are. I hope you enjoy your walk home.* She flipped the woman the bird and burned rubber in her acceleration. The rear window blossomed with its own bullet hole.

Well, Dad, she thought. *I owe you my life on this one, I think. And if I live long enough to get to a hospital, I'll have a story to tell that rivals even yours.*

When Maclyn heard the alarm through the trees, there was no question of going back to the apartment and waiting for the phone call. Rhellen would have to find him, Lianne would have to fend for herself—he armed himself as he ran toward the center of Elfhame Outremer, from whence the alarm came. Even as he ran, he kept thinking *What kind of fool would open a Gate in the heart of an Elfhame?*

Beside him, Dierdre on her elvensteed and Hallara on hers launched themselves toward the battle. :*This is it!*: Dierdre bellowed directly into his brain. :*Get Rhellen.*:

:*I can't! Didn't bring him!*:

Dierdre paused long enough to give him a withering look. :*Idiot.*: She pivoted her mount and leaned down to offer Maclyn an arm up. He took it and swung onto the steed behind Dierdre's saddle.

:*I had to leave Rhellen to listen for the phone.*:

:*Brilliant, oh my son. Riding pillion is not the safest way to go to battle,*: his mother said acidly, :*but you'd be dead in no time on foot. There's nothing to contain those monsters or slow them down here.*:

Dierdre wielded her sword left-handed, Maclyn held his in his right. They charged along the ground paths beneath the singing boughs of the gold-leaved home-trees, past the shimmering curtains of light in the flame-fountains, under the branch-braided arch of the Lover's Trees—and into the melee behind Hallara, who sprayed a broad blanket of machine-gun fire to try to clear them a path. From other sites on the perimeter, reinforcements arrived.

The vortex of a rogue Gate glistened hypnotically from beside the delicate blue-green filigreed sculptures in the Masters' Garden. Three elven mages engaged themselves in battling the Gate itself, trying to close it off. They threw containment spells and reversal spells over the maw that spewed the monsters into their midst—to no avail. Amanda-Anne's hastily-constructed Gate had ripped away part of the spell-formed reality of Elfhame Outremer itself. It fed on the energy of the destruction it caused, creating a direct road from the Unformed Planes to the center of the elves' safe haven. Amanda-Anne's nightmares advanced unchecked.

A horde of giggling, tittering stick-men and multi-legged screamers burst through and launched themselves against the scattered elven forces with bared fangs and razored claws. Initially, there was no strategy to the skirmishing. The elves hacked and slashed and shot, and the monsters failed to die. The grim things pressed forward into the elven ranks, pushed from behind by the larger monsters that moved through the Gate at their backs.

Hallara, Dierdre, and Maclyn joined forces with Felouen and a small phalanx of veteran warriors who were covering an elven spellcaster and one of Outremer's adopted human mages. The mages were mildly successful at individually spelling the nightmare things with the same containment spells that had proven useless on the Gate. But the effort required of them was enormous, while the number of horrors shoving through the Gate far exceeded those being contained.

Then Amanda-Anne's winged creatures arrived in force, lurching through the air like medieval stained glass demons and cathedral gargoyles. They dove on the defenders, howling like the damned, belching fire and dripping acid, diving down to pluck hapless elves from their elvensteeds and ascending far above the trees to fling them back to the ground below.

The defenders of Outremer were forced to retreat beneath the sheltering overhangs of the trees.

Then the trees began to burn.

The entire population of Elfhame Outremer—that part of it, at least, that had managed to survive the initial onslaught—fought back desperately. The few elven children lent their magical energy to parents who cast shielding around Outremer's untouched trees. A contingent of mages battled their way toward the Grove and dug in around the heart-tree. Weapons of every variety, human and magical, were leveled against the invaders. The Oracular Pool, the many fountains, and the Vale River that circled the whole of Elfhame Outremer were drained to feed a storm spell. Rain poured from the smoke-filled sky, and the conflagrations in the tree-homes and shelters of the elven haven began to die. And wet wood did not rekindle as easily.

Maclyn and Dierdre were part of the contingent who fought to protect the Grove. Their losses had been huge— more than half of the Grove's trees were charred stumps, with the bodies of their defenders scattered at their bases like fallen branches. Now, the largest of the monsters seemed to be concentrating on destroying the heart-tree itself. The death of the heart-tree would release the spells of thousands of years that had used it as the focus for maintaining Elfhame Outremer. Without the heart-tree, Elfhame Outremer would disappear back into the nothingness of the Unformed Planes. Mac had seen the movies— the battle to guard the heart-tree was a kind of Masada, an Alamo—there was no question of retreat. If the heart-tree went, there would be nothing to retreat to.

Maclyn had discovered that almost nothing slowed the monsters down, but if he cut off a golem's head, it stopped fighting until it could either locate the missing extremity or grow a new one. He'd passed this information on to the other elves, and the ground around them began to look like a croquet lawn designed by head-hunters.

The monsters became warier, and ground-fighting demons began to time their attacks with those of the airborne gargoyles.

Mac took a two-handed swipe at a winged demon that dove at him. He missed, and the demon sank its claws into a seam in his armor. Maclyn was ripped off of Dierdre's elvensteed, thigh muscles screaming in pain as he struggled vainly to stay horsed. The monster's screech rang in his ears, its breath blasted into his face, burning at his skin and making his eyes water. Then it dropped him. He lay, stunned, while the tides of the fray shifted.

When he was able to stand and wield his sword again, Dierdre was out of sight, and a new horror lurched at him with a grin on its foul face. He had no time to look for allies. His arms felt like lead, but he forced himself to slash again and again as the beast lunged at him. Three times the elven blade bit deep at the monster, yet it continued to giggle maniacally.

Around him, the elves were being herded into a few remaining pockets of resistance, and the toll of the dead mounted.

Amanda-Anne huddled in the hollow of a great silver elven-elm, shivering and miserable. *This* was the only safe place she had known of—this retreat far from the evil Father and the uncaring Step-Mother. This was the place she had thought to come and hide, where no one would hurt her, where nothing could frighten her. She had never thought that her own monsters would follow her—

And when they did, she had been *sure* that the elves would be able to get rid of them.

She had brought hell from her own world and from the Unformed Planes, and visited it here, in the only completely beautiful place she had ever seen. And she had destroyed it, all by herself; ruined it, made it worse than any place she had ever known, worse, even, than the pony barn. She stared out at the devastation that spread before her. Charred and smoking stumps were all that remained of most of the trees; the bodies of elves—so many beautiful, gentle elves—lay bloody and sprawled in the churned mud. The pretty green grass was gone, the sweet music was drowned in the screams of the dying, the bright pennants that had fluttered so briskly in the warm breeze hung in sodden tatters in the pouring rain.

Amanda-Anne, looking at the havoc she had wrought, felt something she had never felt before. She felt pain and guilt for those she had hurt. She felt regret for her actions. She felt responsibility.

She was as bad as the Father.

Maclyn shouldered aside a flailing arm as he cleaved another creature's fleshy skull. They came, still they came. One of the human mages had just been overcome by the monsters, his body clamped in the eight-armed thing's jaws as it laid into a second mage's defenses.

One of the Sidhe who had lived in the humans' world was doubled over near him, as if injured. Her lips moved as she concentrated on a Summoning-spell, and the air before her turned dark. Then a stack of wooden boxes materialized, and another, and finally a wooden rack of firearms with handwritten price tags on them. She stood straight again, pulling thick gauntlets on.

Maclyn hacked at his creature a few more times until he dismembered it, kicked its pieces far from each other, then turned to the female.

"Need help?"

"Could use it." She expertly undid the latch on a case and began loading a grenade launcher. "We need to buy some distance."

Maclyn winced at the amount of Cold Iron in the weapon, but decided that the time for desperate measures had come. "They'll be picking steel chips out of the Grove for years, but at least there *will* be a Grove."

Amanda-Anne huddled in her hidey-hole, and the first tears she had ever cried came to her eyes, scorching her cheeks, etching hot trails down her face.

"I am sorry," she whispered. "Oh, I am . . . so . . . s-s-sorry."

One of her monsters shuffled toward her hiding place, snuffling and casting its head from side to side, following the scent of the living. It looked down into the hollow where she hid, saw her, and chittered in soprano glee. Its bloodstained talons reached in after her.

"G-g-go *away*," Amanda-Anne whispered through her tears. "I d-d-don't want you here anymore!"

The monster vanished with a soft "pop."

:Make them all go away, Anne,: a quiet voice whispered in her head. Amanda-Anne closed her eyes and found her sisters, her other selves, facing her with angry or unhappy faces. Cethlenn stood before her, and Alice, and Abbey. Only the first-born, the real Amanda, was absent.

:Make them go away,: Cethlenn repeated. *:You are the only one who can. Only you have the power. Only you can work the magic—or unwork it.:*

:Please,: Abbey said, piteously, her own tears coursing

down her cheeks. *:Oh, please. They're hurting, they're hurting so much!:*

:You must,: Alice added. *:You can't leave the people in this place to die. You did it, now you have to undo it. It's all your fault.:*

Amanda-Anne felt the hot tears streaking down her cheeks and choking away her breath. *:I know.:* She hugged her arms tighter around herself, and told the three who watched her, *:I'm sorry.:*

But "sorry" didn't fix things. She'd have to do that now, before they got worse. Amanda-Anne crawled out of her shelter and stood exposed to the sharp eyes of the monsters, the startled eyes of the elves. "Go away," she screamed, above the roars of explosions and gunfire, above the skin-crawling chittering laughter, above the howls and the prayers and the oaths and the crying. "Go *away!*" She concentrated on how much she didn't want her monsters, on how much she wished them to disappear. For a moment, there was nothing but silence.

Then the creatures of her imagination vanished, leaving behind only the dead, and the ruin they—*she*—had caused.

And then, miserable and afraid, fearing what the elves would do to her when they realized what she had done to them, and feeling that she would never deserve safety or beauty again, Amanda-Anne raced for the Gate she'd made. She threw herself through it, pulling it shut behind her.

In mid-flight, still spouting flames at the remaining treetops, the three-headed flier popped out of existence. The gothic demons flickered slightly and were gone. Maclyn, fighting a losing battle with a many-legged snake, found himself swinging a rifle-butt at an opponent that had suddenly ceased to exist.

All over Elfhame Outremer, cries of surprise became shouts of elation. The survivors fell together, hugging each other in disbelief and hysterical joy at the sheer miracle of it.

Those who were relatively unscathed soon enough began the grim task of sorting dead from dying, of dying from salvageable. They walked from charred body to mangled body, from one still form to the next, struggling to recognize in death some semblance of those they had known in life. Maclyn rid himself of his gloves and heavy armor with a thought and began that dark walk, too, looking into the faces of survivors, hoping to find his own loved ones, and seeing his own disappointment reflected over and over in each face that was not Dierdre, was not Felouen. He knew that for all of those who stared into his eyes and turned away in despair, his own grimed features represented one less chance that the ones they loved still lived.

He worked his way back to the point where he and Dierdre had become separated. All around him, the Mindshouted calls, the agonized cries for help, the screams of those who recognized the ones they had loved in the features of the dead, blotted out any hope of finding Dierdre or Felouen by Mindcall, or by simple shouting. He kept at his steady examination of each passing face, of each sad corpse, praying to all the gods he'd never believed in that he would recognize his loved ones in those who still stood, and not those who would never stand again.

Suddenly, across a muddied clearing, he recognized a familiar toss of the head, a quick brush of hand through hair.

"FELOUEN!" he roared, and was rewarded by a startled jerk of the head in his direction, by a shriek of "Maclyn!" and by the woman's ungraceful two-legged gallop across the field of the dead.

Felouen threw herself into his arms, careless of her wounds or his, and wept. "By the gods, you're alive. When you fell, I knew I'd lost you, oh, gods I knew—"

She pressed a suddenly tear-streaked face to his, and Maclyn found to his surprise that his own eyes were not dry. He held her tightly, breathing in the scent of her hair and savoring the warmth of her, the hard-muscled strength of her lean body pressed tightly against his. "Thank all the gods you're alive," he whispered. Then he loosened his grip and looked in her eyes. "Dierdre?" he asked.

Felouen's face lost its animation. "She sent me to find you."

Maclyn, ignoring her bleak expression, smiled with relief. "Ha! Then she still lives! I knew she was too tough—"

"Barely," Felouen interrupted grimly. "She waits by the last of the beasts, the ones held in the containment spells. They didn't vanish with the rest of the monsters. She is summoning their thoughts to see where they came from— and why."

He sucked in a breath of dismay. "But if she's injured, using magic will only weaken her further."

She bit her lip, shrugged her helplessness. "Perhaps you can convince her to spare herself—I could not."

Felouen's elvensteed reached them, and Maclyn noted its burden for the first time. A body was slung across the saddle face-down. "Who—?"

Felouen's face tightened. "Hallara. She died trying to put out a fire in the heart-tree. She'd run out of ammunition. The pike line around the mages broke, and one of the things took her when she tranced."

He closed his eyes and fought back despair. "Oh, gods."

"There will be time to count the dead later, Mac. Let's tend the living while we can." Felouen turned away from him and broke into a flat-out run, heading back toward the spot where the Gate had opened.

Maclyn followed.

They found Dierdre propped against one of the contained monsters, her body blood-drenched, her face white with impending shock. But her hands pressed against the thing's skull, and her expression was one of tight concentration.

"Mother!" Maclyn exclaimed as he saw what she was doing. "Lie down! Save your strength."

Dierdre opened pale eyes and quelled him with a single glance. "There is a man who must not be allowed to die," she said. Her voice was a hoarse croak, but her speech never faltered. And her expression was one of implacable hate. "These things were made by an aspect of the child, Amanda."

"What—" Mac was puzzled by her choice of words.

"The child was tormented until she shattered," Dierdre explained tersely, "like a fragile crystal, dropped by a careless hand. She is no longer one, but many. One of her number learned how to weave magic from you, all unwitting. To protect herself and her other selves, she wove these, monsters—fragments of her pain. They are constructs of her fear—her fear, Maclyn, fear so great they nearly leveled Elfhame Outremer and the magic of three thousand Sidhe with it. We did not win the battle, son of mine. Amanda released her fear, and when she did, our foes vanished."

He blinked, uncomprehending. "Mother—"

"Quiet." She pierced him with her eyes. "Do you know what she feared, Maclyn?"

How could he? "No," he replied carefully. Dierdre in this mood was not to be contradicted.

"She feared her father—and with reason. He has tortured her," Dierdre said, at last. "He has raped her—yes, you heard aright. For years, he has done unspeakable things to her—he has shattered her into a handful of strange, fragmented children that do not even communicate with each other. The aspect that created these monsters never knew love, or caring, or kindness. It knew only brutality and pain and hatred and fear—until it came here. This was where that aspect of the child thought it could hide and be safe from the horrors it had created—but because no one had ever been good to it, it feared us as well."

Felouen answered for all of them. "Not the child's fault. She had not the experience, could not have known what she did. Fragment or no, she was a child, and to a child, all adults are gods. She must have thought we could banish these creatures as easily as she. It is her father that has brought this upon us, not her—*he* is the cause that made her create them in the first place. For fear of her father, we have suffered and died."

"I'll kill her father," Maclyn said softly. "For what he has caused here, for what he has done to you—"

Dierdre shook her head. "No, Mac. For my revenge—for her revenge—I want something more." She let herself slip down to the frozen monster's feet. Her skin was the color of snow, waxy and translucent, her lips bloodless. Only her eyes looked alive. Mac stared at her rent armor, at the damage that could not be repaired by the greatest healer of the elves, and covered his face with his hands in grief.

"Listen," she told him.

He knelt and put his ear to her mouth, to hear his mother's dying wish.

Damn them, Belinda thought. *Damn all of them.*

She had never suffered so much or been hurt so badly in pursuit of a target. It seemed as if everything—her target, his feeble girlfriend, even his damned car, for crissakes—had conspired to destroy her. She had been foiled at every turn. She had been made to look like a fool.

Belinda had been through enough.

She leaned wearily against the phone booth's wall, searching the out-of-date phone book's battered pages.

There it is—the Prince Charles! She maneuvered a quarter into the slot and dialed.

A mechanical, but not electronic voice, answered. "Prince Charles, this is Sharon speaking. May I help you?"

"Connect me to Mel Tenner's room," she ordered thickly.

"May I ask who's calling, please?" the polite voice inquired.

Officious bitch. "This is Belinda, and it's an emergency."

The voice did not seem impressed. "Hold please, ma'am."

It was just like that miserable S.O.B. to have his calls screened, Belinda thought. *He'd better decide to take mine—I'll kill him if he doesn't. I don't need this s—*

Sharon returned. "I have Mr. Tenner on the line, ma'am."

"Fine," she said shortly, reining in her temper.

A few clicks, and a moment later Mel drawled, "What is it, Belinda?" He sounded supremely bored.

"Get a pen and some paper," she snarled. "I'm going to give you directions—I want you to come get me. Then we're going to pick up your girl. Bring your gun."

Mel laughed, as if she had made a joke. "I wouldn't leave home without one."

Belinda gave him the directions, tersely, keeping her eyes fixed on the phone.

He made an odd little grunt of surprise. "Belinda, darling, what are you doing at a convenience store out in the middle of nowhere? Slumming?"

"Working. For you," she replied, hoping he *might* feel

a little responsibility. After all, she was still working for him, as he had so pointedly reminded her. "My car got stolen."

"Again?" The laughter in his voice was only too obvious, and he wanted her to hear it. Mel was not going to take on any belated responsibility. Not that she really expected him to. Mel believed that everything that happened to anyone was their own fault—including being caught in earthquakes, high-rise fires, and tornadoes.

She restrained the impulse to scream, and contented herself with shredding the pages of the phone book, one by one. "Sound a little less happy, Mel. I'm having a bad day."

"Why don't you just tell me where to go pick up my little TK," he suggested, with deceptive mildness, "and then you can get a taxi and go home to rest?"

And you can take off with the kid and skip paying me, scumball? I don't think so. "Just come get me, Mel," she growled. "And bring your bankbook."

He sighed, as if with infinite patience. "Fine, sweetheart. If that's what you want. I'll be there in forty-five minutes." *Click.*

Belinda slammed the receiver home and glared at a slip of paper. It was the schoolteacher's phone number. Belinda debated calling. Maybe the woman had gone straight back to her apartment, or maybe she had called first, on the chance that her boyfriend had shown up and found the place trashed. If she had, Belinda wouldn't be able to fool the race-driver—but if she hadn't . . .

Nothing ventured, nothing gained, as they say. She dialed, and the phone rang. Once.

Twice.

Three times.

"Come on, shithead," she muttered. "Pick up."

Four times.

Five times.

Maclyn was alone at the foot of Dierdre's grave beneath the remains of a giant white willow. The tree had protected his mother's Underhill home since she had come over from the Old Country—it was the part of Elfhame Outremer she had missed most when she was in the world of humans.

It was now scarred and burned, and its loving inhabitant had come home forever.

I'm going to miss you, Mother, even more than you would have believed. Maclyn stood alone as the last smatterings of warm rain soaked into his clothes and ran down his face. Her death had destroyed a part of him. He felt suddenly old, watching the loose earth over the grave falling in on itself as the raindrops struck. He had never really given her cause to be proud of him. Unlike the rest of his colleagues on the racing team, he had not been motivated by any higher goals. The others, the elves and human mages of SERRA, had been raising money to finance shelters for teenage runaways, kid-rescue operations, any number of altruistic causes. He had been a member of SERRA only because he liked to drive fast cars, and because he liked to win. If the money he won went to "worthy causes," well, frankly, he hadn't wanted to have to hear about it.

In his own way, he was as much an escapist as any of the elves who lived Underhill permanently, as any of the dilettantes who idled away their days with music, dancing, gaming, loveplay.

Maclyn stiffened as he felt Rhellen's sudden presence in the Elfhame. The elvensteed called out in his blunt mind-images as he galloped, searching on the other side of the Gate for his cohort. He answered the elvensteed with a quick whistle, and the golden beast charged to his side. Rhellen saw the fresh dirt beneath the tree and gave a questioning whicker.

Maclyn shook his head. "Later," he said. "I'll tell you everything later." He sensed the elvensteed's horror at the devastation of Outremer, but there was no time to comfort him, and no time to explain.

Mac leapt to the elvensteed's back, and Rhellen charged back through the Gate. He skidded to a stop in the kitchen next to the phone, bumping against the sink top. Mac leapt off of Rhellen's back and answered the phone.

"Hello?" he said, thinking, *Please, no more bad news. Please.*

"I just about hung up, fella. You took a long time getting to the phone." The voice was the same one he'd talked to earlier—and, in spite of the muffling, he was certain it was Belinda Ciucci he was talking to.

"I was busy," he said. "In the bathroom. I got here as fast as I could."

She snorted. "I don't think calls of nature are as important as my call. Especially since I'm going to let you save your girlfriend's life now."

He spoke carefully, not loosing any of his anger. "What do you want me to do?"

"Meet me out in the woods on the right side of the Bal-A-Shar Stables," she said. "I know you know where. I followed you out there yesterday."

Well, now he had a rendezvous point. "Fine, Belinda. Let me talk to Lianne now."

"Not a chance, buddy—" Then, suddenly, silence.

There was a pause—Maclyn realized from the faint wash of emotions he caught over the phone that he had just tipped the woman to the fact that he knew her real name. Dammit, that was going to make things harder. "You're going to meet me in the woods at five P.M., and then I'll let—ah, Lianne—go," Belinda continued.

"What do you want me to bring?" he asked. "Money?"

There was a bitter, harsh laugh at the other end of the line. "Sure, why not? Write this down."

She paused, and Mac pulled out the pen Lianne kept on the clipboard with the notepad and got ready to write.

Belinda continued. "Bring me a hundred thousand dollars in small, used, non-sequentially marked bills. Pack it all in a little suitcase, drag that with you, and—oh, by the way, don't drive your car. I don't like it. You come in your girlfriend's car—the little yellow Volkswagen convertible. Big racecar stud like you oughta look cute in it. Park in the turn-around next to the dirt road that goes back to the cotton field. Get out of your car, walk along the road until you cross the culvert, and walk across the street and into the woods. I'll have a red ribbon tied around the tree you are to go to. Put the money down beside the tree—when you turn around, you'll see your girlfriend. As long as you follow directions and you're all by yourself, everything will work out fine."

For you or for me? Mac wondered, but he said, "Okay."

The line clicked, and Belinda was gone.

Felouen may come through this Gate, he thought, staring at the dark swirl of energy. *She knows about Lianne, and she knows we have to find Amanda—maybe she'll come through in time to help me. She needs to know what I need, and where to meet me.*

He took paper and pencil, and in flowing elvish script, wrote a note and drew a map to Bal-A-Shar Stables. Then he created a large, elegant leather case out of thin air and filled it full of very real-looking counterfeit bills. He would hand Belinda one-hundred thousand dollars in used-looking twenties, with only eight serial numbers between them. And as soon as she took the case, he decided, the faces on all the bills would abruptly sport matching maniacal, toothy grins. Maybe the motto would read, "Gotcha."

Cethlenn woke in Amanda's room, on Amanda's bed. The child's clothes were soaked and filthy. Bits of the elven domain's dirt and greenery still clung to her. In one hand, she found a silver leaf—crumpled and tattered, it was both beautiful and saddening. Inside her, the children huddled in fear and stared out over her shoulders. Poor children— they had been through so much, and a sixth sense told her the worst was yet to come. Downstairs, she could hear Them arguing.

"Don't you talk to me in that tone of voice! I've been out working with the horses," the Step-Mother yelled. "I haven't had time to watch where your weird kid got to— she was in here with you the last I knew!"

"She isn't in here now! I've been all over the house looking for her." The Father sounded truly furious. "The little liar said she was going up to her room. She isn't up there now, let me tell you."

Fury filled the Step-Mother's voice. "I know where *my* daughter is—and I want to know why the hell she came running out to the barn in tears! What did you do to her, you bastard?"

A pause, and then the Father countered, a hint of something Cethlenn couldn't read in his voice. "I didn't do anything to her—don't change the subject on me!"

The Step-Mother snarled at him, "We agreed when we

got married that your kid would be your responsibility, and my kid would be mine. You remember that? Huh? Well, that means if you want *your* daughter, you find her! *My* daughter and I are going shopping. And from now on, you keep your hands off her!"

Cethlenn heard the Step-Mother's angry footsteps and Sharon's short, light ones clipping across the floor. She heard the door slam so hard the walls shook. She was alone in the house with the Father.

She heard him storm from the front room back to the den. There was a long, silent pause. *Mixin' himself a drink,* Cethlenn thought. *Goin' to feed his anger with a wee drop of the uisge-beatha, no doubt. And then he'll go ragin' through the house until he finds us—and we're in trouble when he does, and sure.*

As if he'd heard her thoughts, the Father bellowed, "I know you're in here somewhere, Amanda! You can come down here right now and spare yourself a lot of trouble. Or I can come find you. I *will* find you. And when I do, I'll break your skinny, ugly little neck."

:*You need to go, Cethlenn,*: Alice urged. :*You have to do what he says. He's our father and we have to obey him.*:

Cethlenn shook her head. :*And if I do what he says, he'll break our neck without having to work to find us first.*:

Abbey said fearfully, :*Daddy wouldn't hurt us, not really. Would he?*:

Cethlenn cocked an eyebrow at Abbey. :*Why don't you ask Anne about that?*:

:*I can't,*: Abbey replied uncertainly. :*Anne's gone.*:

:*Not back into the Unformed Planes, please all the gods!*: Cethlenn felt her pulse race and her breath quicken in dismay at that thought.

Abbey answered slowly. :*I don't think so, Cethlenn. We could feel that she was there, before, even though we didn't let ourselves know about each other. But now there is nothing where she was but an empty place. I think after Alice yelled at her, she went away.*:

In the pit of Cethlenn's stomach, something twisted. :*Alice. What—did you say to her?*: the witch asked Alice. Now that she knew to feel for the emptiness, the place

where Anne should have been nagged like a newly missing tooth.

Alice donned her most self-righteous expression and said,
:*I told her the truth—that she was awful and evil and that
we didn't need her or want her here.*:

And by all the gods, the child had the gall to look
smug—as if she'd done something grand. :*Oh, no! Alice,
Anne is a part of* you! *You can't just get rid of her! You
can't!*:

Alice crossed her arms and glowered at Cethlenn. :*She
did those—things—with our father. Nasty, wicked, sinful
things. She was a bad, bad girl. Our father said so, and
he is our father so he must be right.*:

Cethlenn reacted without thinking. :*Your father is a
vicious brute who ought to be flayed and drawn and
quartered and hung, then burned for good measure,*: she
snapped.

Alice looked shocked. Her mouth opened and closed,
but no sound came out. Her white cheeks flushed momentarily red, and angry tears filled her eyes. :*I'll—I'll—I'll* tell
on *you!*: Alice finally sputtered. She flickered out of sight.

:*Oh, dear,*: Cethlenn told Abbey, with a twinge of guilt.
:*I shouldn't have said that to her.*:

Abbey glared at her. :*You shouldn't have said it to me,
either. I don't believe he's as bad as you and Anne say.
Anne was crazy, and I'm glad she's gone.*:

Abbey followed her sister.

Cethlenn heard the Father coming up the stairs. No time
left to find the children and retract her ill-thought state-
ments. Apologies would have to take second place to survival. She hurriedly jumped off the bed, and noticed as she
did that it was wet and dirty where she had lain on it. A
beating would be the least she got if the Father caught
her. She frowned and slipped out by her secret window
escape. As soon as she pulled the window shut, she dropped
to the roof below. Instead of running to the tree and climbing down to the ground this time, though, she stayed put,
hugging the side of the house and listening to the Father
as he rampaged through her room and then started searching for her through the rest of the house.

There was a drain spout that went right alongside one

of the attic windows. Cethlenn was sure she could climb it. It had fastenings about every two feet that would serve as hand and footholds. It connected along the edge of the roof where she stood and soared to the attic window on the third story without going near any other windows.

The attic wasn't the safest place—the Father would certainly check there for her—but he probably wouldn't check more than once. If she climbed up after she heard him moving around in there, she should be able to buy some time. Perhaps the Step-Mother and Sharon would be home by then. He wouldn't do anything really brutal with them home, surely.

Cethlenn wasn't certain, but the attic plan seemed reasonable in theory. So she scooted down next to the spout and sat with her head pressed against the wood siding, listening for the sounds of the Father's footsteps ascending the stairs above her. Finally, she heard him crashing upward.

She stilled, waiting, and at last she was rewarded with his racket as he clattered back down the uncarpeted stairs. Cethlenn wiped her suddenly-damp palms on her shirt, eased her slender frame onto the gutter, and found the first tiny handhold. Almost afraid to breathe, she began the long ascent.

When Mel picked her up, Belinda flung herself into his car and said, without preamble, "Straight by my hotel—I have something special I need to pick up to finish this job. Then we'll go out and get your kid."

Mel gaped at his employee. Apparently he hadn't thought she'd have sustained any real damage. "You look awful. How did you get all those bruises on your face?"

"I walked into a door." She pulled down the passenger-side visor and looked in the mirror long enough to assess the most recent damage to her appearance, and bit her lip in dismay.

"Not really," he replied, as if he half believed her.

"No," she agreed. "Not really. But I don't want to talk about it." She glanced out at the passing scenery, then over at the speedometer. "Can't you drive any faster? God, you drive like the old coot who used to be my partner."

Mel frowned, disapprovingly. "I'm already going seventy, Belinda. I would just as soon not get pulled over right now. A cop might ask questions, once he gets a look at you, especially if he sees our guns. What are you in such a hurry for?"

She grimaced. "I have an appointment. Move it, okay? If I don't get to my appointment, you won't get your kid."

Neither of them said anything until they arrived at Belinda's hotel. As they pulled into the parking lot, Belinda swore. "Dammit, she took my keys and my fake I.D. I don't think I can get the clerk to give me another key without some identification."

Mel shrugged as if it didn't matter. "Have you done anything to the door or the lock since last night?"

Belinda rolled her eyes. "Oh, yeah, Mel. I installed a bomb so that the first person who opened the door would be blown away. The room is probably coated with Maid-Kibbles by now."

He sighed elaborately. "Hey, I was just asking. If you haven't done anything fancy to the locks, I can still get in."

She decided not to employ any more sarcasm on him; it was obviously wasted effort. "I haven't. Lead on, Macduff."

Mel did as promised. Once in the room, Belinda went to the dresser, crouched with her back to it, and lifted a corner of the heavy furniture a few inches off the floor. "Grab the case," she panted.

Mel, eyebrows well into his hairline, pulled the thinline briefcase out of the tiny space. "Nice hiding place. I haven't seen that one."

Belinda twitched her shoulders in dismissal, then nodded at the case. "That's an expensive toy. I didn't want it to walk off without me." She dropped the dresser, grabbed a bright red excuse for a skirt from a hanger, and with that in one hand and her little case in the other, headed for the door.

"May I ask—"

Belinda cut the question off. "It's a gun."

Mel looked puzzled. "To fit in that case, it couldn't be much of a gun."

Belinda climbed back into the passenger seat of the car.

Mel slipped in. As they backed out of the parking space, she said, "You want specifics? Fine by me." She briefly opened the case to reveal a long, streamlined handgun and a loose scope packed in padded velvet. "It's an XP-100; a single-shot bolt-action handgun that comes tapped and drilled for scope mounting. I use a 12-power quick-mount scope on mine. It shoots a fifty-grain .221 Remington Fireball with a muzzle velocity of about 2650 feet per second. The velocity is still about 1150 feet per second at 300 yards. It delivers an impact over 400 foot/pounds at a hundred yards, and 130 foot/pounds at three hundred yards. It's machine polished, with a hand-carved conforming rosewood handgrip to make it pretty and easy to hold and not look so obvious on x-rays, and a bull-barrel to limit recoil. Best of all, at three-hundred yards, its point-of-aim is only thirteen inches above its target." She gave him a nasty little smile. "Feel better now?"

He only looked bored. "All of that babble means something to you?"

She snarled. "Yeah. It means this is a real nice gun if you want to kill somebody with one bullet from a long way off, but you don't want to drag a rifle around for everybody to see."

"Oh," Mel said, dismissively. "It's an assassination gun."

"It's an assassination gun," Belinda agreed. "An expensive one. I'm about to get my money's worth out of it."

CHAPTER THIRTEEN

By the gods, I had no idea the ground was so far away. A mere strip of wooden ledge was all that separated Cethlenn from the plant beds and pine bark far below. *Och, I'd forgotten how I hated the heights. So, I end up here, in this wee bit of trouble, like a stranded chick and the snake comin'.*

And speaking o' which, I wonder what the bloody bastard's doin' now.

She heard the Father thundering around the lower floors, a bear deprived of his meal—a beast deprived of its prey.

She got eight inches of clearance before the attic window refused to budge further. Amanda was a thin child—Cethlenn could be grateful for that. She squeezed herself through the narrow space and into the cramped confines of the attic.

Boxes and other menacing shapes hulked in the gloom. Cethlenn felt among them, fingers probing for shelter. Her eyes refused to adjust—the darkness wrapped around her like a living cloak. Every breath sounded loud to her; every creak in the floor seemed to scream betrayal to the Father below. And always, it seemed that eyes watched from just over her shoulder.

She found a trunk, half empty, with old dresses and blankets in it. With a muttered prayer of thanks to the gods of her past, Cethlenn clambered in, pulled scratchy, dusty cloth over her head, and went to sleep.

Belinda snapped the sight onto the silver handgun and loaded the single cartridge into the chamber. There was a smooth click as the bolt slid home. She thumbed the safety, then laid the gun on her lap, pointed towards the passenger door.

"I want you to drive down to the other side of the horse stables you'll see on the left," she said to Mel as neutrally as possible. She didn't look at him. She began cutting narrow strips of cloth from her red skirt and tying them together. "Wait for me just down from the intersection. As soon as I'm done with this, I'll hike through the woods and take you to pick up your kid."

"Is she around here somewhere?" Mel asked, unable to conceal his avarice.

"General vicinity," Belinda told him. She knew what he wanted, and she tried to summon up the appropriate wariness—then the wariness melted into her overall exhaustion. *I'm getting paranoid. Mel's been waiting for this TK kid for a long time. It's only natural he should want to know where she is. He won't double-cross me—not after I've done so much for him. And not with all the dirt I have on him.* She smiled at her employer and said slowly, "Sorry I snapped at you. I'm edgy, Mel. I'll feel better when we get the girl and get the hell out of North Carolina. This place is driving me up the wall. I feel like every Billy-Bob G.I. jerk in this state is trying to get in the way of my job."

He nodded, his own smile, thin-lipped and unpleasant. "Don't worry about it, Belinda. I understand."

Belinda got out of the car and watched Mel drive off in the direction she'd indicated. Then she walked well into the woods, tied the red strips around a tree, and paced off two hundred and fifty yards to one side of that point, keeping a clear line of fire in mind. Belinda checked her watch—only fifteen minutes more until Mac Lynn would walk into her sights.

❖   ❖   ❖

Lianne got out of the police car and breathed a sigh of relief. It was over. The cops had found the information in her kidnapper's purse very helpful—they'd traced the aliases back to Berkeley, California, and a woman named Belinda Ciucci, an ex-cop whose record ran to such interesting charges as grand-theft auto, kidnapping, and murder. They'd located her hotel room and staked it out; the woman was going to return to find company waiting. The policemen would be by the apartment later for more information; until they arrived, Lianne had been instructed to take it easy.

Those were pretty much the same instructions the nurse in the E.R. had sent her home with. Her three broken ribs weren't misaligned—and how she'd lucked out there, she had no idea, what with all the twisting and turning and bumping around. The swelling in her face would have to go down before a doctor could tell how much work her nose and cheekbone fractures were going to require—if any. She didn't have any dangerous injuries, only ones that hurt. The folks in the E.R. had been sympathetic and encouraging. They'd given her scrips for an antibiotic and a painkiller, told her to put ice on all the swollen places, and to avoid any further excitement. She'd called her principal—and verified that, yes, she *was* in the emergency room and she wasn't faking all this and that, yes, the police *were* involved, and that she was the victim of something they could not specify. She could only imagine what stories would spread around the teachers' lounge in her absence— everything from rape by her racecar boyfriend to kidnapping by terrorists.

Certainly nice to know I have both medical and legal backing for taking a day or two off. I don't think I could face a class anytime soon. Soon as I let Mac know I'm all right, I'm going to lie down, take my pills, and sleep for the rest of the day.

Lianne felt around inside her mailbox for the spare key taped there, and walked across the quad.

When she put the key into the lock, she realized the door hadn't been locked in the first place. She walked in, ready to take off if anything seemed out of the ordinary. The place was a disaster—Lianne vaguely remembered how it got that way. It was dark inside. She moved quietly through the living room down to the hall and opened all three doors soundlessly. The rooms were undisturbed and nothing was missing. No one was hiding in any of the corners or under the bed. In spite of the mess in the living room, the apartment felt safe and peaceful again. Lianne breathed a sigh of relief. *Thank God for small blessings,* she thought, and headed to the kitchen to fix herself a cup of hot tea to go with her pills.

She noticed a piece of paper taped to the kitchen entryway. She pulled it down and stared at it. It was writing that looked vaguely Arabic or Hebraic or—Her brows knit in puzzlement. Not that—and not anything else she'd ever seen, either. There were lines that were clearly a map to somewhere, but the directions on it weren't anything she could decipher.

With the map in hand, she walked into the kitchen—

Or at least, she intended to. As she stepped across the threshold, her skin tingled and smoke and mist swirled around her. For an instant, she felt nothing under her feet at all. She screamed—and finished the step she had started into the kitchen.

Mac, you scum-sucking worm, what did you do?

She wasn't in the kitchen anymore. The smoke was even thicker here, blown by an intermittent breeze. She landed on her hands and knees in wet, tenacious mud, and caught her breath as her ribs reminded her of their injuries. She looked up at the soaring, sad remains of what had been an ancient forest. The massive ruins of burned trees towered over her, and a few unbelievably beautiful survivors in front of her made her heart ache for the lost glory. *I wish I could have seen this place before the fire,* she thought, surprising herself with the strength of that wish. *It must have been heavenly.*

She pulled the note she'd carried out of the mud, and looked at it gloomily. It was muddied and torn. She considered tossing it out, then decided against it. *Probably Mac's shopping list, written in elvish,* she thought. *But about the time I throw it out, it will be important.*

Lianne heard the quick, faint pounding of horse's hooves, steadily growing louder as she listened. After a moment, she saw a fair-haired man galloping toward her astride a huge chestnut horse. It was an elf—which meant this arrival of burned forest to the middle of her kitchen *was* Mac's doing.

I knew it. Lianne felt a bit smug at how calmly she was taking all this. *I'm getting very rational about facing all these little episodes. Becoming quite the survivor.* She licked her dry lips and told her queasy stomach that this was just business as usual. At least, she thought it was business as usual. *Or else I've gone round the bend entirely, and I'll wake up in a charming little padded room wearing an I-love-me jacket.* She maintained her relaxed facade as the elf reined in his horse in front of her and rested one hand on the butt of a small machine gun, the kind she saw terrorists in news-shots toting.

Machine gun? Oh well, Mac races cars, so what's the difference?

"Hi," she said, wriggling her fingers feebly, in what was supposed to be a friendly, harmless wave. "I've got a note that I'm sure someone here could read." She waved the muddy paper up at him, and the elf took it suspiciously. He scanned it, muttered "Ah, bloody hell!" and reached down to pull Lianne onto the saddle behind him.

He was stronger than he looked. She sailed through the air, shrieking at the pain caused by the rough handling. "Hold on," the elf commanded, ignoring her cries, and launched the horse into a gallop that was closer to flight than any four-legged beast should have been able to manage. The horse's gait wasn't as rough as that of horses Lianne had ridden before, but with her renewed pain, she wasn't inclined towards favorable comparisons.

"I'd rather walk!" she yelled. "My ribs are killing me!"

The elf ignored her. Horse and rider danced through the trees, leaping dark, charred, human-looking forms that Lianne realized with sudden horror were bodies. The destruction wasn't limited to trees.

There had been a fight here—no, not a fight, a war. These were the survivors. No wonder this elf wasn't impressed by a couple of cracked ribs and a broken face.

She decided she didn't want to walk after all.

In quick glimpses through the wreathing smoke and mist,

she caught sight of an open glade where rows of the dead were laid side by side, dreadful wounds visible on most; groups of the fair-haired elves digging beneath the roots of trees, burying their dead; shock and sorrow in pale faces, the grim set to mouths and eyes of people determined to survive and go on.

The destruction was recent; so recent that one or two fires still smoldered. *What's happened here?* she wondered. *What have I walked into—is Mac in this mess somewhere?*

"Felouen," the elf in front of her called. "A note for you from Maclyn. This human brought it."

Felouen, grime-streaked and weary-looking, put down her shovel and took the muddy paper. Lianne saw the paper glow blue, and suddenly it was clean and untorn. Felouen read, and with a puzzled expression, looked directly at Lianne.

She was incredibly beautiful—and vaguely familiar. "You are Lianne, the woman who saved my life yesterday, aren't you?" she asked.

The elf in front of her turned around and stared at his passenger with amazement. Lianne blushed. "Yes. I am."

"Then this letter doesn't make any sense. Maclyn says he's gone to a place near the Bal-A-Shar Stables to pay your ransom and rescue you from the woman who kidnapped you, and that once you're safe, he's going to pick up the little girl who caused all this damage and bring her back here. He wanted my help in rescuing you." She shook her head. "Unless he's already rescued you?"

Now Lianne was just as puzzled. "No. I got away by myself. She was going to kill me, but I clobbered her with a tire iron and stole her car. That was hours ago, uh, hours ago, back there, that is." She waved in the direction she thought her kitchen was. *God, this is like* The Lion, The Witch, and The Wardrobe. *I've got a tunnel to Narnia in my kitchen*, she thought crazily. *Why my kitchen? Was it more convenient than the closet, or is it just because I don't have a wardrobe?*

Felouen rubbed an incongruously dirty finger along the side of her nose. "I don't understand, then. When this abductor spoke to Mac, you must already have escaped her, for he could *not* have spoken to her before this. What can she hope to accomplish if you got away?"

Lianne frowned. "Maybe she thinks she can trick him into giving her money—no!" The real answer hit her, and she groaned. "I was just bait to lure him to her. She hates him. The whole time she was beating up on me last night, she kept saying, 'This is for you, Mac Lynn. Next time it'll be you.' She's crazy. She'll kill him, I swear she will."

Felouen snarled, her face transformed into a mask of anger, no less beautiful but so frightening that Lianne shrank back from her. "No, she won't. I won't lose another of my folk today."

The elven woman whistled, and a black steed materialized out of the smoke-laden mist. "You'll ride with me," she told Lianne, as she leapt into the saddle.

"Oh, God," Lianne whispered, but only to herself. "I don't know if I can take any more of this." But they had plainly endured so much more, she was ashamed of her few piddly broken bones. She slid off the back of one elvensteed and cried out as her feet hit the ground.

"You're hurt," Felouen said in surprise, as Lianne's exclamation of pain penetrated her anger.

Lianne was a little blunter than she would have liked. "No lie. Three broken ribs, a broken nose, a bunch of abrasions, and pain that just won't quit."

Felouen reached for Lianne and muttered under her breath. In an instant, warmth spread through her broken bones, and the pain thinned and paled and sank without a trace. "I have dealt with the pain and strengthened the broken bones—everything else will have to heal naturally. I don't have enough power yet to do much more." The elvish woman sighed. "But I owe you my life—and you'd slow us both down hurt like that."

"Thanks," Lianne said, not quite certain how to react to the elven woman's words, but grateful for the relief. "This is the best I've felt in quite a while."

"Good. Let's get to Mac before that madwoman does." Felouen gave Lianne a hand up and clicked her tongue once. The magnificent black steed raced back to where the devastated splendor of the elven world met Lianne's kitchen.

Amanda-Alice woke with a start. She felt around herself—she was in a box, with cloth over her. It was pitch-dark, and the place where she was smelled musty. She was stiff and sore. She tried to stretch, but the box was too small. She pushed the cloth off of her, and things smelled better immediately. There was some light, too, but not much. Amanda-Alice sat up.

I'm in the attic. Yuck. It's always dusty in the attic. I'll bet I got dust on my clothes.

She climbed out of the box. Father was downstairs, thumping around. From time to time, he'd yell "Amanda! Amanda! Get down here right now!"

That Cethlenn is a bad person, for a grownup, Amanda-Alice thought. *She doesn't mind what she's told. I'm going to tell Father on her. If I don't, he might think I don't mind any better than she does.*

Amanda-Alice walked to the attic stairs and opened the door quietly. She walked out to the steps, and closed the door just as quietly behind her—*I never slam doors like some people do.* She walked down the stairs primly, like a lady, the way Father said to. It sounded like he was going through the bedrooms. Amanda-Alice followed the sound and spotted him in the guest bedroom, digging through the closets.

"Here I am, Father," Amanda-Alice said. "Cethlenn wouldn't let me come when you called."

She saw her father's back stiffen, and he turned. The fury on his face was something Amanda-Alice had never seen before; she backed up, frightened. "I'm sorry," she said. "Cethlenn made me. I couldn't help it. I'm sorry, I really am."

He growled, while his face got redder and redder. "You're sorry?" he breathed. "You're sorry? Not as sorry as you're going to be, you little bitch. Where the hell have you been hiding?"

Amanda-Alice gasped, confusion spreading through her at his tone as much as what he had just said. He had never, ever, spoken to her like that. She responded automatically, in shock, in the only way a good girl could when a grownup said anything so outrageous to her. "Those are bad words! You said never to say bad words."

He grabbed her thin shoulders with his big, thick hands and shook her. In a slow, deliberate voice, he said, "Never correct me." He slapped her across the face once, hard, and Amanda-Alice felt tears spring to her eyes. Why was he acting like this? Hadn't she come as soon as she heard him?

"I asked you where you were," he said slowly, his eyes full of fury.

She pointed timidly toward the attic. "Up there."

"I looked up there," he muttered, as if he didn't believe her.

Hoping to appease him, Amanda-Alice said, "Cethlenn made me climb up the drain spout after you went out. She was being very bad."

In the back of her mind, Amanda-Alice felt Cethlenn wake up and look through her eyes in horror. *Ah, child, what have ye' done? We're in his hands, are we? We're doomed.* She felt Cethlenn moving around in her mind, looking for Abbey and Anne. Suddenly she hoped that the witch would find Anne, the magic-maker, the only one of them with any power. This was not the father she knew. This was a stranger, an angry, unpredictable, frightening stranger. Could he—could Father have people inside him, too. . . . ?

And Cethlenn was afraid of him. That made her even more frightened. What did Cethlenn know that she didn't, that made her so afraid?

Father stared at her. "You're filthy," he whispered. "But it doesn't matter now, does it? You're too big and too ugly and too dirty and too bad—and you're calling attention to yourself. Sharon will have to do in your place. She's younger than you, anyway—and she's not a little slut."

Sharon? What did Sharon have to do with this? Amanda-Alice was even more frightened. She knew she was bad—she had to be, Father said so—but why did he call her a *bad word*?

He grabbed the back of Amanda-Alice's neck and propelled her out of the guest bedroom and down the hall toward the stairs. "I'm going to have to get rid of you," he told her coldly, all of his anger turned inside, but still there for all that it was hidden. "Before that frigid whore Merryl gets home."

Get rid of her? How? Why? What was he going to do?

She resisted a moment, and he shoved her forward, making her stumble. "Come on, you. Don't drag your feet." She looked back over her shoulder and shivered to see his smile. He wasn't talking to her—he was talking to himself. "Whatever it was that happened at the pony barn, it turned out to be good for me. Now the cops are going to look all over hell and gone for my mysterious enemy when they find you."

"F-f-find me?" she faltered. "F-f-father? Where are we going?"

He laughed, and something deep inside her went very small and very still. "We're going down to your step-mother's barn," he said, softly, "with all her precious horses. You're going to make me happy. And then there's going to be an awful accident."

Maclyn stroked Rhellen's dashboard. The elvensteed had been disgruntled to have to impersonate a battered yellow VW Bug. Then his mood had turned playful. He'd let Mac know in every possible way that such vehicles were far beneath his dignity, and he'd better not be asked to humble himself again in such a demeaning way. Mac hadn't had the heart to tell him about D.D.'s death, or about the massacre of the elves of Elfhame Outremer. Not yet. Instead, he took the teasing in silence because he knew the elvensteed was only trying to amuse him. Gradually, though, his mood communicated itself to the great beast, who withdrew into a state of watchful silence.

Mac and Rhellen raced in mounting uneasiness along the back roads to the spot Belinda had indicated. Maclyn thought it odd that she would pick a spot so near the place where he had intended to go next—but he told himself it was about time something worked to his advantage. Certainly the god of Luck had not been with him until now.

There was no sign of a car at the pull-off she'd indicated, nor of a place to hide one. He parked where Belinda had said, watching warily for a sign of long red hair. Then he got out of Rhellen with his case in one hand. He patted the VW on the fender with the other. *:Stay put,:* he said. *:See if you can spot where she's hidden her get-away car.:*

Rhellen communicated anxiety.

He shared it. :*I know, old friend. This is a bad situation. I'll be careful. But remember, this is your old buddy Belinda we're dealing with, okay? She won't get away with anything, especially not sneaking up on me. She moves through the woods like an ox on skis.*:

Rhellen's soft mumbles subsided. Mac turned, counterfeit payoff in hand, and strode confidently across the road. He slipped silently into the woods, eyes open for anything that might be a clue to Lianne's prison, ears alert for the faintest crunch of Belinda's footsteps. He spotted the red marker easily and moved up to it, watching for traps.

Strangely, the woods appeared to be completely devoid of Belinda or Lianne.

He wondered if he could be early. He glanced at his watch, then turned slowly to scan the woods.

She didn't see him until he was in front of the tree. *How the hell does he do that?* she wondered. But how he did it didn't matter. Not really. He wouldn't be doing it anymore.

Belinda lined up the cross-hairs on her scope—a nice, dependable chest shot. The gun had enough punch to kill him from the distance she was at, without being close enough for him to hear or see her, no matter how good his eyes and ears were. Her finger tightened on the trigger. She waited while he dropped the case. Then he turned, slowly, scanning the woods, moving beautifully into a full-face shot.

It was perfect.

At the instant that she pulled the trigger, he spotted her, and through the scope, she could see that his face wore an expression of terrible shock and dismay. And fear. It was beautiful, it was wonderful, it was the sweet taste of revenge.

In the next instant, a red blossom appeared on the white of his shirt, high and to his left. The heart—she couldn't have hit it more perfectly if she had been a surgeon working on an operating table.

Belinda stood and smiled, and ran through the fringe

of woods at the edge of the child's home, on her way to pick up Mel.

God, but revenge was sweet.

Rhellen heard a "crack" from the woods that Mac had walked into, and felt his partner suddenly overcome by pain and fear. He charged toward the sensations that were coming from Maclyn, shape-shifting out of his assumed form on the run. He crashed through the underbrush. To his right, running away, he saw the red-headed woman.

He felt fury, but he didn't dare follow her. He had to find Maclyn.

A clump of white showed up in the dimming light, along with red. Rhellen trotted toward it, smelling blood as he got closer. He tossed his head and snorted. Mac didn't answer, not by voice or in Mindspeech.

The white clump was Mac, all right. The elvensteed put his nose down and nudged the elf, whickering softly and radiating concern.

Mac's eyes didn't open. He didn't respond in any way.

Rhellen grew afraid. He knew he could take Maclyn back to help, though. Lianne's house had a Gate in it—he could go there.

He flattened himself in the middle and slipped under Maclyn like a knife shaving butter, then formed around Mac to prevent moving or jostling him in any way. Then he left the woods, rushing towards Lianne's house, ignoring the roads.

Amanda-Alice felt a jostling in her head, as she was suddenly joined by Amanda-Abbey and Cethlenn. They were tied at wrists and ankles, their mouths gagged, in the unused stall at the end of the stables. The Father stood bent over a little, a few feet away from them, spreading gasoline around the inside of the barn. He ranted under his breath, "This will show Merryl. Let's see how she feels about all of her damned horses going up in smoke."

"Happy, you little whore?" he asked from time to time, looking into the stall where Cethlenn and the Amandas lay. "You won't ever disobey me again. Filthy slut."

Cethlenn struggled with the bonds, trying to work free.

It was no use. The Father had too much practice with this—he knew how to tie up a child so that she couldn't slither free. Both girls were crying and shrieking. Alice was incoherent—she'd been the most sheltered from the Father's abuse—but Abbey was clear enough. *:We're going to die! Help us, Cethlenn! Help us!:*

Cethlenn wanted to weep; she was as helpless as they were. All of her magics required free hands and supplies, neither of which they had. *:If we had Anne, she could get us out of here. We have the bracelet on—she knows how to use the Gate. Can't you find her? Bring her back, tell her we need her.:*

The children cried, and Alice answered for both of them. *:She's gone. She isn't real anymore. I made her go away.:*

Cethlenn steeled herself. She'd passed through this once, already. Surely death could be no harder a second time? *:Och, my darlings, we're all going to cease to be real in a few minutes.:* She held her mental arms out for them, and they huddled inside. *:I cannot protect you, my little ones. Only Anne could do that. But I will be with you. I will not leave you alone.:*

The Father finished spreading the gasoline, and came in and squatted in the straw next to Amanda. He stroked her back in a manner that made Cethlenn's skin crawl and grinned down at them.

"We need to have one last party, little Amanda."

He stared down at her and frowned. "Shit. You look just like your mother, you know that? I killed her, too. Did you know that? I'll bet you didn't." He sat by the child. The smell of gasoline was sharp and overwhelming in the back of their throat. "She found out what I was doing with you— she didn't like it."

He laughed and stood up, and began pulling down his pants. "So I had her committed to a nuthouse, and I hired a woman to go in, pretend she was crazy, and get close to her. That woman slit her wrists for her. Suicide—isn't that great? Everybody felt so sorry for me. And that left me with you."

Pants down, he knelt beside Amanda and smiled. "We've had lots of fun, too, haven't we? You've liked it, huh?

Daddy's little girl. Filthy bitch. Oh, you liked it. You wanted it. You asked for it."

Cethlenn tried to call the bastard something crude, but the gag in her mouth changed her curses to a few weak grunts.

"Yeah," he said, "I'm going to have to take the gag out until we're done, Amanda. My little whore. Just like your mother now—" His eyes got a glazed look to them, and his face reddened. "I want to hear you tell me that you like it. Tell me that you want it."

He pulled Amanda's blue jeans down around her ankles, worked her panties down past her knees. Behind Cethlenn, Alice and Abbey screamed, frightened.

He was breathing hard and obviously very excited. *In my time, you pervert, we'd have cut your balls off and fed them to you raw,* Cethlenn thought.

The Father took the gag out of their mouth. "Tell me you want it," he said thickly. "One last time."

Mel and Belinda had seen the girl and her father go into the barn from their hiding place behind one of the horse troughs in the paddocks. Mel had grinned at her after checking the readings on his own black box. "Good job, Belinda. The kid's as hot as you said she was. I was starting to have some doubts about you."

Belinda felt cheerful and relaxed, now that it was almost over. Within a few hours she'd have her pay. Within twenty-four, she'd be on a beach somewhere. Bermuda, maybe. "I'm sorry about that, Mel. I just couldn't get the racecar driver. From now on, I'll know never to try collecting adults. The real TK's are too dangerous. We'll just have to get 'em while they're kids."

Mel nodded, as if she had just told him something profound. "I'll remember that. It's an important point." He faced Belinda. "You think there will be any danger from this one?"

From a kid? How could there be? She rolled her eyes. "Christ, Mel—she's only ten years old. What the hell could a ten-year-old do?"

He shook his head, as if he hadn't intended to say that. "Yes. You're right, of course. Still, I have my gun with me."

Belinda watched the barn, and with a puzzled glance at Mel, started inching toward it, keeping behind available cover. "They're taking a long time in there," she whispered. "I'm not sure I like this. I think there's something wrong."

Mel followed, nodding, a look of concern on his face. The lovely old post-and-beam wood barn had been moved from another part of the country and restored by real craftsmen, using the original wood wherever possible. The finished building had all the charm of the original, with a few modern amenities required by a modern horse-breeding operation. But the knotholes in the siding had remained. Belinda found one and looked in it.

"Horse's rear end," she whispered. "What a view."

She moved down the side, looking through whatever cracks or gaps came her way. At the far end of the old barn, she stopped and stared.

Jesus Christ. Jesus H. Christ. Her mind babbled obscenities, as her stomach churned. She turned away, the blood draining from her face, struggling to control her sickness.

Mel noticed her expression and pressed his eye to the hole. After a moment, he shrugged and turned to Lianne. "I'm surprised you're squeamish about *that*," he whispered. "Research seems to indicate that that's the sort of thing that brings out TK talents in some of these kids." He watched her, his expression suddenly fascinated. "My God, that really bothers you. I didn't think anything bothered you."

She swallowed. She tried to tell herself it didn't matter; in a few hours Mel would have the kid out of this stinking barn and into a sheltered, cozy environment. She knew that; she knew he'd treat his little prize like the pearl she was, like a precious gem. She'd never even have to think of this again. "I didn't realize we'd be doing her a favor taking her away from here," Belinda whispered. "All of a sudden I feel like a goddamned hero."

Mel chuckled. "Don't let it go to your head," he told her as he climbed over the fence and headed around to the back door of the barn. He tried it and found it locked. He headed toward the front door. "If we have to rape the kid from time to time to keep her talents sharp, we will."

Suddenly, she didn't feel like such a hero. Suddenly, Mel's back was a very attractive target.

Mel disappeared into the barn.

Belinda's head swam, and the sharp burn of vomit hung in the back of her throat. There had been a fat old geezer in the upstairs apartment who'd groped her up when she was a kid. It sure as hell hadn't been her dad. She didn't remember much, and she hadn't ever been able to like men after the little bit she'd been through; now she wondered how this kid felt.

And Mel had nonchalantly said he'd see that the girl was tortured after they got her away from here if that kept her TK magic operating well.

Belinda gritted her teeth and stroked the holster that held her pistol under her jacket. There were financial considerations to be kept in mind, of course, but once she and Mel got the girl out to California, Mel might find that he wasn't going to do that, after all. He might find out it would be a good idea to treat the little girl like a goddamned princess.

Lianne gave directions to Felouen, who passed them on to her elvensteed, who had transformed into a jet-black Lamborghini. The three of them moved along the roads so fast the only scenery that wasn't blurred was that which was directly in front of them.

The topic of what had happened in Elfhame Outremer had been exhausted, and so had the subject of what had happened to Lianne.

The one thing they hadn't discussed was Mac. That subject hung heavily in the air.

Lianne broke the uncomfortable silence. She cleared her throat and said, "He'll be fine, I think." She was trying to offer reassurance to the elven woman, who was wired tighter than a banjo from tension, as best Lianne could tell. She also found that talking was better than silence. It helped keep her mind off of how fast they were going. She couldn't help but be bothered by the fact that Felouen's hands weren't on the steering wheel. "He knows so many tricks—how could a human hurt him?"

Felouen never took her eyes off the road. "My opinion

of the damage a human can cause has gone way up," she said. "And Maclyn is an idiot. I love him," she muttered, "but all that proves is that I'm an idiot, too."

Lianne stared at Felouen. "You love him?"

The elven woman stared stonily out the window. "I have for several hundred years. It's been a most unrewarding occupation."

Lianne folded her hands on her lap and fixed her eyes on the road ahead of them. Her exhaustion must have just caught up with her, because she started speaking before her brain had a chance to clear the words. "I see. But you're beautiful, and you're intelligent, and you're an elf, too. Why—?"

"Why doesn't he love me?" Felouen's lips quirked into a lopsided smile, finishing the question for her. "Why can't you hold the stars in your hands, and why can't you fly if you want to badly enough? The answer is—'Because that is not the way the universe works.' Maclyn is destined to break his heart loving humans, I suppose, and I am destined to break my heart loving him. Just because we are near-immortal in your eyes, it does not follow that we cannot be killed—and just because we have the wisdom of the ages at our disposal, it does not follow that we are wise."

Lianne nodded, but remained silent.

The elven woman suddenly looked over at her. "I never thought I could envy a human," she said, "but I do envy you. I've had his sympathy, but you've had his love."

A familiar-looking golden Chevy roared past them, going in the opposite direction. Felouen's elvensteed bellowed like a foghorn and did a sudden controlled-spin turn that threw Felouen and Lianne around inside.

God, I'm glad this particular elvensteed belted us in, she thought. *A stunt like that in Rhellen would have turned us into tomato paste on the windshield.*

And indeed, Rhellen had slowed cautiously and made a careful turn that Lianne could have imagined her grandmother making. *That isn't how Mac usually drives,* she thought at the same moment that Felouen said, "Moortha just told me Rhellen says Maclyn is hurt."

Lianne shook her head. "No. He'll be fine. I know he will."

Felouen smiled at her, a slow, gentle smile that didn't even begin to hide the pain in her eyes. "You also love him," she said. "I'm glad for that, at least. The woman who broke his heart so long ago never really did." She patted Lianne's hand as the two cars pulled even with each other and came to a stop. "We're allies for now," she said.

The two women got out of the car and ran to the door Rhellen had opened for them. He'd rearranged his interior so that there was nothing inside but a firm, supporting mattress that contoured around the wounded passenger, holding him firmly in place.

"Gunshot," Felouen said, looking critically at the unconscious elf. She pressed her hands against his chest and his shirt faded out of being.

Oh God. Oh my God—Lianne had seen enough cop shows to know where the heart was. And she had seen enough bodies in the past few hours to know what death looked like. Waxy, pale—with a bullet hole in his upper chest that no longer bled. . . . Lianne bit her lip, and felt her eyes fill with tears. "Right through his heart," she whispered. "He must have died instantly."

Felouen turned around with a quizzical expression on her face. "Heart? Not at all. That's down here," she said, pressing her hand low on the center of his chest. "Lucky he wasn't human. That shot was very carefully placed." She suddenly grinned. "Lucky the woman was such a good shot. She hit a lung . . . some big blood vessels . . . we can fix this."

No, I can't believe it. It can't be true, she's just humoring me . . . .

"Really." Lianne tried to smile, but her lip quivered. Felouen gave her a long look—and took both her shoulders in her hard hands, shaking her like a stubborn child.

"*Yes*, you little fool! He'll be fine! I can fix him, I can do it *right now*." She punctuated each word with another shake, until Lianne finally had belief shaken into her.

Felouen let go of her shoulders, with a mutter of "damn fool mortals," and sighed. "Well, I can do a little for him, and there are others Underhill who can do more. Shit, I wish I had my strength back. And you don't even have much you can loan me."

Rhellen rumbled, and Felouen eyed him speculatively. "Well, there is always drawing from you, isn't there?" The car flashed his lights emphatically, and she smiled slightly, and nodded. "We'll do it. Thank you, Rhellen."

Felouen pressed one hand on Rhellen's doorframe, and one on Mac, and sang a soft, minor-key song in a beautiful language Lianne had never heard before. It was hard to believe mere words could be so beautiful, but the teacher felt a poignant sense of loss with each syllable—that this was a world that she could only know briefly from its periphery. The only other time she felt this way was when she watched a Space Shuttle fly. . . .

Lianne rested her hands on Mac's leg and willed him to get better. Felouen's head snapped around, startled, and then she gave the teacher a smile full of gratitude while she sang.

Under their hands, Maclyn groaned and shifted. Felouen kept singing, Lianne kept willing her strength into him—

And he sat up and spoke—dazed, but with only one thing on his mind, and that driving him past all sense or personal injury.

"We have to get to Amanda."

Amanda-Abbey and Amanda-Alice clung to each other and cried. :*I'm sorry, Anne,*: Alice sobbed. :*I didn't know! Please come back. Please help us!*: Gentle Abbey was too much in shock to do anything but weep.

Cethlenn pressed the two of them against her chest and cried helplessly herself, as all three of them shared the pain of the body they lived in. There was no protecting them this time. They were going to die, and before they did, they had to go through this. *Anne could have saved them—Anne would never have been caught by the bastard in the first place,* she thought grimly. *But if she hadn't protected them quite so well, they would have known not to trust him.* Cethlenn wiped viciously at her own tears. "*If only*"—the most useless words in any language. *Limit the damage as best you can,* she told herself.

Abbey, as frightened as her sister, and even more stunned, kept thinking, *Anne saved us from this. She let him hurt her like this so that we wouldn't be hurt. We never even knew.* She wrapped her arms tighter around her remaining "sister" and closed her eyes. *You loved us, and we didn't know enough to love you back. I'm sorry, Anne,* Abbey called. *Wherever you are, I'm sorry. I love you. Please, please come back. I really love you. We really love you.* . . .

Belinda followed Mel into the cavernous barn, stepping softly. She felt her trigger finger twitching. The idea of seeing the child's father with his brains spattered all over the barn wall became increasingly attractive to her with every passing moment. *Funny,* she thought. *I would have figured I had run out of noble motives for doing things a long time ago. It's interesting what you find out about yourself.*

The barn smelled—Belinda reflected that all barns smelled, but this one didn't smell right. The usual animal odors were there, but the place also smelled like—gasoline. Ugh! Just what her already-queasy stomach needed. Lucky she hadn't eaten since—God, sometime yesterday. She decided she was going to take better care of herself as soon as this mess was over.

In front of her, Mel pulled his gun out and shoved the stall door open with his foot.

"Good afternoon," he told the man, leveling his gun at him. "I regret having to interrupt your recreation, but we are in a bit of a hurry. So if you will just put the child down and step away from her, I won't have to shoot you."

The man stared stupidly at them. It took him a moment to see the gun, another few seconds for him to pull away from the child. He stood, pulling up his pants as he did, his face vacant and still.

"Very good. Bend down and pick up the girl while I cover him please, Belinda."

Belinda knelt and began untying the child and trying to rearrange her clothes, while the girl stared at her, disoriented and disbelieving.

"No, don't bother with that," Mel said. "Her father has conveniently packaged her for transport. Just pick her up and let's be going."

Belinda turned and snarled, "For godsakes, Mel, let me fix her clothes, at least."

"Do what I tell you," Mel said, coolly.

Without thinking, Belinda reached into her jacket toward her holster. Mel caught the movement, and his gun wavered for an instant between the man and her.

Lianne followed elves and elvensteeds across the yard toward the barn, running as fast as she could and falling behind again. Mac had paused just long enough to drop Lianne at the edge of the stable-area, then he and Felouen had headed straight for the barn. He'd probably intended for Lianne to stay out of this—but Amanda was her pupil, and she was, by God, going to be there. She'd expected for them to storm the house, but instead, Mac had shouted something about "bad magic at the barn," and the elves and their mounts headed that way.

She saw the elvensteeds hit the barn doors with their hooves. At the first blow, the doors flew open, and Mac, Rhellen, Felouen, and Moortha charged in.

Lianne was just inside the barn when the screaming began.

Andrew knew it was over the second the stranger kicked the door open. His mind raced, even as he feigned shock. He took his time, cultivated his face into a mask of stupidity, and did everything he could to make pulling up his pants seem the harmless actions of a stunned man.

His law career was over. This would get out, and he would find himself in prison. He knew what inmates did to men they found out were child-molesters.

His marriage was over—Merryl and her million-dollar dowry and her pliable, beautiful young daughter were as good as gone already.

He had nothing to lose but his life, and that had ceased to have any value. He decided then that he might as well die—but he wanted the people who had cost him everything to die with him. When the crash at the front of the barn drew everyone's attention away from him, his hand was into his pocket and out again before they could notice. His lighter was in his hand, and no one had seen. He clutched a wad of straw in the same hand.

The man with the gun swore and looked around frantically. "Grab the kid and c'mon," he told the woman.

Pounding hooves clattered at the front of the barn. Whoever was up there would be here in a moment. His daughter looked around at the three of them, a puzzled expression on her face. Andrew noticed that her eyes suddenly looked pale, pale green in the dim light. He'd seen the change before, but never before had he wondered at the cause. Now, though, he had a little time for puzzlement; now, when there were only a few more moments left of his life, and everything was incredibly sharp-edged and clear.

His daughter frowned—an oddly adult frown—and the ropes fell off of her wrists and ankles although no one had untied her. She stood, pulled up her pants, and brushed away the red-headed woman's hand as if no effort were involved.

"You h-h-hurt them," the child said to him, and Andrew felt the chill of unreasoning, senseless fear. "You hurt me—and—I d-d-didn't like it, but I didn't h-h-hurt you back because you left them alone. But now you hurt—them!"

The red-haired woman and the man with the gun both made a grab for her. Two tall blond—rock stars, Andrew thought, for lack of a better term—appeared in the stall and grabbed the man with the gun without pausing for a second.

They threw him. Picked him up, and *threw* him over the stall door.

Odd. The blond bimbo looked like a rock star and dressed like a rock star, but she had pointed ears.

Andrew tried to use the chance to escape, and found himself unable to move. So, apparently, did the battered red-haired woman. She writhed in place, but her feet seemed to be rooted to the ground.

The blond man, who also had those odd pointed ears, walked over and lifted him easily. Andrew found himself slung across the man's shoulders, completely helpless, unable to move at all against the man's unnatural strength. He didn't bother resisting after the initial attempt. It wouldn't change the outcome any.

Andrew thumbed the lighter, felt the straw ignite . . . and he opened his hand.

There was an instant when he wasn't certain it would work—but then the gasoline he'd poured around the inside of the barn caught, and with a satisfying *"whump,"* the inside of the building blossomed into flame.

Horses shrieked, the pale man and the pale woman started in dismay, and Andrew knew he'd won after all.

CHAPTER FOURTEEN

Fire licked within inches of them. The entire barn was in flames, there were strange people and guns and elves all over. None of it mattered—they were all together. Alice, Abbey, Cethlenn—and Anne. Alice and Abbey wiped tears from their eyes, and hugged her with illusory arms.

:*Anne,*: Alice said with real joy, :*you came back, you really came back! You* aren't *bad, you're good, you were right, I was wrong, you're good and you're strong, and—*:

Anne's lip quivered as she interrupted her sister. :*H-h-h-he killed . . . Mommy.*:

Abbey nodded solemnly and put her own arms around her sister, ignoring the flames that crept closer. :*He said so. He was glad about it. We* hate *him. Are you going to feed him to your monsters?*:

Anne shook her head slowly from side to side. :*N-n-no more m-m-m-monsters. That was bad. Th-th-they hurt lots of people, and nobody deserved it. I'm s-s-sorry about the monsters.*:

Alice crossed her snowy arms in front of her chest and pouted. :*But Father is very, very bad. Bad people deserve to be eaten by monsters.*:

Cethlenn rested her hand on Alice's shoulder. :*I don't think Anne wants to be the one to feed people to the*

613

monsters anymore. She hurts inside from all the pain the monsters caused.:

Anne gave the witch a grateful look. :*Yes,:* she said simply.

The flames crackled and reached for the ceiling; horses screamed, including the strange elf-horses. That got their attention, and suddenly Abbey and Alice shrank against Cethlenn in fear. :*Are we all going to die in the fire?:* Abbey asked.

:*No.:* Anne looked at her sisters, and smiled. It was the first time any of them had seen her smile. :*I'm w-w-with you . . . now. We're g-g-going to g-g-g-get better.:*

Belinda backed away from the flames, but there was nowhere to escape. She was really trapped this time, with no place to run, no place to hide. She wasn't alone, but that was no comfort. Even with an escort to Valhalla like this one—Mac Lynn, Miss Teach Lianne, the little girl, her disgusting father, Mel-the-bastard, millions of dollars worth of horses—it was no comfort at all.

All of them trapped in a burning barn, and not one of them had a way out.

So much for noble intentions, Belinda thought, looking at the little girl; for some obscure reason, tears clouded her eyes. *I would have saved you if I could have, kid. But now we're all going to die—because of that shitcan father of yours.*

All of them—including the racecar driver. Nice to know, after all her hard work, that he was finally going to cross the Great Divide. Where the hell did he get the Spock ears, anyway? He looked like some Hollywood director's idea of an elf. *How is he still alive after I put that bullet in his heart? And how did he pick up Mel and throw him like a baseball?*

She was perversely glad that Mel Tanbridge was going to get what was coming to him. She just wished she didn't have to go with him.

The smoke thickened, wreathing around her and making her cough, and she knelt down, sucking for air. Maybe it would be easier to stand and inhale the thick, acrid smoke into her lungs. Get it over with quicker.

I just really don't want to die, she thought, as her eyes streamed tears and her skin started feeling as if she was getting a bad sunburn. Only this sunburn was going to be a real bitch. . . .

Mac stared helplessly at the sudden eruption of flames that penned them in. Lianne grabbed his arm and looked up at him, trusting him to do some wonderful trick to rescue them. But Maclyn had been too badly hurt—he didn't have enough energy left to work the simplest spell, much less create a Gate. When he'd been shot, the energy he'd been using to maintain the Gate in Lianne's apartment had snapped and drained off. That, as much as the bullet, had pushed him near death. Now he was fresh out of tricks.

Felouen, he knew, was no better off; she had drained herself to absolute exhaustion in order to heal the others, and had to borrow power from Rhellen to heal him. She told him with her eyes that she would be no help.

The old wood of the building burned like kindling.

Wait a moment—

There was a chance, Mac thought, looking frantically around, as his eyes lit on the terrified elvensteeds. The elvensteeds weren't immune to fire. But they might be able to transform, to take their riders out, shielded inside them. They probably wouldn't survive—but maybe humans and elves would. He grabbed Rhellen's mane and tried to communicate what he wanted to the terrified beast.

Amanda appeared at his side.

She put her hand on his, and he looked down at her, startled at the upwelling of power from the child. Her green eyes looked up into his. No more hate there, and no more fear. No insanity. He sensed that there were several people, still, inside her little head—but they were all together now, working as one.

"I know—the trick," she said. She pressed the green bead at her wrist between her fingers, her eyes closing in concentration—

In front of them, with a rush of energy, a Gate appeared.

The panicked elvensteeds dove into it. Lianne followed,

with Felouen dragging Amanda's father, and Amanda holding back to maintain the Gate so that Maclyn and Belinda could escape as well. He reached for the child to pull her through.

Belinda suddenly shrieked "No!" and whirled to face them.

Mac froze. Belinda held a gun, leveled at him. "Let the kid go through, but you stay! You aren't getting away again," she shrieked, eyes glittering with madness. He opened his hands to reach for her; she was close enough—when a shape loomed out of the smoke and flames. It was the balding man they'd thrown, and *he* had a gun, too.

"Nobody move," he shouted. Mac and Belinda saw him aim the weapon at the child. "She's mine," he screamed. "You won't have her! Nobody gets her but me!"

Flames roared and circled them; Belinda's eyes flicked from Mac to that son-of-a-bitch Mel. *Why isn't he dead?* she wondered. He should have been. He was going to kill the rest of them—

Including the kid.

The kid didn't deserve it. The kid deserved to go live in fairyland after what had happened to her. Not to die in a goddamn fire.

She bit her lip. Sweat streamed down her face, and she squinted against the worsening smoke.

Dammit. One bullet—why did I leave everything in the car when I got ready to shoot Racer-Boy? One damned bullet—

She could shoot Mac. Or she could save the kid. She couldn't do both.

Belinda made her decision.

"Go!" she yelled to Mac, and the gun in her hands spit fire and bucked—and Mel staggered back, as a crimson dot appeared on his forehead.

:*I couldn't hold the door anymore*,: Anne said sadly, drooping with weariness. :*I couldn't get the lady out. I tried, but I was too tired.*:

Cethlenn looked around the charred remains of Elfhame Outremer, and said softly, :*You did the best you could, Anne.*

*We all know that. I think you've made up for what hap-
pened to the elves.:*

Abbey hugged her, then Alice, trying to reassure her.
:You're our sister,: Alice whispered. *:We aren't mad at you
anymore. You did the right things, and you tried to keep
us safe. You saved all of us!:*

:I'm really glad you came back,: Abbey added shyly. *:We
need you.:*

Anne smiled slowly, as if trying out the feeling for the
first time. *:I need you, too.:*

Maclyn shuddered and took in huge gasps of clean, cool
air. Behind them, the crashes of falling timbers, the roar
of flames, and the anguished screams of horses echoed,
even after the Gate snapped shut.

He could hardly believe their narrow escape. And that
all of it had been caused by—or for—one small girl . . .
that was the least believable of all.

Belinda hadn't made it. Mac straightened and stood in
the forest of Elfhame Outremer, his eyes fixed on the place
where the Gate had been. On the other side of it, she was
dying horribly. She had saved Amanda's life at the last
minute, Mac realized after a moment, and spared his. He
still had no idea why she'd wanted to kill him in the first
place, and he certainly couldn't fathom why she had saved
him in the end. Or had it really been Amanda she was
saving? He wondered if it was the only selfless thing she'd
ever done—or if once she had been someone who had been
worth knowing.

He turned away, saddened by the waste of her life.

Andrew Kendrick figured that he was probably insane.
He should have died—but a blond bimbo with special-
effects ears and eyes had pulled him through a hole in
the air. At first, he'd thought it was some kind of new
firefighting technique, and then he'd thought it was an
hallucination.

He blacked out, and came to surrounded by a crowd
of strangers; he thought then that he might be able to get
away—the only witnesses to what he'd done to Amanda
were dead, except for Amanda herself, and who'd believe

a kid? But all the strangers had those weird ears and eyes, and wherever he was, it wasn't North Carolina.

He·was wrestled to his feet with no consideration for his injuries before he could say a thing and hustled off into captivity. Since then, he'd been kept in a tiny cell, given sparse food and brackish water at odd intervals, and otherwise ignored. He was in some bizarre tree-world, and his cell had been the inside of a tree. That was when he figured he had gone insane, and there was no point in worrying about things.

The tall blond people—Sidhe, elves, he'd been told, and he'd stared at the speaker with disbelief, then laughed at him—had avoided him entirely until several hours ago, when two of them came and told him he was to be tried. He'd laughed at that, too, at the absurdity of it. But they'd hauled him away, and gradually he had to admit that whether or not he was insane, someone had him in their power, and that same someone had plans for him that he probably wasn't going to like.

Now he sat in a high-arching hall whose ceiling had recently been blasted open to the elements. The walls were scarred and pitted and burned. He'd noted that with a sort of detached interest as he'd been led into the hall. He wondered why the place was such a dump. What could possibly have happened here? It looked like a war zone.

The audience wore pointed ears, the jury and judge wore pointed ears—in fact, everyone except his daughter and her damned teacher wore them. The sight of Lianne What's-Her-Name sitting there in the audience stunned him for a moment. Whatever in hell was happening here, she must have a hand in it. Was this the high school drama club's shindig, with the costumes and ears?

He began to think, coldly and with guile. The teacher had him stashed away somewhere. Eventually, he'd get away. Then he'd get her. . . .

As the trial ground on, he was told how this place the "elves" called Elfhame Outremer had come to be destroyed. He was told a litany of dead and injured that made him chuckle in disbelief. He also discovered that the elves maintained that sole responsibility for the damage and all the deaths fell to him.

Even given that these people were loonies, put up to this by Lianne Whatsis, Andrew Kendrick was having some difficulty with that. In the first place, he didn't believe that Amanda had done the things they said she had—if she had been able to make monsters out of thin air, and work "magic" like that, why hadn't she gone after him? Why hadn't she done something about their games?

The memory of what had happened to the pony barn intruded at that moment, but he pushed it resolutely away. Whatever had happened there, Amanda couldn't have been responsible. She was only one little girl, one stupid, sluttish little girl. It must have some rational cause—and surely, surely some adult enemy had done it. Not the brat. Children were helpless, as they should be; property of those who fathered them.

Still, these "elves" insisted that was the truth. It only proved that they were loonies. He didn't know how Lianne Whatever had found them, but she sure fit right in with them.

Even *if* Amanda had been the cause for the "elves'" injuries, he didn't see how he could be legally held responsible for her insane outbreak. *He* hadn't conjured monsters or whatever the hell they were saying she'd done. He couldn't have if he tried—they even admitted that. But they were saying he *made* Amanda do it—and he'd never heard of any charge as crazy as that, not even in the kangaroo courts of Iran and Iraq.

Nuts. They were nutcases, one and all. Maybe Lianne had dragged him off to a nuthouse somehow?

But even nuts responded to some kind of logic, and before he could think about getting away, getting back to Fayetteville, he'd have to convince them that he was innocent. Since Amanda was admittedly as crazy as they were, she must be lying, and he was innocent of whatever they thought he had done. All right, they were trying him as some kind of an accomplice, perhaps. Why should he even have to take the rap for that? The "elves" didn't have any hard evidence. The testimony of a kid the "elves" frankly admitted had serious psychological problems wouldn't have held water for a second back in Fayetteville.

He summoned his best judicial manner and stood up

to speak his piece. But when he'd tried his rebuttal, he'd been firmly silenced and told that in Elfhame Outremer, he had no rights. No speech of any kind on his part would be permitted.

At that point, he was just about ready to explode. He kept his mouth shut only by reminding himself that there were other loonies on the "jury," and that even if they convicted him, he'd be able to get away at some point. And then he'd bring the authorities down on all of them. After silencing Amanda first, of course.

The "trial" took place over most of a day. At the end, he sat, chin erect, eyes firm, expression noble and convincingly innocent. He faced his accusers. Most of the people who had been in the burning barn were there. The blond "elf," who was also the local hero racecar driver Mac Lynn; his own daughter, Amanda—who looked at him from time to time and cried; Amanda's teacher, Miss McCormick; and the tall, skinny "elf" bimbo who had dragged him out of the barn. Felouen? What was that, Jamaican or something?

The kangaroo court prepared for the summing-up.

"Your actions were the direct cause of all of this," the bimbo said. She looked at him as if he were a particularly loathsome form of excrement she'd found on the bottom of her shoe. "Because of your abuse of this child, almost half of the people—innocent people—of Elfhame Outremer are lost to us. The city itself is as you see it now because of you—a ruin that will take hundreds of years to heal. Nothing will heal our many dead, nor the hearts of those who loved them and buried them. There is no punishment that we can give you which will mete out justice fully."

Andrew grinned at her. It was true. The worst they could do was kill him, and he'd been ready to do that himself. And if they didn't kill him, he'd get away, and then he'd come back with the law on his side and ready to deal with them all. Lunatics.

"However," the bimbo "Seleighe Court Lady" continued, "the one of our folk who discovered the true nature of your crimes also declared a fitting sentence for you before she died. In deference to her, and because her demand on the course of your life comes as close as possible to achieving justice, her sentence will be carried out."

Sentence? So they weren't going to kill him. Fine. He was smart, he knew things—he'd learned a lot from some of his less respectable clients. He doubted there was any place they could put him that he couldn't get out of, eventually. He discounted the fact that he hadn't been able to find a way out of the hollow tree they'd put him in at first. He just hadn't had time, that was all. He'd show them.

The bimbo kept right on with her pompous speech. God, how he hated women who got any authority at all, even granted by a pack of nutcases! They got so out of hand. . . .

"We know that you were abused as a child. We discovered this from the Oracular Pool—and we regret that we were not there to intervene for you." A flicker of distant pity passed over her face, and he noted it with resentment. How dared she pity him? "However, your adult life was the result of a long series of choices you made of your own free will—and your decision to abuse your own child was one such choice. You never displayed regret and never sought help. Therefore, there are no mitigating circumstances to soften your punishment."

The bimbo Felouen waved one hand, and a pocket of blackness appeared to her side. The other "elves" watched it with calm interest. Only now did he feel a chill of fear. What the hell was going on?

She turned back to him, with a face as cold as marble. "You are to be banished to a pocket of the Unformed Plane that has been prepared especially for you. It is unlikely that you will ever die in there—it is also unlikely that you will ever be released. In order to be released, you must truly, deeply, and completely come to regret what you inflicted on your daughter, take responsibility for it, and to feel guilt for it. In this pocket of the Unformed, your punishment will fit your crime. We regret this, Andrew Kendrick. But this is the justice you have earned."

Andrew found strong hands clasped over each arm, and although he struggled, suddenly frightened of the dark pool that hung in the air in front of him, he was shoved forward with implacable strength and speed.

"It's not my fault," he screamed. "*She* did it, the little bitch! She made me do it! Little girls are whores, and she was *my daughter* to do with as I pleased, damn it! It's not my fault! It's not my fault!"

He was thrown into that spinning vortex of tenebrous nothingness, and for a brief, disorienting moment, all detail and all sense of existence vanished.

Then he found himself on hands and knees, naked, in a room that glowed disconcertingly red. The room was hot, the light was dim, and a huge creature, as naked as he, stood at the far end. Beside the creature hung ropes, chains, horse tack and other implements that Andrew recognized. Only they were bigger, here, as if he were ten years old again. There was a narrow cot in one corner of the room. In fact, he recognized the room as a much larger version of the special "tack room" he'd kept for his use with Amanda.

The thing moved toward him, smiling. "Come here," it said in a voice so deep Andrew felt it before he heard it. "Come here. You want it. You know you do."

He looked at the monstrous thing's face. It shifted in the dim light, looking first like his father's face, then like Amanda's—and then his own.

"Come here, slut," it crooned. Then it seized him.

In the Oracular Pool, Andrew struggled in the bogan's grip; Amanda—Anne, Abbey, Alice, and Cethlenn together— shuddered and turned away, into Felouen's arms. The elven lady held her. Cethlenn felt Felouen rejoice that the child permitted herself to be held. Felouen banished the vision from the Pool, and led the little girl away, towards the tree-home of the driver Maclyn. He descended from his home to welcome them, with a smile for all of them. All four of them.

The moment that Cethlenn had sensed approaching came, although neither the elven lady nor the children knew it. They were about to become three, not four. It was time for Cethlenn to go.

:*Children*—: she said—and as usual, it was the sensitive Abbey who guessed what was about to happen.

:*No!*: the girl protested; the others understood in an instant and added their protests to hers.

:*You c-c-can't leave,*: Anne wailed. :*Who's g-g-gonna teach me the m-m-magic?*:

:The elves are better teachers than ever I'd be, little Anne,: she said, stroking Anne's hair. *:You're a fast learner, and Felouen will gladly teach you.:*

:But who will—will tell us what to do?: proper Alice asked, completely at a loss. *:You have to stay! We have to know what's right and what's wrong!:*

:Look to Maclyn for that, my dear one,: Cethlenn told her. *:He's learned in a bitter hard school, and he lives what he's learned. He is a most honorable man and a noble elven lord.:*

Abbey crept up beside her and nestled into her side. *:Who will love us?:* she asked piteously. *:You made us see each other, but who is going to make us all better if you go?:*

There her heart nearly broke, but the time was upon her, determined by a higher Power than she could fight. *:Every elf Underhill will love you, my darlings,:* she told them. *:And you will heal yourselves and make yourself whole.:*

They thought about that for a moment, and it was finally Alice who replied. *:You've never lied to us,:* she said. *:How? How are we going to be better?:*

The tugging on her soul became an insistent pull, and she had to fight against it to stay long enough to reply. *:Look for Amanda,:* she said at last, as the answer came to her from the same source as the tugging. *:Look for the littlest of you all, the most frightened, the one in hiding. And when you find her, show her you love her—and show her she is loved. Raise her up. Teach her that there is an end to fear and pain. Then you will find your way home.:*

The two elves with her sensed something going on. Cethlenn looked out of Amanda's eyes and into the eyes of Maclyn. He saw her there, and his lips formed a Word that he did not speak.

She nodded, gravely. "Blessings upon you, Fair One," she said in the most ancient Gaelic. "I give this one into your keeping. See that you deserve her."

Then, with a farewell caress to all three (and was there a hint of a fourth? A tiny, shy, frightened little child?) she spread her wings, and soared into the waiting Light.

❖   ❖   ❖

Lianne and Maclyn stood in the kitchen beside the Gate he'd opened one last time. She'd spent a week healing in Elfhame Outremer, and working with the elves to replant trees and reconsecrate the Grove. But Maclyn assured her that she was going back to the same evening she'd left, that no time would have passed in Fayetteville since she ran through the Gate and out of the burning barn.

He was so handsome, she thought, as if she viewed him from far away. She had spent most of her waking hours with him; she had watched him suffering over his mother's death, she'd worked beside him, had seen the first few smiles he'd managed. She'd seen him with Amanda, who was healing under the tender care of the elves. She knew him now, much better than she had ever known anyone before.

It would be so easy to ignore their differences, to accept the life he offered her straddled between the world of magic and her own mundane existence. Rather, she thought, it would be so easy for a while.

Then it would become impossible. Especially under the carefully uncritical eye of Felouen. Felouen, who loved Mac so desperately. Felouen, who needed him more than she would ever admit.

Then it would become impossible.

"What will I say about Amanda?" she asked, feeling the awkward silence as they looked at each other.

He shrugged. "Nothing. No one knows you were out there. They'll find simulacra in the embers of the barn— burned bodies that look just like hers and her father's. They won't need any more answers. My only regret is that they'll never know what he was doing to her."

Lianne nodded, thinking about the social worker who would never have to make that investigation. Would he be relieved? Or would he spend the rest of his life wondering if he had failed—wondering if he could have saved Amanda's life, if only—if only—"What about her sister, Sharon?" she asked. "*Her* mother is no prize."

Mac considered the question for a moment. "We'll watch the mother, I think. This might be the shock she needed to start taking care of her daughter better. If not—we'll intervene."

They continued to look at each other, and another awkward silence developed.

"Are you sure you won't stay in Elfhame Outremer with me?" Mac asked, softly; the very question she had been dreading.

Lianne looked at the floor, and rolled her foot back and forth across a pencil that lay there. "I can't, Mac. My family is here, my work is here, my past and my future are *here*. People need me in this world, Mac. And Felouen is waiting for you, and hoping the two of you will have a chance together."

He sighed—but was it with regret or relief? As well as she knew him, she still couldn't tell. "I know. I thought that was going to be your answer, but I still hoped—"

"There are some things that really aren't meant to be." Lianne made a stab at a brave smile, and gave it up as useless.

He licked his lips and stared deeply into her eyes. "I understand, or I think I do. You're sure?"

She nodded, not trusting herself to speech. The lump in her throat cut her breath short, and her nose was stuffy from the tears that were waiting to fall. One more word was all it would take.

He rested both hands on her shoulders. "One last kiss, then," he said.

His eyes looked—odd. She pushed him away, tensing with sudden suspicion. "No, Mac," she whispered.

"Just one," he asked.

"I saw *Superman*," she croaked.

That seemed to stump him. "So did I," he said at last.

She spoke with stiff lips. "I *hated* the ending. I always thought that Lois Lane got cheated at the end of the movie." She clenched her hands into fists, to keep from wiping away the tears that slid down her cheeks. "He kissed her and took away her memory of him, of who he was and what he was—and supposedly after that everything was back to normal. But she *earned* her pain. She would have lived without him—she could have kept on going even if she knew the truth."

Was she speaking about a two-dimensional movie character, or herself? Maybe both. "She would have known how special she was, though, if he'd left her alone. She would have known that she had been special enough to be loved by someone like him—and if it couldn't last forever, well . . . so few things do." Her voice turned fierce. "But he stole that from her, stole a part of her life that she couldn't ever replace—all because he thought she wasn't tough enough to handle it."

Maclyn blinked in surprise at her vehemence. "I sort of thought he'd made things easier on her."

She shook her head, angrily, to keep from crying. "Do you think she'd have chosen that if he'd asked her first?"

He hesitated. "Well . . . no. I guess not."

She lowered her voice. "Do you think he couldn't trust her to keep his secret?"

Mac whispered, "No. I think she would have kept his secret."

Lianne lifted her chin and glared at him. "Do you think you can't trust me?"

It was his turn to shake his head violently. "It wasn't that at all. It's just that you've had so much pain—and I thought I could save you some of it. . . ." Mac's eyes widened as he realized she'd caught him.

"That *was* what you were planning." Lianne glared at him with a kind of triumph. "I saw it in your face. You had that same stupid 'pity that poor girl' expression on your face that Christopher Reeve had on his." She kicked the pencil across the kitchen. "Don't do me any favors, Maclyn. I'm smart, and I'll get over you in my own time and in my own way. But I fought as hard for this day as you did—so don't you dare try to take it from me!"

Maclyn nodded and bit his lower lip. He moved toward the Gate, then looked back at her. She saw her own pain reflected in his eyes. "I'll miss you, Lianne McCormick."

"And I'll miss you. Tell Amanda I wish her luck," she added.

He bowed a little, courtly and solemn, offering her the acknowledgement of her own kind of royalty. "I will. She'll find safe haven and healing in Elfhame Outremer. And training for the incredible power she commands."

They gazed at each other from across the distance of the kitchen—from across an abyss than neither could breach—from across the centuries.

"I love you," Mac said into the silence.

Her heart contracted. "I know. I love you, too. It doesn't change anything."

"No. It doesn't." He licked his lips again, and asked, plaintively, "I can still come and see you sometimes, can't I?"

Lianne took a deep breath. "No, Mac. I have to get on with my life—and you have to get on with yours. We can't do that with each other around."

He nodded, as if he had expected that answer, too. "You're right. But maybe . . . sometime . . . you could come out to the track and cheer me on. I could use that . . . all the help I can get. . . ." He leaned over and gave her a gentle kiss on the cheek.

"Good-bye, fair one."

"Good-bye, Mac," she said for the last time, and left unsaid a million more things.

AFTERWORD

Hundreds of children are abducted in this country every year, many by non-custodial parents. We see their faces peering at us from billboards, milk cartons, and on the back of junk-mail ads. The question is: do these pathetic photos work?

The answer is yes. The reason is because of ordinary people, teachers, neighbors, or just passersby, who see something odd in the behavior of a parent and child, and *call*. There are several agencies responsible for helping to find missing children: here are the numbers of two.

CHILD FIND:
1-800-292-9688
MISSING CHILDREN'S HELP CENTER:
1-800-872-5437

Child abuse, whether parental or with parental consent, is *wrong*. Children deserve love, tenderness, and reasonable discipline. They do *not* deserve to be beaten, tied up, starved, abandoned, used, or misused. There are several groups trying to help children who are mistreated: here is the number of one.

CHILDHELP NATIONAL
CHILD ABUSE HOTLINE:
1-800-422-4453

You don't need elves or magic to get a start on helping a child in a desperate situation—you don't even need a quarter. Most pay-phones allow you to call 1-800 numbers completely free of charge, simply by dialing them as written. All you need to start a child back to a decent life is the willingness to get involved.

MERCEDES LACKEY
Hot! Hot! Hot!

Whether it's elves at the racetrack, bards battling evil mages or brainships fighting planet pirates, Mercedes Lackey is always compelling, always fun, always a great read. Complete your collection today!